The Blue Lagoon Trilogy

The Blue Lagoon
The Garden of God
The Gates of Morning

The Blue Lagoon Trilogy

by H. de Vere Stacpoole

THE BLUE LAGOON
Contents

BOOK II
PART I

PART II

BOOK III

BOOK I
PART I

WHERE THE SLUSH LAMP BURNS

Mr Button was seated on a sea-chest with a fiddle under his left ear. He was playing the "Shan van vaught," and accompanying the tune, punctuating it, with blows of his left heel on the fo'cs'le deck.

> "O the *Frinch* are in the bay,
> Says the *Shan van vaught*."

He was dressed in dungaree trousers, a striped shirt, and a jacket baize—green in parts from the influence of sun and salt. A typical old shell-back, round-shouldered, hooked of finger; a figure with strong hints of a crab about it.

His face was like a moon, seen red through tropical mists; and as he played it wore an expression of strained attention as though the fiddle were telling him tales much more marvellous than the old bald statement about Bantry Bay.

"Left-handed Pat," was his fo'cs'le name; not because he was left-handed, but simply because everything he did he did wrong—or nearly so. Reefing or furling, or handling a slush tub—if a mistake was to be made, he made it.

He was a Celt, and all the salt seas that had flowed between him and Connaught these forty years and more had not washed the Celtic element from his blood, nor the belief in fairies from his soul. The Celtic nature is a fast dye, and Mr Button's nature was such that though he had been shanghaied by Larry Marr in 'Frisco, though he had got drunk in most ports of the world, though he had sailed with Yankee captains and been man-handled by Yankee mates, he still carried his fairies about with him—they, and a very large stock of original innocence.

Nearly over the musician's head swung a hammock from which hung a leg; other hammocks hanging in the semi-gloom called up suggestions of lemurs and arboreal bats. The swinging kerosene lamp cast its light forward, past the heel of the bowsprit to the knightheads, lighting here a naked foot hanging over the side of a bunk, here a face from which protruded a pipe, here a breast covered with dark mossy hair, here an arm tattooed.

It was in the days before double topsail yards had reduced ships' crews, and the fo'cs'le of the *Northumberland* had a full company: a crowd of packet rats such as often is to be found on a Cape Horner "Dutchmen" Americans—men who were farm labourers and tending pigs in Ohio three months back, old seasoned sailors like Paddy Button—a mixture of the best and the worst of the earth, such as you find nowhere else in so small a space as in a ship's fo'cs'le.

The *Northumberland* had experienced a terrible rounding of the Horn. Bound from New Orleans to 'Frisco she had spent thirty days battling with head-winds and storms—down there, where the seas are so vast that three waves may cover with their amplitude more than a mile of sea space; thirty days she had passed off Cape Stiff, and just now, at the moment of this story, she was locked in a calm south of the line.

Mr Button finished his tune with a sweep of the bow, and drew his right coat sleeve across his forehead. Then he took out a sooty pipe, filled it with tobacco, and lit it.

"Pawthrick," drawled a voice from the hammock above, from which depended the leg, "what was that yarn you wiz beginnin' to spin ter night 'bout a lip me dawn?"

"A which me dawn?" asked Mr Button, cocking his eye up at the bottom of the hammock while he held the match to his pipe.

"It vas about a green thing," came a sleepy Dutch voice from a bunk.

"Oh, a Leprachaun you mane. Sure, me mother's sister had one down in Connaught."

"Vat vas it like?" asked the dreamy Dutch voice—a voice seemingly possessed by the calm that had made the sea like a mirror for the last three days, reducing the whole ship's company meanwhile to the level of wasters.

"Like? Sure, it was like a Leprachaun; and what else would it be like?"

"What like vas that?" persisted the voice.

"It was like a little man no bigger than a big forked raddish, an' as green as a cabbage. Me a'nt had one in her house down in Connaught in the ould days. O musha! musha! the ould days, the ould days! Now, you may b'lave me or b'lave me not, but you could have put him in your pocket, and the grass-green head of him wouldn't more than'v stuck out. She kept him in a cupboard, and out of the cupboard he'd pop if it was a crack open, an' into the milk pans he'd be, or under the beds, or pullin' the stool from under you, or at some other divarsion. He'd chase the pig—the crathur!—till it'd be all ribs like an ould umbrilla with the fright, an' as thin as a greyhound with the runnin' by the marnin; he'd addle the eggs so the cocks an' hens wouldn't know what they wis afther wid the chickens comin' out wid two heads on them, an' twinty-seven legs fore and aft. And you'd start to chase him, an' then it'd be mainsail haul, and away he'd go, you behint him, till you'd landed tail over snout in a ditch, an' he'd be back in the cupboard."

"He was a Troll," murmured the Dutch voice.

"I'm tellin' you he was a Leprachaun, and there's no knowin' the divilments he'd be up to. He'd pull the cabbidge, maybe, out of the pot boilin' on the fire forenint your eyes, and baste you in the face with it; and thin, maybe, you'd hold out your fist to him, and he'd put a goulden soverin in it."

"Wisht he was here!" murmured a voice from a bunk near the knightheads.

"Pawthrick," drawled the voice from the hammock above, "what'd you do first if you found y'self with twenty pound in your pocket?"

"What's the use of askin' me?" replied Mr Button. "What's the use of twenty pound to a sayman at say, where the grog's all wather an' the beef's all horse? Gimme it ashore, an' you'd see what I'd do wid it!"

"I guess the nearest grog-shop keeper wouldn't see you comin' for dust," said a voice from Ohio.

"He would not," said Mr Button; "nor you afther me. Be damned to the grog and thim that sells it!"

"It's all darned easy to talk," said Ohio. "You curse the grog at sea when you can't get it; set you ashore, and you're bung full."

"I likes me dhrunk," said Mr Button, "I'm free to admit; an' I'm the divil when it's in me, and it'll be the end of me yet, or me ould mother was a liar. 'Pat,' she says, first time I come home from say rowlin', 'storms you may escape, an' wimmen you may escape, but the potheen 'ill have you.' Forty year ago—forty year ago!"

"Well," said Ohio, "it hasn't had you yet."

"No," replied Mr Button, "but it will."

UNDER THE STARS

It was a wonderful night up on deck, filled with all the majesty and beauty of starlight and a tropic calm.

The Pacific slept; a vast, vague swell flowing from far away down south under the night, lifted the *Northumberland* on its undulations to the rattling sound of the reef points and the occasional creak of the rudder; whilst overhead, near the fiery arch of the Milky Way, hung the Southern Cross like a broken kite.

Stars in the sky, stars in the sea, stars by the million and the million; so many lamps ablaze that the firmament filled the mind with the idea of a vast and populous city—yet from all that living and flashing splendour not a sound.

Down in the cabin—or saloon, as it was called by courtesy—were seated the three passengers of the ship; one reading at the table, two playing on the floor.

The man at the table, Arthur Lestrange, was seated with his large, deep-sunken eyes fixed on a book. He was most evidently in consumption—very near, indeed, to reaping the result of that last and most desperate remedy, a long sea voyage.

Emmeline Lestrange, his little niece—eight years of age, a mysterious mite, small for her age, with thoughts of her own, wide-pupilled eyes that seemed the doors for visions, and a face that seemed just to have peeped into this world for a moment ere it was as suddenly withdrawn—sat in a corner nursing something in her arms, and rocking herself to the tune of her own thoughts.

Dick, Lestrange's little son, eight and a bit, was somewhere under the table. They were Bostonians, bound for San Francisco, or rather for the sun and splendour of Los Angeles, where Lestrange had bought a small estate, hoping there to enjoy the life whose lease would be renewed by the long sea voyage.

As he sat reading, the cabin door opened, and appeared an angular female form. This was Mrs Stannard, the stewardess, and Mrs Stannard meant bedtime.

"Dicky," said Mr Lestrange, closing his book, and raising the table-cloth a few inches, "bedtime."

"Oh, not yet, daddy!" came a sleep-freighted voice from under the table; "I ain't ready. I dunno want to go to bed, I— Hi yow!"

Mrs Stannard, who knew her work, had stooped under the table, seized him by the foot, and hauled him out kicking and fighting and blubbering all at the same time.

As for Emmeline, she having glanced up and recognised the inevitable, rose to her feet, and, holding the hideous rag-doll she had been nursing, head down and dangling in one hand, she stood waiting till Dicky, after a few last perfunctory bellows, suddenly dried his eyes and held up a tear-wet face for his father to kiss. Then she presented her brow solemnly to her uncle, received a kiss and vanished, led by the hand into a cabin on the port side of the saloon.

Mr Lestrange returned to his book, but he had not read for long when the cabin door was opened, and Emmeline, in her nightdress, reappeared, holding a brown paper parcel in her hand, a parcel of about the same size as the book you are reading.

"My box," said she; and as she spoke, holding it up as if to prove its safety, the little plain face altered to the face of an angel.

She had smiled.

When Emmeline Lestrange smiled it was absolutely as if the light of Paradise had suddenly flashed upon her face: the happiest form of childish beauty suddenly appeared before your eyes, dazzled them—and was gone.

Then she vanished with her box, and Mr Lestrange resumed his book.

This box of Emmeline's, I may say in parenthesis, had given more trouble aboard ship than all of the rest of the passengers' luggage put together.

It had been presented to her on her departure from Boston by a lady friend, and what it contained was a dark secret to all on board, save its owner and her uncle; she was a woman, or, at all events, the beginning of a woman, yet she kept this secret to herself—a fact which you will please note.

The trouble of the thing was that it was frequently being lost. Suspecting herself, maybe, as an unpractical dreamer in a world filled with robbers, she would cart it about with her for safety, sit down behind a coil of rope and fall into a fit of abstraction: be recalled to life by the evolutions of the crew reefing or furling or what not, rise to superintend the operations—and then suddenly find she had lost her box.

Then she would absolutely haunt the ship. Wide-eyed and distressed of face she would wander hither and thither, peeping into the galley, peeping down the forescuttle, never uttering a word or wail, searching like an uneasy ghost, but dumb.

She seemed ashamed to tell of her loss, ashamed to let any one know of it; but every one knew of it directly they saw her, to use Mr Button's expression, "on the wandher," and every one hunted for it.

Strangely enough it was Paddy Button who usually found it. He who was always doing the wrong thing in the eyes of men, generally did the right thing in the eyes of children. Children, in fact, when they could get at Mr Button, went for him *con amore*. He was as attractive to them as a Punch and Judy show or a German band—almost.

Mr Lestrange after a while closed the book he was reading, looked around him and sighed.

The cabin of the *Northumberland* was a cheerful enough place, pierced by the polished shaft of the mizzen mast, carpeted with an Axminster carpet, and garnished with mirrors let into the white pine panelling. Lestrange was staring at the reflection of his own face in one of these mirrors fixed just opposite to where he sat.

His emaciation was terrible, and it was just perhaps at this moment that he first recognised the fact that he must not only die, but die soon.

He turned from the mirror and sat for a while with his chin resting upon his hand, and his eyes fixed on an ink spot upon the table-cloth; then he arose, and crossing the cabin climbed laboriously up the companion-way to the deck.

As he leaned against the bulwark rail to recover his breath, the splendour and beauty of the Southern night struck him to the heart with a cruel pang. He took his seat on a deck chair and gazed up at the Milky Way, that great triumphal arch built of suns that the dawn would sweep away like a dream.

In the Milky Way, near the Southern Cross, occurs a terrible circular abyss, the Coal Sack. So sharply defined is it, so suggestive of a void and bottomless cavern, that the contemplation of it afflicts the imaginative mind with vertigo. To the naked eye it is as black and as dismal as death, but the smallest telescope reveals it beautiful and populous with stars.

Lestrange's eyes travelled from this mystery to the burning cross, and the nameless and numberless stars reaching to the sea-line, where they paled and vanished in the light of the rising moon. Then he became aware of a figure promenading the quarter-deck. It was the "Old Man."

A sea captain is always the "old man," be his age what it may. Captain Le Farges' age might have been forty-five. He was a sailor of the Jean Bart type, of French descent, but a naturalised American.

"I don't know where the wind's gone," said the captain as he drew near the man in the deck chair. "I guess it's blown a hole in the firmament, and escaped somewheres to the back of beyond."

"It's been a long voyage," said Lestrange; "and I'm thinking, Captain, it will be a very long voyage for me. My port's not 'Frisco; I feel it."

"Don't you be thinking that sort of thing," said the other, taking his seat in a chair close by. "There's no manner of use forecastin' the weather a month ahead.

Now we're in warm latitoods, your glass will rise steady, and you'll be as right and spry as any one of us, before we fetch the Golden Gates."

"I'm thinking about the children," said Lestrange, seeming not to hear the captain's words. "Should anything happen to me before we reach port, I should like you to do something for me. It's only this: dispose of my body without—without the children knowing. It has been in my mind to ask you this for some days. Captain, those children know nothing of death."

Le Farge moved uneasily in his chair.

"Little Emmeline's mother died when she was two. Her father—my brother—died before she was born. Dicky never knew a mother; she died giving him birth. My God, Captain, death has laid a heavy hand on my family; can you wonder that I have hid his very name from those two creatures that I love!"

"Ay, ay," said Le Farge, "it's sad! it's sad!"

"When I was quite a child," went on Lestrange, "a child no older than Dicky, my nurse used to terrify me with tales about dead people. I was told I'd go to hell when I died if I wasn't a good child. I cannot tell you how much that has poisoned my life, for the thoughts we think in childhood, Captain, are the fathers of the thoughts we think when we are grown up. And can a diseased father—have healthy children?"

"I guess not."

"So I just said, when these two tiny creatures came into my care, that I would do all in my power to protect them from the terrors of life—or rather, I should say, from the terror of death. I don't know whether I have done right, but I have done it for the best. They had a cat, and one day Dicky came in to me and said: 'Father, pussy's in the garden asleep, and I can't wake her.' So I just took him out for a walk; there was a circus in the town, and I took him to it. It so filled his mind that he quite forgot the cat. Next day he asked for her. I did not tell him she was buried in the garden, I just said she must have run away. In a week he had forgotten all about her—children soon forget."

"Ay, that's true," said the sea captain. "But 'pears to me they must learn some time they've got to die."

"Should I pay the penalty before we reach land, and be cast into that great, vast sea, I would not wish the children's dreams to be haunted by the thought: just tell them I've gone on board another ship. You will take them back to Boston; I have here, in a letter, the name of a lady who will care for them. Dicky will be well off,

13

as far as worldly goods are concerned, and so will Emmeline. Just tell them I've gone on board another ship—children soon forget."

"I'll do what you ask," said the seaman.

The moon was over the horizon now, and the *Northumberland* lay adrift in a river of silver. Every spar was distinct, every reef point on the great sails, and the decks lay like spaces of frost cut by shadows black as ebony.

As the two men sat without speaking, thinking their own thoughts, a little white figure emerged from the saloon hatch. It was Emmeline. She was a professed sleepwalker—a past mistress of the art.

Scarcely had she stepped into dreamland than she had lost her precious box, and now she was hunting for it on the decks of the *Northumberland*.

Mr Lestrange put his finger to his lips, took off his shoes and silently followed her. She searched behind a coil of rope, she tried to open the galley door; hither and thither she wandered, wide-eyed and troubled of face, till at last, in the shadow of the hencoop, she found her visionary treasure. Then back she came, holding up her little nightdress with one hand, so as not to trip, and vanished down the saloon companion very hurriedly, as if anxious to get back to bed, her uncle close behind, with one hand outstretched so as to catch her in case she stumbled.

THE SHADOW AND THE FIRE

It was the fourth day of the long calm. An awning had been rigged up on the poop for the passengers, and under it sat Lestrange, trying to read, and the children trying to play. The heat and monotony had reduced even Dicky to just a surly mass, languid in movement as a grub. As for Emmeline, she seemed dazed. The rag-doll lay a yard away from her on the poop deck unnursed; even the wretched box and its whereabouts she seemed to have quite forgotten.

"Daddy!" suddenly cried Dick, who had clambered up, and was looking over the after-rail.

"What?"

"Fish!"

Lestrange rose to his feet, came aft and looked over the rail.

Down in the vague green of the water something moved, something pale and long—a ghastly form. It vanished; and yet another came, neared the surface, and displayed itself more fully. Lestrange saw its eyes, he saw the dark fin, and the whole hideous length of the creature; a shudder ran through him as he clasped Dicky.

"Ain't he fine?" said the child. "I guess, daddy, I'd pull him aboard if I had a hook. Why haven't I a hook, daddy?—why haven't I a hook, daddy?— Ow, you're *squeezin'* me!"

Something plucked at Lestrange's coat: it was Emmeline—she also wanted to look. He lifted her up in his arms; her little pale face peeped over the rail, but there was nothing to see: the forms of terror had vanished, leaving the green depths untroubled and unstained.

"What's they called, daddy?" persisted Dick, as his father took him down from the rail, and led him back to the chair.

"Sharks," said Lestrange, whose face was covered with perspiration.

He picked up the book he had been reading—it was a volume of Tennyson—and he sat with it on his knees staring at the white sunlit main-deck barred with the white shadows of the standing rigging.

The sea had disclosed to him a vision. Poetry, Philosophy, Beauty, Art, the love and joy of life—was it possible that these should exist in the same world as those?

He glanced at the book upon his knees, and contrasted the beautiful things in it which he remembered with the terrible things he had just seen, the things that were waiting for their food under the keel of the ship.

It was three bells—half-past three in the afternoon—and the ship's bell had just rung out. The stewardess appeared to take the children below; and as they vanished down the saloon companion-way Captain Le Farge came aft, on to the poop, and stood for a moment looking over the sea on the port side, where a bank of fog had suddenly appeared like the spectre of a country.

"The sun has dimmed a bit," said he; "I can a'most look at it. Glass steady enough—there's a fog coming up—ever seen a Pacific fog?"

"No, never."

"Well, you won't want to see another," replied the mariner, shading his eyes and fixing them upon the sea-line. The sea-line away to starboard had lost somewhat its distinctness, and over the day an almost imperceptible shade had crept.

The captain suddenly turned from his contemplation of the sea and sky, raised his head and sniffed.

"Something is burning somewhere—smell it? Seems to me like an old mat or summat. It's that swab of a steward, maybe; if he isn't breaking glass, he's upsetting lamps and burning holes in the carpet. Bless my soul, I'd sooner have a dozen Mary Anns an' their dustpans round the place than one tomfool steward like Jenkins." He went to the saloon hatch. "Below there!"

"Ay, ay, sir."

"What are you burning?"

"I an't burnin' northen, sir."

"Tell you, I smell it!"

"There's northen burnin' here, sir."

"Neither is there, it's all on deck. Something in the galley, maybe—rags, most likely, they've thrown on the fire."

"Captain!" said Lestrange.

"Ay, ay."

"Come here, please."

Le Farge climbed on to the poop.

"I don't know whether it's my weakness that's affecting my eyes, but there seems to me something strange about the main-mast."

The main-mast near where it entered the deck, and for some distance up, seemed in motion—a corkscrew movement most strange to watch from the shelter of the awning.

This apparent movement was caused by a spiral haze of smoke so vague that one could only tell of its existence from the mirage-like tremor of the mast round which it curled.

"My God!" cried Le Farge, as he sprang from the poop and rushed forward.

Lestrange followed him slowly, stopping every moment to clutch the bulwark rail and pant for breath. He heard the shrill bird-like notes of the bosun's pipe. He saw the hands emerging from the forecastle, like bees out of a hive; he watched them surrounding the main-hatch. He watched the tarpaulin and locking-bars removed. He saw the hatch opened, and a burst of smoke—black, villainous smoke—ascend to the sky, solid as a plume in the windless air.

Lestrange was a man of a highly nervous temperament, and it is just this sort of man who keeps his head in an emergency, whilst your level-headed, phlegmatic individual loses his balance. His first thought was of the children, his second of the boats.

In the battering off Cape Horn the *Northumberland* lost several of her boats. There were left the long-boat, a quarter-boat, and the dinghy. He heard Le Farge's voice

16

ordering the hatch to be closed and the pumps manned, so as to flood the hold; and, knowing that he could do nothing on deck, he made as swiftly as he could for the saloon companion-way.

Mrs Stannard was just coming out of the children's cabin.

"Are the children lying down, Mrs Stannard?" asked Lestrange, almost breathless from the excitement and exertion of the last few minutes.

The woman glanced at him with frightened eyes. He looked like the very herald of disaster.

"For if they are, and you have undressed them, then you must put their clothes on again. The ship is on fire, Mrs Stannard."

"Good God, sir!"

"Listen!" said Lestrange.

From a distance, thin, and dreary as the crying of sea-gulls on a desolate beach, came the clanking of the pumps.

AND LIKE A DREAM DISSOLVED

Before the woman had time to speak a thunderous step was heard on the companion stairs, and Le Farge broke into the saloon. The man's face was injected with blood, his eyes were fixed and glassy like the eyes of a drunkard, and the veins stood on his temples like twisted cords.

"Get those children ready!" he shouted, as he rushed into his own cabin. "Get you all ready—boats are being swung out and victualled. H–l! where are those papers?"

They heard him furiously searching and collecting things in his cabin—the ship's papers, accounts, things the master mariner clings to as he clings to his life; and as he searched, and found, and packed, he kept bellowing orders for the children to be got on deck. Half mad he seemed, and half mad he was with the knowledge of the terrible thing that was stowed amidst the cargo.

Up on deck the crew, under the direction of the first mate, were working in an orderly manner, and with a will, utterly unconscious of there being anything beneath their feet but an ordinary cargo on fire. The covers had been stripped from the boats, kegs of water and bags of biscuit placed in them. The dinghy, smallest of the boats and most easily got away, was hanging at the port quarter-boat davits flush with the bulwarks; and Paddy Button was in the act of stowing a keg of water in her, when Le Farge broke on to the deck, followed by the stewardess carrying Emmeline, and Mr Lestrange leading Dick. The dinghy was rather a larger boat than the ordinary ships' dinghy, and possessed a small mast and long sail. Two sailors stood ready to man the falls, and Paddy Button was just turning to trundle forward again when the captain seized him.

"Into the dinghy with you," he cried, "and row these children and the passenger out a mile from the ship—two miles—three miles—make an offing."

"Sure, Captain dear, I've left me fiddle in the——"

Le Farge dropped the bundle of things he was holding under his left arm, seized the old sailor and rushed him against the bulwarks, as if he meant to fling him into the sea *through* the bulwarks.

Next moment Mr Button was in the boat. Emmeline was handed to him, pale of face and wide-eyed, and clasping something wrapped in a little shawl; then Dick, and then Mr Lestrange was helped over.

"No room for more!" cried Le Farge. "Your place will be in the long-boat, Mrs Stannard, if we have to leave the ship. Lower away, lower away!"

The boat sank towards the smooth blue sea, kissed it and was afloat.

Now Mr Button, before joining the ship at Boston, had spent a good while lingering by the quay, having no money wherewith to enjoy himself in a tavern. He had seen something of the lading of the *Northumberland*, and heard more from a stevedore. No sooner had he cast off the falls and seized the oars, than his knowledge awoke in his mind, living and lurid. He gave a whoop that brought the two sailors leaning over the side.

"Bullies!"

"Ay, ay!"

"Run for your lives—I've just rimimbered—there's two bar'ls of blastin' powther in the hould!"

Then he bent to his oars, as no man ever bent before.

Lestrange, sitting in the stern-sheets clasping Emmeline and Dick, saw nothing for a moment after hearing these words. The children, who knew nothing of blasting powder or its effects, though half frightened by all the bustle and excitement, were still amused and pleased at finding themselves in the little boat so close to the blue pretty sea.

Dick put his finger over the side, so that it made a ripple in the water (the most delightful experience of childhood). Emmeline, with one hand clasped in her uncle's, watched Mr Button with a grave sort of half pleasure.

He certainly was a sight worth watching. His soul was filled with tragedy and terror. His Celtic imagination heard the ship blowing up, saw himself and the little dinghy blown to pieces—nay, saw himself in hell, being toasted by "divils."

But tragedy and terror could find no room for expression on his fortunate or unfortunate face. He puffed and he blew, bulging his cheeks out at the sky as he tugged at the oars, making a hundred and one grimaces—all the outcome of agony of mind, but none expressing it. Behind lay the ship, a picture not without its lighter side. The long-boat and the quarter-boat, lowered with a rush and seaborne by the mercy of Providence, were floating by the side of the *Northumberland*.

From the ship men were casting themselves overboard like water-rats, swimming in the water like ducks, scrambling on board the boats anyhow.

From the half-opened main-hatch the black smoke, mixed now with sparks, rose steadily and swiftly and spitefully, as if driven through the half-closed teeth of a dragon.

A mile away beyond the *Northumberland* stood the fog bank. It looked solid, like a vast country that had suddenly and strangely built itself on the sea—a country where no birds sang and no trees grew. A country with white, precipitous cliffs, solid to look at as the cliffs of Dover.

"I'm spint!" suddenly gasped the oarsman, resting the oar handles under the crook of his knees, and bending down as if he was preparing to butt at the passengers in the stern-sheets. "Blow up or blow down, I'm spint—don't ax me, I'm spint!"

Mr Lestrange, white as a ghost, but recovered somewhat from his first horror, gave the Spent One time to recover himself and turned to look at the ship. She seemed a great distance off, and the boats, well away from her, were making at a furious pace towards the dinghy. Dick was still playing with the water, but Emmeline's eyes were entirely occupied with Paddy Button. New things were always of vast interest to her contemplative mind, and these evolutions of her old friend were eminently new.

She had seen him swilling the decks, she had seen him dancing a jig, she had seen him going round the main deck on all fours with Dick on his back, but she had never seen him going on like this before.

19

She perceived now that he was exhausted, and in trouble about something, and, putting her hand in the pocket of her dress, she searched for something that she knew was there. She produced a Tangerine orange, and leaning forward she touched the Spent One's head with it.

Mr Button raised his head, stared vacantly for a second, saw the proffered orange, and at the sight of it the thought of "the childer" and their innocence, himself and the blasting powder, cleared his dazzled wits, and he took to the sculls again.

"Daddy," said Dick, who had been looking astern, "there's clouds near the ship."

In an incredibly short space of time the solid cliffs of fog had broken. The faint wind that had banked it had pierced it, and was now making pictures and devices of it, most wonderful and weird to see. Horsemen of the mist rode on the water, and were dissolved; billows rolled on the sea, yet were not of the sea; blankets and spirals of vapour ascended to high heaven. And all with a terrible languor of movement. Vast and lazy and sinister, yet steadfast of purpose as Fate or Death, the fog advanced, taking the world for its own.

Against this grey and indescribably sombre background stood the smouldering ship with the breeze already shivering in her sails, and the smoke from her main-hatch blowing and beckoning as if to the retreating boats.

"Why's the ship smoking like that?" asked Dick. "And look at those boats coming—when are we going back, daddy?"

"Uncle," said Emmeline, putting her hand in his, as she gazed towards the ship and beyond it, "I'm 'fraid."

"What frightens you, Emmy?" he asked, drawing her to him.

"Shapes," replied Emmeline, nestling up to his side.

"Oh, Glory be to God!" gasped the old sailor, suddenly resting on his oars. "Will yiz look at the fog that's comin'—"

"I think we had better wait here for the boats," said Mr Lestrange; "we are far enough now to be safe if—anything happens."

"Ay, ay," replied the oarsman, whose wits had returned. "Blow up or blow down, she won't hit us from here."

"Daddy," said Dick, "when are we going back? I want my tea."

"We aren't going back, my child," replied his father. "The ship's on fire; we are waiting for another ship."

"Where's the other ship?" asked the child, looking round at the horizon that was clear.

"We can't see it yet," replied the unhappy man, "but it will come."

The long-boat and the quarter-boat were slowly approaching. They looked like beetles crawling over the water, and after them across the glittering surface came a dullness that took the sparkle from the sea—a dullness that swept and spread like an eclipse shadow.

Now the wind struck the dinghy. It was like a wind from fairyland, almost imperceptible, chill, and dimming the sun. A wind from Lilliput. As it struck the dinghy, the fog took the distant ship.

It was a most extraordinary sight, for in less than thirty seconds the ship of wood became a ship of gauze, a tracery—flickered, and was gone forever from the sight of man.

VOICES HEARD IN THE MIST

The sun became fainter still, and vanished. Though the air round the dinghy seemed quite clear, the on-coming boats were hazy and dim, and that part of the horizon that had been fairly clear was now blotted out.

The long-boat was leading by a good way. When she was within hailing distance the captain's voice came.

"Dinghy ahoy!"

"Ahoy!"

"Fetch alongside here!"

The long-boat ceased rowing to wait for the quarter-boat that was slowly creeping up. She was a heavy boat to pull at all times, and now she was overloaded.

The wrath of Captain Le Farge with Paddy Button for the way he had stampeded the crew was profound, but he had not time to give vent to it.

"Here, get aboard us, Mr Lestrange!" said he, when the dinghy was alongside; "we have room for one. Mrs Stannard is in the quarter-boat, and it's overcrowded; she's better aboard the dinghy, for she can look after the kids. Come, hurry up, the smother is coming down on us fast. Ahoy!"—to the quarter-boat—"hurry up, hurry up!"

The quarter-boat had suddenly vanished.

Mr Lestrange climbed into the long-boat. Paddy pushed the dinghy a few yards away with the tip of a scull, and then lay on his oars waiting.

"Ahoy! ahoy!" cried Le Farge.

"Ahoy!" came from the fog bank.

Next moment the long-boat and the dinghy vanished from each other's sight: the great fog bank had taken them.

Now a couple of strokes of the port scull would have brought Mr Button alongside the long-boat, so close was he; but the quarter-boat was in his mind, or rather imagination, so what must he do but take three powerful strokes in the direction in which he fancied the quarter-boat to be.

The rest was voices.

"Dinghy ahoy!"

"Ahoy!"

"Ahoy!"

"Don't be shoutin' together, or I'll not know which way to pull. Quarter-boat ahoy! where are yiz?"

"Port your helm!"

"Ay, ay!"—putting his helm, so to speak, to starboard—"I'll be wid yiz in wan minute—two or three minutes' hard pulling."

"Ahoy!"—much more faint.

"What d'ye mane rowin' away from me?"—a dozen strokes.

"Ahoy!"—fainter still.

Mr Button rested on his oars.

"Divil mend them—I b'lave that was the long-boat shoutin'."

He took to his oars again and pulled vigorously.

"Paddy," came Dick's small voice, apparently from nowhere, "where are we now?"

"Sure, we're in a fog; where else would we be? Don't you be affeared."

"I ain't affeared, but Em's shivering."

"Give her me coat," said the oarsman, resting on his oars and taking it off. "Wrap it round her; and when it's round her we'll all let one big halloo together. There's an ould shawl som'er in the boat, but I can't be after lookin' for it now."

He held out the coat and an almost invisible hand took it; at the same moment a tremendous report shook the sea and sky.

"There she goes," said Mr Button; "an' me old fiddle an' all. Don't be frightened, childer; it's only a gun they're firin' for diversion. Now we'll all halloo togither—are yiz ready?"

"Ay, ay," said Dick, who was a picker-up of sea terms.

"Halloo!" yelled Pat.

"Halloo! Halloo!" piped Dick and Emmeline.

A faint reply came, but from where, it was difficult to say. The old man rowed a few strokes and then paused on his oars. So still was the surface of the sea that the chuckling of the water at the boat's bow as she drove forward under the impetus of the last powerful stroke could be heard distinctly. It died out as she lost way, and silence closed round them like a ring.

The light from above, a light that seemed to come through a vast scuttle of deeply-muffed glass, faint though it was, almost to extinction, still varied as the little boat floated through the strata of the mist.

A great sea fog is not homogeneous—its density varies: it is honeycombed with streets, it has its caves of clear air, its cliffs of solid vapour, all shifting and changing place with the subtlety of legerdemain. It has also this wizard peculiarity, that it grows with the sinking of the sun and the approach of darkness.

The sun, could they have seen it, was now leaving the horizon.

They called again. Then they waited, but there was no response.

"There's no use bawlin' like bulls to chaps that's deaf as adders," said the old sailor, shipping his oars; immediately upon which declaration he gave another shout, with the same result as far as eliciting a reply.

"Mr Button!" came Emmeline's voice.

"What is it, honey?"

"I'm—m—'fraid."

"You wait wan minit till I find the shawl—here it is, by the same token!—an' I'll wrap you up in it."

He crept cautiously aft to the stern-sheets and took Emmeline in his arms.

"Don't want the shawl," said Emmeline; "I'm not so much afraid in your coat." The rough, tobacco-smelling old coat gave her courage somehow.

"Well, thin, keep it on. Dicky, are you cowld?"

"I've got into daddy's great-coat; he left it behind him."

"Well, thin, I'll put the shawl round me own shoulders, for it's cowld I am. Are y' hungry, childer?"

"No," said Dick, "but I'm drefful—Hi—yow——"

"Slapy, is it? Well, down you get in the bottom of the boat, and here's the shawl for a pilla. I'll be rowin' again in a minit to keep meself warm."

He buttoned the top button of the coat.

"I'm a'right," murmured Emmeline in a dreamy voice.

"Shut your eyes tight," replied Mr Button, "or Billy Winker will be dridgin' sand in them.

> "'Shoheen, shoheen, shoheen, shoheen,
> Sho—hu—lo, sho—hu—lo.
> Shoheen, shoheen, shoheen, shoheen,
> Hush a by the babby O.'"

It was the tag of an old nursery folk-song they sing in the hovels of the Achill coast fixed in his memory, along with the rain and the wind and the smell of the burning turf, and the grunting of the pig and the knickety-knock of a rocking cradle.

"She's off," murmured Mr Button to himself, as the form in his arms relaxed. Then he laid her gently down beside Dick. He shifted forward, moving like a crab. Then he put his hand to his pocket for his pipe and tobacco and tinder box. They were in his coat pocket, but Emmeline was in his coat. To search for them would be to awaken her.

The darkness of night was now adding itself to the blindness of the fog. The oarsman could not see even the thole pins. He sat adrift mind and body. He was, to use his own expression, "moithered." Haunted by the mist, tormented by "shapes."

It was just in a fog like this that the Merrows could be heard disporting in Dunbeg bay, and off the Achill coast. Sporting and laughing, and hallooing through the mist, to lead unfortunate fishermen astray.

Merrows are not altogether evil, but they have green hair and teeth, fishes' tails and fins for arms; and to hear them walloping in the water around you like salmon, and you alone in a small boat, with the dread of one coming floundering on board, is enough to turn a man's hair grey.

For a moment he thought of awakening the children to keep him company, but he was ashamed. Then he took to the sculls again, and rowed "by the feel of the water." The creak of the oars was like a companion's voice, the exercise lulled his fears. Now and again, forgetful of the sleeping children, he gave a halloo, and paused to listen. But no answer came.

Then he continued rowing, long, steady, laborious strokes, each taking him further and further from the boats that he was never destined to sight again.

DAWN ON A WIDE, WIDE SEA

"Is it aslape I've been?" said Mr Button, suddenly awaking with a start.

He had shipped his oars just for a minute's rest. He must have slept for hours, for now, behold! a warm, gentle wind was blowing, the moon was shining, and the fog was gone.

"Is it dhraming I've been?" continued the awakened one. "Where am I at all, at all? O musha! sure, here I am. O wirra! wirra! I dreamt I'd gone aslape on the main-hatch and the ship was blown up with powther, and it's all come true."

"Mr Button!" came a small voice from the stern-sheets (Emmeline's).

"What is it, honey?"

"Where are we now?"

"Sure, we're afloat on the say, acushla; where else would we be?"

"Where's uncle?"

"He's beyant there in the long-boat—he'll be afther us in a minit."

"I want a drink."

He filled a tin pannikin that was by the beaker of water, and gave her a drink. Then he took his pipe and tobacco from his coat pocket.

She almost immediately fell asleep again beside Dick, who had not stirred or moved; and the old sailor, standing up and steadying himself, cast his eyes round the horizon. Not a sign of sail or boat was there on all the moonlit sea.

From the low elevation of an open boat one has a very small horizon, and in the vague world of moonlight somewhere round about it was possible that the boats might be near enough to show up at daybreak.

But open boats a few miles apart may be separated by long leagues in the course of a few hours. Nothing is more mysterious than the currents of the sea.

The ocean is an ocean of rivers, some swiftly flowing, some slow, and a league from where you are drifting at the rate of a mile an hour another boat may be drifting two.

A slight warm breeze was frosting the water, blending moonshine and star shimmer; the ocean lay like a lake, yet the nearest mainland was perhaps a thousand miles away.

The thoughts of youth may be long, long thoughts, but not longer than the thoughts of this old sailor man smoking his pipe under the stars. Thoughts as long as the world is round. Blazing bar rooms in Callao—harbours over whose oily

25

surfaces the sampans slipped like water-beetles—the lights of Macao—the docks of London. Scarcely ever a sea picture, pure and simple, for why should an old seaman care to think about the sea, where life is all into the fo'cs'le and out again, where one voyage blends and jumbles with another, where after forty-five years of reefing topsails you can't well remember off which ship it was Jack Rafferty fell overboard, or who it was killed who in the fo'cs'le of what, though you can still see, as in a mirror darkly, the fight, and the bloody face over which a man is holding a kerosene lamp.

I doubt if Paddy Button could have told you the name of the first ship he ever sailed in. If you had asked him, he would probably have replied: "I disremimber; it was to the Baltic, and cruel cowld weather, and I was say-sick—till I near brought me boots up; and it was 'O for ould Ireland!' I was cryin' all the time, an' the captin dhrummin me back with a rope's end to the tune uv it—but the name of the hooker—I disremimber—bad luck to her, whoever she was!"

So he sat smoking his pipe, whilst the candles of heaven burned above him, and calling to mind roaring drunken scenes and palm-shadowed harbours, and the men and the women he had known—such men and such women! The derelicts of the earth and the ocean. Then he nodded off to sleep again, and when he awoke the moon had gone.

Now in the eastern sky might have been seen a pale fan of light, vague as the wing of an ephemera. It vanished and changed back to darkness.

Presently, and almost at a stroke, a pencil of fire ruled a line along the eastern horizon, and the eastern sky became more beautiful than a rose leaf plucked in May. The line of fire contracted into one increasing spot, the rim of the rising sun.

As the light increased the sky above became of a blue impossible to imagine unless seen, a wan blue, yet living and sparkling as if born of the impalpable dust of sapphires. Then the whole sea flashed like the harp of Apollo touched by the fingers of the god. The light was music to the soul. It was day.

"Daddy!" suddenly cried Dick, sitting up in the sunlight and rubbing his eyes with his open palms. "Where are we?"

"All right, Dicky, me son!" cried the old sailor, who had been standing up casting his eyes round in a vain endeavour to sight the boats. "Your daddy's as safe as if he was in hivin; he'll be wid us in a minit, an' bring another ship along with him. So you're awake, are you, Em'line?"

Emmeline, sitting up in the old pilot coat, nodded in reply without speaking. Another child might have supplemented Dick's enquiries as to her uncle by questions of her own, but she did not.

Did she guess that there was some subterfuge in Mr Button's answer, and that things were different from what he was making them out to be? Who can tell?

She was wearing an old cap of Dick's, which Mrs Stannard in the hurry and confusion had popped on her head. It was pushed to one side, and she made a quaint enough little figure as she sat up in the early morning brightness, dressed in the old salt-stained coat beside Dick, whose straw hat was somewhere in the bottom of the boat, and whose auburn locks were blowing in the faint breeze.

"Hurroo!" cried Dick, looking around at the blue and sparkling water, and banging with a stretcher on the bottom of the boat. "I'm goin' to be a sailor, aren't I, Paddy? You'll let me sail the boat, won't you, Paddy, an' show me how to row?"

"Aisy does it," said Paddy, taking hold of the child. "I haven't a sponge or towel, but I'll just wash your face in salt wather and lave you to dry in the sun."

He filled the bailing tin with sea water.

"I don't want to wash!" shouted Dick.

"Stick your face into the water in the tin," commanded Paddy. "You wouldn't be going about the place with your face like a sut-bag, would you?"

"Stick yours in!" commanded the other.

Mr Button did so, and made a hub-bubbling noise in the water; then he lifted a wet and streaming face, and flung the contents of the bailing tin overboard.

"Now you've lost your chance," said this arch nursery-strategist, "all the water's gone."

"There's more in the sea."

"There's no more to wash with, not till to-morrow—the fishes don't allow it."

"I want to wash," grumbled Dick. "I want to stick my face in the tin, same's you did; 'sides, Em hasn't washed."

"I don't mind," murmured Emmeline.

"Well, thin," said Mr Button, as if making a sudden resolve, "I'll ax the sharks." He leaned over the boat's side, his face close to the surface of the water. "Halloo there!" he shouted, and then bent his head sideways to listen; the children also looked over the side, deeply interested.

"Halloo there! Are y'aslape— Oh, there y'are! Here's a spalpeen with a dhirty face, an's wishful to wash it; may I take a bailin' tin of— Oh, thank your 'arner, thank your 'arner—good day to you, and my respects."

"What did the shark say, Mr Button?" asked Emmeline.

"He said: 'Take a bar'l full, an' welcome, Mister Button; an' it's wishful I am I had a drop of the crathur to offer you this fine marnin'.' Thin he popped his head under his fin and went aslape agin; leastwise, I heard him snore."

Emmeline nearly always "Mr Buttoned" her friend; sometimes she called him "Mr Paddy." As for Dick, it was always "Paddy," pure and simple. Children have etiquettes of their own.

It must often strike landsmen and landswomen that the most terrible experience when cast away at sea in an open boat is the total absence of privacy. It seems an outrage on decency on the part of Providence to herd people together so. But, whoever has gone through the experience will bear me out that in great moments of life like this the human mind enlarges, and things that would shock us ashore are as nothing out there, face to face with eternity.

If so with grown-up people, how much more so with this old shell-back and his two charges?

And indeed Mr Button was a person who called a spade a spade, had no more conventions than a walrus, and looked after his two charges just as a nursemaid might look after her charges, or a walrus after its young.

There was a large bag of biscuits in the boat, and some tinned stuff—mostly sardines.

I have known a sailor to open a box of sardines with a tin-tack. He was in prison, the sardines had been smuggled into him, and he had no can-opener. Only his genius and a tin-tack.

Paddy had a jack-knife, however, and in a marvellously short time a box of sardines was opened, and placed on the stern-sheets beside some biscuits.

These, with some water and Emmeline's Tangerine orange, which she produced and added to the common store, formed the feast, and they fell to.

When they had finished, the remains were put carefully away, and they proceeded to step the tiny mast.

The sailor, when the mast was in its place, stood for a moment resting his hand on it, and gazing around him over the vast and voiceless blue.

The Pacific has three blues: the blue of morning, the blue of midday, and the blue of evening. But the blue of morning is the happiest: the happiest thing in colour—sparkling, vague, newborn—the blue of heaven and youth.

"What are you looking for, Paddy?" asked Dick.

"Say-gulls," replied the prevaricator; then to himself: "Not a sight or a sound of them! Musha! musha! which way will I steer—north, south, aist, or west? It's all wan, for if I steer to the aist, they may be in the west; and if I steer to the west, they may be in the aist; and I can't steer to the west, for I'd be steering right in the wind's eye. Aist it is; I'll make a soldier's wind of it, and thrust to chance."

He set the sail and came aft with the sheet. Then he shifted the rudder, lit a pipe, leaned luxuriously back and gave the bellying sail to the gentle breeze.

It was part of his profession, part of his nature, that, steering, maybe, straight towards death by starvation and thirst, he was as unconcerned as if he were taking the children for a summer's sail. His imagination dealt little with the future; almost entirely influenced by his immediate surroundings, it could conjure up no fears from the scene now before it. The children were the same.

Never was there a happier starting, more joy in a little boat. During breakfast the seaman had given his charges to understand that if Dick did not meet his father and Emmeline her uncle in a "while or two," it was because he had gone on board a ship, and he'd be along presently. The terror of their position was as deeply veiled from them as eternity is veiled from you or me.

The Pacific was still bound by one of those glacial calms that can only occur when the sea has been free from storms for a vast extent of its surface, for a hurricane down by the Horn will send its swell and disturbance beyond the Marquesas. De Bois in his table of amplitudes points out that more than half the sea disturbances at any given space are caused, not by the wind, but by storms at a great distance.

But the sleep of the Pacific is only apparent. This placid lake, over which the dinghy was pursuing the running ripple, was heaving to an imperceptible swell and breaking on the shores of the Low Archipelago, and the Marquesas in foam and thunder.

Emmeline's rag-doll was a shocking affair from a hygienic or artistic standpoint. Its face was just inked on, it had no features, no arms; yet not for all the dolls in the world would she have exchanged this filthy and nearly formless thing. It was a fetish.

She sat nursing it on one side of the helmsman, whilst Dick, on the other side, hung his nose over the water, on the look-out for fish.

"Why do you smoke, Mr Button?" asked Emmeline, who had been watching her friend for some time in silence.

"To aise me thrubbles," replied Paddy.

He was leaning back with one eye shut and the other fixed on the luff of the sail. He was in his element: nothing to do but steer and smoke, warmed by the sun and cooled by the breeze. A landsman would have been half demented in his condition, many a sailor would have been taciturn and surly, on the look-out for sails, and alternately damning his soul and praying to his God. Paddy smoked.

"Whoop!" cried Dick. "Look, Paddy!"

An albicore a few cables lengths to port had taken a flying leap from the flashing sea, turned a complete somersault and vanished.

"It's an albicore takin' a buck lep. Hundreds I've seen before this; he's bein' chased."

"What's chasing him, Paddy?"

"What's chasin' him?—why, what else but the gibly-gobly-ums!"

Before Dick could enquire as to the personal appearance and habits of the latter, a shoal of silver arrow heads passed the boat and flittered into the water with a hissing sound.

"Thim's flyin' fish. What are you sayin'—fish can't fly! Where's the eyes in your head?"

"Are the gibblyums chasing them too?" asked Emmeline fearfully.

"No; 'tis the Billy balloos that's afther thim. Don't be axin' me any more questions now, or I'll be tellin' you lies in a minit."

Emmeline, it will be remembered, had brought a small parcel with her done up in a little shawl; it was under the boat seat, and every now and then she would stoop down to see if it were safe.

STORY OF THE PIG AND THE BILLY-GOAT

Every hour or so Mr Button would shake his lethargy off, and rise and look round for "sea-gulls," but the prospect was sail-less as the prehistoric sea, wingless, voiceless. When Dick would fret now and then, the old sailor would always devise some means of amusing him. He made him fishing-tackle out of a bent pin and some small twine that happened to be in the boat, and told him to fish for "pinkeens"; and Dick, with the pathetic faith of childhood, fished.

Then he told them things. He had spent a year at Deal long ago, where a cousin of his was married to a boatman.

Mr Button had put in a year as a longshoreman at Deal, and he had got a great lot to tell of his cousin and her husband, and more especially of one, Hannah; Hannah was his cousin's baby—a most marvellous child, who was born with its "buck" teeth fully developed, and whose first unnatural act on entering the world was to make a snap at the "docther." "Hung on to his fist like a bull-dog, and him bawlin' 'Murther!'"

"Mrs James," said Emmeline, referring to a Boston acquaintance, "had a little baby, and it was pink."

"Ay, ay," said Paddy; "they're mostly pink to start with, but they fade whin they're washed."

"It'd no teeth," said Emmeline, "for I put my finger in to see."

"The doctor brought it in a bag," put in Dick, who was still steadily fishing—"dug it out of a cabbage patch; an' I got a trow'l and dug all our cabbage patch up, but there weren't any babies—but there were no end of worms."

"I wish I had a baby," said Emmeline, "and I wouldn't send it back to the cabbage patch."

"The doctor," explained Dick, "took it back and planted it again; and Mrs James cried when I asked her, and daddy said it was put back to grow and turn into an angel."

"Angels have wings," said Emmeline dreamily.

"And," pursued Dick, "I told cook, and she said to Jane, daddy was always stuffing children up with—something or 'nother. And I asked daddy to let me see him stuffing up a child—and daddy said cook'd have to go away for saying that, and she went away next day."

"She had three big trunks and a box for her bonnet," said Emmeline, with a far-away look as she recalled the incident.

"And the cabman asked her hadn't she any more trunks to put on his cab, and hadn't she forgot the parrot cage," said Dick.

"I wish I had a parrot in a cage," murmured Emmeline, moving slightly so as to get more in the shadow of the sail.

"And what in the world would you be doin' with a par't in a cage?" asked Mr Button.

"I'd let it out," replied Emmeline.

"Spakin' about lettin' par'ts out of cages, I remimber me grandfather had an ould pig," said Paddy (they were all talking seriously together like equals). "I was a spalpeen no bigger than the height of me knee, and I'd go to the sty door, and he'd come to the door, and grunt an' blow wid his nose undher it; an' I'd grunt back to vex him, an' hammer wid me fist on it, an' shout 'Halloo there! halloo there!' and 'Halloo to you!' he'd say, spakin' the pigs' language. 'Let me out,' he'd say, 'and I'll give yiz a silver shilling.'

"'Pass it under the door,' I'd answer him. Thin he'd stick the snout of him undher the door an' I'd hit it a clip with a stick, and he'd yell murther Irish. An' me mother'd come out an' baste me, an' well I desarved it.

"Well, wan day I opened the sty door, an' out he boulted and away and beyant, over hill and hollo he goes till he gets to the edge of the cliff overlookin' the say, and there he meets a billy-goat, and he and the billy-goat has a division of opinion.

"'Away wid yiz!' says the billy-goat.

"'Away wid yourself!' says he.

"'Whose you talkin' to?' says t'other.

"'Yourself,' says him.

"'Who stole the eggs?' says the billy-goat.

"'Ax your ould grandmother!' says the pig.

"'Ax me ould *which* mother?' says the billy-goat.

"'Oh, ax me——' And before he could complete the sintence ram, blam, the ould billy-goat butts him in the chist, and away goes the both of thim whirtlin' into the say below.

"Thin me ould grandfather comes out, and collars me by the scruff, and 'Into the sty with you!' says he; and into the sty I wint, and there they kep' me for a fortni't on bran mash and skim milk—and well I desarved it."

They dined somewhere about eleven o'clock, and at noon Paddy unstepped the mast and made a sort of little tent or awning with the sail in the bow of the boat to protect the children from the rays of the vertical sun.

Then he took his place in the bottom of the boat, in the stern, stuck Dick's straw hat over his face to preserve it from the sun, kicked about a bit to get a comfortable position, and fell asleep.

"S-H-E-N-A-N-D-O-A-H"

He had slept an hour and more when he was brought to his senses by a thin and prolonged shriek. It was Emmeline in a nightmare, or more properly a day-mare, brought on by a meal of sardines and the haunting memory of the gibbly-gobbly-ums. When she was shaken (it always took a considerable time to bring her to, from these seizures) and comforted, the mast was restepped.

As Mr Button stood with his hand on the spar looking round him before going aft with the sheet, an object struck his eye some three miles ahead. Objects rather, for they were the masts and spars of a small ship rising from the water. Not a vestige of sail, just the naked spars. It might have been a couple of old skeleton trees jutting out of the water for all a landsman could have told.

He stared at this sight for twenty or thirty seconds without speaking, his head projected like the head of a tortoise. Then he gave a wild "Hurroo!"

"What is it, Paddy?" asked Dick.

"Hurroo!" replied Mr Button. "Ship ahoy! ship ahoy! Lie to till I be afther boardin' you. Sure, they are lyin' to—divil a rag of canvas on her—are they aslape or dhramin'? Here, Dick, let me get aft wid the sheet; the wind'll take us up to her quicker than we'll row."

He crawled aft and took the tiller; the breeze took the sail, and the boat forged ahead.

"Is it daddy's ship?" asked Dick, who was almost as excited as his friend.

"I dinno; we'll see when we fetch her."

"Shall we go on her, Mr Button?" asked Emmeline.

"Ay will we, honey."

Emmeline bent down, and fetching her parcel from under the seat, held it in her lap.

As they drew nearer, the outlines of the ship became more apparent. She was a small brig, with stump topmasts, from the spars a few rags of canvas fluttered. It was apparent soon to the old sailor's eye what was amiss with her.

"She's derelick, bad cess to her!" he muttered; "derelick and done for—just me luck!"

"I can't see any people on the ship," cried Dick, who had crept forward to the bow. "Daddy's not there."

The old sailor let the boat off a point or two, so as to get a view of the brig more fully; when they were within twenty cable lengths or so he unstepped the mast and took to the sculls.

The little brig floated very low on the water, and presented a mournful enough appearance; her running rigging all slack, shreds of canvas flapping at the yards, and no boats hanging at her davits. It was easy enough to see that she was a timber ship, and that she had started a butt, flooded herself and been abandoned.

Paddy lay on his oars within a few strokes of her. She was floating as placidly as though she were in the harbour of San Francisco; the green water showed in her shadow, and in the green water waved the tropic weeds that were growing from her copper. Her paint was blistered and burnt absolutely as though a hot iron had been passed over it, and over her taffrail hung a large rope whose end was lost to sight in the water.

A few strokes brought them under the stern. The name of the ship was there in faded letters, also the port to which she belonged. "*Shenandoah. Martha's Vineyard.*"

"There's letters on her," said Mr Button. "But I can't make thim out. I've no larnin'."

"I can read them," said Dick.

"So c'n I," murmured Emmeline.

"S-H-E-N-A-N-D-O-A-H," spelt Dick.

"What's that?" enquired Paddy.

"I don't know," replied Dick, rather downcastedly.

"There you are!" cried the oarsman in a disgusted manner, pulling the boat round to the starboard side of the brig. "They pritind to tache letters to childer in schools, pickin' their eyes out wid book-readin', and here's letters as big as me face an' they can't make hid or tail of them—be dashed to book-readin'!"

The brig had old-fashioned wide channels, regular platforms; and she floated so low in the water that they were scarcely a foot above the level of the dinghy.

Mr Button secured the boat by passing the painter through a channel plate, then, with Emmeline and her parcel in his arms or rather in one arm, he clambered over the channel and passed her over the rail on to the deck. Then it was Dick's turn, and the children stood waiting whilst the old sailor brought the beaker of water, the biscuit, and the tinned stuff on board.

It was a place to delight the heart of a boy, the deck of the *Shenandoah*; forward right from the main hatchway it was laden with timber. Running rigging lay loose on the deck in coils, and nearly the whole of the quarter-deck was occupied by a deck-house. The place had a delightful smell of sea-beach, decaying wood, tar, and mystery. Bights of buntline and other ropes were dangling from above, only waiting to be swung from. A bell was hung just forward of the foremast. In half a moment Dick was forward hammering at the bell with a belaying pin he had picked from the deck.

Mr Button shouted to him to desist; the sound of the bell jarred on his nerves. It sounded like a summons, and a summons on that deserted craft was quite out of place. Who knew what mightn't answer it in the way of the supernatural?

Dick dropped the belaying pin and ran forward. He took the disengaged hand, and the three went aft to the door of the deck-house. The door was open, and they peeped in.

The place had three windows on the starboard side, and through the windows the sun was shining in a mournful manner. There was a table in the middle of the place. A seat was pushed away from the table as if some one had risen in a hurry. On the table lay the remains of a meal, a teapot, two teacups, two plates. On one of the plates rested a fork with a bit of putrifying bacon upon it that some one had evidently been conveying to his mouth when—something had happened. Near the teapot stood a tin of condensed milk, haggled open. Some old salt had just been in the act of putting milk in his tea when the mysterious something had occurred. Never did a lot of dead things speak so eloquently as these things spoke.

One could conjure it all up. The skipper, most likely, had finished his tea, and the mate was hard at work at his, when the leak had been discovered, or some derelict had been run into, or whatever it was had happened—happened.

One thing was evident, that since the abandonment of the brig she had experienced fine weather, else the things would not have been left standing so trimly on the table.

Mr Button and Dick entered the place to prosecute enquiries, but Emmeline remained at the door. The charm of the old brig appealed to her almost as much as to Dick, but she had a feeling about it quite unknown to him. A ship where no one was had about it suggestions of "other things."

She was afraid to enter the gloomy deck-house, and afraid to remain alone outside; she compromised matters by sitting down on the deck. Then she placed the small bundle beside her, and hurriedly took the rag-doll from her pocket, into which it was stuffed head down, pulled its calico skirt from over its head, propped it up against the coaming of the door, and told it not to be afraid.

There was not much to be found in the deck-house, but aft of it were two small cabins like rabbit hutches, once inhabited by the skipper and his mate. Here there were great findings in the way of rubbish. Old clothes, old boots, an old top-hat of that extraordinary pattern you may see in the streets of Pernambuco, immensely tall, and narrowing towards the brim. A telescope without a lens, a volume of Hoyt, a nautical almanac, a great bolt of striped flannel shirting, a box of fish hooks. And in one corner—glorious find!—a coil of what seemed to be ten yards or so of black rope.

"Baccy, begorra!" shouted Pat, seizing upon his treasure. It was pigtail. You may see coils of it in the tobacconists' windows of seaport towns. A pipe full of it would make a hippopotamus vomit, yet old sailors chew it and smoke it and revel in it.

"We'll bring all the lot of the things out on deck, and see what's worth keepin' an' what's worth leavin'," said Mr Button, taking an immense armful of the old truck; whilst Dick, carrying the top-hat, upon which he had instantly seized as his own special booty, led the way.

"Em," shouted Dick, as he emerged from the doorway, "see what I've got!"

He popped the awful-looking structure over his head. It went right down to his shoulders.

Emmeline gave a shriek.

"It smells funny," said Dick, taking it off and applying his nose to the inside of it—"smells like an old hair brush. Here, you try it on."

Emmeline scrambled away as far as she could, till she reached the starboard bulwarks, where she sat in the scupper, breathless and speechless and wide-eyed. She was always dumb when frightened (unless it were a nightmare or a very sudden shock), and this hat suddenly seen half covering Dick frightened her out of her wits. Besides, it was a black thing, and she hated black things—black cats, black horses; worst of all, black dogs.

She had once seen a hearse in the streets of Boston, an old-time hearse with black plumes, trappings and all complete. The sight had nearly given her a fit, though she did not know in the least the meaning of it.

Meanwhile Mr Button was conveying armful after armful of stuff on deck. When the heap was complete, he sat down beside it in the glorious afternoon sunshine, and lit his pipe.

He had searched neither for food or water as yet; content with the treasure God had given him, for the moment the material things of life were forgotten. And, indeed, if he had searched he would have found only half a sack of potatoes in the caboose, for the lazarette was awash, and the water in the scuttle-butt was stinking.

Emmeline, seeing what was in progress, crept up, Dick promising not to put the hat on her, and they all sat round the pile.

"Thim pair of brogues," said the old man, holding a pair of old boots up for inspection like an auctioneer, "would fetch half a dollar any day in the wake in any sayport in the world. Put them beside you, Dick, and lay hold of this pair of britches by the ends of em'—stritch them."

The trousers were stretched out, examined and approved of, and laid beside the boots.

"Here's a tiliscope wid wan eye shut," said Mr Button, examining the broken telescope and pulling it in and out like a concertina. "Stick it beside the brogues; it may come in handy for somethin'. Here's a book"—tossing the nautical almanac to the boy. "Tell me what it says."

Dick examined the pages of figures hopelessly.

"I can't read 'em," said Dick; "it's numbers."

"Buzz it overboard," said Mr Button.

Dick did what he was told joyfully, and the proceedings resumed.

He tried on the tall hat, and the children laughed. On her old friend's head the thing ceased to have terror for Emmeline.

She had two methods of laughing. The angelic smile before mentioned—a rare thing—and, almost as rare, a laugh in which she showed her little white teeth, whilst she pressed her hands together, the left one tight shut, and the right clasped over it.

He put the hat on one side, and continued the sorting, searching all the pockets of the clothes and finding nothing. When he had arranged what to keep, they flung the rest overboard, and the valuables were conveyed to the captain's cabin, there to remain till wanted.

Then the idea that food might turn up useful as well as old clothes in their present condition struck the imaginative mind of Mr Button, and he proceeded to search.

The lazarette was simply a cistern full of sea water; what else it might contain, not being a diver, he could not say. In the copper of the caboose lay a great lump of putrifying pork or meat of some sort. The harness cask contained nothing except huge crystals of salt. All the meat had been taken away. Still, the provisions and water brought on board from the dinghy would be sufficient to last them some ten days or so, and in the course of ten days a lot of things might happen.

Mr Button leaned over the side. The dinghy was nestling beside the brig like a duckling beside a duck; the broad channel might have been likened to the duck's wing half extended. He got on the channel to see if the painter was safely attached. Having made all secure, he climbed slowly up to the main-yard arm, and looked round upon the sea.

SHADOWS IN THE MOONLIGHT

"Daddy's a long time coming," said Dick all of a sudden.

They were seated on the baulks of timber that cumbered the deck of the brig on either side of the caboose. An ideal perch. The sun was setting over Australia way, in a sea that seemed like a sea of boiling gold. Some mystery of mirage caused the water to heave and tremble as if troubled by fervent heat.

"Ay, is he," said Mr Button; "but it's better late than never. Now don't be thinkin' of him, for that won't bring him. Look at the sun goin' into the wather, and don't be spakin' a word, now, but listen and you'll hear it hiss."

The children gazed and listened, Paddy also. All three were mute as the great blazing shield touched the water that leapt to meet it.

You *could* hear the water hiss—if you had imagination enough. Once having touched the water, the sun went down behind it, as swiftly as a man in a hurry going down a ladder. As he vanished a ghostly and golden twilight spread over the sea, a light exquisite but immensely forlorn. Then the sea became a violet shadow, the west darkened as if to a closing door, and the stars rushed over the sky.

"Mr Button," said Emmeline, nodding towards the sun as he vanished, "where's over there?"

"The west," replied he, staring at the sunset. "Chainy and Injee and all away beyant."

"Where's the sun gone to now, Paddy?" asked Dick.

"He's gone chasin' the moon, an' she's skedadlin' wid her dress brailed up for all she's worth; she'll be along up in a minit. He's always afther her, but he's never caught her yet."

"What would he do to her if he caught her?" asked Emmeline.

"Faith, an' maybe he'd fetch her a skelp—an' well she'd desarve it."

"Why'd she deserve it?" asked Dick, who was in one of his questioning moods.

"Because she's always delutherin' people an' leadin' thim asthray. Girls or men, she moidhers thim all once she gets the comeither on them; same as she did Buck M'Cann."

"Who's he?"

"Buck M'Cann? Faith, he was the village ijit where I used to live in the ould days."

"What's that?"

"Hould your whisht, an' don't be axin' questions. He was always wantin' the moon, though he was twinty an' six feet four. He'd a gob on him that hung open like a rat-trap with a broken spring, and he was as thin as a barber's pole, you could a' tied a reef knot in the middle of 'um; and whin the moon was full there was no houldin' him." Mr Button gazed at the reflection of the sunset on the water for a moment as if recalling some form from the past, and then proceeded. "He'd sit on the grass starin' at her, an' thin he'd start to chase her over the hills, and they'd find him at last, maybe a day or two later, lost in the mountains, grazin' on berries, an' as green as a cabbidge from the hunger an' the cowld, till it got so bad at long last they had to hobble him."

"I've seen a donkey hobbled," cried Dick.

"Thin you've seen the twin brother of Buck M'Cann. Well, one night me elder brother Tim was sittin' over the fire, smokin' his dudeen an' thinkin' of his sins, when in comes Buck with the hobbles on him.

"'Tim,' says he, 'I've got her at last!'

"'Got who?' says Tim.

"'The moon,' says he.

"'Got her where?' says Tim.

"'In a bucket down by the pond,' says t'other, 'safe an' sound an' not a scratch on her; you come and look,' says he. So Tim follows him, he hobblin', and they goes to the pond side, and there, sure enough, stood a tin bucket full of wather, an' on the wather the refliction of the moon.

"'I dridged her out of the pond,' whispers Buck. 'Aisy now,' says he, 'an' I'll dribble the water out gently,' says he, 'an' we'll catch her alive at the bottom of it like a trout.' So he drains the wather out gently of the bucket till it was near all gone, an' then he looks into the bucket expectin' to find the moon flounderin' in the bottom of it like a flat fish.

"'She's gone, bad 'cess to her!' says he.

"'Try again,' says me brother, and Buck fills the bucket again, and there was the moon sure enough when the water came to stand still.

"'Go on,' says me brother. 'Drain out the wather, but go gentle, or she'll give yiz the slip again.'

"'Wan minit,' says Buck, 'I've got an idea,' says he; 'she won't give me the slip this time,' says he. 'You wait for me,' says he; and off he hobbles to his old mother's cabin a stone's-throw away, and back he comes with a sieve.

"'You hold the sieve,' says Buck, 'and I'll drain the water into it; if she 'scapes from the bucket we'll have her in the sieve.' And he pours the wather out of the bucket as gentle as if it was crame out of a jug. When all the wather was out he turns the bucket bottom up, and shook it.

"'Ran dan the thing!' he cries, 'she's gone again;' an' wid that he flings the bucket into the pond, and the sieve afther the bucket, when up comes his old mother hobbling on her stick.

"'Where's me bucket?' says she.

"'In the pond,' say Buck.

"'And me sieve?' says she.

"'Gone afther the bucket.'

"'I'll give yiz a bucketin'!' says she; and she up with the stick and landed him a skelp, an' driv him roarin' and hobblin' before her, and locked him up in the cabin, an' kep' him on bread an' wather for a wake to get the moon out of his head; but she might have saved her thruble, for that day month in it was agin— There she comes!"

The moon, argent and splendid, was breaking from the water. She was full, and her light was powerful almost as the light of day. The shadows of the children and the queer shadow of Mr Button were cast on the wall of the caboose hard and black as silhouettes.

"Look at our shadows!" cried Dick, taking off his broad-brimmed straw hat and waving it.

Emmeline held up her doll to see *its* shadow, and Mr Button held up his pipe.

"Come now," said he, putting the pipe back in his mouth, and making to rise, "and shadda off to bed; it's time you were aslape, the both of you."

Dick began to yowl.

"*I* don't want to go to bed; I aint tired, Paddy—les's stay a little longer."

"Not a minit," said the other, with all the decision of a nurse; "not a minit afther me pipe's out!"

"Fill it again," said Dick.

Mr Button made no reply. The pipe gurgled as he puffed at it—a kind of death-rattle speaking of almost immediate extinction.

"Mr Button!" said Emmeline. She was holding her nose in the air and sniffing; seated to windward of the smoker, and out of the pigtail-poisoned air, her delicate sense of smell perceived something lost to the others.

"What is it, acushla?"

"I smell something."

"What d'ye say you smell?"

"Something nice."

"What's it like?" asked Dick, sniffing hard. "*I* don't smell anything."

Emmeline sniffed again to make sure.

"Flowers," said she.

The breeze, which had shifted several points since midday, was bearing with it a faint, faint odour: a perfume of vanilla and spice so faint as to be imperceptible to all but the most acute olfactory sense.

"Flowers!" said the old sailor, tapping the ashes out of his pipe against the heel of his boot. "And where'd you get flowers in middle of the say? It's dhramin' you are. Come now—to bed wid yiz!"

"Fill it again," wailed Dick, referring to the pipe.

"It's a spankin' I'll give you," replied his guardian, lifting him down from the timber baulks, and then assisting Emmeline, "in two ticks if you don't behave. Come along, Em'line."

He started aft, a small hand in each of his, Dick bellowing.

As they passed the ship's bell, Dick stretched towards the belaying pin that was still lying on the deck, seized it, and hit the bell a mighty bang. It was the last pleasure to be snatched before sleep, and he snatched it.

Paddy had made up beds for himself and his charges in the deck-house; he had cleared the stuff off the table, broken open the windows to get the musty smell away, and placed the mattresses from the captain and mate's cabins on the floor.

When the children were in bed and asleep, he went to the starboard rail, and, leaning on it, looked over the moonlit sea. He was thinking of ships as his wandering eye roved over the sea spaces, little dreaming of the message that the perfumed breeze was bearing him. The message that had been received and dimly understood by Emmeline. Then he leaned with his back to the rail and his hands in his pockets. He was not thinking now, he was ruminating.

The basis of the Irish character as exemplified by Paddy Button is a profound laziness mixed with a profound melancholy. Yet Paddy, in his left-handed way, was as hard a worker as any man on board ship; and as for melancholy, he was the life and soul of the fo'cs'le. Yet there they were, the laziness and the melancholy, only waiting to be tapped.

As he stood with his hands thrust deep in his pockets, longshore fashion, counting the dowels in the planking of the deck by the moonlight, he was reviewing the "old days." The tale of Buck M'Cann had recalled them, and across all the salt seas he could see the moonlight on the Connemara mountains, and hear the sea-gulls crying on the thunderous beach where each wave has behind it three thousand miles of sea.

Suddenly Mr Button came back from the mountains of Connemara to find himself on the deck of the *Shenandoah*; and he instantly became possessed by fears. Beyond the white deserted deck, barred by the shadows of the standing rigging, he could see the door of the caboose. Suppose he should suddenly see a head pop out—or, worse, a shadowy form go in?

He turned to the deck-house, where the children were sound asleep, and where, in a few minutes, he, too, was sound asleep beside them, whilst all night long the brig rocked to the gentle swell of the Pacific, and the breeze blew, bringing with it the perfume of flowers.

THE TRAGEDY OF THE BOATS

When the fog lifted after midnight the people in the long-boat saw the quarter-boat half a mile to starboard of them.

"Can you see the dinghy?" asked Lestrange of the captain, who was standing up searching the horizon.

"Not a speck," answered Le Farge. "Damn that Irishman! but for him I'd have got the boats away properly victualled and all; as it is I don't know what we've got aboard. You, Jenkins, what have you got forward there?"

"Two bags of bread and a breaker of water," answered the steward.

"A breaker of water be sugared!" came another voice; "a breaker half full, you mean."

Then the steward's voice: "So it is; there's not more than a couple of gallons in her."

"My God!" said Le Farge. "*Damn* that Irishman!"

"There's not more than'll give us two half pannikins apiece all round," said the steward.

"Maybe," said Le Farge, "the quarter-boat's better stocked; pull for her."

"She's pulling for us," said the stroke oar.

"Captain," asked Lestrange, "are you sure there's no sight of the dinghy?"

"None," replied Le Farge.

The unfortunate man's head sank on his breast. He had little time to brood over his troubles, however, for a tragedy was beginning to unfold around him, the most shocking, perhaps, in the annals of the sea—a tragedy to be hinted at rather than spoken of.

When the boats were within hailing distance, a man in the bow of the long-boat rose up.

"Quarter-boat ahoy!"

"Ahoy!"

"How much water have you?"

"None!"

The word came floating over the placid moonlit water. At it the fellows in the long-boat ceased rowing, and you could see the water-drops dripping off their oars like diamonds in the moonlight.

"Quarter-boat ahoy!" shouted the fellow in the bow. "Lay on your oars."

"Here, you scowbanker!" cried Le Farge, "who are you to be giving directions—"

"Scowbanker yourself!" replied the fellow. "Bullies, put her about!"

The starboard oars backed water, and the boat came round.

By chance the worst lot of the *Northumberland's* crew were in the long-boat—veritable "scowbankers," scum; and how scum clings to life you will never know, until you have been amongst it in an open boat at sea. Le Farge had no more command over this lot than you have who are reading this book.

"Heave to!" came from the quarter-boat, as she laboured behind.

"Lay on your oars, bullies!" cried the ruffian at the bow, who was still standing up like an evil genius who had taken momentary command over events. "Lay on your oars, bullies; they'd better have it now."

The quarter-boat in her turn ceased rowing, and lay a cable's length away.

"How much water have you?" came the mate's voice.

"Not enough to go round."

Le Farge made to rise, and the stroke oar struck at him, catching him in the wind and doubling him up in the bottom of the boat.

"Give us some, for God's sake!" came the mate's voice; "we're parched with rowing, and there's a woman on board."

The fellow in the bow of the long-boat, as if some one had suddenly struck him, broke into a tornado of blasphemy.

"Give us some," came the mate's voice, "or, by God, we'll lay you aboard!"

Before the words were well spoken the men in the quarter-boat carried the threat into action. The conflict was brief: the quarter-boat was too crowded for fighting. The starboard men in the long-boat fought with their oars, whilst the fellows to port steadied the boat.

The fight did not last long, and presently the quarter-boat sheered off, half of the men in her cut about the head and bleeding—two of them senseless.

*

It was sundown on the following day. The long-boat lay adrift. The last drop of water had been served out eight hours before.

The quarter-boat, like a horrible phantom, had been haunting and pursuing her all day, begging for water when there was none. It was like the prayers one might expect to hear in hell.

The men in the long-boat, gloomy and morose, weighed down with a sense of crime, tortured by thirst, and tormented by the voices imploring for water, lay on their oars when the other boat tried to approach.

Now and then, suddenly, and as if moved by a common impulse, they would all shout out together: "We have none." But the quarter-boat would not believe. It was in vain to hold the breaker with the bung out to prove its dryness, the half-delirious creatures had it fixed in their minds that their comrades were withholding from them the water that was not.

Just as the sun touched the sea, Lestrange, rousing himself from a torpor into which he had sunk, raised himself and looked over the gunwale. He saw the quarter-boat drifting a cable's length away, lit by the full light of sunset, and the spectres in it, seeing him, held out in mute appeal their blackened tongues.

*

Of the night that followed it is almost impossible to speak. Thirst was nothing to what the scowbankers suffered from the torture of the whimpering appeal for water that came to them at intervals during the night.

*

When at last the *Arago*, a French whale ship, sighted them, the crew of the long-boat were still alive, but three of them were raving madmen. Of the crew of the quarter-boat was saved—not one.

PART II

THE ISLAND

"Childer!" shouted Paddy. He was at the cross-trees in the full dawn, whilst the children standing beneath on deck were craning their faces up to him. "There's an island forenint us."

"Hurrah!" cried Dick. He was not quite sure what an island might be like in the concrete, but it was something fresh, and Paddy's voice was jubilant.

"Land ho! it is," said he, coming down to the deck. "Come for'ard to the bows, and I'll show it you."

He stood on the timber in the bows and lifted Emmeline up in his arms; and even at that humble elevation from the water she could see something of an undecided colour—green for choice—on the horizon.

It was not directly ahead, but on the starboard bow—or, as she would have expressed it, to the right. When Dick had looked and expressed his disappointment at there being so little to see, Paddy began to make preparations for leaving the ship.

It was only just now, with land in sight, that he recognised in some fashion the horror of the position from which they were about to escape.

He fed the children hurriedly with some biscuits and tinned meat, and then, with a biscuit in his hand, eating as he went, he trotted about the decks, collecting things and stowing them in the dinghy. The bolt of striped flannel, all the old clothes, a housewife full of needles and thread, such as seamen sometimes carry, the half-sack of potatoes, a saw which he found in the caboose, the precious coil of tobacco, and a lot of other odds and ends he transhipped, sinking the little dinghy several strakes in the process. Also, of course, he took the breaker of water, and the remains of the biscuit and tinned stuff they had brought on board. These being stowed, and the dinghy ready, he went forward with the children to the bow, to see how the island was bearing.

It had loomed up nearer during the hour or so in which he had been collecting and storing the things—nearer, and more to the right, which meant that the brig was being borne by a fairly swift current, and that she would pass it, leaving it two or three miles to starboard. It was well they had command of the dinghy.

"The sea's all round it," said Emmeline, who was seated on Paddy's shoulder, holding on tight to him, and gazing upon the island, the green of whose trees was now visible, an oasis of verdure in the sparkling and seraphic blue.

"Are we going there, Paddy?" asked Dick, holding on to a stay, and straining his eyes towards the land.

"Ay, are we," said Mr Button. "Hot foot—five knots, if we're makin' wan; and it's ashore we'll be by noon, and maybe sooner."

The breeze had freshened up, and was blowing dead from the island, as though the island were making a weak attempt to blow them away from it.

Oh, what a fresh and perfumed breeze it was! All sorts of tropical growing things had joined their scent in one bouquet.

"Smell it," said Emmeline, expanding her small nostrils. "That's what I smelt last night, only it's stronger now."

The last reckoning taken on board the *Northumberland* had proved the ship to be south by east of the Marquesas; this was evidently one of those small, lost islands that lie here and there south by east of the Marquesas. Islands the most lonely and beautiful in the world.

As they gazed it grew before them, and shifted still more to the right. It was hilly and green now, though the trees could not be clearly made out; here, the green was lighter in colour, and there, darker. A rim of pure white marble seemed to surround its base. It was foam breaking on the barrier reef.

In another hour the feathery foliage of the cocoa-nut palms could be made out, and the old sailor judged it time to take to the boat.

He lifted Emmeline, who was clasping her luggage, over the rail on to the channel, and deposited her in the stern-sheets; then Dick.

In a moment the boat was adrift, the mast stepped, and the *Shenandoah* left to pursue her mysterious voyage at the will of the currents of the sea.

"You're not going to the island, Paddy," cried Dick, as the old man put the boat on the port tack.

"You be aisy," replied the other, "and don't be larnin' your gran'mother. How the divil d'ye think I'd fetch the land sailin' dead in the wind's eye?"

"Has the wind eyes?"

Mr Button did not answer the question. He was troubled in his mind. What if the island were inhabited? He had spent several years in the South Seas. He knew the people of the Marquesas and Samoa, and liked them. But here he was out of his bearings.

However, all the troubling in the world was of no use. It was a case of the island or the deep sea, and, putting the boat on the starboard tack, he lit his pipe and leaned back with the tiller in the crook of his arm. His keen eyes had made out from the deck of the brig an opening in the reef, and he was making to run the dinghy abreast of the opening, and then take to the sculls and row her through.

Now, as they drew nearer a sound came on the breeze, a sound faint and sonorous and dreamy. It was the sound of the breakers on the reef. The sea just here was heaving to a deeper swell, as if vexed in its sleep at the resistance to it of the land.

Emmeline, sitting with her bundle in her lap, stared without speaking at the sight before her. Even in the bright, glorious sunshine, and despite the greenery that showed beyond, it was a desolate sight seen from her place in the dinghy. A white, forlorn beach, over which the breakers raced and tumbled, sea-gulls wheeling and screaming, and over all the thunder of the surf.

Suddenly the break became visible, and a glimpse of smooth, blue water beyond. Mr Button unshipped the tiller, unstepped the mast, and took to the sculls.

As they drew nearer, the sea became more active, savage, and alive; the thunder of the surf became louder, the breakers more fierce and threatening, the opening broader.

One could see the water swirling round the coral piers, for the tide was flooding into the lagoon; it had seized the little dinghy and was bearing it along far swifter than the sculls could have driven it. Sea-gulls screamed around them, the boat rocked and swayed. Dick shouted with excitement, and Emmeline shut her eyes *tight*.

Then, as though a door had been swiftly and silently closed, the sound of the surf became suddenly less. The boat floated on an even keel; she opened her eyes and found herself in Wonderland.

THE LAKE OF AZURE

On either side lay a great sweep of waving blue water. Calm, almost as a lake, sapphire here, and here with the tints of the aqua marine. Water so clear that fathoms away below you could see the branching coral, the schools of passing fish, and the shadows of the fish upon the spaces of sand.

Before them the clear water washed the sands of a white beach, the cocoa-palms waved and whispered in the breeze; and as the oarsman lay on his oars to look a flock of bluebirds rose, as if suddenly freed from the tree-tops, wheeled, and passed soundless, like a wreath of smoke, over the tree-tops of the higher land beyond.

"Look!" shouted Dick, who had his nose over the gunwale of the boat. "Look at the *fish!*"

"Mr Button," cried Emmeline, "where are we?"

"Bedad, I dunno; but we might be in a worse place, I'm thinkin'," replied the old man, sweeping his eyes over the blue and tranquil lagoon, from the barrier reef to the happy shore.

On either side of the broad beach before them the cocoa-nut trees came down like two regiments, and bending gazed at their own reflections in the lagoon. Beyond lay waving chapparel, where cocoa-palms and breadfruit trees intermixed with the mammee apple and the tendrils of the wild vine. On one of the piers of coral at the break of the reef stood a single cocoa-palm; bending with a slight curve, it, too, seemed seeking its reflection in the waving water.

But the soul of it all, the indescribable thing about this picture of mirrored palm trees, blue lagoon, coral reef and sky, was the light.

Away at sea the light was blinding, dazzling, cruel. Away at sea it had nothing to focus itself upon, nothing to exhibit but infinite spaces of blue water and desolation.

Here it made the air a crystal, through which the gazer saw the loveliness of the land and reef, the green of palm, the white of coral, the wheeling gulls, the blue lagoon, all sharply outlined—burning, coloured, arrogant, yet tender—heart-breakingly beautiful, for the spirit of eternal morning was here, eternal happiness, eternal youth.

As the oarsman pulled the tiny craft towards the beach, neither he nor the children saw away behind the boat, on the water near the bending palm tree at the break in the reef, something that for a moment insulted the day, and was gone. Something like a small triangle of dark canvas, that rippled through the water and sank from sight; something that appeared and vanished like an evil thought.

It did not take long to beach the boat. Mr Button tumbled over the side up to his knees in water, whilst Dick crawled over the bow.

"Catch hould of her the same as I do," cried Paddy, laying hold of the starboard gunwale; whilst Dick, imitative as a monkey, seized the gunwale to port. Now then:

> "'Yeo ho, Chilliman,
> Up wid her, up wid her,
> Heave O, Chilliman.'

"Lave her be now; she's high enough."

He took Emmeline in his arms and carried her up on the sand. It was from just here on the sand that you could see the true beauty of the lagoon. That lake of sea water forever protected from storm and trouble by the barrier reef of coral.

Right from where the little clear ripples ran up the strand, it led the eye to the break in the coral reef where the palm gazed at its own reflection in the water, and there, beyond the break, one caught a vision of the great heaving, sparkling sea.

The lagoon, just here, was perhaps more than a third of a mile broad. I have never measured it, but I know that, standing by the palm tree on the reef, flinging up one's arm and shouting to a person on the beach, the sound took a perceptible time to cross the water: I should say, perhaps, an almost perceptible time. The distant signal and the distant call were almost coincident, yet not quite.

Dick, mad with delight at the place in which he found himself, was running about like a dog just out of the water. Mr Button was discharging the cargo of the dinghy on the dry, white sand. Emmeline seated herself with her precious bundle on the sand, and was watching the operations of her friend, looking at the things around her and feeling very strange.

For all she knew all this was the ordinary accompaniment of a sea voyage. Paddy's manner throughout had been set to the one idea, not to frighten the "childer"; the weather had backed him up. But down in the heart of her lay the knowledge that all was not as it should be. The hurried departure from the ship, the fog in which her uncle had vanished, those things, and others as well, she felt instinctively were not right. But she said nothing.

She had not long for meditation, however, for Dick was running towards her with a live crab which he had picked up, calling out that he was going to make it bite her.

"Take it away!" cried Emmeline, holding both hands with fingers widespread in front of her face. "Mr Button! Mr Button! Mr Button!"

"Lave her be, you little divil!" roared Pat, who was depositing the last of the cargo on the sand. "Lave her be, or it's a cow-hidin' I'll be givin' you!"

"What's a 'divil,' Paddy?" asked Dick, panting from his exertions. "Paddy, what's a 'divil'?"

"You're wan. Ax no questions now, for it's tired I am, an' I want to rest me bones."

He flung himself under the shade of a palm tree, took out his tinder box, tobacco and pipe, cut some tobacco up, filled his pipe and lit it. Emmeline crawled up, and sat near him, and Dick flung himself down on the sand near Emmeline.

Mr Button took off his coat and made a pillow of it against a cocoa-nut tree stem. He had found the El Dorado of the weary. With his knowledge of the South Seas a glance at the vegetation to be seen told him that food for a regiment might be had for the taking; water, too.

Right down the middle of the strand was a depression which in the rainy season would be the bed of a rushing rivulet. The water just now was not strong enough to come all the way to the lagoon, but away up there "beyant" in the woods lay the source, and he'd find it in due time. There was enough in the breaker for a week, and green "cuca-nuts" were to be had for the climbing.

Emmeline contemplated Paddy for a while as he smoked and rested his bones, then a great thought occurred to her. She took the little shawl from around the parcel she was holding and exposed the mysterious box.

"Oh, begorra, the box!" said Paddy, leaning on his elbow interestedly; "I might a' known you wouldn't a' forgot it."

"Mrs James," said Emmeline, "made me promise not to open it till I got on shore, for the things in it might get lost."

"Well, you're ashore now," said Dick; "open it."

"I'm going to," said Emmeline.

She carefully undid the string, refusing the assistance of Paddy's knife. Then the brown paper came off, disclosing a common cardboard box. She raised the lid half an inch, peeped in, and shut it again.

"*Open* it!" cried Dick, mad with curiosity.

"What's in it, honey?" asked the old sailor, who was as interested as Dick.

"Things," replied Emmeline.

Then all at once she took the lid off and disclosed a tiny tea service of china, packed in shavings; there was a teapot with a lid, a cream jug, cups and saucers, and six microscopic plates, each painted with a pansy.

"Sure, it's a tay-set!" said Paddy, in an interested voice. "Glory be to God! will you look at the little plates wid the flowers on thim?"

"Heugh!" said Dick in disgust; "I thought it might a' been soldiers."

"*I* don't want soldiers," replied Emmeline, in a voice of perfect contentment.

She unfolded a piece of tissue paper, and took from it a sugar-tongs and six spoons. Then she arrayed the whole lot on the sand.

"Well, if that don't beat all!" said Paddy.

"And whin are you goin' to ax me to tay with you?"

"Some time," replied Emmeline, collecting the things, and carefully repacking them.

Mr Button finished his pipe, tapped the ashes out, and placed it in his pocket.

"I'll be afther riggin' up a bit of a tint," said he, as he rose to his feet, "to shelter us from the jew to-night; but I'll first have a look at the woods to see if I can find wather. Lave your box with the other things, Emmeline; there's no one here to take it."

Emmeline left her box on the heap of things that Paddy had placed in the shadow of the cocoa-nut trees, took his hand, and the three entered the grove on the right.

It was like entering a pine forest; the tall symmetrical stems of the trees seemed set by mathematical law, each at a given distance from the other. Whichever way you entered a twilight alley set with tree boles lay before you. Looking up you saw at an immense distance above a pale green roof patined with sparkling and flashing points of light, where the breeze was busy playing with the green fronds of the trees.

"Mr Button," murmured Emmeline, "we won't get lost, will we?"

"Lost! No, faith; sure we're goin' uphill, an' all we have to do is to come down again, when we want to get back—ware nuts!" A green nut detached from up above came down rattling and tumbling and hopped on the ground. Paddy picked it up. "It's a green cucanut," said he, putting it in his pocket (it was not very much bigger than a Jaffa orange), "and we'll have it for tay."

"That's not a cocoa-nut," said Dick; "cocoa-nuts are brown. I had five cents once an' I bought one, and scraped it out and y'et it."

"When Dr Sims made Dicky sick," said Emmeline, "he said the wonder t'im was how Dicky held it all."

"Come on," said Mr Button, "an' don't be talkin', or it's the Cluricaunes will be after us."

"What's cluricaunes?" demanded Dick.

"Little men no bigger than your thumb that make the brogues for the Good People."

"Who's they?"

"Whisht, and don't be talkin'. Mind your head, Em'leen, or the branches'll be hittin' you in the face."

They had left the cocoa-nut grove, and entered the chapparel. Here was a deeper twilight, and all sorts of trees lent their foliage to make the shade. The artu with its delicately diamonded trunk, the great breadfruit tall as a beech, and shadowy as a cave, the aoa, and the eternal cocoa-nut palm all grew here like brothers. Great ropes of wild vine twined like the snake of the laocoon from tree to tree, and all sorts of wonderful flowers, from the orchid shaped like a butterfly to the scarlet hibiscus, made beautiful the gloom.

Suddenly Mr Button stopped.

"Whisht!" said he.

Through the silence—a silence filled with the hum and the murmur of wood insects and the faint, far song of the reef—came a tinkling, rippling sound: it was water. He listened to make sure of the bearing of the sound, then he made for it.

Next moment they found themselves in a little grass-grown glade. From the hilly ground above, over a rock black and polished like ebony, fell a tiny cascade not much broader than one's hand; ferns grew around and from a tree above where a great rope of wild convolvulus flowers blew their trumpets in the enchanted twilight.

The children cried out at the prettiness of it, and Emmeline ran and dabbled her hands in the water. Just above the little waterfall sprang a banana tree laden with fruit; it had immense leaves six feet long and more, and broad as a dinner-table. One could see the golden glint of the ripe fruit through the foliage.

In a moment Mr Button had kicked off his shoes and was going up the rock like a cat, absolutely, for it seemed to give him nothing to climb by.

"Hurroo!" cried Dick in admiration. "Look at Paddy!"

Emmeline looked, and saw nothing but swaying leaves.

"Stand from under!" he shouted, and next moment down came a huge bunch of yellow-jacketed bananas. Dick shouted with delight, but Emmeline showed no excitement: she had discovered something.

DEATH VEILED WITH LICHEN

"Mr Button," said she, when the latter had descended, "there's a little barrel"; she pointed to something green and lichen-covered that lay between the trunks of two trees—something that eyes less sharp than the eyes of a child might have mistaken for a boulder.

"Sure, an' faith it's an' ould empty bar'l," said Mr Button, wiping the sweat from his brow and staring at the thing. "Some ship must have been wathering here an' forgot it. It'll do for a sate whilst we have dinner."

He sat down upon it and distributed the bananas to the children, who sat down on the grass.

The barrel looked such a deserted and neglected thing that his imagination assumed it to be empty. Empty or full, however, it made an excellent seat, for it was quarter sunk in the green soft earth, and immovable.

"If ships has been here, ships will come again," said he, as he munched his bananas.

"Will daddy's ship come here?" asked Dick.

"Ay, to be sure it will," replied the other, taking out his pipe. "Now run about and play with the flowers an' lave me alone to smoke a pipe, and then we'll all go to the top of the hill beyant, and have a look round us.

"Come 'long, Em!" cried Dick; and the children started off amongst the trees, Dick pulling at the hanging vine tendrils, and Emmeline plucking what blossoms she could find within her small reach.

When he had finished his pipe he hallooed, and small voices answered him from the wood. Then the children came running back, Emmeline laughing and showing her small white teeth, a large bunch of blossoms in her hand; Dick flowerless, but carrying what seemed a large green stone.

"Look at what a funny thing I've found!" he cried; "it's got holes in it."

"Dhrap it!" shouted Mr Button, springing from the barrel as if some one had stuck an awl into him. "Where'd you find it? What d'you mane by touchin' it? Give it here."

He took it gingerly in his hands; it was a lichen-covered skull, with a great dent in the back of it where it had been cloven by an axe or some sharp instrument. He hove it as far as he could away amidst the trees.

"What is it, Paddy?" asked Dick, half astonished, half frightened at the old man's manner.

"It's nothin' good," replied Mr Button.

"There were two others, and I wanted to fetch them," grumbled Dick.

"You lave them alone. Musha! musha! but there's been black doin's here in days gone by. What is it, Emmeline?"

Emmeline was holding out her bunch of flowers for admiration. He took a great gaudy blossom—if flowers can ever be called gaudy—and stuck its stalk in the pocket of his coat. Then he led the way uphill, muttering as he went.

The higher they got the less dense became the trees and the fewer the cocoa-nut palms. The cocoa-nut palm loves the sea, and the few they had here all had their heads bent in the direction of the lagoon, as if yearning after it.

They passed a cane-brake where canes twenty feet high whispered together like bulrushes. Then a sunlit sward, destitute of tree or shrub, led them sharply upward for a hundred feet or so to where a great rock, the highest point of the island, stood, casting its shadow in the sunshine. The rock was about twenty feet high, and easy to climb. Its top was almost flat, and as spacious as an ordinary dinner-table. From it one could obtain a complete view of the island and the sea.

Looking down, one's eye travelled over the trembling and waving tree-tops, to the lagoon; beyond the lagoon to the reef, beyond the reef to the infinite space of the Pacific. The reef encircled the whole island, here further from the land, here closer; the song of the surf on it came as a whisper, just like the whisper you hear in a shell; but, a strange thing, though the sound heard on the beach was continuous, up here one could distinguish an intermittency as breaker after breaker dashed itself to death on the coral strand below.

You have seen a field of green barley ruffled over by the wind, just so from the hill-top you could see the wind in its passage over the sunlit foliage beneath.

It was breezing up from the south-west, and banyan and cocoa-palm, artu and breadfruit tree, swayed and rocked in the merry wind. So bright and moving was the picture of the breeze-swept sea, the blue lagoon, the foam-dashed reef, and the rocking trees that one felt one had surprised some mysterious gala day, some festival of Nature more than ordinarily glad.

As if to strengthen the idea, now and then above the trees would burst what seemed a rocket of coloured stars. The stars would drift away in a flock on the wind and be lost. They were flights of birds. All-coloured birds peopled the trees below—blue, scarlet, dove-coloured, bright of eye, but voiceless. From the reef you could see occasionally the sea-gulls rising here and there in clouds like small puffs of smoke.

The lagoon, here deep, here shallow, presented, according to its depth or shallowness, the colours of ultra-marine or sky. The broadest parts were the palest, because the most shallow; and here and there, in the shallows, you might see a faint tracery of coral ribs almost reaching the surface. The island at its broadest might have been three miles across. There was not a sign of house or habitation to be seen, and not a sail on the whole of the wide Pacific.

It was a strange place to be, up here. To find oneself surrounded by grass and flowers and trees, and all the kindliness of nature, to feel the breeze blow, to smoke one's pipe, and to remember that one was in a place uninhabited and unknown. A place to which no messages were ever carried except by the wind or the sea-gulls.

In this solitude the beetle was as carefully painted and the flower as carefully tended as though all the peoples of the civilised world were standing by to criticise or approve.

Nowhere in the world, perhaps, so well as here, could you appreciate Nature's splendid indifference to the great affairs of Man.

The old sailor was thinking nothing of this sort. His eyes were fixed on a small and almost imperceptible stain on the horizon to the sou'-sou'-west. It was no doubt another island almost hull-down on the horizon. Save for this blemish the whole wheel of the sea was empty and serene.

Emmeline had not followed them up to the rock. She had gone botanising where some bushes displayed great bunches of the crimson arita berries as if to show to the sun what Earth could do in the way of manufacturing poison. She plucked two great bunches of them, and with this treasure came to the base of the rock.

"Lave thim berries down!" cried Mr Button, when she had attracted his attention. "Don't put thim in your mouth; thim's the never-wake-up berries."

He came down off the rock, hand over fist, flung the poisonous things away, and looked into Emmeline's small mouth, which at his command she opened wide. There was only a little pink tongue in it, however, curled up like a rose-leaf; no sign of berries or poison. So, giving her a little shake, just as a nursemaid would have done in like circumstances, he took Dick off the rock, and led the way back to the beach.

ECHOES OF FAIRY-LAND

"Mr Button," said Emmeline that night, as they sat on the sand near the tent he had improvised, "Mr Button—cats go to sleep."

They had been questioning him about the "never-wake-up" berries.

"Who said they didn't?" asked Mr Button.

"I mean," said Emmeline, "they go to sleep and never wake up again. Ours did. It had stripes on it, and a white chest, and rings all down its tail. It went asleep in the garden, all stretched out, and showing its teeth; an' I told Jane, and Dicky ran in an' told uncle. I went to Mrs Sims, the doctor's wife, to tea; and when I came back I asked Jane where pussy was—and she said it was deadn' berried, but I wasn't to tell uncle."

"I remember," said Dick. "It was the day I went to the circus, and you told me not to tell daddy the cat was deadn' berried. But I told Mrs James's man when he came to do the garden; and I asked him where cats went when they were deadn' berried, and he said he guessed they went to hell—at least he hoped they did, for they were always scratchin' up the flowers. Then he told me not to tell any one he'd said that, for it was a swear word, and he oughtn't to have said it. I asked him what he'd give me if I didn't tell, an' he gave me five cents. That was the day I bought the cocoa-nut."

The tent, a makeshift affair, consisting of two sculls and a tree branch, which Mr Button had sawed off from a dwarf aoa, and the stay-sail he had brought from the brig, was pitched in the centre of the beach, so as to be out of the way of falling cocoa-nuts, should the breeze strengthen during the night. The sun had set, but the moon had not yet risen as they sat in the starlight on the sand near the temporary abode.

"What's the things you said made the boots for the people, Paddy?" asked Dick, after a pause.

"Which things?"

"You said in the wood I wasn't to talk, else—"

"Oh, the Cluricaunes—the little men that cobbles the Good People's brogues. Is it them you mane?"

"Yes," said Dick, not knowing quite whether it was them or not that he meant, but anxious for information that he felt would be curious. "And what are the good people?"

"Sure, where were you born and bred that you don't know the Good People is the other name for the fairies—savin' their presence?"

"There aren't any," replied Dick. "Mrs Sims said there weren't."

"Mrs James," put in Emmeline, "said there were. She said she liked to see children b'lieve in fairies. She was talking to another lady, who'd got a red feather in her bonnet, and a fur muff. They were having tea, and I was sitting on the hearthrug. She said the world was getting too—something or another, an' then the other lady said it was, and asked Mrs James did she see Mrs Someone in the awful hat she wore Thanksgiving Day. They didn't say anything more about fairies, but Mrs James—"

"Whether you b'lave in them or not," said Paddy, "there they are. An' maybe they're poppin' out of the wood behint us now, an' listenin' to us talkin'; though I'm doubtful if there's any in these parts, though down in Connaught they were as thick as blackberries in the ould days. O musha! musha! the ould days, the ould days! when will I be seein' thim again? Now, you may b'lave me or b'lave me not, but me own ould father—God rest his sowl!—was comin' over Croagh Patrick one night before Christmas with a bottle of whisky in one hand of him, and a goose, plucked an' claned an' all, in the other, which same he'd won in a lottery, when, hearin' a tchune no louder than the buzzin' of a bee, over a furze-bush he peeps, and there, round a big white stone, the Good People were dancing in a ring hand in hand, an' kickin' their heels, an' the eyes of them glowin' like the eyes of moths; and a chap on the stone, no bigger than the joint of your thumb, playin' to thim on a bagpipes. Wid that he let wan yell an' drops the goose an' makes for home, over hedge an' ditch, boundin' like a buck kangaroo, an' the face on him as white as flour when he burst in through the door, where we was all sittin' round the fire burnin' chestnuts to see who'd be married the first.

"'An' what in the name of the saints is the mather wid yiz?' says me mother.

"'I've sane the Good People,' says he, 'up on the field beyant,' says he; 'and they've got the goose,' says he, 'but, begorra, I've saved the bottle,' he says. 'Dhraw the cork and give me a taste of it, for me heart's in me throat, and me tongue's like a brick-kil.'

"An' whin we come to prize the cork out of the bottle, there was nothin' in it; an' whin we went next marnin' to look for the goose, it was gone. But there was the stone, sure enough, and the marks on it of the little brogues of the chap that'd played the bagpipes—and who'd be doubtin' there were fairies after that?"

The children said nothing for a while, and then Dick said:

"Tell us about Cluricaunes, and how they make the boots."

"Whin I'm tellin' you about Cluricaunes," said Mr Button, "it's the truth I'm tellin' you, an' out of me own knowlidge, for I've spoken to a man that's held wan in his hand; he was me own mother's brother, Con Cogan—rest his sowl! Con was six fut two, wid a long, white face; he'd had his head bashed in, years before I was barn, in some ruction or other, an' the docthers had japanned him with a five-shillin' piece beat flat."

Dick interposed with a question as to the process, aim, and object of japanning, but Mr Button passed the question by.

"He'd been bad enough for seein' fairies before they japanned him, but afther it, begorra, he was twiced as bad. I was a slip of a lad at the time, but me hair near turned grey wid the tales he'd tell of the Good People and their doin's. One night they'd turn him into a harse an' ride him half over the county, wan chap on his back an' another runnin' behind, shovin' furze prickles under his tail to make him buck-lep. Another night it's a dunkey he'd be, harnessed to a little cart, an' bein' kicked in the belly and made to draw stones. Thin it's a goose he'd be, runnin' over the common wid his neck stritched out squawkin', an' an old fairy woman afther him wid a knife, till it fair drove him to the dhrink; though, by the same token, he didn't want much dhrivin'.

"And what does he do when his money was gone, but tear the five-shillin' piece they'd japanned him wid aff the top of his hed, and swaps it for a bottle of whisky, and that was the end of him."

Mr Button paused to relight his pipe, which had gone out, and there was silence for a moment.

The moon had risen, and the song of the surf on the reef filled the whole night with its lullaby. The broad lagoon lay waving and rippling in the moonlight to the incoming tide. Twice as broad it always looked seen by moonlight or starlight than when seen by day. Occasionally the splash of a great fish would cross the silence, and the ripple of it would pass a moment later across the placid water.

Big things happened in the lagoon at night, unseen by eyes from the shore. You would have found the wood behind them, had you walked through it, full of light. A tropic forest under a tropic moon is green as a sea cave. You can see the vine tendrils and the flowers, the orchids and tree boles all lit as by the light of an emerald-tinted day.

Mr Button took a long piece of string from his pocket.

"It's bedtime," said he; "and I'm going to tether Em'leen, for fear she'd be walkin' in her slape, and wandherin' away an' bein' lost in the woods."

"I don't want to be tethered," said Emmeline.

"It's for your own good I'm doin' it," replied Mr Button, fixing the string round her waist. "Now come 'long."

He led her like a dog in a leash to the tent, and tied the other end of the string to the scull, which was the tent's main prop and support.

"Now," said he, "if you be gettin' up and walkin' about in the night, it's down the tint will be on top of us all."

And, sure enough, in the small hours of the morning, it was.

FAIR PICTURES IN THE BLUE

"I don't want my old britches on! I don't want my old britches on!"

Dick was darting about naked on the sand, Mr Button after him with a pair of small trousers in his hand. A crab might just as well have attempted to chase an antelope.

They had been on the island a fortnight, and Dick had discovered the keenest joy in life—to be naked. To be naked and wallow in the shallows of the lagoon, to be naked and sit drying in the sun. To be free from the curse of clothes, to shed civilisation on the beach in the form of breeches, boots, coat, and hat, and to be one with the wind and the sun and the sea.

The very first command Mr Button had given on the second morning of their arrival was, "Strip and into the water wid you."

Dick had resisted at first, and Emmeline (who rarely wept) had stood weeping in her little chemise. But Mr Button was obdurate. The difficulty at first was to get them in; the difficulty now was to keep them out.

Emmeline was sitting as nude as the day star, drying in the morning sun after her dip, and watching Dick's evolutions on the sand.

The lagoon had for the children far more attraction than the land. Woods where you might knock ripe bananas off the trees with a big cane, sands where golden lizards would scuttle about so tame that you might with a little caution seize them by the tail, a hill-top from whence you might see, to use Paddy's expression, "to the back of beyond"; all these were fine enough in their way, but they were nothing to the lagoon.

Deep down where the coral branches were you might watch, whilst Paddy fished, all sorts of things disporting on the sand patches and between the coral tufts. Hermit crabs that had evicted whelks, wearing the evicted ones' shells—an obvious misfit; sea anemones as big as roses. Flowers that closed up in an irritable manner if you lowered the hook gently down and touched them; extraordinary shells that walked about on feelers, elbowing the crabs out of the way and terrorising the whelks. The overlords of the sand patches, these; yet touch one on the back with a stone tied to a bit of string, and down he would go flat, motionless and feigning death. There was a lot of human nature lurking in the depths of the lagoon, comedy and tragedy.

An English rock-pool has its marvels. You can fancy the marvels of this vast rock-pool, nine miles round and varying from a third to half a mile broad, swarming with tropic life and flights of painted fishes; where the glittering albicore passed beneath the boat like a fire and a shadow; where the boat's reflection lay as clear on the bottom as though the water were air; where the sea, pacified by the reef, told, like a little child, its dreams.

It suited the lazy humour of Mr Button that he never pursued the lagoon more than half a mile or so on either side of the beach. He would bring the fish he caught ashore, and with the aid of his tinder box and dead sticks make a blazing fire on the sand; cook fish and breadfruit and taro roots, helped and hindered by the children. They fixed the tent amidst the trees at the edge of the chapparel, and made it larger and more abiding with the aid of the dinghy's sail.

Amidst these occupations, wonders, and pleasures, the children lost all count of the flight of time. They rarely asked about Mr Lestrange; after a while they did not ask about him at all. Children soon forget.

PART III

THE POETRY OF LEARNING

To forget the passage of time you must live in the open air, in a warm climate, with as few clothes as possible upon you. You must collect and cook your own food. Then, after a while, if you have no special ties to bind you to civilisation, Nature will begin to do for you what she does for the savage. You will recognise that it is possible to be happy without books or newspapers, letters or bills. You will recognise the part sleep plays in Nature.

After a month on the island you might have seen Dick at one moment full of life and activity, helping Mr Button to dig up a taro root or what not, the next curled up to sleep like a dog. Emmeline the same. Profound and prolonged lapses into sleep; sudden awakenings into a world of pure air and dazzling light, the gaiety of colour all round. Nature had indeed opened her doors to these children.

One might have fancied her in an experimental mood, saying: "Let me put these buds of civilisation back into my nursery and see what they will become—how they will blossom, and what will be the end of it all."

Just as Emmeline had brought away her treasured box from the *Northumberland*, Dick had conveyed with him a small linen bag that chinked when shaken. It contained marbles. Small olive-green marbles and middle-sized ones of various colours; glass marbles with splendid coloured cores; and one large old grandfather marble too big to be played with, but none the less to be worshipped—a god marble.

Of course one cannot play at marbles on board ship, but one can play *with* them. They had been a great comfort to Dick on the voyage. He knew them each personally, and he would roll them out on the mattress of his bunk and review them nearly every day, whilst Emmeline looked on.

One day Mr Button, noticing Dick and the girl kneeling opposite each other on a flat, hard piece of sand near the water's edge, strolled up to see what they were doing. They were playing marbles. He stood with his hands in his pockets and his pipe in his mouth watching and criticising the game, pleased that the "childer" were amused. Then he began to be amused himself, and in a few minutes more he was down on his knees taking a hand; Emmeline, a poor player and an unenthusiastic one, withdrawing in his favour.

After that it was a common thing to see them playing together, the old sailor on his knees, one eye shut, and a marble against the nail of his horny thumb taking aim; Dick and Emmeline on the watch to make sure he was playing fair, their shrill voices echoing amidst the cocoa-nut trees with cries of "Knuckle down, Paddy, knuckle down!" He entered into all their amusements just as one of themselves. On high and rare occasions Emmeline would open her precious box, spread its contents and give a tea-party, Mr Button acting as guest or president as the case might be.

"Is your tay to your likin', ma'am?" he would enquire; and Emmeline, sipping at her tiny cup, would invariably make answer: "Another lump of sugar, if you please, Mr Button;" to which would come the stereotyped reply: "Take a dozen, and welcome; and another cup for the good of your make."

Then Emmeline would wash the things in imaginary water, replace them in the box, and every one would lose their company manners and become quite natural again.

"Have you ever seen your name, Paddy?" asked Dick one morning.

"Seen me which?"

"Your name?"

"Arrah, don't be axin' me questions," replied the other. "How the divil could I see me name?"

"Wait and I'll show you," replied Dick.

He ran and fetched a piece of cane, and a minute later on the salt-white sand in face of orthography and the sun appeared these portentous letters:

B U T T E N

"Faith, an' it's a cliver boy y'are," said Mr Button admiringly, as he leaned luxuriously against a cocoa-nut tree, and contemplated Dick's handiwork. "And that's me name, is it? What's the letters in it?"

Dick enumerated them.

"I'll teach you to do it, too," he said. "I'll teach you to write your name, Paddy—would you like to write your name, Paddy?"

"No," replied the other, who only wanted to be let smoke his pipe in peace; "me name's no use to me."

But Dick, with the terrible gadfly tirelessness of childhood, was not to be put off, and the unfortunate Mr Button had to go to school despite himself. In a few days he could achieve the act of drawing upon the sand characters somewhat like the above, but not without prompting, Dick and Emmeline on each side of him, breathless for fear of a mistake.

"Which next?" would ask the sweating scribe, the perspiration pouring from his forehead—"which next? an' be quick, for it's moithered I am."

"N. N.—that's right—Ow, you're making it crooked!—*that's* right—there! it's all there now—Hurroo!"

"Hurroo!" would answer the scholar, waving his old hat over his own name, and "Hurroo!" would answer the cocoa-nut grove echoes; whilst the far, faint "Hi hi!" of the wheeling gulls on the reef would come over the blue lagoon as if in acknowledgment of the deed, and encouragement.

The appetite comes with teaching. The pleasantest mental exercise of childhood is the instruction of one's elders. Even Emmeline felt this. She took the geography class one day in a timid manner, putting her little hand first in the great horny fist of her friend.

"Mr Button!"

"Well, honey?"

"I know g'ography."

"And what's that?" asked Mr Button.

This stumped Emmeline for a moment.

"It's where places are," she said at last.

"Which places?" enquired he.

"All sorts of places," replied Emmeline. "Mr Button!"

"What is it, darlin'?"

"Would you like to learn g'ography?"

"I'm not wishful for larnin'," said the other hurriedly. "It makes me head buzz to hear them things they rade out of books."

"Paddy," said Dick, who was strong on drawing that afternoon, "look here." He drew a bad depiction of an elephant.

"That's an elephant," he said in a dubious voice.

Mr Button grunted, and the sound was by no means filled with enthusiastic assent. A chill fell on the proceedings.

Dick wiped the elephant slowly and regretfully out, whilst Emmeline felt disheartened. Then her face suddenly cleared; the seraphic smile came into it for a moment—a bright idea had struck her.

"Dicky," she said, "draw Henry the Eight."

Dick's face brightened. He cleared the sand and drew the following figure:

```
    1    1
  < [      ] >
    /    \
```

"*That's* not Henry the Eight," he explained, "but he will be in a minute. Daddy showed me how to draw him; he's nothing till he gets his hat on."

"Put his hat on, put his hat on!" implored Emmeline, gazing alternately from the figure on the sand to Mr Button's face, watching for the delighted smile with which she was sure the old man would greet the great king when he appeared in all his glory.

Then Dick with a single stroke of the cane put Henry's hat on.

```
    ===  1
    1    1
  < [      ] >
    /    \
```

Now, no portrait could be liker to his monk-hunting majesty than the above, created with one stroke of a cane (so to speak), yet Mr Button remained unmoved.

"I did it for Mrs Sims," said Dick regretfully, "and *she* said it was the image of him."

"Maybe the hat's not big enough," said Emmeline, turning her head from side to side as she gazed at the picture. It looked right, but she felt there must be something wrong, as Mr Button did not applaud. Has not every true artist felt the same before the silence of some critic?

Mr Button tapped the ashes out of his pipe and rose to stretch himself, and the class rose and trooped down to the lagoon edge, leaving Henry and his hat a figure on the sand to be obliterated by the wind.

After a while, as time went on, Mr Button took to his lessons as a matter of course, the small inventions of the children assisting their utterly untrustworthy knowledge. Knowledge, perhaps, as useful as any other there amidst the lovely poetry of the palm trees and the sky.

Days slipped into weeks, and weeks into months, without the appearance of a ship—a fact which gave Mr Button very little trouble; and even less to his charges, who were far too busy and amused to bother about ships.

The rainy season came on them with a rush, and at the words "rainy season" do not conjure up in your mind the vision of a rainy day in Manchester.

The rainy season here was quite a lively time. Torrential showers followed by bursts of sunshine, rainbows, and rain-dogs in the sky, and the delicious perfume of all manner of growing things on the earth.

After the rains the old sailor said he'd be after making a house of bamboos before the next rains came on them; but, maybe, before that they'd be off the island.

"However," said he, "I'll dra' you a picture of what it'll be like when it's up;" and on the sand he drew a figure like this:

X

Having thus drawn the plans of the building, he leaned back against a cocoa-palm and lit his pipe. But he had reckoned without Dick.

The boy had not the least wish to live in a house, but he had a keen desire to see one built, and help to build one. The ingenuity which is part of the multiform basis of the American nature was aroused.

"How're you going to keep them from slipping, if you tie them together like that?" he asked, when Paddy had more fully explained his method.

"Which from slippin'?"

"The canes—one from the other?"

"After you've fixed thim, one cross t'other, you drive a nail through the cross-piece and a rope over all."

"Have you any nails, Paddy?"

"No," said Mr Button, "I haven't."

"Then how're you goin' to build the house?"

"Ax me no questions now; I want to smoke me pipe."

But he had raised a devil difficult to lay. Morning, noon, and night it was "Paddy, when are you going to begin the house?" or, "Paddy, I guess I've got a way to make the canes stick together without nailing." Till Mr Button, in despair, like a beaver, began to build.

There was great cane-cutting in the cane-brake above, and, when sufficient had been procured, Mr Button struck work for three days. He would have struck altogether, but he had found a taskmaster.

The tireless Dick, young and active, with no original laziness in his composition, no old bones to rest, or pipe to smoke, kept after him like a bluebottle fly. It was in vain that he tried to stave him off with stories about fairies and Cluricaunes. Dick wanted to build a house.

Mr Button didn't. He wanted to rest. He did not mind fishing or climbing a cocoa-nut tree, which he did to admiration by passing a rope round himself and the tree, knotting it, and using it as a support during the climb; but house-building was monotonous work.

He said he had no nails. Dick countered by showing how the canes could be held together by notching them.

"And, faith, but it's a cliver boy you are," said the weary one admiringly, when the other had explained his method.

"Then come along, Paddy, and stick 'em up."

Mr Button said he had no rope, that he'd have to think about it, that to-morrow or next day he'd be after getting some notion how to do it without rope. But Dick pointed out that the brown cloth which Nature has wrapped round the cocoa-palm stalks would do instead of rope if cut in strips. Then the badgered one gave in.

They laboured for a fortnight at the thing, and at the end of that time had produced a rough sort of wigwam on the borders of the chapparel.

Out on the reef, to which they often rowed in the dinghy, when the tide was low, deep pools would be left, and in the pools fish. Paddy said if they had a spear they might be able to spear some of these fish, as he had seen the natives do away "beyant" in Tahiti.

Dick enquired as to the nature of a spear, and next day produced a ten-foot cane sharpened at the end after the fashion of a quill pen.

"Sure, what's the use of that?" said Mr Button. "You might job it into a fish, but he'd be aff it in two ticks; it's the barb that holds them."

Next day the indefatigable one produced the cane amended; he had whittled it down about three feet from the end and on one side, and carved a fairly efficient barb. It was good enough, at all events, to spear a "groper" with, that evening, in the sunset-lit pools of the reef at low tide.

"There aren't any potatoes here," said Dick one day, after the second rains.

"We've et 'em all months ago," replied Paddy.

"How do potatoes grow?" enquired Dick.

"Grow, is it? Why, they grow in the ground; and where else would they grow?" He explained the process of potato-planting: cutting them into pieces so that there was an eye in each piece, and so forth. "Having done this," said Mr Button, "you just chuck the pieces in the ground; their eyes grow, green leaves 'pop up,' and then, if you dug the roots up maybe, six months after, you'd find bushels of potatoes in the ground, ones as big as your head, and weeny ones. It's like a family of childer—some's big and some's little. But there they are in the ground, and all you have to do is to take a fark and dig a potful of them with a turn of your wrist, as many a time I've done it in the ould days."

"Why didn't we do that?" asked Dick.

"Do what?" asked Mr Button.

"Plant some of the potatoes."

"And where'd we have found the spade to plant them with?"

"I guess we could have fixed up a spade," replied the boy. "I made a spade at home, out of a piece of old board, once—daddy helped."

"Well, skelp off with you, and make a spade now," replied the other, who wanted to be quiet and think, "and you and Em'line can dig in the sand."

Emmeline was sitting near by, stringing together some gorgeous blossoms on a tendril of liana. Months of sun and ozone had made a considerable difference in the child. She was as brown as a gipsy and freckled, not very much taller, but twice as plump. Her eyes had lost considerably that look as though she were contemplating futurity and immensity—not as abstractions, but as concrete images, and she had lost the habit of sleep-walking.

The shock of the tent coming down on the first night she was tethered to the scull had broken her of it, helped by the new healthful conditions of life, the sea-bathing, and the eternal open air. There is no narcotic to excel fresh air.

Months of semi-savagery had made also a good deal of difference in Dick's appearance. He was two inches taller than on the day they landed. Freckled and tanned, he had the appearance of a boy of twelve. He was the promise of a fine man. He was not a good-looking child, but he was healthy-looking, with a jolly laugh, and a daring, almost impudent expression of face.

The question of the children's clothes was beginning to vex the mind of the old sailor. The climate was a suit of clothes in itself. One was much happier with almost nothing on. Of course there were changes of temperature, but they were slight.

Eternal summer, broken by torrential rains, and occasionally a storm, that was the climate of the island; still, the "childer" couldn't go about with nothing on.

He took some of the striped flannel and made Emmeline a kilt. It was funny to see him sitting on the sand, Emmeline standing before him with her garment round her waist, being tried on; he, with a mouthful of pins, and the housewife with the scissors, needles, and thread by his side.

"Turn to the lift a bit more," he'd say, "aisy does it. Stidy so—musha! musha! where's thim scissors? Dick, be holdin' the end of this bit of string till I get the stitches in behint. Does that hang comfortable?—well, an' you're the trouble an' all. How's *that*? That's aisier, is it? Lift your fut till I see if it comes to your knees. Now off with it, and lave me alone till I stitch the tags to it."

It was the mixture of a skirt and the idea of a sail, for it had two rows of reef points; a most ingenious idea, as it could be reefed if the child wanted to go paddling, or in windy weather.

THE DEVIL'S CASK

One morning, about a week after the day on which the old sailor, to use his own expression, had bent a skirt on Emmeline, Dick came through the woods and across the sands running. He had been on the hill-top.

"Paddy," he cried to the old man, who was fixing a hook on a fishing-line, "there's a ship!"

It did not take Mr Button long to reach the hill-top, and there she was, beating up for the island. Bluff-bowed and squab, the figure of an old Dutch woman, and telling of her trade a league off. It was just after the rains, the sky was not yet quite clear of clouds; you could see showers away at sea, and the sea was green and foam-capped.

There was the trying-out gear; there were the boats, the crow's nest, and all complete, and labelling her a whaler. She was a ship, no doubt, but Paddy Button would as soon have gone on board a ship manned by devils, and captained by Lucifer, as on board a South Sea whaleman. He had been there before, and he knew.

He hid the children under a large banyan, and told them not to stir or breathe till he came back, for the ship was "the devil's own ship"; and if the men on board caught them they'd skin them alive and all.

68

Then he made for the beach; he collected all the things out of the wigwam, and all the old truck in the shape of boots and old clothes, and stowed them away in the dinghy. He would have destroyed the house, if he could, but he hadn't time. Then he rowed the dinghy a hundred yards down the lagoon to the left, and moored her under the shade of an aoa, whose branches grew right over the water. Then he came back through the cocoa-nut grove on foot, and peered through the trees over the lagoon to see what was to be seen.

The wind was blowing dead on for the opening in the reef, and the old whaleman came along breasting the swell with her bluff bows, and entered the lagoon. There was no leadsman in her chains. She just came in as if she knew all the soundings by heart—as probably she did—for these whalemen know every hole and corner in the Pacific.

The anchor fell with a splash, and she swung to it, making a strange enough picture as she floated on the blue mirror, backed by the graceful palm tree on the reef. Then Mr Button, without waiting to see the boats lowered, made back to his charges, and the three camped in the woods that night.

Next morning the whaleman was off and away, leaving as a token of her visit the white sand all trampled, an empty bottle, half an old newspaper, and the wigwam torn to pieces.

The old sailor cursed her and her crew, for the incident had brought a new exercise into his lazy life. Every day now at noon he had to climb the hill, on the look-out for whalemen. Whalemen haunted his dreams, though I doubt if he would willingly have gone on board even a Royal Mail steamer. He was quite happy where he was. After long years of the fo'cs'le the island was a change indeed. He had tobacco enough to last him for an indefinite time, the children for companions, and food at his elbow. He would have been entirely happy if the island had only been supplied by Nature with a public-house.

The spirit of hilarity and good fellowship, however, who suddenly discovered this error on the part of Nature, rectified it, as will be presently seen.

The most disastrous result of the whaleman's visit was not the destruction of the "house," but the disappearance of Emmeline's box. Hunt high or hunt low, it could not be found. Mr Button in his hurry must have forgotten it when he removed the things to the dinghy—at all events, it was gone. Probably one of the crew of the whalemen had found it and carried it off with him; no one could say. It was gone, and there was the end of the matter, and the beginning of great tribulation, that lasted Emmeline for a week.

She was intensely fond of coloured things, coloured flowers especially; and she had the prettiest way of making them into a wreath for her own or some one else's head. It was the hat-making instinct that was at work in her, perhaps; at all events, it was a feminine instinct, for Dick made no wreaths.

One morning, as she was sitting by the old sailor engaged in stringing shells, Dick came running along the edge of the grove. He had just come out of the wood, and he seemed to be looking for something. Then he found what he was in search of—a big shell—and with it in his hand made back to the wood.

Item.—His dress was a piece of cocoa-nut cloth tied round his middle. Why he wore it at all, goodness knows, for he would as often as not be running about stark naked.

"I've found something, Paddy!" he cried, as he disappeared among the trees.

"What have you found?" piped Emmeline, who was always interested in new things.

"Something funny!" came back from amidst the trees.

Presently he returned; but he was not running now. He was walking slowly and carefully, holding the shell as if it contained something precious that he was afraid would escape.

"Paddy, I turned over the old barrel and it had a cork thing in it, and I pulled it out, and the barrel is full of awfully funny-smelling stuff—I've brought some for you to see."

He gave the shell into the old sailor's hands. There was about half a gill of yellow liquid in the shell. Paddy smelt it, tasted, and gave a shout.

"Rum, begorra!"

"What is it, Paddy?" asked Emmeline.

"*Where* did you say you got it—in the ould bar'l, did you say?" asked Mr Button, who seemed dazed and stunned as if by a blow.

"Yes; I pulled the cork thing out—"

"*Did yiz put it back?*"

"Yes."

"Oh, glory be to God! Here have I been, time out of mind, sittin' on an ould empty bar'l, with me tongue hangin' down to me heels for the want of a drink, and it full of rum all the while!"

He took a sip of the stuff, tossed the lot off, closed his lips tight to keep in the fumes, and shut one eye.

Emmeline laughed.

Mr Button scrambled to his feet. They followed him through the chapparel till they reached the water source. There lay the little green barrel; turned over by the restless Dick, it lay with its bung pointing to the leaves above. You could see the hollow it had made in the soft soil during the years. So green was it, and so like an object of nature, a bit of old tree-bole, or a lichen-stained boulder, that though the whalemen had actually watered from the source, its real nature had not been discovered.

Mr Button tapped on it with the butt end of the shell: it was nearly full. Why it had been left there, by whom, or how, there was no one to tell. The old lichen-covered skulls might have told, could they have spoken.

"We'll rowl it down to the beach," said Paddy, when he had taken another taste of it.

He gave Dick a sip. The boy spat it out, and made a face, then, pushing the barrel before them, they began to roll it downhill to the beach, Emmeline running before them crowned with flowers.

THE RAT HUNT

They had dinner at noon. Paddy knew how to cook fish, island fashion, wrapping them in leaves, and baking them in a hole in the ground in which a fire had previously been lit. They had fish and taro root baked, and green cocoa-nuts; and after dinner Mr Button filled a big shell with rum, and lit his pipe.

The rum had been good originally, and age had improved it. Used as he was to the appalling balloon juice sold in the drinking dens of the "Barbary coast" at San Francisco, or the public-houses of the docks, this stuff was nectar.

Joviality radiated from him: it was infectious. The children felt that some happy influence had fallen upon their friend. Usually after dinner he was drowsy and "wishful to be quiet." To-day he told them stories of the sea, and sang them songs—chantys:

"I'm a flyin' fish sailor come back from Hong Kong,
Yeo ho! blow the man down.

> Blow the man down, bullies, blow the man down,
> Oh, give us *time* to blow the man down.
> You're a dhirty black-baller come back from New York,
> Yeo ho! blow the man down,
> Blow the man down, bullies, blow the man down.
> Oh, give us time to blow the man down."

"Oh, give us *time* to blow the man down!" echoed Dick and Emmeline.

Up above, in the trees, the bright-eyed birds were watching them—such a happy party. They had all the appearance of picnickers, and the song echoed amongst the cocoa-nut trees, and the wind carried it over the lagoon to where the sea-gulls were wheeling and screaming, and the foam was thundering on the reef.

That evening, Mr Button feeling inclined for joviality, and not wishing the children to see him under the influence, rolled the barrel through the cocoa-nut grove to a little clearing by the edge of the water. There, when the children were in bed and asleep, he repaired with some green cocoa-nuts and a shell. He was generally musical when amusing himself in this fashion, and Emmeline, waking up during the night, heard his voice borne through the moonlit cocoa-nut grove by the wind:

> "There were five or six old drunken sailors
> Standin' before the bar,
> And Larry, he was servin' them
> From a big five-gallon jar.
> "*Chorus.*
> —Hoist up the flag, long may it wave!
> Long may it lade us to glory or the grave.
> Stidy, boys, stidy—sound the jubilee,
> For Babylon has fallen, and the niggers are all set free."

Next morning the musician awoke beside the cask. He had not a trace of a headache, or any bad feeling, but he made Dick do the cooking; and he lay in the shade of the cocoa-nut trees, with his head on a "pilla" made out of an old coat rolled up, twiddling his thumbs, smoking his pipe, and discoursing about the "ould" days, half to himself and half to his companions.

That night he had another musical evening all to himself, and so it went on for a week. Then he began to lose his appetite and sleep; and one morning Dick found him sitting on the sand looking very queer indeed—as well he might, for he had been "seeing things" since dawn.

"What is it, Paddy?" said the boy, running up, followed by Emmeline.

Mr Button was staring at a point on the sand close by. He had his right hand raised after the manner of a person who is trying to catch a fly. Suddenly he made a grab at the sand, and then opened his hand wide to see what he had caught.

"What is it, Paddy?"

"The Cluricaune," replied Mr Button. "All dressed in green he was—musha! musha! but it's only pretindin' I am."

The complaint from which he was suffering has this strange thing about it, that, though the patient sees rats, or snakes, or what not, as real-looking as the real things, and though they possess his mind for a moment, almost immediately he recognises that he is suffering from a delusion.

The children laughed, and Mr Button laughed in a stupid sort of way.

"Sure, it was only a game I was playin'—there was no Cluricaune at all—it's whin I dhrink rum it puts it into me head to play games like that. Oh, be the Holy Poker, there's red rats comin' out of the sand!"

He got on his hands and knees and scuttled off towards the cocoa-nut trees, looking over his shoulder with a bewildered expression on his face. He would have risen to fly, only he dared not stand up.

The children laughed and danced round him as he crawled.

"Look at the rats, Paddy! look at the rats!" cried Dick.

"They're in front of me!" cried the afflicted one, making a vicious grab at an imaginary rodent's tail. "Ran dan the bastes!—now they're gone. Musha, but it's a fool I'm makin' of meself."

"Go on, Paddy," said Dick; "don't stop— Look there—there's more rats coming after you!"

"Oh, whisht, will you?" replied Paddy, taking his seat on the sand, and wiping his brow. "They're aff me now."

The children stood by, disappointed of their game. Good acting appeals to children just as much as to grown-up people. They stood waiting for another access of humour to take the comedian, and they had not to wait long.

A thing like a flayed horse came out of the lagoon and up the beach, and this time Mr Button did not crawl away. He got on his feet and ran.

"It's a harse that's afther me—it's a harse that's afther me! Dick! Dick! hit him a skelp. Dick! Dick! dhrive him away."

"Hurroo! Hurroo!" cried Dick, chasing the afflicted one, who was running in a wide circle, his broad red face slewed over his left shoulder. "Go it, Paddy! go it, Paddy!"

"Kape off me, you baste!" shouted Paddy. "Holy Mary, Mother of God! I'll land you a kick wid me fut if yiz come nigh me. Em'leen! Em'leen! come betune us!"

He tripped, and over he went on the sand, the indefatigable Dick beating him with a little switch he had picked up to make him continue.

"I'm better now, but I'm near wore out," said Mr Button, sitting up on the sand. "But, bedad, if I'm chased by any more things like them it's into the say I'll be dashin'. Dick, lend me your arum."

He took Dick's arm and wandered over to the shade of the trees. Here he threw himself down, and told the children to leave him to sleep. They recognised that the game was over and left him. And he slept for six hours on end; it was the first real sleep he had had for several days. When he awoke he was well, but very shaky.

STARLIGHT ON THE FOAM

Mr Button saw no more rats, much to Dick's disappointment. He was off the drink. At dawn next day he got up, refreshed by a second sleep, and wandered down to the edge of the lagoon. The opening in the reef faced the east, and the light of the dawn came rippling in with the flooding tide.

"It's a baste I've been," said the repentant one—"a brute baste."

He was quite wrong; as a matter of fact, he was only a man beset and betrayed.

He stood for a while, cursing the drink, "and them that sells it." Then he determined to put himself out of the way of temptation. Pull the bung out of the barrel, and let the contents escape?

Such a thought never even occurred to him—or, if it did, was instantly dismissed; for, though an old sailor-man may curse the drink, good rum is to him a sacred thing; and to empty half a little barrel of it into the sea, would be an act almost equivalent to child-murder. He put the cask into the dinghy, and rowed it over to the reef. There he placed it in the shelter of a great lump of coral, and rowed back.

Paddy had been trained all his life to rhythmical drunkenness. Four months or so had generally elapsed between his bouts—sometimes six; it all depended on the length of the voyage. Six months now elapsed before he felt even an inclination to look at the rum cask, that tiny dark spot away on the reef. And it was just as well, for during those six months another whale-ship arrived, watered and was avoided.

"Blisther it!" said he; "the say here seems to breed whale-ships, and nothin' but whale-ships. It's like bugs in a bed: you kill wan, and then another comes. Howsomever, we're shut of thim for a while."

He walked down to the lagoon edge, looked at the little dark spot and whistled. Then he walked back to prepare dinner. That little dark spot began to trouble him after a while; not it, but the spirit it contained.

Days grew long and weary, the days that had been so short and pleasant. To the children there was no such thing as time. Having absolute and perfect health, they enjoyed happiness as far as mortals can enjoy it. Emmeline's highly-strung nervous system, it is true, developed a headache when she had been too long in the glare of the sun, but they were few and far between.

The spirit in the little cask had been whispering across the lagoon for some weeks; at last it began to shout. Mr Button, metaphorically speaking, stopped his ears. He busied himself with the children as much as possible. He made another garment for Emmeline, and cut Dick's hair with the scissors (a job which was generally performed once in a couple of months).

One night, to keep the rum from troubling his head, he told them the story of Jack Dogherty and the Merrow, which is well known on the western coast.

The Merrow takes Jack to dinner at the bottom of the sea, and shows him the lobster pots wherein he keeps the souls of old sailor-men, and then they have dinner, and the Merrow produces a big bottle of rum.

It was a fatal story for him to remember and recount; for, after his companions were asleep, the vision of the Merrow and Jack hobnobbing, and the idea of the jollity of it, rose before him, and excited a thirst for joviality not to be resisted.

There were some green cocoa-nuts that he had plucked that day lying in a little heap under a tree—half a dozen or so. He took several of these and a shell, found the dinghy where it was moored to the aoa tree, unmoored her, and pushed off into the lagoon.

The lagoon and sky were full of stars. In the dark depths of the water might have been seen phosphorescent gleams of passing fish, and the thunder of the surf on the reef filled the night with its song.

He fixed the boat's painter carefully round a spike of coral and landed on the reef, and with a shellful of rum and cocoa-nut lemonade mixed half and half, he took his perch on a high ledge of coral from whence a view of the sea and the coral strand could be obtained.

On a moonlight night it was fine to sit here and watch the great breakers coming in, all marbled and clouded and rainbowed with spindrift and sheets of spray. But the snow and the song of them under the diffused light of the stars produced a more indescribably beautiful and strange effect.

The tide was going out now, and Mr Button, as he sat smoking his pipe and drinking his grog, could see bright mirrors here and there where the water lay in rock-pools. When he had contemplated these sights for a considerable time in complete contentment, he returned to the lagoon side of the reef and sat down beside the little barrel. Then, after a while, if you had been standing on the strand opposite, you would have heard scraps of song borne across the quivering water of the lagoon.

"Sailing down, sailing down,
On the coast of Barbaree."

Whether the coast of Barbary in question is that at San Francisco, or the true and proper coast, does not matter. It is an old-time song; and when you hear it, whether on a reef of coral or a granite quay, you may feel assured that an old-time sailor-man is singing it, and that the old-time sailor-man is bemused.

Presently the dinghy put off from the reef, the sculls broke the starlit waters and great shaking circles of light made rhythmical answer to the slow and steady creak of the thole pins against the leather. He tied up to the aoa, saw that the sculls were safely shipped; then, breathing heavily, he cast off his boots for fear of waking the "childer." As the children were sleeping more than two hundred yards away, this was a needless precaution—especially as the intervening distance was mostly soft sand.

Green cocoa-nut juice and rum mixed together are pleasant enough to drink, but they are better drunk separately; combined, not even the brain of an old sailor can make anything of them but mist and muddlement; that is to say, in the way of thought—in the way of action they can make him do a lot. They made Paddy Button swim the lagoon.

The recollection came to him all at once, as he was walking up the strand towards the wigwam, that he had left the dinghy tied to the reef. The dinghy was, as a matter of fact, safe and sound tied to the aoa; but Mr Button's memory told him it was tied to the reef. How he had crossed the lagoon was of no importance at all to him; the fact that he had crossed without the boat, yet without getting wet, did not appear to him strange. He had no time to deal with trifles like these. The dinghy had to be fetched across the lagoon, and there was only one way of fetching it. So he came back down the beach to the water's edge, cast down his boots, cast off his coat, and plunged in. The lagoon was wide, but in his present state of mind he would have swum the Hellespont. His figure gone from the beach, the night resumed its majesty and aspect of meditation.

So lit was the lagoon by starshine that the head of the swimmer could be distinguished away out in the midst of circles of light; also, as the head neared the reef, a dark triangle that came shearing through the water past the palm tree at the pier. It was the night patrol of the lagoon, who had heard in some mysterious manner that a drunken sailor-man was making trouble in his waters.

Looking, one listened, hand on heart, for the scream of the arrested one, yet it did not come. The swimmer, scrambling on to the reef in an exhausted manner, forgetful evidently of the object for which he had returned, made for the rum cask, and fell down beside it as though sleep had touched him instead of death.

THE DREAMER ON THE REEF

"I wonder where Paddy is?" cried Dick next morning. He was coming out of the chapparel pulling a dead branch after him. "He's left his coat on the sand, and the tinder box in it, so I'll make the fire. There's no use waiting. I want my breakfast. Bother——"

He trod the dead stick with his naked feet, breaking it into pieces.

Emmeline sat on the sand and watched him.

Emmeline had two gods of a sort: Paddy Button and Dick. Paddy was almost an esoteric god wrapped in the fumes of tobacco and mystery. The god of rolling ships and creaking masts—the masts and vast sail spaces of the *Northumberland* were an enduring vision in her mind—the deity who had lifted her from a little boat into this marvellous place, where the birds were coloured and the fish were painted, where life was never dull, and the skies scarcely ever grey.

Dick, the other deity, was a much more understandable personage, but no less admirable, as a companion and protector. In the two years and five months of island life he had grown nearly three inches. He was as strong as a boy of twelve, and could scull the boat almost as well as Paddy himself, and light a fire. Indeed, during the last few months Mr Button, engaged in resting his bones, and contemplating rum as an abstract idea, had left the cooking and fishing and general gathering of food as much as possible to Dick.

"It amuses the craythur to pritind he's doing things," he would say, as he watched Dick delving in the earth to make a little oven—island-fashion—for the cooking of fish or what not.

"Come along, Em," said Dick, piling the broken wood on top of some rotten hibiscus sticks; "give me the tinder box."

He got a spark on to a bit of punk, and then he blew at it, looking not unlike Æolus as represented on those old Dutch charts that smell of schiedam and snuff, and give one mermaids and angels instead of soundings.

The fire was soon sparkling and crackling, and he heaped on sticks in profusion, for there was plenty of fuel, and he wanted to cook breadfruit.

The breadfruit varies in size, according to age, and in colour according to season. These that Dick was preparing to cook were as large as small melons. Two would be more than enough for three people's breakfast. They were green and knobbly on the outside, and they suggested to the mind unripe lemons, rather than bread.

He put them in the embers, just as you put potatoes to roast, and presently they sizzled and spat little venomous jets of steam, then they cracked, and the white inner substance became visible. He cut them open and took the core out—the core is not fit to eat—and they were ready.

Meanwhile, Emmeline, under his directions, had not been idle.

There were in the lagoon—there are in several other tropical lagoons I know of—a fish which I can only describe as a golden herring. A bronze herring it looks when landed, but when swimming away down against the background of coral brains and white sand patches, it has the sheen of burnished gold. It is as good to eat as to look at, and Emmeline was carefully toasting several of them on a piece of cane.

The juice of the fish kept the cane from charring, though there were accidents at times, when a whole fish would go into the fire, amidst shouts of derision from Dick.

She made a pretty enough picture as she knelt, the "skirt" round the waist looking not unlike a striped bath-towel, her small face intent, and filled with the seriousness of the job on hand, and her lips puckered out at the heat of the fire.

"It's so hot!" she cried in self-defence, after the first of the accidents.

"Of course it's hot," said Dick, "if you stick to looward of the fire. How often has Paddy told you to keep to windward of it!"

"I don't know which is which," confessed the unfortunate Emmeline, who was an absolute failure at everything practical: who could neither row nor fish, nor throw a stone, and who, though they had now been on the island twenty-eight months or so, could not even swim.

"You mean to say," said Dick, "that you don't know where the wind comes from?"

"Yes, I know that."

"Well, that's to windward."

"I didn't know that."

"Well, you know it now."

"Yes, I know it now."

"Well, then, come to windward of the fire. Why didn't you ask the meaning of it before?"

"I did," said Emmeline; "I asked Mr Button one day, and he told me a lot about it. He said if he was to spit to windward and a person was to stand to loo'ard of him, he'd be a fool; and he said if a ship went too much to loo'ard she went on the rocks, but I didn't understand what he meant. Dicky, I wonder where he is?"

"Paddy!" cried Dick, pausing in the act of splitting open a breadfruit. Echoes came from amidst the cocoa-nut trees, but nothing more.

"Come on," said Dick; "I'm not going to wait for him. He may have gone to fetch up the night lines"—they sometimes put down night lines in the lagoon—"and fallen asleep over them."

Now, though Emmeline honoured Mr Button as a minor deity, Dick had no illusions at all upon the matter. He admired Paddy because he could knot, and splice, and climb a cocoa-nut tree, and exercise his sailor craft in other admirable ways, but he felt the old man's limitations. They ought to have had potatoes now, but they had eaten both potatoes and the possibility of potatoes when they consumed the contents of that half sack. Young as he was, Dick felt the absolute thriftlessness of this proceeding. Emmeline did not; she never thought of potatoes, though she could have told you the colour of all the birds on the island.

Then, again, the house wanted rebuilding, and Mr Button said every day he would set about seeing after it to-morrow, and on the morrow it would be to-morrow. The necessities of the life they led were a stimulus to the daring and active mind of the boy; but he was always being checked by the go-as-you-please methods of his elder. Dick came of the people who make sewing machines and typewriters. Mr Button came of a people notable for ballads, tender hearts, and potheen. That was the main difference.

"Paddy!" again cried the boy, when he had eaten as much as he wanted. "Hullo! where are you?"

They listened, but no answer came. A bright-hued bird flew across the sand space, a lizard scuttled across the glistening sand, the reef spoke, and the wind in the tree-tops; but Mr Button made no reply.

"Wait," said Dick.

He ran through the grove towards the aoa where the dinghy was moored; then he returned.

"The dinghy is all right," he said. "Where on earth can he be?"

"I don't know," said Emmeline, upon whose heart a feeling of loneliness had fallen.

"Let's go up the hill," said Dick; "perhaps we'll find him there."

They went uphill through the wood, past the water-course. Every now and then Dick would call out, and echoes would answer—there were quaint, moist-voiced echoes amidst the trees—or a bevy of birds would take flight. The little waterfall gurgled and whispered, and the great banana leaves spread their shade.

"Come on," said Dick, when he had called again without receiving a reply.

They found the hill-top, and the great boulder stood casting its shadow in the sun. The morning breeze was blowing, the sea sparkling, the reef flashing, the foliage of the island waving in the wind like the flames of a green-flamed torch. A deep swell was spreading itself across the bosom of the Pacific. Some hurricane away beyond the Navigators or Gilberts had sent this message and was finding its echo here, a thousand miles away, in the deeper thunder of the reef.

Nowhere else in the world could you get such a picture, such a combination of splendour and summer, such a vision of freshness and strength, and the delight of morning. It was the smallness of the island, perhaps, that closed the charm and made it perfect. Just a bunch of foliage and flowers set in the midst of the blowing wind and sparkling blue.

Suddenly Dick, standing beside Emmeline on the rock, pointed with his finger to the reef near the opening.

"There he is!" cried he.

THE GARLAND OF FLOWERS

You could just make the figure out lying on the reef near the little cask, and comfortably sheltered from the sun by an upstanding lump of coral.

"He's asleep," said Dick.

He had not thought to look towards the reef from the beach, or he might have seen the figure before.

"Dicky!" said Emmeline.

"Well?"

"How did he get over, if you said the dinghy was tied to the tree?"

"I don't know," said Dick, who had not thought of this; "there he is, anyhow. I'll tell you what, Em, we'll row across and wake him. I'll boo into his ear and make him jump."

They got down from the rock, and came back down through the wood. As they came Emmeline picked flowers and began making them up into one of her wreaths. Some scarlet hibiscus, some bluebells, a couple of pale poppies with furry stalks and bitter perfume.

"What are you making that for?" asked Dick, who always viewed Emmeline's wreath-making with a mixture of compassion and vague disgust.

"I'm going to put it on Mr Button's head," said Emmeline; "so's when you say boo into his ear he'll jump up with it on."

Dick chuckled with pleasure at the idea of the practical joke, and almost admitted in his own mind for a moment, that after all there might be a use for such futilities as wreaths.

The dinghy was moored under the spreading shade of the aoa, the painter tied to one of the branches that projected over the water. These dwarf aoas branch in an extraordinary way close to the ground, throwing out limbs like rails. The tree had made a good protection for the little boat, protecting it from marauding hands and from the sun; besides the protection of the tree Paddy had now and then scuttled the boat in shallow water. It was a new boat to start with, and with precautions like these might be expected to last many years.

"Get in," said Dick, pulling on the painter so that the bow of the dinghy came close to the beach.

Emmeline got carefully in, and went aft. Then Dick got in, pushed off, and took to the sculls. Next moment they were out on the sparkling water.

Dick rowed cautiously, fearing to wake the sleeper. He fastened the painter to the coral spike that seemed set there by nature for the purpose. He scrambled on to the reef, and lying down on his stomach drew the boat's gunwale close up so that Emmeline might land. He had no boots on; the soles of his feet, from constant exposure, had become insensitive as leather.

Emmeline also was without boots. The soles of her feet, as is always the case with highly nervous people, were sensitive, and she walked delicately, avoiding the worst places, holding her wreath in her right hand.

It was full tide, and the thunder of the waves outside shook the reef. It was like being in a church when the deep bass of the organ is turned full on, shaking the ground and the air, the walls and the roof. Dashes of spray came over with the wind, and the melancholy "Hi, hi!" of the wheeling gulls came like the voices of ghostly sailor-men hauling at the halyards.

Paddy was lying on his right side steeped in profound oblivion. His face was buried in the crook of his right arm, and his brown tattooed left hand lay on his left thigh, palm upwards. He had no hat, and the breeze stirred his grizzled hair.

Dick and Emmeline stole up to him till they got right beside him. Then Emmeline, flashing out a laugh, flung the little wreath of flowers on the old man's head, and Dick, popping down on his knees, shouted into his ear. But the dreamer did not stir or move a finger.

"Paddy," cried Dick, "wake up! wake up!"

He pulled at the shoulder till the figure from its sideways posture fell over on its back. The eyes were wide open and staring. The mouth hung open, and from the mouth darted a little crab; it scuttled over the chin and dropped on the coral.

Emmeline screamed, and screamed, and would have fallen, but the boy caught her in his arms—one side of the face had been destroyed by the larvæ of the rocks.

He held her to him as he stared at the terrible figure lying upon its back, hands outspread. Then, wild with terror, he dragged her towards the little boat. She was struggling, and panting and gasping, like a person drowning in ice-cold water.

His one instinct was to escape, to fly—anywhere, no matter where. He dragged the girl to the coral edge, and pulled the boat up close. Had the reef suddenly become enveloped in flames he could not have exerted himself more to escape from it and save his companion. A moment later they were afloat, and he was pulling wildly for the shore.

He did not know what had happened, nor did he pause to think: he was fleeing from horror—nameless horror; whilst the child at his feet, with her head resting against the gunwale, stared up open-eyed and speechless at the great blue sky, as if at some terror visible there. The boat grounded on the white sand, and the wash of the incoming tide drove it up sideways.

Emmeline had fallen forward; she had lost consciousness.

ALONE

The idea of spiritual life must be innate in the heart of man, for all that terrible night, when the children lay huddled together in the little hut in the chapparel, the fear that filled them was that their old friend might suddenly darken the entrance and seek to lie down beside them.

They did not speak about him. Something had been done to him; something had happened. Something terrible had happened to the world they knew. But they dared not speak of it or question each other.

Dick had carried his companion to the hut when he left the boat, and hidden with her there; the evening had come on, and the night, and now in the darkness, without having tasted food all day, he was telling her not to be afraid, that he would take care of her. But not a word of the thing that had happened.

The thing, for them, had no precedent, and no vocabulary. They had come across death raw and real, uncooked by religion, undeodorised by the sayings of sages and poets.

They knew nothing of the philosophy that tells us that death is the common lot, and the natural sequence to birth, or the religion that teaches us that Death is the door to Life.

A dead old sailor-man lying like a festering carcass on a coral ledge, eyes staring and glazed and fixed, a wide-open mouth that once had spoken comforting words, and now spoke living crabs.

That was the vision before them. They did not philosophise about it; and though they were filled with terror, I do not think it was terror that held them from speaking about it, but a vague feeling that what they had beheld was obscene, unspeakable, and a thing to avoid.

Lestrange had brought them up in his own way. He had told them there was a good God who looked after the world; determined as far as he could to exclude demonology and sin and death from their knowledge, he had rested content with the bald statement that there was a good God who looked after the world, without explaining fully that the same God would torture them for ever and ever, should they fail to believe in Him or keep His commandments.

This knowledge of the Almighty, therefore, was but a half knowledge, the vaguest abstraction. Had they been brought up, however, in the most strictly Calvinistic school, this knowledge of Him would have been no comfort now. Belief in God is no comfort to a frightened child. Teach him as many parrot-like prayers as you please, and in distress or the dark of what use are they to him? His cry is for his nurse, or his mother.

During that dreadful night these two children had no comfort to seek anywhere in the whole wide universe but in each other. She, in a sense of his protection, he, in a sense of being her protector. The manliness in him greater and more beautiful than physical strength, developed in those dark hours just as a plant under extraordinary circumstances is hurried into bloom.

Towards dawn Emmeline fell asleep. Dick stole out of the hut when he had assured himself from her regular breathing that she was asleep, and, pushing the tendrils and the branches of the mammee apples aside, found the beach. The dawn was just breaking, and the morning breeze was coming in from the sea.

When he had beached the dinghy the day before, the tide was just at the flood, and it had left her stranded. The tide was coming in now, and in a short time it would be far enough up to push her off.

Emmeline in the night had implored him to take her away. Take her away somewhere from there, and he had promised, without knowing in the least how he was to perform his promise. As he stood looking at the beach, so desolate and strangely different now from what it was the day before, an idea of how he could fulfil his promise came to him. He ran down to where the little boat lay on the shelving sand, with the ripples of the incoming tide just washing the rudder, which was still shipped. He unshipped the rudder and came back.

Under a tree, covered with the stay-sail they had brought from the *Shenandoah*, lay most of their treasures: old clothes and boots, and all the other odds and ends. The precious tobacco stitched up in a piece of canvas was there, and the housewife with the needles and threads. A hole had been dug in the sand as a sort of cache for them, and the stay-sail put over them to protect them from the dew.

The sun was now looking over the sea-line, and the tall cocoa-nut trees were singing and whispering together under the strengthening breeze.

THEY MOVE AWAY

He began to collect the things, and carry them to the dinghy. He took the stay-sail and everything that might be useful; and when he had stowed them in the boat, he took the breaker and filled it with water at the water source in the wood; he collected some bananas and breadfruit, and stowed them in the dinghy with the breaker. Then he found the remains of yesterday's breakfast, which he had hidden between two palmetto leaves, and placed it also in the boat.

The water was now so high that a strong push would float her. He turned back to the hut for Emmeline. She was still asleep: so soundly asleep, that when he lifted her up in his arms she made no movement. He placed her carefully in the stern-sheets with her head on the sail rolled up, and then standing in the bow pushed off with a scull. Then, taking the sculls, he turned the boat's head up the lagoon to the left. He kept close to the shore, but for the life of him he could not help lifting his eyes and looking towards the reef.

Round a certain spot on the distant white coral there was a great commotion of birds. Huge birds some of them seemed, and the "Hi! hi! hi!" of them came across the lagoon on the breeze as they quarrelled together and beat the air with their wings. He turned his head away till a bend of the shore hid the spot from sight.

Here, sheltered more completely than opposite the break in the reef, the artu trees came in places right down to the water's edge; the breadfruit trees cast the shadow of their great scalloped leaves upon the water; glades, thick with fern, wildernesses of the mammee apple, and bushes of the scarlet "wild cocoa-nut" all slipped by, as the dinghy, hugging the shore, crept up the lagoon.

Gazing at the shore edge one might have imagined it the edge of a lake, but for the thunder of the Pacific upon the distant reef; and even that did not destroy the impression, but only lent a strangeness to it.

A lake in the midst of the ocean, that is what the lagoon really was.

Here and there cocoa-nut trees slanted over the water, mirroring their delicate stems, and tracing their clear-cut shadows on the sandy bottom a fathom deep below.

He kept close in-shore for the sake of the shelter of the trees. His object was to find some place where they might stop permanently, and put up a tent. He was seeking a new home, in fact. But, pretty as were the glades they passed, they were not attractive places to live in. There were too many trees, or the ferns were too deep. He was seeking air and space, and suddenly he found it. Rounding a little cape, all blazing with the scarlet of the wild cocoa-nut, the dinghy broke into a new world.

Before her lay a great sweep of the palest blue wind-swept water, down to which came a broad green sward of park-like land set on either side with deep groves, and leading up and away to higher land, where, above the massive and motionless green of the great breadfruit trees, the palm trees swayed and fluttered their pale green feathers in the breeze. The pale colour of the water was due to the extreme shallowness of the lagoon just here. So shallow was it that one could see brown spaces indicating beds of dead and rotten coral, and splashes of darkest sapphire where the deep pools lay. The reef lay more than half a mile from the shore: a great way out, it seemed, so far out that its cramping influence was removed, and one had the impression of wide and unbroken sea.

Dick rested on his oars, and let the dinghy float whilst he looked around him. He had come some four miles and a half, and this was right at the back of the island. As the boat drifting shoreward touched the bank, Emmeline awakened from her sleep, sat up, and looked around her.

BOOK II
PART I

UNDER THE ARTU TREE

On the edge of the green sward, between a diamond-chequered artu trunk and the massive bole of a breadfruit, a house had come into being. It was not much larger than a big hen-house, but quite sufficient for the needs of two people in a climate of eternal summer. It was built of bamboos, and thatched with a double thatch of palmetto leaves, so neatly built, and so well thatched, that one might have fancied it the production of several skilled workmen.

The breadfruit tree was barren of fruit, as these trees sometimes are, whole groves of them ceasing to bear for some mysterious reason only known to Nature. It was green now, but when suffering its yearly change the great scalloped leaves would take all imaginable tinges of gold and bronze and amber. Beyond the artu was a little clearing, where the chapparel had been carefully removed and taro roots planted.

Stepping from the house doorway on to the sward you might have fancied yourself, except for the tropical nature of the foliage, in some English park.

Looking to the right, the eye became lost in the woods, where all tints of green were tinging the foliage, and the bushes of the wild cocoa-nut burned scarlet as haw-berries.

The house had a doorway, but no door. It might have been said to have a double roof, for the breadfruit foliage above gave good shelter during the rains. Inside it was bare enough. Dried, sweet-smelling ferns covered the floor. Two sails, rolled up, lay on either side of the doorway. There was a rude shelf attached to one of the walls, and on the shelf some bowls made of cocoa-nut shell. The people to whom the place belonged evidently did not trouble it much with their presence, using it only at night, and as a refuge from the dew.

Sitting on the grass by the doorway, sheltered by the breadfruit shade, yet with the hot rays of the afternoon sun just touching her naked feet, was a girl. A girl of fifteen or sixteen, naked, except for a kilt of gaily-striped material reaching from her waist to her knees. Her long black hair was drawn back from the forehead, and tied behind with a loop of the elastic vine. A scarlet blossom was stuck behind her right ear, after the fashion of a clerk's pen. Her face was beautiful, powdered with tiny freckles; especially under the eyes, which were of a deep, tranquil blue-grey. She half sat, half lay on her left side; whilst before her, quite close, strutted up and down on the grass, a bird, with blue plumage, coral-red beak, and bright, watchful eyes.

The girl was Emmeline Lestrange. Just by her elbow stood a little bowl made from half a cocoa-nut, and filled with some white substance with which she was feeding the bird. Dick had found it in the woods two years ago, quite small, deserted by its mother, and starving. They had fed it and tamed it, and it was now one of the family; roosting on the roof at night, and appearing regularly at meal times.

All at once she held out her hand; the bird flew into the air, lit on her forefinger and balanced itself, sinking its head between its shoulders, and uttering the sound which formed its entire vocabulary and one means of vocal expression—a sound from which it had derived its name.

"Koko," said Emmeline, "where is Dick?"

The bird turned his head about, as if he were searching for his master; and the girl lay back lazily on the grass, laughing, and holding him up poised on her finger, as if he were some enamelled jewel she wished to admire at a little distance. They made a pretty picture under the cave-like shadow of the breadfruit leaves; and it was difficult to understand how this young girl, so perfectly formed, so fully developed, and so beautiful, had evolved from plain little Emmeline Lestrange. And the whole thing, as far as the beauty of her was concerned, had happened during the last six months.

HALF CHILD-HALF SAVAGE

Five rainy seasons had passed and gone since the tragic occurrence on the reef. Five long years the breakers had thundered, and the sea-gulls had cried round the figure whose spell had drawn a mysterious barrier across the lagoon.

The children had never returned to the old place. They had kept entirely to the back of the island and the woods—the lagoon, down to a certain point, and the reef; a wide enough and beautiful enough world, but a hopeless world, as far as help from civilisation was concerned. For, of the few ships that touched at the island in the course of years, how many would explore the lagoon or woods? Perhaps not one.

Occasionally Dick would make an excursion in the dinghy to the old place, but Emmeline refused to accompany him. He went chiefly to obtain bananas; for on the whole island there was but one clump of banana trees—that near the water source in the wood, where the old green skulls had been discovered, and the little barrel.

She had never quite recovered from the occurrence on the reef. Something had been shown to her, the purport of which she vaguely understood, and it had filled her with horror and a terror of the place where it had occurred. Dick was quite different. He had been frightened enough at first; but the feeling wore away in time.

Dick had built three houses in succession during the five years. He had laid out a patch of taro and another of sweet potatoes. He knew every pool on the reef for two miles either way, and the forms of their inhabitants; and though he did not know the names of the creatures to be found there, he made a profound study of their habits.

He had seen some astonishing things during these five years—from a fight between a whale and two thrashers conducted outside the reef, lasting an hour, and dyeing the breaking waves with blood, to the poisoning of the fish in the lagoon by fresh water, due to an extraordinarily heavy rainy season.

He knew the woods of the back of the island by heart, and the forms of life that inhabited them—butterflies, and moths, and birds, lizards, and insects of strange shape; extraordinary orchids—some filthy-looking, the very image of corruption, some beautiful, and all strange. He found melons and guavas, and breadfruit, the red apple of Tahiti, and the great Brazilian plum, taro in plenty, and a dozen other good things—but there were no bananas. This made him unhappy at times, for he was human.

Though Emmeline had asked Koko for Dick's whereabouts, it was only a remark made by way of making conversation, for she could hear him in the little cane-brake which lay close by amidst the trees.

In a few minutes he appeared, dragging after him two canes which he had just cut, and wiping the perspiration off his brow with his naked arm. He had an old pair of trousers on—part of the truck salved long ago from the *Shenandoah*—nothing else, and he was well worth looking at and considering, both from a physical and psychological point of view.

Auburn-haired and tall, looking more like seventeen than sixteen, with a restless and daring expression, half a child, half a man, half a civilised being, half a savage, he had both progressed and retrograded during the five years of savage life. He sat down beside Emmeline, flung the canes beside him, tried the edge of the old butcher's knife with which he had cut them, then, taking one of the canes across his knee, he began whittling at it.

"What are you making?" asked Emmeline, releasing the bird, which flew into one of the branches of the artu and rested there, a blue point amidst the dark green.

"Fish-spear," replied Dick.

Without being taciturn, he rarely wasted words. Life was all business for him. He would talk to Emmeline, but always in short sentences; and he had developed the habit of talking to inanimate things, to the fish-spear he was carving, or the bowl he was fashioning from a cocoa-nut.

As for Emmeline, even as a child she had never been talkative. There was something mysterious in her personality, something secretive. Her mind seemed half submerged in twilight. Though she spoke little, and though the subject of their conversations was almost entirely material and relative to their everyday needs, her mind would wander into abstract fields and the land of chimerae and dreams. What she found there no one knew—least of all, perhaps, herself.

As for Dick, he would sometimes talk and mutter to himself, as if in a reverie; but if you caught the words, you would find that they referred to no abstraction, but to some trifle he had on hand. He seemed entirely bound up in the moment, and to have forgotten the past as completely as though it had never been.

Yet he had his contemplative moods. He would lie with his face over a rock-pool by the hour, watching the strange forms of life to be seen there, or sit in the woods motionless as a stone, watching the birds and the swift-slipping lizards. The birds came so close that he could easily have knocked them over, but he never hurt one or interfered in any way with the wild life of the woods.

The island, the lagoon, and the reef were for him the three volumes of a great picture book, as they were for Emmeline, though in a different manner. The colour and the beauty of it all fed some mysterious want in her soul. Her life was a long reverie, a beautiful vision—troubled with shadows. Across all the blue and coloured spaces that meant months and years she could still see as in a glass dimly the *Northumberland*, smoking against the wild background of fog; her uncle's face, Boston—a vague and dark picture beyond a storm—and nearer, the tragic form on the reef that still haunted terribly her dreams. But she never spoke of these things to Dick. Just as she kept the secret of what was in her box, and the secret of her trouble whenever she lost it, she kept the secret of her feelings about these things.

Born of these things there remained with her always a vague terror: the terror of losing Dick. Mrs Stannard, her uncle, the dim people she had known in Boston, all had passed away out of her life like a dream and shadows. The other one too, most horribly. What if Dick were taken from her as well?

This haunting trouble had been with her a long time; up to a few months ago it had been mainly personal and selfish—the dread of being left alone. But lately it had altered and become more acute. Dick had changed in her eyes, and the fear was now for him. Her own personality had suddenly and strangely become merged in his. The idea of life without him was unthinkable, yet the trouble remained, a menace in the blue.

Some days it would be worse than others. To-day, for instance, it was worse than yesterday, as though some danger had crept close to them during the night. Yet the sky and sea were stainless, the sun shone on tree and flower, the west wind brought the tune of the far-away reef like a lullaby. There was nothing to hint of danger or the need of distrust.

At last Dick finished his spear and rose to his feet.

"Where are you going?" asked Emmeline.

"The reef," he replied. "The tide's going out."

"I'll go with you," said she.

He went into the house and stowed the precious knife away. Then he came out, spear in one hand, and half a fathom of liana in the other. The liana was for the purpose of stringing the fish on, should the catch be large. He led the way down the grassy sward to the lagoon where the dinghy lay, close up to the bank, and moored to a post driven into the soft soil. Emmeline got in, and, taking the sculls, he pushed off. The tide was going out.

I have said that the reef just here lay a great way out from the shore. The lagoon was so shallow that at low tide one could have waded almost right across it, were it not for pot-holes here and there—ten-feet traps—and great beds of rotten coral, into which one would sink as into brushwood, to say nothing of the nettle coral that stings like a bed of nettles. There were also other dangers. Tropical shallows are full of wild surprises in the way of life—and death.

Dick had long ago marked out in his memory the soundings of the lagoon, and it was fortunate that he possessed the special sense of location which is the main stand-by of the hunter and the savage, for, from the disposition of the coral in ribs, the water from the shore edge to the reef ran in lanes. Only two of these lanes gave a clear, fair way from the shore edge to the reef; had you followed the others, even in a boat of such shallow draught as the dinghy, you would have found yourself stranded half-way across, unless, indeed, it were a spring tide.

Half-way across the sound of the surf on the barrier became louder, and the everlasting and monotonous cry of the gulls came on the breeze. It was lonely out here, and, looking back, the shore seemed a great way off. It was lonelier still on the reef.

Dick tied up the boat to a projection of coral, and helped Emmeline to land. The sun was creeping down into the west, the tide was nearly half out, and large pools of water lay glittering like burnished shields in the sunlight. Dick, with his precious spear beside him, sat calmly down on a ledge of coral, and began to divest himself of his one and only garment.

Emmeline turned away her head and contemplated the distant shore, which seemed thrice as far off as it was in reality. When she turned her head again he was racing along the edge of the surf. He and his spear silhouetted against the spindrift and dazzling foam formed a picture savage enough, and well in keeping with the general desolation of the background. She watched him lie down and cling to a piece of coral, whilst the surf rushed round and over him, and then rise and shake himself like a dog, and pursue his gambols, his body all glittering with the wet.

Sometimes a whoop would come on the breeze, mixing with the sound of the surf and the cry of the gulls, and she would see him plunge his spear into a pool, and the next moment the spear would be held aloft with something struggling and glittering at the end of it.

He was quite different out here on the reef to what he was ashore. The surroundings here seemed to develop all that was savage in him, in a startling way; and he would kill, and kill, just for the pleasure of killing, destroying more fish than they could possibly use.

THE DEMON OF THE REEF

The romance of coral has still to be written. There still exists a widespread opinion that the coral reef and the coral island are the work of an "insect." This fabulous insect, accredited with the genius of Brunel and the patience of Job, has been humorously enough held up before the children of many generations as an example of industry—a thing to be admired, a model to be followed.

H. de Vere Stacpoole

As a matter of fact, nothing could be more slothful or slow, more given up to a life of ease and degeneracy, than the "reef-building polypifer"—to give him his scientific name. He is the hobo of the animal world, but, unlike the hobo, he does not even tramp for a living. He exists as a sluggish and gelatinous worm; he attracts to himself calcareous elements from the water to make himself a house—mark you, the sea does the building—he dies, and he leaves his house behind him—and a reputation for industry, beside which the reputation of the ant turns pale, and that of the bee becomes of little account.

On a coral reef you are treading on rock that the reef-building polypifers of ages have left behind them as evidences of their idle and apparently useless lives. You might fancy that the reef is formed of dead rock, but it is not: that is where the wonder of the thing comes in—a coral reef is half alive. If it were not, it would not resist the action of the sea ten years. The live part of the reef is just where the breakers come in and beyond. The gelatinous rock-building polypifers die almost at once, if exposed to the sun or if left uncovered by water.

Sometimes, at very low tide, if you have courage enough to risk being swept away by the breakers, going as far out on the reef as you can, you may catch a glimpse of them in their living state—great mounds and masses of what seems rock, but which is a honeycomb of coral, whose cells are filled with the living polypifers. Those in the uppermost cells are usually dead, but lower down they are living.

Always dying, always being renewed, devoured by fish, attacked by the sea—that is the life of a coral reef. It is a thing as living as a cabbage or a tree. Every storm tears a piece off the reef, which the living coral replaces; wounds occur in it which actually granulate and heal as wounds do of the human body.

There is nothing, perhaps, more mysterious in nature than this fact of the existence of a living land: a land that repairs itself, when injured, by vital processes, and resists the eternal attack of the sea by vital force, especially when we think of the extent of some of these lagoon islands or atolls, whose existences are an eternal battle with the waves.

Unlike the island of this story (which is an island surrounded by a barrier reef of coral surrounding a space of sea—the lagoon), the reef forms the island. The reef may be grown over by trees, or it may be perfectly destitute of important vegetation, or it may be crusted with islets. Some islets may exist within the lagoon, but as often as not it is just a great empty lake floored with sand and coral, peopled with life different to the life of the outside ocean, protected from the waves, and reflecting the sky like a mirror.

When we remember that the atoll is a living thing, an organic whole, as full of life, though not so highly organised, as a tortoise, the meanest imagination must be struck with the immensity of one of the structures.

Vliegen atoll in the Low Archipelago, measured from lagoon edge to lagoon edge, is sixty miles long by twenty miles broad, at its broadest part. In the Marshall Archipelago, Rimsky Korsacoff is fifty-four miles long and twenty miles broad; and Rimsky Korsacoff is a living thing, secreting, excreting, and growing—more highly organised than the cocoa-nut trees that grow upon its back, or the blossoms that powder the hotoo trees in its groves.

The story of coral is the story of a world, and the longest chapter in that story concerns itself with coral's infinite variety and form.

Out on the margin of the reef where Dick was spearing fish, you might have seen a peach-blossom-coloured lichen on the rock. This lichen was a form of coral. Coral growing upon coral, and in the pools at the edge of the surf branching corals also of the colour of a peach bloom.

Within a hundred yards of where Emmeline was sitting, the pools contained corals of all colours, from lake-red to pure white, and the lagoon behind her—corals of the quaintest and strangest forms.

Dick had speared several fish, and had left them lying on the reef to be picked up later on. Tired of killing, he was now wandering along, examining the various living things he came across.

Huge slugs inhabited the reef, slugs as big as parsnips, and somewhat of the same shape; they were a species of Bech de mer. Globe-shaped jelly-fish as big as oranges, great cuttlefish bones flat and shining and white, shark's teeth, spines of echini; sometimes a dead scarus fish, its stomach distended with bits of coral on which it had been feeding; crabs, sea urchins, sea-weeds of strange colour and shape; star-fish, some tiny and of the colour of cayenne pepper, some huge and pale. These and a thousand other things, beautiful or strange, were to be found on the reef.

Dick had laid his spear down, and was exploring a deep bath-like pool. He had waded up to his knees, and was in the act of wading further when he was suddenly seized by the foot. It was just as if his ankle had been suddenly caught in a clove hitch and the rope drawn tight. He screamed out with pain and terror, and suddenly and viciously a whip-lash shot out from the water, lassoed him round the left knee, drew itself taut, and held him.

WHAT BEAUTY CONCEALED

Emmeline, seated on the coral rock, had almost forgotten Dick for a moment. The sun was setting, and the warm amber light of the sunset shone on reef and rock-pool. Just at sunset and low tide the reef had a peculiar fascination for her. It had the low-tide smell of sea-weed exposed to the air, and the torment and trouble of the breakers seemed eased. Before her, and on either side, the foam-dashed coral glowed in amber and gold, and the great Pacific came glassing and glittering in, voiceless and peaceful, till it reached the strand and burst into song and spray.

Here, just as on the hill-top at the other side of the island, you could mark the rhythm of the rollers. "Forever, and forever—forever, and forever," they seemed to say.

The cry of the gulls came mixed with the spray on the breeze. They haunted the reef like uneasy spirits, always complaining, never at rest; but at sunset their cry seemed farther away and less melancholy, perhaps because just then the whole island world seemed bathed in the spirit of peace.

She turned from the sea prospect and looked backwards over the lagoon to the island. She could make out the broad green glade beside which their little house lay, and a spot of yellow, which was the thatch of the house, just by the artu tree, and nearly hidden by the shadow of the breadfruit. Over the woods the fronds of the great cocoa-nut palms showed above every other tree silhouetted against the dim, dark blue of the eastern sky.

Seen by the enchanted light of sunset, the whole picture had an unreal look, more lovely than a dream. At dawn—and Dick would often start for the reef before dawn, if the tide served—the picture was as beautiful; more so, perhaps, for over the island, all in shadow, and against the stars, you would see the palm-tops catching fire, and then the light of day coming through the green trees and blue sky, like a spirit, across the blue lagoon, widening and strengthening as it widened, across the white foam, out over the sea, spreading like a fan, till, all at once, night was day, and the gulls were crying and the breakers flashing, the dawn wind blowing, and the palm trees bending, as palm trees only know how. Emmeline always imagined herself alone on the island with Dick, but beauty was there, too, and beauty is a great companion.

The girl was contemplating the scene before her. Nature in her friendliest mood seemed to say, "Behold me! Men call me cruel; men have called me deceitful, even treacherous. I—ah well! my answer is, 'Behold me!'"

The girl was contemplating the specious beauty of it all, when on the breeze from seaward came a shout. She turned quickly. There was Dick up to his knees in a rock-pool a hundred yards or so away, motionless, his arms upraised, and crying out for help. She sprang to her feet.

There had once been an islet on this part of the reef, a tiny thing, consisting of a few palms and a handful of vegetation, and destroyed, perhaps, in some great storm. I mention this because the existence of this islet once upon a time was the means, indirectly, of saving Dick's life; for where these islets have been or are, "flats" occur on the reef formed of coral conglomerate.

Emmeline in her bare feet could never have reached him in time over rough coral, but, fortunately, this flat and comparatively smooth surface lay between them.

"My spear!" shouted Dick, as she approached.

He seemed at first tangled in brambles; then she thought ropes were tangling round him and tying him to something in the water—whatever it was, it was most awful, and hideous, and like a nightmare. She ran with the speed of Atalanta to the rock where the spear was resting, all red with the blood of new-slain fish, a foot from the point.

As she approached Dick, spear in hand, she saw, gasping with terror, that the ropes were alive, and that they were flickering and rippling over his back. One of them bound his left arm to his side, but his right arm was free.

"Quick!" he shouted.

In a second the spear was in his free hand, and Emmeline had cast herself down on her knees, and was staring with terrified eyes into the water of the pool from whence the ropes issued. She was, despite her terror, quite prepared to fling herself in and do battle with the thing, whatever it might be.

What she saw was only for a second. In the deep water of the pool, gazing up and forward and straight at Dick, she saw a face, lugubrious and awful. The eyes were wide as saucers, stony and steadfast; a large, heavy, parrot-like beak hung before the eyes, and worked and wobbled, and seemed to beckon. But what froze one's heart was the expression of the eyes, so stony and lugubrious, so passionless, so devoid of speculation, yet so fixed of purpose and full of fate.

From away far down he had risen with the rising tide. He had been feeding on crabs, when the tide, betraying him, had gone out, leaving him trapped in the rock-pool. He had slept, perhaps, and awakened to find a being, naked and defenceless, invading his pool. He was quite small, as octopods go, and young, yet he was large and powerful enough to have drowned an ox.

The octopod has only been described once, in stone, by a Japanese artist. The statue is still extant, and it is the most terrible masterpiece of sculpture ever executed by human hands. It represents a man who has been bathing on a low-tide beach, and has been caught. The man is shouting in a delirium of terror, and threatening with his free arm the spectre that has him in its grip. The eyes of the octopod are fixed upon the man—passionless and lugubrious eyes, but steadfast and fixed.

Another whip-lash shot out of the water in a shower of spray, and seized Dick by the left thigh. At the same instant he drove the point of the spear through the right eye of the monster, deep down through eye and soft gelatinous carcass till the spear-point dirled and splintered against the rock. At the same moment the water of the pool became black as ink, the bands around him relaxed, and he was free.

Emmeline rose up and seized him, sobbing and clinging to him, and kissing him. He clasped her with his left arm round her body, as if to protect her, but it was a mechanical action. He was not thinking of her. Wild with rage, and uttering hoarse cries, he plunged the broken spear again and again into the depths of the pool, seeking utterly to destroy the enemy that had so lately had him in its grip. Then slowly he came to himself, and wiped his forehead, and looked at the broken spear in his hand.

"Beast!" he said. "Did you see its eyes? Did you see its eyes? I wish it had a hundred eyes, and I had a hundred spears to drive into them!"

She was clinging to him, and sobbing and laughing hysterically, and praising him. One might have thought that he had rescued her from death, not she him.

The sun had nearly vanished, and he led her back to where the dinghy was moored recapturing and putting on his trousers on the road. He picked up the dead fish he had speared; and as he rowed her back across the lagoon, he talked and laughed, recounting the incidents of the fight, taking all the glory of the thing to himself, and seeming quite to ignore the important part she had played in it.

This was not from any callousness or want of gratitude, but simply from the fact that for the last five years he had been the be-all and end-all of their tiny community—the Imperial master. And he would just as soon have thought of thanking her for handing him the spear as of thanking his right hand for driving it home. She was quite content, seeking neither thanks nor praise. Everything she had came from him: she was his shadow and his slave. He was her sun.

He went over the fight again and again before they lay down to rest, telling her he had done this and that, and what he would do to the next beast of the sort. The reiteration was tiresome enough, or would have been to an outside listener, but to Emmeline it was better than Homer. People's minds do not improve in an intellectual sense when they are isolated from the world, even though they are living the wild and happy lives of savages.

Then Dick lay down in the dried ferns and covered himself with a piece of the striped flannel which they used for blanketing, and he snored, and chattered in his sleep like a dog hunting imaginary game, and Emmeline lay beside him wakeful and thinking. A new terror had come into her life. She had seen death for the second time, but this time active and in being.

THE SOUND OF A DRUM

The next day Dick was sitting under the shade of the artu. He had the box of fishhooks beside him, and he was bending a line on to one of them. There had originally been a couple of dozen hooks, large and small, in the box; there remained now only six—four small and two large ones. It was a large one he was fixing to the line, for he intended going on the morrow to the old place to fetch some bananas, and on the way to try for a fish in the deeper parts of the lagoon.

It was late afternoon, and the heat had gone out of the day. Emmeline, seated on the grass opposite to him, was holding the end of the line, whilst he got the kinks out of it, when suddenly she raised her head.

There was not a breath of wind; the hush of the far-distant surf came through the blue weather—the only audible sound except, now and then, a movement and flutter from the bird perched in the branches of the artu. All at once another sound mixed itself with the voice of the surf—a faint, throbbing sound, like the beating of a distant drum.

"Listen!" said Emmeline.

Dick paused for a moment in his work. All the sounds of the island were familiar: this was something quite strange.

Faint and far away, now rapid, now slow; coming from where, who could say? Sometimes it seemed to come from the sea, sometimes, if the fancy of the listener turned that way, from the woods. As they listened, a sigh came from overhead; the evening breeze had risen and was moving in the leaves of the artu tree. Just as you might wipe a picture off a slate, the breeze banished the sound. Dick went on with his work.

Next morning early he embarked in the dinghy. He took the hook and line with him, and some raw fish for bait. Emmeline helped him to push off, and stood on the bank waving her hand as he rounded the little cape covered with wild cocoanut.

These expeditions of Dick's were one of her sorrows. To be left alone was frightful; yet she never complained. She was living in a paradise, but something told her that behind all that sun, all that splendour of blue sea and sky, behind the flowers and the leaves, behind all that specious and simpering appearance of happiness in nature, lurked a frown, and the dragon of mischance.

Dick rowed for about a mile, then he shipped his sculls, and let the dinghy float. The water here was very deep; so deep that, despite its clearness, the bottom was invisible; the sunlight over the reef struck through it diagonally, filling it with sparkles.

The fisherman baited his hook with a piece from the belly of a scarus and lowered it down out of sight, then he belayed the line to a thole pin, and, sitting in the bottom of the boat, hung his head over the side and gazed deep down into the water. Sometimes there was nothing to see but just the deep blue of the water. Then a flight of spangled arrowheads would cross the line of sight and vanish, pursued by a form like a moving bar of gold. Then a great fish would materialise itself and hang in the shadow of the boat motionless as a stone, save for the movement of its gills; next moment with a twist of the tail it would be gone.

Suddenly the dinghy shored over, and might have capsized, only for the fact that Dick was sitting on the opposite side to the side from which the line hung. Then the boat righted; the line slackened, and the surface of the lagoon, a few fathoms away, boiled as if being stirred from below by a great silver stick. He had hooked an albicore. He tied the end of the fishing-line to a scull, undid the line from the thole pin, and flung the scull overboard.

He did all this with wonderful rapidity, while the line was still slack. Next moment the scull was rushing over the surface of the lagoon, now towards the reef, now towards the shore, now flat, now end up. Now it would be jerked under the surface entirely; vanish for a moment, and then reappear. It was a most astonishing thing to watch, for the scull seemed alive—viciously alive, and imbued with some destructive purpose; as, in fact, it was. The most venomous of living things, and the most intelligent could not have fought the great fish better.

The albicore would make a frantic dash down the lagoon, hoping, perhaps, to find in the open sea a release from his foe. Then, half drowned with the pull of the scull, he would pause, dart from side to side in perplexity, and then make an equally frantic dash up the lagoon, to be checked in the same manner. Seeking the deepest depths, he would sink the scull a few fathoms; and once he sought the air, leaping into the sunlight like a crescent of silver, whilst the splash of him as he fell echoed amidst the trees bordering the lagoon. An hour passed before the great fish showed signs of weakening.

The struggle had taken place up to this close to the shore, but now the scull swam out into the broad sheet of sunlit water, and slowly began to describe large circles rippling up the peaceful blue into flashing wavelets. It was a melancholy sight to watch, for the great fish had made a good fight, and one could see him, through the eye of imagination, beaten, half drowned, dazed, and moving as is the fashion of dazed things in a circle.

Dick, working the remaining oar at the stern of the boat, rowed out and seized the floating scull, bringing it on board. Foot by foot he hauled his catch towards the boat till the long gleaming line of the thing came dimly into view.

The fight had been heard for miles through the lagoon water by all sorts of swimming things. The lord of the place had got sound of it. A dark fin rippled the water; and as Dick, pulling on his line, hauled his catch closer, a monstrous grey shadow stained the depths, and the glittering streak that was the albicore vanished as if engulfed in a cloud. The line came in slack, and Dick hauled in the albicore's head. It had been divided from the body as if with a huge pair of shears. The grey shadow slipped by the boat, and Dick, mad with rage, shouted and shook his fist at it; then, seizing the albicore's head, from which he had taken the hook, he hurled it at the monster in the water.

The great shark, with a movement of the tail that caused the water to swirl and the dinghy to rock, turned upon his back and engulfed the head; then he slowly sank and vanished, just as if he had been dissolved. He had come off best in this their first encounter—such as it was.

SAILS UPON THE SEA

Dick put the hook away and took to the sculls. He had a three-mile row before him, and the tide was coming in, which did not make it any the easier. As he rowed, he talked and grumbled to himself. He had been in a grumbling mood for some time past: the chief cause, Emmeline.

In the last few months she had changed; even her face had changed. A new person had come upon the island, it seemed to him, and taken the place of the Emmeline he had known from earliest childhood. This one looked different. He did not know that she had grown beautiful, he just knew that she looked different; also she had developed new ways that displeased him—she would go off and bathe by herself, for instance.

Up to six months or so ago he had been quite contented; sleeping and eating, and hunting for food and cooking it, building and rebuilding the house, exploring the woods and the reef. But lately a spirit of restlessness had come upon him; he did not know exactly what he wanted. He had a vague feeling that he wanted to go away from the place where he was; not from the island, but from the place where they had pitched their tent, or rather built their house.

It may have been the spirit of civilisation crying out in him, telling him of all he was missing. Of the cities, and the streets, and the houses, and the businesses, and the striving after gold, the striving after power. It may have been simply the man in him crying out for Love, and not knowing yet that Love was at his elbow.

The dinghy glided along, hugging the shore, past the little glades of fern and the cathedral gloom of the breadfruit; then, rounding a promontory, she opened the view of the break in the reef. A little bit of the white strand was visible, but he was not looking that way—he was looking towards the reef at a tiny, dark spot, not noticeable unless searched for by the eye. Always when he came on these expeditions, just here, he would hang on his oars and gaze over there, where the gulls were flying and the breakers thundering.

A few years ago the spot filled him with dread as well as curiosity, but from familiarity and the dullness that time casts on everything, the dread had almost vanished, but the curiosity remained: the curiosity that makes a child look on at the slaughter of an animal even though his soul revolts at it. He gazed for a while, then he went on pulling, and the dinghy approached the beach.

Something had happened on the beach. The sand was all trampled, and stained red here and there; in the centre lay the remains of a great fire still smouldering, and just where the water lapped the sand, lay two deep grooves as if two heavy boats had been beached there. A South Sea man would have told from the shape of the grooves, and the little marks of the out-riggers, that two heavy canoes had been beached there. And they had.

The day before, early in the afternoon, two canoes, possibly from that far-away island which cast a stain on the horizon to the sou'-sou'-west, had entered the lagoon, one in pursuit of the other.

What happened then had better be left veiled. A war drum with a shark-skin head had set the woods throbbing; the victory was celebrated all night, and at dawn the victors manned the two canoes and set sail for the home, or the hell, they had come from. Had you examined the strand you would have found that a line had been drawn across the beach, beyond which there were no footmarks: that meant that the rest of the island was for some reason *tabu*.

Dick pulled the nose of the boat up a bit on the strand, then he looked around him. He picked up a broken spear that had been cast away or forgotten; it was made of some hard wood and barbed with iron. On the right-hand side of the beach something lay between the cocoa-nut trees. He approached; it was a mass of offal; the entrails of a dozen sheep seemed cast here in one mound, yet there were no sheep on the island, and sheep are not carried as a rule in war canoes.

The sand on the beach was eloquent. The foot pursuing and the foot pursued; the knee of the fallen one, and then the forehead and outspread hands; the heel of the chief who has slain his enemy, beaten the body flat, burst a hole through it through which he has put his head, and who stands absolutely wearing his enemy as a cloak; the head of the man dragged on his back to be butchered like a sheep—of these things spoke the sand.

As far as the sand traces could speak, the story of the battle was still being told; the screams and the shouting, the clashing of clubs and spears were gone, yet the ghost of the fight remained.

If the sand could bear such traces, and tell such tales, who shall say that the plastic æther was destitute of the story of the fight and the butchery?

However that may have been, Dick, looking around him, had the shivering sense of having just escaped from danger. Whoever had been, had gone—he could tell that by the canoe traces. Gone either out to sea, or up the right stretch of the lagoon. It was important to determine this.

He climbed to the hill-top and swept the sea with his eyes. There, away to the south-west, far away on the sea, he could distinguish the brown sails of two canoes. There was something indescribably mournful and lonely in their appearance; they looked like withered leaves—brown moths blown to sea—derelicts of autumn. Then, remembering the beach, these things became freighted with the most sinister thoughts for the mind of the gazer. They were hurrying away, having done their work. That they looked lonely and old and mournful, and like withered leaves blown across the sea, only heightened the horror.

Dick had never seen canoes before, but he knew that these things were boats of some sort holding people, and that the people had left all those traces on the beach. How much of the horror of the thing was revealed to his subconscious intelligence, who can say?

He had climbed the boulder, and he now sat down with his knees drawn up, and his hands clasped round them. Whenever he came round to this side of the island, something happened of a fateful or sinister nature. The last time he had nearly lost the dinghy; he had beached the little boat in such a way that she floated off, and the tide was just in the act of stealing her, and sweeping her from the lagoon out to sea, when he returned laden with his bananas, and, rushing into the water up to his waist, saved her. Another time he had fallen out of a tree, and just by a miracle escaped death. Another time a hurricane had broken, lashing the lagoon into snow, and sending the cocoa-nuts bounding and flying like tennis balls across the strand. This time he had just escaped something, he knew not exactly what. It was almost as if Providence were saying to him, "Don't come here."

He watched the brown sails as they dwindled in the wind-blown blue, then he came down from the hill-top and cut his bananas. He cut four large bunches, which caused him to make two journeys to the boat. When the bananas were stowed he pushed off.

For a long time a great curiosity had been pulling at his heart-strings: a curiosity of which he was dimly ashamed. Fear had given it birth, and Fear still clung to it. It was, perhaps, the element of fear and the awful delight of daring the unknown that made him give way to it.

He had rowed, perhaps, a hundred yards when he turned the boat's head and made for the reef. It was more than five years since that day when he rowed across the lagoon, Emmeline sitting in the stern, with her wreath of flowers in her hand. It might have been only yesterday, for everything seemed just the same. The thunderous surf and the flying gulls, the blinding sunlight, and the salt, fresh smell of the sea. The palm tree at the entrance of the lagoon still bent gazing into the water, and round the projection of coral to which he had last moored the boat still lay a fragment of the rope which he had cut in his hurry to escape.

Ships had come into the lagoon, perhaps, during the five years, but no one had noticed anything on the reef, for it was only from the hill-top that a full view of what was there could be seen, and then only by eyes knowing where to look. From the beach there was visible just a speck. It might have been, perhaps, a bit of old wreckage flung there by a wave in some big storm. A piece of old wreckage that had been tossed hither and thither for years, and had at last found a place of rest.

Dick tied the boat up, and stepped on to the reef. It was high tide just as before; the breeze was blowing strongly, and overhead a man-of-war's bird, black as ebony, with a blood-red bill, came sailing, the wind doming out his wings. He circled in the air, and cried out fiercely, as if resenting the presence of the intruder, then he passed away, let himself be blown away, as it were, across the lagoon, wheeled, circled, and passed out to sea.

Dick approached the place he knew, and there lay the little old barrel all warped by the powerful sun; the staves stood apart, and the hooping was rusted and broken, and whatever it had contained in the way of spirit and conviviality had long ago drained away.

Beside the barrel lay a skeleton, round which lay a few rags of cloth. The skull had fallen to one side, and the lower jaw had fallen from the skull; the bones of the hands and feet were still articulated, and the ribs had not fallen in. It was all white and bleached, and the sun shone on it as indifferently as on the coral, this shell and framework that had once been a man. There was nothing dreadful about it, but a whole world of wonder.

To Dick, who had not been broken into the idea of death, who had not learned to associate it with graves and funerals, sorrow, eternity, and hell, the thing spoke as it never could have spoken to you or me.

Looking at it, things linked themselves together in his mind: the skeletons of birds he had found in the woods, the fish he had slain, even trees lying dead and rotten—even the shells of crabs.

If you had asked him what lay before him, and if he could have expressed the thought in his mind, he would have answered you "change."

All the philosophy in the world could not have told him more than he knew just then about death—he, who even did not know its name.

He was held spellbound by the marvel and miracle of the thing and the thoughts that suddenly crowded his mind like a host of spectres for whom a door has just been opened.

Just as a child by unanswerable logic knows that a fire which has burned him once will burn him again, or will burn another person, he knew that just as the form before him was, his form would be some day—and Emmeline's.

Then came the vague question which is born not of the brain, but the heart, and which is the basis of all religions—where shall I be then? His mind was not of an introspective nature, and the question just strayed across it and was gone. And still the wonder of the thing held him. He was for the first time in his life in a reverie; the corpse that had shocked and terrified him five years ago had cast seeds of thought with its dead fingers upon his mind, the skeleton had brought them to maturity. The full fact of universal death suddenly appeared before him, and he recognised it.

He stood for a long time motionless, and then with a deep sigh turned to the boat and pushed off without once looking back at the reef. He crossed the lagoon and rowed slowly homewards, keeping in the shelter of the tree shadows as much as possible.

Even looking at him from the shore you might have noticed a difference in him. Your savage paddles his canoe, or sculls his boat, alert, glancing about him, at touch with nature at all points; though he be lazy as a cat and sleeps half the day, awake he is all ears and eyes—a creature reacting to the least external impression.

Dick, as he rowed back, did not look about him: he was thinking or retrospecting. The savage in him had received a check. As he turned the little cape where the wild cocoa-nut blazed, he looked over his shoulder. A figure was standing on the sward by the edge of the water. It was Emmeline.

THE SCHOONER

They carried the bananas up to the house, and hung them from a branch of the artu. Then Dick, on his knees, lit the fire to prepare the evening meal. When it was over he went down to where the boat was moored, and returned with something in his hand. It was the javelin with the iron point—or, rather, the two pieces of it. He had said nothing of what he had seen to the girl.

Emmeline was seated on the grass; she had a long strip of the striped flannel stuff about her, worn like a scarf, and she had another piece in her hand which she was hemming. The bird was hopping about, pecking at a banana which they had thrown to him; a light breeze made the shadow of the artu leaves dance upon the grass, and the serrated leaves of the breadfruit to patter one on the other with the sound of rain-drops falling upon glass.

"Where did you get it?" asked Emmeline, staring at the piece of the javelin which Dick had flung down almost beside her whilst he went into the house to fetch the knife.

"It was on the beach over there," he replied, taking his seat and examining the two fragments to see how he could splice them together.

Emmeline looked at the pieces, putting them together in her mind. She did not like the look of the thing: so keen and savage, and stained dark a foot and more from the point.

"People had been there," said Dick, putting the two pieces together and examining the fracture critically.

"Where?"

"Over there. This was lying on the sand, and the sand was all trod up."

"Dick," said Emmeline, "who were the people?"

"I don't know; I went up the hill and saw their boats going away—far away out. This was lying on the sand."

"Dick," said Emmeline, "do you remember the noise yesterday?"

"Yes," said Dick.

"I heard it in the night."

"When?"

"In the night before the moon went away."

"That was them," said Dick.

"Dick!"

"Yes?"

"Who were they?"

"I don't know," replied Dick.

"It was in the night, before the moon went away, and it went on and on beating in the trees. I thought I was asleep, and then I knew I was awake; you were asleep, and I pushed you to listen, but you couldn't wake, you were so asleep; then the moon went away, and the noise went on. How did they make the noise?"

"I don't know," replied Dick, "but it was them; and they left this on the sand, and the sand was all trod up, and I saw their boats from the hill, away out far."

"I thought I heard voices," said Emmeline, "but I was not sure."

She fell into meditation, watching her companion at work on the savage and sinister-looking thing in his hands. He was splicing the two pieces together with a strip of the brown cloth-like stuff which is wrapped round the stalks of the cocoa-palm fronds. The thing seemed to have been hurled here out of the blue by some unseen hand.

When he had spliced the pieces, doing so with marvellous dexterity, he took the thing short down near the point, and began thrusting it into the soft earth to clean it; then, with a bit of flannel, he polished it till it shone. He felt a keen delight in it. It was useless as a fish-spear, because it had no barb, but it was a weapon. It was useless as a weapon, because there was no foe on the island to use it against; still, it was a weapon.

When he had finished scrubbing at it, he rose, hitched his old trousers up, tightened the belt of cocoa-cloth which Emmeline had made for him, went into the house and got his fish-spear, and stalked off to the boat, calling out to Emmeline to follow him. They crossed over to the reef, where, as usual, he divested himself of clothing.

It was strange that out here he would go about stark naked, yet on the island he always wore some covering. But not so strange, perhaps, after all.

The sea is a great purifier, both of the mind and the body; before that great sweet spirit people do not think in the same way as they think far inland. What woman would appear in a town or on a country road, or even bathing in a river, as she appears bathing in the sea?

Some instinct made Dick cover himself up on shore, and strip naked on the reef. In a minute he was down by the edge of the surf, javelin in one hand, fish-spear in the other.

Emmeline, by a little pool the bottom of which was covered with branching coral, sat gazing down into its depths, lost in a reverie like that into which we fall when gazing at shapes in the fire. She had sat some time like this when a shout from Dick aroused her. She started to her feet and gazed to where he was pointing. An amazing thing was there.

To the east, just rounding the curve of the reef, and scarcely a quarter of a mile from it, was coming a big topsail schooner; a beautiful sight she was, heeling to the breeze with every sail drawing, and the white foam like a feather at her fore-foot.

Dick, with the javelin in his hand, was standing gazing at her; he had dropped his fish-spear, and he stood as motionless as though he were carved out of stone. Emmeline ran to him and stood beside him; neither of them spoke a word as the vessel drew closer.

Everything was visible, so close was she now, from the reef points on the great mainsail, luminous with the sunlight, and white as the wing of a gull, to the rail of the bulwarks. A crowd of men were hanging over the port bulwarks gazing at the island and the figures on the reef. Browned by the sun and sea-breeze, Emmeline's hair blowing on the wind, and the point of Dick's javelin flashing in the sun, they looked an ideal pair of savages, seen from the schooner's deck.

"They are going away," said Emmeline, with a long-drawn breath of relief.

Dick made no reply; he stared at the schooner a moment longer in silence, then, having made sure that she was standing away from the land, he began to run up and down, calling out wildly, and beckoning to the vessel as if to call her back.

A moment later a sound came on the breeze, a faint hail; a flag was run up to the peak and dipped as in derision, and the vessel continued on her course.

As a matter of fact, she had been on the point of putting about. Her captain had for a moment been undecided as to whether the forms on the reef were those of castaways or savages. But the javelin in Dick's hand had turned the scale of his opinion in favour of the theory of savages.

LOVE STEPS IN

Two birds were sitting in the branches of the artu tree: Koko had taken a mate. They had built a nest out of fibres pulled from the wrappings of the cocoa-nut fronds, bits of stick and wire grass—anything, in fact; even fibres from the palmetto thatch of the house below. The pilferings of birds, the building of nests, what charming incidents they are in the great episode of spring!

The hawthorn tree never bloomed here, the climate was that of eternal summer, yet the spirit of May came just as she comes to the English countryside or the German forest. The doings in the artu branches greatly interested Emmeline.

The love-making and the nest-building were conducted quite in the usual manner, according to rules laid down by Nature and carried out by men and birds. All sorts of quaint sounds came filtering down through the leaves from the branch where the sapphire-coloured lovers sat side by side, or the fork where the nest was beginning to form: croonings and cluckings, sounds like the flirting of a fan, the sounds of a squabble, followed by the sounds that told of the squabble made up. Sometimes after one of these squabbles a pale blue downy feather or two would come floating earthwards, touch the palmetto leaves of the house-roof and cling there, or be blown on to the grass.

It was some days after the appearance of the schooner, and Dick was making ready to go into the woods and pick guavas. He had all the morning been engaged in making a basket to carry them in. In civilisation he would, judging from his mechanical talent, perhaps have been an engineer, building bridges and ships, instead of palmetto-leaf baskets and cane houses—who knows if he would have been happier?

The heat of midday had passed, when, with the basket hanging over his shoulder on a piece of cane, he started for the woods, Emmeline following. The place they were going to always filled her with a vague dread; not for a great deal would she have gone there alone. Dick had discovered it in one of his rambles.

They entered the wood and passed a little well, a well without apparent source or outlet and a bottom of fine white sand. How the sand had formed there, it would be impossible to say; but there it was, and around the margin grew ferns redoubling themselves on the surface of the crystal-clear water. They left this to the right and struck into the heart of the wood. The heat of midday still lurked here; the way was clear, for there was a sort of path between the trees, as if, in very ancient days, there had been a road.

Right across this path, half lost in shadow, half sunlit, the lianas hung their ropes. The hotoo tree, with its powdering of delicate blossoms, here stood, showing its lost loveliness to the sun; in the shade the scarlet hibiscus burned like a flame. Artu and breadfruit trees and cocoa-nut bordered the way.

As they proceeded the trees grew denser and the path more obscure. All at once, rounding a sharp turn, the path ended in a valley carpeted with fern. This was the place that always filled Emmeline with an undefined dread. One side of it was all built up in terraces with huge blocks of stone. Blocks of stone so enormous, that the wonder was how the ancient builders had put them in their places.

Trees grew along the terraces, thrusting their roots between the interstices of the blocks. At their base, slightly tilted forward as if with the sinkage of years, stood a great stone figure roughly carved, thirty feet high at least—mysterious-looking, the very spirit of the place. This figure and the terraces, the valley itself, and the very trees that grew there, inspired Emmeline with deep curiosity and vague fear.

People had been here once; sometimes she could fancy she saw dark shadows moving amidst the trees, and the whisper of the foliage seemed to her to hide voices at times, even as its shadow concealed forms. It was indeed an uncanny place to be alone in even under the broad light of day. All across the Pacific for thousands of miles you find relics of the past, like these scattered through the islands.

These temple places are nearly all the same: great terraces of stone, massive idols, desolation overgrown with foliage. They hint at one religion, and a time when the sea space of the Pacific was a continent, which, sinking slowly through the ages, has left only its higher lands and hill-tops visible in the form of islands. Round these places the woods are thicker than elsewhere, hinting at the presence there, once, of sacred groves. The idols are immense, their faces are vague; the storms and the suns and the rains of the ages have cast over them a veil. The sphinx is understandable and a toy compared to these things, some of which have a stature of fifty feet, whose creation is veiled in absolute mystery—the gods of a people for ever and for ever lost.

The "stone man" was the name Emmeline had given the idol of the valley; and sometimes at nights, when her thoughts would stray that way, she would picture him standing all alone in the moonlight or starlight staring straight before him.

He seemed for ever listening; unconsciously one fell to listening too, and then the valley seemed steeped in a supernatural silence. He was not good to be alone with.

Emmeline sat down amidst the fears just at his base. When one was close up to him he lost the suggestion of life, and was simply a great stone which cast a shadow in the sun.

Dick threw himself down also to rest. Then he rose up and went off amidst the guava bushes, plucking the fruit and filling his basket. Since he had seen the schooner, the white men on her decks, her great masts and sails, and general appearance of freedom and speed and unknown adventure, he had been more than ordinarily glum and restless. Perhaps he connected her in his mind with the far-away vision of the *Northumberland*, and the idea of other places and lands, and the yearning for change the idea of them inspired.

He came back with his basket full of the ripe fruit, gave some to the girl and sat down beside her. When she had finished eating them she took the cane that he used for carrying the basket and held it in her hands. She was bending it in the form of a bow when it slipped, flew out and struck her companion a sharp blow on the side of his face.

Almost on the instant he turned and slapped her on the shoulder. She stared at him for a moment in troubled amazement, a sob came in her throat. Then some veil seemed lifted, some wizard's wand stretched out, some mysterious vial broken. As she looked at him like that, he suddenly and fiercely clasped her in his arms. He held her like this for a moment, dazed, stupefied, not knowing what to do with her. Then her lips told him, for they met his in an endless kiss.

THE SLEEP OF PARADISE

The moon rose up that evening and shot her silver arrows at the house under the artu tree. The house was empty. Then the moon came across the sea and across the reef.

She lit the lagoon to its dark, dim heart. She lit the coral brains and sand spaces, and the fish, casting their shadows on the sand and the coral. The keeper of the lagoon rose to greet her, and the fin of him broke her reflection on the mirror-like surface into a thousand glittering ripples. She saw the white staring ribs of the form on the reef. Then, peeping over the trees, she looked down into the valley, where the great idol of stone had kept its solitary vigil for five thousand years, perhaps, or more.

At his base, in his shadow, looking as if under his protection, lay two human beings, naked, clasped in each other's arms, and fast asleep. One could scarcely pity his vigil, had it been marked sometimes through the years by such an incident as this. The thing had been conducted just as the birds conduct their love affairs. An affair absolutely natural, absolutely blameless, and without sin.

It was a marriage according to Nature, without feast or guests, consummated with accidental cynicism under the shadow of a religion a thousand years dead.

So happy in their ignorance were they, that they only knew that suddenly life had changed, that the skies and the sea were bluer, and that they had become in some magical way one a part of the other. The birds on the tree above were equally as happy in their ignorance, and in their love.

PART II

AN ISLAND HONEYMOON

One day Dick climbed on to the tree above the house, and, driving Madame Koko off the nest upon which she was sitting, peeped in. There were several pale green eggs in it. He did not disturb them, but climbed down again, and the bird resumed her seat as if nothing had happened. Such an occurrence would have terrified a bird used to the ways of men, but here the birds were so fearless and so full of confidence that often they would follow Emmeline in the wood, flying from branch to branch, peering at her through the leaves, lighting quite close to her—once, even, on her shoulder.

The days passed. Dick had lost his restlessness: his wish to wander had vanished. He had no reason to wander; perhaps that was the reason why. In all the broad earth he could not have found anything more desirable than what he had.

Instead now of finding a half-naked savage followed dog-like by his mate, you would have found of an evening a pair of lovers wandering on the reef. They had in a pathetic sort of way attempted to adorn the house with a blue flowering creeper taken from the wood and trained over the entrance.

Emmeline, up to this, had mostly done the cooking, such as it was; Dick helped her now, always. He talked to her no longer in short sentences flung out as if to a dog; and she, almost losing the strange reserve that had clung to her from childhood, half showed him her mind. It was a curious mind: the mind of a dreamer, almost the mind of a poet. The Cluricaunes dwelt there, and vague shapes born of things she had heard about or dreamt of: she had thoughts about the sea and stars, the flowers and birds.

Dick would listen to her as she talked, as a man might listen to the sound of a rivulet. His practical mind could take no share in the dreams of his other half, but her conversation pleased him.

He would look at her for a long time together, absorbed in thought. He was admiring her.

Her hair, blue-black and glossy, tangled him in its meshes; he would stroke it, so to speak, with his eyes, and then pull her close to him and bury his face in it; the smell of it was intoxicating. He breathed her as one does the perfume of a rose.

Her ears were small, and like little white shells. He would take one between finger and thumb and play with it as if it were a toy, pulling at the lobe of it, or trying to flatten out the curved part. Her breasts, her shoulders, her knees, her little feet, every bit of her, he would examine and play with and kiss. She would lie and let him, seeming absorbed in some far-away thought, of which he was the object, then all at once her arms would go round him. All this used to go on in the broad light of day, under the shadow of the artu leaves, with no one to watch except the bright-eyed birds in the leaves above.

Not all their time would be spent in this fashion. Dick was just as keen after the fish. He dug up with a spade—improvised from one of the boards of the dinghy—a space of soft earth near the taro patch and planted the seeds of melons he found in the wood; he rethatched the house. They were, in short, as busy as they could be in such a climate, but love-making would come on them in fits, and then everything would be forgotten. Just as one revisits some spot to renew the memory of a painful or pleasant experience received there, they would return to the valley of the idol and spend a whole afternoon in its shade. The absolute happiness of wandering through the woods together, discovering new flowers, getting lost, and finding their way again, was a thing beyond expression.

Dick had suddenly stumbled upon Love. His courtship had lasted only some twenty minutes; it was being gone over again now, and extended.

One day, hearing a curious noise from the tree above the house, he climbed it. The noise came from the nest, which had been temporarily left by the mother bird. It was a gasping, wheezing sound, and it came from four wide-open beaks, so anxious to be fed that one could almost see into the very crops of the owners. They were Koko's children. In another year each of those ugly downy things would, if permitted to live, be a beautiful sapphire-coloured bird with a few dove-coloured tail feathers, coral beak, and bright, intelligent eyes. A few days ago each of these things was imprisoned in a pale green egg. A month ago they were nowhere.

Something hit Dick on the cheek. It was the mother bird returned with food for the young ones. Dick drew his head aside, and she proceeded without more ado to fill their crops.

THE VANISHING OF EMMELINE

Months passed away. Only one bird remained in the branches of the artu: Koko's children and mate had vanished, but he remained. The breadfruit leaves had turned from green to pale gold and darkest amber, and now the new green leaves were being presented to the spring.

Dick, who had a complete chart of the lagoon in his head, and knew all the soundings and best fishing places, the locality of the stinging coral, and the places where you could wade right across at low tide—Dick, one morning, was gathering his things together for a fishing expedition. The place he was going to lay some two and a half miles away across the island, and as the road was bad he was going alone.

Emmeline had been passing a new thread through the beads of the necklace she sometimes wore. This necklace had a history. In the shallows not far away, Dick had found a bed of shell-fish; wading out at low tide, he had taken some of them out to examine. They were oysters. The first one he opened, so disgusting did its appearance seem to him, might have been the last, only that under the beard of the thing lay a pearl. It was about twice the size of a large pea, and so lustrous that even he could not but admire its beauty, though quite unconscious of its value.

He flung the unopened oysters down, and took the thing to Emmeline. Next day, returning by chance to the same spot, he found the oysters he had cast down all dead and open in the sun. He examined them, and found another pearl embedded in one of them. Then he collected nearly a bushel of the oysters, and left them to die and open. The idea had occurred to him of making a necklace for his companion. She had one made of shells, he intended to make her one of pearls.

It took a long time, but it was something to do. He pierced them with a big needle, and at the end of four months or so the thing was complete. Great pearls most of them were—pure white, black, pink, some perfectly round, some tear shaped, some irregular. The thing was worth fifteen, or perhaps twenty thousand pounds, for he only used the biggest he could find, casting away the small ones as useless.

Emmeline this morning had just finished restringing them on a double thread. She looked pale and not at all well and had been restless all night.

As he went off, armed with his spear and fishing tackle, she waved her hand to him without getting up. Usually she followed him a bit into the wood when he was going away like this, but this morning she just sat at the doorway of the little house, the necklace in her lap, following him with her eyes until he was lost amidst the trees.

He had no compass to guide him, and he needed none. He knew the woods by heart. The mysterious line beyond which scarcely an artu tree was to be found. The long strip of mammee apple—a regular sheet of it a hundred yards broad, and reaching from the middle of the island right down to the lagoon. The clearings, some almost circular where the ferns grew knee-deep. Then he came to the bad part.

The vegetation here had burst into a riot. All sorts of great sappy stalks of unknown plants barred the way and tangled the foot; and there were boggy places into which one sank horribly. Pausing to wipe one's brow, the stalks and tendrils one had beaten down, or beaten aside, rose up and closed together, making one a prisoner almost as closely surrounded as a fly in amber.

All the noontides that had ever fallen upon the island seemed to have left some of their heat behind them here. The air was damp and close like the air of a laundry; and the mournful and perpetual buzz of insects filled the silence without destroying it.

A hundred men with scythes might make a road through the place to-day; a month or two later, searching for the road, you would find none—the vegetation would have closed in as water closes when divided.

This was the haunt of the jug orchid—a veritable jug, lid and all. Raising the lid you would find the jug half filled with water. Sometimes in the tangle up above, between two trees, you would see a thing like a bird come to ruin. Orchids grew here as in a hothouse. All the trees—the few there were—had a spectral and miserable appearance. They were half starved by the voluptuous growth of the gigantic weeds.

If one had much imagination one felt afraid in this place, for one felt not alone. At any moment it seemed that one might be touched on the elbow by a hand reaching out from the surrounding tangle. Even Dick felt this, unimaginative and fearless as he was. It took him nearly three-quarters of an hour to get through, and then, at last, came the blessed air of real day, and a glimpse of the lagoon between the tree-boles.

He would have rowed round in the dinghy, only that at low tide the shallows of the north of the island were a bar to the boat's passage. Of course he might have rowed all the way round by way of the strand and reef entrance, but that would have meant a circuit of six miles or more. When he came between the trees down to the lagoon edge it was about eleven o'clock in the morning, and the tide was nearly at the full.

The lagoon just here was like a trough, and the reef was very near, scarcely a quarter of a mile from the shore. The water did not shelve, it went down sheer fifty fathoms or more, and one could fish from the bank just as from a pier head. He had brought some food with him, and he placed it under a tree whilst he prepared his line, which had a lump of coral for a sinker. He baited the hook, and whirling the sinker round in the air sent it flying out a hundred feet from shore. There was a baby cocoa-nut tree growing just at the edge of the water. He fastened the end of his line round the narrow stem, in case of eventualities, and then, holding the line itself, he fished.

He had promised Emmeline to return before sundown.

He was a fisherman. That is to say, a creature with the enduring patience of a cat, tireless and heedless of time as an oyster. He came here for sport more than for fish. Large things were to be found in this part of the lagoon. The last time he had hooked a horror in the form of a cat-fish; at least in outward appearance it was likest to a Mississippi cat-fish. Unlike the cat-fish, it was coarse and useless as food, but it gave good sport.

The tide was now going out, and it was at the going-out of the tide that the best fishing was to be had. There was no wind, and the lagoon lay like a sheet of glass, with just a dimple here and there where the outgoing tide made a swirl in the water.

As he fished he thought of Emmeline and the little house under the trees. Scarcely one could call it thinking. Pictures passed before his mind's eye—pleasant and happy pictures, sunlit, moonlit, starlit.

Three hours passed thus without a bite or symptom that the lagoon contained anything else but sea water, and disappointment; but he did not grumble. He was a fisherman. Then he left the line tied to the tree and sat down to eat the food he had brought with him. He had scarcely finished his meal when the baby cocoa-nut tree shivered and became convulsed, and he did not require to touch the taut line

116

to know that it was useless to attempt to cope with the thing at the end of it. The only course was to let it tug and drown itself. So he sat down and watched.

After a few minutes the line slackened, and the little cocoa-nut tree resumed its attitude of pensive meditation and repose. He pulled the line up: there was nothing at the end of it but a hook. He did not grumble; he baited the hook again, and flung it in, for it was quite likely that the ferocious thing in the water would bite again.

Full of this idea and heedless of time he fished and waited. The sun was sinking into the west—he did not heed it. He had quite forgotten that he had promised Emmeline to return before sunset; it was nearly sunset now. Suddenly, just behind him, from among the trees, he heard her voice, crying:

"Dick!"

THE VANISHING OF EMMELINE (continued)

He dropped the line, and turned with a start. There was no one visible. He ran amongst the trees calling out her name, but only echoes answered. Then he came back to the lagoon edge.

He felt sure that what he had heard was only fancy, but it was nearly sunset, and more than time to be off. He pulled in his line, wrapped it up, took his fish-spear and started.

It was just in the middle of the bad place that dread came to him. What if anything had happened to her? It was dusk here, and never had the weeds seemed so thick, dimness so dismal, the tendrils of the vines so gin-like. Then he lost his way—he who was so sure of his way always! The hunter's instinct had been crossed, and for a time he went hither and thither helpless as a ship without a compass. At last he broke into the real wood, but far to the right of where he ought to have been. He felt like a beast escaped from a trap, and hurried along, led by the sound of the surf.

When he reached the clear sward that led down to the lagoon the sun had just vanished beyond the sea-line. A streak of red cloud floated like the feather of a flamingo in the western sky close to the sea, and twilight had already filled the world. He could see the house dimly, under the shadow of the trees, and he ran towards it, crossing the sward diagonally.

Always before, when he had been away, the first thing to greet his eyes on his return had been the figure of Emmeline. Either at the lagoon edge or the house door he would find her waiting for him.

She was not waiting for him to-night. When he reached the house she was not there, and he paused, after searching the place, a prey to the most horrible perplexity, and unable for the moment to think or act.

Since the shock of the occurrence on the reef she had been subject at times to occasional attacks of headache; and when the pain was more than she could bear, she would go off and hide. Dick would hunt for her amidst the trees, calling out her name and hallooing. A faint "halloo" would answer when she heard him, and then he would find her under a tree or bush, with her unfortunate head between her hands, a picture of misery.

He remembered this now, and started off along the borders of the wood, calling to her, and pausing to listen. No answer came.

He searched amidst the trees as far as the little well, waking the echoes with his voice; then he came back slowly, peering about him in the deep dusk that now was yielding to the starlight. He sat down before the door of the house, and, looking at him, you might have fancied him in the last stages of exhaustion. Profound grief and profound exhaustion act on the frame very much in the same way. He sat with his chin resting on his chest, his hands helpless. He could hear her voice, still as he heard it over at the other side of the island. She had been in danger and called to him, and he had been calmly fishing, unconscious of it all.

This thought maddened him. He sat up, stared around him and beat the ground with the palms of his hands; then he sprang to his feet and made for the dinghy. He rowed to the reef: the action of a madman, for she could not possibly be there.

There was no moon, the starlight both lit and veiled the world, and no sound but the majestic thunder of the waves. As he stood, the night wind blowing on his face, the white foam seething before him, and Canopus burning in the great silence overhead, the fact that he stood in the centre of an awful and profound indifference came to his untutored mind with a pang.

He returned to the shore: the house was still deserted. A little bowl made from the shell of a cocoa-nut stood on the grass near the doorway. He had last seen it in her hands, and he took it up and held it for a moment, pressing it tightly to his breast. Then he threw himself down before the doorway, and lay upon his face, with head resting upon his arms in the attitude of a person who is profoundly asleep.

He must have searched through the woods again that night just as a somnambulist searches, for he found himself towards dawn in the valley before the idol. Then it was daybreak—the world was full of light and colour. He was seated before the house door, worn out and exhausted, when, raising his head, he saw Emmeline's figure coming out from amidst the distant trees on the other side of the sward.

THE NEWCOMER

He could not move for a moment, then he sprang to his feet and ran towards her. She looked pale and dazed, and she held something in her arms; something wrapped up in her scarf. As he pressed her to him, the something in the bundle struggled against his breast and emitted a squall—just like the squall of a cat. He drew back, and Emmeline, tenderly moving her scarf a bit aside, exposed a wee face. It was brick-red and wrinkled; there were two bright eyes, and a tuft of dark hair over the forehead. Then the eyes closed, the face screwed itself up, and the thing sneezed twice.

"Where did you *get* it?" he asked, absolutely lost in astonishment as she covered the face again gently with the scarf.

"I found it in the woods," replied Emmeline.

Dumb with amazement, he helped her along to the house, and she sat down, resting her head against the bamboos of the wall.

"I felt so bad," she explained; "and then I went off to sit in the woods, and then I remembered nothing more, and when I woke up it was there."

"It's a baby!" said Dick.

"I know," replied Emmeline.

Mrs James's baby, seen in the long ago, had risen up before their mind's eyes, a messenger from the past to explain what the new thing was. Then she told him things—things that completely shattered the old "cabbage bed" theory, supplanting it with a truth far more wonderful, far more poetical, too, to he who can appreciate the marvel and the mystery of life.

"It has something funny tied on to it," she went on, as if she were referring to a parcel she had just received.

"Let's look," said Dick.

"No," she replied; "leave it alone."

She sat rocking the thing gently, seeming oblivious to the whole world, and quite absorbed in it, as, indeed, was Dick. A physician would have shuddered, but, perhaps fortunately enough, there was no physician on the island. Only Nature, and she put everything to rights in her own time and way.

When Dick had sat marvelling long enough, he set to and lit the fire. He had eaten nothing since the day before, and he was nearly as exhausted as the girl. He cooked some breadfruit, there was some cold fish left over from the day before; this, with some bananas, he served up on two broad leaves, making Emmeline eat first.

Before they had finished, the creature in the bundle, as though it had smelt the food, began to scream. Emmeline drew the scarf aside. It looked hungry; its mouth would now be pinched up and now wide open, its eyes opened and closed. The girl touched it on the lips with her finger, and it seized upon her fingertip and sucked it. Her eyes filled with tears, she looked appealingly at Dick, who was on his knees; he took a banana, peeled it, broke off a bit and handed it to her. She approached it to the baby's mouth. It tried to suck it, failed, blew bubbles at the sun and squalled.

"Wait a minute," said Dick.

There were some green cocoa-nuts he had gathered the day before close by. He took one, removed the green husk, and opened one of the eyes, making an opening also in the opposite side of the shell. The unfortunate infant sucked ravenously at the nut, filled its stomach with the young cocoa-nut juice, vomited violently, and wailed. Emmeline in despair clasped it to her naked breast, wherefrom, in a moment, it was hanging like a leech. It knew more about babies than they did.

HANNAH

At noon, in the shallows of the reef, under the burning sun, the water would be quite warm. They would carry the baby down here, and Emmeline would wash it with a bit of flannel. After a few days it scarcely ever screamed, even when she washed it. It would lie on her knees during the process, striking valiantly out with its arms and legs, staring straight up at the sky. Then, when she turned it on its face, it would lay its head down and chuckle and blow bubbles at the coral of the reef, examining, apparently, the pattern of the coral with deep and philosophic attention.

Dick would sit by with his knees up to his chin, watching it all. He felt himself to be part proprietor in the thing—as indeed he was. The mystery of the affair still hung over them both. A week ago they two had been alone, and suddenly from nowhere this new individual had appeared.

It was so complete. It had hair on its head, tiny finger-nails, and hands that would grasp you. It had a whole host of little ways of its own, and every day added to them.

In a week the extreme ugliness of the newborn child had vanished. Its face, which had seemed carved in the imitation of a monkey's face from half a brick, became the face of a happy and healthy baby. It seemed to see things, and sometimes it would laugh and chuckle as though it had been told a good joke. Its black hair all came off and was supplanted by a sort of down. It had no teeth. It would lie on its back and kick and crow, and double its fists up and try to swallow them alternately, and cross its feet and play with its toes. In fact, it was exactly like any of the thousand-and-one babies that are born into the world at every tick of the clock.

"What will we call it?" said Dick one day, as he sat watching his son and heir crawling about on the grass under the shade of the breadfruit leaves.

"Hannah," said Emmeline promptly.

The recollection of another baby once heard about was in her mind; and it was as good a name as any other, perhaps, in that lonely place, notwithstanding the fact that Hannah was a boy.

Koko took a vast interest in the new arrival. He would hop round it and peer at it with his head on one side; and Hannah would crawl after the bird and try to grab it by the tail. In a few months so valiant and strong did he become that he would pursue his own father, crawling before him on the grass, and you might have seen the mother and father and child playing all together like three children, the bird sometimes hovering overhead like a good spirit, sometimes joining in the fun.

Sometimes Emmeline would sit and brood over the child, a troubled expression on her face and a far-away look in her eyes. The old vague fear of mischance had returned—the dread of that viewless form her imagination half pictured behind the smile on the face of Nature. Her happiness was so great that she dreaded to lose it.

There is nothing more wonderful than the birth of a man, and all that goes to bring it about. Here, on this island, in the very heart of the sea, amidst the sunshine and the wind-blown trees, under the great blue arch of the sky, in perfect purity of thought, they would discuss the question from beginning to end without a blush, the object of their discussion crawling before them on the grass, and attempting to grab feathers from Koko's tail.

It was the loneliness of the place as well as their ignorance of life that made the old, old miracle appear so strange and fresh—as beautiful as the miracle of death had appeared awful. In thoughts vague and beyond expression in words, they linked this new occurrence with that old occurrence on the reef six years before. The vanishing and the coming of a man.

Hannah, despite his unfortunate name, was certainly a most virile and engaging baby. The black hair which had appeared and vanished like some practical joke played by Nature, gave place to a down at first as yellow as sun-bleached wheat, but in a few months' time tinged with auburn.

One day—he had been uneasy and biting at his thumbs for some time past—Emmeline, looking into his mouth, saw something white and like a grain of rice protruding from his gum. It was a tooth just born. He could eat bananas now, and breadfruit, and they often fed him on fish—a fact which again might have caused a medical man to shudder; yet he throve on it all, and waxed stouter every day.

Emmeline, with a profound and natural wisdom, let him crawl about stark naked, dressed in ozone and sunlight. Taking him out on the reef, she would let him paddle in the shallow pools, holding him under the armpits whilst he splashed the diamond-bright water into spray with his feet, and laughed and shouted.

They were beginning now to experience a phenomenon, as wonderful as the birth of the child's body—the birth of his intelligence: the peeping out of a little personality with predilections of its own, likes and dislikes.

He knew Dick from Emmeline; and when Emmeline had satisfied his material wants, he would hold out his arms to go to Dick if he were by. He looked upon Koko as a friend, but when a friend of Koko's—a bird with an inquisitive mind and three red feathers in his tail—dropped in one day to inspect the newcomer, he resented the intrusion, and screamed.

He had a passion for flowers, or anything bright. He would laugh and shout when taken on the lagoon in the dinghy, and make as if to jump into the water to get at the bright-coloured corals below.

Ah me! we laugh at young mothers, and all the miraculous things they tell us about their babies. They see what we cannot see: the first unfolding of that mysterious flower, the mind.

H. de Vere Stacpoole

One day they were out on the lagoon. Dick had been rowing; he had ceased, and was letting the boat drift for a bit. Emmeline was dancing the child on her knee, when it suddenly held out its arms to the oarsman and said:

"Dick!"

The little word, so often heard and easily repeated, was its first word on earth.

A voice that had never spoken in the world before, had spoken; and to hear his name thus mysteriously uttered by a being he has created, is the sweetest and perhaps the saddest thing a man can ever know.

Dick took the child on his knee, and from that moment his love for it was more than his love for Emmeline or anything else on earth.

THE LAGOON OF FIRE

Ever since the tragedy of six years ago there had been forming in the mind of Emmeline Lestrange a something—shall I call it a deep mistrust. She had never been clever; lessons had saddened and wearied her, without making her much the wiser. Yet her mind was of that order into which profound truths come by short cuts. She was intuitive.

Great knowledge may lurk in the human mind without the owner of the mind being aware. He or she acts in such or such a way, or thinks in such and such a manner from intuition; in other words, as the outcome of the profoundest reasoning.

When we have learned to call storms, storms, and death, death, and birth, birth; when we have mastered the sailor's horn book, and Mr Piddington's law of cyclones, Ellis's anatomy, and Lewer's midwifery, we have already made ourselves half blind. We have become hypnotised by words and names. We think in words and names, not in ideas; the commonplace has triumphed, the true intellect is half crushed.

Storms had burst over the island before this. And what Emmeline remembered of them might be expressed by an instance.

The morning would be bright and happy, never so bright the sun, or so balmy the breeze, or so peaceful the blue lagoon; then, with a horrid suddenness, as if sick with dissimulation and mad to show itself, something would blacken the sun, and with a yell stretch out a hand and ravage the island, churn the lagoon into foam, beat down the cocoa-nut trees, and slay the birds. And one bird would be left and

123

another taken, one tree destroyed, and another left standing. The fury of the thing was less fearful than the blindness of it, and the indifference of it.

One night, when the child was asleep, just after the last star was lit, Dick appeared at the doorway of the house. He had been down to the water's edge and had now returned. He beckoned Emmeline to follow him, and, putting down the child, she did so.

"Come here and look," said he.

He led the way to the water; and as they approached it, Emmeline became aware that there was something strange about the lagoon. From a distance it looked pale and solid; it might have been a great stretch of grey marble veined with black. Then, as she drew nearer, she saw that the dull grey appearance was a deception of the eye.

The lagoon was alight and burning.

The phosphoric fire was in its very heart and being; every coral branch was a torch, every fish a passing lantern. The incoming tide moving the waters made the whole glittering floor of the lagoon move and shiver, and the tiny waves to lap the bank, leaving behind them glow-worm traces.

"Look!" said Dick.

He knelt down and plunged his forearm into the water. The immersed part burned like a smouldering torch. Emmeline could see it as plainly as though it were lit by sunlight. Then he drew his arm out, and as far as the water had reached, it was covered by a glowing glove.

They had seen the phosphorescence of the lagoon before; indeed, any night you might watch the passing fish like bars of silver, when the moon was away; but this was something quite new, and it was entrancing.

Emmeline knelt down and dabbled her hands, and made herself a pair of phosphoric gloves, and cried out with pleasure, and laughed. It was all the pleasure of playing with fire without the danger of being burnt. Then Dick rubbed his face with the water till it glowed.

"Wait!" he cried; and, running up to the house, he fetched out Hannah.

He came running down with him to the water's edge, gave Emmeline the child, unmoored the boat, and started out from shore.

The sculls, as far as they were immersed, were like bars of glistening silver; under them passed the fish, leaving cometic tails; each coral clump was a lamp, lending its lustre till the great lagoon was luminous as a lit-up ballroom. Even the child on Emmeline's lap crowed and cried out at the strangeness of the sight.

They landed on the reef and wandered over the flat. The sea was white and bright as snow, and the foam looked like a hedge of fire.

As they stood gazing on this extraordinary sight, suddenly, almost as instantaneously as the switching off of an electric light, the phosphorescence of the sea flickered and vanished.

The moon was rising. Her crest was just breaking from the water, and as her face came slowly into view behind a belt of vapour that lay on the horizon, it looked fierce and red, stained with smoke like the face of Eblis.

THE CYCLONE

When they awoke next morning the day was dark. A solid roof of cloud, lead-coloured and without a ripple on it, lay over the sky, almost to the horizon. There was not a breath of wind, and the birds flew wildly about as if disturbed by some unseen enemy in the wood.

As Dick lit the fire to prepare the breakfast, Emmeline walked up and down, holding her baby to her breast; she felt restless and uneasy.

As the morning wore on the darkness increased; a breeze rose up, and the leaves of the breadfruit trees pattered together with the sound of rain falling upon glass. A storm was coming, but there was something different in its approach to the approach of the storms they had already known.

As the breeze increased a sound filled the air, coming from far away beyond the horizon. It was like the sound of a great multitude of people, and yet so faint and vague was it that sudden bursts of the breeze through the leaves above would drown it utterly. Then it ceased, and nothing could be heard but the rocking of the branches and the tossing of the leaves under the increasing wind, which was now blowing sharply and fiercely and with a steady rush dead from the west, fretting the lagoon, and sending clouds and masses of foam right over the reef. The sky that had been so leaden and peaceful and like a solid roof was now all in a hurry, flowing eastward like a great turbulent river in spate.

And now, again, one could hear the sound in the distance—the thunder of the captains of the storm and the shouting; but still so faint, so vague, so indeterminate and unearthly that it seemed like the sound in a dream.

Emmeline sat amidst the ferns on the floor cowed and dumb, holding the baby to her breast. It was fast asleep. Dick stood at the doorway. He was disturbed in mind, but he did not show it.

The whole beautiful island world had now taken on the colour of ashes and the colour of lead. Beauty had utterly vanished, all seemed sadness and distress.

The cocoa-palms, under the wind that had lost its steady rush and was now blowing in hurricane blasts, flung themselves about in all the attitudes of distress; and whoever has seen a tropical storm will know what a cocoa-palm can express by its movements under the lash of the wind.

Fortunately the house was so placed that it was protected by the whole depth of the grove between it and the lagoon; and fortunately, too, it was sheltered by the dense foliage of the breadfruit, for suddenly, with a crash of thunder as if the hammer of Thor had been flung from sky to earth, the clouds split and the rain came down in a great slanting wave. It roared on the foliage above, which, bending leaf on leaf, made a slanting roof from which it rushed in a steady sheet-like cascade.

Dick had darted into the house, and was now sitting beside Emmeline, who was shivering and holding the child, which had awakened at the sound of the thunder.

For an hour they sat, the rain ceasing and coming again, the thunder shaking earth and sea, and the wind passing overhead with a piercing, monotonous cry.

Then all at once the wind dropped, the rain ceased, and a pale spectral light, like the light of dawn, fell before the doorway.

"It's over!" cried Dick, making to get up.

"Oh, listen!" said Emmeline, clinging to him, and holding the baby to his breast as if the touch of him would give it protection. She had divined that there was something approaching worse than a storm.

Then, listening in the silence, away from the other side of the island, they heard a sound like the droning of a great top.

It was the centre of the cyclone approaching.

A cyclone is a circular storm: a storm in the form of a ring. This ring of hurricane travels across the ocean with inconceivable speed and fury, yet its centre is a haven of peace.

As they listened the sound increased, sharpened, and became a tang that pierced the ear-drums: a sound that shook with hurry and speed, increasing, bringing with it the bursting and crashing of trees, and breaking at last overhead in a yell that stunned the brain like the blow of a bludgeon. In a second the house was torn away, and they were clinging to the roots of the breadfruit, deaf, blinded, half-lifeless.

The terror and the prolonged shock of it reduced them from thinking beings to the level of frightened animals whose one instinct is preservation.

How long the horror lasted they could not tell, when, like a madman who pauses for a moment in the midst of his struggles and stands stock-still, the wind ceased blowing, and there was peace. The centre of the cyclone was passing over the island.

Looking up, one saw a marvellous sight. The air was full of birds, butterflies, insects—all hanging in the heart of the storm and travelling with it under its protection.

Though the air was still as the air of a summer's day, from north, south, east, and west, from every point of the compass, came the yell of the hurricane.

There was something shocking in this.

In a storm one is so beaten about by the wind that one has no time to think: one is half stupefied. But in the dead centre of a cyclone one is in perfect peace. The trouble is all around, but it is not here. One has time to examine the thing like a tiger in a cage, listen to its voice and shudder at its ferocity.

The girl, holding the baby to her breast, sat up gasping. The baby had come to no harm; it had cried at first when the thunder broke, but now it seemed impassive, almost dazed. Dick stepped from under the tree and looked at the prodigy in the air.

The cyclone had gathered on its way sea-birds and birds from the land; there were gulls, electric white and black man-of-war birds, butterflies, and they all seemed imprisoned under a great drifting dome of glass. As they went, travelling like things without volition and in a dream, with a hum and a roar the south-west quadrant of the cyclone burst on the island, and the whole bitter business began over again.

It lasted for hours, then towards midnight the wind fell; and when the sun rose next morning he came through a cloudless sky, without a trace of apology for the destruction caused by his children the winds. He showed trees uprooted and birds lying dead, three or four canes remaining of what had once been a house, the lagoon the colour of a pale sapphire, and a glass-green, foam-capped sea racing in thunder against the reef.

THE STRICKEN WOODS

At first they thought they were ruined; then Dick, searching, found the old saw under a tree, and the butcher's knife near it, as though the knife and saw had been trying to escape in company and had failed.

Bit by bit they began to recover something of their scattered property. The remains of the flannel had been taken by the cyclone and wrapped round and round a slender cocoa-nut tree, till the trunk looked like a gaily-bandaged leg. The box of fishhooks had been jammed into the centre of a cooked breadfruit, both having been picked up by the fingers of the wind and hurled against the same tree; and the stay-sail of the *Shenandoah* was out on the reef, with a piece of coral carefully placed on it as if to keep it down. As for the lug-sail belonging to the dinghy, it was never seen again.

There is humour sometimes in a cyclone, if you can only appreciate it; no other form of air disturbance produces such quaint effects. Beside the great main whirlpool of wind, there are subsidiary whirlpools, each actuated by its own special imp.

Emmeline had felt Hannah nearly snatched from her arms twice by these little ferocious gimlet winds; and that the whole business of the great storm was set about with the object of snatching Hannah from her, and blowing him out to sea, was a belief which she held, perhaps, in the innermost recesses of her mind.

The dinghy would have been utterly destroyed, had it not heeled over and sunk in shallow water at the first onset of the wind; as it was, Dick was able to bail it out at the next low tide, when it floated as bravely as ever, not having started a single seam.

But the destruction amidst the trees was pitiful. Looking at the woods as a mass, one noticed gaps here and there, but what had really happened could not be seen till one was amongst the trees. Great, beautiful cocoa-nut palms, not dead, but just dying, lay crushed and broken as if trampled upon by some enormous foot. You would come across half a dozen lianas twisted into one great cable. Where cocoa-nut palms were, you could not move a yard without kicking against a fallen nut; you might have picked up full-grown, half-grown, and wee baby nuts, not bigger than small apples, for on the same tree you will find nuts of all sizes and conditions.

One never sees a perfectly straight-stemmed cocoa-palm; they all have an inclination from the perpendicular more or less; perhaps that is why a cyclone has more effect on them than on other trees.

Artus, once so pretty a picture with their diamond-chequered trunks, lay broken and ruined; and right through the belt of mammee apple, right through the bad lands, lay a broad road, as if an army, horse, foot, and artillery, had passed that way from lagoon edge to lagoon edge. This was the path left by the great fore-foot of the storm; but had you searched the woods on either side, you would have found paths where the lesser winds had been at work, where the baby whirlwinds had been at play.

From the bruised woods, like an incense offered to heaven, rose a perfume of blossoms gathered and scattered, of rain-wet leaves, of lianas twisted and broken and oozing their sap; the perfume of newly-wrecked and ruined trees—the essence and soul of the artu, the banyan and cocoa-palm cast upon the wind.

You would have found dead butterflies in the woods, dead birds too; but in the great path of the storm you would have found dead butterflies' wings, feathers, leaves frayed as if by fingers, branches of the aoa, and sticks of the hibiscus broken into little fragments.

Powerful enough to rip a ship open, root up a tree, half ruin a city. Delicate enough to tear a butterfly wing from wing—that is a cyclone.

Emmeline, wandering about in the woods with Dick on the day after the storm, looking at the ruin of great tree and little bird, and recollecting the land birds she had caught a glimpse of yesterday being carried along safely by the storm out to sea to be drowned, felt a great weight lifting from her heart. Mischance had come, and spared them and the baby. The blue had spoken, but had not called them.

She felt that something—the something which we in civilisation call Fate—was for the present gorged; and, without being annihilated, her incessant hypochondriacal dread condensed itself into a point, leaving her horizon sunlit and clear.

The cyclone had indeed treated them almost, one might say, amiably. It had taken the house—but that was a small matter, for it had left them nearly all their small possessions. The tinder box and flint and steel would have been a much more serious loss than a dozen houses, for, without it, they would have had absolutely no means of making a fire.

If anything, the cyclone had been almost too kind to them; had let them pay off too little of that mysterious debt they owed to the gods.

A FALLEN IDOL

The next day Dick began to rebuild the house. He had fetched the stay-sail from the reef and rigged up a temporary tent.

It was a great business cutting the canes and dragging them out in the open. Emmeline helped; whilst Hannah, seated on the grass, played with the bird that had vanished during the storm, but reappeared the evening after.

The child and the bird had grown fast friends; they were friendly enough even at first, but now the bird would sometimes let the tiny hands clasp him right round his body—at least, as far as the hands would go.

It is a rare experience for a man to hold a tame and unstruggling and unfrightened bird in his hands; next to pressing a woman in his arms, it is the pleasantest tactile sensation he will ever experience, perhaps, in life. He will feel a desire to press it to his heart, if he has such a thing.

Hannah would press Koko to his little brown stomach, as if in artless admission of where his heart lay.

He was an extraordinarily bright and intelligent child. He did not promise to be talkative, for, having achieved the word "Dick," he rested content for a long while before advancing further into the labyrinth of language; but though he did not use his tongue, he spoke in a host of other ways. With his eyes, that were as bright as Koko's, and full of all sorts of mischief; with his hands and feet and the movements of his body. He had a way of shaking his hands before him when highly delighted, a way of expressing nearly all the shades of pleasure; and though he rarely expressed anger, when he did so, he expressed it fully.

He was just now passing over the frontier into toyland. In civilisation he would no doubt have been the possessor of an india-rubber dog or a woolly lamb, but there were no toys here at all. Emmeline's old doll had been left behind when they took flight from the other side of the island, and Dick, a year or so ago, on one of his expeditions, had found it lying half buried in the sand of the beach.

He had brought it back now more as a curiosity than anything else, and they had kept it on the shelf in the house. The cyclone had impaled it on a tree-twig near by, as if in derision; and Hannah, when it was presented to him as a plaything, flung it away from him as if in disgust. But he would play with flowers or bright shells, or bits of coral, making vague patterns with them on the sward.

All the toy lambs in the world would not have pleased him better than those things, the toys of the Troglodyte children—the children of the Stone Age. To clap two oyster shells together and make a noise—what, after all, could a baby want better than that?

One afternoon, when the house was beginning to take some sort of form, they ceased work and went off into the woods; Emmeline carrying the baby, and Dick taking turns with him. They were going to the valley of the idol.

Since the coming of Hannah, and even before, the stone figure standing in its awful and mysterious solitude had ceased to be an object of dread to Emmeline, and had become a thing vaguely benevolent. Love had come to her under its shade; and under its shade the spirit of the child had entered into her—from where, who knows? But certainly through heaven.

Perhaps the thing which had been the god of some unknown people had inspired her with the instinct of religion; if so, she was his last worshipper on earth, for when they entered the valley they found him lying upon his face. Great blocks of stone lay around him: there had evidently been a landslip, a catastrophe preparing for ages, and determined, perhaps, by the torrential rain of the cyclone.

In Ponape, Huahine, in Easter Island, you may see great idols that have been felled like this, temples slowly dissolving from sight, and terraces, seemingly as solid as the hills, turning softly and subtly into shapeless mounds of stone.

THE EXPEDITION

Next morning the light of day filtering through the trees awakened Emmeline in the tent which they had improvised whilst the house was building. Dawn came later here than on the other side of the island which faced east—later, and in a different manner—for there is the difference of worlds between dawn coming over a wooded hill, and dawn coming over the sea.

Over at the other side, sitting on the sand with the break of the reef which faced the east before you, scarcely would the east change colour before the sea-line would be on fire, the sky lit up into an illimitable void of blue, and the sunlight flooding into the lagoon, the ripples of light seeming to chase the ripples of water.

On this side it was different. The sky would be dark and full of stars, and the woods, great spaces of velvety shadow. Then through the leaves of the artu would come a sigh, and the leaves of the breadfruit would patter, and the sound of the reef become faint. The land breeze had awakened, and in a while, as if it had blown them away, looking up, you would find the stars gone, and the sky a veil of palest blue. In this indirect approach of dawn there was something ineffably mysterious. One could see, but the things seen were indecisive and vague, just as they are in the gloaming of an English summer's day.

Scarcely had Emmeline arisen when Dick woke also, and they went out on to the sward, and then down to the water's edge. Dick went in for a swim, and the girl, holding the baby, stood on the bank watching him.

Always after a great storm the weather of the island would become more bracing and exhilarating, and this morning the air seemed filled with the spirit of spring. Emmeline felt it, and as she watched the swimmer disporting in the water, she laughed, and held the child up to watch him. She was fey. The breeze, filled with all sorts of sweet perfumes from the woods, blew her black hair about her shoulders, and the full light of morning coming over the palm fronds of the woods beyond the sward touched her and the child. Nature seemed caressing them.

Dick came ashore, and then ran about to dry himself in the wind. Then he went to the dinghy and examined her; for he had determined to leave the house-building for half a day, and row round to the old place to see how the banana trees had fared during the storm. His anxiety about them was not to be wondered at. The island was his larder, and the bananas were a most valuable article of food. He had all the feelings of a careful housekeeper about them, and he could not rest till he had seen for himself the extent of damage, if damage there was any.

He examined the boat, and then they all went back to breakfast. Living their lives, they had to use forethought. They would put away, for instance, all the shells of the cocoa-nuts they used for fuel; and you never could imagine the blazing splendour there lives in the shell of a cocoa-nut till you see it burning. Yesterday, Dick, with his usual prudence, had placed a heap of sticks, all wet with the rain of the storm, to dry in the sun: as a consequence, they had plenty of fuel to make a fire with this morning.

When they had finished breakfast he got the knife to cut the bananas with—if there were any left to cut—and, taking the javelin, he went down to the boat, followed by Emmeline and the child.

Dick had stepped into the boat, and was on the point of unmooring her, and pushing her off, when Emmeline stopped him.

"Dick!"

"Yes?"

"I will go with you."

"You!" said he in astonishment.

"Yes, I'm—not afraid any more."

It was a fact; since the coming of the child she had lost that dread of the other side of the island—or almost lost it.

Death is a great darkness, birth is a great light—they had intermixed in her mind; the darkness was still there, but it was no longer terrible to her, for it was infused with the light. The result was a twilight sad, but beautiful, and unpeopled with forms of fear.

Years ago she had seen a mysterious door close and shut a human being out for ever from the world. The sight had filled her with dread unimaginable, for she had no words for the thing, no religion or philosophy to explain it away or gloss it over. Just recently she had seen an equally mysterious door open and admit a human being; and deep down in her mind, in the place where the dreams were, the one great fact had explained and justified the other. Life had vanished into the void, but life had come from there. There was life in the void, and it was no longer terrible.

Perhaps all religions were born on a day when some woman, seated upon a rock by the prehistoric sea, looked at her newborn child and recalled to mind her man who had been slain, thus closing the charm and imprisoning the idea of a future state.

Emmeline, with the child in her arms, stepped into the little boat and took her seat in the stern, whilst Dick pushed off. Scarcely had he put out the sculls than a new passenger arrived. It was Koko. He would often accompany them to the reef, though, strangely enough, he would never go there alone of his own accord. He made a circle or two over them, and then lit on the gunwale in the bow, and perched there, humped up, and with his long dove-coloured tail feathers presented to the water.

The oarsman kept close in-shore, and as they rounded the little cape all gay with wild cocoa-nut the bushes brushed the boat, and the child, excited by their colour, held out his hands to them. Emmeline stretched out her hand and broke off a branch; but it was not a branch of the wild cocoa-nut she had plucked, it was a branch of the never-wake-up berries. The berries that will cause a man to sleep, should he eat of them—to sleep and dream, and never wake up again.

"Throw them away!" cried Dick, who remembered.

"I will in a minute," she replied.

She was holding them up before the child, who was laughing and trying to grasp them. Then she forgot them, and dropped them in the bottom of the boat, for something had struck the keel with a thud, and the water was boiling all round.

There was a savage fight going on below. In the breeding season great battles would take place sometimes in the lagoon, for fish have their jealousies just like men—love affairs, friendships. The two great forms could be dimly perceived, one in pursuit of the other, and they terrified Emmeline, who implored Dick to row on.

They slipped by the pleasant shores that Emmeline had never seen before, having been sound asleep when they came past them those years ago.

Just before putting off she had looked back at the beginnings of the little house under the artu tree, and as she looked at the strange glades and groves, the picture of it rose before her, and seemed to call her back.

It was a tiny possession, but it was home; and so little used to change was she that already a sort of home-sickness was upon her; but it passed away almost as soon as it came, and she fell to wondering at the things around her, and pointing them out to the child.

When they came to the place where Dick had hooked the albicore, he hung on his oars and told her about it. It was the first time she had heard of it; a fact which shows into what a state of savagery he had been lapsing. He had mentioned about the canoes, for he had to account for the javelin; but as for telling her of the incidents of the chase, he no more thought of doing so than a red Indian would think of detailing to his squaw the incidents of a bear hunt. Contempt for women is the first law of savagery, and perhaps the last law of some old and profound philosophy.

She listened, and when it came to the incident of the shark, she shuddered.

"I wish I had a hook big enough to catch him with," said he, staring into the water as if in search of his enemy.

"Don't think of him, Dick," said Emmeline, holding the child more tightly to her heart. "Row on."

He resumed the sculls, but you could have seen from his face that he was recounting to himself the incident.

When they had rounded the last promontory, and the strand and the break in the reef opened before them, Emmeline caught her breath. The place had changed in some subtle manner; everything was there as before, yet everything seemed different—the lagoon seemed narrower, the reef nearer, the cocoa-palms not nearly so tall. She was contrasting the real things with the recollection of them when seen by a child. The black speck had vanished from the reef; the storm had swept it utterly away.

Dick beached the boat on the shelving sand, and left Emmeline seated in the stern of it, whilst he went in search of the bananas; she would have accompanied him, but the child had fallen asleep.

Hannah asleep was even a pleasanter picture than when awake. He looked like a little brown Cupid without wings, bow or arrow. He had all the grace of a curled-up feather. Sleep was always in pursuit of him, and would catch him up at the most unexpected moments—when he was at play, or indeed at any time. Emmeline would sometimes find him with a coloured shell or bit of coral that he had been playing with in his hand fast asleep, a happy expression on his face, as if his mind were pursuing its earthly avocations on some fortunate beach in dreamland.

Dick had plucked a huge breadfruit leaf and given it to her as a shelter from the sun, and she sat holding it over her, and gazing straight before her, over the white, sunlit sands.

The flight of the mind in reverie is not in a direct line. To her, dreaming as she sat, came all sorts of coloured pictures, recalled by the scene before her: the green water under the stern of a ship, and the word *Shenandoah* vaguely reflected on it; their landing, and the little tea-set spread out on the white sand—she could still see the pansies painted on the plates, and she counted in memory the lead spoons; the great stars that burned over the reef at nights; the Cluricaunes and fairies; the cask by the well where the convolvulus blossomed, and the wind-blown trees seen from the summit of the hill—all these pictures drifted before her, dissolving and replacing each other as they went.

There was sadness in the contemplation of them, but pleasure too. She felt at peace with the world. All trouble seemed far behind her. It was as if the great storm that had left them unharmed had been an ambassador from the powers above to assure her of their forbearance, protection, and love.

All at once she noticed that between the boat's bow and the sand there lay a broad, blue, sparkling line. The dinghy was afloat.

THE KEEPER OF THE LAGOON

The woods here had been less affected by the cyclone than those upon the other side of the island, but there had been destruction enough. To reach the place he wanted, Dick had to climb over felled trees and fight his way through a tangle of vines that had once hung overhead.

The banana trees had not suffered at all; as if by some special dispensation of Providence even the great bunches of fruit had been scarcely injured, and he proceeded to climb and cut them. He cut two bunches, and with one across his shoulder came back down through the trees.

He had got half across the sands, his head bent under the load, when a distant call came to him, and, raising his head, he saw the boat adrift in the middle of the lagoon, and the figure of the girl in the bow of it waving to him with her arm. He saw a scull floating on the water half-way between the boat and the shore, which she had no doubt lost in an attempt to paddle the boat back. He remembered that the tide was going out.

He flung his load aside, and ran down the beach; in a moment he was in the water. Emmeline, standing up in the boat, watched him.

When she found herself adrift, she had made an effort to row back, and in her hurry shipping the sculls she had lost one. With a single scull she was quite helpless, as she had not the art of sculling a boat from the stern. At first she was not frightened, because she knew that Dick would soon return to her assistance; but as the distance between boat and shore increased, a cold hand seemed laid upon her heart. Looking at the shore it seemed very far away, and the view towards the reef was terrific, for the opening had increased in apparent size, and the great sea beyond seemed drawing her to it.

She saw Dick coming out of the wood with the load on his shoulder, and she called to him. At first he did not seem to hear, then she saw him look up, cast the bananas away, and come running down the sand to the water's edge. She watched him swimming, she saw him seize the scull, and her heart gave a great leap of joy.

Towing the scull and swimming with one arm, he rapidly approached the boat. He was quite close, only ten feet away, when Emmeline saw behind him, shearing through the clear, rippling water and advancing with speed, a dark triangle that seemed made of canvas stretched upon a sword point.

Forty years ago he had floated adrift on the sea in the form and likeness of a small shabby pine-cone, a prey to anything that might find him. He had escaped the jaws of the dog-fish, and the jaws of the dog-fish are a very wide door; he had escaped the albicore and squid: his life had been one long series of miraculous escapes from death. Out of a billion like him born in the same year, he and a few others only had survived.

For thirty years he had kept the lagoon to himself, as a ferocious tiger keeps a jungle. He had known the palm tree on the reef when it was a seedling, and he had known the reef even before the palm tree was there. The things he had devoured, flung one upon another, would have made a mountain; yet he was as clear of enmity as a sword, as cruel, and as soulless. He was the spirit of the lagoon.

Emmeline screamed, and pointed to the thing behind the swimmer. He turned, saw it, dropped the oar and made for the boat. She had seized the remaining scull and stood with it poised, then she hurled it blade foremost at the form in the water, now fully visible, and close on its prey.

She could not throw a stone straight, yet the scull went like an arrow to the mark, balking the pursuer and saving the pursued. In a moment more his leg was over the gunwale, and he was saved.

But the scull was lost.

THE HAND OF THE SEA

There was nothing in the boat that could possibly be used as a paddle; the scull was only five or six yards away, but to attempt to swim to it was certain death, yet they were being swept out to sea. He might have made the attempt, only that on the starboard quarter the form of the shark, gently swimming at the same pace as they were drifting, could be made out only half veiled by the water.

The bird perched on the gunwale seemed to divine their trouble, for he rose in the air, made a circle, and resumed his perch with all his feathers ruffled.

Dick stood in despair, helpless, his hands clasping his head. The shore was drawing away before him, the surf loudening behind him, yet he could do nothing. The island was being taken away from them by the great hand of the sea.

Then, suddenly, the little boat entered the race formed by the confluence of the tides, from the right and left arms of the lagoon; the sound of the surf suddenly increased as though a door had been flung open. The breakers were falling and the sea-gulls crying on either side of them, and for a moment the ocean seemed to hesitate as to whether they were to be taken away into her wastes, or dashed on the coral strand. Only for a moment this seeming hesitation lasted; then the power of the tide prevailed over the power of the swell, and the little boat taken by the current drifted gently out to sea.

Dick flung himself down beside Emmeline, who was seated in the bottom of the boat holding the child to her breast. The bird, seeing the land retreat, and wise in its instinct, rose into the air. It circled thrice round the drifting boat, and then, like a beautiful but faithless spirit, passed away to the shore.

TOGETHER

The island had sunk slowly from sight; at sundown it was just a trace, a stain on the south-western horizon. It was before the new moon, and the little boat lay drifting. It drifted from the light of sunset into a world of vague violet twilight, and now it lay drifting under the stars.

The girl, clasping the baby to her breast, leaned against her companion's shoulder; neither of them spoke. All the wonders in their short existence had culminated in this final wonder, this passing away together from the world of Time. This strange voyage they had embarked on—to where?

Now that the first terror was over they felt neither sorrow nor fear. They were together. Come what might, nothing could divide them; even should they sleep and never wake up, they would sleep together. Had one been left and the other taken!

As though the thought had occurred to them simultaneously, they turned one to the other, and their lips met, their souls met, mingling in one dream; whilst above in the windless heaven space answered space with flashes of siderial light, and Canopus shone and burned like the pointed sword of Azrael.

Clasped in Emmeline's hand was the last and most mysterious gift of the mysterious world they had known—the branch of crimson berries.

BOOK III

MAD LESTRANGE

They knew him upon the Pacific slope as "Mad Lestrange." He was not mad, but he was a man with a fixed idea. He was pursued by a vision: the vision of two children and an old sailor adrift in a little boat upon a wide blue sea.

When the *Arago*, bound for Papetee, picked up the boats of the *Northumberland*, only the people in the long-boat were alive. Le Farge, the captain, was mad, and he never recovered his reason. Lestrange was utterly shattered; the awful experience in the boats and the loss of the children had left him a seemingly helpless wreck. The scowbankers, like all their class, had fared better, and in a few days were about the ship and sitting in the sun. Four days after the rescue the *Arago* spoke the *Newcastle*, bound for San Francisco, and transhipped the shipwrecked men.

Had a physician seen Lestrange on board the *Northumberland* as she lay in that long, long calm before the fire, he would have declared that nothing but a miracle could prolong his life. The miracle came about.

In the general hospital of San Francisco, as the clouds cleared from his mind, they unveiled the picture of the children and the little boat. The picture had been there daily, seen but not truly comprehended; the horrors gone through in the open boat, the sheer physical exhaustion, had merged all the accidents of the great disaster into one mournful half-comprehended fact. When his brain cleared all the other incidents fell out of focus, and memory, with her eyes set upon the children, began to paint a picture that he was ever more to see.

Memory cannot produce a picture that Imagination has not retouched; and her pictures, even the ones least touched by Imagination, are no mere photographs, but the work of an artist. All that is inessential she casts away, all that is essential she retains; she idealises, and that is why her picture of a lost mistress has had power to keep a man a celibate to the end of his days, and why she can break a human heart with the picture of a dead child. She is a painter, but she is also a poet.

The picture before the mind of Lestrange was filled with this almost diabolical poetry, for in it the little boat and her helpless crew were represented adrift on a blue and sunlit sea. A sea most beautiful to look at, yet most terrible, bearing as it did the recollections of thirst.

He had been dying, when, raising himself on his elbow, so to say, he looked at this picture. It recalled him to life. His willpower asserted itself, and he refused to die.

The will of a man has, if it is strong enough, the power to reject death. He was not in the least conscious of the exercise of this power; he only knew that a great and absorbing interest had suddenly arisen in him, and that a great aim stood before him—the recovery of the children.

The disease that was killing him ceased its ravages, or rather was slain in its turn by the increased vitality against which it had to strive. He left the hospital and took up his quarters at the Palace Hotel, and then, like the General of an army, he began to formulate his plan of campaign against Fate.

When the crew of the *Northumberland* had stampeded, hurling their officers aside, lowering the boats with a rush, and casting themselves into the sea, everything had been lost in the way of ship's papers; the charts, the two logs—everything, in fact, that could indicate the latitude and longitude of the disaster. The first and second officers and a midshipman had shared the fate of the quarter-boat; of the foremast hands saved, not one, of course, could give the slightest hint as to the locality of the spot.

A time reckoning from the Horn told little, for there was no record of the log. All that could be said was that the disaster had occurred somewhere south of the line.

In Le Farge's brain lay for a certainty the position, and Lestrange went to see the captain in the "Maison de Sante," where he was being looked after, and found him quite recovered from the furious mania that he had been suffering from. Quite recovered, and playing with a ball of coloured worsted.

There remained the log of the *Arago*; in it would be found the latitude and longitude of the boats she had picked up.

The *Arago*, due at Papetee, became overdue. Lestrange watched the overdue lists from day to day, from week to week, from month to month, uselessly, for the *Arago* never was heard of again. One could not affirm even that she was wrecked; she was simply one of the ships that never come back from the sea.

THE SECRET OF THE AZURE

To lose a child he loves is undoubtedly the greatest catastrophe that can happen to a man. I do not refer to its death.

A child wanders into the street, or is left by its nurse for a moment, and vanishes. At first the thing is not realised. There is a pang and hurry at the heart which half vanishes, whilst the understanding explains that in a civilised city, if a child gets lost, it will be found and brought back by the neighbours or the police.

But the police know nothing of the matter, or the neighbours, and the hours pass. Any minute may bring back the wanderer; but the minutes pass, and the day wears into evening, and the evening to night, and the night to dawn, and the common sounds of a new day begin.

You cannot remain at home for restlessness; you go out, only to return hurriedly for news. You are eternally listening, and what you hear shocks you; the common sounds of life, the roll of the carts and cabs in the street, the footsteps of the passers-by, are full of an indescribable mournfulness; music increases your misery into madness, and the joy of others is monstrous as laughter heard in hell.

If some one were to bring you the dead body of the child, you might weep, but you would bless him, for it is the uncertainty that kills.

You go mad, or go on living. Years pass by, and you are an old man. You say to yourself: "He would have been twenty years of age to-day."

There is not in the old ferocious penal code of our forefathers a punishment adequate to the case of the man or woman who steals a child.

Lestrange was a wealthy man, and one hope remained to him, that the children might have been rescued by some passing ship. It was not the case of children lost in a city, but in the broad Pacific, where ships travel from all ports to all ports, and to advertise his loss adequately it was necessary to placard the world. Ten thousand dollars was the reward offered for news of the lost ones, twenty thousand for the recovery; and the advertisement appeared in every newspaper likely to reach the eyes of a sailor, from the *Liverpool Post* to the *Dead Bird*.

The years passed without anything definite coming in answer to all these advertisements. Once news came of two children saved from the sea in the neighbourhood of the Gilberts, and it was not false news, but they were not the children he was seeking for. This incident at once depressed and stimulated him, for it seemed to say, "If these children have been saved, why not yours?"

The strange thing was, that in his heart he felt a certainty that they were alive. His intellect suggested their death in twenty different forms; but a whisper, somewhere out of that great blue ocean, told him at intervals that what he sought was there, living, and waiting for him.

He was somewhat of the same temperament as Emmeline—a dreamer, with a mind tuned to receive and record the fine rays that fill this world flowing from intellect to intellect, and even from what we call inanimate things. A coarser nature would, though feeling, perhaps, as acutely the grief, have given up in despair the search. But he kept on; and at the end of the fifth year, so far from desisting, he chartered a schooner and passed eighteen months in a fruitless search, calling at little-known islands, and once, unknowing, at an island only three hundred miles away from the tiny island of this story.

If you wish to feel the hopelessness of this unguided search, do not look at a map of the Pacific, but go there. Hundreds and hundreds of thousands of square leagues of sea, thousands of islands, reefs, atolls.

Up to a few years ago there were many small islands utterly unknown; even still there are some, though the charts of the Pacific are the greatest triumphs of hydrography; and though the island of the story was actually on the Admiralty charts, of what use was that fact to Lestrange?

He would have continued searching, but he dared not, for the desolation of the sea had touched him.

In that eighteen months the Pacific explained itself to him in part, explained its vastness, its secrecy and inviolability. The schooner lifted veil upon veil of distance, and veil upon veil lay beyond. He could only move in a right line; to search the wilderness of water with any hope, one would have to be endowed with the gift of moving in all directions at once.

He would often lean over the bulwark rail and watch the swell slip by, as if questioning the water. Then the sunsets began to weigh upon his heart, and the stars to speak to him in a new language, and he knew that it was time to return, if he would return with a whole mind.

When he got back to San Francisco he called upon his agent, Wannamaker of Kearney Street, but there was still no news.

CAPTAIN FOUNTAIN

He had a suite of rooms at the Palace Hotel, and he lived the life of any other rich man who is not addicted to pleasure. He knew some of the best people in the city, and conducted himself so sanely in all respects that a casual stranger would never have guessed his reputation for madness; but when you knew him better, you would find sometimes in the middle of a conversation that his mind was away from the subject; and were you to follow him in the street, you would hear him in conversation with himself. Once at a dinner-party he rose and left the room, and did not return. Trifles, but sufficient to establish a reputation of a sort.

One morning—to be precise, it was the second day of May, exactly eight years and five months after the wreck of the *Northumberland*—Lestrange was in his sitting-room reading, when the bell of the telephone, which stood in the corner of the room, rang. He went to the instrument.

"Are you there?" came a high American voice. "Lestrange—right—come down and see me—Wannamaker—I have news for you."

Lestrange held the receiver for a moment, then he put it back in the rest. He went to a chair and sat down, holding his head between his hands, then he rose and went to the telephone again; but he dared not use it, he dare not shatter the newborn hope.

"News!" What a world lies in that word.

In Kearney Street he stood before the door of Wannamaker's office collecting himself and watching the crowd drifting by, then he entered and went up the stairs. He pushed open a swing-door and entered a great room. The clink and rattle of a dozen typewriters filled the place, and all the hurry of business; clerks passed and came with sheaves of correspondence in their hands; and Wannamaker himself, rising from bending over a message which he was correcting on one of the typewriters' tables, saw the newcomer and led him to the private office.

"What is it?" said Lestrange.

"Only this," said the other, taking up a slip of paper with a name and address on it. "Simon J. Fountain, of 45 Rathray Street, West—that's down near the wharves—says he has seen your ad. in an old number of a paper, and he thinks he can tell you something. He did not specify the nature of the intelligence, but it might be worth finding out."

"I will go there," said Lestrange.

"Do you know Rathray Street?"

"No."

Wannamaker went out and called a boy and gave him some directions; then Lestrange and the boy started.

Lestrange left the office without saying "Thank you," or taking leave in any way of the advertising agent—who did not feel in the least affronted, for he knew his customer.

Rathray Street is, or was before the earthquake, a street of small clean houses. It had a seafaring look that was accentuated by the marine perfumes from the wharves close by and the sound of steam winches loading or discharging cargo—a sound that ceased not night or day as the work went on beneath the sun or the sizzling arc lamps.

No. 45 was almost exactly like its fellows, neither better nor worse; and the door was opened by a neat, prim woman, small, and of middle age. Commonplace she was, no doubt, but not commonplace to Lestrange.

"Is Mr Fountain in?" he asked. "I have come about the advertisement."

"Oh, have you, sir?" she replied, making way for him to enter, and showing him into a little sitting-room on the left of the passage. "The Captain is in bed; he is a great invalid, but he was expecting, perhaps, some one would call, and he will be able to see you in a minute, if you don't mind waiting."

"Thanks," said Lestrange; "I can wait."

He had waited eight years, what mattered a few minutes now? But at no time in the eight years had he suffered such suspense, for his heart knew that now, just now in this commonplace little house, from the lips of, perhaps, the husband of that commonplace woman, he was going to learn either what he feared to hear, or what he hoped.

It was a depressing little room; it was so clean, and looked as though it were never used. A ship imprisoned in a glass bottle stood upon the mantelpiece, and there were shells from far-away places, pictures of ships in sand—all the things one finds as a rule adorning an old sailor's home.

Lestrange, as he sat waiting, could hear movements from the next room—probably the invalid's, which they were preparing for his reception. The distant sounds of the derricks and winches came muffled through the tightly-shut window that looked as though it never had been opened. A square of sunlight lit the upper part of the cheap lace curtain on the right of the window, and repeated its pattern vaguely on the lower part of the wall opposite. Then a bluebottle fly awoke suddenly into life and began to buzz and drum against the window pane, and Lestrange wished that they would come.

A man of his temperament must necessarily, even under the happiest circumstances, suffer in going through the world; the fine fibre always suffers when brought into contact with the coarse. These people were as kindly disposed as any one else. The advertisement and the face and manners of the visitor might have told them that it was not the time for delay, yet they kept him waiting whilst they arranged bed-quilts and put medicine bottles straight—as if he could see!

At last the door opened, and the woman said:

"Will you step this way, sir?"

She showed him into a bedroom opening off the passage. The room was neat and clean, and had that indescribable appearance which marks the bedroom of the invalid.

In the bed, making a mountain under the counterpane with an enormously distended stomach, lay a man, black-bearded, and with his large, capable, useless hands spread out on the coverlet—hands ready and willing, but debarred from work. Without moving his body, he turned his head slowly and looked at the newcomer. This slow movement was not from weakness or disease, it was the slow, emotionless nature of the man speaking.

"This is the gentleman, Silas," said the woman, speaking over Lestrange's shoulder. Then she withdrew and closed the door.

"Take a chair, sir," said the sea captain, flapping one of his hands on the counterpane as if in wearied protest against his own helplessness. "I haven't the pleasure of your name, but the missus tells me you're come about the advertisement I lit on yester-even."

He took a paper, folded small, that lay beside him, and held it out to his visitor. It was a *Sidney Bulletin* three years old.

"Yes," said Lestrange, looking at the paper; "that is my advertisement."

"Well, it's strange—very strange," said Captain Fountain, "that I should have lit on it only yesterday. I've had it all three years in my chest, the way old papers get lying at the bottom with odds and ends. Mightn't a' seen it now, only the missus cleared the raffle out of the chest, and, 'Give me that paper,' I says, seeing it in her hand; and I fell to reading it, for a man'll read anything bar tracts lying in bed eight months, as I've been with the dropsy. I've been whaler man and boy forty year, and my last ship was the *Sea-Horse*. Over seven years ago one of my men picked up something on a beach of one of them islands east of the Marquesas—we'd put in to water—"

"Yes, yes," said Lestrange. "What was it he found?"

"Missus!" roared the captain in a voice that shook the walls of the room.

The door opened, and the woman appeared.

"Fetch me my keys out of my trousers pocket."

The trousers were hanging up on the back of the door, as if only waiting to be put on. The woman fetched the keys, and he fumbled over them and found one. He handed it to her, and pointed to the drawer of a bureau opposite the bed.

She knew evidently what was wanted, for she opened the drawer and produced a box, which she handed to him. It was a small cardboard box tied round with a bit of string. He undid the string, and disclosed a child's tea service: a teapot, cream jug, six little plates—all painted with a pansy.

It was the box which Emmeline had always been losing—lost again.

Lestrange buried his face in his hands. He knew the things. Emmeline had shown them to him in a burst of confidence. Out of all that vast ocean he had searched unavailingly: they had come to him like a message, and the awe and mystery of it bowed him down and crushed him.

The captain had placed the things on the newspaper spread out by his side, and he was unrolling the little spoons from their tissue-paper covering. He counted them as if entering up the tale of some trust, and placed them on the newspaper.

"When did you find them?" asked Lestrange, speaking with his face still covered.

"A matter of over seven years ago," replied the captain, "we'd put in to water at a place south of the line—Palm Tree Island we whalemen call it, because of the tree at the break of the lagoon. One of my men brought it aboard, found it in a shanty built of sugar-canes which the men bust up for devilment."

"Good God!" said Lestrange. "Was there no one there—nothing but this box?"

"Not a sight or sound, so the men said; just the shanty abandoned seemingly. I had no time to land and hunt for castaways, I was after whales."

"How big is the island?"

"Oh, a fairish middle-sized island—no natives. I've heard tell it's *tabu*; why, the Lord only knows—some crank of the Kanakas, I s'pose. Anyhow, there's the findings—you recognise them?"

"I do."

"Seems strange," said the captain, "that I should pick 'em up; seems strange your advertisement out, and the answer to it lying amongst my gear, but that's the way things go."

146

"Strange!" said the other. "It's more than strange."

"Of course," continued the captain, "they might have been on the island hid away som'ere, there's no saying; only appearances are against it. Of course they might be there now unbeknownst to you or me."

"They *are* there now," answered Lestrange, who was sitting up and looking at the playthings as though he read in them some hidden message. "They *are* there now. Have you the position of the island?"

"I have. Missus, hand me my private log."

She took a bulky, greasy, black note-book from the bureau, and handed it to him. He opened it, thumbed the pages, and then read out the latitude and longitude.

"I entered it on the day of finding—here's the entry. 'Adams brought aboard child's toy box out of deserted shanty, which men pulled down; traded it to me for a caulker of rum.' The cruise lasted three years and eight months after that; we'd only been out three when it happened. I forgot all about it: three years scrubbing round the world after whales doesn't brighten a man's memory. Right round we went, and paid off at Nantucket. Then, after a fortni't on shore and a month repairin', the old *Sea-Horse* was off again, I with her. It was at Honolulu this dropsy took me, and back I come here, home. That's the yarn. There's not much to it, but, seein' your advertisement, I thought I might answer it."

Lestrange took Fountain's hand and shook it.

"You see the reward I offered?" he said. "I have not my cheque book with me, but you shall have the cheque in an hour from now."

"No, *sir*," replied the captain; "if anything comes of it, I don't say I'm not open to some small acknowledgment, but ten thousand dollars for a five-cent box—that's not my way of doing business."

"I can't make you take the money now—I can't even thank you properly now," said Lestrange—"I am in a fever; but when all is settled, you and I will settle this business. My God!"

He buried his face in his hands again.

"I'm not wishing to be inquisitive," said Captain Fountain, slowly putting the things back in the box and tucking the paper shavings round them, "but may I ask how you propose to move in this business?"

"I will hire a ship at once and search."

"Ay," said the captain, wrapping up the little spoons in a meditative manner; "perhaps that will be best."

He felt certain in his own mind that the search would be fruitless, but he did not say so. If he had been absolutely certain in his mind without being able to produce the proof, he would not have counselled Lestrange to any other course, knowing that the man's mind would never be settled until proof positive was produced.

"The question is," said Lestrange, "what is my quickest way to get there?"

"There I may be able to help you," said Fountain, tying the string round the box. "A schooner with good heels to her is what you want; and, if I'm not mistaken, there's one discharging cargo at this present minit at O'Sullivan's wharf. Missus!"

The woman answered the call. Lestrange felt like a person in a dream, and these people who were interesting themselves in his affairs seemed to him beneficent beyond the nature of human beings.

"Is Captain Stannistreet home, think you?"

"I don't know," replied the woman; "but I can go see."

"Do."

She went.

"He lives only a few doors down," said Fountain, "and he's the man for you. Best schooner captain ever sailed out of 'Frisco. The *Raratonga* is the name of the boat I have in my mind—best boat that ever wore copper. Stannistreet is captain of her, owners are M'Vitie. She's been missionary, and she's been pigs; copra was her last cargo, and she's nearly discharged it. Oh, M'Vitie would hire her out to Satan at a price; you needn't be afraid of their boggling at it if you can raise the dollars. She's had a new suit of sails only the beginning of the year. Oh, she'll fix you up to a T, and you take the word of S. Fountain for that. I'll engineer the thing from this bed if you'll let me put my oar in your trouble; I'll victual her, and find a crew three quarter price of any of those d~d skulking agents. Oh, I'll take a commission right enough, but I'm half paid with doing the thing—"

He ceased, for footsteps sounded in the passage outside, and Captain Stannistreet was shown in. He was a young man of not more than thirty, alert, quick of eye, and pleasant of face. Fountain introduced him to Lestrange, who had taken a fancy to him at first sight.

When he heard about the business in hand, he seemed interested at once; the affair seemed to appeal to him more than if it had been a purely commercial matter, such as copra and pigs.

"If you'll come with me, sir, down to the wharf, I'll show you the boat now," he said, when they had discussed the matter and threshed it out thoroughly.

He rose, bid good-day to his friend Fountain, and Lestrange followed him, carrying the brown-paper box in his hand.

O'Sullivan's Wharf was not far away. A tall Cape Horner that looked almost a twin sister of the ill-fated *Northumberland* was discharging iron, and astern of her, graceful as a dream, with snow-white decks, lay the *Raratonga* discharging copra.

"That's the boat," said Stannistreet; "cargo nearly all out. How does she strike your fancy?"

"I'll take her," said Lestrange, "cost what it will."

DUE SOUTH

It was on the 10th of May, so quickly did things move under the supervision of the bedridden captain, that the *Raratonga*, with Lestrange on board, cleared the Golden Gates, and made south, heeling to a ten-knot breeze.

There is no mode of travel to be compared to your sailing-ship. In a great ship, if you have ever made a voyage in one, the vast spaces of canvas, the sky-high spars, the *finesse* with which the wind is met and taken advantage of, will form a memory never to be blotted out.

A schooner is the queen of all rigs; she has a bounding buoyancy denied to the square-rigged craft, to which she stands in the same relationship as a young girl to a dowager; and the *Raratonga* was not only a schooner, but the queen, acknowledged of all the schooners in the Pacific.

For the first few days they made good way south; then the wind became baffling and headed them off.

Added to Lestrange's feverish excitement there was an anxiety, a deep and soul-fretting anxiety, as if some half-heard voice were telling him that the children he sought were threatened by some danger.

These baffling winds blew upon the smouldering anxiety in his breast, as wind blows upon embers, causing them to glow. They lasted some days, and then, as if Fate had relented, up sprang on the starboard quarter a spanking breeze, making the rigging sing to a merry tune, and blowing the spindrift from the forefoot, as the *Raratonga*, heeling to its pressure, went humming through the sea, leaving a wake spreading behind her like a fan.

It took them along five hundred miles, silently and with the speed of a dream. Then it ceased.

The ocean and the air stood still. The sky above stood solid like a great pale blue dome; just where it met the water line of the far horizon a delicate tracery of cloud draped the entire round of the sky.

I have said that the ocean stood still as well as the air: to the eye it was so, for the swell under-running the glitter on its surface was so even, so equable, and so rhythmical, that the surface seemed not in motion. Occasionally a dimple broke the surface, and strips of dark sea-weed floated by, showing up the green; dim things rose to the surface, and, guessing the presence of man, sank slowly and dissolved from sight.

Two days, never to be recovered, passed, and still the calm continued. On the morning of the third day it breezed up from the nor'-nor'west, and they continued their course, a cloud of canvas, every sail drawing, and the music of the ripple under the forefoot.

Captain Stannistreet was a genius in his profession; he could get more speed out of a schooner than any other man afloat, and carry more canvas without losing a stick. He was also, fortunately for Lestrange, a man of refinement and education, and what was better still, understanding.

They were pacing the deck one afternoon, when Lestrange, who was walking with his hands behind him, and his eyes counting the brown dowels in the cream-white planking, broke silence.

"You don't believe in visions and dreams?"

"How do you know that?" replied the other.

"Oh, I only put it as a question; most people say they don't."

"Yes, but most people do."

"I do," said Lestrange.

He was silent for a moment.

"You know my trouble so well that I won't bother you going over it, but there has come over me of late a feeling—it is like a waking dream."

"Yes?"

"I can't quite explain, for it is as if I saw something which my intelligence could not comprehend, or make an image of."

"I think I know what you mean."

"I don't think you do. This is something quite strange. I am fifty, and in fifty years a man has experienced, as a rule, all the ordinary and most of the extraordinary sensations that a human being can be subjected to. Well, I have never felt this sensation before; it comes on only at times. I see, as you might imagine, a young baby sees, and things are before me that I do not comprehend. It is not through my bodily eyes that this sensation comes, but through some window of the mind, from before which a curtain has been drawn."

"That's strange," said Stannistreet, who did not like the conversation over-much, being simply a schooner captain and a plain man, though intelligent enough and sympathetic.

"This something tells me," went on Lestrange, "that there is danger threatening the—" He ceased, paused a minute, and then, to Stannistreet's relief, went on. "If I talk like that you will think I am not right in my head: let us pass the subject by, let us forget dreams and omens and come to realities. You know how I lost the children; you know how I hope to find them at the place where Captain Fountain found their traces? He says the island was uninhabited, but he was not sure."

"No," replied Stannistreet, "he only spoke of the beach."

"Yes. Well, suppose there were natives at the other side of the island who had taken these children."

"If so, they would grow up with the natives."

"And become savages?"

"Yes; but the Polynesians can't be really called savages; they are a very decent lot. I've knocked about amongst them a good while, and a kanaka is as white as a white man—which is not saying much, but it's something. Most of the islands are civilised now. Of course there are a few that aren't, but still, suppose even that 'savages,' as you call them, had come and taken the children off—"

Lestrange's breath caught, for this was the very fear that was in his heart, though he had never spoken it.

"Well?"

"Well, they would be well treated."

"And brought up as savages?"

"I suppose so."

Lestrange sighed.

"Look here," said the captain; "it's all very well talking, but upon my word I think that we civilised folk put on a lot of airs, and waste a lot of pity on savages."

"How so?"

"What does a man want to be but happy?"

"Yes."

"Well, who is happier than a naked savage in a warm climate? Oh, he's happy enough, and he's not always holding a corroboree. He's a good deal of a gentleman; he has perfect health; he lives the life a man was born to live face to face with Nature. He doesn't see the sun through an office window or the moon through the smoke of factory chimneys; happy and civilised too—but, bless you, where is he? The whites have driven him out; in one or two small islands you may find him still—a crumb or so of him."

"Suppose," said Lestrange, "suppose those children had been brought up face to face with Nature—"

"Yes?"

"Living that free life—"

"Yes?"

"Waking up under the stars"—Lestrange was speaking with his eyes fixed, as if upon something very far away—"going to sleep as the sun sets, feeling the air fresh, like this which blows upon us, all around them. Suppose they were like that, would it not be a cruelty to bring them to what we call civilisation?"

"I think it would," said Stannistreet.

Lestrange said nothing, but continued pacing the deck, his head bowed and his hands behind his back.

One evening at sunset, Stannistreet said:

"We're two hundred and forty miles from the island, reckoning from to-day's reckoning at noon. We're going all ten knots even with this breeze; we ought to fetch the place this time to-morrow. Before that if it freshens."

"I am greatly disturbed," said Lestrange.

He went below, and the schooner captain shook his head, and, locking his arm round a ratlin, gave his body to the gentle roll of the craft as she stole along, skirting the sunset, splendid, and to the nautical eye full of fine weather.

The breeze was not quite so fresh next morning, but it had been blowing fairly all the night, and the *Raratonga* had made good way. About eleven it began to fail. It became the lightest sailing breeze, just sufficient to keep the sails drawing, and the wake rippling and swirling behind. Suddenly Stannistreet, who had been standing talking to Lestrange, climbed a few feet up the mizzen ratlins, and shaded his eyes.

"What is it?" asked Lestrange.

"A boat," he replied. "Hand me that glass you will find in the sling there."

He levelled the glass, and looked for a long time without speaking.

"It's a boat adrift—a small boat, nothing in her. Stay! I see something white, can't make it out. Hi there!"—to the fellow at the wheel "Keep her a point more to starboard." He got on to the deck. "We're going dead on for her."

"Is there any one in her?" asked Lestrange.

"Can't quite make out, but I'll lower the whale-boat and fetch her alongside."

He gave orders for the whale-boat to be slung out and manned.

As they approached nearer, it was evident that the drifting boat, which looked like a ship's dinghy, contained something, but what, could not be made out.

When he had approached near enough, Stannistreet put the helm down and brought the schooner to, with her sails all shivering. He took his place in the bow of the whale-boat and Lestrange in the stern. The boat was lowered, the falls cast off, and the oars bent to the water.

The little dinghy made a mournful picture as she floated, looking scarcely bigger than a walnut shell. In thirty strokes the whale-boat's nose was touching her quarter. Stannistreet grasped her gunwale.

In the bottom of the dinghy lay a girl, naked all but for a strip of coloured striped material. One of her arms was clasped round the neck of a form that was half hidden by her body, the other clasped partly to herself, partly to her companion, the body of a baby. They were natives, evidently, wrecked or lost by some mischance from some inter-island schooner. Their breasts rose and fell gently, and clasped in the girl's hand was a branch of some tree, and on the branch a single withered berry.

"Are they dead?" asked Lestrange, who divined that there were people in the boat, and who was standing up in the stern of the whale-boat trying to see.

"No," said Stannistreet; "they are asleep."

THE END

The Garden of God
Contents

BOOK I—ON THE ISLAND

BOOK II—THE CHILDREN RETURN

BOOK I
ON THE ISLAND

THE CORMORANT

"No," said Lestrange, "they are dead."

The whale boat and the dinghy lay together, gunnels grinding as they lifted to the swell. Two cable lengths away lay the schooner from which the whale boat had come; beyond and around from sky-line to sky-line the blue Pacific lay desolate beneath the day.

"They are dead."

He was gazing at the forms on the dinghy, the form of a girl with a child embraced in one arm, and a youth. Clasping one another, they seemed asleep.

From where had they drifted? To where were they drifting? God and the sea alone could tell.

A Farallone cormorant, far above, wheeling and slanting on the breeze, had followed the dinghy for hours, held away by the awful and profound knowledge, born of instinct, that one of the castaways was still alive. But it still hung, waiting.

"The child is not dead," said Stanistreet. He had reached forward and, gently separating the forms, had taken the child from the mother's arms. It was warm, it moved, and as he handed it to the steersman, Lestrange, almost upsetting the boat, stood up. He had glimpsed the faces of the dead people. Clasping his head with both hands and staring at the forms before him, mad, distracted by the blow that Fate had suddenly dealt him, his voice rang out across the sea: "My children!"

Stanistreet, the captain of the schooner, Stanistreet, who knew the story of the lost children so well, knelt aghast just in the position in which he had handed the child to the sailor in the stern sheets.

The truth took him by the throat. It must be so. These were no Kanakas drifted to sea; the dinghy alone might have told him that. These were the children they had come in search of, grown, mated and—dead.

His quick sailor's mind reckoned rapidly. The island they were making for in hopes of finding the long-lost ones was close to them; the northward running current would have brought the dinghy; some inexplicable sea chance had drifted them from shore; they were here, come to meet the man who had sought them for years—what a fatality!

Lestrange had sunk as if crushed down by some hand. Taking the girl's arm, he drew it towards him. "Look!" he cried, as if speaking to high heaven. "And my boy—oh, look! Dick—Emmeline—oh, God! My God! Why? Why? Why?"

He dashed his head on the gunnel. Far away above the cormorant watched.

It saw the whale boat making back from the schooner with the dinghy in tow; it saw the forms it hungered for taken on board; it saw the preparations on deck and the bodies of the lost ones committed to the deep. Then, turning with a cry, it drifted on the wind and vanished, like an evil spirit, from the blue.

DAWN

It was just on daybreak and the *Ranatonga*, running before an eight-knot breeze, was boosting the star-shot water to snow.

Bowers, the bo'sun, an old British Navy quartermaster, was at the wheel and Stanistreet, the captain, had just come on deck.

"Gentleman goin' on all right, sir?" asked Bowers.

"Mr. Lestrange is still asleep, and thank God for it," said Stanistreet, "and the child's well. It woke and I gave it a pannikin of condensed and water and it's in the starboard after-bunk asleep again."

"I thought the gentleman was dead when you brought him back aboard, sir," said Bowers. "I never did see such a traverse, them pore young things and all; we goin' to hunt for them, as you may say, and them comin' off to meet us like that—why, that dinghy was swep' clean down to the bailer—no oars, nuthin—and what were they doin' with that dinghy? Where'd they get that dinghy from's what I want to know."

"Curse the dinghy," said Stanistreet. "Only for her I wouldn't believe this thing true—but I've got to, there's no getting away from it. I'll tell you about that dinghy. It's just like this. It belonged to a hooker that Mr. Lestrange was coming up to Frisco in long years ago. She got burnt out way down here somewhere, the boats got separated in a fog that came on them and the ship's dinghy, with his two kids and an old sailor man, was never seen again. He never believed them dead; he's been hunting all these years up and down the ports of the world on chance of finding news of them. He had it in his head some chap had picked them up—not a sign; then, a bit ago, a friend of mine, Captain Fountain, struck one of his advertisements, and gave news of indications he'd found on this island we're seeking for; he'd picked up a child's toy box, but he hadn't made a search of the place, being after whales and knowing nothing of the story, so Mr. Lestrange, when he got the news, put the *Ranatonga* in commission. That's what we started on this voyage for, and now you know."

"How far's that island from here, sir?" asked Bowers.

"When we struck the dinghy yesterday it was a hundred and fifty south; we're not more than sixty from it now. We'll reach it before noon."

"And them pore things came driftin', father, mother and child, a hundred and fifty mile without bite or sup?"

"God knows," said Stanistreet, "what food they had with them. There was nothing in the boat but a bit of tree branch with a red berry on it."

Bowers spun the wheel and shifted the quid in his mouth.

"And the child stood the batter of the business better than them," said he. "I've known that happen before; kids take a lot of killing as long as the cold don't get at them. They weren't both his children, was they, sir?"

"No," said Stanistreet. "The young fellow was his son, the girl was his niece."

The old quartermaster lay silent for a moment, while in the east a line of turbulent and travelling gold marked the horizon of the lonely sea. The slash of the low wash and the creak of block and cordage remained the only sounds in that world of dawn above which Canopus and the Cross were fading.

There was no morning bank; nothing to mar the splendour of the sunburst across the marching swell; far away a gull had caught it and showed wings of rose and gold against the increasing azure.

Bowers saw nothing but the binnacle cord. Without letting her half a point from her course, the mind of this perfect steersman was travelling far afield. He had signed on not knowing and not caring whither the *Ranatonga* was bound. He thought Lestrange was taking a voyage for the good of his health. He liked the thin, nervous man with grey eyes who always had a good word for every one, and, now that he knew his story, he pitied him. The whole business was plain before him: he could see the burning ship of long years ago, the escape in the boats, the separation in the fog, the children landed on some island, growing up together, mating, and then in some unaccountable manner being drifted out to sea with the child that had been born to them. Maybe they had been fishing and caught in a storm—who could tell? It was easy to be seen that chance had only half a hand in the meeting between the father and his dead children, seeing that Captain Fountain's information had brought him right to the spot. All the same, the thing gripped the battered and sea-stained and case-hardened mind of Bowers as ivy grips an old wall. Bowers was close on seventy, British-born. Sixty years of sea and tossing from ship to ship, from port to port, from hemisphere to hemisphere, had left him just what he was, a man heavy with years, yet in some extraordinary fashion young.

In all his time he had never risen to a command or found himself in the after-guard, he was ignorant as the mainmast of literature and art, politics and history, and he signed the pay sheet with a cross; all the same the fate of the children had perhaps made a deeper impression on this amphibian than it had on the more educated Stanistreet; the sight of the girl and her companion brought on board, so young, beautiful—yet dead, like stricken flowers, had given his simple mind a twist from which it had not recovered.

Down in the fo'c'sle, when the matter had been turned over and turned over and discussed, the dinghy had been talked of as much as its occupants. Where had it come from? To what ship had it belonged, and what ship could have set adrift two people like those with scarcely any clothes on? A rum business, surely.

Bowers had contributed scarcely anything to the discussion. It did not seem to interest him.

Stanistreet snuffed out the binnacle light; the day was now strong, the wind tepid, yet fresh from a thousand miles of ocean, bellying the sails, golden in the level sun blaze.

Before going below he came to the after-rail for a moment and stood looking at the swirl of the wake.

The thought of Lestrange was troubling him. Lestrange, since yesterday, had fallen into a sleep profound as though Nature had chloroformed him. As a matter of fact she had, but the cruelty of Nature lies in the fact that she uses her anæsthetics after instead of during the operations performed by Fate. When man can endure no more she puts the sponge to his nose, lest he should die and escape more suffering. Stanistreet was thinking somewhat like that. He was a good-hearted man who had seen more than enough of tragic happenings, and this last business seemed to him beyond the limit. He was telling himself it would have been better to have put a revolver to the head of the man below and have shot him as one does a maimed animal. He frankly dreaded Lestrange's awakening. What would he do, what would he say? Would it be a repetition of the terrible scene of yesterday?

Leaning on the rail, he spat at the gold-tinged foam as though to get some bitter taste from his mouth.

Then came the thought, had he done right in holding on south for the island since yesterday? What would be the effect on Lestrange of the traces surely left there by the children?

He was thinking this when from below came a sound, some one was moving about in the saloon, and Stanistreet, taking his courage in both hands, turned to the cabin hatch and went below.

THE VISION

He entered the saloon.

The place was gay with the morning beams shining through the ports and skylight. Lestrange, who had been looking into the starboard after-bunk, turned, and as the two men came face to face, Stanistreet saw at once that his fears were groundless. Lestrange had quite recovered himself. That was the first impression; then came another—the thin, nervous Lestrange, always brooding and dreaming as with the air of one possessed by some pressing anxiety, had become altered. He looked cheerful, younger, no longer anxious.

Stanistreet felt almost shocked for a moment, contrasting the vision of the distraught man of yesterday with the figure before him; but a weight was taken from his mind and the next moment, impulsively, his hand went out to grip the hand of the other.

"We are still keeping south?" said Lestrange.

"Yes," said the captain. "I carried on. I thought it best, but what's your wishes in the matter?"

"South," said Lestrange. "Come up on deck, I want to talk to you."

Stanistreet followed, wondering what was to happen next. There was a contained vivacity in the voice and manner of the other that, to the logical and matter-of-fact mind of the sailor, seemed a portent of troubles to come.

He followed closely, and when Lestrange walked to the port rail and stood with his hands upon it fronting the blazing east, the captain of the *Ranatonga* came and stood beside him, elbow touching elbow, and ready for any emergency. But his mind was soon put at rest. Lestrange, quite calm and cheerful in manner, stood contemplating the splendour before him and breathing in the fresh sea air with evident delight.

Then he turned and glanced along the deck to where Peterson, one of the hands, had succeeded Bowers at the wheel.

"What is she doing?" asked he.

"Ten knots," replied Stanistreet.

"And the island?"

"Less than sixty miles from here."

"Good," said Lestrange. He turned again to the rail. A land gull passed them flying topmast high, drifted a bit on the wind, lit on the water and rose again, making north.

Lestrange watched it for a moment. Then he spoke.

"Stanistreet, I said down below I had something to tell you. It's difficult, and I would not say it to any other man. It's just this. I am happy—for the first time in twelve years I am happy."

The captain made no reply.

"That sounds strange, does it not?" went on the other; "and maybe you will think my mind has been unhinged by all that has occurred, especially when you hear me out. It has not, and I will just tell you why I am happy. Happy! that is no name for it. I am joyful, jubilant, praising God, who knows all things and does all things right! You believe in God, Stanistreet?"

"Yes, sir," replied the sailor, not at all happy at the turn things were taking. "I believe in God; ought to, anyway, seeing what I've seen."

"Well, then, listen," said the other. "For twelve long years, as you know, I sought for the children I loved, always sure that they were alive, always uncertain as to their fate. It is the uncertainty that kills. I suppose I am more imaginative than most people. I conjured up visions of them falling into the hands of Chinese, falling into the hands of the ruffians that infest these seas, finding sin and misery as their portion in life; but worse than that were the things I could not conjure up. There were times when I said to myself, 'There is surely no God,' but always I was driven back to prayer, which was my only hope. I prayed that I might meet the children again. I prayed and prayed, and searched and sought, and yesterday my prayer was granted.

"My children were handed back to me by a merciful God—but they were dead! What a mockery! What an answer to the humble and heartfelt prayer of one of His poor creatures! Yesterday as I lay broken in the cabin below whilst you were committing them to the deep, I blasphemed His name, whilst He sat smiling in the Infinite—He who knows all things and does all things right.

"Listen. Grief, when it rises to its true stature, is a magician. I fell asleep and grief drove me beyond sleep into a world of visions where I met the children. It was no dream. I saw them as I see you. Dick and Emmeline, just as they were long years ago, pure and sweet and happy and childlike, but knowing all things. Stanistreet, as sure as there is a God in heaven, what I am telling you is no fiction of the imagination. I have seen the children and I am to see them again, for they are about to return."

"Return!"

"Yes, return. They have told me the place, but not the time. I am to go to the island and they will come to me. I am to wait for them and they will come to me."

"But how, sir?" said Stanistreet, for a moment almost believing what the other said, so intense was the conviction in Lestrange's manner and voice.

"How, I do not know, but they will come to me. It is permitted them for my sake and to save my reason, for otherwise I would have gone mad; also for some other purpose they would not say.—Do you not believe me?"

"Yes, yes," said the other soothingly. "It's strange, but there's no telling—no telling." He felt that Providence or Nature had possibly used the dream device to save the poor gentleman from, at all events, violent insanity, but he doubted if he had gained much by the exchange.

"No telling," said Lestrange. "We know as little of this life as our shadows know of us, but there it is, and now you know why I am happy. My mind is free from all care and my loved ones are coming to meet me."

He turned from the rail and went below. Stanistreet saw the steward come along with breakfast things—the *Ranatonga* had a deck galley—and vanish down the cabin hatch. Then he heard the voice of a child and the voice of the steward as if talking to it.

Then Bowers rose like a sea elephant from the fo'c'sle and came along the deck. Bowers had handed over the wheel to Peterson just before Lestrange came up. He had dodged below to light a pipe, risen to see Lestrange and Stanistreet in confabulation and then lain doggo, waiting.

"How's the gentleman taking it now, sir?" asked Bowers, speaking in a lowered voice. "I popped my head up when you was talkin' and he looked to have got back to his self."

"God help me, I don't know," said Stanistreet; "but if there's any sense in the world he's gone crazy, plain crazy—but he's happy."

"Well, thank the Lord he's gone the laughin', not the howlin' kind," said Bowers. "Happy, is he? Well, it's fortunit for him. That's all I have to say."

"Maybe. Anyhow, dodge down, will you, and bring up that kid. The steward's fooling with it and wasting his time, and I want to see it on deck—after-bunk you'll find it."

Bowers dived.

A minute later he reappeared with the "kid" wrapped in a bunk blanket and clasped in one huge arm.

Plump, brown as a berry, auburn-haired and laughing, it was a very different child from the child that had come aboard yesterday.

"It pulled me beard," said Bowers. "It's as strong as Ham, b'gosh.—There, out you get and play in the sun, where you used to."

He turned the naked child out of the blanket on to the deck. "Called me Dick as I was comin' up with him," said Bowers, now on his knees beside it, tickling it and rolling it over with his huge hand. "Called me Dick, did you—where's your pants? Eh? Where's your pants, you little devil, sold them, did you?—Hand's a belaying pin, sir, till I knock the brains out of him."

Stanistreet handed the pin.

"Now," said Bowers, putting it in the two hands of the child, "bang the deck and be happy."

He had no need to give directions.

"Well, sir, what do you think of that?" said the sailor, rising to his feet. "Looked like dying of wantin' to go to sleep yesterday afternoon, and hark at it now!"

"It's a fine kid," said Stanistreet, contemplating it. "I'd make it to be getting on for two years, but I'm no judge of children. But I'll tell you what, Bowers; it's my opinion it wasn't so much asleep when we got it aboard as doped. Did you see that sprig of a tree lying in the dinghy? Well, I'll bet my hat that was arita. I've seen the stuff growing in some of the islands and it's more poisonous than oap; a couple of berries will do for any man. I believe those two ate some of the berries, not knowing what they were, maybe, and maybe the child took the poison through the mother's milk. I'm dead sure that's how the thing went, for them two showed no signs of dying of starvation or thirst and they'd come a long way."

"Maybe," said Bowers, his eyes on the child. "Now then, now then, where are you rollin' that pin to?—Come out of it or you'll be tumblin' down the hatch—God's truth, I'll have to hobble you before I've done with you."

He was leading the child away from the companion hatch, when Lestrange reappeared and joined Stanistreet near the wheel. Lestrange glanced at the sailor and his charge but seemed to take little interest in it, or only that benign interest which he seemed, now, to bestow on everything animate and inanimate; it might have been the child of Bowers for all he seemed to care. Stanistreet tried to draw the conversation to it, and the other did not resist, but he let the subject drop as though it was of little account, and then, the steward announcing breakfast, they went below.

DICK EM

Meanwhile the fo'c'sle had got wind of happenings on deck and even the watch that had turned in, turned out. Eight men, all told, schooner men of the old South Sea type, hard-bitten, berry-brown, and, save for their pants, as naked to the hot morning as the "kid."

The *Ranatonga* had sailed without a mate; drink and the police combined had seized him the night before she sailed. There was no one of the afterguard on deck to keep order, and the criticism was free.

"Lord save us and love us," cried one of the ruffians, "look at Bob playin' nursery-maid!—Where's your apron, Bob?"

"He's stole the pore infant's clothes," put in another, "and pawned the p'rambulator. Len's a dollar, Bob, if you haven't bust it on drink."

A gentleman peeling a banana offered part of it to the charge and was repulsed.

"Now then, now then," cried Mr. Bowers, "scatter off an' clean yourselves—take your damn bananas where they're wanted! Jim, fetch me that old tin butt tub outa the galley, the one the doctor sticks his 'tatoes in, and there's an old sponge in the locker behind the door. Grease yourself and then b—r off down and tell Jenkins to send's a tow'l."

He filled the bath with sea water dipped up in a bucket, and began the scrubbing and sponging, Jim, a long wall-eyed son of perdition, standing by with the towel, and the others looking on.

"What's his name?" asked Jim.

"Name!" cried Bowers. "How the blazes do you think I know what his name is?—Hasn't got one—" Then as an afterthought, "Dick's his name, ain't it, bo? Dick—hey! Dick, ain't that your name, hey?"

"Dick," repeated the laughing child, splashing the water. "Dick! Dick!"

"And Dick you'll be," said Bowers, with a last squeeze of the sponge, baptismal in its significance, though such a thought was far from the mind of the baptiser. "Now, hold me the tow'l—and there you are."

He finished off the drying and released the child, who at once made for Jim, of all people in the world, clasped him round the legs with his chubby little arms, and looked up in his face. Innocence adoring the biggest blackguard that ever footed Long Wharf.

Then Stanistreet appeared from the saloon hatch and the fo'c'sle crowd melted, all but Jim.

"Bowers!" cried Stanistreet.

"Comin', sir," replied the bo'sun. He shoved the bath away, shot the sponge into the locker, and came forward.

"So Dick's your name, is it?" said Jim, unclasping the tiny hands and lifting the "kid" in his arms. "And what's your other name? Tell's your other name, or up ye go over the rail, up ye go over the rail!" He danced the child in his arms, making pretence to throw it overboard. "Em," cried Dick, the warm arms of Jim maybe waking in his misty mind the name of Emmeline, who had danced him so often. "Em—Em."

"Here, drop the child," said Bowers, coming forward again. "What are you foolin' like that with him for? Sick you'll make him before he's had his breakfast.—What's he sayin'?"

"Says his other name's M," replied Jim. "Sure as there's hair on his head, he's been tellin' me. Dick M's his name. Ain't it, bo?"

"Em—Em," cried Dick, stretching out his arms to Bowers.

"And Dick M you'll be if you wants to," said that worthy as he hoisted him on his shoulder and went aft in search of Jenkins the steward and condensed milk.

Seven bells had struck, when along the blazing deck came the voice of the look-out, plaintive as the voice of a gull.

"Land ho-o-o."

It was Ericsson the Swede who gave the cry, and Stanistreet, pacing the deck, hands behind his back, suddenly became galvanised into activity. He sprang with one foot on the port bulwarks and a hand clutching the main ratlins, then, shading his eyes with the other hand, he looked.

Yes, far away ahead, danced void by the sea shimmer, vague, indeterminate, lay something that was not sea and was not sky. The swell, building higher with the flood just setting in, now wiped it away, now showed it again.

Yes, it was the island, far, far away, but surely there, the thing unmapped, uncharted, known only to the gulls and the whale men, and even to the whale men scarcely known.

Away down in Stanistreet's mind had always lain the shadow of a doubt, a doubt removed by the finding of the dinghy, but somehow illogically returning and lingering. Was the island a figment of old Captain Fountain's imagination? a vision of the mind, useful only to shipwreck Hope? No, it was there, right before his eyes and true to place.

He dropped on deck. Lestrange was still below and the port watch was forward lazing in the sun. One fellow was standing looking with shaded eyes to get a sight of the land-fall, but the rest seemed indifferent. Then Bowers, rising from the fo'c'sle, broke up their talk, setting them to work on the fore planking with a deck beam. Having seen them busy, he took a glance forward, and then came aft to the captain.

"It's liftin', sir," said Bowers. "You haven't a chart of the soundin's by any chance?"

"Oh, Lord, no," said Stanistreet; "it's mile-deep water off the reef all round and there's a clear run through the break. That's all Fountain said and we've got to take his word. Where's the kid?"

"I've give him his breakfast and he's in the bunk asleep," said Bowers. "The gentleman was down there reading a book, but he didn't seem to be takin' much notice, not of the kid or anything."

"No," said the other, "everything's nothing to him now but just what's on his mind. You'd have thought their child would have been more to him than them,

166

even, seeing they are dead—but he's got them fixed in his head—he's got it screwed down in his nut that he's going to meet them on that island."

"Good Lord, sir!" said Bowers. "D'ye mean to say he's thinkin' to meet them, knowin' they're dead an' all?"

"I can't say what he thinks," replied the other. "He's had a dream or something, and he's got it in his head they're going to meet him on that island. Maybe if you and me had been through the mill he's been through we'd be just as crazy, but I wish to the Lord he'd chosen some other skipper for this cruise. It's a heavy responsibility. If he was fighting mad, I could clap him in his cabin and put about for Frisco; but there you are, he's mild as milk and sensible as Sam on everything but that point, and what's going to happen when he gets to that infernal island and maybe finds traces of them I don't know. Bowers, what would you do if you were in my place?"

"I'd carry on, sir," said Bowers. "Crazy folk are like children. I remember old Sam Hatch; he used to be sittin' all day watching Sydney Harbour, sittin' on Circular Wharf waitin' for his son's ship to come in, and she lost beyond the Heads and he knowing it. Cross him in his ideas and he'd be the devil, but leave him be and he'd make no trouble. Carry on, sir—there he is."

Lestrange had come on deck. He took the news from Stanistreet, walked forward a bit, and then, with arm upon the starboard rail, he stood and watched.

The wind had shifted almost dead aft, came stronger and the vast trapezium of the mainsail loomed out, stood rigid against the blue, whilst the *Ranatonga*, running with swell and wind, laid the knots behind her, swift, gracile, and silent as the gulls that followed on the wind, land gulls that seemed escorting her like spirits white as snow.

And now, minute by minute, rising like Aphrodite from the sea, the island before them bloomed to life. With every lift of the swell, the gull-strewn barrier reef showed its foam, whilst ever more distinctly beyond the reef, green and fair, grew the foliage, changing in depth of emerald to the touch of the wind.

Stanistreet had taken the wheel, Bowers the lookout, and the *Ranatonga*, no longer dead before the wind, was travelling on a bow line that would take her a mile to eastward of the land. The break in the reef lay to the east.

They held on. The breeze still freshened, and the splendour of the day and the blueness of the sea took on an extraordinary freshness and gaiety. Under the lash of the wind and the sun, the diamond dash and sparkle of northern summer seas lent a heart-catching subtlety to the vision of the island with its coral reef and far trembling palms; and now, across the foam-broken swell, came a sound like the voices of voyage-weary sailor men howling in chorus—it was the gulls of the reef, and another sound like the hush of a mother to her child—the voice of the reef itself.

It was near high tide and the sleeting foam could be seen racing on the coral, as now, with the island almost on the starboard beam, the break came slowly to view, with the palm tree on its northern pier.

A moment more the *Ranatonga* held on, then, as the wheel went over to the rattle of the rudder chains, the main boom swung, hung for a moment supported by the topping lifts, and then lashed out to port, the bowsprit pointing straight for the break.

Lestrange, his hand on the starboard rail, stood with his eyes fixed on the vision before him—the home of his children. He had never dreamed of anything like this, all his visions of paradise fell to dust before what he saw, what he heard, what he felt, as the schooner, heeling to the wind, made like an arrow for the break.

Gulls raced them and the foam roared aft, rail-high and dashing the decks with spray. Wind, flood, sun and sea, gulls and the waving palm trees—all, with the shifting of the helm, had broken into new life. The glass-green rollers on the outer beach were breaking now to port and starboard, and now, in one miraculous moment, the break was passed and the great sea was gone—transformed into a silent lake of azure.

THE GARDEN OF GOD

The *Ranatonga* on a level keel, and spilling the wind from her sails, came round in a great curve on the dazzling water, her great shadow following her across the coral gardens of the lagoon floor. Then the rumble of the anchor chain echoed and passed away in the woods, and ship and shadow swung slowly to the tide and came to rest.

To port lay the reef booming to the blue and to starboard the island beach of white coral sand, answering the reef with a thudding song, whilst north and south the two arms of the lagoon, curving, lost themselves beyond capes where the banyans and palms trooped to the very water.

"Its emerald shallows calling to the deep

168

Blue soundings where the soul of Man might sleep
For ever undisturbed but for the song
Of reef and sea—"

Away beyond the hill-borne trees of the island a flight of coloured birds passed like a scarf across the brilliant sky and vanished. Other sign of life there was none.

Stanistreet, having given his last orders, stood for a moment looking around him, the men, grouped forward, stood without a word, some gazing overside at the coral gardens and flights of fish, others with their faces turned shorewards to the groves of cocoanuts and the coloured gloom where the great bread-fruit leaves waved to the wind and the yellow of cassia and scarlet of hibiscus fought for the eye through the foliage shadows.

The schooner and all on board her seemed for a moment waiting, silent, expectant. Lestrange, leaning on the rail, had not turned his head; one might have fancied them waiting for the shore people to put off, watching the canoes taking to the water. But shore people there were none, nor canoes; neither voices of men nor the forms of women, nor the laughter of children; nothing but the untrodden sands and the foliage, fresh as when the world was young.

Stanistreet moved beside Lestrange, who turned, his face lit as if with the reflection of all the beauty around.

"Well, sir," said the captain, "we're in harbour at last. Shall I order the shore boat out?"

"Yes," said the other, turning again to the rail. "Yes—but look, Stanistreet, look!"

"It's fine," said the sailor. "I never struck a prettier bit of beach—ay, it's grand!"

"It is the Garden of God," said Lestrange. "He made it and He has kept it, in all the wide world the one spot undefiled. He made it and He kept it for my children, and now He has led me to it that I should meet them once again and, dying, praise His name."

The idea that the God who made the great world to receive man should make a tiny island to receive and protect two innocent children, should furnish it with beauty and hide it with sea, might not seem strange to a true believer in the omniscience of a benevolent deity, but to Stanistreet the words of Lestrange brought back the dread of a few hours ago—what would happen on landing?

He went forward a bit and gave Bowers the order for the boat. The whaler was dropped and, leaving Bowers in charge of the deck, Stanistreet got in, following Lestrange.

Lestrange was of the nervous type that does not show its age. Dying of consumption years ago, his spirit had triumphed over disease; he had said to himself, "I will not die till I have found my children." The mental strength that had defied disease refused age. Though well over sixty, he did not look it, and since yesterday a decade seemed to have fallen from his shoulders.

The boat pushed off and again, just as on passing the break, dreamland cast its magic upon them. The *Ranatonga* on whose solid decks they had trod a moment ago, showed now as a ship floating on air, air liquid and tinted with emerald and aquamarine. So clear was the lagoon water, they could see her copper and the weeds upon it and the anchor chain, now slack with the turn of the tide and lying like a conger on the coral. As the oars drove them shoreward the illusion held, for, glancing over-side, the brains of coral and sand patches, though fathoms deep, seemed likely to scrape the keel.

The boat touched the sand where wavelets were breaking scarce a foot high, and Stanistreet, getting out, helped Lestrange over the gunnel.

"Take her back," said the captain to the fellow who had been rowing stern oar. "You can stream her on a line. I'll signal when I want you."

The boat put back and the two men stood watching it.

Here on the beach was a new prospect and a new enchantment. Fair as the vision of the island seemed from the water, who could say that this was not fairer? For distance stood on the far reef beyond the lonely and unutterable blue of the broad lagoon, and beyond the reef break distance led the eye to the rim of an almost purple sea. There was nothing to break the charm or fetter the eye, not even the *Ranatonga* mirroring herself near the reef, nor the boat, the creak of whose oars came lazily across the water; they had become, in some way, part and parcel of the desolation.

Stanistreet, turning from the sea, cast his eyes about. The extraordinary thing was that the mind of the sailor was perturbed, anxious, eager for any traces of the children, whilst the mind of Lestrange seemed absolutely at peace. Stanistreet had dreaded some outbreak on landing, he had dreaded trouble should they discover traces, some instinct told him that this quietude might mean something graver than any outburst could foreshadow.

170

But Lestrange, despite his placidity and brightness of eye, showed no sign of alienation from the normal. Having gazed his fill, he turned and took his companion's arm as one might take the arm of a brother. They walked towards the trees.

HERE ONCE THEY DWELT

The wind had died to a fitful breeze that tossed the foliage to the rainy patter of the palm fronds.

Just before entering the shadow of the trees, Stanistreet paused. His quick eye had noticed something lying on the sand a little to the left. A great banana bunch half eaten by the birds, half ruined by the sun, something that must have lain there for days and got there—how?

There were no banana trees in sight, nothing but the level line of the coco-palms, like the first ranks of an army suddenly halted.

He bent to examine it. The stalk had been cut with a knife.

Straightening himself, he found that Lestrange had noticed the fact.

"Look," said Lestrange, "it has been cut. Dick must have cut it from the tree, but there are no banana trees round here. Let us go on." He was as much unconcerned by this, the first trace of the lost ones, as though Dick and Emmeline were alive out there, fishing in the lagoon and due to return any moment, out there on the lagoon where the blue beyond blue of the distant sea spoke at the reef break through a silence troubled only by the lamentation of the gulls.

It was a living fact that the eyes of Stanistreet were blurred and dimmed by this first find, whilst the eyes of Lestrange remained clear of sight. He followed the other, who had suddenly taken the lead, and as they passed into the shadow of the trees the whole business for Stanistreet took a new complexion, and the island a tinge of romance beyond the power of words to express.

Just that bunch of cut bananas had linked in some strange way in his mind the forms of the lost ones with the trees they had left and the ground they had trodden on. Haunted! Oh, yes, the island was haunted, if only in the imagination of the sailor man who, disbelieving in ghosts, heard voices in the wind that stirred the foliage and fancied forms moving in the coloured gloom of the groves.

Lestrange was following a path that led uphill, less a path than a trail; to right and left the narrow pillars of the coco-palms showed alleys broken by vast bread-fruits and bays of shadow, and now the voice of a little rivulet came tinkling and lisping and the palms broke, disclosing a glade, fern-haunted and showered with light from the moving leaves.

Here, over the face of an age-worn rock, a little cascade flashed to lose itself amidst the ferns, and above, like great candelabra, stood the banana trees, holding their full-ripe fruit to the sky.

"Look!" said Lestrange. He was pointing to a bunch of the fruit that had been cut and thrown down and was lying close to the ferns. Then he pointed to a diamond-trunked artu close to them on the left. A knife was sticking in the tree, left there by the banana-cutter—till his return.

Lestrange walked up close to the tree, glanced at the knife, and, without touching it, led the way on, past the waterfall, uphill and as if sure of his ground.

The trees fell away and past a coco grove, whispering in the wind, the hill-top broke to view, a sun-lit space, dome-like and surmounted by a great rock, broken and worn by a thousand years of weather.

They climbed the rock, warm as a living thing from the sun, and, resting on its upper face, looked.

The wind had freshened again from the nor'west, billowing the foliage far below and breezing the sea beyond the reef, and from here the whole island world lay beneath them alive with the wind in changing hues of emerald.

They could trace the azure-amethyst ring of the lagoon, here broad, here narrow, and the reef with its blinding outer beach bombarded by the swell of a sea consumed with light.

Sometimes a smoke of gulls would burst from the reef spurs to northward of the break and the wind would bring a chanting sound mixed with the faint murmur of the surf, a murmur ceaseless as the whisper of a shell.

Lestrange, leaning on his elbow, gazed far and wide. Just at this hour of the westering sun the shadow of the island was beginning to steal seaward, venturing timidly across the lagoon to pass the reef and lose itself in the evening sea.

Stanistreet was watching the spreading shadow that had touched the *Ranatonga* lying far below like a toy ship, when his companion roused him.

"Look!" said Lestrange. He was pointing to the west, to a place where the trees broke towards the lagoon bank, leaving an open space green to the water.

"Look!" said Lestrange. "Can you not see their house?"

"I see nothing," replied the sailor, shading his eyes against the sun. "House! No, sir, I can see nothing."

"There by the clearing, the shadow of the trees has taken it, not far from the water's edge, close to that tree cluster that stands out a bit into the open."

The sailor gazed again in the direction pointed out. Ah, yes, now that it was pointed out he could see something that was neither rock nor bush nor tree. Even at full moon it would not have attracted the eye of a casual gazer, small as it was and elusive, like a nest in a branch.

Yes, it was a structure of some sort, and even at this distance he thought he could make out a roof, but why, if it was a house, had the builders chosen their habitation in a spot so remote, so far from the break? The wind could not say, nor the untroubled sea, nor the great sun that builds everything from his habitation to the dreams of men.

"Come!" said Lestrange. He rose from his half recumbent position and began to descend from the rock. On the sward, where the rock's shadow was lengthening itself, he stood for a moment with head bowed and eyes half closed; then, turning, he led the way downhill towards the west.

For quarter of a mile the cocoanut groves held, then came a great belt of mammee-apple, pandanus trees and bread-fruit, through which they passed to find a valley where the ferns grew high—the strangest surprise—for here great blocks of hewn stone lay cast about and terraces of stone stood in ruin, disrupted by the rains of the ages and the roots of screw pines working beneath them.

Fallen from its place, half prone amidst the ferns, lay a great stone idol, an island god of the long ago. The heat of the day lingered here where no wind came and where the ferns stood in stereoscopic stillness in a silence broken only by the faint hum of insects.

Stanistreet had seen temple places like this amongst the islands, but the sight was new to Lestrange. He stood for a moment gazing at the fallen god, the blocks strewn about, the terraces lit by the amber light of evening. Then he passed on down the valley and beyond, where a trodden path showed them the way past a grove of hootoo trees to the sward they had seen from the hill-top and where stood the house.

Close to the left-hand belt of trees and with a little garden beside it where toro grew, it stood, leaf-thatched and built of cane. It had no door. The light of evening entered, exposing all the simple contents, mats carefully and neatly rolled up, a shelf where stood bowls cut from cocoanut shell, a ball of twine, an old pair of scissors—all arranged neatly and in order. Some fish spears stood, leaning against a corner, and in a small bowl at the extreme end of the shelf some flowers, once bright but now withered. Yet for all the cunning of the construction the house had an unfinished look, as though the builders had been called away before its full completion.

Lestrange stood before the open door of the house, so trustful, so naive, so like a nest, this house built by the lost children whose forms he had seen but a day ago, whose voices he had not heard for so many years. It was the sight of the neatly rolled mats, the bowl of withered flowers and the carefully arranged things on the shelf that shattered for a moment the great contentment born of his vision and the surety that he was to meet the children soon. These things said "Emmeline" as plainly as a voice—Emmeline so neat, so careful of things, so fond of flowers.

The ghost child came running to him across the sands of memory, those sunlit sands that swallow so many and such great things.

He broke down and, leaning his arm against the door-post, hid his face.

Stanistreet turned on his heel and walked rapidly down to the lagoon edge, he was hit nearly as badly as the other. That house, coming after all the other things, would have moved the most callous heart.

He stood with his arms folded, looking across the lagoon water to the reef. The lagoon here was broad and shallow, corallised here and there by ridges of coral, the reef so low and far that he could see the evening light on the Pacific, the sound of whose surf on the far outer beach came like the voice of sleep.

Ah, well, it was the fate of everything and they had lived their day and been happy; there was no use in a man letting his feelings get the better of him—no use in snivelling; just as well they had come on the house: it would cure Lestrange of that madness about meeting them, it had broken down that terrible contentment—a bitter medicine, but better than the disease that threatened him.

He stood for a long while to give the other time to recover, then he turned.

Lestrange had recovered. He was standing before the house with one of the fish spears in his hand, examining it. Stanistreet walked up to him.

"Look," said Lestrange, "how cleverly he has made the barbs; he was always clever with his hands."

He placed the spear back where he had found it and then, with a last look at the house, turned away.

"Come," said he, "we must get back to the ship, for there is much to be done before she sails, and I want her to sail to-morrow. I will go to her with you now and return in the morning."

"Return?" said Stanistreet. "Are you not going with us?"

"I will never see San Francisco again," replied Lestrange. "My home is here with my children who are coming to meet me, who have met me, for I feel them on either side of me. I cannot see them yet, but they will show themselves to me in time."

Stanistreet made no reply for a moment. He stood looking round him at the fading lagoon soon to be showered with starlight, and the trees stirring to the wind in the ghostly light of evening.

"And the child?" said he at length.

"Their child will remain with me," said Lestrange.

THE KEEPER OF THE LAGOON

When Lestrange and Stanistreet had been rowed ashore, Bowers set the lads to work clearing up and putting things straight.

The *Ranatonga* was a schooner of the old Pacific type built at Velego and for the sandalwood trade by men who recognised that speed and cargo space are almost synonymous terms. Her lines were lovely, and her character; never would she play a man false and, to use Bowers' words, a child might have steered her. He had fallen in love with her and the fo'c'sle hands cursed his passion, which kept them Flemish-coiling, polishing and deck-scrubbing—all but Jim, bo'sun's mate and second in importance after Bowers.

Kearney was his other name, but it was never used. He had no letters; like Bowers, he could not write his name, but he was great with his fists in an emergency, and he could do anything with his hands.

Jim had been in the gold rush—there were dead men lying in One Horse Gulch and on Dows Flat that had known him, and the scars on his hide were many—but he had made no profit out of the business. Then the sea took him, and drink, and the sandalwood traders used him, so that he was never out of employment one way or another—always in schooner work and escaping by some miracle the whalemen's crimps at a time when shanghaied men were bringing thirty dollars a head.

When Bowers had bathed and dried off Dick, the child had run to this scamp, clasped him round the legs and looked up into his hard-bitten face laughing and with evident approval.

It was a new moment in the life of Jim and the start of what almost amounted to a quarrel between him and Bowers, for Jim had danced the child in his arms, to say nothing of the fact that the child had shown a predilection for Jim.

Jealousy! No man would ever have suspected such a thing in connection with a leathery old salt like Bowers, yet there it was, the jealousy of a nursery-maid, patent and plain and exhibiting itself now in words.

Work had knocked off, darkness was stealing over the lagoon and the lads were lying on deck, down below, the child was asleep in its bunk, and with his back against the rail, filling a pipe, Bowers was telling off Jim.

"I didn't say nuthin' of the sort," said Jim. "I said Gord A'mighty had given it teeth to chaw with, and you fillin' it up with pap like that, that's what I said and that's what I sticks to."

"Then what were you sayin' about goats?" fired Bowers. "Where's the chawin' to be done with goat's milk—"

"Goats, nuthin'! I was talkin' of Kanakas feedin' their young uns on goat's milk. Can't a man talk without bein' took up and havin' his words shoved down his throat?"

"I ain't shovin' no words down no throats," replied the bo'sun, lighting his pipe, "and we'll leave it there. Bill, ain't you goin' to get that ridin' light fixed?" He stumped forward and the discussion dropped, but the tension remained. Then, as the anchor light cast its amber on the waving lagoon water and the moon was raising her forehead across the reef, a hail came from the shore.

Lestrange and Stanistreet had returned, taking their way along the lagoon bank. The boat put off to their hail, and they came on board.

After supper, and on the moonlit deck, the captain of the *Ranatonga* went back to the subject they had been discussing on their way to the ship.

"No, sir," said he. "I don't like it and nothing will make me like it, sailing off like that and leaving you here. I'm talking as man to man, and you're not as young as you were. Well, I've said my say, and as I was saying on the beach there, I'm willing to take your orders up to a point, and that point is leaving some one with you. Bowers I can't part with, so it must be one of the others. Question is, which?"

"But what is to harm me?" said Lestrange. "You see a man who only craves for solitude. It is true I am not as young as I was, but I am active and, as you know, I have the simplest tastes. I can get my food without trouble here where there is food on every hand. Before going on that voyage years ago, when the consumption first threatened me, I camped out all alone away in the Adirondacks and kept myself with a gun and a rod. I am more vigorous now than then."

"Well, sir," said the sailor, "it's just myself I'm thinking of. You say I'm to come back in a year, but I wouldn't have any peace of mind till then, and a year's a long time."

"Well, be it so," said the other, "leave me one of your sailors; after all, these honest fellows are more like children than men, and I would prefer one of them to any other companion—if companion I must have."

Stanistreet smiled as he mentally reviewed "those honest fellows." All the same, it was a fo'c'sle tough or nothing, and he had gained his point. Besides, in the depths of his mind he felt that the innocence of Lestrange had touched something of the truth; the worst of those rascals had the salt of the sea on him, and the question was, would any of them remain? Bowers would—he felt that—but he could not run the schooner without him.

He let the question be whilst they discussed other matters. Lestrange, knowing his man and trusting him implicitly, was giving him very wide powers over his affairs. Most of his money was in real estate, and his bankers and lawyers had things in hand, but Stanistreet would have power to draw what money he wanted for the return trip, and he was to receive a salary for the year, or until he left Lestrange's service, twice the amount of what he was now receiving.

They talked till the moon far above them was preparing to cross the hill-top. The wind had fallen dead and the lagoon water lay still as glass. Under the moonlight the trooping trees, the salt-white beach and the far reef lay clearly visible, as by day, yet ghostly, bathed in the light of dreamland—which is the light of memory.

Stanistreet, when the other had gone below, leaned on the rail, looking at the picture before him. The Garden of God. Yes, if any spot on earth deserved that sacred name, it was this, where sin was not, nor cruelty, nor visible sign of death.

As he gazed, his eyes were drawn to something pale and phosphorescent moving swiftly through the water astern; it vanished, and then across the moon track hinted of itself again in the form of something dark and rapidly moving that passed, leaving a ripple on the glittering surface.

SUNSET

Morning was coming into the lagoon, where a nautilus fleet was putting out on the land wind that breezed the sea to broken gold.

The tide was at half-full and the *Ranatonga*, swinging to it, showed a ripple at her stern and a ripple where the anchor chain broke the luminous blue of the water.

On the sunlit deck Stanistreet, with his back to some fellows who were cleaning brass-work, was talking to Bowers. He had explained the position, and the bo'sun, as he had expected, was ready, though not very willing, to stay.

"I'm not botherin' about myself so much as the gentleman," said Bowers. "If he's fixed on staying, well, there's no more to be said, but supposin' he took sick—and it isn't as if his mind was as right as it might be—then there's the kid."

"I know—I know—" replied the other. "It's crazy—but there's some sense in it all the same. His mind is sick, but he's happy here; if he went back to Frisco wouldn't he always be troubling over these children? He doesn't trouble here—I've lain awake half the night thinking it out. I can't leave you, can't run the old hooker without you, unless"—he paused for a moment and looked over the water—"unless none of the others will take the job on—which is the most likely of them, do you think?"

"Well, sir," said the bo'sun, "they're a tough lot, but there's no harm among them. Jim's the ablest and he's took a fancy to the kid, but God help it if he ever had the handlin' of it; wanted to give it a chunk of beef when you were off the ship yesterday—no sense in his head. But, whether or no, he wouldn't stop, he's a long sight too fond of his pleasures ashore."

"Well, I'll get the chaps aft and put it to them," said Stanistreet. "Tell Jenkins to hurry along with the breakfast, and we'll muster them then."

An hour later, led by Bowers, they came trooping aft, a coloured crowd in striped shirts or plain, open at the chest, canvas breeches, and not a shoe amongst them. One fellow had a red handkerchief tied round his head, Spanish fashion, and several wore the big buckled belts seen now only in the pictures adorning pirate stories and in melodrama.

They shuffled along, halted, swayed uneasily and then stood whilst Bowers ran them over with his eye as if counting them.

The fellow by the starboard rail sent a squirt of tobacco juice overside and then wiped his mouth with the back of his hand apologetically whilst Stanistreet, who had been standing talking to Lestrange, wheeled on them.

178

"Got them all here, Bowers?" said the captain of the *Ranatonga*. "Good. Now, you chaps, I've called you aft just to have a word with you. It's soon said. Mr. Lestrange here is staying behind on the island for his health, him and the child. I'm taking the ship back to port, and I want a man to stick here with him till my return.

"I want a chap to sign up for a year on this job, double pay and fifty dollars bonus when the time's up. That's good pay, but I'm not deceiving you; there'll be no drink or strikes for the fellow that takes the job on, but he'll have a good time. You all know Mr. Lestrange, and you can see for yourself what the island is like, plenty of grub, fishing, and nothing to do. Now then, step aft, one of you."

Dead silence, and eyes cast everywhere but at the after-guard.

"Lots of time," said Stanistreet. "Get a bit more forward and talk it over together."

He turned and paced the deck with his hands behind his back, whilst the crowd shifted forward and broke into several groups, the grumble of their voices coming on the wind.

The fellow with the red handkerchief broke away from the others and came aft touching his forehead.

"Ax your pardon, sir," said he, "but the chaps wants to know what's a bolus?"

"A present," said Stanistreet, "fifty dollars for nothing into the hand of the chap that stays."

The meeting resumed, but, it was plain to be seen, without enthusiasm. Then, at last, all in one group they came aft and halted, whilst the spokesman gave their decision to the skipper.

"The chaps ain't unwillin' to oblige you or the gentleman, sir, but it's the lonesomeness."

"None of you will stay?"

"Well, sir, it's not the stayin', but the keepin' here."

"Of course you'd have to keep here—but that's enough—get forward."

Then, suddenly, came a voice of mockery, the voice of Jim. Jim had taken little part in the discussion, leaving to abler speakers the handling of the affair, but he had made no objection to the general verdict. It was a characteristic that, whilst one with the others, he was always a bit apart; illiterate as any of them, his mind was of a different stamp.

"Lonesomeness be sugared, it's the booze they're thinkin' of, sir."

For a moment the presence of the after-guard was forgotten and voices were raised.

"You're thinkin' of, you mean, or why don't you stay yourself?" enquired the man with the red handkerchief.

"And who says I won't?" asked Jim.

That is how it happened, all of a sudden. I doubt if a moment before he had made up his mind or whether the necessity of answering back smart had done the business. At all events it was done, and Jim Kearney, long, red-headed, lantern-jawed and trailing behind him his tattered past, was enlisted the third inhabitant of the Garden of God.

Stanistreet had pointed out to Lestrange the impossibility of the schooner putting out that day: stores had to be landed, and not only landed, but brought round to the house away at the other side of the lagoon.

Lestrange did not want stores, and Jim Kearney, who was a small eater for all his size and strength, and who in these latitudes was indifferent to meat, despite his advocacy of beef as a food for children, only wanted tobacco. All the same, the captain of the *Ranatonga* had his own ideas on the subject. A cask of flour was broken out of the hold, the medicine chest was ransacked of pain-killer, opium and Epsom salts; needles, thread, scissors, carpenter's tools, lines and fish-hooks—nothing was forgotten.

A shack had to be run up in the trees behind the house to hold the stores, and it was not till the morning of the third day that all was finished.

The old dinghy was overhauled and condemned, but Lestrange wished to keep it, so it was left, together with the dinghy of the *Ranatonga*, for practical purposes, and they were towed round by the whale boat to the sward by the house and tied up to the bank.

It was eleven o'clock in the morning when all was finished. Dick was playing about in the sun under the eye of Kearney, pipe in mouth and hands in pockets, and Lestrange was saying good-bye to his skipper.

Stanistreet was downcast. The very beauty of the morning, the loveliness of the sward with its protecting trees, the lagoon with its coloured shadows and depths, the remote reef and the perfect sky above it, all this only served to deepen the depression that had come upon him.

Now, at the moment of parting, the feeling came to him that he would never see Lestrange again, that on the child playing on the sward, Kearney, and the grey-haired man with those strange eyes that seemed fixed upon another world, Fate was preparing to drop a curtain that it would never be his part to lift.

For a moment and to his plain, simple mind the tragedy of the lost children seemed part of this new happening and the hand that had shaped their fate not yet finished with its work.

The fellows in the whale boat that was hanging onto the bank ready to take him round the lagoon back to the ship, seemed under the same blanket; Jim, for all his rating them over the drink business, had been a favourite, and here they were leaving him, marooned, so to speak. Bowers, who had left the boat to give some last instructions to Jim, returned to his place in the stern sheets, and Stanistreet cast his eye over the house with its open doorway, over the child, over Jim.

"Well, sir," said he, "I don't think we've forgotten anything, and I've got your orders safe in mind and pocket—and—" He held out his hand and gripped that of the other.

"Good luck," said Lestrange.

The boat shoved off, some of the fellows shouting, "Bye, Jim!" others nodding their heads at him.

Then, just before rounding the cape to the right, the oars came in and the crew, scrambling to their feet, gave a cheer that roused the echoes in the trees. Then the boat passed away for ever beyond the cape.

"Kearney," said Lestrange, "those are good men—would that there were more like them in this strange world."

"Yes, sir," said Kearney. "They ain't bad—off the wharfside."

But Lestrange, fallen into a dream, scarce heard, and hearing would not have understood this profound and comprehensive summary of the ethical condition of the departed ones.

He cared for nothing. He was at peace. The presence of Stanistreet, the very decks of the *Ranatonga* were ties connecting him with the misery of the last twelve years, things disturbing that perfect new mood of mind, born of his vision and the surety that here in this paradise, at their own good time, his children would come to him, be with him.

Leaving the child to Kearney, he turned to the house and began to put things in order. This dreamer was no idler; he had brought all his books with him, some dozen volumes or so, and he arranged them on the shelf already prepared for him by the children, taking care that none of the other objects were disturbed.

He examined the walls, still incomplete in parts, and the roof all but finished, but not quite; the thought that the children had left it for him to complete came to him suddenly and made him pause in his work. It was only a fancy, yet his mind held it and dwelt on it as though it had been a fact of the first importance. It was to be his house as well as theirs.

As he stood like this, idle for a moment and gazing out across the sunlit sward, his eyes fell on Kearney and the child. The sailor's hands were out of his pockets and he was standing, knife in one hand and a bit of stick in the other, whittling away and evidently making some sort of toy. Dick, seated on the ground, naked as the sun, was looking up at the work in progress.

Bowers had decided not to force clothes upon the child, firstly, because Dick, like some form of insane people, fought against any covering, even a blanket; secondly, because the child's skin was already clothed, covered with a lovely golden brown tinge, a suit given him by the sea. He didn't look naked, and the simple and logical mind of the sailor decided to let him be, and there he sat, perhaps the most beautiful object on earth, whilst above him stood Kearney whittling his stick—and Lestrange, casting his benevolent eye upon them, saw nothing but a little child waiting for a toy at the hands of a sailor man.

For Dick was almost nothing to Lestrange, he had no part in his obsession. Stanistreet had reckoned him half crazy partly because of his indifference to this grandchild—but he had forgotten that the forms for ever in the mind of the "poor gentleman" were the forms of the children of the past, that the vision that had brought him what seemed the peace of madness was the vision of two little children of six and seven. "Dick and Emmeline, just as they were long years ago, pure and sweet and happy and childlike, but knowing all things." The fact that they had mated in life, the very fact of Dick, were alien to the consuming dream that here at their own chosen time little hands would push the leaves aside and that in some twilight he would see again the forms of the lost ones.

Poor gentleman!

"There you are and play about," said Mr. Kearney, delivering up the finished article to the chubby hand reaching for it. "Yes, sir." He came to Lestrange, who had called him, and between them they set about the work of making things shipshape. Some bunk bedding had been brought ashore, and Jim's scanty wardrobe that had never been increased out of the slop chest lay in a bundle by the shack amongst the trees.

Stanistreet had wanted to leave a tent, but Jim said the shack was good enough for him. There was lots of room for him besides the stores; Lestrange and the child would have the house.

They worked away at the little jobs to be finished and then came dinner, a sort of picnic on cold stuff brought from the *Ranatonga* and eaten seated on the sward, Dick sharing with them in the way of bananas and scraps just as a dog might have done.

In some extraordinary way the common sailor and the sensitive, super-civilised Lestrange had almost at once become companions, yet without any alteration in status.

It was always "Yes, sir," with Jim, with Lestrange it was always "Kearney," and the power of little things was never more evidenced than in the case of Jim relabelled by the gentle-voiced Lestrange in the first hours of this island life. He had always been "Jim" to himself and others. "Jim" had placer-mined on the hills of California, drunk himself blind, killed a "Chink" in a tong dust-up he had joined in for the fun of the thing, worked for the sandalwood traders and always had come out, to use his own expression, at the little end of the horn. There were rare moments of heart-searching with Jim when he accused himself not of crimes committed but of opportunities let slip, opportunities with women and with Fortune. In those rare moments which yet tinged in some manner his conscious life, the man he knew was "Jim"; the inconsiderable name summoned up his failures. "Kearney" was something new, didn't seem to fit, yet in some way was not distasteful—almost a title.

Towards evening that day Kearney, who had been prospecting about in the woods and who with his island-trained eye had discovered and noted the places of all sorts of fruit-bearing trees, to say nothing of a patch of yams that showed evidence of cultivation—Kearney, chewing a long straw of maya grass, appeared before Lestrange, who was seated in front of the house reading a book.

"The old hooker was due out at the half ebb, sir," said he. "She'll be well to sea by this and bearing north, and I was thinking you'd maybe like to go over to the reefs to have a last look at her."

"The schooner?" said Lestrange, closing his book. "Yes, I would like to see her on her way. Can you row me over?"

"Yes, sir," said Kearney, with a half smile, "I can row you all right." He took a glance into the house where Dick in a corner was asleep under a half kicked off blanket. "And the kid won't take no harm, he's sleepin' like a Dutchman. Ain't you goin' to take your coat, sir? It's breezin' up out there an' fresher than here."

"Yes, Kearney," replied Lestrange, putting the book and his reading glasses away on a little shelf by the door, a quaint little shelf that the lost ones had put up for who knows what purpose. "Yes, perhaps I had better take my coat." He put it on and they went down to the water's edge, where Kearney pulled the new dinghy close up whilst he got in.

Then they pushed off, the sailor sculling with his eye over his shoulder for the reefs.

As I have said, the lagoon here was very broad and broken by coral ridges that made navigation difficult; great ponds and narrow passages of diamond-bright water showed a floor ablaze with live or dingy dead and rotten coral. Coloured fish, haliotis shells, crabs and jellyfish showed as clearly as seen through air, and as they rowed, Lestrange, leaning over, gazed as interested as a child.

"Oh, them," said Jim, his attention being called to a school of jellyfish, disc-shaped, adorned with purple buttons and projecting themselves through the water by the simple act of opening and closing like umbrellas. "Them's pikers, seen 'em as big as a ship's tops'l in the waters over by Howland—Howland, sir, it's one of them line islands, east of the Gilberts.—Yes, sir, there's fish to feed the fleet in this lagoon and I'll be getting busy with the lines to-morrow. Fond o' fishin', are you, sir? Well, you'll have your choice and plenty when we get the lines rigged. Step careful."

He held the boat up to the reef coral whilst Lestrange got out. Then, having fastened her by tying the painter to a spike of rock, they stood looking.

The sound of the surf had been loudening as they crossed from the land. Here, facing the fresh sea breeze, the full roar of the breakers came to them, whilst to right and left the great low-tide outer beach lay bombarded by the ocean, flown across by gulls and showing in the golden light of early evening the rock pools left like bits of mirror by the retreating sea. Coral sings, and mixed with the voices of the waves the inner voice of the reef could be heard, a vague, chanting sound, remote and bell-like.

Here, standing with the sound of the sea and the reef in one's ears, the island world took a new colour and a new atmosphere, altering according to the time of day from the gaiety of morning to the loneliness of evening.

"Look!" cried the sailor. "That's her."

He pointed away to where far at sea the white sails of the *Ranatonga* showed the sun full on them. There was a lump of coral worn smooth by weather just here. Lestrange took his seat on it and whilst Kearney pottered about examining the contents of the rock pools, the cuttle-fish bones and reef debris, he sat, his eyes fixed on the distant sail and his thoughts travelling far beyond.

A long time passed till footsteps roused him from his reverie. It was Kearney, a vast and edible crab—its claws bound with seaweed—in one hand, a crawfish in the other.

"Look!" said Lestrange, as he rose to his feet. "She is nearly gone."

The sailor looked. Hull down, almost washed from sight by evening and distance, the *Ranatonga* showed her canvas to the sunset like a flake of golden spar. Less and less it grew, till at last the eye that chanced to lose it failed to find it again.

"Kearney," said Lestrange, as he turned to the boat, and speaking without any sadness in his tone, "I may be wrong, but it has just come to me that I will never see that ship any more."

The sailor, taking advantage of the fact that the dinghy had slipped her moorings in the last few minutes and had to be captured where she had grounded against a spur further along, made no reply.

Bowers, instructed by Stanistreet, had given him the hint that Lestrange's compasses wanted correcting, and that he wasn't to be "crossed" if he put up strange ideas about things, more especially if those ideas had anything to do with his lost children.

"Which children are you meanin'?" had asked Kearney.

"Them two in the boat we found," replied Bowers.

"Children! What are you talkin' about?" had asked the other.

"Maybe you'll get it into your thick head he's always seein' them same as when they were little," replied Bowers, "and he's got it fixed in his nut he's to find them again, that they're somewhere hid on the island, not them but their sperrits; that's how the land lays with him, and now you know."

Kearney had thought a good deal on this matter. He had a fair charge of superstition in his make-up and no wish to increase his education in psychic affairs, reckoning bad luck, ghosts, omens, and all such things on the same string and to be avoided.

THE ROLLERS

Next morning Lestrange, asleep in the house, was awakened by a child's laughter.

Dick had vanished from the corner where he slept, fetched out by Kearney, whose voice could be heard in admonition.

"Now then, Dick M, now then lave that down or I'll put you back in the house. Lave that down, I tell you." Silence.

Lestrange peeped out and saw the man and the child.

Kearney must have been up a good while, for a fire was alight in a little slip to the right where there was evidence that the old occupants of the place had often done their cooking, a kettle was on the fire and crockery-ware from the *Ranatonga* graced the sward close by, and a coffee pot. Kearney was getting breakfast ready whilst the child stood by him; on the sward, a bit away, hopping about and watching the preparations with bright eyes, was a newcomer, a bird with brilliant plumage.

Lestrange dressed himself and came out whilst the coffee was being made, filling the air with its perfume.

"Why do you call him Dick M?" asked Lestrange, taking his seat on the sward as the other went on with his preparations, whilst the child, who had lost interest in the business, was stalking the bird.

"Well, sir," said Kearney, "it's just a name he give himself on board the ship. Bowers labelled him Dick and I says to him, 'What's your name?' I says, and 'Dick M,' says he, and then he closed up. He's the silentest kid I've ever struck—and I'm thinking those that brought him up mustn't have had much use for their tongues." Mr. Kearney, led away by his own tongue, suddenly closed up himself, but Lestrange did not notice; his mind was on other matters. He had taken his seat with his face to the house, and as the meal progressed his thoughts showed themselves.

"Kearney," said he, "look at that roof and those walls. Can you cut me some canes and get me some of those leaves for thatching? I have been examining the thatch from the inside and it is quite simple. The leaves seem stitched to the big canes that form the beams."

"Lord, sir," said Kearney, "you needn't trouble about that. I'll do the job when I get things a bit more ship-shape; canvas would be better than them leaves, and there's a big roll of spare canvas Captain Stanistreet left, thinkin' I'd like to make a tent."

"No," said Lestrange. "I want to do this business myself. There is no hurry about it, but I would like to do it myself. You know, Kearney, all about my children and how they lived here."

"Yes, sir," said Kearney. "I've heard it from Bowers."

"They lived here and grew up together," went on Lestrange, "lived here in the open and in the woods the happy life that people knew before cities were built. I do not know, but I some day shall know, what fatality carried them out to sea; but I do know that shortly before it occurred they began to build that house. Why?"

Kearney, who knew the tropics better than Lestrange, had an answer on his tongue, pat, the sensible answer that maybe a storm had destroyed their first house, but he said nothing, wishing to keep clear of the subject of the children as much as possible, and Lestrange went on:

"Well, it is just my fancy, but it has come to me that they built it unconsciously, instinctively knowing that I was coming, knowing that death was approaching them, leaving it unfinished for me to finish—to complete for them—"

Kearney, distinctly uncomfortable at the turn the talk was taking, still remained mute. From what Bowers had said, and from his own observation, he knew that Lestrange was sane on every point but this. Instinct told him, or hinted to him, that craziness covered with sanity in this fashion might be a worse proposition if it burst loose than the open and general sort of craziness—like that of old Sam Fisher, with whom he had sailed years ago, a man clean cracked, yet harmless and able to do his duty. He had no fear of violence from Lestrange, but visions of the poor gentleman "dashing into the lagoon," if crossed, made him hold his tongue.

Just at that moment the bird that Dick had been stalking rose in the air and passed over their heads and lit on the roof edge of the house. The child came running after it and, standing beneath, held up his hand.

"Koko!" cried Dick.

But the bird, evidently disturbed and puzzled by the newcomers, resisted all blandishments and after a moment of indecision rose into the air and passed away across the trees.

Lestrange did not notice, he had risen and walked down to the lagoon edge, where the dinghies were moored, the old battered dinghy of the *Northumberland* and the dinghy of the *Ranatonga*.

He seemed to have forgotten all about the house-building, a fact comforting to the mind of Mr. Kearney, who didn't want to cut canes and hunt for palmetto leaves, but to fish.

Lighting his pipe, he followed down to the water's edge and ten minutes later he had his charge safe out on the lagoon, anchored over a vast deep pool and within eyeshot of Dick.

The child was busy. He had toys of his own hidden in some hole behind the house and which he had unearthed: stones and lumps of coloured coral and oyster shells, with which he was making patterns on the sward. He seemed quite happy and content.

Just at first, on board the *Ranatonga*, on awakening from that strange dead sleep induced, perhaps, as Stanistreet had suggested, by the poison of the berries, he had seemed to miss his parents, calling out "Daddy" and stretching out his arms to some imaginary person; but whether the drug had drawn some curtain or whether he had been used to long absences of his parents in their wild life on the island, who can say?—but, content with the moment, he seemed soon to forget the burning interest of the decks of the schooner, the masts and sails and crew occupying his mind.

Lestrange, with a piece of crab on his hook, leaned over the gunnel, gazing at the painted world below; just as the child was occupied with its play, so was he and so was Jim Kearney with their fishing. A shoal of tiny fish, the whole school not bigger than one's hand, would pass like a silver cloud, its shadow following across the coral and sand patches; then a scarus with moving gills would circle, nose the bait and pass, fish and shadow suddenly and utterly dissolved from sight. Everything that moved within a certain distance of the lagoon floor had its shadow, a thing inseparable, blind, yet endowed with movement and duplicating the object that cast it in all things but solidity and colour. These fish shadows seen through water were things quite new to Lestrange, different in some subtle way from terrestrial shadows seen through air. He remarked on them to Kearney, who agreed that they looked rum when you weren't used to them.

"And who knows," said Lestrange, remembering a conversation he had had with Stanistreet, "whether we aren't the shadows of our real selves, Kearney? Knowing nothing, and just following the movements and the dictates of our souls; have you ever thought of these matters, Kearney?"

"No, sir," replied the sailor. "I was never any good at l'arnin'."

Lestrange was about to reply when a fish took his bait, a thing like a rock cod with a bright red band across its back, weighing four or five pounds, and beating the water to spray as it was hauled up.

Lestrange, as he brought this "soul" on board, to Kearney's relief, seemed to have cast speculative philosophy over the other gunnel. Excited as a boy with his catch, he rebaited and the fishing resumed.

Here on this island there was one thing steadfast as the sun, insistent as hunger and merciful as death—sleep. Sleep with no bad taste in its mouth, no feverish dreams in its hand. Sleep as God made it and before man spoiled it.

Dick on board the *Ranatonga* had astonished Bowers by his capacity for slumber and his facility in "dropping off" even in the midst of play. Here it was the same. This afternoon, dinner over, there was not a conscious soul on the island. Lestrange had retired with a book, and a half a page had drowned him in oblivion; Kearney, under a tree, was lost to the world, and Dick, curled like a leaf, was gripping in oblivion the toy the sailor had cut for him, a tiny boat no bigger than a forefinger, rough-hewn in a few minutes, but still a boat.

Just before sunset that evening the wind fell to a dead calm. Living in the open the faintest breathing of wind makes itself felt; there is no anemometer like the sense of man, and a dead calm affects not only the sense of man, but his soul.

You feel it below decks just as you feel it above. It is the one unnatural thing in Nature whose soul is movement, stress, storm.

The groves stood in stereoscopic stillness and the great sea beyond the reef had lowered its song. The rumour of the surf seemed far away, yet in reality was only diminished.

Lestrange, before going to bed, was sitting having a talk with the sailor.

Kearney, well fed, with a pipe in his mouth and his back to a tree, was in the mood for talk, unknowing of the things that might come, released from that fear of life and the future which is the birthright of every man who changes a dollar. Released from the drudgery of shipboard life, Jim Kearney was as communicative as though he had been in a bar on the Bombay coast. The push of whisky was absent, but—and as this is a story which would fall to pieces at once if truth were absent—the push of Lestrange was present. Lestrange to Kearney was not only a poor gentleman who had to be looked after, but "a wonderful rich man." A man who could commission a schooner like the *Ranatonga* was in himself a person to command respect, but the fo'c'sle had embroidered on this, true to the instincts of the mass that will debase an individual or exalt him beyond fact and truth. The fo'c'sle of the *Ranatonga* had elevated Lestrange to the height of Nobs Hill. He wasn't as high as this, and—give Kearney his due—the height of Lestrange in the financial world had had nothing to do with his decision to remain with him. That decision had been born in a moment, and maybe sickness of the sea and love of Dick had been the core. All the same, the "richness" of Lestrange was a powerful underlying factor in his present contentment with his surroundings.

The amber glow of the sunset had faded as these two people, drawn from poles apart, sat towards one side of the little house, Kearney with his back to a bread-fruit, Lestrange more in the open, leaning on his side, plucking at the grass, talking.

"Ain't you ever used tobacco, sir?" said Kearney, apropos of some remark of the other.

"No, Kearney," replied Lestrange. "I tried it once, many years ago, and it didn't suit. I like the smell of it, but I can't smoke. It's the same with whisky. I've tried whisky. I tried it once. I said to myself, 'I'll forget things,' and I went into the Palace at San Francisco—you know that big hotel they have built—and I drank."

"Yes, sir," said the interested Kearney.

"I did not mean to get tipsy," went on the other, "but I drank in company with other men, and I forgot. Yes, whisky is a wonderful thing to make you forget for the moment. I remember quite well and quite distinctly the whole of that evening, up to a point. We talked of horse racing—and I knew nothing of horse racing, but it was just as though I knew. It interested me. We talked of other things far worse. I found myself in a billiard room and I was talking to two men and making bets on players and waging money, and then, Kearney, I awoke next morning—I awoke—and there was nothing but a filthy taste on my tongue and the feeling that I had betrayed those I loved—in having forgotten them, if even for a moment."

"Well, sir, it ain't much use to a man, and that's the truth," said the sailor, tapping the dottle from his pipe.

Then the meeting adjourned, leaving the rising moon to rule the unrippled sea.

The moon was full up when Lestrange, who was asleep in the house, was awakened by a booming sound, measured and rhythmical, that filled the night like the solemn beating of a great drum.

He rose and, passing the sleeping child, came out on the sward.

Kearney was out and standing in the moonlight, shading his eyes and staring towards the sea.

"It's breakers on the reef, sir!" cried the sailor. "Lord! Look at it!"

Away over the reef the spray was flying to the even-spaced and ever loudening thunder of the great rollers. The reef seemed on fire and fuming under the moon, whilst jets of spume-drift rose like sheeted ghosts from the hurricane seas bursting on the outer beach—rose and dissolved and vanished in an atmosphere windless and still as crystal.

It was the dead calm of the night that made the vision appalling, together with the fact that the anger of the sea was still rising. Above the sheeting spray the gulls were flying wildly in the moonlight, and above their voices louder and louder came the thunder of the breakers.

The woods were now echoing to the sound of it, and now, like a line of crystal above the reef, showed the head of the first beaching wave.

It broke in snow and smoke, sheeting into the lagoon, and was followed by two others. That was the climax. As the terror came, so it went, dying gradually down, till at last nothing was left but the old eternal murmur of the surf.

"Well," said Kearney, "that beats all.—Earthquake?—No, sir. I'm thinking there's been some big storm up north there, one of them cyclones, and the push of it has come down pilin' up against tide an' current. Lord help the schooner if she's met it. The sea's big still; listen to that surf. Shall us run over to the reef, sir, and have a look?"

They took the dinghy. The passage was easy in the moonlight, and on the reef, when they reached it, the coral was still drenched and the rock pools over-flooded.

On the outer beach the rollers were still coming in, no longer gigantic, yet great, marching beneath the moon to break in thunderbursts that seemed ruled by the beat of a metronome; marching from the north, where, against the sunset of the day before, the sails of the *Ranatonga* had passed from sight beyond the sea-line.

BOOK II
THE CHILDREN RETURN

TIME PASSES

For weeks after that night Kearney, though busy and contented enough, was possessed by the uneasy feeling that maybe they were marooned for good and all.

If the *Ranatonga* never came back, why, then God help them, it might be years before a ship came along.

Working in the patch of yams, fishing, or what not, he worried over this business in private. Not caring to speak of it to Lestrange, he sometimes spoke of it to Dick. Dick, almost as dumb as a dog, had words, but no use for connected speech as yet; sometimes thoughtful, nearly always busy, the child seemed to live a life of his own and, though fast friends with the man, was quite happy when left by himself. All the same, Mr. Kearney would talk to the child sometimes as if he understood, and it was a relief to give voice to his doubts if it was only to Dick.

Sometimes the man would take him out in the dinghy when he went fishing and Lestrange was otherwise employed, and the child with its chin over the gunnel would watch without a word, or crooning to itself, while the bright-coloured fish passed or nosed the bait.

"Ay, them's big fish," said Mr. Kearney one morning as three grampuses went by in line of battle and vanished into the world of crystal beyond. "Hullo!" A rock cod had taken the bait; he hauled it, fighting, on board and as it foundered on the bottom boards Dick caught it in his chubby hands.

"Fish!" said Dick.

"Ay, now you're talking," said the other, pleased to hear the word he had uttered repeated back to him, and holding up the fish with a finger through the gills. "What'll you give me for 'm, answer up now, eh? What'll you give me for 'm, or I'll chuck him overboard? Answer up now."

"Sivim!" cried Dick. He had risen and was standing, balancing himself, and holding up his hands for the coloured fish.

Mr. Kearney roared with laughter, so that Lestrange, who was weeding in the taro patch, heard the sound borne to him across the water.

He handed the fish to the child, who, clutching it by the tail and through the gills, placed it carefully in the shadow of the thwart, where the sun could not get at it.

"Well, I'm damned," said Kearney to himself. If Dick had suddenly made a long oration in Latin the sailor would not have been very much more surprised than he was at this revelation of care and free thought. It was like a flash of light revealing the child's upbringing and the fact that the people of the wild begin their education in the school of necessity, which is not a school of languages.

He rebaited and dropped his hook, talking to the child as he did so.

"Did your daddy teach you that, eh? Well, you're a cleverer chap than I thought—don't be tanglin' the line; there, you can hold it if you want." He let the little hand clutch the line without letting go of it himself and they fished in partnership, Dick between his knees and helping to haul in the catches. But from that day he began to take a different and more lively interest in the child, and as the weeks passed the bother about the *Ranatonga* began to fade. There was no use in bothering, for one thing, and for another the island life was beginning to clutch him.

Time measured by the shadow of a palm tree, days so like that they slipped by uncounted, no watches to be kept, no worry, and food which was just a pleasant exercise to collect, no home to regret—in a month the thought of the *Ranatonga* had passed away even as the ship herself had passed beyond the sea-line. In two months the fo'c'sle had receded, a dark vision that seemed separated from him by years.

Then, as time went on, the sprouting of Dick became for this common sailor man an interest that beat fishing, spearing grampus on the reef, beating the woods for new fruit patches or speculating on the rumness of Lestrange, whose mild peculiarities seemed spreading in a new direction, to be noted presently.

He heard his own words repeated by the child. It was like teaching a parrot to talk, only with a difference, for under the influence of this conversationalist Dick was beginning to string his words together. He had a little stock of old words collected in his past life—"Dick"—"Em"—"Koko"—"Daddy"—but, whether the strange, new experience of waking to find himself on the schooner had broken the threads or whether his parents had almost forgotten language, he had nothing of connected speech.

The man who takes an interest in a thing has two sets of eyes, and Kearney's interest in Dick made him see things lost to Lestrange, whose indifference to the child, so far from diminishing, seemed to increase as time went on; one might say that it almost amounted to a dislike—as though the presence of a living child here was distasteful to him who was waiting for the children who were dead.

During the first few months his mind was so busy, so intrigued with the new surroundings, so intent on completing the house, clearing the yam patch of weeds and finishing what the lost children had left undone, that time passed as it passed for Kearney. Then, gradually, and as though time were losing the feathers of his wings one by one, the days began to lengthen for Lestrange.

The glorious vision that had brought him such assurance and comfort, had it been born after all of dementia, of that compensating madness which turns grief sometimes into indifference or laughter? Was it a toy produced by Nature to soothe his mind? He did not ask himself this, he questioned nothing, but fishing began to lose its interest for him and, now that the house was finished, there seemed nothing more to do.

How the children were to come to him he had never tried clearly to imagine—perhaps in dreams—perhaps in a vision or stealing to him as ghosts. Perhaps he would die and they would come to lead him into that glorious country where he had met them—he could not tell, he had only been sure that they would come.

But now, as time went on, it was as though the vaguest tinge of darkness had come upon the blessed assurance—a tinge so vague at first that it only changed contentment into expectancy. The first chill touch, perhaps, of that sanity whose home is the commonplace, the sanity that knows nothing of visions, that questions, turns over and doubts. Who knows? But as time went on, expectancy began to take on the tinge of doubt.

Sitting reading by the house you might have seen Lestrange pause in his reading and glance round—a step—no, only a leaf blown by the wind. Sometimes at night Kearney would see him wandering by the lagoon side, a figure clearly defined in the starlight, walking with head bowed and hands behind its back, not a happy figure.

He talked little nowadays and his face had lost something of that other-world look, but what he said was always definite and to the point, his manner was more normal, and if the sailor had been questioned as to his condition, he would have given it as his opinion that the gentleman was "coming round."

All the same, this coming-round business made it a dull time for Mr. Kearney, and only for Dick he might have grumbled. As I have said, his interest in the child made him see things lost to Lestrange.

Dick had a hole behind the house where he used to hide his toys, just as a dog hides bones. He was very secretive about this business, putting the things away when no one was looking. Kearney found the cache one day and must have left some marks behind him, for next day the hiding-place was changed. Another queer thing about Dick was the way, changing from one mood to another, he would alter.

Sometimes he would be racing along the lagoon bank or trying to climb trees, full of life and energy. Again, sometimes he would be seated, quiet and brooding, often with his hands folded, as if contemplating some abstract matter—day-dreaming.

A rum child.

THE RETURN OF THE CHILDREN

One day, moved by a spirit of restlessness, Lestrange went off by himself through the woods, making towards the hill-top. It was the first time he had gone there alone, and when he reached the great boulder that crowned the rise he climbed it. Resting on its upper face, he looked far and wide across the sea, northward where the *Ranatonga* had vanished and westward where the sun would vanish that evening, the vast blue sea so beautiful from here, the sea that had taken his children—for ever.

Nothing broke the wheel of that sea-line; in the sou'west one could see a faint blur in the sky above it as though another island might be there, but the line itself was perfect, like the ring of a pentagram imprisoning Loneliness.

Then his eyes wandered to the reef, the hush of whose surf reached him here with an occasional breath of sound from the wind-touched trees below.

From here he could see the sward and the little house half shaded by the trees. That darker spot was the patch of taro, and just by that great breadfruit whose leaves were beginning to turn lay the patch of yams. He could not see it, for it was hidden in a bay of the trees.

Well, there it all lay as they had left it—never to return.

The exaltation born of the vision that had saved his reason had departed, yet as he sat here to-day feeling in his heart sure that never, never would the dead return visibly, as he had dreamed, to this mortal place, the promise of the vision, in some curious way, did not seem quite broken.

The children might be with him even now without his knowing it—even in the house they had built, and the evidence of their handiwork—were they not with him after a fashion? When he died he might meet them—who could tell? He only felt that they never would return as he had hoped. Never come out from amidst the trees to meet him, or steal to him at night. Then came a new thought. He said to himself as he sat there, with the island before him, "How could they? The dead, if they could return, would come back as they were when they died.—They had grown up; their childish selves vanished long ago, existing only in my memory. Even had they lived, even were they with me here instead of lying there beneath that blue sea, they would be grown up. The children I loved vanished when we parted long years ago. They did not die—they grew up. And yet it is always those children that I have been seeking—what madness!"

Quite clear now in his mind, reasoning without any trace of delusion, it seemed to him that nothing dies so utterly as childhood. That growing up separates a parent from a child with a barrier more invincible than death, stronger, often more sad.

And yet, in his vision, the children had appeared to him just as they had been, and against logic, against reason, came the feeling that the promise of the vision was not to be utterly broken.

The question, did they ever really grow up, ever lose their childhood here in this place where the birds were the only other inhabitants and where sin was not?—this question, unasked, unanswered, scarcely nascent in his mind, may have worked upon him subconsciously, perhaps answering itself in the negative, or leaving the door open to doubt.

It was a brilliant and breezy day, just like the day on which they had made the lagoon. The *Ranatonga* had listed over to port under the press of the wind, the main boom lifting, and the foam roaring aft, gunnel high.

Out of the rainy seasons it was always bright here, yet there were days when the north seemed to come south in some great blue ship whose sails were filled by the winds of the north spilling over in zephyrs that touched the palms with fingers scented by the pine—fresh breezes that whipped the lagoon to amethyst and spread meadows of tourmaline on the coloured swell of the ocean beyond.

To-day the horizon was curiously hard, like the rim of a great jewel, and to-day in the south that pale indication of another island was more distinct.

There were days when the horizon was hot, the azure of sea dimming off into a luminous haze flowing up to the blue of the sky.

Lestrange, with his eyes fixed on the sea-line, seemed fallen into a dream. Then, slowly recovering himself, he rose from his half-recumbent position, climbed down the rock and began the descent of the hillside.

To reach the sward he had to pass through a bad patch where the ground was moist and where things grew with a luxuriance unknown on any other part of the island. Trees living, trees dead and rotting, unknown sappy plants and cables of liantasse, rope convolvulus and python lianas made this place difficult; the air was like the air of a conservatory and to lose oneself here would be easy, but it had never troubled him; his sense of direction was keen and the slight downhill trend of the ground was guide enough.

There was about this place the vague, uncanny something that clings to the rooms of an old deserted house. One felt oneself closed in, yet not alone.

Here, as on the other side of the island, there was a little stream, a thing scarcely a foot broad that passed chuckling, half hidden by ground leaves, and making on either side of it a zone of marsh. Lestrange was stepping across this stream when something clutched the side of his coat. It was as if a tiny hand had been put out to draw him back. It was only a thorn branch, a green tendril armed with thorns an inch long, curved like the claws of a cat.

He disentangled it and passed on, reaching the valley where the great stone blocks lay strewn about and where the idol of a thousand years ago lay amidst the ferns; the thing that had once been a god, omnipotent in the minds of a people long vanished.

Here, to rest himself, he sat down on a boulder and, leaning forward with his elbows on his knees and his chin in the cup of his hands, fell into a reverie.

The name he had given to this island came back to him as he sat there surrounded by those ruins, perhaps two thousand years old: "The Garden of God."

Ages ago men with hearts and minds, men who loved their children and hated their enemies, had worshipped here—generations of them—and there lay their god, thrown down, and his impotence confessed in stone; and not only here. All across the world stretched the fireless altars and the broken figures of gods that had been, the graveyards of futile faiths—gardens of derision.

The great stone figure of the god that had been held his mind in this train of thought: What was the use? All those ancestors of his whom he had never seen, whose forms he could not imagine—of what use had been their sufferings, their religions; what remained of them and their worship, their tears and their laughter?

"You." It was as though the ferns had answered him, the ferns that seemed trying to hide the debasement of the great figure, the ferns still green for all the passage of the years, immortal because they were alive.

The very pines that had broken the blocks apart took up the tale, the pines whose ancestors were green when the blocks were hewn. "The God of this garden knows nothing of ghosts or ruins, cares for nothing but the one untarnishable thing, life;

the spirit that repeats itself through the centuries in the forms of the ferns and the trees, in the guise of the insect on the man: you."

Near by a pine was standing dead and withered, a half-grown tree that had fallen victim to disease. Close to it shoots were springing, its children, born of seeds cast maybe a year ago, children of its spirit as well as its body.

Lestrange's eyes wandered from the stricken parent to the children green and striking towards the sun; then, rising from his seat, he went on through the valley, reaching the sward and the house.

It was a couple of hours after midday, Kearney was nowhere visible, and Dick, down by the waterside, was busy with a cane Kearney had cut for him in imitation of a fish spear. Kearney had taken to spearing fish in the reef pools during the past six months, taking Dick with him sometimes, an apt pupil, to judge by his imitative performances.

An hour later, when Lestrange was seated by the house door reading a book, Dick, who had given up imitation fish-spearing and had fetched some toys from his cache, took his place on the sward near by. Lestrange, who had taken more notice of the child in the last few days, watched him for a bit and then relapsed into his book.

He was busy for a while, and the clink of oyster shells and bits of coral kept the reader aware of the fact. Then he ceased play and Lestrange, looking up again from his book, saw before him, seated on the sward, Emmeline.

*

The child, having lost interest in its play, was seated with hands folded, gazing away across the lagoon, gazing wide-pupiled beyond the world, just as Emmeline had often sat, caught away suddenly into daydream-land. The folded hands were the hands of Emmeline, and the attitude of the body, and, just in that moment, the expression of the face was as if the shade of little Emmeline's sweet soul had reappeared vaguely braving the glances of the sun.

This was no illusion. The likeness was there, evanescent, independent of feature, yet distinct.

Expression, gaze, attitude of body and carriage of hands all said to Lestrange: Here is Emmeline reborn, living again—her gaze, her expression, her attitude, her very self. It was only lately that Mr. Kearney had noticed the child falling into what he called "moody fits." It was only now that the negligent eye of Lestrange, sharpened maybe by his return to the normal, saw what Kearney had missed. Nothing supernatural, something as common as the ground he stood on, and as strange—the parent reappearing in the child.

Then, as Lestrange gazed on this wonder which was yet so commonplace, it passed away. Kearney broke from the trees on the opposite side, carrying a bunch of bananas he had been to fetch, and Emmeline, sighting him, vanished—turned, as if touched by a magic wand, into Dick, who went running towards the sailor across the sward.

IN THE GARDEN OF GOD THERE IS TRUTH

Yes, the promise of the vision had not been entirely broken, but that night, as he lay sleepless in the house, Lestrange almost wished it had.

If you have been waiting years for the return of someone you love, will you be satisfied with a likeness, however vivid and living, even if that likeness is wrought from flesh and blood and spirit?

In the days that followed, watching closely now, he saw that not only had heredity given the child the attributes of the mother, but of the father. Perhaps to the absolute isolation of the parents from the world was due this more than ordinary duplicity and simplicity of mind-structure in the child—he could not tell—but the fact was there. Racing about like a dog, following Kearney, imitating him in the things he did, the child was the Dick of long ago, different somewhat in face, but Dick to the life; tired of play or seized with a fit of day-dreaming, Emmeline would peep forth. Even in play, sometimes, Lestrange would notice the characteristics of the mother in the child's love for coloured things, flowers, bits of coral and bright shells, and in the careful way the toys would be collected and hidden.

Sometimes so vivid was the impression that he could have thrown out his arms and cried: "Emmeline!" only that he knew Emmeline would know him not.

One day, suddenly moved by an impulse he could not resist, he caught the child up in his arms. It let itself be held unresisting, and then, sighting Kearney, who had suddenly appeared, it struggled free and ran to the sailor.

It cared far more for Kearney than for him—no wonder, seeing how he had neglected it, yet, even though it ran to the sailor, Lestrange noted that its interest was not so much in the man as the object he was carrying, a little turtle that he had found trapped in a pool.

"Kearney," said Lestrange, as they sat talking after supper that night, "you remember a long time ago my asking you about the other name you gave Dick—Dick M you called him."

"Yes, sir," said Kearney, "that's what he labelled himself."

"His mother's name was Emmeline," said Lestrange; "he used to call her Em. He was repeating his mother's name, which he would have often heard from the lips of his father, but the strange thing is that he used both names. It was only the other day that I noticed the likeness, Kearney."

"Which, sir?" asked Kearney.

"The likeness he bears to his mother and to his father as well. Sometimes when he is at play or when he sits quiet, it is just exactly as if I were looking at his mother when she was a tiny child, and sometimes when he is running about busy, it is just as if I were watching little Dick of long ago; the thing has given me a shock, Kearney, and I don't know how to take it."

"Well, sir," said the sailor, "children are apt to take after their fathers and mothers. I've seen it often meself, an' I wouldn't be worryin' about that, if I were you."

"I know," said the other, "but it's a bit different in my case, Kearney. I have been waiting and hoping so long—and then to see them at last like—like reflections in a mirror—that's what it is to me, Kearney—just like reflections in a mirror, things that I know and love, but that do not know me and do not love me."

Now Kearney knew only of one child, the solid and redoubtable Dick M, and to hear Lestrange talking of two children and reflections in a mirror gave him a touch of the old uneasiness. Not knowing what to say, he said nothing, and the subject dropped.

It would have been better if Lestrange could have thrashed the whole thing out in conversation with someone of a more philosophic bent than the sailor. Thinking, in a case like this, leads to brooding.

One night the strange thought came to him: Do children really care? Did Dick and Emmeline long ago love me? Have I been all these years breaking my heart for the loss of two beings who, caring for me after their way, had no enduring love, were incapable of enduring love—being children?

The thought was born of Dick's indifference towards him and of his apparent affection for Kearney. Watching closely it seemed to Lestrange that this affection was less for Kearney than for the things Kearney did and the things Kearney handled. Kearney stripped the dinghy of the fishing lines, fish spears; Kearney unable to climb trees or carve toys would not have been the Kearney loved by Dick; the great size of the sailor probably had something to do also with the business, maybe was the cause that made Dick run to him first on the *Ranatonga*.

Then, when Dick in his moody fits turned into Emmeline, he seemed to care for nobody at all.

Lestrange, casting his mind years back, and with his eyes made clear by this new revelation, tried to remember any one instance that would show him Dick or Emmeline's love for him—he could not.

The sweet, dreamy little figure of Emmeline sat before him on the deck of the long lost Northumberland, hunted for its lost box of toys, was carried off to bed by the stewardess, came, as a matter of routine, to kiss him good-night—but it was her charm that she seemed to live in a world of her own.

Dick, an affectionate child enough, had called him "Daddy" and sat on his knee only to wriggle off at the first enticement—had, indeed, shown more affection and interest for an old sailor on board, one Paddy Button, than for his father.

Lestrange, looking back across the years, could still see him riding round the deck on Mr. Button's back, and recalled his own pleasure in seeing the child amused. Then they had vanished with Mr. Button, and he, Lestrange, had broken his heart for them, and they had grown up without him, surely and absolutely forgetting him—never having loved him as he loved them.

It was only now, here in the Garden of God, as he had chosen to call this land of Nature, only here, and taught by Nature herself, that the truth was borne to him: the truth that for years he had been wandering in the world of illusion searching for what was not there—searching for what he told himself, perhaps truly, perhaps falsely, could not be there—the love of a child for a parent equal to the love of a parent for a child.

Nature said to him: You must grow up to love, Love is the blossom of the mind, not the green tendril. Children do not love as men love, they only twine. Would you have it otherwise? Would you have condemned Dick and Emmeline to endless regret for your loss and have made them suffer what you have suffered—even in part?

"Dick," cried Kearney, "kim along, *aisy*! That's no way to be gettin' into a boat. Now set steady and give over handlin' them spears."

The tide was on the ebb and he was going over to the reef to hunt in the rock pools.

Since the revelation that had come to Lestrange, six months and more had passed, making over twelve months since the *Ranatonga* sailed, and with the passing of the months the child had grown.

He was now perhaps three and a half years of age, yet he was big as a civilised child of five, the germ of a man full of vigour and daring, restless, a thing actuated entirely by the moment, except when now and then a broody fit would take him.

Kearney had made him a little kilt of grass such as he had seen worn by the natives of Nauru, and Dick in his kilt sat now in the stern sheets watching every movement of the man as he cast off from the bank.

They had only one boat now, for a little while ago the old dinghy of the *Northumberland* had given up the ghost, opening her seams, which they had no means of caulking, and filling with lagoon water.

It was nine o'clock in the morning, and when they reached the reef and tied up, the sea was half out and the pools showed, flashing like shields in the morning sun.

Spray and the fume of beach filled the air, and the crying of gulls, and the everlasting murmur of the surf. Out here one's environment was completely altered: the still lagoon, the mirrored trees, the foliage and earth scents changing to thunderous sea, blinding coral and sea breeze scented by beach and wave. There the coloured birds passed softly across the groves, here the sea gulls charged down the wind.

With the breeze blowing their hair about, the man and the child stood for a moment. Kearney was looking about him to right and left; then, deciding on the eastern pools, he turned to the right.

Dick followed, avoiding the sharp places in the coral, disdaining to notice the small scuttling crabs or to pick up the stray shells and cuttle-fish bones that a civilised child would have pounced on; they were after fish, not futilities of that sort, and he carried the cane, cut for him by Kearney, over his right shoulder in exact imitation of the man before him with the fish spears.

The first pool they reached was lovely, like a jeweller's shop window for colour; rose-red and amber coral, pink and purple sea anemones, tiny shells like golden buttons, and strips of emerald fucus showed up through the diamond-clear water, but there was no game, only a little fish like a sardine that flitted here and there, and a "piker" no bigger than a saucer pumping itself along. Dick took aim at the jellyfish with his pointed cane and speared it plumb through the centre.

"Now then," said Kearney, noting the fact, and not for the first time, that the child had allowed for refraction, "shoulder your stick an' come along. We've no time to be playin'—Christmas!"

A crab with a body the size of a penny bun and legs three feet long had elevated itself from a cleft in the coral after the fashion of a camera when set up; it seemed to take a snapshot of the oncomers and then, legs in a hurry and body wobbling as if on springs, passed over into the water on the lagoon side.

"Crab!" cried Dick.

The length of the legs differentiated the creature from its fellows. It looked more like a huge spider than a crab, but the reef craft born in the child was not to be deceived. The movement of the creature was enough for him.

The pool beyond held a trapped Jew-fish which fell a victim to Mr. Kearney, owing to the fact that the pool itself was small. In the great pools, floored with sand and showing the silvery gleam of mullet and the scarlet of rock cod, little or nothing could be done with the spear.

It did not matter; the lines gave them all the fish they wanted from the lagoon, and this business was more in the nature of sport.

They wandered along in the blazing sunshine inspecting the pools and exploring the pot-holes, killing squids and turning over the heaps of coloured fuci left by the outgoing tide. A polished rock would sometimes move, disclose itself as a hawk-bill turtle and plunge into a pool. Shells of crabs and whelks lay everywhere, and great haliotis shells empty of everything but the whisper of the sea. Here, amongst the weeds, you could find the sucker claws of octopi, big as the claws of a tiger, and there, on the slab coral polished like window glass by the washing of the sea, huge sea-slugs the size of parsnips.

Kearney preferred the reef to the island. There was "more air" and, as a rule, out here he was lost to everything but the interests around him, pleased as the child with the ever-varying wonders of the place. There was always something new left by the tide. Last time in the biggest of the pools a chambered nautilus was sailing like a lost galleon, the most exquisite dream of Nature; a bit beyond they had come upon the skull of a whale, whose tongue had been torn out by orcas and whose body had been devoured by sharks.

To-day, however, Mr. Kearney seemed to have little interest in the business of the reef. He was bothered. Lestrange had been going very much to pieces of late, physically more than mentally. His heart was troubling him. Sometimes he would be all right, and sometimes he would have to sit down to rest after a little exertion. He had "gone baggy" under the eyes and wasn't himself at all. The fact that the schooner was getting long overdue did not help matters.

Kearney, as he prodded about in the pools, would sometimes stand erect and gaze away off into the north, but in the north there was nothing but the brimming sea, broken only by the wing of a distant gull.

About eleven o'clock they turned back. Lestrange was nowhere to be seen, but he often went wandering in the woods, and Kearney, having put the spears aside, set to work preparing the midday meal.

When it was ready and the fish cooked to a turn, Lestrange had not yet come back. However, he was sometimes late, and the child was hungry, so they set to, the sailor grumbling to himself like a housewife whose cooking has been slighted.

"Wonder where he can have got to," said Mr. Kearney to himself. "Tomfoolin' about in them woods."

After the meal he sat down with his back to a tree and lit a pipe. The pipe finished, he lay on his back with his hands behind his head, looking up at the leaves moving gently in the wind. Next moment he was asleep.

He slept several hours, and when he awoke Lestrange had not yet come back. He was nowhere to be seen, and Kearney, now seriously alarmed, after a glance into the house, stood looking about him, now towards the lagoon, now towards the woods. Then, seeing Dick, who had roused from sleep and was playing about, he caught the child by the hand and made towards the trees.

The act was unconscious; it was as though the sudden sense of loneliness had made him seize the child's hand for companionship.

Dick, nothing loath, and divining some new game, trotted beside him till they reached the trees, amidst which Mr. Kearney plunged, child in hand.

He halted after a few yards and began to shout: "Hi! Are ye there?—Are ye there?—Hi!—Hi!" The child, laughing, took up the call, his small voice sounding through the woods:

"Hi—hi—hi!"

No answer.

They plunged deeper into the groves, and the twilit alleys of the coco-palms and the stretches of pandanus and bread-fruit heard the calling of the man and the child, to which only the wind in the branches made reply.

THE FIRST GLIMPSE OF THE DEMON

"He's gone," said Kearney.

The child was asleep in the house, and he had taken his seat alone by the water's edge. The tide was running out of the lagoon under the sunset and a faint chuckle of water against the ribs of the tied-up dinghy was the only response.

Tired out, he had taken his seat near the little boat as if for the sake of company and, with his pipe in his mouth, was chucking bits of coral at the water. Dick had left them kicking about on the sward; they had been his playthings, but he had outgrown them.

"Gone west," said Kearney, chucking the last of them far out and watching the ripples as they spread, "and Lord knows where he's dropped in them woods." He had done his best, beating the trees and shouting and hallooing, hunting right up to where the groves halted before the rise of the summit, and returning with the tired-out Dick on his shoulder.

There was no chance that the missing man was lying somewhere disabled with a sprained ankle or broken leg. He would have heard the shouting and made answer. Lestrange had gone west; he had dropped, maybe by reason of his heart giving out, and was lying somewhere in those woods, lost beyond discovery.

Leaning now on his elbow, with his pipe, which had gone out, between his teeth, Kearney stared at the water before him.

The swirls in it as it moved gently with the outgoing tide seemed part of his trouble. The *Ranatonga* had not returned, Lestrange was sure dead somewhere or other in those woods, and here he was left alone with the child. What was to be the end of it all?

The sound of the reef was loud to-night, and his mind, travelling back, caught again the sound of the rollers on that night so long ago. He could hear them still, even-spaced, solemn, funereal—yes, the *Ranatonga* was gone beyond any manner of doubt, Lestrange was gone like the ship, and here he was left alone with the child—and what was to be the end of it all?

Too tired for concentrated thought, the general proposition framed itself loosely and vaguely in his mind, unanswerable, expecting an answer no more than that other proposition Nature had once or twice placed before him, making him ask himself, "What are them stars?"

Then a frightful yawn sounded through the dark, the sound of someone spitting into the lagoon, and a voice, grumbling and deep, addressing itself to the gathering night.

"That bloody hooker!"

Kearney had risen. He also seemed to have shoveled all his troubles on to the back of the *Ranatonga*. It is a way with sailors—complaints of misfortunes on shipboard, bad food, hazing officers or Cape Horn weather are rarely addressed to the proper quarters—the ship takes it all—"That — hooker!" If he hadn't sailed on the *Ranatonga* all this wouldn't have happened.

Dusk, almost in a moment, had turned to night, and, just as though a door had been closed, the breeze from the sea died off, leaving the lagoon water unruffled.

Right before Kearney lay the west pool, from ten to six fathoms deep, beyond which lay the broken water that made navigation to the reef so difficult. The pool lay black as ebony, ebony polished and silvered with starlight. As the sailor cast his eyes over it, he saw moving beneath the surface a long thin line of light. It was a deep-sea pala, six feet in length, narrow as a sword, a fish that rarely enters lagoon waters, and never unless at night.

This phosphorescent ghost from the outer sea circled the pool in a grand curve and then, followed by a train of silvery-golden bubbles, vanished.

At night, especially when the moon was away, you could see the lagoon fish, like ghostly shadows, beneath the water. The phosphorescence varied. To-night it was intense, and as the pala vanished, a garfish flashed along, chased by a bream thrice its size. The bream seized the garfish in a whirl of phosphorescent light.

It was like a fight between fireworks, fading off in a luminous mist. As the attacked and attacker drove farther up the pool, the mist remained for a moment, slowly fading and dispersing. It was blood.

Kearney, forgetting everything else for the moment, stood watching as the night life of the lagoon disclosed itself, showing visions never revealed to the day. Great eels passed, filled with fire, and a whip-ray, a yard across, turning, as it went, over and over, like a leaf blown by a leisurely wind.

Then, looking up from the deep entrance to the pool came something that was not a fish—something that walked the floor of the lagoon to-night spreading terror before it as it went, so that in an instant the pool flashed black, free of all fish traces and showing nothing but the newcomer.

What Kearney saw was exactly like the bole of a great oak-tree sawed off at the branches and roots, glowing and pulsating with phosphorescence and crawling like a cat on the floor of the pool. In its forefront two broad lamps burned with an emerald light, now brilliant, now smoky, and from around the lamps serpentine tendrils a foot thick at the base spread and twined through the water, searching, feeling, exploring, now radiating out like a fan, now up-writhing like the locks of Medusa.

It was a barrel-shaped decapod twenty-five feet in length and over ten feet in circumference.

It had risen with the night from some cave far below the outer reef and strayed into the lagoon, either across the reef or by way of the break.

When he had got a full view of the thing, one glance was enough for Kearney. He turned away and made for the house. The child was fast asleep and he crept in beside it. Dick was company, after that sight, and though the child slept without a sound or a stir, the knowledge that it was there lessened the feeling of lonesomeness. Lying on his side on Lestrange's bedding, he could see the doorway, and beyond the doorway the star-showered night stood as if watching him.

If that thing were to come out of the "lagun" and appear at the doorway with those two lamps—God! He tried to forget it by thinking of Lestrange, and then tried to forget Lestrange by thinking of the *Ranatonga*.

Bowers, Bully Stavers, Jerdein, all the fo'c'sle crowd appeared before him, individually, then collectively, and they were leading him off into dreamland, when a voice hailed him.

It was Lestrange's voice, thin and far away like a voice in a gramophone.

Leaning upon his elbow, he listened—nothing. Then he sank back, still listening—nothing.

Next morning, when he awoke and turned out into the bright, early morning sunshine, he looked around him as though in search of someone or some sign that would tell him of the vanished one's fate.

But the lagoon lay as blue in the morning light as though it had never shown him the spectre of the night before, and the trees of God's Garden gave no hint of the form that lay amidst the groves, dead of a worn-out heart.

OUT OF THE GLOOM

"God bless my soul!" cried Kearney. "Come in! What are you doin' there? Get an oar over if you can. Get an oar over, I tell ye."

It was three weeks or so after the departure of Lestrange. Kearney, busy over something near the house, and looking up, had caught sight of Dick.

Dick had got into the dinghy, untied her and pushed out with the boat hook. That the tide was on the ebb didn't matter to Dick.

Hanging over the stern and pretending to fish, Kearney's voice had roused him and he stood, now, balancing himself and considering the situation created by his own act.

A little over three and a half years of age, he was as strong and big as a child of five, but he was neither big nor strong enough to man the sculls, and the dinghy was drifting towards the cape of wild cocoanuts beyond which lay the lagoon stretch reaching to the break and the sea. Then, attending to Kearney's directions, he got a scull over on the port side, got it into the cup of the rowlock and, still standing up, tried to pull, making a terrible mess of the business.

"God's truth!" cried Kearney. "You've done it now—pull it in; that ain't no good, you're getting her farther out." He came running along the bank to the little cape, hoping the boat would drift close enough for him to catch it by the gunnel. He couldn't swim.

Dick had pulled the scull in and was standing, showing no sign of fear, as the dinghy which had twisted sideways a bit, owing to the efforts with the scull, altered its position and came along, bow on, nearing the cape now, but at least a yard too far away to be seized.

"Boat huk!" cried Kearney. "Stick out the boat huk! Lord alive, look slippy!"

Before the words were spoken Dick had grasped the idea. He seized the boat hook, raised it aloft with a mighty effort, and, as the dinghy closed with the cape, let the end drop into the hands of the sailor.

Kearney drew the boat to the bank. Then getting into the little craft, he took the sculls and rowed back.

He neither scolded nor shook the child as another might have done. Dick had acted so sensibly and so pluckily that the sailor had no heart to "be harsh with him," but the incident had a profound effect upon the mind of Kearney and the future of Dick.

The question "what would have happened to the little devil if he'd gone drifting off" suggested another question to the mind of the sailor: the question what would happen to the child if he, Kearney, were drifted off in the dinghy, or if he went west suddenly, like Lestrange.

He knew himself to be in full health and strength. All the same, the question presented itself and made him consider it.

He pictured to himself Dick starving to death in the midst of plenty and, unpleasant as the picture was, it gave him something to think about and something to do. The whole thing was a godsend, in a way, to Kearney, for the vanishing of Lestrange had begun to weigh on his mind. If he had seen Lestrange drop dead and had buried him, it would not have been nearly so bad. It was the thought of him lying somewhere in those woods, unburied, just as he was, that weighed on him.

The thought poisoned the groves; it maybe would have poisoned the lagoon and reef, only for Dick.

That evening, an hour or so before sunset, he took the child out in the boat.

"Now," said Kearney, "I'm goin' to teach you how to scull if you ever get adrift again."

He drew in the sculls and then put one over the stern, resting it in the notch in the transom, and began to instruct his pupil how to scull a boat with a single oar.

Dick watched attentively, and then the sailor, with one hand on the oar, let his pupil grasp it to show him how it was done. The whole business was hopeless, for the child had neither the height nor strength for the work, though he had the spirit. But Kearney was not the man to cast cold water on a pupil. "That's grand," said he; "couldn't be doin' it better meself—that's the way we do it—"

"Lemme—lemme!" cried Dick, trying to push the other aside and get the whole business in his own hands, and nearly losing the scull when he did.

"Ay," said Kearney, recovering it, "I'll let you when you're a bit bigger—there now, let hold of it and maybe I'll make you a little one to-morrow you can get a proper grip of. Now get forward and play with the boat huk—that's more your size."

Next morning, Kearney, pursuing his educational course, made Dick light the fire. Tried to, at all events. Stanistreet had left two tinder-boxes with them and a supply of flints, also matches, but the matches had almost given out, and as Kearney was an expert in the old method, he generally, now, used the flint and steel. Dick, gravely striking away with the flint, made a poor hand of the business, though he seemed to enjoy it, and it took two to do the business at last. All the same it was a beginning—and something new to do. There was lots to be done in the ordinary way of life, between fishing and cooking and what not, but it had grown monotonous from repetition. Teaching Dick gave everything a new tinge and supplied an impetus that was beginning to fail.

Then, after breakfast, Kearney bethought him of the little paddle he had promised to make. He had no wood to make it of and the problem of what to do gave him a comfortable half hour's meditation over his pipe till he solved it by rooting out the saw and sawing off one of the rail-like branches of a dwarf arm that grew near the water.

Here was a piece of straight wood eight inches thick and over four feet long. It only wanted thinning and shaping, and with a knife in his hand down he sat, Dick disposed before him in various postures as the work went on, sometimes standing, sometimes kneeling or sitting—always absorbed, sometimes helping.

The feature that was beginning to strike out individually in the child was his mouth. Dick was a nose-breather and only opened his mouth to eat, and sometimes to talk in two- or three-word sentences. You could chase him round the sward and his way of breathing would be just the same, and, like the Red Indians, when he laughed he rarely opened his lips. It was a beautiful mouth, firm, well curved and showing the dawn of decision upon it.

"Hold it tight now," said Mr. Kearney, and he gave one end of the piece of branch to Dick.

"Am," said Dick.

He held it whilst the man with the knife attacked the bark, the pungent smell of the wood filling the air.

"That's the way of it," said Mr. Kearney, talking as he worked; "off with the bark first and then we'll slope it. That'll do, I can hold it meself now." He continued to work, and Dick to watch. Then, getting tired of the monotony of the business, Dick sat down. Presently, folding his hands in his lap, one of his moody fits came on him; his eyes, wide-pupiled, seemed contemplating things at a vast distance, and Kearney, happening to glance up and notice his condition, called to mind what Lestrange had said about the child taking after the mother when he was quiet. He had often noticed the thing before, but now, from what Lestrange had said, it seemed to the simple mind of Kearney that Dick as he sat there was more like a little girl than a boy, that the "mother in him was coming out too much."

But Kearney, as he worked over the paddle, had other things to think of besides Dick. The tobacco was showing signs indicating that it would not last for ever, and the pipe he was smoking was, so to speak, on its last legs. Stanistreet had left him two beautiful new American briars of the sort they used to sell in Frisco in those days, ornately mounted with chased silver. They had been given to Stanistreet in a moment of expansion by a rich and bibulous friend. The sailor, who was mostly a cigar-smoker, had never used them and as a parting gift had presented them to Kearney.

"There you are, Jim," said he; "they'll last you till we come back. No use having tobacco and running short of pipes."

The sailor had used them, but could never take to them. They didn't smoke right. The old wooden pipe he had brought off from the *Ranatonga* was always sweet as a nut, never got plugged, was always cool and "fitted his mouth." Now it was cracking all down one side, and might go any time. It was like contemplating the death of a wife.

Then there was the bother about Lestrange. It had only just come to him that, supposing by any chance the *Ranatonga* were to turn up, months overdue as she was, might they think by any chance there had been foul play and that he had done Lestrange in?

He spent half the morning working over the paddle and, later that day, urged by the spirit of restlessness, he determined on an expedition over to the eastern side of the island in search of bananas. He could have gone in the dinghy or have taken his way along the lagoon bank, but at the last moment he decided to make a short cut through the woods, taking Dick along with him.

They started, taking their way through the trees on the side of the sward opposite to the house, Kearney leading. The trees were not dense and the wind from the sea stirred their fronds and branches, bringing with it the murmur of the reef. The twilight was alive with dancing lights and sun-sparkles moving as the foliage stirred to the breeze, and now and then, as they passed along, a bird resting on some branch would take flight with the sound of a fan flirted open.

Then came some giant trees with trunks buttressed like the matamata. They stood in two rows, making an alley across which swung cables of liantasse powdered here and there with the star-like blossoms of some lesser vine, and here and there orchids like vast butterflies and birds in arrested flight.

The trees like the pillars of a cathedral, the twilight and the incense-like odours of tropical flowers gave to this place a solemnity and character all its own. Lestrange, in his wood wanderings, had found it out and had often come here to meditate and dream and sometimes forget, for here the great trees cast their presence as well as their shadow on a man's soul. Half-way down this alley Kearney halted.

A breath of wind came stealing towards him, stirring the tendrils of the liantasse and bearing with it suddenly an odour of corruption from the flower-decked gloom ahead.

He stood just as though a bar had been placed across his path. Then, taking the child by the hand, he turned and retraced his path to the house.

KATAFA

Standing on the summit of Palm Tree Island and gazing sou'west, one saw above the horizon line something that was not land; the sky just then altered in colour, as though dimmed by a fingerprint, and sometimes, just before sunset, this mysterious spot in the sky took on a vague glow.

Any old South Sea man would have known at once that this spot was the mirror blaze from a great lagoon reflected in the sky. Kearney recognised the fact at once when he saw it. "There's a big low island somewheres down there," had been his verdict, and he was right.

Karolin was the name of this atoll island; even the whalemen called it by its native name instead of dubbing it with some outlandish term of their own after their custom with islands not on the chart. But they never entered the lagoon. The place had a bad name, wood and water being scarce and the natives untrustable.

But the birds of Palm Tree cared nothing for the scarcity of wood or water or the trustability of the natives, and the great gulls, when fancy took them, would spread their wings for the south, thinking little of the journey of fifty miles. League after league they would lay behind them with nothing in view but the blaze of the sea till, like a trace of pale smoke, the birds of Karolin showed circling in the sky. Then the line of the reef sent its murmur to meet them, but, unheeding reef or surf, they would pass over to poise above the lagoon before slanting down to rest and fish.

H. de Vere Stacpoole

The lagoon was forty miles in circumference and the containing reef nowhere higher than six feet; standing on the reef, you could not see the opposite shore, except when mirage lifted it, showing across the great pond brimming with light a line dotted with palm clumps. There was no water source on Karolin, only ponds cut in the coral and filled by the rains; no taro, only puraka; no bread-fruit; cocoanuts, puraka, pandanus-fruit and fish were the main support of the inhabitants, and though Palm Tree, with all its vegetation lay within reach, they never went there for food.

The fishing canoes, in the bad seasons when fish were poisonous at Karolin, would push out with the northward-running current and sometimes even skirt the reef of the northern island, but they never landed, and for three reasons. The high island, with its dense trees and narrow lagoon, was an abomination to the minds of the atoll-bred people. In the remote past, for some reason, they had emigrated en masse, but had returned in less than three months, broken in spirit and yearning for the great spaces and the sun blaze on the lagoon. Again, years ago there had been a tribal war and the remnants of the defeated tribe had made north and had been pursued and killed on the beach of Palm Tree to a man, and their ghosts were supposed still to haunt the beach. Lastly, Palm Tree, though invisible from Karolin by direct vision, was sometimes at long intervals raised by the witchery of mirage, showing as a picture in the sky, and an island that could raise itself like this was a place to be avoided. Katafa had only seen this vision twice, though she was thirteen years of age.

Eleven years ago a ship had come into the lagoon of Karolin, a Spanish ship, the *Pablo Poirez*, Spanish-owned and out of Valparaiso. Valores was the captain's name, and he had his wife and little daughter on board, a child two years old, named Chita.

He came in for water. There had been a drought, and the wells of Karolin were low, and Le Juan, the sorceress and rain expert, in a temper, and Uta Matu, the chief man of the northern tribe, spoiling for a fight. When the wells were low there was always trouble on Karolin—offerings to the god Nanawa, rejuvenations of old vendettas and the general nerve-tension and gloom of a people who feel that the Fates are against them.

In the middle of all this the Spaniards came on shore with their water barrels and were met by Le Juan and Uta Matu, who barred the way to the wells only to be pushed aside by Valores and his men. In a moment the beach was in a turmoil;

daggers and shark's-teeth spears were whipped from beneath mats and from clefts in the rock; attacked on all sides, and with the fury of a typhoon, the Spaniards fell, butchered like sheep—slaughtered to a man.

Then the canoes put out for the ship, Uta Matu boarding her to starboard and his son Laminai to port. There were six Spaniards on board. They had knocked the shackle off the anchor chain and were trying to handle the sails, forgetting that the tide was flooding and that the wind was coming from the break—working like maniacs and falling like cattle before the spearmen. The wife of Valores fell defending her child. Stricken on the back with a coral-headed club, she fell with it in her arms, covering it so that they had to turn her over to tear it from her.

Now the ship, free of the anchor, had been drifting with the flood and wind, and just as Laminai was holding the child aloft before dashing it on the deck, the keel took a submerged reef that rose from the lagoon floor just there. The shock made him slip on the blood-soaked deck and as he fell Uta caught the child.

His blood lust was satiated and the gods had spoken, at least so it seemed to Uta Matu, and when Laminai got on his feet again and tried to seize his prey he received a clip on the side of the head from the old man's right fist, strong to save as to kill.

But the chief had reckoned without Le Juan. The sight of the rescued Chita filled the priestess of Nanawa with the most dismal forebodings. It was a girl-child, belonging to the murdered papalagi whose spirits, through it, would surely find revenge. Le Juan, despite her devotion to sorcery or maybe because of it, was a very clever woman. She foresaw in the growing up and mating of this alien with some young man of the tribe danger to the people of Karolin. It might be that the ghosts of the murdered ones would work through her and the children she bore; Le Juan could not tell, she only knew that there was danger in the thing, and that night, squatting in Uta Matu's house whilst the rest of the tribe lay about on the beach drunk with carnage and kava, she so worked on the mind of the chief that he was about to assent to the strangling of Chita, when of a sudden a noise filled the air, first a whisper, then a murmur, then a roar—the rain, the long deferred rain, beating the lagoon to foam and washing the coral free of blood-stains.

"How now about the ill luck?" asked Uta Matu. "The child is lucky; it has brought us rain. Take her and do what you will with her, put spells upon her or what you like, but if you injure one hair of her head I will have you choked with a wedge of raw puraka and I will cast your body to the sharks, Le Juan."

"As you please," said the old woman; "I will do what I can."

She did.

She christened Chita, Katafa, or the "Frigate Bird," a creature associated with wanderings and great distances, and then gradually and year by year she isolated Katafa from the tribe, absolutely and in all but speech.

Now, how can you isolate human beings from their fellows so that whilst living, talking, eating and moving amongst them they are as much apart as though ringed round with a barrier of steel? It seems impossible, but it was not impossible to Le Juan. She imposed upon Chita the rarest of all the forms of tabu, *taminan*. There were men and women on Karolin tabued from touching the skin of a shark, from eating certain forms of shell-fish, and so forth, and so on, but the terrible tabu of *taminan* debarred its victims from touching any human creature or *being touched*.

From her earliest infancy the mind of the Spanish child had been worked upon by Le Juan until the tabu had taken a firm hold and become part and parcel of her brain processes, and evasion an instantaneous reflex act. You might suddenly have put out your hand to grasp or touch Katafa—you would have touched nothing but air; like an expert fencer, she would have evaded you if only by the twentieth part of an inch. To understand the tremendous grasp of this thing upon the mind, it is enough to say that had she wished you to touch her, desired with all her heart that you should touch her, wish or desire would have been fruitless before the impassable barrier erected by the subliminal mind.

On no grown person could the tabu of *taminan* be imposed. Only on the plastic mind of childhood could it obtain its grip strong as hypnotism and lasting till death.

At six years of age Le Juan's work was accomplished and Katafa was immune, isolated for ever from her kind. The work had been helped by the fact that every creature on Karolin had avoided her, but on the day when Le Juan proclaimed her free, she was taken into the tribe, men, women and children no longer held apart, and she mixed with them, played with them, fished with them, talked with them, a ghost in everything but speech.

BLOWN TO SEA

This evening, just before sunset, Katafa was standing on the beach waiting for Taiofa, the son of Laminai. They were going out to fish for palu beyond the reef.

Straight as a dart, naked but for a girdle of dracæna leaves, she stood, her eyes sweeping the lagoon water where the gulls were fishing.

Near by some native girls were helping to unload a canoe that had come over from the southern beach, and as they talked and laughed over the work, flat-nosed and plain, muscular and full of the joy of life, they formed the strangest contrast to the Spanish girl in the dawn of her beauty. Slim, graceful as a young palm tree, Katafa stood separate from the others in spirit as in body.

The work of Le Juan had been well done and the result was amazing, for Katafa from all other human beings stood apart, ringed by the mystic charm of *taminan*.

One might have said of her that here was a living, breathing human being who yet was divorced from humanity. Every movement of her body, her glance, her laughter, spoke of a spirit irresponsible, thoughtless, light as the spirit of a bird. She who touched nothing but the food she ate, the ground she trod on and the water she swam in, who had never grasped a living thing since the tragedy of the Spanish ship so long ago, had seemingly failed to find the hold upon life given to the least of the Kanaka girls amongst whom she had grown up—creatures almost animal, yet human in affection and tied together by the common bonds of joy and hope and fear. One of the strangest effects of the terrible law under which Katafa lived was her insensibility to fear.

The natural law of compensation gave to the isolated one fearlessness and the power to stand alone, and to the one who had no use for a soul the lightness of spirit and waywardness of a bird, the irresponsibility of the flower moved by the wind. Katafa—well was she named as she stood there, her mind roving with the frigate birds across the sunset-tinged waters of the lagoon.

"O he, Katafa!"

It was Taiofa, sixteen years of age and strong as a grown man. He was carrying a big basket containing food and several young drinking cocoanuts, the lines and bait; the canoe that was to take them lay on the beach, the water washing its stern, and between them they put off, Taiofa running up the sail to catch the favouring westerly wind.

Katafa steered with a paddle. The tide was running out and they cleared the break just as the setting sun touched the far-off invisible western reef.

Out here they met the swell and, with the wind blowing up against the night and the last of the sunset on the sail, they steered for the fishing bank and the forty-fathom water that lay three miles to the northeast.

The water off Karolin is a mile deep; then the soundings vary towards the bank, the floor of the sea rising in terrace-like steps to within forty fathoms of the surface.

Neither Katafa nor her companion spoke, or only a word now and then. Steering an outriggered curve required attention, for if the outrigger dips too deep there may be disaster; as for Taiofa, he was busy overhauling the tackle, the anchor which was simply a chipped lump of coral, and the mooring rope.

The Spanish ship had been a blessing to Karolin. Before burning and scuttling, the natives had looted her. The rope Taiofa was handling had been made from part of her running rigging unwoven and retwisted, the fishing hooks beaten out of some of her metal. Having placed everything in order, he crouched, brooding, his eyes fixed on the last tinge of sunset, and then raised to the outjetting stars.

A three-days-old moon hung, half tilted, like a boat rising on a steep wave, its light trickling on the swell and turning the outrigger spume to silver. A last fishing gull passed them making for the land, and now, as though assured of their position by chart, compass, and sounding lead, the sail was hailed and the anchor dropped, the canoe riding to it bow to swell.

Whilst the boy fished, the girl watched, a heavy maul beside her for the stunning of the palu when caught; from far away, and borne on the wind, came the voice of the reef, a confused indefinite murmur from the vastness of the night, answered only by the slap of the water on the planking as the northward-running current strained the anchor line.

An hour passed, during which the fisherman hauled in a few small schnappers whilst the girl, perched now on the pole of the outrigger, watched the seas go by flowing up out of the night ahead and passing in long rhythmical columns of swell, star-shot and rippling on the anchor rope; the schnappers lay where they were cast, like bars of silver leaping now and again to life, whilst on the wind the invisible beach of Karolin still sent the murmur of the breakers on the coral.

"The palu are not," said Taiofa, "but—who knows?—they may come before dawn."

"Better then than not at all," said the girl, "but it is not the palu, O he, Taiofa; we should have waited for a bigger moon."

The fisherman made no reply and the girl relapsed into herself in a silence broken only by the far-off beach.

Hours passed and then at last came the reward, the line ran out and the boy, calling to the girl to steady the canoe, hauled whilst the great fish fought, now darting ahead till the bow overran the anchor rope, now zigzagging astern. Now they could see it fighting below the surface and now thrashing the starlit water to foam;

it was nearly alongside, and Taiofa was shouting to his companion to get ready to strike, when of a sudden the night went black; the squall was on them.

They had not noticed it coming up from the south. The smash of the rain and the rush of the wind took them like the stroke of a hand.

Taiofa, dropping the line which ran out, flung his weight to the outrigger side, whilst the girl, instinctively and at once, dropped the maul and sprang aft to the steering paddle. Her thought was to keep the canoe head to sea, but the anchor rope had parted and the canoe, instead of broaching to, was running in some mysterious manner before the squall stern on to the leaping swell.

It was the palu. The end of the line was tied to the bow and the great fish driving north was towing them.

Then, with a last roaring cataract of rain, the squall passed and the stars appeared, showing the tossing sea and Taiofa gone! He had been on the forward outrigger pole and the sea had taken him, leaving neither trace nor sound. The canoe had possibly overrun him; she did not know, nor did she care: Taiofa was less to her than an animal, and the devouring sea was feeling for her to devour her.

Something hit her like the stroke of a whip. It was the sheet of the mast sail that had broken loose. She seized it, fastened it, and then, as the sail filled before the wind, steered. The palu, feeling the slackening of the line, made a dash at right angles to their course. She saw the line tauten out to starboard and countered with the paddle before the bow could be dragged round. Then the line went slack; it had either broken or the fish had unhooked.

Then she steered, the big waves following her, and the wind that had fallen to a strong breeze filling the sails.

To turn was impossible in that sea, and even with the bow to the south she could never have made Karolin against the wind with a single paddle and that clumsy sail.

In the hands of the God who sends the seeds of the thistle adrift on the wind, fearless, and grasping the paddle, she steered with only one object—to keep the little craft from broaching to.

Blown to sea! For ages across the Pacific the seeds of life have passed like that from island to island, borne in lost canoes blown off the land at the mercy of chance and the wind.

H. de Vere Stacpoole

AT DAWN

At dawn the wind had sunk to a steady sailing breeze and the swell had lost its steepness, as the great blaze came in the east and the brow of the sun shattered the horizon. Katafa reached for the basket of food tied to the after-pole of the outrigger and opened it.

As she ate, her eyes roamed far and wide from sea-line to sea-line—nothing! Karolin had vanished far from sight and Palm Tree was too far off to show—nothing but the vales and hills of the marching swell, the following wind and the sun now breaking from the sea that seemed to cling to him.

To beat back against the wind and the current was impossible to her. It was impossible even to turn the canoe with a single paddle, and in that swell there was nothing to do but steer.

Then gulls came up on the wind, birds that had left Karolin before dawn and were bound for the fishing grounds off Palm Tree. They passed her, low-flying and honey-coloured against the sun, to vanish snowflake-white in the distant blue.

Far to the westward lay the Paumotus, with their reefs and races and utterly unaccountable currents; behind, Karolin and the vacant sea stretching to the Gambiers; to the east, the South American coast, a thousand miles and more away; to the north, Palm Tree and the vacant sea stretching to the Marquesas—and all around, silence. This new, strange thing for which she had no name almost daunted her. She had lived with the eternal sound of the reef in her ears, it had been part of her world like the ground beneath her feet, and now that it was withdrawn she was at a loss. The occasional flap of the sail, the whisper and chuckle of the bow wash, the fizz of the foam as the outrigger broke the gloss of the swell—all these sounds came to her strange against the silence.

A great sea current is a world of its own and, like the *Kuro Shiwo*, this northern drift carried with it its own peculiar people. Jellyfish from the far south, albacores from the Gambier grounds, turtle drowsing or asleep on its surface, sometimes a shoal of flying fish, like shaftless arrow-heads of silver shot by invisible marksmen, would pass, flittering into the water ahead; once, uprunning a steeper wall of the swell, she glimpsed a shark cradled in the glossy green like a fish in ice or a faun in amber. At noon a reef showed away to starboard, razor-backed and spouting like a whale, and then, just before sunset, gulls began to pass her, flying north; away across the water she could see more gulls in full flight, all making north.

Standing up in the last blaze of the sunset, she strained her eyes—nothing. Once she thought that she could see a point breaking the far horizon, land or gull's wing she could not be sure. Then, with the dark, the wind sank to a dead calm and the swell to a gentle heave of the sea, and, crouching in the bottom of the canoe, Katafa, her head resting against the outrigger pole, closed her eyes.

She awoke at dawn with the whole eastern sky flushed like the petal of a vast rose on which the day-star glittered like a point of dew. A faint breathing of wind from the north brought a whisper with it, the whisper of the reef, and for a second, just as she opened her eyes, the picture of Karolin came before her. Had she drifted back? Rising and grasping the mast, she turned her face to the wind, and there, far away still but breathing at her with the perfumed breath of the land wind, lay the form she had seen in mirage as a dreamer sees his fate.

Moment by moment, as the light increased, it grew clearer and more definite, till now, struck by the first level beams of the sun, it bloomed to full life across the blue.

OUT OF THE SEA

That morning, three hours after sun-up and half an hour after breakfast, Fate and Mr. Kearney had a difference of opinion.

The bananas were ripe on the eastern side of the island and he had arranged in his mind to go and fetch a bunch, taking the quickest way—that is to say, right over the hill-top instead of round by the lagoon edge—but he was lazy and disposed to put the business off to a more convenient time. He would have made Dick row him round in the dinghy, only that Dick wanted the boat for purposes of his own beyond on the reef.

Sitting with his back against a tree bole, he could see the figure of the boy away out on the coral; the amethyst and azure lagoon, the reef with the moving figure upon it and a touch of purple sea beyond, all made a picture as soothing as it was lovely on that perfect and almost windless morning.

But Kearney was not thinking of the beauty of the scene. Bananas were bothering him; he did not want to move, and they were calling on him to get on his legs, cross the island, cut them and fetch them.

Ten years of island life had altered Kearney almost as much as they had altered Dick. Always on the look-out for a ship during the first three years, he would not have left the island to-day unless shifted with a derrick. He had grown into the life, grown lazy and stout and grizzled—and moral. A most extraordinary type of beach-comber. The child and the island, the sun and the easy way of life, had all conspired in this work upon him. He had no hankerings now after bar-rooms; without tobacco for years, he had taken to chewing gum, finding plenty of it in the woods, and he had devised several innocent and non-laborious amusements for himself and the child, among others, ship building. The very first act of Kearney when they had landed on the island had been the cutting of a little boat for Dick from a bit of wood. He could do anything with a knife and one day, some six years ago, when time was hanging heavy, the saving idea came to him of constructing a model of the lost *Ranatonga*. It took him nearly eight months to accomplish, but it was a beauty when finished, with sails of silk made from an old shirt of Lestrange's and a leaden keel constructed from the lead wrappings of a tea chest which he managed to melt down.

They took it over and sailed it on the reef pool where the nautilus fleet had once floated, and next day he set to work on another, a frigate this time. Four ships altogether had left the stocks of the Kearney-Dick combination, and meanwhile three real ships had touched the island, two whalers and a sandalwood schooner. The whalers Kearney had carefully avoided; the sandalwood schooner had come up in the arms of a hurricane, smashed herself to pieces on the reef, drowned every soul on board of her and left the coral littered with trade goods, bolts of cloth enough to clothe a village, boxes of beads, cheap looking-glasses, dull Barlow knives—everything but tobacco.

Having contemplated the lagoon, the reef and the moving figure of Dick for a while, Kearney suddenly shifted his position, rose, stretched himself and, fetching a case knife from the shelf in the house, turned towards the trees. The bananas had conquered. Passing through the woods, he struck uphill till he reached the summit, where he paused for a moment to rest, a figure not unlike that of Robinson Crusoe, standing with his hand on the great summit rock and gazing far and wide across the ocean.

Then he shaded his eyes. Far off on the dead calm sea a canoe was drifting; two miles away it might have been to the south and perhaps half a mile to the east. The land wind had died off completely and the tiny sail hung without a stir. He could not tell at that distance whether it had any occupants. Brown, like a withered leaf on the water, it lay drifting with the current that would take it past the island just as it had taken the dinghy with the lost children of Lestrange.

Kearney gazed for a full minute, then, turning, he came running downhill and back through the trees to the lagoon edge. Dick was still in view; Kearney hailed him, waving his arms, and the boy, understanding that he was wanted, left the business he was on, ran to the dinghy and, untying her, pushed across.

Dick was worth looking at as he came alongside, standing up in the dinghy, the boat hook in his hands. Nearly thirteen, yet tall and big as a boy of fourteen or more, naked but for a kilt of leaves, with the forthright gaze of an eagle and a face where decision met daring, a philosopher, looking at him, might have said, "Here is the making of the world's finest man, here is the perfect human being, neither savage nor civilised, swift as a panther, graceful as a tree, yet endowed with mind, decision and character."

Kearney saw only the red-headed boy whom he had watched growing up, and who had been a handful in his way ever since he had been big enough to row the dinghy.

"There's a boat beyond the reef," cried Kearney, stepping into the dinghy. "Now get aft with you and give me the sculls. I'm go'n' to try 'n' fetch it in."

"A boat—where y' say?" asked the boy.

"Out beyond the reef," replied the other, pushing off. "Ship the tiller an' keep us close to the bank. I've not time for talkin'!"

Dick shipped the tiller and steered whilst the other put all his strength into his stroke. They passed the little cape, nearly brushing the trees, and then down the long arm of the lagoon stretching to the east. It was slack tide, just before the flood, and the water was calm at the break. They shot through, taking the heave of the glassy swell, and there, drifted now quarter of a mile to the north, was the canoe, the sail still hanging without a stir.

"There's someun in her," cried Dick.

Kearney took a glance over his shoulder and saw the figure of the girl, who had tried to make the break with her single paddle and failed. She was standing, holding on to the mast and looking towards them, a form graceful as the new moon, naked but for her girdle of dracæna leaves and with her free hand sheltering her eyes against the sun.

As they drew closer her voice came across the water clear as a bell and hailing them in some unknown language.

"It's a girl!" cried Kearney.

"What's a girl?" asked Dick, so filled with excitement over this new find that he was forgetting to steer.

"It's a female—mind your steerin'—you're a mile to starboard—there, let it be and I'll manage meself."

The girl, as they drew close, ran forward and seized the anchor rope; it had parted a good way from its fastening and there were some four fathoms of it left. She stood with it coiled in her hand and as the dinghy approached, she sent the coil flying towards them, straight and sure. Then, as Kearney caught it, she darted aft and seized the steering paddle, crying out in answer to the sailor's questions in the same strange bell-like voice, but in a tongue dark to her saviours as Hebrew.

"Kanaka," said Kearney, "but she knows her business. Dick, leave that boat huk down—we aren't boardin' her. We'll tow her in—catch hold of the rope."

He got the sculls in, fastened the rope end to the after-thwart, and then started to work towing the canoe's head round.

Though Dick had asked Kearney what a girl was, it was the word he was enquiring about, not the thing. The stupid old story of the boy who saw girls for the first time at a fair, was told that they were ducks, and then expressed his desire for a duck, has no foundation in psychology. Life is cleverer than that. Dick saw in Katafa a young creature something like himself. Descended from a thousand generations of people who knew all about girls, his subconscious mind accepted Katafa's structural differences without question; she was far less strange to him than the canoe. His ancestors had never seen a South Sea canoe. This strange, savage, mosquito-like structure, with its bindings of cocoanut sennit and its mat-sail, fascinated the boy far more than its occupant. To him, truly, it was like nothing earthly; the outrigger alone was a mystery and the whole thing a joy, a joy delightfully tinged with uneasiness, for the absolutely new is disturbing to the soul of man or beast. As he rowed, Kearney noticed that the girl was chewing something in the way of food, and once he saw her bend and take up a drinking cocoanut and put it to her mouth, a fact that eased his mind, bothered by the idea that she might be starving. The tide was beginning to flood. It swept them through the break and as the dinghy turned up the right arm of the lagoon, the tow rope now tautening, now smacking the water, it was the girl's turn to be astonished. The tall trees from outside the reef had seemed monstrous to her eyes, accustomed only to the flat circle of the atoll, but here, inside the reef, the density of the foliage, the unknown plants, the unknown smells, the trees sweeping up to heaven almost terrified her, brave though she was; the only familiar and comforting thing was the reef and its voice—but those trees in their hundreds and thousands, climbing on each other's shoulders!

Steering with her paddle, she kept the canoe in line with the dinghy, the wild cocoanut almost brushing her as they turned the little cape; then, as they came alongside the bank, she sprang out and stood, her arms crossed and a hand on each shoulder, watching, whilst the others landed and Kearney tied the boats up.

"Now then, Kanaka girl," said Mr. Kearney, as he rose from this business and approached her, followed cautiously by the boy, "what's yer name?—Jim," pointing to his breast with his thumb. "I'm Jim—Jim.—What's yourn, eh?"

She understood at once.

"Katafa," came the reply; then, swift as a rippling stream, "Te tataga Karolin po uli agotoimoana—Katafa."

"Ain't no use," replied Mr. Kearney. "Tie a clove hitch in it and we'll call you Jimmy. Want some food? God bless my soul, where's the use in talkin' to her? Here you, Dick, come along an' get the fire goin'. Come along, Kanaka girl." He clapped her on the shoulder—made to do so, but his hand touched nothing but empty air.

"Well, I'm damned," said Kearney. He had got the shock of his life. It was not the fact that she had evaded him, but the manner of the evasion. His hand had missed the shoulder, driven it away, seemingly, as wind moves a curtain; yet she had scarcely moved and her face and attitude had not altered in the least. She seemed quite unconscious of what had happened, and the man who has ever tried to touch a taminanite will know exactly the feeling of Mr. Kearney as he turned to make the fire, followed by Dick.

Katafa drew closer; then, at a certain distance, she squatted down and watched them at work. She had no fear of men or ghosts. Human beings and ghosts were things equally remote to Katafa, who could touch or be touched by neither.

Infected by Le Juan and filled with wild fancies, or maybe endowed with psychic powers, she had seen the "men who leave no footprints" walking in the sun-blaze of Karolin. There was a sandy cove eight or nine miles from the break and here with Taori, the second son of Laminai, she had watched them walking like people astray and bewildered.

She had flung stones through them, Taori wondering and seeing nothing. At night, had you possessed the eyes of the Spanish girl, you would have seen in the dark of the moon, and at a certain hour, a man swimming in the starlight from the old anchorage of the Pablo Poirez towards the break, leaving a trail in the starlight, always at the same hour and always in the same direction; and sometimes on these nights fires would spring up on the reef where it trended to the west, lit by no man's hand, for no man was there.

But Palm Tree to her eyes seemed free of anything like this. Amongst the gifts presented by the wreck were three or four tin cases of Swedish matches, enough to last for years. Kearney had discarded the tinder-box and he was lighting the fire with a box of matches, a fact more interesting than bonnets to Katafa as she squatted, watching his every movement.

Then, when the food was ready and Dick had fetched some water from the little spring at the back of the yam patch, Kearney called to the "Kanaka girl" to pull in her chair.

She came within a couple of yards, but would come no further, squatting on her heels in an attitude that gave her freedom to spring away at a moment's notice. Kearney stretched over with some food on a plate for her, then he handed a cocoanut bowl with some water in it. Then he began on his own meal. He seemed put out.

"She ain't right," said Mr. Kearney, as though communing with himself.

"What ain't right, Jim?" asked the boy, a fish in his fingers. "Why ain't she right, Jim? What's the matter she can't talk?"

The only things he had ever heard Kearney address as "she" were the ships they made. Katafa had in some way taken in his mind a tinge from those delightful ships; she was a "she." The canoe helped; it was hers. Now that the canoe was half out of sight, hidden by the bank, and Katafa sitting there close to him, she fascinated him. His passionate love of the sea, of the dinghy, of the little ships, of everything connected with the water, all lent colour to this strange new being who had come up out of the sea in that thing—it was almost as if she had a keel on her. He would have loved to make friends, but he was too shy as yet and she couldn't talk so that he could understand.

He set his teeth in the fish.

"Lord, I dunno," said Kearney, his recent experience hot in his mind, yet unable to explain it in speech. "She ain't like other folk. There, don't be askin' questions, but get on with your dinner. Maybe it's just she's a Kanaka."

"What's a Kanaka, Jim?"

"You get on with your dinner and don't be askin' questions."

The sociable meal proceeded, Katafa "tuckin' into the food" with a good appetite, but with an eye ever on Kearney. Kearney, by his attempts to clap her on the shoulder, had laid the foundation of a lot of trouble for himself. He had raised against him the something that Le Juan had bred in the subconscious mind of the girl.

No man, woman or child on Karolin had ever tried to touch her. She was tabu to them, as they to her. The art of avoidance, which was as natural and unconscious to her as the art of walking, had always been exercised against an accidental touch. Kearney had done what no one else had ever done, tried to touch her.

But if you think that she reasoned this out in her mind, you would be far from the truth. Whatever Le Juan's means of tuition may have been—a hot iron was one of them—they had left all but no mark on the conscious mind of the grown girl. Otherwise her life would have been as impossible as the life of a person who has to think over each step he takes, each movement of the body and each respiration he makes. Le Juan had made the tabu not a direction to be obeyed, but a law of being, living like a watchdog in the dark chambers of the girl's mind, a watchdog baring its teeth at Kearney.

Katafa had evaded the friendly blow of Kearney just as on Karolin she had often evaded the touch of hands in the pulling in of a fishing net, instantaneously and all but unconsciously, but the difference was vast. Kearney had placed himself among a new order of beings by his act. His clothes helped. She had never seen any one in trousers and shirt before. Decidedly this strange bearded man required watching.

Dick was different. For all his red head and straight nose and strange-coloured eyes he might have been a boy of Karolin.

She finished her food. Kearney had given her a plate, one of the few unbroken of those Stanistreet had left behind for them. It had flowers painted on it and the thing intrigued her vastly. It seemed to her a new sort of shell, and when the sailor rose, replete and drowsy, and went off for his siesta in a comfortable spot amidst the trees, Dick, who had received instructions to "clear up them things an' give's a call if she tries to meddle with the boats," saw Katafa furtively trying to scratch one of the flowers off the plate.

"They're painted on," said Dick, suddenly losing his shyness. "You can't get them things off." Finding his voice gave him courage, and getting on his legs, he ran off to the house, returning in a minute with one of the ships, a frigate. Kearney had made rests for each one to stand on, and he carried the frigate, rest and all, and placed it close by her on the ground.

"Ain't like yours," said Dick, reclining beside it and handling the tiny spars so that she might see how they swung. "It's a fridgit."

The girl, appealed to in the language of ships and sitting on her heels, regarded the little vessel with interest. In Karolin lagoon, two miles beyond the break and in ten-fathom water, lay the hull of a sunk ship that the Kanakas had burnt. She had knocked a hole in herself by drifting on a reef, and the flames had only time to bring the masts down before she sunk, and there she lay on an even keel, clear to be seen in the crystal water and with the fish playing round her stern post.

The Karolin boys called her the big canoe of the papalagi. Katafa knew nothing of her history or of its connection with herself, but the shape was the same as the shape of the "fridgit"; only the masts were wanting.

"Look!" said Dick, showing how the yards were swung. "She's square-sailed, all but the mizzen, same's your boat. You could reef 'em up, only there ain't any reef points; she's too small, Jim says. This is the rudder an' tiller. You ain't got no rudder to yours." He looked up at her. From her face and the interest in it, she seemed to understand. She leaned forward and moved the tiny tiller with her finger tip. A wheel was beyond Kearney's art and the steering gear of Sir Cloudesley Shovel's ships had to suffice. Then she leaned further forward and blew hard at the tiny main topsail, slinging the yard round.

"Matagi," cried she, "O he amorai—Matagi."

"That's the way it goes!" cried Dick, pleased to find her so apt, and talking just as though she were able to understand every word. "And when you're sailin' close to the wind you haul it that way. That square rig—wait a minit."

He rushed off to the house and returned with the schooner, dumping it before her.

"That's fore 'n' aft."

Katafa looked at the model of the *Ranatonga*; with her head slightly on one side, she seemed admiring it. Dick, watching her, felt pleased. Many a grown-up English person, able to talk, would have failed in this business or blundered in their appreciation of these important things, but Katafa was one of the craft—seemed so, anyway—and Dick, old friends with her now and free and easy as though she were Kearney, proceeded to demonstrate the action of the throat and peak halyards in raising the gaff, the topping lifts in supporting the boom, and how the head canvas was set. Then, suddenly remembering duty, he ran back to the house with the ships and set to work to clear away the remains of the food and the three plates.

He did not wash the plates; he was too anxious to get busy again with Katafa.

She had become all of a sudden the first great event of his life. She could neither speak in ordinary language to him nor he to her—but she was youth.

Though he had lived ten years with Kearney and though Kearney had practically taught him to talk, the sailor had never got so close to him as this creature of his own age who had suddenly appeared as if at the lift of a curtain.

The instant Kearney had withdrawn, the spell had begun to work. It might have been weeks before Dick would have shown those treasured ships to a grown person.

As he bustled about, filled with a new energy and interest, Katafa, who had risen to her feet, watched him. Light-minded and irresponsible as the boy, there still lay between her and him an abyss that even youth could not cross, the abyss that had lain between her and the children of Karolin, with whom, yet, she had played, but as a person might play with shadows. All the same, youth could gaze across the abyss, over which, despite everything, the little ships had sailed. These things had fascinated her; she could see more of them in the house, attractive as toys, yet mysterious as fetishes—maybe having something to do with the gods of Dick and Kearney.

Dick knew nothing of this. Duty done with, he made another dash for the house, producing no ship this time, but a stick three feet long and a ball made of tia wood.

Kearney had invented a game for him, a sort of cross between baseball and cricket. The trunk of a jack-fruit tree on the grove edge did for wickets, and the run was from this to an artu trunk and back.

Kearney, since he had grown lazy, had held off from this game, saying it was "too much of a bother."

"Catch!" cried Dick, throwing the ball to Katafa. She caught it, and he held out his hands, and she flung it back hard and swift and sure. She could throw a stone a hundred yards and throw it like a man.

He showed her the stick and, tossing the ball back to her, ran to the tree, pointed to it, and then stood with the stick, ready to defend it.

She understood at once.

When Kearney came forth from his afternoon rest he found Dick tired out, sitting by the house, and the girl by the lagoon bank, dabbling her feet in the water. It looked almost as though they had quarrelled, but they had not in the least. One of Dick's moody fits had come on him, as they often did after excitement or strenuous exertion. He was a different creature from the Dick of only a moment ago, and when these fits took him, it was always the same; he seemed caught away to another world, and liked to sit by himself.

If ever a mother "came out" in a child, the lost Emmeline came out in Dick during these moods. It was almost as though he had changed sex.

"What have you been doin' with the stick?" asked Kearney.

"Playin'," said Dick, waking from his reverie.

A FIRE ON THE REEF

Kearney had put shelves in the house to hold the ships so that they did not interfere with the floor space where he slept with Dick.

The shack behind the house where the provisions had been stored still held, though the roof had gone pretty much to pieces, and here the sailor had fixed the sleeping quarters of Katafa.

Blankets had been given to them by the wreck, supplementing those left behind by Stanistreet, and, getting along for sundown, Kearney, with three blankets on his arm, two for a bed and one for a quilt, beckoned the girl to follow him.

She stopped short at the entrance to the shack and then took a step backwards, standing and watching him at his work.

Then, when he came out, he pointed to the blankets.

"There ain't no pilla," said Kearney, "but you won't be mindin' that. Now then, Kanaka girl, there's your bunk. Ain't you likin' the look of it?"

She had drawn back another step.

"I'm with you," said Kearney, pointing to the couch.

She shook her head. Ask a fox to enter a trap.

"Well, then, you can just sleep in the trees," said he, and off he went round the house, leaving her to her choice.

Dick, tired out with the day, was in the house and sound asleep, and the sailor, who had a fishing line to overhaul, sat down by the door and set to work on it. As he sat, busy with his fingers and reviewing with his mind Kanakas and their unaccountable ways, he saw the girl coming out from the trees. She had fished two of the blankets out of the shack, and she was crossing the sward with them towards the canoe that was tied to the bank. She got into the canoe with them and vanished from sight—all but her head, visible in the sunset light above the bank.

Now Kearney had old-fashioned ideas as to how young people should behave towards their elders, and Dick had received many a "clip" from him for disobedience. He was starting to "go after" the girl, when he saw two hands go up to her head; she was arranging her hair. One might have fancied her before a mirror.

This sight checked him. He finished his work, put the line away, and retired to the house. During their ten years of residence the house had almost been destroyed by a big blow from the northwest and Kearney, in rebuilding, had enlarged it.

There was plenty of room for him and Dick, and to-night, as he lay there, the four ships on their shelves above him and Dick sound asleep by the wall, he could see through the open doorway a new picture: the mat sail of the canoe still unfurled, and, just distinguishable in the fast-rising twilight, the head of the girl above the bank.

Kearney was worried. Living in ease and quietude, one might fancy worry his last visitant, but that was not so; quite small things, things he would never have given a second thought to on shipboard, had the power to upset him here, and though he would not have changed his mode of life for worlds, a broken fishing line or a leak in the dinghy would make him grumpy for hours, cursing his fate and wondering what was going to happen next.

Katafa was worrying him now; she was unlike any Kanaka he had ever seen. Where had she come from? Was it from that island he guessed to be lying down south there? And if so, might she not bring others of her kind after her? Then the way she had slipped from under his hand, and those eyes of hers which she kept fixed on him—she wasn't right.

He dropped off to sleep with this conviction in his mind and dreamt troublous dreams, awaking about two in the morning to wonder what she was doing and whether everything was secure. Then, sleep driven away, he came out into the windless, starry night, where a six days' old moon was lolling above the trees.

Away out to sea a red flicker met his gaze. A fire was burning on the reef. Trumpets blowing in the night could not have astonished him more.

He watched for a moment as the flame waxed and waned, now casting a trail of red light on the lagoon water, now dying down only to leap up again. Then he came running to the canoe. The girl was not there and the dinghy was gone; the paddle was gone from the canoe also; she must have taken it to paddle herself over to the reef, not being able to use the sculls.

There was plenty of dried weed and bits of wreckage on the reef to make a fire with, but how had she got a light? He came back to the house and searched for the box of matches on the little shelf outside, where it was always put when done with. It was gone.

She must have come "smelling round" when they were asleep. She must have noticed where the matches had been put and treasured up the fact in her dark mind!

"But what in the nation's she done it for?" asked Kearney of himself, as he stood scratching his head. "What's she up to, anyway?"

The night made no reply—only the rumble of the reef, now loud, now low, and the mysterious light of the fire, now waxing, now waning, flaring up only to die down again.

He came to the trees on the other side of the sward and watched for an hour, till at last the fire died to a spark and the spark vanished.

Then came the sound of the paddle as the dinghy stole like a beetle across the star-shot lagoon water and tied up at the bank. A figure passed along the bank towards the house. She was putting the matchbox back; then she came along towards the canoe, slipped into it and vanished from sight.

Kearney waited ten minutes. Then he stole back to the house and turned in again.

"You wait till the mornin', and I'll l'arn you," said he to himself as he closed his eyes, composing his mind to slumber with the thought of the whacking in store for the Kanaka girl.

A FIRE ON THE REEF (Continued)

Katafa, when she had arranged her hair and made her bed of blankets in the bottom of the canoe, lay down, but she did not close her eyes. She lay watching the last glow of the sunset, and then the instantly following stars held her gaze, talking to her of Karolin and the great sea spaces she had been suddenly caught away from.

The atoll island has never been adequately described by pen or brush—never will be. What brush or pen could paint the starlight on the great lagoons, the sunrises and sunsets, the vastness of the distances unbroken by any land but just the low ring of reef? Life on an atoll is like life on a raft: immensity on every side—and the sea.

Here the girl felt herself suddenly shut in, the groves rising to the hill-top fretted her spirit, the bit of lagoon was nothing, and even the reef was different from the reef of Karolin. Kearney had raised something deep down in her mind against him and he seemed somehow now the centre and core of all her trouble. Dick she scarcely thought of; he, like other human beings, was of little account to her.

Thoughts came to her of trying to get the canoe out and escaping back to the freedom which was the only thing she loved, but it was hopeless. She could never do the business single-handed; she was trapped and she knew it.

Now, when Le Juan wanted help from Nanawa, the shark-toothed god, she had several methods of invoking the deity. One of the simplest was by fire. She would go off, build a little fire and, as she fed it, repeat over it a formula, always the same string of words representing the wish of her heart, which was never spoken.

Something generally happened after that. Sometimes the wish would be granted, long overdue rain would come, or some enemy already dying would die, or the palu that had forsaken for a while the palu bank would come back.

But the shark-toothed one was a tricky deity and had a habit of sending other gifts along by way of Laggniappe.

For instance, in that great drought long years ago, Le Juan had sacrificed stacks of fuel to the god, and weeks after he had sent the rain, but he also sent the Spanish ship with Katafa on board of it, and Katafa had given Le Juan a lot of trouble and heart-searching.

Again, two years ago, he had sent the palu back to the bank but at the same time he had extended the season in the lagoon when the fish were poisonous by a fortnight.

Sometimes he was quite amiable and would cure an indigestion without killing the patient as well—but it was all a toss-up. He was a dark force, and even Le Juan recognised in a dim way that she was playing with evil, and was never easy till the effects of her invocations were over and done with.

Katafa had often helped to stoke the little fires and she knew the ritual in all its simplicity. The thing had never interested her much till now.

Maybe Nanawa could help her, take the island away or knock it to pieces without hurting her, or lift it like a dish cover to the sky as she had seen it lifted by mirage, or free her in some way—any way.

She brooded for an hour or more over this business. Then, having made up her mind, she rose, skipped lightly on to the bank and, moving silently as a shadow, approached the house. She could tell by their breathing that the occupants were asleep, and she could see the box of matches on the little shelf in the moonlight.

She took it and, as she held the strange fire box in her hand, the sudden impulse came to her, maybe from the shark-toothed one, to fire the house. The mysterious antagonism against Kearney urged her to destroy him; it seemed also a way out of her trouble.

The little ships saved the sleepers.

The remembrance of them suddenly came to the girl, and the thought that some god of whom they were the insignia might be on the watch. She could not see them in the darkness of the house, but they were doubtless there on their shelves, put there to protect the sleepers just as Le Juan hung over her bed place a shrunken human hand.

Maybe she was right; maybe Kearney, without knowing, had placed them there under higher direction, but, right or wrong, the things acted as efficiently as a spell.

She turned away and, taking the paddle from the canoe, unmoored the dinghy and pushed off for the reef.

She found, as she had expected, plenty of fuel, and the match-box gave her no trouble. She had watched the process of striking a match carefully with those eyes from which no detail escaped, and in a minute the stuff she had collected was alight and burning.

Then, standing in the windless night and piling on dead weed, bits of wood and dried fish fragments that popped and blazed like gas jets, Katafa, with hands pressed against her ridi so that the flames might not catch its dracæna leaves, put up her prayers to the shark-toothed one, repeating the old formula of Le Juan and backing it with the unspoken wish that the island might be taken away and freedom restored to her.

An hour later she returned across the lagoon, tied up the dinghy and, snuggling down in the canoe, went to sleep.

NANAWA SPEAKS

"Now then, Dick, l'ave her alone and don't get lookin' at her," said Mr. Kearney. "She's been misbehavin'."

"What's she been doin', Jim?" asked the boy.

"Playin' with the matches," replied the other, thinking it just as well not to go into full particulars that were sure to bring a string of Dick's endless questions.

They were seated at breakfast and Katafa had drawn close for her food. Katafa could be ugly, she could be pretty; never was anything more protean than the looks of this Spanish girl who was yet in all things but birth and blood a Kanaka. This morning, as she sat in the liquid shadow of the trees, she was unpaintably beautiful. She had run away beyond the cape of wild cocoanuts and taken a dip in the lagoon, and now, fresh from sleep and her bath, with a red flower in her hair and her hands folded in her lap, she sat like the incarnation of dawn, her luminous eyes fixed on Kearney.

But Kearney had no eye for her beauty.

"When was she playin' with them, Jim?" asked the boy, a piece of baked bread-fruit in his fingers.

"Never you mind," replied the other. "Get on with your breakfast and hand us that plate—I'll l'arn her."

He passed a plateful of food to the girl and then helped himself and the meal proceeded, Dick attending to business, but with an occasional side-glance at the criminal.

Playing with the matches was a hideous offence for which he had been whacked twice in earlier days. He reckoned Kearney would whack her, and he looked forward to the business with an interest tinged, but not in the least unsharpened, by his sneaking sympathy with the offence and the offender.

But, the meal finished, the sailor, instead of setting to, simply walked to the dinghy, beckoning the girl to follow him. He got in, took the sculls, and as she stepped after him, taking her seat gingerly in the stern sheets, pushed off.

The pair landed on the reef, Kearney leading the way and glancing about him till they came on the remains of the fire.

"Now," said Kearney, halting and pointing to the ashes and the scorched coral, "that's what you've been doin', is it? What made you light that fire for, eh?"

Although the language of Kearney was to her as Double Dutch to a Chinese, she knew quite well his drift. He had discovered the fact that she had lit the fire. How? Maybe the god of the little ships had told him. She said nothing, however, as he went on, his voice rising in anger with every word.

"What made you touch them matches for, smellin' round when I was asleep and makin' off with the matches? I'll l'arn you."

He picked up a stalk of seaweed and make a "skelp" at her. She was quite close and it was impossible to miss her. All the same, the stalk touched nothing; she had skipped aside.

Trees had once grown here on the reef and the coral was smooth, and round and about this smooth patch Kearney, blazing with righteous wrath, pursued her. It was like trying to whip the wind. He tried to drive her on to the rough coral, but she wasn't to be caught like that. She kept to the smooth, and in three or four minutes he was done.

Flinging the stick of seaweed away, he wiped his brow with his arms. Dick was watching them from the sward, and he felt that he had been making a fool of himself.

"Now never you do that no more!" said Mr. Kearney, shaking his finger at her. "If you do, b'gosh, I'll skelp you roun' the island." He nodded his head to give force to this tremendous threat and was turning to the dinghy when something caught his eye.

Away to the east, across the sparkling blue, stood a sail.

The dead calm had broken an hour ago and a merry breeze was whipping up the swell. The ship, lying beyond the northern drift current, must have been within sight of the island all night. Had she seen the fire?

Kearney, shading his eyes, stood watching her. A splash from the lagoon made him turn. Katafa had taken to the water, ridi and all, and was swimming back to the shore, evidently determined not to trust herself with him in the dinghy. He looked at her for a moment as she swam; then he turned his gaze back to the ship.

She showed, now, square-rigged and close-hauled. Yes, she was beating up for the island. Would she put in at the break? Was she a whaler, a sandalwood trader, or what?

In those days of Pease and Steinberger, a ship in Pacific waters had many possibilities, and if Kearney had known that he was watching the *Portsoy*, captained by Collin Robertson, who feared neither God nor the Paumotus, he would not have waited on the reef so calmly.

No, she was not making for the break, but to pass the island close to northward. She was no whaler, and, relieved of this dread, he stuck to his post as she came, every sail drawing, listed to starboard with the press of the wind and the foam bursting from her forefoot.

Now she was nearly level with him, less than a quarter of a mile away. He could see the busy decks and a fellow running up the ratlins, and at the sight of the striped shirts and the old familiar crowd, the sticks and ropes, the white-painted deck-house and the sun on the bellying canvas, Kearney, forgetting ease and comfort and the hundred good gifts God had bestowed on him, sobriety included, sprang into the air and flung up his arms and yelled like a lunatic.

The answer came prompt in a burst of sound, like the outcrying of gulls. The helm went over and the brig, curving under the thrashing canvas, presented her stern to the damned castaway on the reef.

He saw the glint of a long brass gun, a plume of smoke bellying over the blue sea, and, as the wind of the shot went over him the report shook the reef like the blow of a giant's fist, passing across the lagoon to wake the echoes of the groves.

Aimed at nothing, fired for the fun of the thing, the shot had yet found its mark, bursting the canoe of Katafa into fifty pieces.

THE WISH

Island life had not quickened Mr. Kearney's intellectual powers, and for eight or nine months after that day things happened to him that he could not account for. Sometimes fishing lines broke that ought not to have broken. He would leave a bit of chewing gum on the shelf outside the house and it would be gone, taken by the birds, maybe—but why did the birds suddenly develop a desire for gum? The dinghy sprang a leak that took him two days to mend, and fish spears would become mysteriously blunted though put away apparently sharp enough.

He never thought of the girl. The feud between them had died down, at least on his part, and she and Dick seemed getting on well together. Too well, perhaps, from a civilised person's point of view. She and Dick would chatter away together now in the native; the girl had picked up at first enough English to help them along, but at the end of nine months it was always the language of Karolin they spoke, and even to Kearney's heavy intelligence it was funny to hear them "clacking away" and to think that she had made him talk her lingo instead of the other way about. More than that, the boy was altering, losing the fits of abstraction that had made him seem at times almost the reincarnation of his mother, losing also the light-heartedness of the child; laughing rarely, and desperately serious over the little things of life, the moment seemed to him everything, as it is to the savage.

236

"She's turning him into a — Kanaka," grumbled Kearney one day as he watched them starting for the reef, Dick with his fish spears over his shoulder, the girl following him. "Ain't to hold on to these days, and sulks if he's spoke to crooked or crossed in his vagaries. Well, if he ain't careful I'll l'arn him for once and all."

But he never put the threat in action—too lazy, maybe, or too dispirited, feeling himself a back number. He was. The reins had gone out of his hands, youth had pushed him aside, and the boy, moving away towards savagery, had left this relict of high civilisation a good piece astern.

But one day Kearney was roused out of his apathy. Resting in the tree shadows at the opposite side of the sward, he saw the girl, who fancied herself alone and unobserved, cautiously approaching the house.

Never for one single day since her landing had she lost the desire to escape, to find freedom and the great spaces of the sea. Her intercourse with Dick had attached her neither to Dick nor the island, yet beyond playing tricks upon Kearney she had shown no sign of the fret that lay in her soul.

The cannon shot from the *Portsoy* that had burst the canoe in pieces, and the report of the gun that had rolled in echoes from the woods—these, in her firm belief, were the manifestations of the power and the voice of the shark-toothed one. Just as firmly she believed that some other god had intervened, frustrating the doings of Nanawa and spoiling the canoe out of spite.

The idea had come to her that maybe it was the god who presided over the little ships, that if she got rid of them—not all at once, for that might make a disturbance with the god, but one by one—the way might be clear. Kearney had never suspected her of stealing and throwing away his gum, of breaking the fishing lines or blunting the spears, and if she took these things off into the wood one by one and smashed them he would be equally stupid and unsuspicious—perhaps.

It was worth trying, and to-day, finding herself alone, she stole up to the house and peeped in. There they stood in the twilight on their shelves, the things whose god had broken her canoe. Impudent, unbroken themselves, and no doubt manned by sprites, they stood, the schooner, the frigate, a full-rigged ship and a tiny whaleman with bluff bows, wooden davits, crow's nest and try-works, all complete.

An old knife of Kearney's lay on the little shelf by the door beside the box of matches. She could not resist that. Leaving the matches untouched, she picked up the knife and flung it into the lagoon. Then she entered the house and lifted the whaleman from its shelf. It was the smallest, and it was just as well to begin with the smallest. She turned to the door with it and saw Kearney running across the sward, dropped the whaler, sprang from the doorway, and ran. Another half minute and she would have been trapped.

Kearney, on seeing her entering the house, had made a bolt from the trees on the opposite side, thinking he had her bottled, but he was too late and, as for chasing her, he might as well have tried to course a hare. Stopping suddenly and picking up Dick's tia wood ball, which was lying in his way, he took aim at her as she ran, catching her full in the small of the back as she dived into the trees.

The sound of the smack of the ball, followed by a gasping cry, came back to him. Then she vanished, traceless but for the swaying leaves.

"That will l'arn you," said Mr. Kearney, turning to the house and picking up the whaler, undamaged but for a broken main-topmast. He knew now who had stolen his gum, blunted the spears and outraged the dinghy. The flinging of that knife into the lagoon had told him everything, and as he sat down by the door to repair the broken spar he took an oath to be even with her.

"Break the fish lines, would you?" said he as he sat with the whaler clipped between his knees as in a vise, and his fingers busy unrigging the mast. "Fling me knife into the water? Well, you wait. Not another bite or sup will you have that you don't get yourself, or me name's not Jim Kearney. Not another bite or sup till you go down on your marrow bones and beg me pardon." He worked away, his soul raging in him, his mind fumbling round and remembering other things to be laid to her account. Gum that had vanished, a saw that had gone west, spirited off as if by pixies—he had put these levitations down to his own carelessness or forgetfulness, quite unable to imagine a human being's tricky malevolence as the agent.

As he worked, the splash of oars came from the lagoon, and Dick landed with three red-backed bream strung on a length of liana. Seeing Kearney alone, he looked round for Katafa, but could see no sign of her.

"Where's she gone?" asked Dick.

Kearney looked up; the back number had taken fire at last. "Get off with you and don't be askin' me questions!" he shouted, just as if he were speaking to a man, not a boy. "Go 'n' look for her if you want to find her, throwin' me knife in the water and smashin' me lines! The pair of you is one as bad as the other, always tinkerin' together, you and her."

The boy drew back, staring at the other with wide-pupilled eyes.

"What's she been doin'?" he asked.

"Doin'!" cried Kearney. "I've told you what she's been doin'. Go 'n' hunt for her in the wood if you want to know what she's been doin'! Well you know what she's been doin', standin' there like the — Kanaka she's turned you into and askin' me what she's been doin'—clear off with you!"

The boy flung down the fish and started off, running towards the trees to the right of the sward. As he vanished, Kearney heard his voice crying out in the native: "Katafa, hai amanoi Katafa, hai, hai!"

"Bloody Kanaka," grumbled Kearney.

Katafa, deep in the gloom of the groves, heard the call but she made no answer. Her mind was in a turmoil.

Once, long ago on Karolin, a stone thrown by a child had struck her accidentally, rousing in the dark part of her mind a confusion and resentment that almost upset her reason. As in the case of Kearney, the child had been behind her, she had not seen the stone coming, and the sudden blow was as though some one had struck her with a fist. It was the same now. Though she had recognised instantly that it was only the ball that had struck her, the shock remained.

She stood for a while listening to the far-off calling of Dick. "Katafa, hai! amanoi Katafa! hai!" It grew fainter; he was taking the wrong direction and now, with the suddenness of a clapped door, silence cut him off.

That was a trick of the woods caused maybe by the upward trend of the land; a person calling to you and moving away in a horizontal direction would suddenly be cut off.

Katafa had never been alone in the woods before this; she had always gone accompanied by either the boy or Kearney. Never had she grown accustomed to these vast masses of trees, their gloom, their congregated perfumes, the strange lights and shadows made by the moving branches and fronds, the sense of being surrounded; always amongst them the great distances of the atoll cried louder to her to come back, and the heartache and homesickness grew more intense.

But to-day she had lost her fear of the trees, and the call of Karolin had lost for a while its power. The outrage committed by Kearney had shaken her away from all other considerations, all other pictures but that of the first man who had struck her.

She moved away to the right and entered an alley formed by a double line of matamata trees. Ferns grew here on either side, and above in the liquid gloom cables of liantasse swung, powdered with starry blossoms.

She stood for a moment glancing up at the orchids that seemed like birds in flight, the bugles of the giant convolvuli and the far-off roof of leaves moving to the wind in trembles of shattered light and shadow.

Then she went on, reaching at last a little bay in the trees, ferns and bushes, where the glint of something white caught her eye. It was a skull. She pushed the leaves aside; the whole skeleton was there, the ribs still articulated, the vertebrae intact. Flame lit by mortal hand could not have calcined the bones more whitely, destroyed the flesh more completely than the slow fire of time burning here through the years amidst the cool green ferns.

Katafa, holding the leaves aside, gazed at the skull. Amongst Le Juan's properties had been a man's skull, used when she was invoking the dark powers against some enemy.

As Katafa gazed at the skull, the thought of Kearney came to her, and the vision of him lying like that—and the wish.

OUT OF THE GLOOM

When Dick came back to the house, the girl had not returned.

Kearney seemed to have recovered his temper, and presently, putting the ship away on the shelf till to-morrow, he helped the boy to prepare supper. They scarcely spoke over this business; the shadow of the quarrel still hung between them, and that supper, as they sat silent opposite one another, was a mark in the life of Dick. It was his coming-of-age party, for Kearney was treating him as a man with whom he had a difference, not as a boy to be threatened and skelped.

Neither of them saw that far-away scene of the Dick of the *Ranatonga*, the tall sailor dancing the tiny child in his arms and crying out to Bowers: "Says his other name's M. Sure as there's hair on his head, he's been tellin' me Dick M's his name. Ain't it, bo?"

Neither of them saw the early island days when Dick M, left entirely in the sailor's charge by his grandfather, fished in the lagoon with thread for line and played at fish-spearing on the reef and tried to scull the dinghy, guided and assisted by his big companion.

Dick, sitting there in the sunset this evening, was no longer a child. Not quite a man, he was greater than a man. Fresh from the hand of Nature that had moulded and wrought on his father and mother, not quite civilized, not quite a savage, a poet

240

might have seen in him the youth of the world, the dawn of man before cities arose to cast their shadows on him, before civilisation created savages.

Neither of them saw the long years of companionship during which they had worked as shipbuilders together, the storms and incidents by shore and reef—it was all as nought. Katafa had brought a new interest to Dick. Age and laziness had done their work with Kearney.

As they sat like this, the meal nearly finished, they saw the girl. She had come out from among the trees away on the other side of the sward. She was carrying something under her arm. She stood for a moment shading her eyes against the sunset and looking towards them. Then she vanished back amongst the trees, and Dick, rising to his feet, came running across the sward. He knew where to find her. Since the breaking of the canoe, she had made a shack for herself amongst the trees, and there she was crouched now and dimly to be seen in the fading light.

At the sound of the parting of the leaves, she moved suddenly as if trying to hide something with her body.

"Katafa," said the boy, speaking in the native, "the food is waiting for you and he is no longer angry."

"It does not matter, Taori," replied her voice from the shadows. "I will eat to-morrow."

"What is that you have beneath you there?"

"A bread-fruit, Taori—I want no better food."

"Ahai—but you have no fire to cook it."

"It does not matter, Taori. I will cook it to-morrow."

"Then eat it raw," said he, angry with her, and off he went.

Taori was the name she had given him.

When he had gone she took the skull which she had been hiding and placed it beside her. Then she lay down with her eyes fixed on the ruddy-tinted light of the sunset visible through the spaces of the leaves.

There was no moon that night, and a dead calm had set in an hour before sunset. The heat was oppressive. Even the great Pacific seemed drugged and drowsy, and the sound of the surf on the reef like the breathing of a sleeper uneasy in his sleep.

Kearney, awaking about midnight, came out for a breath of air. It was almost as oppressive out of doors as in the house, and above the trees the sky, heavy with stars, stood like the roof of a jewelled oven. The fronds of a palmetto by the water stood without a tremor and the lagoon lay like a fallen sky of stars, tremorless as space itself.

Kearney came down to the bank and sat bathing his feet in the water, the ripples waving out and shattering the reflected firmament. He heard the rustle of robber crabs feeding on the fallen drupes of a pandanus near by, the splash of a heavy fish beyond the cape of wild cocoanut, the fall of a nut from the grove behind the house, the fret and murmur of the reef—no other sound from land and sea and all that wilderness of stars.

Then, as he lay on his elbow yawning and half asleep, a spark of light that was not a star struck his sight. It was on the reef line. It died out, came to life again, flickered and grew. Some one was lighting a fire on the reef. He sat up, glanced at the dinghy lying safely at her moorings, then out away at the far-off fire.

"She ain't taken the boat," said he to himself. "She must have got over smimmin', curse that Kanaka! What trick is she up to anyway, signalling? That's what she's after—signalling. That's her game, maybe to bring a hive of niggers atop of us."

He rushed off to see if the box of matches had been taken; no, it was there, but he knew she could light a fire with a fire-stick. She had taught Dick to do it. He came running back to the dinghy, got in, unmoored her, and pushed out.

He had always had it in his mind that the fire she had lit long ago was a signal made to attract her people, whoever they might be.

The absurdity of this idea never struck him; he just "had it in his mind" as an easy way of accounting for the matter, and to-night, in face of this second offence, his wrath rose up against the girl as it had never risen before. Everything conspired—the heat, the want of sleep, the quarrel with Dick, and the long hump-backed antagonism she had constructed against herself by snatching Dick away into Kanaka land and making him talk her lingo—her very youth was against her to-night. It was her youth that had made her companion with Dick. Kearney had killed men in his time, and the years of soft island life, the companionship of the child, the absence of drink, whilst softening him, had not destroyed the fierce something which was not Kearney and which could wake under stimulus to strike, regardless of consequences.

Guiding the dinghy across the water, he was steering straight for murder. Not intentional murder, but the murder we come on in the slums when men of Kearney's type, urged to the deed by a nagging wife or gone-wrong daughter, and assisted maybe by alcohol, suddenly give loose to themselves and maim or kill.

His project was to land unobserved if possible, and then go for her with a scull, bowl her over, and then beat the devil out of her once and for all with his fists. He'd "l'arn" her this time, sure.

Less than half-way across, he drew in his sculls and then, with a single scull at the stern, began working the boat almost noiselessly towards the reef. He could see her now standing by the fire and feeding it, the cairngorm light of the flames upon her face and arms. It was a big fire and lit the reef, the lagoon water and the foam of the gently curling waves. Great fish, attracted by the light, were swimming in the waters of the lagoon, nosing about the reef. The news had gone far and wide that something was doing, and could Nature, who has her own methods of warning men and beasts, have expressed herself in writing, with fire for ink, above the breaking foam would have appeared the words: "The Reef Is Dangerous To-night."

Then, as Kearney drew closer, the girl, who had suddenly turned and sighted him, broke away from the fire and ran.

He drew in the scull, took his seat, and, seizing the other scull, rowed as if rowing a race. The nose of the dinghy crashed against the coral. He sprang out, secured her, and turned, scull in hand.

The girl was gone.

Beyond the fire-glow he thought he saw her for a moment, but the light dazzled his eyes, and when he put it behind him he could see nothing but the starlit coral, its humps and dips and pools, the foam of the waves and the tranquil mirror of the lagoon.

He knew quite well what had become of her—she had dipped into one of the reef pools; they were the only possible places of concealment. She had not taken to the lagoon—he could see that at a glance—for the water lay unrippled and a swimmer's head would have shown even more clearly than by day. He came along, grasping the scull, with the anger of the balked hunter now at his heart. He looked into the first great pool—nothing, only a trapped fish flitting like a ghost here and there, its shadow ghost following it across the white coral sand of the bottom.

He rose and was moving on, when a great undulation came in the lagoon water, flowing from behind him and spreading to the west.

Kearney turned. The fire still gave a good light, and between him and the fire something had heaved itself on to the coral. Attracted by the firelight, it had left the lagoon, soundless as a crawling cat, yet tons in weight. It was only some thirty feet away from him, yet it seemed formless, a long heaped mass covered with shiny

243

tarpaulin. Then suddenly it took form, extending itself like a slug; lamps, like the headlights of a locomotive, blazed out, and around the lamps great serpents curled like the locks of Medusa.

For one fatal moment he stood staring at the thing before him. Then a rope slashed round his waist and tightened.

He was caught.

Katafa had taken refuge in the second great pool, a pool some four feet deep and large enough for a person to swim in. The water was tepid and the floor of soft sand, and as she slipped into it, gracile as a serpent, she did not look to see what fish there might be there.

A small whip-ray, an electric eel or a stinging jellyfish would have made the pool untenable, she knew, but chanced it, and, lying submerged to the chin, waited and listened.

She felt an eel pass like a cold waving ribbon over her thighs; it touched the outer side of her left leg as it made its way along the sand and was gone. Then she felt the tap of small sharp-pointed fingers here and there on her body. Fish were nuzzling her, yet she dared not move for dread of setting the water waving. Instinct told her that Kearney was more to be feared than fish or eels or the great crab of the reef, and even when a sting like a hot needle sticking in her side told her that a banda fish had attacked her flesh, her only movement was the drift of her right hand like floating seaweed towards her side, and the sudden snap of the fingers as the banda fish, caught by the hand, was crushed to death.

She kneaded the fragments viciously between her fingers. Then, as she released them, sudden and sharp came a cry, the piercing cry of a man who has been speared or stabbed with a shark-toothed dagger. Raising her head swift as a lizard, she glanced, shuddered and dived again. She had seen Nanawa.

Katafa knew the seas and its creatures with an intimacy given to few naturalists. She had seen great fleets of giant whip-rays enter Karolin lagoon disporting under the stars and filling the night with a sound like the thunder of big guns at battle practice. She had seen a cachalot driven by destroyers to its death, and an octopus with sixty-foot tentacles floating like a burst balloon near the palu bank, driven up from mile-deep water by some submarine disturbance, the sharks tearing at it and the eyes still living, lugubrious, and staring at the sky as if in astonishment. But she had never seen the most terrible of all sea things, the giant decapod, barrel-shaped, great as an oak-tree, with two beaks, a tongue armed with teeth, eyes a foot broad and ten tentacles, two of thirty or forty feet in length.

Snuggling into the tepid water, she lay listening—nothing. Only the sound of the surf rising and falling to the pulse of the sea whilst the untroubled stars shone down on her and the minutes passed, bringing not another sound to tell of what was happening—of what had happened.

Then, raising herself gently, she looked again. The reef showed nothing but the last embers of the fire. The dinghy was lying still just where she had been moored, but of the man who had brought her across there was no trace.

NAN

"Jim!" cried Dick. "Hai amonai—Jim—where you gone to?"

He was standing before the house in the early sunlight; he had just come out and Kearney was nowhere to be seen. A breeze had broken the heat, and the absolute loveliness of the morning found reflection in the soul of the boy.

The far-off sea that would be purple at noon lay like smashed sapphires beyond the reef. The lagoon, whipped by the breeze, showed colours unimaginable by man, colours that seemed to live by their own intrinsic brilliancy, stretching from the luminous blue of the near pools to the purples and mauves of the submerged rotten coral beyond which lay the dancing sapphire that washed the reef line.

Over all, the breeze, the flower-blue sky and the gulls.

But Kearney was nowhere to be seen.

Then, as Dick called again, the girl came out from the trees at the opposite side of the sward, fresh from a dip in the lagoon beyond the cape, and with a scarlet flower in her hair, which was tied back with a bit of thread liana.

She crossed the sward, and the boy, seeing her, bothered himself no longer about Kearney, and set to preparing for breakfast. Had he not been so busy he might have noticed a difference in her. She walked assuredly and with a carelessness and an ease that were new to her. In ordinary times she would come for her food as an animal might come, an animal not quite tamed, and vaguely distrustful, take her seat at a little distance, and wait meekly, yet watchfully, for the dispensations of Providence. It was different now. She came close up to Dick and, without offering in the least to help, stood watching him, taking her seat when the meal was ready as close as "Kea'ney" had sat, and helping herself to the food without waiting to be helped.

Even Dick, satisfying his voracious appetite, noticed the change in her now. He did not know what it was in the least and he didn't bother to think, yet in some curious way it disturbed him.

With Kearney there, he and Katafa had always been subordinates; between subordinates there is always a bond, a league, however vague and unwritten, against the master. Youth had helped, and the two had made a little society of their own, with Dick as leader. This relationship had been strangely disturbed this morning by the absence of Kearney and by the actions of Katafa, who was doing things she had never done before, sitting in a different attitude and speaking in a new tone of assurance and indifference. Dick almost felt that something had happened to himself—something had.

She had been accustomed to help in clearing away after meals, but this morning she just sat and watched. There was not much clearing to be done, but Kearney had always been particular that no scraps or fish bones were left about to bring the robber crabs round scavenging or the gulls. A dirty camp has always followers, so the scraps were shot into the lagoon; then the plates had to be cleaned and put away on their shelf in the house.

Dick, thinking she was maybe lazy or tired, did not bother. He finished his business and stamped out the fire, reckoning that if Kearney wanted food when he came back he could cook it for himself—but where had Kearney gone to, and why was he so long away?

He had not taken the dinghy. The little boat was moored at its usual place by the bank. He must have gone off in the woods.

"Katafa," said Dick, after running to the boat to see if Kearney had taken the fishing tackle, always kept in a little locker in the stern sheets, "what makes Kearney so long away? He has not taken the lines to fish with from the boat."

"Perhaps," said Katafa, "he is on the reef."

"No," replied the boy, "for he has not taken the boat."

"Perhaps he is amongst the tall trees."

Dick half shook his head as if in doubt. Then, raising his voice, he cried again:

"Hai, amonai—Jim! Hai! Hai!"

A far-off echo in the trees caught the hail and sent it back. "Hai! hai!"—faint, yet clear came the echo, dying off to a silence troubled only by the sound of the reef.

"He answers," said Katafa, "but he is too far away, he cannot come."

There was a grove on the south beach of Karolin that had an echo; call there and you would hear the spirits of the departed answering you, jeering you in your own voice. She did not believe that the spirit of Kearney was answering Dick; some old spirit of the grove, maybe, but not Kearney. She knew that Kearney was not among the trees, and she spoke in mockery.

Dick knew that it was only an echo. He gave another shout and then, dropping the business as a bad job and Kearney from his mind, ran off to the boat to overhaul the fishing tackle. When he had finished he came back for her to go fishing and found her busy with a huge old grandfather cocoanut and one of the Barlow knives salved from the wreck.

She must have gone into the house to get the knife, but Dick never thought of that; the work she was on held him. She had frayed away the brown husk into a sort of frill and was busy now on the face of it, making eyes in it and the semblance of a nose and mouth.

A new idea had come to Katafa, a common-sensical idea, and it was this. Nanawa was the active god of Karolin; frightful, capricious, striking right and left when invoked, and sometimes hitting the invoker. She had brought him to her twice, and the first time he had roared over the lagoon and broken her canoe, angry no doubt at having been balked by the god of the little ships; the second time, last night, he was much more satisfactory in his behaviour. But Katafa had a dim suspicion that, had he not found Kearney and taken him to himself, he would have found her, and this suspicion was perfectly well founded—he would. She determined not to deal with him again.

Now, on Karolin there was another god, Nan, very old, amiable, the president of the cocoanut groves, the puraka patches and the pandanus trees; a sort of minister of agriculture, but much beloved, honoured and fêted. Nan, in fact, was more than a god; he was the symbol of Karolin, just as the British flag is the symbol of Britain. His old carved-cocoanut face was to be found in all the houses, and the sight of it to a Karolinite was as the sight of the Union Jack to an Englishman.

Katafa's idea was to make a symbol of Nan and stick it up on the southern reef. The common-sensical part of the business was the idea of using the deity as a signal. If any fishing canoe from Karolin were to sight that effigy erected on the reef, it would come in to explore, and, if Katafa knew anything of the Karolinites, it would not leave till the whole place had been searched for the persons who had dared to erect the image of the cocoanut god on an alien shore. For not only would they consider that the god had been trifled with, which was bad, but that his virtue had been diluted, which was worse. He belonged exclusively to Karolin, and if he went spending his powers on other islands it would be all the worse for Karolin.

Dick watched the girl as she sat working away on a business as bloody and desperate as that of filling a shell with high explosive. Any little trifling thing beyond the routine of daily life would interest Dick, and now, squatting on his heels, the fishing utterly forgotten, he followed every movement of the knife as it worked away at the mouth of the deity, which was anything but an imitation of a rosebud.

"What are you doing that for?" asked he.

"You were saying but yesterday that the fish were growing smaller in the lagoon," replied she, glancing with head aside at the progress of her work, as a woman might glance at a picture she is painting.

"I know," he replied, "but what are you doing that for?"

"This will bring big fish to the lagoon," replied she darkly.

She saw, as she spoke, not the grotesque ju-ju she was gazing at, but the sun-blaze on the waters of Karolin, the azure and chatoyancy of those depths where the gulls were always fishing, the great distances, where a mind could soar in freedom, resting on nothing, caring for nothing, heedless of everything. She saw the wind and the sun and the breakers falling on the coral. For the people there she had no more feeling than she had for Dick or the departed Kearney; they were to her only as shadows or ghosts. The place was everything.

Perhaps the old Egyptians knew how to practise the *taminan* tabu and used it on cats with partial effect or an effect that has worn out through the ages—cats, for whom places are more real than people, who live in so strange a world of their own, almost beyond human touch.

She could see, as she worked, the big canoes landing and taking her back. As for what they might do to Dick, she neither thought nor cared.

"But how?" asked Dick.

"I will show you," said she; "but first get me what I want."

She gave him some directions and off he went to the groves, taking the axe with him, returning in half an hour or so dragging after him an eight-foot sapling, straight as a fishing rod, four inches thick at the base and tapering gradually to its extremity.

She examined the point of the sapling. Then, making a hole at the base of the cocoanut, she drove the point in so that the thing was fixed on tight. Then between them they carried the affair to the dinghy, placed it long-ways with the frightful face staring down at the water over the stern, got in, and pushed off.

Dick sculled under her direction, using the oars with a will, and, vastly intrigued with this new game of attracting big fish, he half expected to see them coming after the boat or coming up the lagoon, lured by this strange bait. Nothing appeared, however; the dinghy passed unfollowed down the long arm of the lagoon, passed the break and the vision of blazing sea beyond, reached the southern part of the reef, and tied up.

The wind was fresh this morning and the waves on the outer beach of the reef came in curving and clear as if cut from aquamarine, bursting in snow and thunder, sheeting over the coral and sucking back only to form and burst again. The breeze brought the spray and the mewing of the gulls and the scent of a thousand square leagues of sea. Katafa, her hair blowing in the wind, stood for a moment looking south—south, where Karolin lay—the great lagoon, in its forty-mile clip of reef, sending its fume and song to the sky, and the sun making haze of the distances.

Then she turned to Dick, who was standing beside her, supporting Nan.

He could not tell yet how the bait was to be used. With the common sense born in him from his father, he was beginning to suspect the whole business as being unpractical. However, he said nothing, and when she began to search about for a crack in the coral or some convenient hole to take the base of the sapling, he helped. They found one some three feet deep, erected the pole, secured it from rocking with lumps of loose coral and sand, and then stood to look at their work. The thing was hideous, fantastic and stamped with the seal of the South Seas. The breeze blew the frill on the thing's head and, as the sapling swayed slightly in the wind, the grotesque and grinning head seemed nodding towards Karolin.

"Ehu!" cried Dick. "But how will that bring the big fish?"

"They will come from there," said Katafa, pointing south.

Dick looked towards the south. He saw nothing but sea, gulls and sky. Then he turned to the dinghy, the girl following him.

THE MONTHS PASS

Under the sea surface lies a world ruled by laws of which we know little or nothing. We know that the shoals have roads that they follow, and that some master law keeps the balance so that the ocean's population is checked and restrained to certain limits; that the palu change their feeding ground for some mysterious reason, and that for some other reason equally mysterious the lagoons are poisoned periodically so that the fish become uneatable; but no man knows how or why the poisoner uses his art, or why, as in the instance of Palm Tree, some lagoons are immune.

No one can tell why the fish run small at times, as they had been running in Palm Tree lagoon, where the big bream had taken themselves off of late, and the schnapper and garfish rarely scaled more than a few pounds.

Nan, on the southern reef, grinning out to sea, had done nothing, and as the months passed, sliding away in long ribbons of coloured days, Dick from time to time rubbed the fact in, Katafa saying nothing. She was not expecting bream. She was expecting the long canoes from Karolin, and as the months passed and they did not come, she might have lost heart, only that she had something else to think about—Dick.

The relationship between the two had altered subtly.

For a long time—some three months or so—Dick had remembered Kearney, wondering what had become of him, even hunting about the woods spasmodically in the chance of coming on him. Dick knew nothing of death. Kearney had gone, that was all. But where?

This incessant reference to "Kea'n'y" had stirred something in the girl's mind against Dick, a vague antagonism of the type that had been bred by Kearney before he hit her on the back with the tia wood ball.

On Karolin she had never felt antagonism or hatred to any one of the human phantoms that surrounded her. It had been reserved for Kearney, by his attempt to hit her with the seaweed stick and his success in hitting her with the ball, to humanise her to the point of being able to feel aversion and hate.

This antagonism against Dick was helped by the fact that he had put her in her place. Without a direct word, yet in a hundred little ways, he made her feel that he was the superior being, or thought himself so.

Keeping still to her shack in the trees, she yet came to meals just as she had done on the morning after Kearney's disappearance, taking her seat boldly, close to the boy, and showing no trace of the old diffidence and humility, but, unchivalrous as a dog, Dick gave her the worst of the fish and, whilst reserving to himself the high office of cleaning the plates, gave her the rubbish on a leaf to fling into the lagoon. Fishing, out in the boat and on the reef, it was the same. Dick first, Katafa nowhere.

That is perhaps how sex first came between these two, making a foot-mat of the female for the use of his lordship, Dick; sex, a law of Nature from the workings of which Katafa was for ever barred out by *taminan*. The law which Le Juan had implanted in her subconsciousness, condemning her to eternal isolation, had shown its teeth at Kearney because he had attempted to touch her. Was it showing its teeth at Dick because he was a man?

Katafa only knew that Dick was going the way of Kearney in her mind, turning from an almost abstraction into something she could resent and dislike for some reason that she could not fathom, for he had never made any attempt to touch her.

One day, when Dick had taken the dinghy fishing away beyond the cape, he returned elate and triumphant.

"Katafa!" shouted he as he brought the boat up to the bank. "The big fish have come!"

The girl, lying in the shade of the trees by the house, sprang to her feet. The vision of Karolin flashed before her eyes, destroying everything for a moment; then she came running to the bank.

"Where are they?" cried she.

"There," replied Dick, pointing to the boat, where a brace of big bream lay, red and silver in the sunlight.

It was like a blow between the eyes.

She sat crouched on the bank, watching him with a dark look on her face as he hauled them on shore. Nan had fooled her nicely, but her animosity was not against Nan but Dick, and next day, when he went off gaily with a single fish spear to the reef, he found that the point had been blunted, the fishing lines began to break without apparent reason, and a lobster hung up one night was gone in the morning.

If he had chewed gum, his gum would have gone into the lagoon after the lobster. It was the same old game she had played with Kearney, and, like Kearney, Dick suspected nothing of what it all meant—or what it portended.

THE FIGHT ON THE BEACH

The rainy season came and made Dick busy mending a hole that had suddenly come in the roof of the house. It passed, leaving the island greener than ever and the birds preparing to mate.

Nan, on his stick on the southern reef, was beginning to show signs of wear and weather. Gulls roosting on his crown had left a white patch that did not add to his beauty, and the winds, for ever bending and straightening the sapling, had loosened his head so that it waggled a bit, making at times a click-clocking noise, as though he were clucking his tongue with impatience. But all things have their time and season, and had he been god of the lagoon instead of the cocoanut trees and puraka patches, he might have known that the poisonous season had arrived at Karolin.

They had fish ponds there stocked with sea fish to tide them over the bad time, but these pond fish were never quite as good as fresh fish from the sea, and adventurous spirits would put out sometimes long distances after the real article and, unable to carry fire with them, eat their catches raw.

"A raw sea fish is better than a cooked pond fish," was a proverb with them, and one morning, when Dick took the dinghy round to the eastern beach after bananas, the proverb bore fruit. He had secured his bananas and placed them on the sand ready for shipment, when the idea suddenly took him of having a look at the gollywog on the reef. He rowed over, and no sooner had he landed on the coral than away across the sea he saw a canoe. It was longer than the canoe of Katafa, it was standing in towards the reef, and when the occupant caught sight of him a cry came across the water, fierce and sharp like the tearing of a sheet.

Dick didn't wait. He dropped into the dinghy, rowed off to where an aoa tree jutted over the water, just beyond the beach sand, and hid the dinghy under its branches. Then he took to the trees. He had forgotten the bananas. They lay there on the sand, shouting to the sun, and it was too late now to secure them, for the canoe was coming into the lagoon. The sail was brailed up and paddles were flashing, and Dick, peeping through the branches, could see the forms and faces of the four rowers, fierce faces utterly unlike the face of Katafa, and forms brown and polished like mahogany.

The canoe passed the break and took the quiet undulations of the lagoon, the paddles now scarcely touching the water. Gliding and silent as a stoat it came, the faces of the paddle men turning to right, to left, to left, to right, the eyeballs showing, white as the shark's-teeth necklaces on the breast of the bow paddle.

The bow touched the sand. Two of the men jumped out, made for the bananas, turned them over, and gave a shout. The bunches had been cut—no ghost had done that—and assured of this fact, the powwow began, the fellows on the beach shouting to the fellows in the canoe, evidently urging them to land.

But the boatmen were coy. Land! not they! It was well known that this beach was haunted by the spirits of the ancients and the men who had fallen in battle. They were unarmed, they were too few, they would come at another season with more men to follow them.

"Go, then, and search in the trees thyself, O Sru, son of Laminai," cried the stern paddler; "if there is nought to fear, why fear it?"

"Dogs!" cried Sru. He bent, picked up the two banana bunches, and turned to the boats with them.

"They come!" yelled the canoe men.

Dick had burst from the trees, fear flung to the winds at the sight of his precious bananas being spirited away from him. Swift as a panther, flexible as india-rubber, he was almost on Sru, when the other man caught him, tripped, fell with him, and lay flattened for a moment with a blow on the nose.

Then, as Dick bounded to his feet, Sru had him—almost.

Kearney had always clipped Dick's hair, and since the vanishing of Kearney Dick had done his own clipping when the hair worried him by getting too long, using Lestrange's folding mirror for the purpose.

Sru had caught him by the hair and the hair was just an inch too short for the grip to hold, but long enough to hurt. With a yelp of pain like a dog when kicked, Dick struck out and Sru fell.

The lightning-swift blow had been given just below the chin point. Sru fell like a pole-axed steer and next moment Dick, a banana stalk in each hand, was running for the trees, trailing the clusters after him and diving amidst the foliage.

He had saved the bananas, but he was still ready for battle. Rage filled his mind, and a curious musky smell—it was the smell of Sru, cocoanut oil and Kanaka mixed. The smell kept his anger blazing; game as a terrier who scents a badger, he stuck his head from the leaves, ready to renew the fight armed only with the weapons of his race, but Sru had not risen. Sru was lying just where he fell; the other man bending over him and trying to lift him was chattering and crying to the fellows in the canoe who had pushed away a bit off the beach, their voices mixed with his like the clanging of sea-gulls.

"Tia kau—Tia kau—Matadi hai matadi."

The broken sentences came up on the breeze. It was the language of Katafa. What were they saying about the reef and the wind? What was the matter with Sru?

Then Dick saw the bending Kanaka rise, race through the water, and scramble on board the canoe. The paddles flashed and the bow turned towards the break. They were leaving Sru, who still lay on the sand with arms outspread, staring up at the sky.

Now what was the meaning of that?

Dick knew all about traps, from the trap of the great spider of the woods to the trap which he and Kearney had constructed for catching crawfish on the reef. He was a fisherman and knew the ways of sea creatures that assume the appearance of sleep whilst watchful and waiting to snap; absolutely brave, he was yet no fool, and remained amongst the leaves waiting for developments.

He had no fear of Sru, but great fear of the thing he did not understand. The fellows in the canoe were under the same obsession; they had suddenly come on something they did not understand and, the foam dashing from their paddles, they drove out, the paddle swirls and the shearing ripple of the outrigger marking their track across the azure-satin surface of the lagoon.

At the break, they found their voices, shrill with rage. "Kara! Kara! Kara!" "War! War! War!" The cry came like the clang of sea fowl, and they were gone.

Dick watched. He was standing. He squatted, sitting on his heels, and continued to watch. The bananas were safe and on that fact he sat contented as on the top of a tower, his eyes travelling from the man on the beach to the opening of the break, and from there to the reef and back again.

He was capable of sitting there watching till Sru rotted—almost; capable of anything but playing into the hands of these strange folk, the first enemies he had met, the first robbers.

Sometimes the man on the beach seemed to move, but it was only the heat-shaken air blanketing over him; now a cry came from the reef as though the canoe men had landed there from the outer beach and were threatening him. No, it was only a sea bird.

Then a shadow passed over the sand and a great predatory gull circled over the beach, swept out across the lagoon, returned, and lit on the sand.

Sru had fallen near low-tide mark and the great gull, after a moment's rest, came towards him, hop, hop, hop, across the hard sand, paused, and, as if frightened, took a flight and returned to its original position.

It was not afraid of the man, but it sensed Dick and was nervous in the face of something it did not understand. Then, gaining courage, it rose and lit on the chest of the man, spread its wings slightly, steadying itself, and then struck its beak, sharp as a dagger, into the stomach just below the ribs—plong! Like a dropped stone, another great gull lit on the man's throat, steadied itself, and struck—extracting an eye.

Dick knew now that Sru was out of count, like the big fish when they went stiff, and he knew he had knocked him like that just with a blow.

He came out pulling the bananas after him, the birds flew away, and Dick, approaching the body, touched it with his toe. The creature with the broken neck was stiff now as a board, and his slayer stood looking at him, a boy no longer, but a man.

Dick knew nothing about death except its effect upon fish, eels, lobsters and crabs. Some of these fought him like the big eel he had hooked a month ago in the northward stretch of the lagoon and which he had killed just as he had killed Sru, the second son of Laminai, whom Katafa, without intention and through Fate, had brought to his death.

He touched the body again with his toe. Then, seizing his precious bananas, he took them to the dinghy hidden in the branches of the aoa and embarked with them.

As he turned the cape he heard the quarrelling of great gulls, sharp and fierce as the voices of the canoe men. One might almost have fancied it to be their voices rising and falling on the breeze.

"Kara! Kara! Kara!" "War! War! War!"

WAR

"Katafa," said Dick that night as they sat after supper, idle, watching the dusk rise over the lagoon, "men came to-day in a boat like yours."

Katafa heaved a great sigh; then she sat as if the breath were stricken out of her, without a word, her eyes fixed on the other.

He had said nothing of the affair till now, a fact that spoke volumes as to their mental relationship. Between Dick and Kearney there had been little of what we call conversation, between Dick and Katafa none. The inanimate things around them had the time of their lives; they did the talking or supplied the talk. Abstractions had no place in this strange community of two where the actual moment was everything, at least to Dick.

"Men?" said the girl, breaking the silence at last. "Where are they?"

"Gone," said Dick. "I struck one and they went away, all but the one."

Some instinct checked him, helped by dislike of the labour of talking. Dick could think up things from the past easily enough if they were recent, but to arrange them in the order of thought, dressed in and connected by words, was becoming a hateful labour.

It was extraordinary. The things he saw or touched gave him no trouble, but the things he had seen or touched, even though it were only an hour ago, were bothersome when they had to be turned into talk.

He lay back and yawned. Then, rising up, he went down to the lagoon bank, and the girl, watching in the dusk, saw him getting into the dinghy. He was bailing water out of her. That done, he busied himself for a few minutes overhauling the lines and putting them back in the locker. Then he walked off to the house and turned in, without a word, just as a cave man might have done in the days before speech was invented.

The girl, left to herself, turned on her side and then on her face, lying with her forehead on her crossed arms, brooding, suffering, dumb.

Karolin had drawn close to her and drawn away again, perhaps for ever, but Karolin was only a thought. Something deeper than thought had her in its grip, something that had risen in her mind to destroy Dick just as Nanawa had risen from the sea to destroy Kearney.

Once a law becomes part of the human mind, it becomes a living thing capable of good and evil, and the law of *taminan* implanted in the mind of Katafa, though simple as the law of gravity, became capable of profound effects—became, in fact, a beast of prey.

Thou shalt not touch another nor be touched. What law could be simpler than that or more seemingly innocent? Yet of Katafa it had made a creature beyond human sympathy and appeal. It lay in her soul as the barrel-shaped decapod lay in the sea, watchful, ever waiting to strike, ever fearful of being itself destroyed.

To clearly understand the power of *taminan*, one must recognise that its hold was not upon conscious thought but on the subconscious basis of thought beyond the power of will and reason, and yet capable of rousing will and reason into action, capable of inspiring the mind with aversion and hatred.

It had roused her thinking mind against Kearney, who had threatened it, and now as she lay with her face on her crossed arms, it was rousing her against Dick, calling on her to destroy him. Why? Dick had never tried to touch her, never threatened her, yet the beast of Le Juan in her soul dreaded Dick even more than it had dreaded Kearney.

Up to this, just as in the case of Kearney at first, her conscious mind had set itself against Dick in all sorts of trivial ways, breaking fishing lines and blunting the spears, but now, as in the case of Kearney when he hit her in the back with the ball, it had something definite to cling to. Dick had sent the canoes back to Karolin.

It was full night now, and as she rose and came down to the lagoon bank, the wind from the sea came warm and strong, breezing up the water and bringing with it the sound of the reef and the scent of the outer beach.

It was low tide. She cast her eyes on the dinghy where it lay moored to the bank. Dick, inspired by the sapling he had cut for the support of Nan, had made a little mast for the boat. The sail of Katafa's canoe, which had not been destroyed, was lying in the shack behind the house and he intended using it for the purpose of cruising about the lagoon. She looked at the mast and the trivial thought of destroying or hiding it crossed her mind only to be dismissed.

Then, turning from the bank, she drew near the house and, close to the doorway, sank down, sitting on her heels, her face towards the doorway, listening.

She could hear nothing for a moment but the gently stirring foliage as it moved to the wind. Then, as she listened, clasped in the sound of the softly moving leaves, she heard the breathing of Dick in his sleep.

The interior of the house was dark except for a few points of starlight piercing the roof, but, as she gazed, her eyes growing accustomed to the darkness, the little ships began to show on their shelves, guarding the dreams of the sleeper beneath.

Once, long ago, on the very first night she had passed on the island, the prompting had seized her to set fire to the house, but the ships had saved Kearney and the boy. Now, darkly rising from the recesses of her mind, the prompting came again and the ships were no longer potent against it. She had handled one of them and though its god had brought Kearney running to its rescue, the god had done nothing else—could not even protect Kearney when Nanawa had seized him on the reef—a futile sort of deity, surely.

She could see the little shelf in the starlight and the match-box upon it. She rose to her feet without a sound and was moving towards the shelf, when a voice struck her motionless.

It was the voice of Dick fighting his battle with Sru over again in his dreams.

"Katafa!" came the voice, "hai amonai Katafa—help! He is seizing me!" Then a mumble of unintelligible words dying off to silence and the sound of Dick tossing uneasily in his sleep.

She stood with the starlight showering on her and the wind stirring her hair. Something had come between her and the deathly prompting to destroy him. Perhaps it was the voice suddenly shattering the silence and her purpose, or the appeal for help, the first that had ever reached her from human being.

She stood with her head uptilted as a person stands who is trying to catch some far-away sound. Then she drifted away, crossing the sward and vanishing among the trees.

Lying in her shack, she knew that the shark-toothed god had been about to seize Taori with claws of fire—as indeed he had. Taori had called to her for help, and she had helped by not firing the thatch. She could not understand in the least why she had held her hand, or why the appeal for help had so shattered her purpose. She didn't try. She only knew that something had balked her for the moment.

DAYBREAK

For a moment only.

Next day and for days after, Katafa, drawing apart from Dick, would sit brooding, watchful, waiting, but wherever she might be, by the wood edge or lagoon bank, if Dick were in sight her face would be turned towards him, her eyes stealthily watching him.

She had forgotten Karolin. There was only one thing in the world now that mattered to her—Dick.

Since the night when he had cried to her in his sleep for help, everything else had ceased to matter, and her light-thinking mind had become the wrestling-ground of two opposing forces.

The impulse to destroy Dick came at times in great waves up from the darkest recesses of her mind, like the rollers from the storm that had destroyed the *Ranatonga*. Yet the impulse always just failed of effect. The terrible desire to destroy, and destroy with her own hand, had less relationship to hatred than to irritation. Dick vexed her soul, or the something dark that lay in her soul, and time and again she would almost stretch out her hand towards the fish spear or the knife that, once clasped, would have been driven into his heart.

Taminan cried to her, "Seize it and destroy him!" and then the voice of *taminan* would turn into the voice of Dick: "Hai, amonai, Katafa! Help!" and her hand would lose its power.

One day, when Dick was off hunting for turtle on the reef, the crisis came and the evil thing in her heart triumphed.

The fear of Nanawa and danger to herself vanished and, rising up from where she had been sitting beside the house, she put fresh fuel on the cooking fire they had used for the midday meal and which had not been put out.

Then, swift as Atalanta, she crossed the sward, dived amongst the leaves and, fetching the skull from where she had hidden it, close to her shack, returned with it, placed it on the ground before the fire, and, piling on more fuel, stood like a beautiful priestess, her eyes on the skull and her lips moving, repeating the old formula. "Come now, Nanawa, powerful to kill or save, come now and fulfil the wish of my heart—the wish of my heart—the wish of my heart—"

The formula ran from her lips, a string of meaningless words. The something that had checked her hand was checking now her thinking power. She could not put into thought the wish to destroy; just as yesterday, she could not put the will into action.

Nanawa, that figment of a Kanaka's fancy, was powerless against a real god more terrible and cruel than any deity of man's imagination—a god that held Katafa now in his grip.

She put the fire out and hid the skull in the leaves. Then casting herself down in the shadow of the trees, she lay balked, demagnetised, impotent, looking at the lagoon water, the far-off reefs and the sky beyond.

Above the house two birds were building, two blue parua birds, exquisite in colour and form, fearless of man, and making their house again in the same position they had chosen for numberless years.

These birds, long-lived as parrots, had seen the father and mother of Dick build, mate, bring forth their young and depart; they had seen the arrival of Lestrange, the growth of Dick, the coming of Katafa. They had seen Lestrange waiting for his lost children, they had seen him vanish, and now they had seen his skull laid on a strange altar. Verily they had seen strange things, but the strangest lay below them on the sward in the tree shadows of that slumbrous afternoon, for Katafa might have been Emmeline, who had often lain there just like that, Emmeline with the faithful flower still in her hair and her dark eyes fixed across the lagoon on the mysterious sea beyond.

The birds, whilst friendly, had always held aloof, the noisy and restless Dick managing to break somehow that thread of confidence which had drawn them sometimes to swoop down and light on Emmeline's shoulder or hand.

Now, Dick away and Katafa lying absolutely motionless, one of the birds, stirred, maybe, by some old memory, fluttered down on the sward close to her, looked at her with bright eyes, picked up a bit of dried grass, and flew up with it to the nest.

Again it came down and, the girl stretching out her hand to it, it lit on her thumb, hopping at once back to the ground. She put her hand on its blue, warm back, clasping it for a moment. It was the first warm-blooded living thing she had ever touched, the first thing she had handled without intent to kill, the first thing that had come to waken the warmth of humanity in her heart—except that cry of Dick: "Hai, amonai, Katafa! Help!"

THE TREE

We see in nature forms of which perhaps the highest images of men are only compound reflections and symbols. If there had never been birds, would men ever have imagined angels? If there had never been serpents, would men ever have imagined Satan? Are the things about us—which we grossly believe to be the properties of a vast stage set for man to strut on—are these things the real actors in a drama of which man is only a property? A mirror exceedingly complex, built and set up by them for their reflections to fall on. Subtract from man all that he has ever seen, touched, smelt, heard or tasted, and what is left? Bar the road of any of these five senses—will he be complete?

Katafa, who had never touched a warm-blooded sentient thing till now, released the bird and it flew up to the branch where the nest was building, but it had left

260

with her something that had become part of her for ever—something strange and new and sweet, yet disturbing, something from the universal soul of sentient things that had reached her, vaguely perhaps in the cry for help, but more fully now.

A great longing came on her to clasp the bird again, but it was far from her reach, busy in the branches above. She sat up and, with her hands folded in her lap, gazed away out to sea, perplexed, troubled, listening to the sound of the surf on the reef, the movements of the birds above and the gentle stirring of the wind in the leaves.

All the tenderest voices of the Garden of God, all the voices that had brought comfort to Lestrange and promise to his tired heart, seemed conspiring now to augment the message of the bird, the message from a world of compassion, tenderness and pity.

A clap of thunder shattered the silence of the cloudless day and roused the echoes of the woods; another, and another, swiftly following like drum strokes on some Gargantuan drum.

Katafa sprang to her feet.

The mirror-still water of the lagoon was broken and boiling with fish, fish driven and in flight, great bream tossing themselves into the air, palu driving like swords through the water, schnapper, garfish, all as if pursued by some enclosing net, whilst louder now came the thunder and turmoil of a battle that was drawing closer, a battle between Titans of the sea.

A bull cachalot, cruising alone and exploring the great depths to southward of the island for octopods, had fallen in with four bandits.

The first was a Japanese swordfish, a ferocious samurai of the sea who had come on the Kjiro Shiwo current from Japan to Alaska and from Alaska down the Pacific Coast, past Central America, then skirting Humboldt's Current, striking west for Gambier and up past Karolin to its fate.

Close on to Palm Tree, sighting the cachalot, a dusky bloom in the green ahead, it reversed its gear and then charged. Swift as a dagger stroke the appalling sword got home and stuck like a nail in a barn door.

Now, that sword, driven by energy to be calculated in foot tons, would have passed through the planking of a ship as easily as a knife through cheese and have been withdrawn as easily; for twenty years it had ripped and slain living creatures from Honda to Ducie, but never before had it stuck.

Embedded to the hilt under the backbone of the whale, the sword resisted all the efforts of the tail and great sail-like fins of the swordsman, the cachalot shearing through the water, terrified less by the pain of the blow than the fact that its steering gear was upset by the frantic evolutions of the fins and tail of its assailant.

Then, tearing through the sea, came the orcas, three of them from miles away. They did the steering. Like bulldogs clinging to the head of the leviathan, they piloted it into the lagoon, the cachalot springing into the air and falling back in foam and thunder. Up the left arm of the lagoon the fighters came, driving everything before them, palu, garfish, bream, turtle, rays and eels all rushing to escape, the orcas like tigers to left and right and ahead, sharks and giant dogfish following after, tearing at the swordfish, whose fins were in ribbons and whose tail was gone.

Then the great sight broke before the eyes of Katafa, the monstrous bulk of the cachalot rounding the cape, and the water leaping in waves over the bank as it drove into the pool. Above, a blanket of wheeling, screaming gulls followed the battle, whilst from far at sea the great burgomasters and bo'suns were coming in swift, wide of wing and all converging to one point—the cachalot.

She heard a shout. It was Dick, who had just come back from the woods. He was running down to the lagoon bank, wild with excitement and not regarding her in the least as he stood watching, whilst the orcas, steadfast as death, clinging to left and right, hung, thrashing, till the great barn-door mouth of the cachalot opened at last and, swift as ferrets, they began to root and tear out the tongue.

Then, suddenly, the body of the cachalot bent and, with the snap of a released spring, it turned, dashing the spray tree-high, and drove back down the lagoon with the rush of a torpedo boat, sharks and dogfish following after to be lost beyond the cape.

Dick, shouting like a maniac, followed through the trees to see the end. Katafa, gazing with wide-pupilled eyes at the blood-stained waters of the pool, shivered.

She had seen orcas hunting and destroying a cachalot from the outer beach of Karolin and the sight had left her without emotion, but the mind of Katafa had changed, and the world around her had found voices telling her of things unguessed and undreamed of till now.

The great fight had brought matters to a head with her, coupling itself in some extraordinary way, by antithesis, with the warm tenderness revealed by the birds and with Dick, who had just vanished heedless of her.

262

What the bluebirds had whispered, the battle had suddenly shouted: "You stand alone. A world lies around you of which you know nothing. It belongs to Taori; never shall you enter it."

She looked up at the birds, happy and building, heedless of the terror that had just passed and vanished. She looked at the pool, still murky, its surface spangled with prismatic colours where streaks of oil had spread. She looked at the far-off reef and the sea beyond, and she saw nothing but Taori, that beautiful lithe form, that face, fearless and ever seeming to look upwards, those eyes full of sight for all things but her. Until now she had never really seen him. She heard again his voice calling on her for help.

Like a person wandering in sleep, she passed along the lagoon bank towards the eastern trees, seeing nothing, moving by instinct, scarcely alive, terribly, suddenly and mortally stricken. Sounds filled her ears like the chiming of the reef coral when the breakers of the high tide were coming in, sounds now broken and diffuse, now calling his name, gull-clear: "Taori! Taori! Taori!"

Then, breaking away from the dream state and turning to a great tree, she cast her arms about it, embracing it like a living thing and resting her cheek against its smooth, sun-warmed bark, clinging to it and the great momentary peace that had come to her tormented heart.

THE GREAT KILL

Dick, who had heard the first thunder of the battle in the woods, running from the trees had seen Katafa standing watching the cachalot come into the pool, but he had no eyes for her. The excitement of the fight and the fear of injury to the dinghy moored by the bank held him from thought of anything else.

Then, when the cachalot broke away, he followed, running through the trees, hallooing, mad with excitement and the desire to be in at the death.

He could see, through the branches overhanging the water, the foam in the wake of the fight and a long line of following gulls.

The gulls were coming down already. The high cloud of them had broken, and, as if on a moving stairway, they were coming down in a great curve that broke and flittered about the nearly dead leviathan, surging now slowly, tongueless, torn, half eviscerated, towards the break of the reef.

It seemed as though scarce consciously it was making a last attempt to get to sea to the freedom it had lost. The sharks grazing on it, tearing into it, were indifferent. It might get to sea or remain in the lagoon, it was all the same to them; it was theirs. The burgomasters and the bo'suns, clanging and wheeling and swooping, were indifferent. As long as it did not sink, it was theirs.

Dick, knocking himself against trees and tripping on the undergrowth, followed till he reached the banana beach opposite the bank. Here, where he had slain Sru, son of Laminai, whose body the tides and gulls and sharks had long dispersed, he stood to watch whilst the cachalot, practically dead, moved in a great ring on the water, a ring described beneath a vortex of birds.

Never had the lagoon looked more beautiful, glass-smooth, except where the vast bulk moved half submerged, escorted by the gulls whose reflection flew white on the surface, and whose shadows on the floor seemed phantom birds circling amidst the shark shadows and the shadows of the dogfish.

Then, as Dick watched, little by little the dying cachalot gained speed; rising on the water as the momentum increased, the great bulk showed clear, moving in the circle that Nature has prescribed for all creatures dazed or confused.

As the speed increased, the sharks held off for a moment, dozens of dark fins breaking the surface of the water. The gulls, ceasing their clamour, circled like a coil of smoke, and silence fell on the lagoon, broken only by the rush of the fish and the murmur of the reef tinged with the first fires of sunset.

Dick watched without moving till the flurry passed, the leviathan, like a ship turned turtle, moving ever more slowly whilst the shark fins vanished and a gull lit on it as the gull had lit on the chest of Sru.

When he returned to the house, Katafa was nowhere in sight. He did not trouble about her; his mind was too full of the things he had seen. He ate his supper and turned in, but he could not sleep. Katafa, supperless in her shack, gazing with wide-open eyes at the starlight seen through the leaves, could not sleep. She had seen him come back, cook his food, and vanish into the house. He had never called for her as he usually did were she absent at meal time; he never had called for her unless he wanted her for something, to help in the cooking, to carry his spears, to work the boat. She was less to him than the fish he had just eaten or the mat he was lying on.

It was only now that she recognised this. Steadily, bit by bit, strand by strand, the clutch of *taminan* on her conscious mind had been broken so that her heart could beat as the human heart beats and her eyes could show her heart what it desired. Powerful as ever in her subconscious self, the spell remained capable of separating her for ever from the touch of human being, but her conscious mind had found release, an object to grasp with all the pent-up passion of her nature—and its indifference to her.

THE CRISIS

Next morning Dick, who had spent the night hunting cachalots in dreamland, came out to find Katafa lighting the fire for breakfast. She seemed just the same as ever, save for the fact that she had no flower in her hair, but a third person, had one been present, would have noticed that her eyes evaded him, that she ate scarcely anything, and sat mumchance as though some bitter quarrel had arisen between them.

Dick noticed nothing of all this. He did not even help to clear away and tidy the place. He was off to see if there was anything left of the cachalot, and as he picked up a spear and made away towards the opposite trees, he shouted some words of directions to her which she did not reply to. She seemed deaf as well as dumb, and when he was gone, instead of clearing away the remains of the food and putting out the fire, she turned on her side and lay with eyes half closed, scarcely breathing, seemingly asleep. Her half-closed eyes were fixed on the point where Dick had vanished among the trees—Dick, who, without a thought of her, was making his way through the woods, now skirting the water side, now plunging through the growths of mammee-apple and fern.

When he reached the beach, all traces of the cachalot were gone. Not a sign remained of the great fight of yesterday. The gulls were fishing just as of old, and the lagoon lay placid and untroubled, blue and breezed and happy, to where the reef line whispered its eternal message to the shore.

He saw Nan on his post away to the south. He remembered the "big fish," and a sudden respect for Nan and his power—perhaps the first dawn of a religious feeling—came into his mind. Nan had brought the cachalot into the lagoon as well as the big bream and schnapper, and as he stood by the creaming ripples on the sand, he gave a nod of his head in the direction of the gollywog as if in recognition.

Then he came plunging back through the trees. Nan had suddenly reminded him of the sapling he had cut for his elevation, and the sapling of the mast he had made for the dinghy.

He must get busy on that mast and sail—he had neglected them for days—and, full of the fury of the newly released idea, he came bursting out of the wood across the sward, making for the house and shack where the sail was stowed. He would be able to sail the dinghy out beyond the reef and hunt for bigger things. Unhappy Dick, he did not know of the bigger thing that was feeling for him to grip him, of the hunting awaiting him on that day.

Full of this idea, heedless of earth, sea, sky or Katafa, he came running across the sward. The girl saw him coming and half rose, sitting on her heels, a lovely picture in the tree shadows; a picture that might have driven an artist to despair or drawn an anchorite from his cell; a picture only to be matched by that of Dick as he ran, sunny-haired and light of foot and swift as the wind.

One might have fancied him running towards her and have pictured the embrace of these two most lovely of God's creatures, but he passed her as though she were a tree stump, vanished behind the house, and reappeared in a minute dragging after him the ugly old mat sail. Casting it on the ground, he made for the dinghy, seized the mast which he had left lying in it, and came back with it on his shoulder, still running.

That was just like him. He would leave a thing undone for days, maybe for weeks, and then, of a sudden, start on it, forgetful of everything else.

There was some old rope and signal halyard line that Kearney had salved from the wreck. This had to be fetched, also some tools from the tool box; he fetched them himself and then, sitting down, happy and content, he set to work and found his work cut out for him.

The sail was too big, it and the spar that carried it. With the sail and spar spread out on the ground, he crawled about it on his hands and knees, measuring it as against the mast.

Sometimes he would say a few words to the girl, heedless whether she replied or not. Then, when he had been working some half hour or so, looking up, he caught her eyes.

He was sitting with the sail spread on his knees and she was lying opposite to him, resting on her arm. She had looked in his face a thousand times before, straight as the sun looked at him or the lagoon, but now, just before her eyes could evade him, he caught their glance, caught the look on her face—something that vanished and became nothing before his mind could fully seize it.

Pausing in his work, he looked at her for a moment without speaking. She seemed to have forgotten his presence; her eyes, cast down under their long lashes, were following some pattern her finger was tracing on the ground, and her face showed no expression.

He went on with his business mechanically. His mind, so far from straying, focused on the work in his hands. Every fibre of the mat that differed in colour from the others impressed itself on his sight and understanding. The stitches went in evenly spaced, as though made by some unerring mechanism; Katafa might seemingly have been a thousand miles away, and yet every fibre of the sail, every stitch he put in, seemed part of the something strange that had suddenly come to him from Katafa.

He worked with head bent as if lost in thought; then, pausing in his work, he raised his head and looked at her, his lips pursed ever so slightly, the trace of a wrinkle on his forehead.

She heard the stitches cease. Slowly raising her face, her eyes met his fully, without flinching, steadfast, whilst with her eyes still clinging to his, her breast rose with a sigh that died to a shudder. He had dropped the needle from his hand and the sail from his knees. Leaning forward with half-parted lips, his respiration ceased whilst her gaze fell away languorously like the gaze of a dying person, only to be raised again and plunged into his very soul.

They were standing now, the mat between them, Katafa flushed, shuddering, half laughing, as one might fancy a being new-dead and on the threshold of Paradise. Dick, his nostrils wide-spread, his pupils broad with new-born desire, flinging out his arm, tried to seize her, and grasped—nothing. She had evaded him as though some wind had blown her aside. The attempt to seize her had thrown her into the world we enter when we fall asleep.

THE PRISON OF THE TREES

Just as a person in some phases of the state we call the dream condition has to run or finds himself rooted to the spot, Katafa bent aside with no more volition than a reed possesses when moved by the wind.

The very intensity of her longing and her passion cast her more completely into the grasp of the subconscious power that had her in its charge.

Dick, with a sharp cry as if someone had struck him, sprang across the mat, grasped at her again, and missed. She had bent and, springing erect again, all her soul craving for the embrace, with arms outspread like a drowning person, she in turn tried to grasp. Then, turning, she ran, as the dreamer runs followed by the viewless, across the sward. Pursued, yet untouched, she passed with the speed of Atalanta. The leaves divided before her, yet still she ran, unharmed by bramble, unhurt by tree, seeing nothing, protected by instinct.

Then, far in the woods, where the tall matamatas tossed their broad green leaves to the wind, she crouched amidst the ferns like a hare in its form.

The great crisis had come and passed and *taminan* had triumphed.

KARA! KARA! KARA!

There was a girl of the islands, Nalia by name, who, living under the tabu of *taminan* and pursued by a lover, found refuge in the sea. Swimming far out, she could not return, for the place of refuge had in some way, by association, linked itself with the spell and she could not leave it. She was swept away and drowned. Katafa, crouching amidst the ferns, heard the wind in the matamata leaves, the flutter of birds, the murmur of the reef, muted by the woods. Then a voice faint and far away, the voice of Taori:

"Katafa, hai, amonai, Katafa."

She listened—nothing more. Nothing but the wind, the reef murmur and the birds.

Time passed, sunset bloomed and the dusk rose, and then, as the starlight fell, silvering the lagoon and the sea, she came gliding through the trees.

Dividing the leaves, she looked and saw the sward and the house with the starlight upon it. There in the house, with the little ships above him, Taori was sleeping, far from her as any star.

She could no more leave the protection of the trees than Nalia could have left the sea. The open space repelled her as it might have repelled an agoraphobiac, only with infinitely greater power. She was bound to the woods for ever.

In the old romances we read of women spell-bound by witches and black magic. Le Juan had used no black magic; working with no material but Katafa's self, she had moulded into it a law that had become part of self. Passion could not fight with or break that law; nothing could break it but something higher than self, something not yet fully existent in her still nebulous soul.

Like an animal held from its mate, she crouched now, her eyes fixed on the house, the very depth of her passion forging her bonds more securely in so far as it destroyed reason. Dead to thought, her senses were yet acutely alive.

She heard with miraculous clearness the thousand little noises of the night, the moving of leaves, the faint creak of branches, the rustle of a lizard. She heard the surf on the outer beach and the far-off splash of a fish from the lagoon water. Then, as the wind from the sea died to the faintest stirring of air, the moon rising across the eastern trees struck the house, and the air, as though some crystal door had been closed, grew still. Not a leaf moved. Katafa, crouched amidst the leaves, seemed part of the silence that had taken the world, a silence reaching from the furthest sea stars to the trees, a silence suddenly broken by a sound more terrible than the voice of any beast. Suddenly through the utter silence of the night it came, howling, bubbling, bellowing, echoing through the trees from the distant eastern beach, raising the birds in screaming flocks, waking roosting gulls on the reef.

She knew that sound. It was the blowing of a lambai shell, the great conch shell of Karolin, blown only for war.

"We have come!" cried the shell. "The long canoes have come from the south, from the south, from the south! Kara! Kara! Kara! War! War! War!"

SOUTH

When the squall took Katafa's canoe that night, sweeping Taiofa overboard, he was not drowned, but the sea killed him all the same.

The canoe, driving north free of its anchor rope and towed by the fish, left him far behind, and without a moment's hesitation he struck due west, swimming for his life.

He was making for the water to leeward of the atoll, where the current would be broken in its force, and the waves. Here he landed after hours of swimming and with his left leg gone below the knee. The sea is full of hungry mouths and to leeward of Karolin that night there were many sharks. He had just time to reach his people and tell his story before he died.

A great wind had struck the canoe and capsised it. He and Katafa had been thrown into the water. A shark had taken her. He had struck out for the reef. That was the story he told and he had told it in all good faith. He had seen Katafa pulled to pieces by sharks, though how he had seen it Heaven and the Kanaka imagination alone could tell.

When Dick struck Sru dead on the beach, Talia, Manua and Leopa, paddling off across the lagoon, had with equal imagination seen the island alive with Dicks, potential Dicks, stirring amidst the trees. The canoe men had yelled their war cry and, once clear of the lagoon, the potential Dicks became real figures thronging the beaches of their imaginations.

Nan's head waggling on its stick became the size of a house full of speech and proclaiming to high heaven that his deityship had taken up forced residence on Palm Tree, that his power and protection had been filched from Karolin, the fecundity of whose women, cocoanut trees and puraka plants would be now a thing of the past.

Beyond the reef and heading south, the wind changed, blowing gently at first, and then steadily and strongly from the north, a favourable wind and a good omen.

The paddles dashed the water to spray and the great sail bellied to the breeze. Evening came, the dusk rose and the stars broke out, and southward still they flew, tireless as the wind, taking no heed of the current. All night long they paddled, whilst the turning dome of stars rotated above them, the Cross and Canopus and the great streak of the Milky Way all moving mysteriously in one piece till suddenly, in the east, like a dropped rose-leaf, came the dawn.

Away ahead lay Karolin, and the paddle men, who had taken a spell of rest, leaving all the work to the wind, resumed their paddles.

As they came through the reef opening, the sun was behind them and broad on the lagoon, lighting the white beach that swept curving away to invisibility, the cocoanut trees, the canoe houses, and the houses of the village; and scarcely had they passed the reef opening than the sands began to swarm, for eager eyes had reported that they had lost a man, and that of the four who had started three only were returning.

Now this canoe was in no wise of importance except for the fact that Sru, the son of the king's son, was on board of it. Still, it was only one of the fishing canoes of which several that had put out in search of floating turtle were due to put in that morning. It flew no signal of disaster, yet instantly the news was known by this little nation of fishers and hunters of the sea to whom sight was life and swift deduction bread.

Before beaching, it was known that Sru was the missing man, and Laminai himself was standing to meet them as the keel took the sand.

It was Laminai who had tried to dash Katafa to death on board of the Spanish ship; it was Laminai who had killed her mother with the blow of a coral-headed club. Better for him and his sons had he killed the child as well, for Taiofa had gone with her to his death and Sru would never have fallen but for the image of Nan which she had erected to bring the big fish to the lagoon.

Laminai was tall and slight and subtle and exceedingly strong, with a forthright and ferocious expression and a permanent hard double wrinkle between the eyes, eyes that seemed always skimming great distances in search of prey.

Talia, Manua and Leopa, when they saw Laminai standing there with his shark-tooth necklace on his breast, were hit of a sudden by the forgotten fact that this terrible man would most likely visit on them the death of Sru. Visions of being staked out on the reef for sharks to devour drove them half crazy with fright, but not crazy enough to forget Nan as a stand-by.

"Nan! Nan! Nan!" they yelled as the keel drove ashore. "He has been taken from us by a new people who have slain thy son, O Laminai. For half a day we fought with them, but Sru was slain and Nan stands on the reef of Marua [Palm Tree], and never will our crops flourish again."

This news, delivered so convincingly, hit the whole beach dumb. Laminai, at a stroke, seemed to have forgotten Sru. The people automatically drew back, making a semi-circle, and in this arena the three survivors of the great fight stood facing Laminai and his last son, Ma, a youth of some nineteen years.

He questioned them with a word or two and then, turning, led the way to the great house of the village where, in the shadow of the door, Uta Matu was lying on a mat with his back to the sun.

Uta was an old man now, very different from the man who years ago had led the attack on the Spanish ship. He was so fat and indolent that he had to be turned by his women like a feather bed, and there he lay puffing out his cheeks whilst the three canoe men stood before him and one told their tale of the ravishing of Nan, the great fight and the death of Sru.

Having heard them out, Uta did an astonishing thing. He sat up.

This old gentleman, despite his fat, his indolence, the blood-lust that still clung to him amidst the other lusts, and the fact that his only dress was a gee string, was a statesman of a sort. It was quite easy to call for revenge, to set the village buzzing like a beehive, sharpening spears, and rolling the long canoes out of the canoe houses; yet when the murmur that marked the conclusion of the canoe men's story began to swell and spread and threatened to break into a roar, Uta Matu raised his hand and cut it off as one cuts off water at the main.

He had to do two things: consult the priestess of Nanawa to see if the war gods were propitious, and consult Ma, admiral-in-chief and dockyard superintendent of the Karolin navy. Being what he was, Uta decided not to worry the gods till he was sure of the navy. He called Ma, and the son of Laminai came and stood before his grandfather and king.

The fleet was ready. That was the report of Ma. The four great canoes, each capable of holding thirty men, were safe in the canoe houses, seaworthy and only recently caulked; the paddles were in their places and the masts and mat sails in readiness.

Now, these canoes were useless for fishing, or at least never used. They were too large and cumbersome and were kept for war. They had been used for the attack on the Spanish ship, and they had been used when the present northern ruling tribe of Karolin had fought the southern tribe living across the lagoon, nearly exterminating it, and chasing the remnants to the beach of Palm Tree. Long before that, the navy of Karolin had resisted an attack from a fleet that broke the waters one pink and pearly dawn, a fleet of dusk-sailed canoes from the Paumotus that had vanished for ever, sunk and burnt before the crimson sunset died.

Karolin was a sea power ever ready for eventualities.

Having received the report, Uta, to confirm it, caused himself to be carried to the canoe houses. Not content with hearing, he must see, and he saw, as he sat facing the open doorways of the houses, that Ma was no liar. In the gloomy interiors beneath thatched roofs supported by ridge poles, the great canoes slewed on their rollers, ready for the sea.

Even here on land they were moored by innumerable shore fasts in case of accident. Twice had hurricanes blown the houses to fragments, leaving the canoes unharmed.

Uta, having seen that all was right, ordered himself to be carried back to the door of his palace, but the order for war did not come yet. Le Juan had to be consulted.

"Call Le Juan," commanded Uta.

THE PRIESTESS OF NANAWA

Le Juan had seen the canoe men land and heard their story. She had been on the outskirts of the crowd and, having got the gist of the matter, retired to her hut, waiting for the call she knew would come.

Whether Nanawa was a false god or not, she believed in him just as she believed in Nan.

Never laugh at the gods nor sneer at them. The form of history has been moulded by them and man's destiny arranged by them, and the meanest African idol is the emblem of something that, if not real, was at all events powerful.

An interesting thing about these gods of Karolin was their individuality; each was a distinct character—Nan mild and benevolent, Nanawa ferocious, capricious and always ready to strike. Nan would never have been willing or able to reduce Le Juan to the condition in which she appeared before Uta when they found her and led her to him. Naturally ugly, her face was now appalling, rigid as a face carved from stone, and with only the whites of the eyes showing.

Standing before Uta, and supported on either side, she remained dumb for a moment. Then her mouth opened and a voice issued from it.

The words flowed over out of it, almost adhering together, the very saliva of speech.

"Set forth, strike, destroy," commanded the voice. "Destroy utterly, O Uta, and thou Laminai, his son, and thou Ma, the son of Laminai." The words became thicker, lost meaning, became a shout, a prolonged bray, more terrific than the bellowing of a conch. Convulsions seized her, foam ran from her mouth and then, collapsing, she was carried off, whilst Ma seized the great lambai shell passed to him out of the king's house by one of the wives, and filled the air with its howling.

The bellowing of the shell, echoing over beach and lagoon, roused the gulls; their cries came back like the echoes of the cries of the people. "Kara! Kara! Kara!" "War! War! War!" Then silence fell and the fighting men, the women and the very children set to work, marshalled by Laminai, on the great business that had suddenly entered their lives like a sword.

It was still early morning. At that moment the cachalot was passing Karolin to find the swordfish, the orcas, and destruction! But it was not till early morning of the next day that the preparations were complete and the four great canoes ready for launching.

Each canoe held thirty men, one hundred and twenty men all told, and every man of the tribe was of that expedition except Uta, who was long past war, and three old men, dwellers on the southern beach, useless for anything but fishing in a small way.

In two hours after launching, such was the readiness of response of Karolin to danger or aggression, the provisions were on board, and in another hour the fleet, led by the canoe of Laminai, was paddling towards the break.

THE SHADOWS AND THE ECHOES

The wind had changed and was blowing now dead from the south, and as they passed the break the mat sails went up and the four great canoes shot away to the north, urged by wind, current and paddles, like hawks released on their prey.

An hour after the start the wind failed them, but still the paddles kept on. They passed turtles asleep on the ceaseless swell and great belts of fucus carried by the current, the outriggers tangling and lifting kelp fish and fathom-long ribbons of kelp gemmed with sea growths and clung to by crabs.

The drinking nuts secured to the outrigger gratings were passed round under the blazing sun of noon, and as the fleet drifted for a moment, it was saluted by the thunder of a school of giant whip-rays playing away across the blue. Warriors saluting warriors. The whip-rays were a good omen, Karolin being one of their haunts, and Ma, seizing the great conch shell, returned the salute. Then, before sunset, the paddle men ceased work for a moment to shout and wave their paddles at Palm Tree, far off still, but clearly to be seen on the northern horizon.

Half an hour later the landward flying gulls began to take the light of sunset on their wings, and the sun to dip towards a sea blazing with light, and now, as the sun vanished and the dusk brimmed over from the east, a wind rose, blowing towards the land, and the paddle men, at the command of Laminai, ceased work.

Silence fell almost complete, broken only by the wash of the canoe bows, the straining of a rope to the tug of a sail and the shifting of a steering paddle, and now in the pauses of the wind could be heard the surf on the reef, like the breathing of the far-off island in its sleep.

The moon would not rise yet, but the stars gave them light—light enough to see, as they closed with the land, the breakers on the outer beach and the head of Nan on its post. Keeping away to the east, they sought the reef opening where the palm tree stood bowed like a sentinel fallen asleep, and as it came in view, Laminai giving an order, the sails were taken in and the paddles flashed into work.

At that moment the brow of the moon broke the sea.

The tide was just at the slack after full, and on the long river of light from the moon the canoes came like dark drifting leaves; past the break, the paddles working with scarcely a sound, across the lagoon, moving ever more slowly, till again came an order from Laminai and, the stone anchors going over without a splash, the fleet rode at its moorings, silent as the moon that now stood above the reef.

They were brave with a courage that nothing could destroy but defeat or superstition, that nothing could dent but the unknown.

Had they been attacking a known tribe they would have beached the canoes, shouting defiance. As it was, they anchored, feeling their courage and their shark-tooth spears, listening, looking, whilst the moon rose higher, lighting more fully the fairyland they were about to attack, whose only defenders were a youth fast asleep, and a girl the prisoner of illusion, and the trees.

Then, of a sudden, the lagoon became dotted with heads. The whole army of Karolin had disembarked. Swimming like otters, they made for the shore and, leaving the canoes with a man apiece for anchor watch, formed on the beach.

Nothing but their long shadows, drawn on the salt-white beach by the moon, opposed them, shadows that swung clubs and brandished spears, threatening who knows what in shadow-land.

The silent woods stood firm; the reef beyond the lagoon sent the selfsame whisper; the wind lifting the foliage failed and died. Nature, before the terrific threat of Karolin, seemed to have fallen asleep till Ma, like the knight before the enchanted castle, seizing the great conch, blew the signal for war, blew with one mighty and prolonged breath till the whorls of the conch nearly split asunder, till the howling, bubbling echoes came back from strand and hill-top and wind and sea.

Like the response of the shadows came the response of the echoes—nothing more.

IN THE NIGHT

Dick, when sleep took him that night, passed straight into dreamland. He rarely dreamed. When he did, his dreams had always one origin, some vexation or irritation experienced during the day. He would be trying to light a fire that would not light, or the dinghy would be sinking under him, or, going to cut bananas, the banana trees would be gone; those were the sort of dreams that came to Dick. Katafa had never entered them till to-night, when suddenly he found himself chasing her over the sands of sleep, chasing her, spear in hand, till she dashed into the lagoon and became a fish, the most beautiful fish in the world, glimpsed for a moment like a flash of silver.

He had hunted for her till dusk through the trees, beside the lagoon, right to the eastern beach, and now in dreamland he was hunting her again. Ye gods and writers of the old romance, creators of the lovesick swain! Hunting her like an animal, possessed with one overmastering desire, the desire to seize her.

Suddenly the dream was shattered. Sitting up, he saw the world outside the house clearly in the moonlight as though seen by day. A sound filled his ears. It was the sound of the conch.

He was master of all the sounds of his world. The island was always talking to him—the reef and the sea. Here was something new and unknown and inimical.

It came from the eastern beach, that beach which faced the gateway to the world beyond. The sound ceased, the echoes died, and the night reserved its silence. Dick, still listening without a movement, heard the reef speaking to the first waves of the ebb, the fall of a leaf on the roof, and the furtive sound of a robber crab by the house wall on the right. Then, rising, he came out into the moonlight, moving silently as his own shadow.

A fish spear was standing against the house wall. He took it and came along by the trees, listening, pausing every now and then, seeming to scent the air like a hound. Nothing. He turned his face towards the lagoon. Nothing. The great mirror lay unruffled to the reef, and beyond the reef the sea stars shone paled by the moonlight but steadfast and untroubled.

The island said to him: "There is nothing here at all but the things you have always known. That voice was the voice of some sea beast that came like the big fish and has gone."

Yet still he listened.

276

Ah, what was that? A branch stirred and, turning, he saw, like a ghost amidst the trees, Katafa.

She was standing, the moonlight on her face and her arms outstretched. Next moment she had turned, vanished, and he was in pursuit. The woods, one vast green glow under the moon, were lit almost as brilliantly as by day, and as she ran he could see, now a glossy shoulder, now her whole form, now nothing but swaying leaves above which the convolulus flowers seemed the bugles of aerial huntsmen joining in the chase.

He was not hunting alone. The woods to-night were full of armed men, men who at the sound of the conch had spread and entered the groves like a bunch of shadows, beating the trees and glades, dumb as hounds when hot on the scent.

The line Katafa had taken was towards these. Pitcher plants cascaded their water as she ran dashing them aside, and branches foiled him as he pursued; great perfumed flowers hit him in the face. Now he had almost seized her, and now she was gone, saved by a branch or tangle of liana.

The trees broke to a glade carpeted with slippery moss spread like a snare to betray her. Crossing it, she fell. She was his, he flung himself upon her, and fell on the hard ground. He had not even touched her. By a last miracle she had saved herself and was gone, doubling back through the trees.

The fall half stunned him for a moment. Then, getting on his feet, he seized the spear; all through the chase he had carried it slanted over his shoulder, carried it unconsciously or instinctively, just as he had carried it in dreamland. Balked and furious, not knowing what he did, he brandished it now as if threatening some enemy; then, reason returning, he stood resting on it and listening.

He knew she had escaped. To lose sight of a person for half a minute in that place was to lose him. Dick's only chance was to track her by sound, but he could hear nothing. Not the breaking of a twig or the rustle of a leaf came to tell him of where she might be or what line she was taking. He did not even know whether she had dived into the trees, to right or left, or before or behind him; the fall had blotted out everything for a moment, and in that moment she had vanished.

With head uptossed, and leaning on the spear, he stood like a statue, more beautiful than any statue ever hewn from marble, the tropical trees still as the moon above him, the sound of the far-off reef a confused murmur on the windless air.

Then his chin sank ever so slightly. A sound had come to him, something that was not the reef.

It was—she. He could hear the leaves moving—a step—louder now; she was coming towards him and coming swiftly; she had lost her direction and was blundering back to the place she had started from.

He waited without a movement. The foliage dashed aside and into the glade broke, not Katafa, but Ma, the son of Laminai, with the moon full upon him.

Ma, club in hand, the shark-tooth necklace showing white as his eyeballs in the strong light. Ma, lithe and fierce as a tiger, and petrified for the moment by the sight before him.

The two faced one another without a word. Then the figure of Ma seemed to shrink slightly, relaxed itself suddenly, sprang, slipped on the treacherous moss, and fell with the cruel fish spear bedded in its back and heart.

The club shot away across the carpet of moss, and Dick was in the act of turning to seize it, when out from the trees broke Laminai—Laminai, with twenty others behind him. Ma had been the vanguard of these.

Dick turned and ran. Dashing among the leaves, he ran, weaponless, defenceless, with sure death on his heels and only one craving, to free himself from the woods, to find an open space, to escape from the branches that checked him, the flowers that hit at him, the veils and veils and veils of leaves. Instinctively he made uphill, the pursuit almost touching him, the groves ringing now to the cries of the pursuers and of Talia, Manua and Leopa, who had recognised him as the slayer of Sru and were shouting the news to Laminai.

THE BREAKING OF THE SPELL

Katafa, amidst the trees, pausing half dazed from the pursuit, and released for a moment from the spell that had made her fly, stood listening.

She had taken the upward way towards the hill-top. The great sward, moon-stricken and surmounted by the rock, gleamed at her through the trees on her right; below, and to her left, the green gloom of the woods showed in luminous depths marked vaguely by the outlines of trees and sagging lianas.

The glass-house atmosphere of the woods rose around her like an incense. Coco-palm, artu, bread-fruit and pandanus, vanilla and hoya, husk, bark, foliage and flower all blent their perfumes undisturbed by any wind.

Then, as she stood listening, just at the moment when Ma, bursting from the trees, stood face to face with Dick, she heard a sudden loudening of the surf on the reef.

The sound of a single great tumbling wave heaving up from the glacial sea to burst on the coral in foam. Silence, and then through the heat of the night another sound far away and vague, the chanting of gulls disturbed from their sleep and made uneasy by some voice or sign they alone could interpret.

Then, shattering the silence of the woods, came the yell of Laminai as he sprang after Dick, the voices of Talia, Manua and Leopa, and then the tongue of the whole pack in full cry, the sound of branches broken and leaves cast aside, footfalls, all rising towards her like a tide, and breaking through the trees so close to her that she could see the parting of the leaves and the forms of the pursuers and pursued.

Dick, reaching the sward, made one last effort. Breaking from the rock, he would have reached it and rounded it and dived into the thickness of the woods beyond, where the bog land lay and where he might have found refuge, but the uphill path was treacherous as the moss on the sward. He slipped, fell on one knee, and was surrounded and lost.

A spearman raised his spear to pierce him but Laminai dashed him aside.

Sure now of his vengeance, the son of Uta Matu wished to taste it alone, and, waving the others off with a sweep of his arm, and standing with his back to the trees, signed to his enemy to rise.

Dick sprang to his feet and stood facing the other with folded arms. He was lost and he knew it. He had no ideas about death. He only knew that as the speared fish was, so he would be, and that at once. He heard without at least heeding the words pouring out of the mouth of the other, and his gaze never flinched when Laminai, reaching with the spear, touched him on the left breast with the sharp brown point.

On the left breast, just below the nipple, Laminai laid the point of the spear. Just there the point would enter, piercing the beating heart. Then, swift as light, the father of Ma flung his arm back from the thrust and fell, struggling, with Katafa about his neck.

THE GREAT WIND

Creeping close to the wood edge, she had watched like a person in a dream whilst Dick rose to his feet and faced the spearman. She had heard the words of Laminai, she had seen him point the spear, and in those few seconds she had seen death and she had known love, the real love that heeds nothing, even death.

In those few seconds self vanished, and with it the spell that had bound her since childhood, the spell that passion or hatred could not break, that nothing could have broken in the mind of a Kanaka.

As the arm flung back for the fatal stroke, she launched herself, Laminai came crashing to earth, the spear flew from his hand, and Dick caught it. Useless, but for one thing, the cry that went up from Laminai's men as Dick, seizing the spear, cried: "Katafa." Instantly they recognised her, the girl who was dead, the taminanite whom no man dare touch, who dared touch no man. They saw her ghost clinging to Laminai and, breaking, they ran like curs, filling the woods with their cries.

But Laminai did not run. Rolling on the ground, fighting and struggling to free himself from the creature that had him in its grip, teeth in his hair and arms round his neck and legs locked in his, screaming like a horse in terror or rage, he tried to rise, whilst Dick, the spear held short, not daring to thrust, called on Katafa to release him. Then, as with a great and mighty effort the brute half rose, Dick, seeing his chance, drove the spear into his gaping mouth, raising the butt with the stroke so that the point emerged from the neck.

Then, with Katafa in his arms, Katafa clinging to him almost as tightly as she had clung to the other, he made upwards across the sward till he reached the rock. He was making for the southern woods, where the bad lands would give them a hiding place and protection, but as he reached the summit something seized him and wrestled with him and tried to drive him back. It was the wind.

Hot as the breath of a tiger, blowing up from southward, through the clear night it had come, tremendous and sudden, like a giant springing on the island; shouting and dashing the trees together, clashing the branches, stripping the leaves and sending the nuts flying like cannon balls.

It took Nan from his post and sent him flying into the lagoon, the post after him; it stripped the mat sails from the anchored fleet and sent them sailing off like dish cloths; it drove the limp, dead body of Laminai up against the trees, the spear still sticking in its throat.

Dick, with Katafa's hair streaming across his face, half bent, nearly blown from his feet, took shelter to leeward of the rock. Here there was peace though the whole island beneath them was yelling and tossing under an absolutely cloudless sky and in the strong, clear light of the moon. It was the Naya e Matadi, the great wind without rain that once in a decade swept Karolin and the sea for a hundred miles beyond, coming always at night and always at the full of the moon, lasting only an hour, and more dreaded than a hurricane, because more mysterious.

Here, sheltered in the cup of the wind, they lay in the light of the quiet moon, the fight, the killing of Laminai, the still imminent presence of death, all as remote from them as the tossing trees below, the thundering reef and the infinite moonlit sea.

DEBACLE

When the fighting men of Karolin began their assault on the woods, they broke into two companies, one under Laminai and Ma, the other under Utah, a son of Makara, once chief of the southern tribe. When the southern tribe had been destroyed Utali, a boy of some fourteen years, had been spared—he, and a few old men, and several women past childbearing. He had grown up with the northern tribe, become one of them, fought in their wars and fished in their waters, and forgotten and forgiven. He knew that Makara had been slain by the followers of Uta Matu, and slain on Palm Tree beach. That did not matter a bit to him; he bore no grudge. He had always been well treated by Uta, and his father, as he remembered him, had been a brute—"a mouth to shout, a foot to kick and a hand to strike."

He had bravely set off with the others, thinking of nothing but the work in hand; as the finest and most powerful man after Laminai the command of the second division had been given to him, and, leading it, he went off through the trees by the bank of the left arm of the lagoon, whilst Laminai's men struck due west.

Now, Utali carried no love for his father, but he carried still the fear of him, a much more enduring possession if a parent gives it to his offspring, and it was not till the woods of Palm Tree surrounded him that Utali remembered that Makara was a ghost and that he had been made a ghost here, on this island, by the chief whom he, Utali, was now serving.

A nice complication!

"Suppose," thought Utali, "my father were to appear at the head of his men armed as of old and thirsting to kill!"

His mind drew the picture and cast it aside as he drove forward, trampling the ground lianas and shouldering the branches aside.

Suddenly he bolted. The boom of the great wave that Katafa had heard came through the trees, followed by the garrulous chanting of the gulls. He stood listening. He knew every sound of the sea and the meaning of each. A storm of some sort was approaching and his first thought was of the canoes.

Then he heard Laminai giving tongue, and the sound of the chase as it swept to the hill-top, and, turning, leading his men, he began to climb. Laminai had evidently taken no heed of the warning from the sea.

It had been arranged that the two divisions should join up should the illusive enemy give battle to either; each division considered itself all-powerful and ready to meet any contingency, and it was right, for the spears were poisoned with angara, a species of oap, deadly and instantaneous in its effects. So Utali did not hasten his steps unduly, keeping his men fresh for whatever might be to do, and going cautiously with an eye and ear for surprises.

The shouting suddenly ceased as if cut off by a closed door, and Utali, holding up his hand in the green twilight, halted.

The cries he had heard had been the sounds of pursuit, not of battle. Why had they ceased so suddenly?

He listened and waited—not a sound. He stood still listening, his mind filled with wild conjectures, whilst up above, Laminai, spear in hand, stood fronting Dick, touching his breast with the spear-point, flinging back his arm for the thrust.

A yell split the night above as Laminai's division caught sight of Katafa, and Utali, taking it for the shout of battle, charged upwards through the trees, followed by his men, to the assistance of Laminai.

They had not gone twenty paces when they found that they were being charged. Down through the trees, towards them, a host was pouring—there was only one instantaneous solution: Laminai's division had been utterly and silently destroyed and the destroyers were coming, ghosts and evil spirits, no doubt, led by the ghostly Makara.

"Makara's men are coming! Makara's men are coming! Death! Death!" shrieked Utali, not daring to turn and run as he might have done from a living enemy. Then thrusting with his spear at a dark form that sprang at him out of the gloom ahead, he missed and fell, pierced to death, whilst the form, yelling with fright and rage, pressed over him.

The whole of Laminai's followers, stampeded by the vision of the ghost of the girl who had been eaten by sharks, charging down through the trees of a place now filled with ghosts, only wanted the cry that Makara's men were coming to finish them—Makara, that terrible chief who had been slain here by their fathers and brothers.

The yell of the new-risen wind from the south, the dashing about of the trees, and the great alternating splashes of moonlight and shadow raised their rage and terror to dementia, and as they saw Utali and his warriors, and charged them and were charged in turn, imaginary ghosts attacking imaginary ghosts, nothing on earth could be compared to the fight, and nothing in dreamland.

Twenty men alone escaped from that psychological battle, twenty of Laminai's men, spearless, daggerless, torn by brambles, gasping and running for the canoes, whilst the trees roared above them and tossed them out to the shouting beach where three of the canoes, dragged from their anchorage, lay broken and ruined.

One canoe alone remained straining at its rope, the fellow in her waving his arms and shouting, screaming as he saw the survivors taking the water. "Karaka! Karaka! Karaka!" "Sharks! Sharks! Sharks!"

The lagoon was full of sharks driven in by the storm, but the survivors neither heard the cries of the anchor watch nor would they have heeded. Worse things were behind them than sharks. Makara and his ghostly followers were on their heels. They struck out across the tossing water, the moonlight steady on the bobbing heads that vanished one by one till ten only were left, saved by the number and rapacity of the sharks.

Thick as women at a bargain counter, the brutes foiled themselves by getting in each other's way, and the ten survivors, scrambling on board, some over the outrigger gratings, some over the side, cut free from the anchor rope, seized the paddles, and headed for the break.

No sooner had they cut the rope and struck the water with the paddles than they saw their blunder.

The tide had caught them. The full ebb tide, rushing from the two arms of the lagoon, had them in its grip, bearing them to the break, beyond which the out-boiling water had set up a terrible cross-sea.

The heavy canoe was undermanned. They could do nothing but steer and shout as they went, swept as a toboggan on the sheeting foam, stern lifting, bow lifting, shooting through the break into the lumping sea that turned them turtle.

A wave took the canoe and smashed it on the coral, destroying the outrigger, and a great king wave festooned with foam took the remains and hove it onto the reef high and dry, stern stuck in a cleft and bow in air, a last touch of the fantasy of the sea, that sister of Fate.

So, at a stroke, went the navy of Karolin and all her fighting men, destroyed by their own imaginations and the child of the woman they had slain long years ago.

AFTER THE BATTLE

The gulls were crying above the reef, and away in the east, below the sea-line, a rose-red fire was burning, paling gradually, passing into the starless, infinite distance of the true dawn.

Then, as the ripple of light on the horizon waters turned to a ripple of fire and the birds in the groves chattered out in answer to the gulls, Dick, flinging sleep off suddenly as one flings a blanket, sat up, striking out at the vision of Laminai—Laminai, spear in hand and ready to lunge. For a moment the dead chief stood before him, hard in the imagination as a real figure; then it vanished and his eyes fell on Katafa.

She was lying on her side fast asleep, her face buried in her arms. He watched her, his eyes consuming her in the strengthening light.

He knew nothing of love; he only knew that the something that had revealed itself to him and evaded him was his—his—and the whole unearthly world that surrounded it.

The voices of the gulls and the sound of the reef were part of her, and the strengthening light part of her; the rising sun, his own very life, were part of her—and she was his.

Had she suddenly been snatched from him, the voices of the gulls and the sound of the reef, the rising sun—every bit of the old world she had made new would have fallen in on him and crushed him with despair; and yet only yesterday he had run past her bent on the business of making a sail for the dinghy, run past her heedless as though she had been a tree stump, and, had she been taken from him then, would he have cared?

As the sun struck Katafa full, from her night-black hair to her little feet, she moved. Then, suddenly casting sleep away, she sat up.

Just as Dick's waking vision had been the man he had fought with, hers was Dick.

She saw him, with wide-pupilled eyes that saw nothing of this world, and, holding out her arms to the vision, cried: "Taori!"

H. de Vere Stacpoole

It faded as her arms clasped themselves round the reality.

*

They had climbed the sun-warmed rock.

The vast columnar swell was marching across the Pacific, smooth as though the Naya e Matadi had never blown, and nothing to tell of the great wind remained but a few broken trees in the groves and the up-ended canoe on the reef. Dick could see it as they sat, the sun now high above the horizon, and the land breeze fanning out across the sea in spaces of violet shadow.

He pointed it out to Katafa and she nodded her head. She knew.

Instinct told her that the men of Karolin had been destroyed, that something had happened, something that came with that wind which she remembered now like a wind that had blown in dreamland.

The sense of security was everywhere ringed and completed by the peace of the violet sea.

Here, high above the world as the birds, they could see a thousand square leagues of the blue Pacific from the limitless north to the far pale sky trace that was Karolin, the world of the sea-gulls ever clanging and clanging about the reef, the lagoon, and, rising up towards them from the lagoon, the trees. Not a trunk, not a stem, nothing but the glory of the foliage; the dancing, feathery palm fronds, the still dark spread of the bread-fruits, the piercing green of the new-leaved artus, and here and there lords of the forest and the groves, the matamatas striking boldly to the sky.

Over all, the breeze dancing light-footed as a faun, and coloured birds like blossoms blown from the trees.

Some drinking nuts had been blown right from the mid-zone of trees up to the sward; he had fetched them and they had drunk the contents. Neither of them had eaten since the day before, but Dick, who had not the sure instinct for safety that possessed Katafa, had no idea of returning to the house till he was sure that the enemy was gone. He wanted to explore and see. The wrecked canoe filled his mind with a thrill. From it came a waft of the battle of the night before, bringing up the vision of Ma, the man he had speared like a fish, and with the recollection his nostrils broadened as the sound of pursuit came again to his ears, and the feel of the branches he had dashed aside in his escape; he tripped again on the sward, and again he faced Laminai and death; again he thrust the spear into the gaping mouth.

He almost forgot Katafa; love and passion were nothing for a moment as the blaze of anger broke up again in his mind—the fury of the man who has been attacked and who has killed his attacker, the rage of the defenceless man who, being unarmed, has had to run.

Telling Katafa not to move from the hill-top till his return, he slipped down from the rock and ran towards the groves. Laminai, spear and all, had been blown by a last gust of the great wind in amongst the trees. Dick, coming on the body, disengaged the spear and, carrying it slanted over his shoulder, came along down, taking the track that Manua, Leopa and Talia had taken the night before as they raced howling with terror and driven by imagination to their death.

Nothing could be more peaceful than the woods this morning. The great wind, broken by the hill, had left scarcely a trace, the morning breeze left scarcely a sound louder than the rainy patter of leaf on leaf. Bursting from beneath the great apron leaves of a bread-fruit, Dick suddenly found his path barred by a brown, naked man on all fours.

The man seemed crawling on hands and knees. In the merry dancing lights that showered as the breeze footed it in the foliage overhead, he seemed to move, but he was dead, and supported in his position by a decayed tree stump across which he had fallen.

The rigor mortis, setting in instantly from the poison of some spear or dagger, had turned his limbs stiff as the legs of a table. On his back the siftings of the forest had already fallen, the white droppings of a bird, a leaf, a single, gummy, coloured petal of the hootoo.

Beyond this man who crawled, yet never moved, stood a man clasping a tree bole tightly with head thrown back and a light, wand-light spear through his shoulder. He had caught at the tree before falling and clung; still clinging in the death rigour, his face, turned back, with eyes wide open and mouth agape, seemed gazing wildly in search of the man who had struck him, yet there was nothing in his line of sight but an orchid swinging in the perfumed air on a loop of liantasse.

Beyond, men were lying in heaps, singly, in pairs, on their backs with arms outspread, clasped together in a deadly embrace, petrified by the poison that kills like a pole-axe, half hidden, half revealed by the trees and the brambles and the still green beauty of the ferns.

Makara and his men, slain long ago on the eastern beach, had taken their revenge in full, and as Dick passed swiftly, glancing to left and right, by the mounds of the dead and glades that told their tale, the knowledge came to him that there was nothing more to fear; all the men in the world seemed lying here stricken to nothingness. Done for.

As he broke onto the eastern beach he saw the three canoes that had been driven upon the sands. Two lay on their sides and one bottom up with out-rigger smashed; away on the reef the fourth stuck up just as he had seen it from the hill-top.

A coral-headed club lay near one of the canoes. He cast away the spear he was holding and seized the club. That was a weapon worth carrying, yet, having handled it and swung it in the face of the quiet lagoon and desolate eastern sea, he lost interest in it and let it drop, and turned to examine the canoes. There was no one here to use a weapon against, no one but the men in the woods, those strange brown men so stiff, yet so seemingly alive, so full of anger, rage and terror, so swiftly running, so furiously hitting, yet so still.

As he overhauled the canoes, pictures from the woods came before him: a man who had been stricken running just as he had dashed into a tangle of vines, still erect, upheld and preserved in position by the vines; a green glade where ferns grew, and out of the ferns a brown leg, stiff as the leg of a table, making as if to kick at the sky through the roof of foliage and merry dancing lights and liquid shadows.

But he did not think of those things long. He was too much interested in the canoes and their make and their huge size.

Nothing born of the sea is more fascinating than a native canoe with its outrigger, outrigger poles and grating, its mast and yard and mat sail, its paddles, the perfume of its wood, the cunning of its cocoanut fibre lashings, the mystery of its whole being.

What an antiquity lies behind it, and what a history! Whilst the galleys and caravels of the eastern world were in evolution, it was as now, a thing never to develop like the boat that carries the seed of the plant on the wind.

Dick saw that the construction was identical with that of the canoe of Katafa. The old smashed canoe had engraved itself upon his memory in every detail; nothing was different but the size and the number of paddles that would be used. He examined the broken mast and the sail of the only one from which the wind had not stripped the sail. It was the same as Katafa's.

Then, as he turned away, something that had been washed up on the sand caught his eye. He stooped and picked it up. It was Nan.

Nan's head, which the wind had blown into the lagoon, and the lagoon had faithfully delivered to the sands; Nan looking terribly debauched and battered, but still Nan.

How Katafa had created so much personality with a few cuts of a knife must remain a mystery. She had, and the thing was Itself. Every moment was making it more so, for its fuzzy head was drying rapidly in the sun and Dick, recognising this, placed it on the hot sand higher up and started to hunt for the pole.

There was no pole to be seen on the reef, and he reckoned that if it had been blown into the lagoon after the head, it would come ashore on the same drift.

He was right. He found it just where the tree roots on the left of the beach came into the water like great claws, and, fetching it, fixed Nan again on its tip.

Then, with the pole on his shoulder, he came running along the lagoon side through the trees. Canoes, clubs, dead men, even Nan himself, were forgotten. The memory of Katafa had rushed suddenly out at him from the trees, and the sudden passionate desire to get to her nearly drove him back along the road he had come—would have done so but for the fact that his main purpose, after scouting, that morning, was food.

There was food at the house, a crab he had put by and some baked fish and taro, and the quickest way to the house was by the lagoon bank.

Arrived there, he stuck Nan against the house, fetched out the food from where he had hidden it to protect it from the robber crabs, and sat down to eat.

Katafa must have been as hungry as himself, but his hunger made him forget that fact, although all the time he was eating he was thinking of her; when he reached her at last, labouring up the hillside with the remains of the food wrapped in a great leaf, she was in the shelter of the rock, asleep, and, placing the leaf on the ground, he sat down beside her.

THE CALL OF KAROLIN

If the blue parua birds resting above the house were indeed the birds of long ago, they might have fancied nothing changed since those days when the father of Dick returned from the valley of the idol with Emmeline.

Love never alters, and the forms of the lovers were almost the same, and the incidents of their simple and humble lives made beautiful by love and the absolute innocence which is Nature.

H. de Vere Stacpoole

The joyous awakenings to mornings of new life, the sudden and passionate embraces, the sudden and seeming forgetfulness of one another, as when the figure of Dick could be seen far away on the reef, heedless of everything but the fish he was hunting for, followed by the figure of Katafa, faithful as his shadow—all was the same and yet, touched by the wizard spell of Karolin beyond the southern sea, all was vaguely different. The spell of Karolin had seized Dick through Katafa; though he had never seen the reef and the gulls and the forty-mile sweep of lagoon, the great atoll island had begun its work upon him even before Kearney had died.

It had made him talk its language; it had made him forget his past; little by little, and strand by strand, it had broken him away from all things connecting him with the world, drifting him farther than his parents had ever drifted from civilisation and its fantastic labours, its hopes, dreams and ambitions.

And this it had done through Katafa.

He was no longer Dick but Taori. The language of his early childhood had gone from him like a bird flown. Kearney was the recollection of something that had once been part of a dream; Nan, on his pole by the house, was far more potent and living.

At night sometimes now Katafa, as they sat under the stars, would talk to him in an extraordinary way. It was as though Karolin were speaking and trying to tell of itself.

Karolin had never released its hold on her, and in some strange manner the coming of love, the breaking of the spell of *taminan*, the new meaning of life, all revived in his mind the memory of the environment of her childhood. She told him of Le Juan, the priestess of Nanawa, and of Nanawa, and of Uta Matu, the king, so old that his skin was beginning to scale off in white scales like the scales of the alomba. She told him that at Karolin there was nothing but reef—no island—nothing but reef.

Dick laughed at this, a short, hard laugh that struck through the starlight like the cough of a stabbing spear. She took his hand as they lay there side by side, as if to lead his imagination.

At Karolin there was nothing but reef, a reef so great that sight could not follow it; on one side the lagoon—the quiet water—and on the other the sea. Were you to follow it on foot you would walk for days before it led you round back to the break. Two days' journey it was, and you had to sleep at night without a roof under the

289

stars. The lagoon was so wide that it held all the stars, even the Milky Way—the great smoke—and the moon, travelling all night, could not cross it.

She told of the great fish that came in from the outer sea and made thunder, whip-rays tossing themselves into the air and falling back in fountains of foam, the coral ringing to the echo of the concussions.

Then, in a voice more remote and as if telling a secret: "There are no trees there, only the palms."

It was Karolin speaking, not Katafa—Karolin the treeless, Karolin that had become part of her through the magic of environment. If the great sea spaces, the forty-mile reef, the lagoon mirror and the snow of surf had found voices to tell of themselves, could they have spoken more clearly than they spoke through her?

Her antagonism to the trees, felt when she first viewed them in their great masses, had become increased by the part they had played in trapping her; yet at base it was the antagonism of Karolin expressed by the human mind.

In all these talks there was no word of herself or the spell that had been put upon her by Le Juan. She herself scarcely knew the meaning of it, or why for years she had lived in the world as a shadow amongst shadows, or how it was that she had awakened to this new world in the arms of Dick. Yet deep in her heart a light had pierced, showing something vague and monstrous, something nameless that named itself Le Juan.

And now, as though Karolin had placed its finger upon the very woods themselves and upon the trees it hated because it had no trees, sometimes, when the wind was in a certain quarter, the dead men from Karolin would hint of their presence vaguely and dreadfully, driving Dick and Katafa to the reef to escape them.

The rigor had long since lost its grip and the fantastic show had collapsed, figures falling apart and in pieces like waxworks melted by heat in the furious corruption of the tropics.

Then, in a month, the woods were sweet again, but the stain remained in memory.

Dick had never loved the woods. His passion was all for the sea and the reef, and the stories of the girl about Karolin, whilst only half believed in, had left their mark on his mind. She had never indicated where the island lay, only conveying to him that somewhere there was a place where she had come from where nothing existed but sea and reef and lagoon; it was just a story, yet it dwelt with him and, working in the inner recesses of his mind, it joined itself with vague recollections of what

Kearney had said about the place where she had come from. Kearney had shown him one day the stain on the southern horizon, telling him that another island lay there and that the girl had come from it in all likelihood.

The thing had passed almost out of recollection.

One morning, a month or so after the woods had regained their sweetness, Dick, who had completed the sail for the dinghy, was standing by the little boat as she lay moored to the bank, when suddenly a whole lot of things grouped themselves together in his mind—the dinghy, the mast and sail, the open sea, recollections of Katafa's stories about the great reef and the lagoon where fish made thunder.

Katafa was in the boat, ready to push off, but instead of joining her he beckoned her on shore again and saying, "Come," led the way off towards the trees. She followed him through the woods and up to the hill-top. There, on the southernmost side of the great rock, he stood and pointed south across the morning sea. She gazed and saw nothing.

"I see nothing, Taori, but the water and the wind on the water and the sea birds on the wind. Ah! There!"

Her eyes had caught the stain.

Out on the fishing bank, long ago, she had seen the full blaze of the lagoon striking upwards to the sky, making a vague, pale window in the blue; this was the same, though remote.

"Karolin," said Dick.

She stood, the wind lifting her hair, and her eyes fixed on the stain, which grew and spread in her imagination till the song of the reef came round her, and the freedom of the infinite spaces of sea and sky. All she longed for lay there, and all she loved stood beside her. She said nothing. Never once in her talk of her old home had she expressed the wish to go back. The place where she had found Dick was antagonistic to her, yet it was the place where she had found him, and was in some way part of him, and she could not put her dislike of it in speech, nor her desire to leave it. Even now she said nothing.

She did not know that the craving for adventure, for movement, for change, and the desire for newness were stirring in Dick's heart.

He scarcely knew it himself. The thing that had come in his mind was scarcely formed as yet, or, being formed, had not yet developed its wings.

They left the hill-top and came down through the trees, scarcely speaking. One might have thought that they had quarrelled but for the fact that his arm was about her neck.

Before leaving the hill-top, had they turned their eyes to the north, they might have seen across the blue morning sea a vision that seemed cast on the screen of things by the gods in opposition to the far, faint vision of Karolin.

There, on the northern horizon, white as the wing of a gull, stood a sail, remote, lonely, only visible from this height—the sail of the first copra trader in these waters.

THE MORNING LIGHT

When the *Portsoy* had turned her stern to the reef long ago, she had done more than fire the shot that smashed the canoe of Katafa. She had logged the position of Palm Tree, and her captain, in his drunken brain, had logged the fact that it was "full of copra." He was no trader, but he drank where traders were, and in Pacific bar-rooms, in a blue haze of smoke, the fact made itself known after a time. That is how islands were discovered in the old days that are not so very old; through chance and schooner captains and the dingy pages of logs, through memories and conversations and the haze of bar-rooms, the islands unknown came into the world of the known, and not only the islands but their qualities.

For years Nauru in its desolate beauty laughed at the sun till chance betrayed it and the phosphates that lay beneath its surface, and for years the Garden of God might have remained unknown but for what its palm trees had said to the *Portsoy*, and the fact that copra had taken the place of sandalwood in the world of trade.

It was from Papeete that the *Morning Light* set out, a topsail schooner of a hundred and fifty tons with enough native labour to work the island if found. Owing to a slight error in the *Portsoy's* reckoning, she nearly missed it and was about to give up the hunt, when one morning, just as the sun broke above the sealine, it showed, far to the south, just a point on the new-born blue of the sky.

For an hour and more the favourable wind held strong and the island grew apace. Then the wind failed and faded, as if in regret at the ruin it was helping on, the ruin of Nature by trade.

All day long the *Morning Light* held south under the play of light and variable winds, making the lagoon only at dusk and entering with the first of the stars.

292

Dick had put out the cooking fire; it was after supper, and they were talking of the day's work. Over on the southern bank, at certain times of the tide the fishing was better than anywhere else in the lagoon. The water was deep there and you could reach the place either by striking across through the woods or going round the lagoon in the dinghy. This was the longer way but they generally used it for the convenience of the boat in bringing back the fish. They had seen nothing of the *Morning Light*, nor had they exchanged a word about Karolin.

Night was the time for talking, as a rule, unless the business of the day had tired them out, as it had this evening.

Dick, having put out the fire, turned on his side and was just about to speak to Katafa, when through the woods, from the direction of the eastern beach, came a sound, a long low rumble, suddenly beginning and suddenly ceasing, the sound of the anchor chain of the *Morning Light* running out.

Instantly he was on his feet.

Every sound of the island was known to him. This was something new, new as the voice of the conch that had roused him from sleep to face Laminai and his tribe.

"Did you hear?" said Dick.

"Yes," said Katafa, "I heard." She was standing close to him, her head thrown back, listening.

The moon in its first quarter had risen above the trees and a wan, rosy light fell on Dick, on Katafa, on the house beside which Nan leaned on his pole and within which could be dimly discovered the outline of the little ships.

Dick, as though fearful of listeners, raised his finger and then motioned to Katafa to follow him, leading the way towards the trees on the opposite side. He had not gone a dozen paces when, remembering his spear, he turned back for it and then, resuming the lead, plunged amongst the trees, keeping along the lagoon bank, the glitter of the water showing through the branches, and the green glow of the forest lighting them as they walked in single file and silent as Indians on the war path in a hostile country.

As they drew close to the eastern beach, a red spark of light showed through the leaves ahead. A fire was burning on the beach and as Dick parted the last branches and stood, Katafa beside him, the fire blazed up till the trunks of the coco-palms took the light.

A boat was beached near the fire, around which half a dozen dark, nearly naked men were busy cooking, whilst two white men, dressed as Kearney had been dressed, were seated on the sands, knees up and with a bottle before them. Some drinking nuts lay close to the man on the left.

Away out on the lagoon the *Morning Light* lay at her moorings, the ebb showing a silver streak where the chain met it and where it passed away astern.

Katafa drew closer and drew her arm round Dick.

The dark, naked men swarming about the cooking fire fascinated her. Never had she seen such faces. The people of Karolin, owing to a Melanesian taint, were fierce enough, and some of them were plain enough, but the ugliest man of Karolin would have been handsome compared with any of these.

Recruited from the New Hebrides and beyond, naked but for a gee string, with slit ear lobes and nose rings all complete, they seemed less like men than apes, less like apes than devils.

Sometimes one of the two seated men would cry out a harsh order or rise to boot one of the ape men, and now, as Katafa watched, something broke the lagoon near the schooner—another boat, a boat laden with stores, tent poles, canvas, crawling slowly across the lagoon to beach where the zone of firelight met the ripples of the outgoing tide.

Dick drew Katafa away, the branches closed, and, turning, they made their way back through the clear, clean night of the woods, the green gloom of the thickets, the glades where the young moon lit the ferns.

What had happened to the island, to the night, to the very trees, to life itself? How and in what way did they sense the fact that what they had seen was bad—they who knew not even the name of evil—and how and in what way did they know that what had come had come to stay? That something had broken in on them, incomprehensible but loathsome, that the island would never be the same again?

Not a word did they speak the whole way back to the house, Dick leading, Katafa following. The most extraordinary thing in their strange life alone and cut off from the world was the fact that though they spoke little to each other with their tongues, they were always conversing together. A movement, a look, a touch, a change of expression could convey what would have taken a dozen words to convey, and above and beyond that they had a mind relationship perhaps purely psychic. They could think together. Often some wish or want of Dick would be understood by Katafa, and before he could stretch out his hand for something it would be handed to him. Or a wish of Katafa's would become known to Dick without a word conveying it.

Arrived at the house, they consulted together for a moment.

"From where have they come?" asked Katafa—as though Dick could know.

He shook his head. Then standing, his eyes fixed on the house and his brow wrinkled, he came to a sudden decision. Everything must be hidden, even the dinghy; they must take to the trees—and before he had finished speaking, Katafa, who knew his mind, turned to the house whilst he ran down to the lagoon bank where the dinghy was moored, saw that the mast and sail were in her, and that the fishing gear was safe in the locker. There were three fish spears in the boat; he let them lie. Then running back to the house, he helped in the removal of the things.

The dinghy of the *Ranatonga* was an outsized boat of her type, carvel-built, broad of beam and with plenty of space for their wants. They brought nearly everything down—Nan and the little ships, which they placed in the bow, the two mats on which they slept, the axe and saw, a knife, and a huge bunch of bananas that Dick had cut two days before. Everything they treasured they took away, leaving everything else—the plates, the cooking utensils and all the stuff in the shack behind the house. Then, when they had finished, they got in and Dick, taking the sculls, brought the boat to the cape, where the wild cocoanut and arita bushes spread out over the water. Then, taking in the sculls and seizing the branches, he dragged the boat in, far in, till the branches and bushes covered her entirely and tied up to a root. Then, avoiding the house, they made their bed amidst the trees where Katafa had slept once.

Neither of them spoke of the thing that had been in the depths of their minds since, standing on the hilltop yesterday morning, Dick had pointed to the stain on the southern sky—Karolin. The call that had come to them had remained unspoken of; mysterious as the call of the south to the northern swallow, the call of the great lagoon island would have fetched them at last, as the suck of the whirlpool fetches flotsam remote from it and seemingly beyond attraction, but the scene on the eastern beach to-night had brought them leagues closer to their goal. The instinct to seek Karolin had been joined to the desire for flight. The *Morning Light* and her crew had acted as the touch of cold that intensifies the swallow's vision of the palm trees and the south. It was only when, the dinghy loaded and securely hidden, they laid themselves down in the nest of fern that Dick spoke.

"If they stay," said Dick, "we will go there."

"Karolin?" said Katafa. "But if the big canoe is not gone, how can we pass it?"

"We will pass it," said Dick.

He had brought some bananas from the dinghy for their supper. He divided them, and as they ate he sketched the plan that had formulated itself in his mind.

If the new people left to-morrow, it would make no difference—they would start for Karolin; if the new people remained, it would make no difference—they would start all the same. With the slack of the tide to-morrow night, late, when the newcomers were asleep, they would put down the lagoon and make past the big canoe for the break; the big canoe would not stop them.

He spoke with the assurance of daring and power, but quietly, as though he were speaking of some ordinary matter.

They would sail for the south, "é Naya." The wind from the north that had been dying and waking again all day was blowing strong again. It would last like that for days; it was the prevailing wind of the year and the moon was a fair-weather moon.

Then he went calmly to sleep, with Katafa's arm across him, but she could not sleep.

She was already in her imagination on her way to her old home. The men of Karolin were all dead, their bones were whitening in the trees up there, there was nothing to fear. Only the women and children were left, and Uta Matu, the old king, worn out and approaching his end.

With her woman's imagination, she saw Dick, the man she loved and gloried in, standing on the beach of Karolin, king and ruler.

Perhaps it was a prevision of this and the whitening bones of the men of Karolin that had made Le Juan years ago urge Uta Matu to destroy Katafa, and, failing, made her segregate the girl under the tabu of *taminan*. Who knows?

THE DEATH OF A SEA KING

On the morning when Laminai and all his host set out, never to return, Uta Matu, sitting where his women had placed him on the sand of the beach, watched the canoes depart.

It was a glorious morning and the waters of the lagoon, stirring to the first of the ebb, were sweeping towards the break beyond which lay the outer sea like a vision of shattered sapphires.

He saw the paddles flashing, and the sheening foam of the outriggers; he watched the mat sails take the wind. Gulls followed the canoes, escorting them, wheeling, sweeping and clanging on the wind. Then the gulls passed away and the sails vanished beyond the reef, and Uta found himself alone.

Alone with the women and the children and the crabs of the beach, he who had always led the fight and directed the rowers and dispensed the laws of Karolin for sixty long years! Alone, and useless as the smallest child! Uta had been a hard and stern ruler, merciless to enemies, yet just according to his lights. He had known three gods—himself, Nanawa, the shark-toothed one, and Nan of the cocoanuts.

He had only worshipped the first.

Just as a clever man believes in ghosts without letting the belief interfere in the least with his renting a house supposed to be haunted, Uta believed in his co-gods without letting his belief worry him much.

Even if the verdict of Le Juan had been against the expedition, it is highly probable that he would have sent it off all the same; his fighting instincts had been roused and the death of his grandson, Sru, had vexed his soul.

Having sat for a while contemplating the ripples breaking on the sand and the gulls flighting above the water, the king of Karolin called to his women to carry him back to his house.

That night the great hot wind from the south blew, and whilst Laminai and his men were slaughtering each other and the waves were roaring on the reef of Karolin, Le Juan, full of kava and the fear that Nanawa had taken it into his head to play them some dirty trick, instead of running straight, was clinging to a tree before the house of the king, shouting that Karolin was triumphant and her enemies slain, that Nanawa was riding the great south wind, hastening to fight with the men of Karolin.

Then came the peaceful morning, and after that came the next day, and the next, and a week passed, and a fortnight, and still the men of Karolin did not return, and still another fortnight.

Uta would cause himself to be carried on his litter down to the canoe houses and there, resting and reviewing things, he would gaze into the great half-lit interiors of the houses where the long canoes had once rested. He could see the ridge poles and the thatch of the roofs, the rollers and the tackle that had once held the canoes. The great hot wind, broken by a cocoanut grove, had left the houses almost undamaged, but the canoes—where were they? "Of what use are the houses without the canoes?" Uta would say to himself. "Or of what use is life without the men who made the life of Karolin—and my son, Laminai, and my grandsons, where are they?"

He ordered three women to take a fishing canoe and start for the north, find Palm Tree, and see what they could see, but never to come back unless they brought news of the missing ones; and the three women he chose were the wives of Talia, Manua and Leopa, the three men who had been with Sru and who had brought the news of his death to Karolin.

The three wretched women started with food enough for four days and they never came back. Weeks vanished, the days flighting from east to west like gorgeous birds, born in purple dawns and vanishing in amber sunsets, but no word came—nothing but the voice of the bearded sea mumbling on the reef, and the wind in the coco-palms, and the challenge of the gulls.

Uta lost touch with life. For days he would neither speak nor eat. Then, one morning, he called for Le Juan, and she came, her knees knocking together.

"Well," said Uta in a voice suddenly grown strong again, "what have you done with my men? What have you done with Laminai, my son, with his son and the men who went with him? Speak!"

The wretched creature stood without a word. She had been honest; born of a priestess to Nanawa, and brought up in the faith, she had always served faithfully her belief and her god.

She knew his trickery, his capriciousness; how sometimes he would answer a wish favourably and sometimes he would do exactly the reverse of what was desired. He had let her down now once and for all. She could tell that by the light in Uta's eye, which meant death to her.

But though honest, her heart was wicked, and her wicked heart came now to her assistance and she found her voice.

"It is not my fault, O Uta," said Le Juan, "nor the fault of him who speaks through me. Last night in my dreams he revealed his form, and his voice was like the voice of the reef when the great waves come in. The men of Karolin are held by Nanawa, the shark-toothed one, nor will he let them go till a woman of Karolin is given to him, O Kai O fai kanaka [to be staked out on the reef for the sharks to eat]."

"And the name of the woman?" asked Uta.

"It has not been told to me yet," replied the wretched creature, fighting for time in the presence of imminent death.

But Uta had suddenly failed and lost interest. The spurt of energy had passed and the light of rage had faded from his eyes. Perhaps in his inmost heart he knew that nothing availed, that his men had gone where the dead men go, and that all the women of Karolin staked out on the reef for the servants of the shark-toothed one to devour would be a sacrifice offered in vain.

He moved his hand as if dismissing Le Juan. "To-morrow," said Uta. Then, turning on his side, he seemed to forget things, and Le Juan took her departure, saved for the moment.

But the king's women had heard, and in an hour there was not a woman of Karolin who did not know that their men were held by Nanawa and that nothing would free them but the great sacrifice which might fall to the lot of any one of them.

Never for a moment did it occur to any of these unfortunates that, since Nanawa wanted a woman and since Le Juan was a woman, the simplest way out would be to stake Le Juan on the reef.

Not a bit. She was sacred, being a priestess. On Karolin there was not enough morality to divide in two pieces, but there was enough religion of a sort to furnish a world.

By sunset, from Le Juan sweating in her hut, word went forth that the victim had been revealed to her. Nalia, the wife of Leopa, and failing Nalia, her daughter Ooma, a half-witted girl of fourteen.

Never was fox cuter than Le Juan. Nalia was one of the women sent in the canoe to scout for the lost expedition; she had not come back, but she might still come back, so nothing would be done for a while, and in the meantime Uta might die and, Uta once dead, she would have no fear of anything. Having sent this pronouncement abroad, Le Juan set to work whole-heartedly to light a fire and wish Uta dead, and dead quickly.

She might have saved her fire. Uta was dying. The king of Karolin's time had come, and by midnight the fact was known.

It was the night before the new moon, a hot breathless night, and round the king's house the air was filled with the piping and whistling of little shells, tiny varieties of the conch, blown to keep away evil spirits. The surf on the reef sounded low and its respirations were long-spaced, like the breathing of the dying man.

Not a soul was in the house with him, though the whole population of Karolin, every woman and every child, was seated outside in rows and rings beneath the stars.

The chief wife sat by the right doorpost listening, waiting to signal the fact of death, and though not a breath of wind stirred, a vague whispering came and went like the sound the sand makes when the wind blows over it. It was the whispering of the women.

All Uta's life was running about that night outside his house from lip to lip, from memory to memory. The battles he had fought, the children he had begotten, the men he had executed with his own hand or caused to be killed. The fight with the Spanish ship people and the people of the Paumotus. Katafa's name was mentioned—the child whom he had saved from Laminai and who had been drowned and devoured by the sharks. And as they whispered and talked, the lagoon water whispering on the beach seemed telling also of the deeds of the departing one, and in the far rumble of the reef the voice of the outer sea seemed joining in.

If Uta had never loved a human being, he had loved the sea, as the gulls love it, and the fish. It was part of him.

Then suddenly the whispering ceased. The chief wife had risen and was standing erect and motionless, like a brown statue, by the door.

Deceived by a cessation of the breathing in the house, she gave the signal that her lord and master was dead, but scarcely had she raised her arm to lower it again when a voice from the house made her jump as though she had received a slap behind.

The king of Karolin was not the man to depart from this world like a sickly child. He who had entered it shouting eighty-one years ago was not the man to leave it without saying good-bye.

He was calling for his women, calling them to carry him down to the water's edge. "It is hot here," cried Uta. "I wish to be cool. I want the wind."

There was no wind, but they carried him, four women, one at each shoulder and one at each thigh, and lo! as they reached the lagoon edge and placed him on the sand facing the water and propped in their arms, the air stirred with a breath that shivered the star reflections on the lagoon.

The wind of dawn had begun to blow, and in the east beyond the break the dawn itself showed a dubious light that brightened and burned as though day were hurrying to greet Uta and crown him for the last time with the only crown he had ever worn. With the strengthening light the tide could be seen sweeping into the lagoon. It had turned half an hour ago and was coming strong, sweeping past the coral piers from the dim violet sea above which the high flying gulls showed bright with the day.

Uta watched. He was not the man to go out with the tide. The full flood was the time for him when, bravely swimming, his soul might go fearless to the God who made the sharks and the gulls and the kings and peoples of the sea.

He watched the light break on the water, and the brow of the sun rise from the ocean. Then, as the morning lit the lagoon in the whole of its forty-mile stretch, Uta, straightening in the arms of the women, gave a shout.

"They come!"

Past the piers of the break they were coming, the whole fleet of Karolin, sailing against the wind and with all the paddles flashing, gulls wheeling and crying above them, and the flood tide boiling in their wake.

Rising like a young man and swift as a boy, he ran where, curving inwards, they made to beach on the cream-white sand. Laminai, shouting his name, sprang on the outrigger gratings to meet him—and as he sprang on board and they grasped each other, the great canoe, turning, shot up into the eyes of the sun.

But the women saw nothing of this—nothing but the monstrous dead body of Uta that had fallen together, supported in the arms of his wives.

THE CLUB OF MA

"Taori!"

The birds were twittering on the branches above, and the first sunbeams breaking through the leaves.

"Taori!" whispered Katafa, her arm round the neck of the sleeper and her lips close to his ear.

He stirred, raised himself on his elbow, and sat up, sleep dropping from him suddenly, like a cloak.

"Listen!" said Katafa.

Awakening with the first beam of light, she had heard vague and far-away sounds, sounds caught and repeated by the echoes of the hated woods—the woods that had imprisoned her once, that seemed in league against her again—the woods she had always hated, that had always hated her, barring her from the freedom she craved for and the wide spaces that were part of her soul.

301

Karolin was calling and the sea was open and the boat was there ready; nothing was wanting but the dark of the next night, and just in that first clear minute of waking from sleep, with her arm around the man she loved, came a sense of oppression, imprisonment and evil—the woods.

The vision of the copra traders and the great canoe guarding the lagoon was almost forgotten. The sense of hate and imprisonment came from the trees, and maybe in that waking moment her mind had glimpsed the core of things, for it was the trees that had brought the traders.

Then came the far-away sounds: shouts and vague, indefinite noises heard through the movement of the wind in the leaves, now dying to nothing, now more clear and purposeful, almost like the sound of pursuit—it was the sound of search.

The copra traders were combing the groves. The remains of the canoes broken on the beach had given them pause before taking full possession of the place, and they wished to see what might possibly be lurking amidst the trees.

Even as Dick listened, the sounds grew clearer. They would die away as though finished and done with, and then they would break out, of a sudden, closer. There is nothing more deceptive than the trees with their dense patches, their winding runways, their echo-haunted dells, their draughts and stillnesses. Sound enters here like a runner and gets lost, and goes far or fails or drops dead, according to the road it takes, according to the wind it meets, or the absence of wind.

A shout came from the sward. Dick parted the leaves and there, running across the sward towards the house, was a man, a red-bearded man, gun in hand.

Four others came after him, brown and naked, with frizzy black beards, and Dick, whose piercing eyes noted everything, saw the marks on their bodies, marks of old wounds and ringworm sores.

He stooped and picked up the coral-headed club he had found that day on the eastern beach and, resting his hands lightly on it, continued to watch.

They made for the house and surrounded it whilst the red-bearded man went in. Dick could see him inside looking here and there at the shelves, at the walls, and round on the floor as if searching for trace of the owners; then he came out and the whole party disappeared into the grove to the left.

Ten minutes later they reappeared, recrossed the sward, and entered the woods, again making, evidently, for the eastern beach.

"They are gone," said Katafa, "but let us still keep hidden, for they may return."

Dick, without answering, stood listening. "No," said he; "they are gone, but they will not return yet."

He pushed his way through the branches to where the boat was hidden, fetched out a fishing line, caught a robber crab, and, using its flesh for bait, came out and began to fish from the bank in the full light of day. A bream was in the hook in a couple of minutes, and, leaving it for Katafa to clean and prepare, he went straight across the sward to the old fire-hole and began to light a fire.

Then, putting some bread-fruit to bake, he made off behind the house to the shack that the search party had missed, found the old water beaker of the dinghy, filled it at the little well at the back of the yam patch, and returned with it on his shoulder.

He placed it carefully in the boat; then he came back to where Katafa was cooking the fish, and stood with his brow knotted, watching, but scarcely seeing her.

He was reviewing everything in his mind, that mind so simple, yet so straight-thinking and clear-sighted; another person might have been bothering about the strangers and the possibility of their return to the sward, he was thinking of nothing but the journey ahead and the meal in hand.

Having determined to risk being found, he dismissed the matter from his mind.

After standing for a moment like this he suddenly turned, went back to the bank and, having rebaited the hook with the remains of the crab, began to fish again, landing in the course of five minutes or so a three-pound schnapper and another bream. "For to-morrow," said he as he threw them on the ground by the girl and sat down to the meal she had prepared.

Katafa said nothing. Fear was at her heart, she could scarcely eat; every breath of the breeze was a footstep, and the hateful woods that surrounded the sward seemed only waiting to seize her, but she said nothing. The calm, certain courage of Dick bore her along with it, his coolness became part of her, but without destroying the fear that breathed on her from the woods.

Then when the meal was over and Dick, picking up the club that had never left him even when fishing, gave her directions to cook the remaining fish, place them in the boat and stay in the boat till his return, she made no objection, though the fear of being alone was like the fear of death.

"I am going to look," said Dick, "to see if the big canoe is still there and how it lies, and count how many of them there are, and see what they are doing. Wait for me." He swept the sward, the trees and the lagoon with a glance; then he made off, trailing the club towards the eastern trees.

She had played her part so well that he did not guess her terror. He himself had no fear even of the ape-like men; fear had been left out of his composition when he was born in those same woods he was treading now, light of foot, silent as a panther, and as swift on the trail.

Katafa, left to herself, bent her head for a moment as though a heavy hand were pressing it down. Then, straightening herself and flinging out her arms as though casting fear away, she set to on the work before her.

In half an hour it was finished, the fish cooked and wrapped in leaves and placed in the boat, the fire put out, and all traces of the meal cast into the lagoon.

Then, snuggling down in the dinghy, she waited.

Nothing could be more hidden than her position, nothing more secure, yet fear lay with her, clawing at her heart. Never had she felt such fear as this fear, not for herself now, but for Dick.

It was their first parting. She had not known at all what Dick was to her till now, how every fibre of her being was tied to him, and the true and awful meaning of love—the sexless love that is akin to mother love, the one thing deathless, if there is no death.

For a moment she had felt it on that night when the point of Laminai's spear killed *taminan* and self in her and she had flung passion away only to be seized by it again in the arms of Taori.

Since then life had been a dream almost without thought, a happiness whose only stain was the far-off vision of Karolin.

Now alone, with the branches moving above her in the wind, she knew what love really was, the crudest gift the gods ever gave to man, and the most beautiful; the most terrible, and yet the most benign.

As the embryo passes through the forms of all things once embryonic, even of the fish, before it takes the form of man, so had the soul of Katafa passed through all the forms of human soul states in its change from the nebulous to the formed.

Antagonism when Kearney tried to hit her with the whip of seaweed, hatred when he hit her with the tia wood ball, the longing for revenge which brought him death, the boundless irritation that had been born in her from Dick, the mad desire to destroy him, pity born in her at his cry for help, tenderness brought to her by the bird, passion full-grown in a moment and casting her to embrace the living tree, love that turned all other things to nothing, even the spell of *taminan*.

Who finds a soul finds sorrow, and who finds love finds death. Death surely and at last, and almost as surely a hundred little deaths in imagination, absence or estrangement.

She heard the movement of the leaves in the wind and the eternal voice of the surf on the reef, and beyond them the silence so full of possibilities.

Katafa knew more of the world than Dick. Dick was the child of two people who had gone far to a state of savagery, Katafa had been born in civilisation. On Karolin, when she had walked as a ghost amongst ghosts, she had seen terrible things that had left her unmoved owing to the gulf that had separated her from humanity, and now from that past came all sorts of half-formless imaginings threatening Dick.

Time and again she would have left the boat and made for the eastern beach to see what had happened, but for his order. She was to stay in the boat and wait for him. She could not resist that order and, fortunately for them both, she did not try.

As she lay there listening, waiting, loathing her own security and inaction, the one thing giving her comfort and strength was the fact that she was obeying his order. It was as though he had left with her part of his mind, warm, living and sustaining.

An hour passed, and then from the trees came a sound, the sound of something moving swiftly and moving towards her. A form dashed the leaves and branches aside—it was Dick.

The club was trailing from his left hand; his right, grasping a branch, was holding it thrust aside; around his neck a tendril of convolvulus twined as though the woods, worshipping, had wreathed him, and his face was lit with battle, triumph and the light of something terrible that was almost laughter. For a moment he stood there like a god of old time before his worshipper; then, letting the branches close behind him, he slipped into the boat and lay holding her in his arms, his lips almost to her ear.

He had stolen through the trees to spy on the strangers and, drawing towards the eastern beach, had heard the sound of axes at work. The men with holes in their ears and slit noses were cutting down trees away to the right of the beach, in amongst the trees and invisible from the beach. Having watched them through the leaves without being seen, he made for the beach itself. The great canoe was in the lagoon, just as she had been on the night before, and on the sands, walking up and down, were two white men. Men the same as Kearney, only different in face; men with hair on their faces, one red, the other black.

What happened then he told in few words.

Watching the bearded men walking up and down and talking together, the wish came on him to go up to them and look them in the face and speak to them. His pride had somehow risen against the fact that he was hiding there in concealment whilst they were walking free with command of the beach, and besides that there was the wish to speak to them, to hear them speak, to see them closer. Yet something held him back. Caution, maybe—who knows?—but it did not hold him long. Just as though something were pushing him from behind, out he came from the trees and, crossing the sands, approached the two men. They stopped in their walk, turned and stared at him.

Dick's description of the two men was succinct. They stank—gin probably, but whatever it was, it offended his fine sense of smell and the memory of it made him spit over the side of the dinghy as he told of it.

One can fancy that the disgust was written on his beautiful and expressive face as he came towards the strangers, chin uptilted and with level eyes, like an object lesson in what man ought to be, contrasted with what man is; and one may fancy what the products of high civilisation may have felt at the sight of a bloody Kanaka walking as if the world belonged to him as well as the beach, and with a look like that on his mug.

Nothing is so infectious as dislike and distaste, and the gentlemen from the ship exchanged remarks and laughed, and, though Dick had all but forgotten the language of his birth, he knew. An animal would have known what they said and what they thought, for the language of insult is universal, and Dick, standing before them, forgetting Katafa, forgetting everything, replied. Just one word: "Panaka!"

"Panaka" in Karolinese means a dogfish, just as "kanaka" means a shark. Do the Karolinites know the relationship between the two creatures, since they use only a single letter to differentiate one name from the other? Who knows? But the single letter concludes the business as far as insult is concerned, for the shark is feared and respected, the dogfish loathed and despised; it steals the bait, it bites the fish on the hook, it will sometimes attack a man if he is defenceless, or a child. It was Katafa's term of dishonour and reproach for the robber crabs, and scavenger gulls, and the bula fish, all spines and snap, the ink-jetting octopods and the green eels that tangled the lines when caught.

The word heaped with insult had scarcely left Dick's mouth when the red man struck. Dick nearly fell, recovered himself and, with a great half-moon sweep of the club, brought the red man low. Then he chased the black-bearded man for half a hundred yards till reason returned and he remembered the ape-men, Katafa and all the things he ought never to have forgotten.

Shouts from the anchored schooner did not delay his steps as he took cover in the trees, making with all speed for the hidden dinghy.

That was the story he told into Katafa's ear.

"Remembering you, I came back," he finished.

That was the truth. Only for Katafa he would have no doubt done to the black-bearded man what he had done to the red. Heaven knows what the end of the whole adventure might have been, or the end of that dominant and fearless spirit—whether he would have fallen beneath the weight of numbers and been trodden out on the sand, or whether he would have brought the New Hebrideans to heel, taken the schooner, sailed and found civilisation and risen to Napoleonic heights. No one knows where a human rocket may go, once fired, but Katafa and Fate interposed—at least to delay the firing and alter the direction of the line of energy.

They lay listening, yet hearing nothing but the wind and the surf; but they knew that this silence was absolutely deceptive—the woods were full of trickery and the altering of a few points in the wind would cut off or increase sound travelling from a distance.

More, the altering of the time of day made a difference. Here, in the twenty-four hours of a day, leaves, twigs, branches, the very trees themselves, altered in pose or position, and every alteration of the great green curtain interposed or removed barriers to sound. The energy expended in the opening and closing of earth flowers—what mill might it not drive if "properly directed"? And the energy Palm Tree Island expended in a day—who could measure it? It was unknown, or only instinctively known, to Dick and Katafa in the recognition that the sound-carrying qualities of the woods varied with morning, noon and night.

As they lay secure, hidden and listening, Katafa, whose left arm was about the neck of her companion, let her right hand rest on the club that lay beside her.

The cocoanut fibre always wrapped round the club handles in war time, so as to give a better grip, had unwound a bit, and her fingers, straying, felt a ring surrounding the wood, lower down another ring, and lower down another. It was the three-ringed club of Karolin, the sacred pasht always carried by the eldest son of the king or his representative in battle. It had been carried by Laminai in the attack on the Spanish ship long years ago, and recently by Ma, the only son of Laminai. When Dick had killed Ma in the glade, it had lain there in the moonlight and had been picked up by one of the fugitives from the battle, who cast it away on the beach before plunging into the water in his vain attempt to escape.

Katafa knew that it was the royal club, a thing equivalent to a sceptre. She had seen it naked of its cocoanut-fibre wrapping, carried in state, worshipped.

No woman of Karolin dared handle it on pain of death, and as her fingers touched the sacred rings and the fact became clear to her that it was it, a thrill of pride went through her.

It was Dick's.

Karolin's symbol of power and success in war had fallen into the hands of Taori.

She did not know that she was handling the weapon that had slain her mother—the weapon that had fallen into the hands of Taori, not through coincidence, but the iron logic of events.

THE CLUB OF MA (Continued)

Dismiss the clumsy and brutal affair that sculptors have placed in the hand of Hercules, and which inevitably is recalled to mind by the word "club."

The pasht of Karolin might almost have been called a sword, almost likened to a hockey stick. Four feet two inches from extremity to extremity, curved and broadened and flattened at the striking end, with a tip rim of coral morticed to the wood, it could strike with the convexity, the concavity or the flat. It could sever a head if properly used, or make a gash half a foot deep in a man, or simply stun. No man knew its age; the fire-hardened wood of which it was made had ceased to grow on Karolin, and the art by which the coral tip had been morticed to the wood was a forgotten art.

There is no doubt that this terrible weapon had a history as blood-stained as it was long, but it was the blood of battle it had spilt, not the blood of sacrifice and superstition, not the blood of greed and trade. Laminai alone had disgraced it by killing a woman with it. But Laminai was dead, and his sons and his seed destroyed for ever.

Lying by Dick, Katafa told him what she knew about it, showed him the rings on the handle, told him that now, since Ma and all the fighting men of Karolin were gone and Uta of no account, it was his to keep and hold and wield above the heads of all other men.

Talking to him, her voice suddenly ceased. The wind through the branches had brought a sound. Now it came clear, a sound like the cry of hounds in pursuit of game; it died off, grew louder, ceased. Then came another sound, sudden and close, and, bursting through the branches and between the trees so close to the lagoon bank that Dick could have hit him with a biscuit, came a man. He was the black-bearded man of the beach, and he was running for his life. Dick, concealed by the branches, just glimpsed him, but the glimpse was enough. Right on the heels of the fugitive came three of the ape-men, the leader armed with an axe.

They were no longer giving tongue, but he could hear their breath coming as they ran. "Waugh—waugh—waugh."

They passed, then came a shriek from the sward, and then pandemonium.

Dick, listening, with Katafa's arm about him, knew what had happened, but he did not know all, or how that the red-bearded man, the owner of the schooner and the terrible personality that had dominated the expedition, being put out of count, the New Hebrideans, armed with their tree-cutting axes, had risen in revolt. That of the four white men and the dozen Polynesian sailors of the schooner, not one man remained alive; that a hundred and forty Nahanesians held the island in their grasp, the schooner and the trade goods and rum on board of her.

At one stroke the club of Ma had done this work of magic with no magic to help it but that of its own perfect balance and the personality of its wielder.

Safe-hidden in the bushes, they heard the sounds from the sward die down. Then came silence, broken only by the old tune of the reef, the whisper of the wind and the sounds of the birds in the branches.

THE FÊTE OF DEATH

It was close on midnight and the ebb, running strong, showed through the branches an occasional lazy swirl on the moonlit lagoon water.

At the break it was racing strong, but here the water seemed hardly to move. The wind still held from the north, and as Dick untied from the tree roots, it parted and closed the branches above, showering Katafa with moonlight and shadow. He pushed off with a scull and before he could take his seat again, the current, lazy though it looked, had slewed the bow of the little boat right round.

They had settled to get away when the schooner people were asleep, but sleep was far from the island that night, to judge by the vague sounds that came from the east between the breathings of the wind.

But the tide was outrunning and the hour was come, and Dick was not of the order that waits for a better opportunity.

Stepping the mast with the sail lightly brailed and ready to break out, he took the sculls, and the moonlit glade and the cape of wild cocoanuts passed behind them out of sight for ever.

And now as they moved swiftly, great ripples running out from the divided water and spreading towards bank and reef, Katafa, who was steering, saw something beyond the tree-tops, a rose-red, pulsating light that seemed fighting the light of the moon, and, above the light, smoke like blown hair streaming on the wind towards the south; and now as the dinghy, driven by sculls and current, drew on to the great curve that led to the eastern beach, the sounds that had reached them by the sward loudened and became more shrill, and through the voices of men outshouting gulls, and gulls outshouting men, came a new sound, sudden, sonorous and without cease, the roar of flame triumphant.

The dinghy turned the last cape into a world of light. The schooner, fired by accident or design and straining at her anchor chain, was blazing against the night like a bonfire. Lagoon, reef and woods were lit broad as by day and, crossing the roar of the flames, the shouting of the reef gulls came mixing with the yelling from the beach, where a hundred black forms danced and sang and screeched, mad with the black joy of rum and destruction.

It was like breaking into a fête.

At a stroke the desolation of the Island was shattered and the world, holding clamorous festival, had taken the beach. Katafa, half standing up for a moment with the red light shining on her face, gazed fascinated with the terrible glamour of the thing. Then she sank back, steadily steering right for the broad fairway between ship and shore.

Dick shouted to her, she knew, and, leaving the tiller for a moment, leaned over him, unbrailed the sail, and gave it to the following wind.

Then, as the boat raced for salvation and without releasing the tiller, she saw two things; to left, and for a moment, the blazing schooner pouring flame to the sky, roaring at her, scorching her, and with its bowsprit festooned with wretches who dared not drop into the shark-filled lagoon, to right the white beach a stone's throw away, and, racing the boat along the beach, shouting at her, threatening her, a great crowd of men naked, black and mad with rum.

Then, in a flash, all this was wiped out and the fire-lit concave of the sail was before her, outlined on the calm night beyond.

Dick, who had spoken no word since his order to her, half rose. She saw his face lit by the retreating blaze, and the rage and hatred in it. She saw him fling out his arm at the beach and schooner, and she heard his voice shrill against the cries that followed him. It was the cry that the companions of Sru had hurled at him long ago.

"Kara! Kara! Kara!" "War! War! War!"

Turning, he brailed the sail and seized again the sculls. The dinghy was rocking and racing in the confluence of the floods from the arms of the lagoon.

They passed the palm tree in the northern pier of the break as an arrow passes the mark, tossed to the meeting of current and flood, and with sail filling again headed south against the long heave of the Pacific. Behind them lay the glow of the still burning wreck, which was seen that night at Karolin.

FROM GARDEN TO GARDEN LIKE SEEDS ON THE WIND

Here there was peace. The great dark swell coming up and passing in the moonlight, the following wind, the stars—nothing remained but these, these and the whisper of the reef far astern, and the far glow of the burning ship.

Katafa steered, the great bunch of bananas up against her legs, Nan on his stick beside her, the head of Nan hanging over the transom like the head of a person contemplating seasickness.

They had never thought of dishonouring him by taking him off his stick. He was something real to them, and, without thinking back and putting things together, they felt that he was an influence in their lives.

He was. Only for him Sru would not have landed to be killed, the army and navy of Karolin would never have sailed to break the charm of *taminan*. Only for him the idea of making a mast for the dinghy would never have occurred to Dick, for it was the cut sapling that gave him the idea. Only for the mast the idea of journeying to Karolin would never have arisen.

Nan had literally put the club of Ma into the hands of Dick; the blazing schooner, the dread white men, the revolt of the Melanesians, all these were part of the work of Nan, who seemed only a cocoanut, but was yet an idea. The fish, the bread-fruit, the water beaker, and all the odds and ends they had brought away were stowed some in the stern sheets and some amidships, whilst in the bow reposed the little ships, like the toys of these children who had never learned to play with toys, but with men and events and with Destiny itself.

The wind blew steady and strong from the north.

Palm Tree had never depended on the trades. Owing to the influence of the Low Archipelago, the Trade Law did not hold either here or at Karolin; neither could the strength of the northern-runnning current be depended on—south winds increased its rate of flow. North winds decreased it. To-night the dinghy had to face only a knot-and-a-half current.

Towards ten o'clock in the morning the far glow of the burning schooner suddenly vanished from the northern sky. The sound of the reef had been left long ago astern. Nothing remained but the sea, the wind and the stars.

Dick, who had not spoken for some time, had slipped down into the bottom of the boat and was leaning his arm on the thwart and his head on his arm. He was asleep. Katafa did not awaken him. She was almost glad to be alone in these first solemn hours of return to all that her heart desired. The frigate bird had found its home again among the infinite sea distances, and the wide-spaced columns of the swell, as they passed, saluted her.

Now to port the tremendous vagueness and secrecy of the night began to give before something that seemed less like light than life; the sky showed scarcely a change, yet the sea had altered and now, low in the east, dim, red and luminous, like the banked smoke of burning cities, a line of mist lay suddenly revealed above the line of sea.

A gull passed the boat, soaring on the wind, and the wind whipped the sea with renewed life and freshness, and the sea cast its spray at Katafa as she steered, her eyes wandering from the sail to the old and accustomed glory, the wild, triumphant splendour of the east aflame.

Two great zones of light, like the knees of the angel of the dawn, showed, and, far above, wings in tumultuous colour and wide-spread arms of light struggling as if to smash down the crystal doors—and then, tumult dying and colour fading, at a stroke the western sky showed not a single star and in the eastern sky stood day.

Dick awoke from sleep with the sun half lifted above the horizon. Creeping aft, he took his place beside Katafa, but though she gave the tiller to him and, slipping down, rested her head against her knee, she could not sleep.

The island they had left vanished utterly from sight; they were alone with the sea, and now for the first time came doubt.

She knew the sea and its absolute infidelity, its traps and surprises, should they not find Karolin; should some storm rise suddenly and blow them into the unknown east, or the west where the dead men warm themselves round the dying sun!

She glanced up at Dick—Dick, beautiful as the god of youth and as serene—Dick, who had only known the waters of the lagoon and the sea beyond the reef and who was gazing now at the sea itself, untroubled by its vastness and unafraid.

Whilst her eyes held him she knew no fear, but when her eyes left him doubt returned. She had been so long separated from the sea that the guiding sense and instinct that served the fishermen for compass had all but deserted her. She felt lost.

She had forgotten the guiding sign placed long ago above the great lagoon by God, whose garden is Nature and whose rivers are the currents of the sea. Dick, perhaps divining her trouble by that subtle sense which enabled them to communicate without words, leaned sideways towards her as he steered and, letting the boat a few points off her course, pointed to where, far ahead, the light of the great lagoon formed its wan, miraculous window in the sky.

THE BIRTH OF A SEA KING

They had with them food and water enough for a week. Dick had left little to chance. When a tiny child, he had almost frightened Kearney by putting the fish away in the shadow of the thwart to prevent the sun from spoiling it, and this natural ability for dealing with things, which had been a gift from his parents, had not been decreased by life on the island.

Now, with all he had ever known taken away from him by distance, facing a new world and the unknown sea, this ability to deal with things showed itself in his fearlessness and absolute confidence in himself, the boat and the course they were steering.

By noon they had been twelve hours on their journey, making two and a half knots against the current. Thirty miles to the north lay Palm Tree, whilst in the south, like a beacon, the forty-mile lagoon of Karolin signalled to them from the blue; and now, as it drew towards sunset, Katafa, who had fallen asleep, awoke and, sitting up, seemed listening as though to catch the sound of something she had heard in her dreams.

There was nothing, nothing but the slap of the bow wash and the creak of the mast and the lapping of the long swell as it kissed the planks, nothing but the cry of a gull that passed them. It was flying south.

Yet still she listened, resting her head against the gunnel, her eyes fixed on the space of sky beneath the sail. Nothing.

Then, as the sun, now far down in the west, was reaching to the sea that boiled up in gold to meet him, Katafa raised her head.

Dick heard it now, a faint, far breathing, a murmur that came and passed and came again, a voice that was not the wind.

It was Karolin—Karolin invisible but singing, calling the gulls home across the evening sea.

Far away they could be seen flying from east and west towards the invisible land, and now as the sun went down like a ship on fire and a single great star broke out above the purple west, the whisper of the great forty-mile reef loudened and changed to a definite murmur like the voice of a far-off multitude.

Katafa, standing up for a moment and steadying herself with her hand on the mast, seemed to have forgotten Dick. Karolin was still a great way off, but its voice was enough to dispel all doubt and fear. She knew these waters, and all the old sea instincts that had given her distance and direction when out in the fishing canoes returned, led by memory and the voice of the reef.

The fishing bank where the squall had struck her canoe, blowing Taiofa overboard, lay straight before them. They could anchor there for the night; it was safer to make the lagoon entrance in the morning.

She told him this, and then, resting in the bottom of the boat with her elbow on a thwart, she watched and listened whilst the moon and the stars took the sky, and the voice of the distant reef came louder against the wind.

The tide was beginning to flood on Karolin, and the air was filled with the rumour of it; it seemed the wind and tide were building the sea on the coral, to come from everywhere around, from the very stars that lit the night.

Then the running swell, looming up and passing in the gloom, altered in character, and away to starboard something showed white—something that came

314

and went like the flicker of a handkerchief, a natural sea beacon, the foam on the Kanaka rock.

Katafa knew. They were on the fishing bank.

The Kanaka rises sharp, like the spire of a cathedral, from the great mountain range that forms the palu bank. At full flood it is submerged entirely, but even then it will break if there is a heavy swell on. It is the only sign of the bank and the only danger to ships, but to Katafa it was a friend.

Crawling forward, whilst Dick let go the sheet, she dropped the anchor they had so often used when fishing off Palm Tree; it fell in twelve-fathom water and held.

It was near here that she had anchored when the squall struck the canoe, driving her from Karolin, but to-night there was no danger of squalls. The wind had sunk to a steady breathing from the north, and the swell had fallen to a gentle heave that rocked the little boat like a cradle to the lullaby of the surf.

Dick, tired out, had fallen asleep lying in the bottom of the boat, clasped by the girl, just as his father had fallen asleep long years ago clasped by Emmeline and death.

But death was far away to-night. Life ringed the sleepers with its charm, and the future spoke in the voice of the reef.

"Taori, Karolin has called you to be her king and rule her people and make her laws and break her chains of error; for this you were born, for this you still live, and war shall be your portion whilst you live, and peace shall crown your victories and lead you at last to the eternal peace which is Freedom."

With his head on the pasht, unconscious as the dead, he slept whilst the sea wind blew and the great reef sang, mourned, murmured and spoke.

HIS KINGDOM

Broad as the reef break was at Karolin, no ship under sail could enter at the full ebb. Sweeping with an eight-knot clip and boiling round the coral piers, the waters of the great lagoon met the northward-running current in a leaping cross-sea of aquamarine and emerald whipped to snow when the wind was in the east. At slack all this died away; a child might have swum the passage and a leaf would have drifted with scarce a change of place. This was the sea gate of Karolin, and the keepers of the gate were the sun and the moon.

The sun and the moon and the wind and the sea—these four held the great atoll between them and had here a significance unguessed by dwellers on the continents and lands of the world; for here the new and the full moons were manifestly the letters-in of the great spring tides, and the first- and third-quarter moons the admitters of the neaps. Here the sun was seen from his rising to his setting, from his leap to his plunge, and storm and halcyon cast their spells on life, unbroken and uninterfered with by hills or walls or mountains or forests.

Here for undated ages man had lived alone with the sea and the gulls and the fish, and had remained man, learning little, forgetting nothing, with a memory and tradition kept alive by the necessities of the moment that urged him to build canoes as his forefathers had built them, and houses to shelter the canoes, and houses to protect him from the rains and winds.

Here there was nothing that did not date from the remote past, nothing that was not of use in the immediate present.

So is it with the beavers and the ants and the bees, whose work ever advances from the time of Nineveh and beyond, yet never advances to the future, who build as they built, who live as they lived, who die as they died, and as first they built and lived and died in the garden of God, which is Nature.

Only man can change, only man can live for ages without change, yet remain capable of change, only man can be sealed away in the land of instinct, yet remain capable of entering the land of reason.

So was it with the people of Karolin gathered together this morning on the beach by the gridiron of coral where for ages past victims had been sacrificed to Nanawa, the shark-toothed one, by his priests and through the agency of his servants, the sharks.

Le Juan, after the death of Uta Matu, had temporised. She did not in the least mind sacrificing the half-witted girl Ooma, but she greatly dreaded barren results.

Including the king's wives, there were over two hundred women on Karolin, all wanting their men back, and close on three hundred children, more than half of which were boys. Of these boys a large number were over twelve and a good number over fourteen, all ripe for mischief, without much fear of Nanawa, and with the antagonism of all boys towards old women of Le Juan's type.

Le Juan had sent the fathers and husbands of this terrible population to a war from which they had not returned, and, worse than that, she had made herself responsible, under Nanawa, for their return.

316

She had declared that they were "held" by Nanawa till the great sacrifice of a woman had been offered to him, yet, feeling that the tricky shark god had played her another trick, she simply dared not make the sacrifice. She knew what would happen if it failed; she felt the temper of the people as a man feels the sharp point of a dagger against his breast, so, as before said, she temporised, fell into pretended trances, had pretended visions, declared that nothing was to be done until it was absolutely sure that the mother of Ooma would not return, and sweated consumedly at night as she lay in her shack listening to the sounds of the village and the shouting of the ribald boys and the boom of the surf on the reef, whilst Ooma, half-witted and happy, slept protected from death by the ferocious beast that was the soul of Le Juan and whose one dread was extinction—through failure.

But the time had come, and the death warrant was sealed by the far red speck of light on the northern sky caused by the burning of the schooner.

A boy had seen it, two minutes later the whole village was watching it, and next day it had got into the minds of the people. It was looked on as a sign—of what, no one could say—but it was an angry sign, and that night Nalia, the chief wife of the dead Uta, had a dream.

She dreamt that Uta appeared to her and that the red light was his wrath that the great sacrifice had not been made. He also declared that if it was not made at once, worse would befall Karolin. That was the end. Before dawn Le Juan, dragged from her hut to hear the news, gave in, and as the sun broke above the lagoon the preparations began.

Ooma, awakening to another happy day of life, was anointed and rubbed with palm oil to make her acceptable to the god. She laughed with pleasure. She was of the happy half-witted kind with sense enough to know that she was being fêted; when they put flowers in her hair she laughed and laughed, and when they led her by the hand to a suddenly prepared banquet where she alone was the guest, she went laughing, the boys dancing around her and shouting: "Karak, O he, Ooma, karaka."

The last of the tide was flowing out of the lagoon when, the banquet over, Le Juan, taking the hand of Ooma, led her along by the waterside, followed by the whole population of Karolin.

By the break great sheets and coils of glass-smooth water, pale as forget-me-nots, could be seen moving between the wind-flaws where a half-dead breeze touched the surface; ahead of the advancing crowd the gridiron of coral lay almost entirely uncovered by the tide.

Nature, with that assistance which she sometimes lends to inhumanity, had tilted this terrible shelf so that the gradually rising water would take the victim to the waist at greater flood; art had driven in iron bars for the binding.

At quarter-flood or before, the sharks, who always knew what was going on, instructed maybe by Nanawa, would begin their struggle for the prize.

As the procession approached the gridiron, Ooma suddenly began to hold back.

Some instinctive warning had come to her that danger lay ahead, that all things were not as they pictured themselves to be; that the flowers and the feasting and all the splendours of that most glorious morning of her life were veils of illusion behind which lay Terror.

She stopped, trying to release her hand from the grip of Le Juan, then, struggling with her captor, she began to scream. They seized her, still screaming, and brutally cast her on the coral, binding her to it by each thigh, by the wrist and by the shoulders. Then, as she lay there half-stunned, voiceless, and staring the sky, suddenly from the great ring of the atoll rising to heaven like a protest, came a sigh, profound from the very heart of the sea. It was the turning of the tide.

CHAPTER THE LAST

At sunrise that morning Katafa had awakened to find the wind fallen to a gentle breeze. Away to the south she could see the palms of Karolin, and across the scarcely ruffled swell she could hear the song of the surf on the coral.

The Kanaka rock spouting to starboard told her the state of the tide; it was falling. Hours must elapse before they could make the break with the flood, so, instead of waking Dick, who was still soundly asleep, she sat watching the gulls and the wind-flaws on the water, listening, dreaming.

Far away over the past her mind flitted like the frigate bird, her namesake, tireless, covering vast distances. She saw again the reef where she had wandered as a child, that endless sunlit coral road, the sea wrack and the shells and the gulls always flying, the beaches where she had played like a ghost child with children untouchable as ghosts. The vast sunsets, the tumultuous dawns, the nights when, under the coil of the great snake, she had watched the torches of the fish-spearers on the reef, and the night when, under the sickle moon, the sea had taken her and swept her away to find love and a soul.

A gull sweeping past saluted the boat with a cry and Dick, stirring in his sleep, awoke, stretched, held out his arms and then clasped them around Katafa, gazing as she pointed away to the south, where every lift of the swell showed the palms of the great atoll whose mirror blaze was paling the sky.

Then hauling in the anchor and setting the sail to the light wind that had shifted to the west of north, Katafa steered, heading for the east, whilst Dick handed her food and water from the beaker, eating scarcely anything himself.

His eyes were fixed on the far-off shore to starboard, the endless shore that showed nothing but gulls and palms, foam jets when a greater breaker broke on the coral, all seen against air luminous with the dazzle of the vast lagoon.

And now, still following the turn of the reef, Katafa pointed ahead where, far away past the northern pier of the break, the whole sea danced as the outpouring waters met the current, the last of the ebb rushing like a river, foam dashed, jubilant, green against blue, white against green and gulls over all, gulls wheeling and shouting and diving and drifting on the wind like turbulent spirits on the sun blaze. Katafa held on still steering due east as though to leave Karolin behind, on and on till the vast sea disclosed itself to the south and the turmoil at the break died and oiled away into the slack. Deep in the knowledge of those waters, she held on steering now to the southwest against the current; then, turning the boat at last, she made due west. The wind had freshened and backed to the east of north as if to help them, yet it was half-flood before the piers of the break showed clear before them, the water pouring in and lashing the coral, leaping on the outer beach and filling the air with its fume and song; great fish went with them, albacores leaping like whirled swords, bream, garfish, all in the grip of the mighty river of the flood.

And now the blue and blazing lagoon, where the fleets of the world might have harboured, flung out its mighty arms, the roar and thunder and spray of the breakers saluted them, and then, under a storm of gulls, the spray and thunder and torrent of the sea passed like a dream, and before them, across the untroubled waters, lay the white beach where Uta Matu had watched the dawn and the return of the fleet that never more could return.

The beach was crowded. It was half-flood, and the sharks had snatched away the last of the last offering ever to be made to the great god Nanawa. Steering for the beach, Katafa saw nothing but the crowd—women, children, boys, all lined by the water's edge, dumb, with scarcely a movement, watching the approaching boat that had appeared as if in answer to the sacrifice of Ooma.

Amongst them stood Le Juan, and as she watched, wondering like the others and as dumb, the rapidly approaching boat called up in her mind a vision from far away—the boat of the Spanish ship of years ago, the ship that had brought Katafa and whose timbers lay sunk ten fathoms deep, crusted by the ever-building coral.

She saw in the boat the answer of Nanawa, the evil god who was to play her one last trick, for, as the prow dashed on the sand, and as though the god had suddenly stripped a curtain aside, she saw Katafa.

Ah, the spirit of prophecy had not been denied to her those long years ago when, urging Uta Matu to destroy the child, she saw in her the agent of revenge for the murdered papalagi. Katafa, who had brought Taiofa to his death and Sru, Laminai, and all the men of Karolin. Katafa, who had destroyed half a nation to re-create it. Katafa, who had vanished to return, a woman beautiful like a star risen from the sea.

She saw nothing else, neither Taori, who stood on the sands beside the girl, nor the people, who had surged back as the cry rang along the beach: "Katafa, from the dead she has returned, Katafa!"

She saw neither the boat that the lagoon waves were driving broadside on to the sand, nor the lagoon, nor the sky beyond; like a beast the spirit that had dwelt with her always swelled and seized her and shook her and spoke, spoke in words that were strange and unknown as though it had flung human speech aside for the language of the devils.

Then, as though the great hand that had used her was crushing her and dropping her, she fell, and with her the power of Nanawa for ever.

The sun was near his setting, and in the evening light Nan stood on his post erected by the house of Uta, once king of Karolin, and in the house, dimly to be seen, were the little ships of Taori, toys of the long ago, symbols now of the sea power that he dreamed of vaguely as he stood in the sunset on the reef with Katafa, and facing the line of the empty canoe houses.

Only yesterday he had stood armed with the pasht by the dead body of Le Juan whilst the people, listening to the words of Katafa, proclaimed him their chief; yet by this evening he had visited the canoe houses and had sent fisher-boys to the southern beach to fetch Aioma, Falia and Tafuta, the three old men, too old for war, but canoe-builders all of them, and holding between them the secret of the construction of the great war canoes.

For to Dick, standing with uptilted chin before the women and the children and the boys who, with the sure instinct of children and women and boys, had seen in him their ruler, a vision had come, God-sent, of the world that lay beyond the world he knew. He had seen again Ma in the moonlight, and the spear of Laminai, the red-bearded man he had put to death, and, the black-bearded man chased through the woods, the burning schooner and the ape-men who still held the beach of Palm Tree; and as he looked on Katafa, on the women and helpless children, on the boys growing towards war age but still unripe, the great knowledge came to him, as it came to the earliest men who fronted the wolf, that strength is possession, and that without possession love is a mockery—that dreams based on unreality are dreams.

They turned from the canoe houses and came along the reef. Here, on the outer beach, the village far behind them, they sat down to rest.

It was the first time they had found themselves alone since leaving Palm Tree. All last night the village had hummed around them, bonfires burning all along the coral and bonfires answering from the southern beach, conch answering conch, whilst the great stars watched and the breakers thundered as they had thundered at the coming of Uta Matu to power, of Uta Maru, his father, and all the line of the kings of Karolin stretching to the remote past, but never beyond the voice of the sea.

Here they were at last alone, all trouble done with for the moment, the past like a tempestuous sea, the future veiled and vague, but great and full of the splendours of Promise.

For a moment neither of them spoke, their eyes following the spray clouds of the breakers and the flighting gulls wheeling above the flooding sea. Then as they turned one to the other, and as he seized her by the shoulders, to Katafa for the first time fully came the knowledge of the splendour of man crowned with power—man triumphant, mighty, kingly and dominant. For in the past few hours Taori had changed from the passionate boy to a man fit to be the ruler of men.

Holding her from him for a moment, his head drawn back like the head of a cobra, he consumed her with his eyes.

Then he struck, crushing her with his arms, his lips to her lips, her throat, her breast, whilst the full-flooding sea shook the coral with its thunder and the gulls in great circles swung chanting above the haze of the spray.

321

As the sea touched the horizon, pouring its gold across the outgoing tide, Katafa, turning from her lover and sweeping the sea with her eyes, saw floating far above the northern sky-line something that was not cloud, that was not land, that was not sea. The ghost of an island, lonely and illusive as the land where in his dream Lestrange had met his vanished children.

Palm Tree, far lifted above all things earthly—by mirage.

THE END

The Gates of Morning
Contents

BOOK IV

BOOK I

THE CANOE BUILDER

Dick standing on a ledge of coral cast his eyes to the South.

Behind him the breakers of the outer sea thundered and the spindrift scattered on the wind; before him stretched an ocean calm as a lake, infinite, blue, and flown about by the fishing gulls—the lagoon of Karolin.

Clipped by its forty-mile ring of coral this great pond was a sea in itself, a sea of storm in heavy winds, a lake of azure, in light airs—and it was his—he who had landed here only yesterday.

Women, children, youths, all the tribe to be seen busy along the beach in the blazing sun, fishing with nets, playing their games or working on the paraka patches, all were his people. His were the canoes drawn up on the sand and his the empty houses where the war canoes had once rested on their rollers.

Then as he cast his eyes from the lagoon to the canoe houses his brow contracted, and, turning his back to the lagoon he stood facing the breakers on the outer beach and the northern sea. Away there, beyond the sea line, invisible, lay Palm Tree, an island beautiful as a dream, yet swarming with devils.

Little Tari the son of Le Taioi the net maker, sitting on the coral close by, looked up at him. Tari knew little of life, but he knew that all the men of Karolin swept away by war had left the women and the boys and the children like himself defenseless and without a man or leader.

Then, yesterday, from the northern sea in a strange boat and with Katafa, the girl who had been blown to sea years ago when out fishing, this strange new figure had come, sent by the gods, so the women said, to be their chief and ruler.

The child knew nothing of whom the gods might be nor did he care, alone now with this wonderful new person, and out of earshot of his mother, he put the question direct with all the simplicity of childhood.

"Taori," said little Tari, "who are you?" (é kamina tai)

Could Dick have answered, would the child have understood the strange words of the strange story Dick might have told him? "Tari, I come of people beyond the world you know. My name is Dick Lestrange, and when I was smaller than you, Tari, I was left alone with an old sailor man on that island you call Marua (Palm Tree), which lies beyond sight fifty miles to the north. There we lived and there I grew to be a boy and Kearney, that was his name, taught me to fish and spear fish, and he made for me things to play with, little ships unlike the canoes of the islands. And then, Tari, one day long ago came Katafa, the girl who was blown away from here in a storm. She lived with us till Kearney died and then we two were alone. She taught me her language, which is the language of Karolin. She named me Taori; we loved one another and might have lived forever at Marua had not a great ship come there filled with bad men, men from the eastern islands of Melanesia. They came to cut the trees. Then they rose and killed the white men with them and burned the ship and in our boat we escaped from them, taking with us everything we loved, even the little ships, and steering for Karolin, we came, led by the lagoon light in the sky."

But he could not tell Tari this, or at least all of it, for the very name of Dick had passed from his memory, that and the language he had spoken as a child; Kearney, the sailor who had brought him up, was all but forgotten, all but lost sight of in the luminous haze that was his past.

The past, for men long shipwrecked and alone, becomes blurred and fogged, for Dick it began only with the coming of Katafa to Marua, behind and beyond that all was forgotten as though consumed in the great blaze of tropic light that bathed the island and the sea, the storms that swept the coconut groves, the mists of the rainy seasons. Kearney would have been quite forgotten but for the little ships he had made as playthings for the boy—who was now a man.

He looked down at the questioning child. "I am Taori, Tari tatu, why do you ask?"

"I do not know," said the child. "I ask as I breathe but no big folk—madyana—will ever answer the questions of Tari— Ai, the fish!" His facile mind had already dropped the subject, attracted by the cries of some children, hauling in a net, and he rose and trotted away.

Dick turned his gaze again to the north. The question of the child had stirred his mind and he saw again the schooner that had put in to Palm Tree only to be burned by the Melanesian hands, he saw again Katafa and himself as they made their escape in the old dinghy that Kearney had taught him to handle as a boy. He saw their landing on this beach, yesterday, and the women and, children swarming round him, he the man whom they considered sent by the gods to be their chief and leader.

Then as he gazed towards the north the memory of the men from whom he had escaped with the girl stained the beauty of sea and sky.

H. de Vere Stacpoole

There was no immediate fear of the men who had taken possession of Palm Tree; the men of Palm Tree had no canoes, but they would build canoes—surely they would build canoes, and as surely they would see the far mirror blaze of Karolin lagoon in the sky, just as he had seen it, and they would come. It might be a very long time yet, but they would come.

Dick was an all but blook, a kanaka, a savage, and yet the white man was there. He could think forward, he could think round a subject and he could imagine.

That was why he had sent a canoe that morning across to the southern beach to fetch Aioma, Palia and Tafata, three old men, too old for war, but expert canoe-builders, that was why when gazing at the tribe in full congregation, his eyes had brightened to the fact that nearly a hundred of the youths were ripening to war age, but under all, lighting and animating his mind, raising daring to eagle heights, lay his passion for Katafa, his other self more dear to him than self, threatened, ever so vaguely, yet still threatened.

War canoes! Did he intend fighting any invaders in the lagoon or as they drew towards shore, or did he vaguely intend to be the attacker, destroying the danger at its source before it could develop? Who knows?

*

A hand fell upon his shoulder and turning, he found himself face to face with Katafa, a lock of her dark hair escaped from the thread of elastic vine that bound it, blew right back on the breeze like an eagle's feather, and her eyes, luminous and dark instead of meeting his, were fixed towards the point where he had been gazing—the due-north sea line.

"Look!" said Katafa.

At big intervals and in certain conditions of weather Palm Tree, though far behind the sea line, became visible from Karolin through mirage. Last evening they had seen it and now again it was beginning to live, to bloom, to come to life, a mysterious stain low down in the southern sky, a dull spot in the sea dazzle, that deepened by degrees and hardened till as if sketched in by some unseen painter, the island showed beautiful as a dream, diaphanous, yet vivid.

With her hand upon his shoulder they stood without speaking, their minds untutored, knowing nothing of mirage, their eyes fixed on the place from which they had escaped and which was rising now so strangely beyond the far sea line as if to gaze at them.

327

They saw again the horde of savages on the beach, figures monstrous as the forms in a nightmare, they felt again the wind that filled the sail as the dinghy raced for safety and the open sea, and again they heard the yells of the Melanesians mad with rum stolen from the schooner they had brought in, and which they had burnt. And there, there before them lay the scene of the Tragedy, that lovely picture which showed nothing of the demons that still inhabited it.

Then as Dick gazed on this loveliness, which was yet a threat and a warning, his nostrils expanded and his eyes grew dark with hate. They had threatened him—that was nothing, they had threatened Katafa, that was everything—and they still threatened her.

Some day they would come. The vision of Palm Tree seemed to repeat what instinct told him. They would build canoes and seeing the lagoon mirror-light in the sky, they would come. They had no women, those men, and here were women, and instinct half whispered to him that just as he had been drawn to Katafa, so would these men be drawn to the women of Karolin. They would scan the horizon in search of some island whose tribe might be raided of its women and seeing the lagoon light they would come.

Ah, if he had known, danger lay not only to the north, but wherever greed or desire or hatred might roam on that azure sea, not only amongst savages, but the wolves of civilization.

To Dick there was no world beyond the world of water that ringed the two islands; no Europe, no America, no history but the history of his short life as the life of Katafa, and yet even in that life, short as it was, he had learned to dread men and he had envisaged the foundation of all history—man's instinct for war, rapine and destruction.

Then gradually the vision of Palm Tree began to fade and pass, suddenly it vanished like a light blown out and as they turned from the sea to the lagoon, Katafa pointed across the lagoon water to a canoe approaching from the southern beach.

It was the canoe Dick has sent for the canoe builders and, leaving the coral, they came down to the white sand of the inner beach to meet it.

H. de Vere Stacpoole

THE REVOLT OF THE OLD MEN

Two women were in it, and as they drove it ashore beaching it with the outrigger a-tilt, Dick, followed by Katafa, approached, and resting his hand on the mast stays attached to the outrigger gratings, he turned to the women, who, springing out, stood, paddles in hand, looking from him to Katafa.

"And the builders?" asked he, "where are they?" The shorter woman clucked her tongue and turned her face away towards the lagoon, the taller one looked Dick straight in the face.

"They will not come," said she. "They say Uta Matu alone was their king and he is dead, also they say they are too old. 'A mataya ayana'—they are feeble and near past the fishing, even in the quiet water."

The shorter woman choked as if over a laugh, then she turned straight to Dick.

"They will not come, Taori, all else is talk."

She was right. The express order had gone to them to cross over and they refused; they would not acknowledge the newcomer as their chief, all else was talk.

Several villagers, seeing the canoe beaching, had run up and were listening, more were coming along. Already the subject was under whispered discussion amongst the group by the canoe, whilst Dick, his foot resting on the slightly tilted outrigger, stood, his eyes fixed on the sennit binding of the outrigger pole as if studying it profoundly.

The blaze of anger that had come into his eyes on hearing the news had passed; anger had given place to thought.

This was no ordinary business. Dick had never heard the word "revolt," nor the word "authority," but he could think quite well without them. The only men who could direct the building of the big war canoes refused to work, and from the tone and looks of the women who brought the message, he saw quite clearly that if something were not done to bring the canoe-builders to heel, his power to make the natives do things would be gone.

Dick never wasted much time in thought. He turned from the canoe, raced up to the house where the little ships were carefully stored and came racing back with a fish spear.

Then, calling to the women, he helped to run the canoe out, sprang on board and helped to raise the mat sail to the wind coming in from the break.

329

"I will soon return," he cried to Katafa, his voice borne across the sparkling water on a slant of the wind; then the women crouched down to ballast the canoe, and with the steering paddle in his hand he steered.

The canoe that had brought Katafa drifting to Palm Tree years ago had been the first South Sea island craft that the boy had seen. The fascination of it had remained with him. This canoe was bigger, broader of beam and the long skate-shaped piece of wood that formed the outrigger was connected with it not by outrigger poles but by a bridge.

Dick, as he steered, took in every little detail, the rattans of the grating, the way the mast stays were fixed to the grating and how the mast itself was stepped, the outrigger and the curve of its ends, the mat sail and the way it was fastened to the yard.

Though he had never steered a canoe before, the sea-craft inborn in him carried him through, and the women crouching and watching and noting every detail saw nothing indicative of indecision.

Now there are two ways in which one may upset a canoe of this sort by bad handling, one is to let the outrigger leave the water and tilt too high in the air, the other is to let the outrigger dip too deep in the water.

Dick seemed to know, and as they crossed the big lift of sea coming in with the flood from the break, he avoided both dangers.

The beach where the remnants of the southern tribe lived, was exactly opposite to the beach of the northern tribe, and as both beaches were close to the break in the reef, the distance from one to the other was little over a mile. Then as they drew close, Dick could see more distinctly the few remaining huts under the shelter of a grove of Jack-fruit trees; beyond the Jack-fruit stood pandanus palms bending lagoonward, and three tall coconut palms sharp against the white up-flaring horizon.

As the canoe beached, Dick saw the rebels. They were seated on the sand close to the most easterly of the huts, seated in the shadow of the Jack-fruit leaves; three old men seated, two with their knees up and one tailor fashion, whilst close to them by the edge of a little pool lay a girl.

As Dick drew near followed by the taller of the boat women, the girl, who had been gazing into the waters of the pool, looked up.

She was Le Moan, granddaughter of Le Juan, the witch woman of Karolin now dead and gone to meet judgment for the destruction she had caused. Le Moan was only fourteen. She had heard of the coming of the new ruler to Karolin and of his bringing with him Katafa, the girl long thought to be dead. She had heard the order given to her grandfather Aioma that morning to come at once to the northern beach as the new chief required canoes to be built, and she had heard the old man's refusal. Le Moan had wondered what this new chief might be like. The monstrous great figure of Uta Matu, last king of Karolin, had come up in memory at the word "chief," and now, as the canoe was hauled up and the women cried out "He comes," she saw Dick.

Dick with the sun on his face and on his red-gold hair, Dick naked and honey-coloured, lithe as a panther and straight as a stabbing spear. Dick with his eyes fixed on the three old men of Karolin who had turned their heads to gaze on Dick.

Le Moan drew in her breath, then she seemed to cease breathing as the vision approached, passed her without a word and stood facing Aioma, the eldest and the greatest of the canoe-builders.

Le Moan was only fourteen, yet she was tall almost as Katafa, she was not a true Polynesian; though her mother had been a native of Karolin, her father, a sailor from a Spanish ship destroyed years ago by Uta Matu, had given the girl European characteristics so strong that she stood apart from the other islanders as a pine might stand amongst palm trees.

She was beautiful, with a dark beauty just beginning to unfold from the bud and she was strange as the sea depths themselves. Sometimes seated alone beneath the towering Jack-fruits her head would poise as though she were listening, as though some voice were calling through the sound of the surf on the reef, some voice whose words she could not quite catch; and sometimes she would sit above the reef pools gazing deep down into the water, the crystal water where coralline growths bloomed and fish swam, but where she seemed to see more things than fish.

The sharp mixture of two utterly alien races sometimes produces strange results—it was almost at times as if Le Moan were confused by voices or visions from lands of ancestry worlds apart.

She would go with Aioma fishing, and with her on board, Aioma never dreaded losing sight of land, for Le Moan was a pathfinder.

Blindfold her on the coral and she would yet find her way on foot, take her beyond the sea-line and she would return like a homing pigeon. Like the pigeon she had the compass in her brain.

331

This was the only gift she had received from her mother, La Jennabon, who had received it from seafaring ancestors of the remote past.

Crouching by the well she saw now Dick standing before Aioma and she heard his voice.

"You are Aioma?" said Dick, who had singled the chief of the three out by instinct.

The three old men rose to their feet. The sight of the newcomer helped, but it was the singling out of Aioma with such success by one who had never seen him that produced the effect. Surely here was a chief.

"I am Aioma," replied the other. "What want you with me?"

"That which the woman had already told you," replied Dick, who hated waste of words or repeating himself.

"They told me of the new chief who had come to the northern beach—*e uma kaio tau*, and of how he had ordered canoes to be built," said Aioma, "and I said, 'I am too old, and Uta is dead, and I know no chief but Uta; also in the last war on that Island in the north all the men of Karolin fell and they have never returned, they nor their canoes.' So what is the use of building more canoes when there are no men to fill them?"

"The men are growing," said Dick.

"Ay, they are growing," grumbled Aioma, "but it will be many moons before they are ready to take the paddle and the spear—and even so, where is the enemy? The sea is clear."

"Aioma," said Dick, "I have come from there," pointing to the north; "the sea is not clear."

"You have come from Marua (Palm Tree)?"

"I have come from Marua, where one day Katafa came, drifted from here in her canoe; there we lived till a little while ago when men landed, killing and breaking and burning—burning even the big canoe they had come in. Then Katafa and I set sail for Karolin, for Karolin called me to rule her people."

"And the men who landed to kill and burn?" asked Aioma.

"They are still on Marua; they have no canoes but they will build them, and surely they will come."

Neither of Aioma's companions said a word whilst Aioma stood looking at the ground as if consulting it, then his eyes rose to Dick's face. Age and war had made Aioma wise, he knew men and he knew Truth when he saw her.

332

"I will do your bidding, Taori," said he quite simply, then he turned to the others, spoke some words to them, giving directions what to do till his return, and led the way to the canoe.

Le Moan, still crouching by the well, said nothing. Her eyes were fixed on Dick, this creature so new, so different from any one she had ever seen. Perhaps the race spirit was telling her that here was a being of her father's race miraculously come to Karolin, perhaps she was held simply by the grace and youth of the newcomer—who knows?

Dick, as he turned, noticed her fully for the first time and as their eyes met, he paused, held by her gaze and the strangeness of her appearance, so different from that of the other natives. For a moment his mind seemed trapped, then as his eyes fell he passed on and taking the steering paddle pushed off, the wind from the reef-break filling the sail of the canoe.

Le Moan, rising and shading her eyes, stood watching as the sail grew less across the sparkling water, watching as the canoe rose and fell on the swell setting in from the break, watching as it reached the far white line of the northern beach where Katafa was waiting for the return of her lover.

THE LITTLE SHIPS

The primitive canoe of the Pacific is a dugout—the trunk of a tree hollowed and shaped into the form of a boat, so narrow in proportion to its length as to be absolutely unstable but for the outrigger.

The outrigger, a long skate-shaped piece of wood fixed to port—always to port—by poles on a central bridge, is an apology to the sea for want of beam, and the sea accepts it—on conditions. But for the outrigger, no canoe of any size would dare the sea, but for it the islands would have been sealed as between themselves, war made impossible, and the drift of people between island and island and between island and continent.

Far away in the remote past some man once stood, the father of this daring invention; little dreaming of the vast consequences of the work to which he had put his hand.

Dick at the steering paddle saw a figure on the northern beach' as they drew near. It was Katafa, waiting for him, the wind blowing her girdle of dracaena leaves and her hand sheltering her eyes against the sun. Standing just as Le Moan was stand-ins on the southern beach sheltering her eves and watching the canoe that carried the first man who had ever made her turn her head.

Some children were playing near Katafa and a fishing canoe was putting out nearby, but he saw only Katafa.

"Katafa," said Aioma, who was crouched by the after outrigger pole. "It is she sure enough, and they said she was dead and that her ghost had returned bringing you with her, Taori, but the dead do not return. Katafa, she was the girl under the taboo of Taminan, the girl no man or woman might touch, and then one day she went fishing beyond the reef and a storm took her and she was drowned, so they said."

"She was not drowned," replied Dick. "The wind blew her to Marua where I was—I and another whose face I have near forgotten, Kearney, he was called, and he made canoes but not like these, then one day he went among the trees and did not return. Then the god Nan came to the island and after him the men of Karolin who fought together so that all were killed, and then came the bad men as I have told you and would have killed us but we left Marua in the night. . . . Look, there is the canoe we came in." He pointed to the dinghy hauled up on the beach.

"O he! Taori!" It was Katafa's voice hailing them from the shore, glad, sweet, clear as a bell, yet far-carrying as the voice of a gull.

As Dick sprang out on the sands he seized her in his arms; parted only a few hours, it seemed to them that they had been weeks apart.

In the old days, even before he was born, his mother Emmeline had never been at ease when separated from his father even by the breadth of the lagoon, the demon that hints of mischance seemed always at her ear.

Dick seemed to have inherited with his power of love for Katafa, something of the dread of mischance for the beloved.

He embraced her, heedless of onlookers, though the only eyes to see were the eyes of the children and of Aioma who had eyes for nothing but the dinghy.

As soon as his foot touched sand, the canoe-builder made for it running like a boy, clapped his hand on the gunnel and then ran it over the planking.

The boats of the Spanish ship of long ago had been clinker-built and had been destroyed in the fight, but he had seen bits of them washed ashore on the southern beach. The dinghy was carvel-built and entire, a perfect specimen of eastern boat-building over which the canoe designer brooded forgetful of Dick and Katafa, the beach he stood on and the sun that lit it.

The idea of a boat built of planking and not hollowed out of a tree trunk had been presented to him by the charred and shattered fragments of the Spanish boats, but how to get planking and how to bend it to the form he desired was beyond his imagination and beyond his means. He saw vaguely that these boats of the papalagi were made somewhat after the fashion of a man, with a backbone and ribs and a covering for the ribs, he saw that by this means enough beam could be obtained to enable the builder to dispense with the outrigger—but then speed, where was there sign of speed in this thing squat and ugly?

In the early ages of the world in which Aioma still dwelt, ugliness had only two expressions, the lines that indicated want of speed and the lines that indicated want of strength.

Dick, though brown as the canoe-builder and almost to be mistaken for a true islander, was perhaps a million years younger than Aioma, just as the dinghy was a million years younger than the fishing canoe that had just brought him across the lagoon. In Dick, Aioma saw the lines that indicated speed and strength, nothing more—he was blind to the nobility of type expressed by that daring face, to the far sight of the eyes and the breadth of the brow; in the dinghy Aioma saw want of speed—he was blind to the nobility of type that made this bud the sister of a battleship, made it a vertebrate as against the dugout which has neither keel nor ribs.

Then Aioma, standing in the sun, a plain canoe-builder and workman in the sight of God and a critic as every true workman is, began to deride the dinghy, at first with chuckles deep down in his throat, then with a sound like the clacking of a hen, then with laughter long and loud and words of derision.

"Which end is which of this pig fish?" inquired Aioma of heaven and Dick, "and he who made her, how many more did he make like her?"

Dick, who had always connected the dinghy with Kearney, and who had a sort of faith that Kearney had made her just as he had made the little model ships, winced at the laughter of the old man. Perhaps it was the white man in him revolting at the derision of a savage over the works of the white man. However that may be, he turned and ran up the beach to the house of Uta Matu which he and Katafa had made their own. There in the shadow, on a hastily constructed shelf stood the little model ships he had so carefully salved from Palm Tree: the frigate, the schooner, the full-rigged ship and the whale man, the last thread connecting him with civilization; toys of the long ago, but no longer toys—fetishes from a world whose very language he had lost, a world of sun and tall trees where like a ghost in the sun dazzle moved a memory that was once a man—Kearney.

He took the schooner from its rest and coming out with it, ran to a great pool in the coral, calling Aioma to come and see what he who made the dinghy had also made.

The pool thirty feet long by twenty broad was ruffled by the breeze from the sea, it was clear as crystal, coral floored—and a trapped school of tiny fish no larger than needles, passed like a silver cloud here and there. Dick on his knees launched the schooner and Aioma standing bent with a hand on each knee watched her as she floated on an even keel. Then on the merry west wind with helm properly set and main boom guyed out she went sailing down the pool to the east where Katafa had run to receive her.

Aioma watched, then Dick running to the other end showed him how she could sail almost against the wind. Dick knew every stick and string of her, how to hoist and lower main and fore and how to set the head sails,—had you placed him on a real schooner, he could have worked her from his knowledge of the model, and Aioma watched vastly intrigued; then, taking a hand, he got on his knees and the great sun saw the builders of the future fleet of Karolin playing like children, whilst the little schooner on its imitation sea sailed from port to port, bowing to the ripples of the pool as the lost *Rarotonga*, of which it was the model, had bowed to the swell of the great Pacific.

THE GATES OF MORNING

The break on the reef of Karolin faced due east. Like a harbour mouth it stood, the only entrance to the lagoon, and through it at ebb and flood the sea raced dancing round the coral piers, pouring in and out swift as a river in spate.

When the sun rose he looked straight through the break, and the river of gold from him came level across the dancing waves of the outer sea, rose at the break, as a river rises to flood the coral piers and palms, passed through and spread on the quiet waters of the lagoon.

Mayay amyana—(the way—or the gates—of morning). Ages ago the name had been given to the break and the people who gave it were not speaking in the language of poetry, but of truth, for the one great thing that entered these gates was not the moon, now shriveled, now full, now absent; nor the tides that altered in time and size; but the morning, eternal, changeless and triumphant.

This great sea gate was more to the people of Karolin than a way of ingress and outgoing; it had a significance deep, almost religious, and based on the experiences of a thousand years, for it was the way to an outer world of which they knew little or nothing, and through it came not only the tides of the sea and the first light of the sun, but also whatever they knew or had known of the world beyond.

The Spanish ship had come in, strange beyond belief, and canoes from the Paumotus had brought war through it—trouble came through the gates of morning no less than joy, and all the dead who had died at sea had passed through them never to return.

To Le Moan just as to Aioma and the others, the sea gate of Karolin was a way and a mystery, a road, yet almost a temple.

But through the gates of morning came other things than ships and men.

Sometimes on a dead calm night and generally at full of moon Karolin lagoon would wake to the sound of thunder, thunder shaking the coral and rolling back in echoes from the far reef, not the thunder of nature, but the thunder of big guns as though fleets were at war on the outer sea.

Then if you came out on the beach you would see the shells bursting in the lagoon, columns of spray rising ghostlike and dissolving in the moonlight whilst the gulls, absolutely indifferent and roosting, stirred never a feather, and the pirate crabs, white as ivory, stood like carved things or went on their business undisturbed.

Natives waking from their sleep, if they woke at all, would turn on the other side and close their eyes again. It was only the *Matura*.

Whip rays twenty feet broad and four feet thick, a school of them at play, flinging themselves ten feet in the air and falling back in a litter of foam and with a concussion striking the lagoon floor and the reef; circling, pursuing one another in their monstrous play, they would keep the echoes rolling beneath the stars, till, as if at a given signal, silence would fall and the great fleet put out to sea again bound for where no man could know.

*

Awakened from sleep one night, Dick came out on the beach with Katafa. Used to the Matura from childhood, she knew and told him, and standing there beside her he had to believe that all this thunder and disturbance was caused by fish.

It was his first real initiation into the wonders of Karolin and the possibilities of the lagoon water. Then, as time went on, in the intervals of the treefelling, a business in which nearly all the women and boys took part, he would put out by himself to explore the depths and shallows of this great lake that was yet a sea in itself.

On the mind of Dick, almost unstained by the touch of civilization, yet vigorous and developed owing to his civilized ancestry, the world of Karolin exercised a fascination impossible to describe.

Sight, that bird of the soul, could roam here unchecked through the vast distances of sky or rest on a coral branch in the emerald shallows of sea, pursue the frigate mackerel in its rush or the frigate bird in its flight. Out on the lagoon he would crouch sometimes with the paddle across his knees, drifting, idle, without connected thought, environment pressing in upon him till his mind became part of the brilliancy of sea and sky, of the current drift and the wind that blew.

All to the west of a line drawn from mid-reef to mid-reef lay oyster beds, acres in extent and separated by great streaks of hard sand where the fish cast black shadows as they swam, and the crabs scuttered away from the drifting shadow of the canoe; near the northern beach, in ten-fathom water lay the Spanish ship of long ago, coral crusted, with the sea fans waving in the green and the mullet flitting in the shadow of her stem, a thing almost formless, yet with a trace of man's handiwork despite all the work of the coral builders, and still as death in a world where everything was adrift and moving, from the fish sharks that lurked in her shadows to the fucus blown as if by some submarine wind. But the strangest thing in this world of water was the circular current which the outflowing and incoming tides established in its centre, a lazy drift of not more than two knots which was yet sufficient to trap any floating thing and keep it prisoner till a storm broke the spell.

One day Dick ventured so far out that he lost sight of land. Sure of his sense of direction this did not trouble him; he kept on allured by clumps and masses of focus tom loose by the last storm, and drifting with the current, weed alive with sea creatures, tiny crabs, ribbon fish and starry sea-growths brilliant with colour.

Then he put back. But an hour's paddling did not raise the reef; the current was just sufficient to turn the nose of the canoe and he was moving in that fatal circle in which all blind things and things without sense of direction move.

It was noon and the position of the sun gave him no help; sunset or starlight would have put him all right but he had not to wait for these. Then away off beyond a great patch of floating kelp and on his port bow he suddenly saw a dark spot in the sea dazzle. It was a canoe.

Le Moan, as fearless as himself and with a far greater knowledge of these waters, had been fishing along the bank that ran like a spar from the southern beach straight out, shoaling the lagoon water to four fathoms and at some places three. The Karaka bank it was called, and in great storms the lagoon waves broke on it and it showed like a pillow of snow. In ordinary weather nothing marked it but a slight change of colour in the water indicating want of depth.

Away beyond the spur of the Karaka bank, Le Moan saw a canoe adrift and put towards it, guessing from its position and the fact that the paddle was not at work that it was in the grip of the central current.

As she drew near she saw that the canoe man was Taori. She hailed him and he told her that he had lost direction, then, telling him to follow, she put her canoe about and struck the water with the paddle. Though from the elevation of a canoe the horizon showed nothing of the girding reef, her instinct for direction told her exactly how they lay with regard to all the reef points. The marvelous compass in her brain that never failed, and could have steered a ship on the high seas as well as a canoe in Karolin lagoon, told her that the village on the north beach lay over there, and over there her home on the south beach, that the matamata trees lay in such a position and the great palm clump just there.

But as she steered she made not for the north beach where Dick had launched forth and where he lived, but for the south beach where her own home was situated. She said no word but steered, and presently Dick following her saw across the narrowing lagoon the far off Jack-fruit trees showing across the water. He knew them and that this was the south beach and anxious to get back to Katafa, he would have turned and made for the northern village where trees were also vaguely, visible, but he felt tired, the paddle was heavy in his hands—he wanted food and he was being led.

Just as the circular current of the lagoon had been sufficient to steer the canoe into a circular course, so was the leading of Le Moan sufficient to bring him to the south beach. A canoe was lying on the south beach and as Dick drew nearer he saw Palia and Tafuta, the two old men companions of Aioma and fellow craftsmen in the art of canoe building.

They were standing by the canoe, in which a woman was seated, and behind them stood the last habitable houses of the village, and behind the houses three coconut trees, hard against the dazzling pale blue of a sky that swept up to burning cobalt. Not a soul was to be seen on all that beach but the two old men.

Then came Le Moan's voice as she hailed them. "O he, Palia, where are the people, and what are you doing with that canoe?"

And Palia's voice answering.

"The word came after you put out this morning calling us to the northern beach for the building. We go. The rest have gone already in the big canoe that brought the word."

Dick at once knew. Aioma yesterday had declared the work far enough advanced to call in all hands including Palia and Tafuta, and the remaining people of the southern tribe.

"Then go," came Le Moan's voice as her canoe stranded on the shelving sand, "but leave me those things and a knife." She went to the canoe and took out some matting, a basket made of coconut sennit and a knife; as Dick brought his canoe ashore Palia and the others were putting off.

"You will follow us?" cried Palia as the paddles struck the water.

"Some time," replied Le Moan. She turned and began to build a fire to cook the fish she had caught and a breadfruit. Dick, seated on the sand with his knees up and his eyes following the far-off canoe, scarcely noticed her. She was one of the island girls, and though different from the others, of no account to him. An ordinary man would have been struck by her beauty, by her grace, and the fact that she was different from the others, but Katafa had blinded him to other women; it was as though she had put a charm round him, a ring rendering him inviolate to all female approach.

Le Moan, building the fire and preparing the fish and putting the breadfruit to bake, never glanced at him. He was there. The being who had in some extraordinary way suddenly become part of her life was there. This was no ordinary passion of a girl for a man, but something far more recondite and rare; perhaps something half evolved from the yearning of the civilization hidden in her for the civilization in him, perhaps the recognition of race, and that he and she were apart from the island people, those animals man and woman shaped, but destitute of the something that moved like a flame in her mind, lighting nothing—till now.

He was hers just as the sun was hers.

In this first dawn of a love that was to consume her being, she would have died rather than tell him by glance or word the something that filled her mind.

The smoke of the little cooking fire went up like the smoke of an altar.

Who knows but perhaps woman cooking for man was the first priest, the camp fire the first altar, man the first god, his food—the first burnt offering.

An hour later Dick fed, and rested, was pushing his canoe into the water helped by his worshipper.

Then she got into her canoe and accompanied him till the northern beach showed clear before them, the village, and to right of the village the great clump of matamatas, less by three than on the day she had sighted them last.

Here they parted company with the wave of a paddle, Le Moan returning to the desolation of the southern beach, Dick not knowing and not caring whither she went.

CIVILIZATION PEEPS IN

Without looking back, she turned the nose of her canoe straight for the southern beach. To left of her as she pad- died lay the sea gate where the tide was flooding round the coral and the breeze blowing the gulls like snowflakes against the blue; to right the limitless expanse of the lagoon; ahead the desolate beach, the ruined village and the wild tangle of pandanus trees, their limbs wide-spreading as the limbs of an elm, their fronds tossing like ill-kempt hair.

She hauled the light canoe above tide mark, then, turning to the right along the sands, she passed the trees and climbed the coral, standing for a moment facing the south and the empty sea. Then, turning, she gazed across the lagoon to where the far-away northern beach showed its trees above the water 'dazzle.

It was near full flood and the lagoon was brimming, the outer sea coming in great sheets of smoky blue, whirls of amethyst and streaks of cobalt between the piers of the break. Le Moan could hear the suck of the water through the gates as distinct from the sound of the breakers on the coral, beyond the sound of the breakers the voices of the gulls, beyond the gulls the silence reaching to the white trade clouds on the rim of the purple sea.

She was alone, but for the matter of that, she had always been alone, Aioma and the two old men and the women and children who formed the last remnant of the southern tribe had never been her companions; she had fished with them and helped in the cooking and mat-making, talked with them, lived with them, yet in a way, dwelt apart.

It was the race difference, perhaps, or some bent of soul owing to the fusion of races in her that made her a being quite alone, relying on no one but herself—a creature apart, almost a spirit. She had the power to lose herself utterly when gazing down into clear water as on the day when Dick first saw her gazing into the pond by the trees. Great distances held her in the same way should she give herself over to them, and that strange flair for direction which she shared with the gulls was less perhaps instinctive than psychic, for the mind of Le Moan, eternally in touch with the wind, the sea, the sun and the stars, was clairvoyant to the coming of storm and the sea changes that brought the great tiger sharks into the lagoon, altered the course of the mullet or drove the palu far from the fishing banks to northward of the reef.

Having stood for a while gazing to the north, she came back towards the deserted houses and began to prepare herself some food; after that there were lines to be mended and oap to be cleared from the paraka patch and then came sunset and then the stars, and sleep deeper than the great depths beyond the palu bank.

Had Le Moan looked back across her past, she would have seen a succession of days coloured like the day just dead, brilliancy stretching away into years and opalled by rainy seasons and storms, nights when dreams were unhaunted by human form till to-night, when, towards dawn, a ghostly canoe man showed in the mirror of sleep paddling towards her across a shimmering lagoon.

Then as the dream broke up and the vision vanished, Le Moan awoke beneath the last of the stars, awoke suddenly with fear clutching at her heart and with eyes wide but still half-blinded with sleep.

She sat up. The dawn was breaking and the fishing gulls were putting out to sea; she could hear their voices through the sound of the breakers on the reef. Nothing more, yet she listened, listened with her eyes fixed on the great fan of light showing in the eastern sky against which the gulls showed like withered leaves tossed on the wind.

Nothing. The sea breeze stirred the leaves of the bread-fruit and the branches of the pandamus palms and then fell flat, died out and changed to the first stirring of a land breeze, the highest flying gulls took colour and the ghostly lagoon took form.

The girl rising to her feet swept the lagoon water with her eyes. Nothing. Then, turning, she passed between the trees to the coral of the outer beach and there, out on the ghostly sea and touched by the light of dawn, she saw a ship.

Years after the destruction of the Spanish ship, which had happened before her birth, a whale man had put into the lagoon, cut wood, taken on water, been attacked by Uta Matu, the chief of Karolin, and escaped to the outer sea by a miracle.

Uta would have sent her to the bottom of the lagoon after the Spaniard, for in the depth of his ignorant but instinctive heart lay the knowledge that the black man's burden is the white man and that civilization to the savage means death.

Le Moan could still see as in a glass darkly the fight and the escape of the whale man, and here again was a ship, different in shape from the one of long ago, but arousing in her mind, from association, an instinct of antagonism and dread.

The ship, which had been standing off and on all night, was a schooner, and now as the great sun heaved himself higher and golden ripples broke the sea line, Le Moan watched her take fire, sail after sail catching the light till on the newborn blue of the sea a golden ship lay heaving to the swell, flown round by golden gulls, whose voices came chanting against the breeze like the voices of ghostly sailormen hauling in chorus.

Then as she altered her helm and the wind shivered out of her canvas, a boat was dropped, it ran up a sail and Le Moan, her eyes shaded against the risen sun, saw the boat heading for the break. She ran back amongst the trees and stood for a moment, her hand pressed against her forehead, her mind in confusion, with one idea only fixed and steadfast—Taori.

Here was danger, recollection backed instinct, the powerful instinct of a mind that could tell the north from the south without star or compass, the coming changes of weather, the movement of the fish shoals—the instinct that had awakened her with fear clutching at her heart.

Here was danger to Taori, and now as she stood her hand clasped on her forehead, came the recollection, not only of Uta Matu's fight against the whale man, but of Taori's words to Aioma about the bad men on Marua and the necessity of building the war canoes and of how the young men of Karolin would soon be ripe for war.

But the canoes were not built and the warriors were not ready, and here, suddenly from out of nowhere, had come this great canoe with sails spreading to the sky. Uta Matu and his warriors and fleet were vanished and Taori was unprepared. Then came the thought that the boat making for the break was like the pilot fish that scouts ahead of the tiger shark, it would come into the lagoon and if it found food worth devouring, the tiger shark would follow.

The village on the northern beach was invisible from the break, owing to the trees and the crafty way Uta Matu had set it amongst the trees. She remembered that.

Then her heart suddenly took flame. She would save Taori.

She left the trees and, taking the sand of the inner beach, she began running towards the break. She would attract the boat to her.

You have seen a bird attracting a man away from its nest, heedless of its own fate, thinking only of the thing it loved; just so Le Moan, facing the unknown, which was more terrible than the terrible, sought now to save the being she loved with the love that casts out fear.

She had not run a hundred yards when the boat entered the lagoon, heeling to the breeze and carried by the first of the flood, she flung up her arms to it, then she stood watching as it changed its course making straight towards her.

It was an ordinary ship's quarter boat, painted white, fitted with a mast and lug sail, and Le Moan as she stood watching paralyzed and waiting for her fate, saw that she held four men, three kanakas, whose naked shoulders showed above the gunnel, and a huge man, black bearded and wearing a broad-brimmed white straw hat beneath which his face showed dark and terrible as the face of the King of Terrors.

He wore a shirt open at the throat and his shirt sleeves were rolled up showing arms white yet covered with black hair. As the boat grounded and the kanakas sprang out Le Moan scarcely saw them; her eyes were fixed on the great man now standing on the beach, Colin Peterson, no less, one of the last of the sandalwood traders, master and owner of the *Kermadec*—Black Peterson, terrible to look at, swift to strike when roused, yet a man with kindness in his heart and straightness in his soul.

Poor Le Moan, had she only known!

Peterson, sweeping his eyes over the empty and ruined houses and the desolate beach, fixed them on the girl, spoke to her in a tongue she did not understand and then called out:

"Sru!"

A kanaka stepped forward. He was a Paumotuan, a yellow man, and half Malanesian, fierce of face, frizzy headed and wearing a necklace of little shells. After a word with Peterson, he turned to Le Moan and spoke to her and she understood. The language of Karolin was the language of the Paumotas; those far-off islands in the distant days had raided and fought with Karolin, in days still further removed the first inhabitants of Karolin had drifted from the Paumotas but neither Le Moan nor Sru knew aught of this nor of the common ancestry which gave them power of speech.

"I am here alone," said Le Moan answering Sru. "My people are gone—a storm took them all. There is no one here." As she spoke her eyes left Sru and wandered northward to the far trace of the northern beach, the dread at her heart was lest Taori might, by some ill-chance, put out fishing, show himself and be lost, but nothing appeared, nothing but the far- distant trees above the sun blaze on the water.

She knew that the schooner was too far off and too much sheltered by the southern reef for the people on the north beach to see her, that Taori would be busy with the canoe building, yet the dread at her heart drove her to repeat the words automatically like a parrot. "There is no one here but me—my people are gone; a storm took them—I am here alone." As she spoke, she watched Peterson with side glances. She had never seen a bearded man before, and this man with the black curling hair reaching almost to his eyes seemed a monster.

Whilst she was speaking, the other kanakas taking two large water breakers from the boat began to fill them at the well, the well into which she had been looking on the day on which she had first seen Taori.

Colin Peterson stood looking at them, he had half turned from Le Moan and seemed to have forgotten her existence; then, shading his eyes, he looked across and about the lagoon, but he was thinking neither of the kanakas nor the lagoon. He was cursing Le Moan.

He had no use for this girl. He had come ashore for water at this uncharted island thinking maybe to find natives, never dreaming that he would be faced by a problem like this. It was impossible to leave the forlorn creature to her fate, yet what was he to do with her on board of the *Kermadec*? Had it been a man or a boy the matter would have been simple enough, but a girl? If he took her off he would have to find her a home somewhere among the kanakas on one of the northern islands. He was bound for Amao but he reckoned that place was of no use—the kanakas were a bad lot.

As he stood like this thinking and staring about her, Le Moan still watched him, this terrific man who seemed searching with his eyes for Taori.

Would he believe her story—would he kill her? Old tales of the terrible *papalagi* chased through her mind like bats in the dusk that had fallen upon her powers of thought—she did not know. She only knew that she did not care whether he killed her or not as long as he believed her story and departed without hurting Taori.

Then, suddenly, the last breaker of water in the boat, Peterson turned on Sru and shouted to him to fetch her on board. Perplexity in Peterson generally expressed itself in blasphemy, and when Big Feller Mass'r Peterson began to talk like that, Sru never waited for the toe of the boot that was sure to follow.

He seized Le Moan by the arm and pushed her to the boat; for a moment she resisted, then she gave up, tumbled in and squatting forward of the mast saw as one sees in a dream the straining shoulders and tense arms of the kanakas, as, bending and clutching the port and starboard gunnels, they ran the boat out; she saw them tumble on board, felt the grating of the sand and then the balloon-like lift of the waterborne keel; she saw the sail above her take the wind and bulge hard against the blue of the sky; she saw the flying gulls and the wheeling lagoon and the trees of the southern beach vanishing to starboard as the boat headed for the break, but always and above everything she saw the massive hand of Peterson as he sat in the stern sheets with the tiller in the crook of his elbow and his eyes fixed towards her and beyond.

*

Ai, the sea! What tragedies has it not been partner in? The sea of storms, the blue laughing sea, the sea that now, lovely in the light of morning was flooding gently with the first of the flood through the gates of Karolin, lifting the boat to the outer swell as it passed the coral piers where the gulls cried above the foam of the breakers and the breakers answered to the crying gulls.

If Peterson had killed Le Moan on the beach, she would have met her death without flinching. Seated now watching Karolin drop astern, her eyes never wavered nor softened—even her fear of Peterson had vanished. It was as though she had died on passing the gates of the great atoll and entered a land where personality was not, only perception. A land of pictures that had no relationship to herself or anything she had ever known. She saw as they came alongside the white painted side of the *Kermadec* with the ladder cast down, the rail, and above the rail the great white sail spaces all a-shiver in the wind. The faces of men looking down at the boat, the face of Rantan the mate, and Carlin, a beachcomber picked up at Soma and working his passage north.

Then she was on the deck, which seemed to her broad and white as a beach, and the extraordinary newness of this strange place took on a cutting edge which pierced the deadness that had fallen upon her– this place so vast to her mind that it seemed land of a sort. A moment before, in the boat, the sea had been around her, but here the sea was nothing, this place was everything. Taori, Karolin, the reef, the ocean itself, all for a moment vanished, consumed by the *Kermadec* as by a flame.

And not a soul took notice of her after the first few words of Peterson to the Mate. They were busy getting in the boat and now as the rumbling and threshing of the canvas above died out and the sails filled hard against the blue came the voices of gulls, gulls from the reef and deep-sea gulls flitting in the wake of the *Kermadec* that was now under way.

Le Moan, feeling herself unnoticed, and moving cautiously, came to the weather rail. She saw the reef and the distant trees of Karolin and the following gulls now flying north and south as if giving up the chase. Then the reef line passed from sight beneath the sea dazzle and the voice of the reef and the crying of the gulls died far off, whilst the tree-tops vainly fought with the ever-growing distance, now clinging to the sight, now washed utterly away.

THE MEN OF THE KERMADEC

Now on board that ship there were three men set there by circumstance as pawns in a game of which Taori was king, Katafa queen, and Le Moan perhaps the hand of the player, and these men were Rantan the mate, Carlin the beachcomber, and Sru, bo'sun and chief of the kanakas.

Rantan, a narrow slip of a man, hard bitten and brown as a hickory nut, was a mystery. Perfect in the art of handling a schooner, he knew next to nothing of navigation. Peterson had picked him up as an extra hand and, the mate dying of fever, Rantan had taken his place, making up in general efficiency for his want of higher knowledge. He had spent all his life amongst the islands and natives, he could talk to Sru in his own tongue like a brother born, could pick up the dialect of any island in a week, but had little to say in English. A silent man who never drank, never smoked and never cursed.

Peterson disliked him for no apparent reason whatsoever; he could have got rid of him, but he didn't. Sobriety is a jewel in the Pacific, especially when it is worn by schooner mates.

Carlin had come on board the ship just before she sailed from Soma. He was a big red-headed man useless for anything but beachcombing, he wanted to get up to "them Northern islands" and Peterson out of the heart kindness that had made him take Le Moan on board, took him. He made him work, yet gave him a bunk aft, thus constituting him in a way one of the ship's officers.

Carlin was one of the unfortunates born with a thirst, but in his case it only broke out on land, on board ship he had no wish for liquor but the beach felled him as if with a pole-ax.

Sru, the last of the three men, stood over six feet, stark naked except for a gee-string. He was a man from the beginning of the world. He could cast a spear and find his mark at fifty yards, his nose was flattened, his cheek-bones broad and his face, especially when his eyes were accommodated for distance, wore an expression of ferocity that yet had nothing evil in it. Le Moan had no fear of him. Indeed at the end of her second day on the schooner, she had no fear of anyone on board. Instinct told her that whatever these men might have done to Taori and the tribe, they would not hurt her. Fortunately she never recognized how utterly useless had been her sacrifice, never recognized the fact that Colin Peterson, so far from hurting Dick, would have been his friend—otherwise she might have cast herself overboard, for her sorrow was heavy on her and wanted no extra weight.

Peterson had given her over to Sru to look after and Sru had made her a shake-down in the long boat. She fed with the kanaka crew, who took their meals on deck, and became part of their family and tribe, but she would not go into the foc'sle, nor would she go into the cabin; those holes in the deck leading down below were, for her, mysterious and terrific; she had peeped down the saloon hatchway and seen the steps going down as into a well and the polish of the handrail and a light below shining on a mat. It was light reflected from the saloon, yet none the less mysterious for that and the whole thing struck her with the enchantment that quite commonplace things sometimes possess for little children, but it was an enchantment tinged with the shadow of dread.

She had no fear of the men on board yet she had a dread of the saloon companionway, of the main boom, till it explained itself to her, of the windlass with its iron teeth. The men, in spite of their clothes and strange ways, shook down as human beings, but the wheel that steered the schooner and the binnacle into which the steersman gazed as he stood moving the spokes, forever moving the spokes of the mysterious wheel, those things were mysterious and their mystery was tinged with the shadow of dread. They were part of the unknown that surrounded her: to the savage the thing unknown is a thing to be feared.

One day when Sru was at the wheel and the deck was empty, she ventured to peep into the binnacle and saw beneath the glittering glass like a star-fish in a rock pool the compass cord trembling like a living thing. Had not the deck been empty so that she dared to speak to Sru on this matter and had not he been in a mood to answer her, the whole life of Le Moan would have been altered and never again might she have seen Taori.

"What is it," asked she, glancing across her shoulder at the steersman, "and why do you look at it so?"

"This," said Sru, indicating the wheel for which he had no word in the native, "moves the steering paddle (*e caya madyara*) and into that I look to find my way."

Now when Karolin had sunk beneath the sea rim the conviction had come to Le Moan that never would she see Karolin again; her instinct told her where it lay and, given a canoe, she could have found it even at this great distance, but her knowledge of where it lay was no comfort to her—she felt that the great hand that had seized her would never let her go and that a door had closed forever between this new world and the old where Taori dwelt safe owing to the closing of the door.

She glanced again at the binnacle and then speaking like a person in reverie she said: "Without that I could find my way though the sea were dark and no stars shone, as I have found my way often in the fishing canoes when the land was so far it could not be seen."

Sru knew what she meant; at Soma in the Paumotus from where he had come the directional instinct, shared more or less by all savages, was especially marked in some of the children, and the deep-sea canoes in those waters where the currents run in an unaccountable manner and where the trade winds are not, depended on the instinct of the steersman.

He bade her close her eyes and turn and turn. "Where now lies the land we have left?" asked Sru. Without opening her eyes and not knowing east from west or north from south, she pointed aft almost dead south.

Sru laughed. She was right, the mysterious compass in her brain that worked without error or deviation would have pointed to Karolin, though a thousand miles away; then as he spun the wheel having let the *Kermadec* a point or two off her course, Le Moan went forward and he forgot her, but he did not forget what she had told him. It remained in his tenacious mind like a pebble in molasses, hidden, but there till three days later when towards evening, the kanakas were eating their supper on deck, Sru was brought face to face and for the first time in his life with a great idea, an idea that included tobacco not by the stick, but in cases, rum in casks, women, barlow knives, chalk pipes and patent leather boots, also canned salmon and seidlitz powders.

Sru, an old pearler, had been in the last of the pearling at Soma before the banks gave out. He knew the value of pearls.

THE PEARL

They were seated on the main deck near the galley, their coffee mugs beside them and their plates on their knees and the *Kermadec* on a steady seven-knot clip was heeled slightly to starboard almost rigid as a board, save for the sound of the sea as she dipped to the swell.

For days she had run so with the port rail raised against the white fringe of trade clouds on the far horizon, a steady list from a steady breeze warm and winged with the silver fins of flying fish, a tepid sea-scented wind such as the north can never know, less a wind than a revelation such as men try to express when they speak of the breath of the tropics.

The cook had served out the food, and as they ate he talked; he was a big man with the voice of a child and he was talking of his native village apropos of nothing and to nobody in particular, which is a way kanakas have.

Of the world around them, save for Soma and the southern islands and the island in the north which a few of them knew, Sru, Peroii and the rest of them were as ignorant as Le Moan.

As they talked, the rosy light of sunset falling on them and reflected by the fore canvas. Sru, who was seated by Peroii, saw the wind lift Le Moan's dark hair exposing the pearl charm she wore behind the left ear—the double pearl, lustrous and beautiful, tied in the hair so cunningly and betrayed by the wind.

Le Jennabon had given it to her daughter as a protection against drowning and mischance. More than that it was a love amulet, making sure for the girl a happy married life with a man who would not misuse her. Love amulet or not Le

Jennabon had given to her daughter a talisman of extraordinary power. Exposed by the wind for a moment, it had spoken to Sru. It said clearly as tongue could speak, "Karolin is a pearl lagoon." Then as Le Moan raised her hand and tucked the hair back behind her ear, Sru, who had paused in his eating, went on with his food, his dark eyes fixed beyond Peroii, beyond the vision of deck and mast and standing rigging, beyond all things visible, upon wealth: cases of tobacco and rum in many bottles, girls, clay pipes, a gun, and boxes of Swedish matches to strike at pleasure. Karolin lagoon held all these things, the pearl behind Le Moan's ear told him that for a certainty, but Karolin was far astern and he would never see it again, that also was a certainty and before it the heart of Sru became filled with bitterness. A few minutes ago he had been happy and free of care, now his soul was dark as the sea becomes dark with a squall suddenly rising and blowing up out of a clear sky. He had discovered a pearl lagoon—too late. Leaving the others to finish their meal, he rose up and dropped below into the foc'sle, there curled up in his bunk in the gloom he lay to consider this matter.

It was useless to speak of it to Peterson, he would never put the ship back; even if he did he, Sru, would profit little by the matter. He would maybe get a few sticks of tobacco for telling of it, or a knife. Peterson, though kind-hearted enough to rescue Le Moan, was a hard man where bargaining with natives was concerned. Sru had an intimate knowledge of white men, or at least white traders and their ways, and Peterson was a white man to the core.

Then as he lay facing this fact, the idea of Rantan came before him.

Rantan who could talk to him in his own tongue like a brother, who was half a native as far as language and ideas went, and yet was a white man.

Though Rantan had no power to put the ship back, it came into Sru's mind that somehow or in some way this man, clever as all the papalagi were, might be able to do something in the matter. Eased by this idea he turned out of the bunk and came on deck.

The sunset was just vanishing from the sky where in the pansy dusk the constellations were sketching themselves above the vague violet of the sea. Then, suddenly, like the closing of a door, the west went dark and the stars blazed out and bloomed in full sight. The wind, moist, and warm, blew steadily, and Sru, standing in the draught from the head sails, looked about him, forward at the bowsprit rising and falling against the sea stars and aft where the white decks showed, the man at the wheel clearly visible and someone leaning on the weather rail, Carlin to judge by his bulk.

Rantan was nowhere to be seen.

Close to Sru and hunched against some rope coiled by the windlass he saw a figure. It was Le Moan. She was seated with her knees up and her hands round her knees, and she seemed asleep—but she was not asleep, for as Sru's eyes fell on her, her face lifted and he saw the glint of her eyes in the starlight. Those mournful eyes that ever since her departure from Karolin seemed like the eyes of a person in trance, of a dreamer who was yet conscious of some great and real disaster.

Sru instantly forgot Rantan. It seemed that somewhere deep in his shadowy mind something had linked Le Moan with the pearl lagoon and any chance of success in finding it again, raiding it, and turning milk-white chatoyant pearls into sticks of tobacco, bottles of rum, clay pipes and beads to buy love with.

She had given him the indication of what was there, but it seemed to him that she could do more than that.

He crumpled up and sat down beside her on the deck and spoke soft words, asking her what ailed her that she looked so sorrowful. "For," said Sru, "the storm that took your people has without doubt taken many more in the island and will not give them back, not though men weep forever—it is so, and it is so, and ever will be so, and to eat the heart out for that which has been, is to feed foolishly, for," said Sru, "the coral waxes, the palm grows, but man departs." He was repeating the old Island proverb and for a moment he had forgotten Karolin, pearls, gin bottles and the glory of seidlitz powders in effervescence like the foam on the reef; he had forgotten all little things and his words and voice broke up the depths of Le Moan and the cause of her grief came forth. Otherwise and soon she might have died of it. Conscious that Karolin was so far in the past that it was safe to speak, she told Sru that no storm had overtaken her people, that she had lied to Peterson so that he might not discover and perhaps kill the being she loved; and there, sitting in the showering starlight, she did that which she had never done before even for her own inspection, opened her heart, told, as a sleeper might tell in sleep, of her love for Taori and of his beauty and strength and swiftness and of everything except that which she did not know—the fact that Taori had a lover already, Katafa.

She spoke and Sru listened, absorbing her words and her story as a kanaka will absorb any sort of tale he can understand. Then this amazing savage who had spoken so poetically about the waxing of the coral and the passing of man, this sympathizer who had spoken so softly in addressing grief, leaning on his elbow began to shake with laughter.

He knew that big feller Mas'r Peterson would not have hurt a hair of Taori's head, that he did not want to take Le Moan off the beach and had only done so because he imagined her unable to fend for herself. He saw that Le Moan, trying to protect her lover against imaginary perils had allowed herself to be sacrificed and snatched away from everything she loved and cared for, that she had prepared for herself the trap into which she had fallen—and all this to the mind of Sru seemed a huge joke, almost as good as the joke of the drunken man he had once seen, who, trying to cut wood with his foot on a log had cut off his foot with the axe he was wielding.

Sru giggled like a girl being tickled, then he burst out in snorts like a buffalo in a temper, choked as though he had swallowed a fish-bone and then began to explain.

Began to explain and failed to hit the mark simply because Le Moan could not understand why big feller Mas'r Peterson had taken her away from Karolin. He did not want to take her away yet he had taken her away. Le Moan could not understand that in the least.

Le Moan could not understand pity, she had never come across it in others and she had never felt it for herself. Had she been able to pity herself, she would have flung herself on the deck weeping and wailing when the *Kermadec* turned her stem to the south and dropped Karolin beyond the horizon. She had sacrificed herself for the sake of the being who dominated her existence, she had dared the most terrible of all things, the unknown, yet she could not in the least understand why Peterson should do what he did not want to do for the sake of a being, a stranger whom he had never seen before.

To tell the truth Sru did not quite comprehend it either, he knew it was so and he left it at that. It was one of the strange and unaccountable things that white men were always doing. What intrigued him was the fact that Le Moan had fooled herself in fancying Peterson a dangerous man capable of injuring her lover and that Peterson had fooled himself in believing her story.

So he talked till Le Moan at last understood the fact that, whatever Peterson's object in taking her away may have been, he would not have injured Taori, that if she had said nothing he would have gone off after having filled the water breakers at the well, and as he talked and as she listened dumb before the great truth that she had sacrificed everything for nothing, slowly up from the subconscious mind of Sru and urged by his talk, came an idea.

"You will go back," said Sru. "Listen, it is I, Sru, who am talking—we will go back, you and I, and what tells me is that which lies behind thy left ear."

Le Moan put her hand up to the amulet hidden beneath her hair.

"We will go back," went on Sru, "you and I and another man, and perhaps more, all good men who will not hurt Taori—but Pete'son, no—no," he murmured as if communing with some dark spirit. "He would swallow all. He alone knows the way across the sea, so that setting the steering paddle this way or that he can go straight as the frigate bird to Soma or to Nalauka or to what island or land he chooses, he alone of the men on board this ship. But thou art wise as he. Wise as the frigate bird that leaves the land far from sight yet can return. You will guide us to Karolin. Can your eyes still see that beach and where it lies?"

Le Moan threw out her arms.

"Though I were blind as the sand worm, I could find it," said Le Moan, "through night and storm— but when?"

"No man can hurry the rising of the day," said Sru, "but soon it will come and soon your eyes shall fall upon Taori—that which lies behind your left ear has told me, and it has told me more. Answer so that I may know if it speak the truth. It has told me that thick in that lagoon lie the shells of the *iyama* (oyster) from whence it came—is that true talk?"

"Thick and far they lie," said Le Moan, "from the *kaaka* far as one can paddle from the coming in to the middle of the tide."

"So," said Sru, "it spoke the truth. When we make our return you will go to meet Taori and we to find the *iyama* for the sake of the stones they hold, brethren of that which lies . . . there."

He touched her hair behind her left ear and rose gliding off aft, whilst Le Moan, whose life had suddenly come back to her, sat gazing through night and beyond the stars at a sunlit beach where spear in hand and lovely as the morning stood Taori.

Taori who at that moment tired out with the labour of canoe-building was lying asleep with his arm across the warm body of Katafa.

H. de Vere Stacpoole

THE MIND OF SRU

Now the mind of Sru had sat down to talk with Le Moan, having in it no plan—nothing but a desire for pearls and what pearls would bring, and the knowledge sure and instinctive that Karolin was a pearl lagoon. It had risen up armed with a plan.

This plan had come to him from his close contact and talk with Le Moan. Brooding alone with nothing for his mind to cling to, it is doubtful if Sru could have evolved a plan; the presence of the girl, her connection with Karolin, her story, her wish to get back, the fact that she was a pathfinder and the fact that Peterson, even if he took the *Kermadec* back, would take all the profit of the business for himself—all these thoughts and considerations came together in Sru's mind and held together like a cluster of bees, owing to the presence of the girl who was the core and center of everything. He would speak of the matter to Rantan. Sru understood that Karolin was not on the charts, those mysterious pieces of paper that enabled Peterson to find his way about, he understood that Rantan had little knowledge of navigation, he only knew that were they to steer south for as many days as they had steered north and then hand the steering over to Le Moan, she would bring them to the place desired.

Give her the wheel right away and she would steer them back, but she could not stand at the wheel for days and days; no, it would be enough to steer south by the compass and then when close on the latitude hand the wheel to her. The instinct that led the birds over unmarked sea spaces and the palu from hundreds of miles away to the self-same breeding grounds, that would be sufficient.

Going aft he hung about for a while close to the fellow at the. wheel, but there was no sign of Rantan and Peterson coming on deck. Sru went forward again and dropped below to the foc'sle. It was in the morning watch that he found his opportunity, only Rantan and the steersman were aft and Sru coming along, stood with the mate by the rail.

The dawn was full on the sea.

They spoke for a minute on the prospect of the wind holding, and then Sru, with a glance at the steersman to make sure he was out of hearing, came to his subject.

"That land we have left," said Sru, "is Karolin—the girl has told me the name, but much more as well. That lagoon is a pearl lagoon. This is a private matter between us. I tell you because I could not tell anyone else and because I think we may profit by it."

"A pearl lagoon," said Rantan. "Is she speaking the truth?"

"The truth. She wears behind her ear two pearls in one, so," said Sru, joining his closed fists in the dawn light, "they are tied in her hair and the wind lifting her hair I saw them; then I spoke and she told me. Now listen, Ra'tan, we know of this matter, you and I, we two alone will get those pearls—Pete'son, no. He would swallow them all and give us the shells to eat, but how we are to go has not been shown to me, it is for you to see to that matter."

All this he said in the native and Rantan, listening, tapped out the ashes from his pipe against his heel, and then, pipe in hand, leaned against the rail, his eyes fixed on the deck.

In the increasing light he could see the deck planking clearly even to the dowels. Plunged fathoms deep in thought he said nothing for a while, then raising his eyes he spoke.

"What you say is true, but Pete'son is the wisest of us. How can we find that island again without him? As you know, my life has been spent mostly among the islands—shore along and between island and island as they lie in the Paumotas ten to a space as broad as your palm. I can handle this ship or any ship like this or any canoe, as you know, but to look at the sun at noon as Pete'son looks, and to say 'I am here, or here,' that art has not been given me. I have not lived my life on the deep sea, but only in shallow waters. Then again Pete'son is not the full owner of this ship, there is another man who owns a part and without talking to him he cannot break a voyage, he cannot say, I will go here or here without the other man saying yes."

"That is the more reason," said Sru, "that we must go without him."

"And without him we cannot find our way," replied Rantan.

Then Sru told of Le Moan's power of direction finding. Rantan understood at once, he had seen the thing often amongst the natives of Soma and other islands and the fact came suddenly on his mind like the blow of a hammer riveting things together.

But he said nothing to show exactly what was in his mind, he heard Sru out, and told him to go forward and not speak of the matter to anyone. "For," said Rantan, "there may be something in what you say. I do not know yet, but I will think the matter over."

Left alone he stood, his eyes on the sun blaze creeping upon the eastern horizon. He was a quick thinker. The thing was possible, and if Karolin lagoon was a true pearl lagoon the thing was a fortune.

By taking the *Kermadec* there with the kanaka crew for divers, eight months or a year's work would give the profit of twenty voyages. Well he knew that if Colin Peterson were the chief of that expedition, there would be little profit for anyone but Peterson and his partner. Peterson would have to be eliminated if there was any work to be done in this business.

Sru had not said a word about Taori or Le Moan's untruth as to Karolin being uninhabited.

It would have tangled the story for one thing, and for another might not Ra'tan say to himself. "If this girl has lied on one matter, may she not be lying about the pearls?" Sru knew instinctively that she spoke the truth, and he left it at that, and Rantan watching now the glory of the rising sun, stood, his plan crystallizing into full shape, his eyes gazing not on the sunlit sea, but on Karolin, a desolate atoll, uninhabited, with no eyes to watch what might be done there but the eyes of the seagulls.

CASHI

Le Moan had never known pity. She had lived amongst the pitiless, and if any seed of the divine flower lay in her heart it had never grown nor come to blossom. She had seen her tribe raided and destroyed and the remnants chased to sea by the northern tribe under Uta Matu, she had seen battle and murder and sudden death, storm and destruction; she had seen sword-fish at war and the madness and blood-lust of fish, bow-head whales destroyed by orcas and tiger sharks taking men—all these things had left her unmoved by pity as they would have left Rantan. Yet between these two pitiless ones lay a distance greater than that between star and star.

Le Moan had sacrificed herself for the sake of Taori; had faced what was more terrible than death— the unknown, for the sake of the man who had inspired her with passion; and had found what was more terrible than death—separation.

To return and find Taori she would, if necessary, have destroyed the *Kermadec* and her crew without a second thought, just as to save him she would have destroyed herself. Rantan could not have understood this, even if it had been carefully explained to him with diagrams exhibiting the savage soul of Le Moan, all dark, save where at a point it blazed into flame.

All that day working out his black plan he reviewed his instruments, Sru, Carlin, the crew, the ship, and last and least the kanaka girl who would act as a compass and a navigator. A creature of no account save the instinct she shared with the fish and the birds, so he fancied.

The *Kermadec* had loaded some turtle shell at Soma and at Levua she was to pick up a cargo of sandalwood. San Francisco was the next port of call, but to Rantan's mind it did not seem probable that she would ever reach San Francisco. It all depended on Carlin. Rantan could not do the business alone even with the help of Sru; Carlin was a beachcomber and to leave him with a full whiskey bottle would have been fatal for the whiskey bottle, but he was a white man; he would have been fired off any ship but the *Kermadec*, but he was a white man. Rantan felt the necessity of having a white man with him on the desperate venture which he had planned, and taking Carlin aside that night he began to sound him.

"We're due at Levua to-morrow," said Rantan. "Ever been to Levua?"

"Don't know it," replied the other, "don't want to neither; by all accounts, listening to the old man, there's nothing there but one dam' sandalwood trader and the karakas he uses for cutting the wood. I want to beach at Tahiti, that's where I'm nosing for when I get to 'Frisco; there's boats in plenty running down from 'Frisco to Tahiti."

"Maybe," said Rantan, "but seems to me there's not much doing at Tahiti. Hasn't it ever hit you that there's money to be made in the islands and better work to be done than bumming about on the beach? I don't mean hard work, handling cargo or running a ship—I mean money to be picked up, easy money and plenty of it."

The big red man laughed and spat over the rail.

"Not much," said he, "not by the likes of me or you; clam shells is all there's to be picked up by the likes of me and you when the other chaps have eaten the chowder."

"How'd you like ten thousand dollars in your fist?" asked Rantan, "twenty—thirty—there's no knowing what it might come to, and all for no work at all but just watching kanakas diving for pearls."

Carlin glanced sideways at his companion.

"What are you getting at?" asked he.

"Well, I'll tell you," said Rantan, "I know of a pearl island and it's not far from here. It's a sealed lagoon, never been worked, and there's enough there to make a dozen men rich, but to get there I'd want a ship, but I haven't got one nor the money to charter one; I'm like you, see?"

"What are you getting at?" asked Carlin again, a new tone in his voice.

"I'm just saying I haven't a ship," replied the other, "but I know where to get one if I could find a chap to help me in the taking of her."

Carlin leaned further over the rail and spat again into the sea. With terrible instinct he had taken up the full meaning of the other.

"And how about the kanakas?" asked he, "kanakas are dam' fools, but get them into a court of law and they're bilge pumps for turning up the evidence. I've seen it," he finished, wiping his mouth with the back of his hand. "A sinking job it was, and the chap that did it got ten years, on kanaka evidence."

Rantan laughed. "Leave the kanakas to me," said he, "I'm putting it to you—if I've the sand to do the job, would you help?"

"I'm not saying I wouldn't," said Carlin, "but what about the navigating? You aren't much good on that job . . . or are you? I'm thinking maybe you've been holding it up your sleeve."

"I'm good enough to get there," replied Rantan. "Well, think it over, we've time in our hands and no need to hurry. But remember there's no knowing the money in the business, and if it comes to doing it, don't you worry about risks; I'm not a man to take more than ordinary risks and I'll fix everything."

Then he turned away and walked aft leaving Carlin leaning on the rail.

Whatever Carlin's start in life may have been, he was now beach-worn like one of the old cans you find tossing about the reef flung away by the kanakas—label gone, and nothing to indicate its past contents. The best men in the world would wilt on the beach, and that's the truth; the beach, that is to say sun and little to do—the sun kills or demoralizes more men than whiskey; to be born to the sun, you must be born in the sun, like Katafa, like Dick, like Le Moan; you must never have worn clothes.

Sometimes a white man is sun proof inside and out, but rarely. Carlin was sun proof on the outside, his skin stood the pelting of the terrible invisible rays; he throve on it; but internally he had gone to pieces.

He had one ambition, whiskey—or rum, or gin, or even samshu, but whiskey for choice.

There was whiskey on the *Kermadec*, but not for Carlin. Peterson, as sober a man as Rantan, kept it, just as he kept the Viterli rifles in the arms rack, for use in an emergency. It was under lock and key, but Carlin had smelt it out.

Its presence on board was like the presence of an evil genius, invisible, but there and exercising its power; it kept reminding him of Rantan's words at supper that night, and when he turned in and even in his sleep its work went on; he saw in his dreams the vessel heading for the unknown pearl island towards the golden light of fortune and unlimited whiskey, he was on her deck with Rantan in command and Peterson was not there.

The dream said nothing about Peterson, totally ignored him, and Peterson, on deck at that moment, had no idea that the beachcomber was dreaming of the *Kermadec* off her course and without her skipper.

Next day in the morning watch, Sru was at the wheel and Rantan, a pipe in his mouth, stood by the weather rail, the sun had just risen shattering the night and spreading gold across the breezed up blue of the swell.

The sunrise came to the *Kermadec* like the sudden clap of a hot hand: Sru felt it on his back and Rantan on his cheek. From away to windward came the cry of a gull, a gull passed overhead with domed wings circled as if inspecting the schooner and drifted off on the wind. Almost at the same moment, came the cry of the kanaka lookout. "Land!"

Rantan walked forward. Right ahead, rosy above the brimming sea, lay the cloud scarf of Levua.

Still a great way off, facing the blazing east, the island, clear of any trace of morning bank, seemed to float between the blue of sea and sky, remote, more lovely than any dream.

When Rantan turned aft again he found Le Moan standing by Sru at the wheel. Sru was explaining to her how the wheel worked the "steering paddle" in the stem. The *Kermadec* was close hauled, every sail drawing, Sru was explaining this matter and showing how the least bit closer to the wind would set the sails shivering and take the way off the ship. Le Moan understood. Sea craft was born in her, and used now to the vast sail spaces of the schooner, she felt no fear—the *Kermadec* was only a canoe after all, of a larger build and different make.

He let her hold the spokes for a moment, governing the wheel with a guiding hand, then at the risk of the schooner being taken aback, he stood aside and the girl had the helm.

The *Kermadec* for a moment showed no sign that the wheel had changed hands, then, suddenly, a little warning flutter passed through the canvas from the luff of the mainsail, passed and ceased and the sail became hard again. Le Moan had understood, understood instinctively, that ceaseless pressure against the lee bow which tends to push a vessel's head up into the wind.

For a moment Taori, Karolin, the very presence of Sru were forgotten, the words that Sru had spoken to her only a little while before, "You will soon see Taori, little one, but first you must learn to use the steering paddle." Everything was forgotten in the first new grip of the power that was in her to hold all those great sail spaces filling, to play such a great game with the wind and the sea.

Aioma had taught her to steer her fishing canoe, but so long ago that she could not remember the first time she had the paddle to herself; but this was different, different as the kiss of a lover from the kiss of a friend—something that reached her soul; it was different as the sight of Taori from the sight of other men, great, thrilling, lifting her above herself, creative.

Utterly ignorant of the mechanism that moved the rudder as a man is ignorant of the mechanism that moves his arm, after the first few minutes of the great new experience she could not do wrong. She knew nothing of the compass, she only knew that she was to keep the ship close hauled as Sru had been keeping her, so close that a fraction nearer the wind would spill the sails. Sru watched her and Rantan, forgetting his pipe, stood with his eyes fixed on her. Both men recognized that the ship was safe for the moment. One might have thought them admiring the picture that she made against the blue sky and the glory of morning, but the interest in their eyes was neither the interest of the roused aesthetic sense, nor of love, nor of passion, nor of seamanship.

As they stood, suddenly, and as though Tragedy had staged the scene for some viewless audience, the head and shoulders of Peterson appeared at the saloon hatch opening.

Rantan, his face mottled with white, stared at Peterson, Sru drawing the back of his hand across his nose as if wiping it, stood on one foot, then on the other, confused, looking like a dog that has been misbehaving itself. Le Moan saw nothing.

Without losing its alertness on the touch of the wheel her mind had gone off for a momentary flight. She saw herself steering the *Kermadec* towards Karolin, she saw in imagination the distant reef, the gulls and the thrilling blue of the great lagoon beyond the reef opening.

Peterson, without coming further on deck, watched her for a moment without comprehending anything but the fact that the girl had been allowed to take the wheel. Then as Sru took the spokes from her and pushed her forward, the captain of the *Kermadec* turned on Rantan, but the abuse on his lips was half shriveled by the face of the mate.

"Don't you never do a thing like that again," said Peterson. "Dam' tomfoolery." He snorted and went forward, kicked a kanaka out of his way and then stood, his eyes fixed on the distant vision of Levua opal tinted in the blue, blue north.

THE HIGH ISLAND

They came in on a dying wind, the outlying reefs creaming to the swell and the great high island opening its canons and mountain glades as they drew towards it pursued by the chanting gulls.

Le Moan, who had never seen a high island or only the vision of Palm Tree uplifted by mirage, stood with her eyes fixed on the multitude of the trees. Palms, breadfruit, tree ferns, aoas, sandalwood groves, trees mounting towards the skies, reaching ever upwards, changing in form and misted by the smoke of torrents.

Here there was no freedom, the great spaces of the sea had vanished, Levua like an ogre had seized her mind and made it a prisoner.

For the first time in her life something came to her heart, terrible as her grief for the loss of Taori, yet even more far searching and taking its bitterness from the remote past as well as the present. It was the homesickness of the atoll-bred islander encompassed by the new world of the high island; of the caged gull taken from the freedom of the wind and the sea.

At Karolin you could see the sun from his rising to his setting, and the stars from sea line to sea line; the reef rose nowhere to more than twice the height of a man, the sea was a glittering plain of freedom and a sound and a scent.

Worse even than the monstrous height of Levua, its strange canons and gloomy woods, was the scent of the foliage, cossi and vanilla and sandalwood, unknown flowers, unknown plants, all mixed with the smell of earth and breathing from the glasshouse atmosphere of the groves.

An extraordinary thing was the way in which the forms and perfumes of Levua permeated the *Kermadec* itself, so that, turning her eyes away from the land, the deck of the schooner, the rails, masts and spars, all seemed hostile to her as the land itself. Sru alone gave her comfort as she watched him superintending the fellows busy with the anchor—Sru, who had promised that she would return.

The anchor fell in twelve-fathom water and as the rumble-tumble of the anchor chain came back in echoes from the moist-throated woods, a boat put out from the beach. It was Sanders the white trader, the man who lived here alone year in, year out, taking toll of the sandalwood trees, paying the natives for their labour in trade goods; cut off from the world, without books, without friends, and with no interest beyond the zone of sea encircling the island, except the interest of his steadily accumulating money in the hands of his agents—the Bank of California.

The face of the white man showed thin and expressionless as a wedge of ice as he came over the rail like a ghost and slipped down to the cabin with Peterson to talk business.

Rantan and Carlin leaned over the side and watched the kanakas in the boat pulling forward to talk to the schooner crew congregated at the rail by the foc'sle head.

The beach lay only a cable length or two away, empty except for a couple of fishing canoes drawn up beyond tide mark; no house was to be seen, the village lying back among the trees, and no sound came from all that incredible wealth of verdure—nothing, but the far voice of a torrent, raving yet slumberous and mixed with the hush of the surf on the reefs and beach.

"Notice that chap," said Carlin, "didn't look to right or left of him, same's if he'd been doped. Reckon he's full of money too if he's the only trader here—notice his white ducks and his dandy hat and the mug under it? I know the sort. Drink turns to vinegar in a chap like that and that's the sort that makes money in the islands."

"Or the fellows that aren't afraid to put their hands on the stuff when they see it," replied Rantan. "Well, what about that pearl island I was speaking of?"

"And that hooker you were going to take to get there," cut in Carlin. "Put me on her deck and I'm with you."

"You're on it," replied Rantan.

Carlin laughed. He had known Rantan's meaning all along and this strange game of evasion between the two had nothing to do with the *Kermadec*, but with something neither dared to discuss one with the other: Peterson, and what was to be done with Peterson.

"You're on it," continued Rantan, "and now what do you say?"

363

"I'm with you," replied Carlin, "but I don't see how you're to do it. I'll have no hand in doing it."

"Leave that to me," said the other, "you've only to help work the ship when I've taken her."

"You say Sanders is the only white man here," said Carlin.

"So Peterson tells me," replied Rantan.

"Well, one white man is enough to turn on us," said Carlin.

"He won't turn on us," replied Rantan grimly, and Carlin glancing at him sideways wondered for a moment if he hadn't the devil in tow with Rantan. But Carlin was of the type that will take profit and not care so long as its own hands are clean. I wonder how many of us would eat meat if we had to do the killing ourselves or make money from poisonous industries if we had ourselves to face the poison. What Rantan chose to do was nothing to Carlin so long as he himself had not to do it or to plan it, but he was cautious.

"How about that chap Sru?" he asked. "He's boss of the crew and the only thinking one of them— suppose . . ."

"Nothing," replied the other. "He's with me."

Fell a silence filled with the voice of the far torrent and the murmur of the sea, a hush-a-bye sound through which vaguely came the murmur of voices through the skylight of the saloon where Peterson and the trader were discussing prices and freights, each absorbed by the one sole idea, profit at the expense of the other.

THE TRAGEDY

The Pacific has many industries but none more appealing to the imagination than the old sandalwood trade, a perfumed business that died when copra found its own, before the novelist and the soap boiler came to work the sea of romance, before the B. P. boats churned its swell or Honolulu learned to talk the language of San Francisco.

In those days Levua showed above the billowing green of the breadfruit, the seaward nodding palms, and the tossing fronds of the dracaenas, a belt, visible from the sea, where the sandalwood trees grew and flourished. Trees like the myrtle, many branched and not more than a foot thick in the trunk, with a white deliciously perfumed wood deepening to yellow at the root.

Sanders, the trader of Levua who exported this timber, paid for it in trade goods, so many sticks of tobacco at five cents a stick, so many coloured beads or pieces of hoop iron wherewith to make knives, for a tree. He paid this price to Tahuku the chief of the tribe and he paid nothing for the work of tree felling, barking, and cutting the wood into billets. Tahuku arranged all that. He was the capitalist of Levua, though his only capital was his own ferocity and cunning, the trees rightfully belonged to all. The billets already cut and stored in go-downs were rafted across the lagoon in fragment heaps to the *Kermadec* and shot on board from hand to hand, piled on deck and then stowed in the hold, a slow business watched by Le Moan with uncomprehending eyes. She knew nothing of trade. She only knew what Sru had promised her, that soon, very soon, the ship would turn and go south to find Karolin once again. She believed him because he spoke the truth and she had an instinct for the truth keen as her instinct for direction, so she waited and watched whilst the cargo came leisurely and day by day and week by week, the cargo bound for nowhere, never to be sold, never to be turned into incense, beads, fancy boxes and cabinets; the cargo only submitted to by the powers that had taken command of the *Kermadec* and her captain, because until the cargo was on board, the ship would not take on her water and her sea-going stores in the shape of bananas and taro.

Down through the paths where the great tree ferns grew on either side and the artu and Jack-fruit trees cast their shadows, came the men of Levua, naked, like polished mahogany, and bearing the white perfumed billets of sandalwood; as they rafted them across the diamond-clear emerald-green water to where the *Kermadec* stood in the sapphire blue of twelve fathoms their songs came and went on the wind, the singers unconscious that all the business of that beach was as futile as the labour of ants or the movement of shadows, made useless by the power of the pearl Le Moan carried behind her left ear.

The night before sailing, the water and fruit were brought on board and Peterson went ashore to have supper with Sanders taking Rantan with him. Carlin remained behind to look after the ship.

It was a lovely evening, the light of sunset rose- gold on the foam of the reefs and gliding the heights of Levua, the trees and the bursting torrent whose far-off voice filled the air with a mist of sound. Carlin, leaning on the rail, watched the boat row ashore, Sru at the stem oar, Peterson steering. He watched Peterson and the mate walk up the beach and disappear amongst the trees; they had evidently given orders that the boat was to wait for them on the beach, for, instead of returning, Sru and his men squatted on the sands, lit their pipes and fell to playing su-ken, tossing pebbles and bits of coral in the air and catching them on the backs of their hands.

Carlin lit his pipe. What he was watching was more interesting than any stage play, for he knew that the hour had struck, that the water and stores were on board and the ship due to raise her anchor at sunrise.

He stood with his eyes fixed on the beach. The trader's house and store lay only a few hundred yards back among the trees and the native village quarter of a mile beyond and close to the beginning of the sandalwood groves; would any trouble in the trader's house be heard by the people of the village? He put this question to himself in a general way and the answer came "No." Not unless shots were fired; but then without shooting—how—how—how?

How what?

He did not enter into details with himself. He stood watching the men on the beach and then he saw Sru as if suddenly tired of the game they were playing, rise up, stretch himself and stroll towards the boat. Near the boat a fishing canoe was beached and Sru having contemplated the boat for a minute or so turned his attention to the canoe. He examined the outrigger, pressed his foot on it and then bending over the interior picked out something—it was a fish spear with a single barb. Carlin remembered that Rantan on landing had looked into the canoe, as though from curiosity or as if to make sure there was something in it. Who could tell?

The fish spear seemed to interest Sru. He poised it as if for a throw, examined the barb and then, spear in hand, came back to the fellows who were still playing their game and sat down. Carlin saw him exhibiting the spear to them, poised it, talking, telling no doubt old stories of fish he had killed on the reef at Soma; then, as if tired, he threw the thing on the sand beside him and lay back whilst the others continued their endless game.

Then came dark and the steadily increasing shower of star-light till the coal sack showed in the Milky Way like a hole punched in marble and the beach like a beach in ghost-land, the figures on it clearly defined and especially now the figure of Sru, who had suddenly risen as though alarmed and was standing spear in hand.

Then at a run he made for the trees and vanished.

*

Carlin turned away from the rail and spat. The palms of his hands were sweating and something went knock, knock, knock, in his ears with every beat of his heart. The kanakas on board were down in the foc'sle from which a thin island voice rose singing an endless song, the deck was clear only for the figure of Le Moan—and Carlin, half crazy with excitement, not daring to look towards the beach, walking like a drunken man up and down began to shout and talk to the girl.

"Hi, you kanaka girl," cried Carlin, "something up on the beach—Lord God! she can't talk, why can't you talk, hey? Whacha staring at me dumb for? Rouse the chaps forward, we'll be wantin' the anchor up". . . He went to the foc'sle head and kicked— calling to the hands below to tumble up, tumble up, and to hell with their singing for there was something going on on the beach. Ruining everything, himself included, if they had been a white crew; then making a dash down to the saloon he beat and smashed at the store cupboard where he knew the whiskey was kept, beat with his naked fists till the panels gave and he tore them out, and breaking the neck of a whiskey bottle, drank with bleeding lips till a quarter of the bottle was gone.

Then he sat at the table still clutching the bottle by the neck but himself again. The nerve crisis had passed suddenly as it had come.

Yes, there was something going on upon the beach that night when, as Le Moan and the crew crowding to the port rail watched, the figure of Rantan suddenly broke from the trees and came running across the sands towards the boat followed by Sru.

She heard the voice of Sru shouting to the boat kanakas: "Tahuku has slain the white man, the trader and Pete'son have been slain." She saw the boat rushed out into the starlit water and as it came along towards the ship, she saw some of the crew rush to the windlass and begin heaving the anchor chain short whilst others fought to get the gaskets off the jib and raise the mainsail. Already alarmed by Carlin the words of Sru completed the business. Tahuku was out for killing and as they laboured and shouted, Carlin hearing the uproar on deck, put the whiskey bottle upstanding in a bunk and came tumbling up the ladder and almost into the arms of Rantan who came tumbling over the rail.

THEY MAKE SOUTH

Then from the shore you might have seen the *Kermadec* like a frightened bird unfolding her wings as the boat came on board and the anchor came home, mainsail, foresail and jib filling to the steady wind coming like an accomplice out of the west, the forefoot cutting a ripple in the starlit waters of the lagoon and the stern swinging slowly towards Levua, where two white men lay dead in the trader's house and where in the village by the sandal grove Tahuku and his men lay asleep, unconscious of what civilization had done in their name.

Rantan, steering, brought the ship through the broad passage in the reefs where the starlight lit the spray of the breaking swell, the vessel lifting to the heave of the sea caught a stronger flow of wind and with the main boom swung to port headed due south.

Rantan handed the wheel to Sru and turned to a bundle lying in the port scuppers. It was Carlin sound asleep and snoring; the mate touched the beachcomber with his foot and then turning, went below.

He saw the locker smashed open and the whiskey bottle in the bunk, he opened a porthole and flung the bottle out and then turning to the locker, searched it. There were two more bottles in the locker and having sent them after the first, he closed the port and sat down at the table under the swinging lamp.

Kermadec, cargo, crew and ship's money were his; the crew knew nothing except that Tahuku had killed Pete'son and the white trader; there was no man to speak except Sru, who dared not speak, and Carlin who knew nothing definite. In time and at a proper season it was possible that these might be rendered dumb and out of count, and this would be the story of the *Kermadec*.

*

Without her captain, murdered by the natives of Levua, and navigated by her mate, who knew little or nothing of navigation, she had attempted to make back to Soma; had missed Soma and found a big lagoon island, Karolin, which was not on the charts. There Sru, the bo'sun, and Carolin, a white man, had died of fish poisoning, and there she had lain for a year—doing what . . . ?

"And what were you doing all that time, Mr. Rantan?" The question was being put to him before an imaginary Admiralty court, and the answer "Pearling" could not be given.

It was only now, with everything done and the ship his, that the final moves in the game were asking to be solved; up to this the first moves had claimed all his mental energy.

H. de Vere Stacpoole

The *Kermadec* could be lost on some civilized coast quite easily, everything would be quite easy but the accounting for that infernal year—and it would take a year at least to make good in a pearl lagoon.

No, the *Kermadec* must never come within touch of civilization again, once he was sure of the pearl ground being worth working; the vessel must go; with the longboat he might get at last back to Soma or some of the Paumotuan islands—might.

The fact of his ignorance of navigation that had helped his story so far, hit him now on the other side, the fact so useful before a Board of Trade enquiry would help him little with the winds and tides and to the winds and tides he had committed himself in the long run.

He came on deck. The crew, all but the watch, had crowded down into the foc'sle where all danger over and well at sea, they had turned in. Sru was still at the wheel and Le Moan, who had been talking to him, vanished forward as the mate appeared in the starlight and stood watching for a moment the far-off loom of the land.

Carlin still slept. He had rolled over on his back and was lying, mouth open and one hand stretched out on the deck planking, his snores mixed with the sound of the bow wash and the creaking of the gaff jaws and cordage.

Rantan looked into the binnacle, then with a glance at Carlin he turned to Sru.

The Paumotuan did not speak, he did not seem to see the mate or recognize his presence on deck, the whites of his eyeballs showed in the starlight; and as he steered, true as a hair to the course, his lips kept working as he muttered to himself.

He looked like a man scared, and steering, alone, out of some imminent danger, that appearance of being isolated was the strangest thing. It made Rantan feel for a moment as though he were not there, as though the *Kermadec* were a ship deserted by all but the steersman.

Sru was scared. Steering true as an automaton, his mind was far away in the land of vacancy and pursued by white feller Mas'r Pete'son. It had come on him like a stroke when Le Moan, approaching him, had asked where the bearded man was who had gone ashore and not returned. He had no fear of Le Moan or her question, but out of it Peterson had come, the white man whom he had always feared yet whom he had dared to kill. The appalling power that had strengthened his arm and mind, the power of the vision of tobacco unlimited, Swedish matches, knives, gin and seidlitz powders, was no longer with him—Peterson was on his back, worse than any black dog, and now he steered, his head began to toss from side to side and like a man exalted by drink he began to sing and chatter, whilst Rantan, who knew the Paumotuan mind and that in another minute the wheel would be dropped and the steersman loose and running amok, drew close.

Then suddenly, and with all the force of his body behind the blow, he struck and Sru fell like a pole- axed ox whilst the mate snapping at the spokes of the wheel steadied the vessel and stood, his eye on the binnacle cord holding the ship on her course.

Sru lay where he fell, just as Carlin lay where drink had struck him down; the fellows forward saw nothing, or if they did they made no movement, and the schooner, heeling deeper to the steadying breeze held on full south, whilst behind her the wake ran luminous with the gold of phosphorus and the silver of star-light.

Presently Sru sat up, then he rose to his feet. He remembered nothing, nothing of his terror or of the blow that had felled him; it seemed to him he must have fallen asleep at the wheel and that Rantan had relieved him.

SOUTH

The stars faded, the east grew crimson and the sun arose to show Levua gone; a sky without cloud, a sea without trace of sail or gull.

Le Moan, crouching in the bow with the risen sun hot on her left shoulder, saw the long levels of the marching swell as they came and passed, the *Kermadec* bowing to them; saw the distant southern sea line and beyond it the road to Karolin.

With her eyes shut and as the needle of the compass finds the north magnetic pole, she could have pointed to where Karolin lay; and as she gazed across the fields of the breeze-blown swell no trace of cloud troubled her mind, all was bright ahead. Sru had made it clear to her that no hurt would come to Taori, and with Peterson, had gone any last lingering doubt that may have been in her mind. She trusted Sru and she trusted Rantan, who had spoken kindly to her, Carlin, and the kanaka crew; of Peterson, the man who had terrified her first and the only trustable man on that ship, she had always had her doubts, begotten by that first impression, by his beard, his gruff voice and what Sru had said about Peterson and how he would "swallow all"—that is to say the pearls of Karolin; those mysterious pearls that the white men treasured and of which the charm hidden behind her ear had spoken to Sru.

She had always worn it as a protection and she had not the least doubt that it had spoken to Sru, just as a person might speak, and told him of those other pearls which she had often seen and played with when oysters were cast to rot on the beach for the sake of their shells. She had not the least doubt that to the talisman behind her ear was due this happy return and the elimination of Peterson. Was she wrong?

As she crouched, the back draught from the head sails fanning her hair, the ship and her crew, the sea and its waves, all vanished, dissolved matter from which grew as by some process of recrystallization the beach of Karolin. The long south beach where the sand was whispering in the wind, the hot south beach where the sun-stricken palms lifted their fronds to the brassy sky of noon and the tender skies of dawn and evening, the beach above which the stars stood at night all turning with the turning dome of sky.

She saw a canoe paddling ashore and the canoe man now on the beach, his eyes crinkled against the sun—eyes coloured like the sea when the grey of the squall mixes with its blue. The sun was on his red-gold hair and he trod the sands lightly, not as the kanaka walks and moves; one might have fancied little wings upon his feet.

His naked body against the blazing lagoon showed like a flame of gold against a flame of blue. It was Taori. Taori as she had seen him first, on that day when he had come to bid Aioma to the canoe building.

It was as if Fate on that day had suddenly stripped away a veil showing her the one thing to be desired, the only thing that would ever matter to her in this life or the next.

As she leaned, the breeze in her hair and her mind like a bird fleeting far ahead into the distance, flying fish like silver shaftless arrow-heads passed and flittered into the blue water, and now a turtle floating asleep and disturbed by the warble of the bow wash and the creak of the onrushing schooner, sank quietly fathoms deep leaving only a few bubbles on the swell.

Carlin had come on deck. Rantan had said not a word about the broken open cupboard or the whiskey; the ship was cleared of drink and that was enough for him; when he came on deck a few minutes after the other, he found the beachcomber leaning on the after rail.

A shark was hanging in the wake of the schooner. A deep-sea ship does not sail alone. She gives company and shelter to all sorts of fish from the remora that hangs on for a whole voyage, to the bonito that follows her maybe for a week. In front of the shark, moving and glittering like spoon bait, a pilot fish showed in flashes of blue and gold.

Carlin turned from contemplation of these things to find Rantan at his side.

On going below for a wash after his night on deck, Carlin had found the other at breakfast. Neither man had spoken of the events of the night before, nor did they now.

"Following us steady, isn't he?" said Carlin, turning again to contemplate the monster in the wake— "don't seem to be swimming either and he's going all of eight knots. What's he after, following us like that?"

"Haven't you ever seen a shark before?" asked Rantan.

"Yes, and I've never seen good of them following a ship," replied Carlin, "and I'm not set on seeing them, 'specially now."

"Why now?" asked the mate.

But Carlin shied from the subject that was in both their minds.

"Oh, I don't know," said he, "I was thinking of the traverse in front of us. . . . Say, now we're set and sailing for it, are you sure of hitting that island?"

"Sure," said the mate.

"Then you're better at the navigating job than you pretended to be," said Carlin. "What I like about you is the way you keep things hid."

"I've kept nothing hid," replied the other. "I'm crazy bad on the navigation, but I've got a navigator on board that'll take us there same as a bullet to a target."

"Sru?"

"Sru nothing—the kanaka girl, she's a Marayara. Ever heard of them? You get them among the kanakas; every kanaka has a pretty good sense of direction, but a Marayara, take him away from his island and he'll home back like a pigeon if he has a canoe and can paddle long enough. That island we took the girl from is the pearl island. Born and bred there she was, and it's her centre of everything. Sru got it all out of her and about the pearls and fixed up with her to take us back. Don't know what he's promised her, I reckon a few beads is all she wants and all she'll get, but that's how it lies: we've only got to push along due south by the compass and she'll correct us, leeway or set of current or any tomfool tricks of the needle don't matter to her. She never bothers about the compass, she sees where she wants to go straight before her nose, same's when land's in sight you see it and steer for it."

"Can she steer?" asked Carlin, who had not been on deck the day Sru set her at the wheel.

Rantan turned to where the girl was standing in the bow, called her aft and gave the wheel over to her. When she had felt the ship, standing with her head slightly uptilted, she altered the course a few points; the *Kermadec* had been off her path by that amount owing to leeway or set of current.

From that moment the ship was in the hands of Le Moan, tireless as only a being can be who exists always in the open air, she lived at the wheel with intervals for sleep and rest, always finding on her return the ship off her course, still heading south, but no longer on that exact and miraculous line drawn by instinct between herself and Karolin.

Error in the form of leeway or the influence of swell or the set of current could never push the vessel to east or west of that line, for the line moved with the ship, and as the journey shortened, like a steadily shortening string tied to a ball in centrifugal motion, it would bring the *Kermadec* at last to Karolin, no matter how far she was swung out of her course—blown fifty, a hundred, two hundred miles to east or west it would not matter, her head would turn to Karolin. The only flaw in that curious navigational instrument, the mind of Le Moan, was its blindness to distance from Karolin, the pull being the same for any distance, and had the island risen suddenly before them on some dark night, she would have piled the craft upon it unless warned by the sound of the reef.

*

Rantan kept the log going, he had a rough idea of the distance between Karolin and Levua, but he did not try to explain the log to Le Moan. If he had done so, his labour would have been wasted. Le Moan had no idea of time as we conceive it, cut up into hours, minutes and seconds. Time for her was a thing, not an abstract idea; a thing ever present yet shifting in appearance—energy.

The recognition of Time is simply the recognition of the rhythm of energy by energy itself. Le Moan recognized the rhythm in the tides, in the sunrises and sunsets, in the going and coming of the fish shoals, in slumber and waking life, but of those figments of man's intellect, hours, minutes, years, she had no idea. Always in touch with reality, she had come in vague touch with the truth that there is no past, no future—nothing ever but rhythmic alternations of the present.

But, though unable to grasp the division of the real day into empirical fractions, the compass, that triumph of man's intellect, presented no difficulties to her. When Rantan explained its pointing to her she understood, the needle pointed away from Karolin.

The fleur-de-lys on the card, which seemed to her vaguely like the head of a fish spear, pointed away from Karolin, that is away from the south.

The compass card moved, she did not know that the compass card was absolutely steady, that this appearance of movement was a delusion caused by the altered course of the ship, that the ship pivoted on the card not the card on the ship.

If she let the ship off her course to the east, the card moved and her sense of direction told her at once that the fleur-de-lys was still pointing away from Karolin. She spoke on this matter to Sru. Sru, who had made the two voyages on ships and who was yet a capable steersman, had quite taken for granted his first captain's explanation to him of the compass; there was a god in it that held it just so and if Sru let the card wobble from the course set down, the god would most likely come out of the binnacle and kick Sru into the middle of next week. He was a Yankee skipper and he had made an excellent steersman of Sru.

Le Moan understood; she believed in gods, from Naniwa the shark-toothed one to Nan the benign: believed in them, just as white men believe in their Gods—with reservations; but this was different from anything she had hitherto conceived of a deity. He must be very small to be contained in the binnacle, very small and set of purpose always pointing with the spear head away from Karolin. Why?

Rantan had pointed down to the spear head and away north and told her it always pointed there, always away from the direction of Karolin. Why?

She had not asked him why the card moved, or seemed to move, Sru having already told her.

The feeling came to her that the little imprisoned something was against going to Karolin, but no one seemed to mind it, yet they were always consulting it, Rantan when he took the wheel and Sru and Maru, who was also a good steersman.

Every day at noon Rantan would appear on deck and take an observation of the sun with Peterson's sextant, whilst Carlin, if he were on deck, would cuff himself on the thigh and turn and lean over the rail to laugh unobserved.

Rantan was only fooling—keeping up appearances, so that the crew might fancy him as good as Peterson in finding his way on the sea. Sru had never told the others that they depended entirely on Le Moan, the fact that she was a way-finder was known to them, but it is as well for the after guard to keep up appearances. Rantan might as well have been looking at the sun through a beer bottle for all he knew of the matter, but the crew could not tell that. So, as a navigator, he held a place in their minds above the girl.

At night when the binnacle lamp was lit and she happened to be at the wheel, her eyes would wander to the trembling card. She would put the ship a bit off its course just to see it move, noticing that it always moved in the same manner in a reverse direction to the alteration in course. If the head of the schooner turned to starboard, the card would rotate to port and vice versa. She studied its doings as one studies the doings of a strange animal, but she never caught it altering its mind or its action.

At night it always seemed to her that the thing in the binnacle, whether god or devil, was inimical to her, or at all events warning her not to take the ship back to Karolin; by day it did not matter.

So under the stars and over the phosphorescent sea the *Kermadec* headed south, ever south, the blazing dawns leaping over the port rail and the gigantic sunsets dying with the blood of Titans the skies to starboard, till one morning Le Moan, handing the wheel to Rantan, pointed ahead and then walked forward. Her work was done. Far ahead, paling the sky, shone the lagoon blaze of Karolin.

BOOK II

THE MAID OF AIOMA

Le Moan had left Karolin as a gull leaves the reef, unnoticed.

Not a soul had seen her go and it was not for some days that Aioma, busy with the tree felling, recollected her existence, and the fact that she had not followed him to the northern beach; then he sent a woman across and she had returned with news that there was no trace of the girl though her canoe was beached, also that there was no trace of food having been recently cooked, and that the girl must have been gone some days as there were no recent sand traces. The wind even when it is only moderately strong blurs and obliterates sand traces, and the woman judged that no one had been about on the southern beach for some days. She had found tracks, however, for which she could not account. The marks left by the boots of Peterson, also the footsteps of the kanakas who had carried the water casks disturbed her mind; they had nearly vanished, but it seemed to her that many people had been there, a statement that left Aioma cold.

Aioma had no time for fancies. If the girl were alive, she would come across in her canoe, if death had come to her in any of the forms in which death walked the reef, there was no use in troubling. The call to the canoe building, resented at first, had given him new youth, the spirit of the sea sang in him and the perfume of the new-felled trees brought Uta Matu walking on the beach, and his warriors.

Aioma, like Le Moan, had no use for the past or the future, the burning present was everything.

Things that had been were to Aioma things floating alongside at a greater or less distance, not astern. It was not the memory of Uta Matu that walked the beach, but Uta Matu himself, untouchable, because of distance, and only able to talk as he had talked in life, but still there. Aioma had not to turn his head to look backwards at him as we have to turn our heads to see our dead, he had only to glance sideways, as it were. The things of yesterday, the day before yesterday and the day before that, were beside Aioma at greater or less distances, not behind him—all like surf riders on the same wave with him and carried forward by the same flowing, yet ever separating one from the other though keeping in line.

In the language of Karolin there was no word indicating our idea of the past except the word *akuma* (distance) which might mean the distance between a canoe and a canoe or between a happening of to-day and of yesterday, and to the woman who judged that Le Moan had not trod the beach for some days, "days" meant measures of distance, not of time. Le Moan had been travelling, moving away from the beach, not returning, whilst so many sunrises had occurred and so many sunsets. She had been away a long distance, not a long time.

The speed of a man running a mile on Karolin had nothing to do with the time occupied, it was a measure of his strength; the race was a struggle between the man and the mile, and of the runners the swiftest to a Karalonite was not the quickest but the strongest and most agile; this profound truth was revealed to their instinctive sight undimmed by the *muscæ volitantes* which we call minutes, seconds and hours, also the truth that when the race was over it was not extinct but merely removed to a distance—just as a canoe drifting from a canoe is not extinct though untouchable and out of hail, and fading at last from sight through distance.

A dead man on Karolin was a man who had drifted away; he was there, but at a distance, he might even return through the distance in a stronger way than memory sight could reveal him! Many had. Uta Matu himself had been seen in this way by several since he had drifted away—he had come back once to tell Nalia the wife of

Oti where the sacred paddle was hid, the paddle which acted as the steer oar of the biggest war canoe. He had forgotten that the war canoe had been destroyed. Still he had returned. Though with a Melanesian strain in them, unlike the Melanesians the men of Karolin had no belief that the souls of ancestors become reincarnated in fish or birds, nor did they believe in the influence of *Mana*, that mysterious spiritual something believed in so widely by Polynesians and Melanesians alike.

Memory, to the Karolinite, was a sort of sight which enabled the living to look not over the past but the present, and see the people and things that floated, not behind in a far-off past, but to right and left in a far-off present.

Just as the surf rider sees his companions near and far, all borne on the same wave, though some might be beyond reach of voice, and some almost invisible through distance, the return of a spirit was an actual moving of a distant one towards the seer, as though a surf rider were to strike out and swim to a far-off fellow at right angles to the flow of the wave.

So Aioma, as he worked, saw Uta Matu and his warriors and the old canoe-builders, not as dead and gone figures, but as realities though beyond touch and hail of voice and sight of the eye of flesh.

*

Since the war, years ago, between the northern and southern tribes, a large proportion of the children born on the island had been boys, whilst most of the women had developed manly attributes in accordance with that natural law which rules in the remotest island as well as in the highest and broadest civilization.

Aioma had no need of helpers, leaving out the boys, some dozen or so, who could wield an ax as well as a man; but Aioma though his heart and soul were in his work was no mere canoe-builder. He had in him the making of a statesman. He would not let Dick work at the building or do any work at all except fishing and fish spearing.

"You are the chief (Ompalu)," said Aioma as he sat of an evening before the house of Uta Matu, now the house of Dick. "You are young and do not know all the ways of things, but I love you as a son; I do not know what is in you that is above us, but the sea I love is in your eyes. The sea, our father, sent you, but you have still to learn the ways of the land, where the chief does no work." Then he would grunt to himself and rock as he sat, and then his voice rising to a whine, "Could the people raise their heads to one who labours with them, or would they bow their heads so that he might put his foot on their necks?" Then casting his eyes down he would talk to himself, the words so run together as to be indistinguishable; but always, Katafa noticed, his eyes would return again and again to the little ships in the shadow of the house, the model ships made by Kearney long ago—the vestiges of a civilization of which Dick and Aioma and Katafa knew nothing, or only that the ships, the big ships of which these were the likenesses, were dangerous and the men in them evil and to be avoided or destroyed if possible.

The *Portsey* of long ago that had fired a cannon shot and destroyed Katafa's canoe, the schooner that had brought the Melanesians to Palm Tree, the Spanish ship that had been sunk in Karolin lagoon and the whaler that had come after her, all these had burnt into the minds of Dick, Aioma and Katafa; the fact that something of which they did not know the name (but which was civilization), was out there beyond the sea line, something that, octopus-like, would at times thrust out a feeler in the form of a ship, an *ayat* destructive and, if possible, to be destroyed.

Ayat was the name given by Karolin to the great burgomaster gulls that were to the small gulls what schooners are to canoes, and so anything in the form of a ship was an *ayat*, that is to say, a thing carrying with it all the propensities of a robber and a murderer; for the great gulls would rob the lesser gulls of their food and devour their chicks and fight and darken the sunshine of the reef with their wings.

The comparison was not a compliment to the Pacific traders or their ships or the civilization that had sent them forth to prey on the world, but it was horribly apposite.

And yet the little *ayats* in the shadow of the house had for Aioma an attraction beyond words. They were as fascinating as sin. This old child after a hard day's work would sometimes dream of them in his sleep; dream that he was helping to sail them on the big rock pool, as he sometimes did in reality. The frigate, the full-rigged ship, the schooner and the whale man, all had cruised in the rock pool which seemed constructed by nature as a model testing tank; indeed the first great public act of Dick as ruler of the Karolinites had been a full review of this navy on the day after he had fetched Aioma from the southern beach. Aioma, fascinated by the sight of the schooner which Dick had shown him on his landing, had insisted on seeing the others launched and the whole population had stood round ten deep with the little children between the women's legs, all with their eyes fixed on the pretty sight. The strangest sight;—for Kearney the illiterate and ignorant had managed to symbolize the two foundations of civilization, war and trade; and here in little yet in essence lay the ships of Nelson and the ships of Villeneuve: the great wool ships, the *Northumberland* that had brought Dick's parents to Palm Tree, the whalers of Martha's Vineyard and the sandalwood schooners, those first carriers of the disease of the white man.

To Aioma the schooner was the most fascinating. He knew the whaler with her try works and her heavy davits and her squat build; he had seen her before in the whaler whose brutal crew had landed and been driven off. He knew the ship, he had seen its likeness in the Spanish ship of long ago; the frigate intrigued him, but the schooner took his heart—it was not only that he understood her rig and way of sailing better than the rig and way of sailing of the others, it was more than that. Aioma was an instinctive ship lover, and to the lover of ships, the schooner has most appeal, for the schooner is of all things that float the most graceful and the most beautiful; and in contrast to her canvas, the canvas of your square rigged ship becomes dishcloths hung out to dry.

He brooded on this thing over which Kearney had expended his most loving care, and in which nothing was wanting. He understood the topping lifts that supported the main boom, the foresail, the use of the standing rigging. Kearney, through his work, was talking to him and just as Kearney had explained this and that to Dick, so Dick was explaining it to Aioma. Truly a man can speak though dead, even as Kearney was speaking now.

The method of reefing a sail was unknown to Aioma; a canoe sail was never reefed, reduction of canvas was made by tying the head of the sail up to spill the wind. Fore canvas was unknown to Aioma, but he understood.

The subconscious mathematician in him that made him able to build great canoes capable of standing heavy weather and carrying forty or fifty men apiece, understood all about the practice of the business, though he had never heard of centres of rotation, absolute or relative velocities, of impelling powers, or the laws of the collision of bodies; of inertia or pressures of resistance or squares of velocity or series of inclinations.

Squatting on his hams before the little model of the *Rarotonga*, he knew nothing of these things and yet he knew that the schooner was good, that she would sail close to the wind with little leeway when the wind was on the beam, that the rudder was better than the steering paddle, that the sail area though great would not capsize her, that she was miles ahead of anything he had ever made in the form of a ship. That the maker of the *ayat* was a genius beside whom he was a duffer, unknowing that Kearney was absolutely without inventive genius, and that the schooner was the work of a million men extending over three thousand years.

Katafa sitting beside Dick would watch Aioma as he brooded and played with the thing. It had no fascination for her. The little ships had always repelled her if anything. They were the only dividing point between her and Dick—she could not feel his pleasure or interest in them, and from this fact possibly arose a vague foreboding that perhaps some day in some way the little ships might separate them. When a woman loves, she can become jealous of a man's pipe, of his tennis racket, of his best friend, of anything that she can't share and which occupies his attention at times more than she does.

But the essence of jealousy is concentration, and Katafa's green eye was cast not so much on the whole fleet as on the little schooner. This was Dick's favourite, as it was Aioma's.

*

One night, long after the vanishing of Le Moan, so long that everyone had nearly forgotten her, Aioma had a delightful dream.

He dreamt that he was only an inch high and standing on the schooner's deck. Dick reduced to the same stature was with him, and half a dozen others, and the schooner was in the rock pool that had spread to the size of Karolin lagoon. Oh, the joy of that business! They were hauling up the mainsail and up it went to the pull of the halyards just as he had often hauled it with the pull of his finger and thumb on the tiny halyards of the model; but this was a real great sail and men had to pull hard to raise it and there it was set. Then the foresail went up and the jib was cast loose and Aioma, mad with joy, was at the tiller, the tiller that he had often moved with his finger and thumb.

Then pressed by the wind she began to heel over and the outrigger—she had taken on an outrigger— went into the air; he could see the outrigger gratings with drinking-nuts and bundles of food tied to it after the fashion of sea-going canoes, and he shouted to his companions to climb on to it and bring it down. Then he awoke, sweating but dazzled by the first part of the dream.

Two days later a boy came running and shouting to him as he was at work; and turning, Aioma saw the fulfilment of his vision. Borne by the flooding tide with all sails drawing and a bone in her teeth, the little schooner swelled to a thousand times her size, was gaily entering the lagoon. It was the *Kermadec*.

H. de Vere Stacpoole

WAR

Rantan was at the wheel, and Le Moan forward, with swelling heart, stood watching as they passed the break, the Gates of Morning, through which the tide was flooding like a mill-race. She saw the southern beach still deserted and the northern beach where the trees sheltered the village from sight. Not a sign of life was to be seen in all that vast prospect of locked lagoon and far- running reefs till from the distant trees a form appeared—Aioma.

After him came others till the beach close to the trees was thronged by a crowd even in movement like a colony of ants disturbed and showing now against the background of the trees the glint of spears. Le Moan's heart sank under a sudden premonition of evil. She turned and glanced to where Rantan at the wheel was staring ahead and Carlin close by him was shading his eyes.

Rantan had not expected this. He had fancied Karolin deserted. Sru had said nothing of what Le Moan had told him about Taori and he said nothing now as he stood with eyes wrinkled against the sun blaze from the lagoon. Taori, he had gathered to be some kanaka boy, a love of Le Moan's who, so far from giving trouble, would welcome her back—but that crowd, its movements and the flash of the thready spears! He made vague answers to the questions flung at him by the mate, then at the order to let go the anchor he ran forward whilst Carlin dived below, returning with two of the Viterli rifles and ammunition. Then as the anchor fell and the *Kermadec* swung to her moorings on the flood, nose to the break, Rantan, leaving the wheel and standing with compressed lips, his hand on the after rail and his eyes on the crowd, suddenly broke silence and turned to Carlin.

"We don't want any fighting," said he. "We've got to palaver them. It's a jolt. Peterson said the place was empty, and I reckon he lied or else he didn't keep his eyes skinned, but whether or no we've got to swallow it. Worst is we've no trade to speak of, nothing but sandalwood. No matter—we don't want nothing but to be left alone. Order out the boat and we'll row off to them, and keep those guns hid."

He went below for Peterson's revolver which Carlin had forgotten, and when he returned, the boat was down with four kanakas for crew and Carlin in the stern sheets; he followed and took his place by the beachcomber and the boat pushed off.

He had made a great blunder, absolutely forgotten the existence of Le Moan and her use as an ambassador, but the mind of Rantan was working against odds.

381

He had never consciously worried about Peterson. The dead Peterson was done with out of count, and yet away in the back of his mind Peterson existed, not as a form, not even as a shadow, but as the vaguest, vaguest hint of possible trouble, some day. Steering, or smoking below, or enjoying in prospect the profits to be got out of the venture, Rantan would be conscious of a something that was marring his view of things; something that, seizing it with his mind, would prove to be nothing more than just a feeling that trouble might come some day owing to Peterson.

On sailing into the lagoon, the wind across that great blue pearl garden had swept his mind clear of all trace of worry. Here was success at last, wealth for the taking and no one to watch the taker or interfere with his doings. No one but the gulls. A child on that beach would have shattered the desolation and destroyed the feeling of security and detachment from the world.

Then the trees had given up their people and to Rantan it was almost as though Peterson himself had reappeared.

He had reckoned to get rid of the crew of the *Kermadec* in his own given time after he had worked them for his profit, to get rid of Carlin, of his own name, of everything and anything that could associate him with this venture, and here Were hundreds of witnesses where he had expected to find none but the gull that cannot talk.

Truly it was a jolt!

As the boat drew on for the shore, the crowd on the beach moved and spread and contracted and then became still, the spears all in one clump.

There were at least thirty of the boys of Karolin able to hurl a spear with the precision of a man, and when Aioma had sighted the schooner and given the alarm, Dick, who had been on the outer beach, had called them together. Taiepa, the son of Aioma, had distributed the spears and Aioma himself in a few rapid words had fired the hearts of the tribe.

The strangers must not be allowed to land. For a moment, but only a moment, he took the command of things from Dick's hands. "They came before," said Aioma, "when I was a young man, and the great Uta knowing them to be men full of evil would not allow them to land but drove them off, and yet again they came in a canoe bigger than the first (the Spanish ship), and they landed and fought with Uta and he killed them and burnt their great canoe—and yet again they have come and yet again we must fight. We are few, but Taori in himself is many."

"They shall not land," said Dick, "even if I face them alone."

That was the temper of Karolin and it voiced itself as the boat drew closer to the beach in a cry that rang across the water, harsh and sudden, making the kanaka rowers pause and turn their heads.

"They mean fighting," said Carlin, bending towards one of the rifles lying on the bottom boards.

"Leave that gun alone," said Rantan.

He ordered the rowers to pull a bit closer, rising up and standing in the stern sheets and waving his hand to the beach crowd as though intimating that he wished to speak to them.

The only answer was a spear flung by Taiepa that came like a flash of light and fell into the water true of aim but short by a few yards. The rowers stopped again and backed water. Whilst Carlin picked up the floating spear as a trophy and put it with the rifles, Rantan sat down. Then he ordered them to pull ahead altering the helm so that the bow turned away from the shore and to the west.

As they moved along the beach the distant crowd followed, but the mate did not heed it; he was busy taking notes of the lie of the land, and the position of the trees. The trees, though deep enough to hide the village from the break, were nowhere dense enough to give efficient cover; the reef just here was very broad but very low. A man would be a target—the head and shoulders of him at least—even if he were on the outer coral.

Rantan having obtained all the information he required on these matters altered the course of the boat and made back for the ship.

"Aren't you going to have one single shot at them?" asked the disgusted Carlin.

"You wait a while," replied the other.

When they reached the *Kermadec* he ordered the men to remain in the boat, and going on board dropped down below with his companion. He went to the locker where the ammunition was stored and counted the boxes. There were two thousand rounds.

"I reckon that will do," said Rantan. "You said you were a good shot. Well, you've got a chance to prove your words. I'm going to shoot up this lagoon."

"From the ship?"

"Ship, no, the boat's good enough; they have no cover worth anything and only a few old fishing canoes that aren't good enough to attack us in."

"Well, I'm not saying you're wrong," said Carlin, "but seems to me it will be more than a one-day job."

"We aren't hustled for time," replied the other, "not if it took weeks."

They came on deck, each carrying a box of ammunition, the spear salved by Carlin had been brought on board by him and stood against the rail. Neither man noticed it, nor did they notice Le Moan crouched in the doorway of the galley and seeming to take shelter from the sun.

Carlin who had ordered a water breaker to be filled, lowered it himself into the boat, then getting in followed by the mate the boat pushed off, Sru rowing stern oar and Rantan at the yoke lines.

It was close on midday and the great sun directly overhead poured his light on the lagoon; beyond the crowd and the trees on the northern beach the coral ran like a white road for miles and miles, to be lost in a smoky shimmer, and from the reef came the near and far voice of the breakers on the outer beach.

The crew left on board, some six in number, had dropped into the foc'sle to smoke and talk. Le Moan could hear their voices as she rose and stood at the rail, her eyes fixed on the boat and her mind divided between the desire to cast herself into the water and swim to the reef and the instinct which told her to stay and watch and wait.

She knew what a rifle was. She had seen Peterson practicing with one of the Viterlis at a floating bottle. There were rifles in the boat, but it was not the rifles that filled her mind with a foreboding amounting to terror, it was Rantan's face as he returned and as he left again. And she could do nothing.

Carlin, before lowering the water breaker had handed an ax into the boat. Why? She could not tell, nor why the water breaker had been taken. It was all part of something that she could not understand, something that was yet evil and threatening to Taori.

She could not make his figure out amongst the crowd, it was too far, and yet he was surely there.

She watched.

The boat drew on towards the beach. Then at the distance of a couple of hundred yards the oarsmen ceased rowing and she floated idly and scarcely drifting—for it was slack water, the flood having ceased. One might have thought the men on board of her were fishing or just lazing in the sun—anything but the truth.

Then Le Moan saw a tiny puff of smoke from the boat's side, a figure amongst the crowd on the beach sprang into the air and fell, and on the still air came the far-off crack of a rifle.

Carlin had got his man. He was an indifferent shot but he could scarcely have missed as he fired into the brown of the crowd. Rantan, no better a shot, fired immediately after and by some miracle nobody was hit.

Then as Le Moan watched, she saw the crowd break to pieces and vanish amongst the trees, leaving only two figures on the beach, one lying on the sands and one standing erect and seeming to threaten the boat with upflung arm. It was Taori. Her sight as though it had gained telescopic power told her at once that it was Taori.

She saw him bend and catch up the fallen figure in his arms and as he turned to the trees with it, the boat fired again, but missed him. Another shot rang out before he reached the trees, but he vanished unscathed, and quiet fell on the beach and lagoon, broken only by the clamour of gulls disturbed by the firing.

Le Moan changed her place, the ebb was beginning to run and the schooner to swing with it. She came forward and took her position near the foc'sle head, her eyes still fixed on the boat and beach. From the foc'sle came the sound of an occasional snore from the kanakas who had turned in and were sleeping like dogs.

Four fishing canoes lay on the sands near the trees, and now as she watched, she saw the boat under way again pulling in to the beach. The rowers tumbled out and the boat pushed off a few yards with only the two white men in her whilst the landing party made for the canoes and began to smash them up.

Sru—she could tell him by his size—wielded the ax, two others helped in the business with great lumps of loose coral, whilst the fourth stood watch.

It took time, for they did their work thoroughly, breaking the outriggers, breaking the outrigger poles, breaking the canoe bodies, working with the delight that children take in sheer destruction.

The god Destruction was abroad on Karolin beach and lagoon. Though without a temple or a place in mythology of all the gods, he is the most powerful, the most agile and quick of eye, and the swiftest to come when called.

Le Moan watching, saw the four men on the beach stand contemplating their work before returning to the boat.

Then she saw one of them throw up his hands and fall as if felled by an ax. The others turned to run and the foremost of them tripped as a man trips on a kink in a carpet and fell; of the two others one pitched and turned a complete somersault as though some unseen jiu-jitsu player had dealt with him, and the fourth crumpled like a suddenly closed concertina.

Le Moan's heart sprang alive in her. She knew. The terrible arrows of Karolin poisoned with argora that kills with the swiftness and more than certainty of a bullet had, fired from the trees, done their work.

The spear was the favourite weapon of Karolin, not the bow. The bow was used only on occasions and at long distances. When they came down to resist the landing of Rantan, they had come armed with spears; driven to the shelter of the trees, Aioma, the artful one, had remembered the bows stowed in one of the canoe houses. It was years since the arrows had been poisoned, but the poison of argora never dies, nor does it weaken with time.

In four swings of a pendulum the arrows had done their work, and four upstanding men lay stretched on the beach, motionless, for this terrible poison striking at the nerve centres kills in two beats of the pulse.

Rantan and Carlin, close enough to see the flight of the arrows, put wildly out, tugging at the heavy oars and rowing for their lives; a few hundred yards off shore they paused, rested on their oars and took counsel.

It was a bad business.

Armed with rifles and with easy range they had only managed to bag one of the enemy, whereas. . . !

"Hell," said Carlin.

The sweat was running down his broad face. Rantan, brooding, said nothing for a moment. Then suddenly he broke silence.

"We've dished their canoes, they can't come out and attack us; we've got the range over them, those arrows are no use at any distance; they live mostly on fish, those chaps, and they can't come out and fish, having no canoes, and we aren't hurried for time." He seemed talking to himself, adding up accounts, whilst Carlin, who had picked up one of the rifles, sat with it across his knees, his face turned shoreward where on the beach lay the four dead men, and save for the gulls not a sign of life. The boat on the ebb tide was drifting slowly back in the direction of the schooner.

"We've just got to row up along," went on Rantan, "and get lével with the trees. Those trees don't give much shelter across the reef. Their houses wouldn't stop a bullet from a popgun. Take your oar, when we've got our position we can anchor and take things quiet."

Carlin, putting his gun down, took his oar and they began pulling the heavy boat against the current till they got opposite the village and the trees.

Then within rifle shot, but beyond the reach of arrow flight, they dropped the anchor and the boat swung to the current and broadside to the shore.

Rantan was right—the trees though dense enough in patches were not a sufficient cover for a crowd of people, and the houses were death traps. From where they lay they could see the little houses clear marked against the sky beyond and the house of Uta Matu with the post beside it on top of which was the head of Nan, god of the coconut trees, Nan the benign watching over his people, the puraka beds and the pandanus palms.

Of old there had been two gods of Karolin, Nan the benign and Naniwa the ferocious.

Le Moan's mother had been Le Jennabon, daughter of Le Juan, priestess of Naniwa the shark-toothed god. On the death of Le Juan, Naniwa had seemed to depart, for Karolin. Had he? Do the gods ever die whilst there is a human heart to give them sanctuary?

Nan the benign, grinning on his post—he was carved from a coconut—was set in such a way that his face was turned to the east, that is to say towards the gates of morning. He was placed in that way according to ritual. Chance had anchored the schooner in his line of vision. Hand helpless, as are most benign things, poor old Nan could do nothing to protect the people he no doubt loved. He could keep the weazle-teazle worms away from the puraka plants and he could help a bit in bringing up rain, and it was considered that he could even protect the canoes from the cobra worms that devour planking; but against the wickedness of man and Viterli rifles he was useless.

And yet to-day as he gazed across at the schooner, his grin was in no way diminished, and as the wind stirred the cane post he waggled his head jauntily, perhaps because on the deck of the schooner he saw the granddaughter of the priestess of the sharktoothed god and said to himself with a thrill and a shudder: "Naniwa has returned."

In the old days when a man revenged himself for some wrong, or, going mad, dashed out the brains of another with a club, he was supposed to be possessed by Naniwa, for just as Nan was the minister of agriculture, the shark-toothed one was the minister of justice. He was in a way the law executing criminals and also making criminals for execution, just as the law does with us.

Anyhow and at all events and bad as he may have been, he was the sworn enemy of foreigners; he had inspired Uta Matu to attack the whaler and he had inspired

Le Juan in calling for the attack on the Spanish ship of long ago and to-day perhaps he had inspired Aioma in resisting the landing of these newcomers. The battle was still in the balance, but there on the deck of the anchored schooner stood the granddaughter of his priestess darkly brooding, helpless for the moment, but watching and waiting to strike.

No wonder that Nan grinned and waggled his head at her with a click-clocking noise, for the coconut had worked a bit loose on its stick.

*

Rantan took his seat on the bottom boards in the stern, resting his rifle comfortably on the gunnel; Carlin, going forward, did the same. The wind which had risen and which was moving Nan on his post, stirred the foliage, and between the boles and over the bushes of mammee apple the shifting shadows danced and the shafts of light showered, but sign of human being there was none.

The crafty Aioma, through the mouth of Dick, had ordered all the children and young people into the mammee apple and the women into the houses whilst he and Dick had taken shelter behind trees, two vast trees that stood like giants amidst the coconuts and pandanas palms, brothers of the trees growing further along the reef that were being used for canoe building.

Aioma knew from old experience what white men could do with guns, but he did not know that a house wall capable of stopping an arrow was incapable of stopping a rifle bullet.

Rantan seeing nothing else to fire at aimed at one of the houses, fired, and as the smoke cleared saw, literally, the house burst open.

The women poured out through the broken canes, made as if to run along the reef to the west and were suddenly headed back by a figure armed with a canoe paddle. It was Dick. He drove them into the mammee apple, where they took cover with the others, then running to the second house of refuge, whilst the bullets whizzed around him, he bade the women in it lie down, calling to the other hidden women to do the same, and then taking shelter himself.

But the blunder of Aioma was fatal. The men in the boat knew now for certain that the mammee apple thickets were packed, that there were no pot holes or crevasses of any account on the seaward side of the reef, that they had the population of Karolin corralled.

Resting his rifle carefully on the gunnel, Rantan led off. He couldn't well miss, and the deafening explosion of the rifle was followed by a shriek and a movement in the distant bushes where some unfortunate had been hit, and, striving to rise, had been pulled down by his or her companions.

Carlin laughed and fired and evidently missed, to judge by the silence that followed the shot.

Rantan had some trouble with a cartridge. His face had quite changed within the last few minutes and since the corralling of the natives was assured. It was like a mask and the upper lip projected as though suddenly swollen by some injury. He flung the defective cartridge away, loaded with another and fired.

The shot was followed by the cry of a woman and the wailing of a child. One could guess that the child had been hit, not the woman it belonged to, for the wailing kept on and on, a sound shocking in that solitude where nothing was to be seen but the empty beach, the line of mammee apple and the glimpse of empty sea beyond and through the trees.

Carlin, more brutal but less terrible than Rantan, laughed. He was about to fire when a form suddenly moving and breaking from the trees took his eye and stayed his hand.

It was Dick. In his left hand he held a bow and in his right a sheaf of arrows. Aioma had directed that before taking cover the bows and arrows should be laid by the westermost of the two big trees that he and Dick had chosen for shelter. Dick had only to stretch out his arm to seize the weapons and armed with them he came, leaving shelter behind him, right into the open and on to the sands.

At the cry of the first victim, he had started and shivered all over like a dog; at the voice of the child thought left him, or only the thought that there, amongst the bushes with the children and the women, was Katafa; seizing a bow and a handful of the arrows, he left the tree and came out on to the beach and right down to the waterside.

There were seven arrows. He cast them on the sand, picked up one and fixed it with the notch in the bow-string; as he did so Carlin, altering his aim from the bushes to this new target, fired. The sand spurted a yard to the right of the bowman, who, drawing the arrow till the barb nearly touched the bow shaft, loosed it.

It fell true in line but yards short, and as it flicked the water, Rantan's bullet came plunge into the sand and only three inches from Dick's right foot.

Dick laughed. Like Rantan's, his face was transfigured.

He had come with no instinct but to draw the fire away from the bushes to himself. Now, in a moment, he had forgotten everything but the boat and the men in the boat and the burning hatred that, could it have been loosed, would have destroyed them like a thunderbolt.

Bending and picking up another arrow he loosed it, increasing the elevation. This time it did not fall short, it went over the boat, zipping down and into the water from the blue several yards away in the lagoon side.

"Hell," said Carlin.

He dropped the rifle in his hands and seized on the anchor rope, dragging up the anchor, whilst Rantan, firing hurriedly and without effect, seized an oar.

Poisoned arrows even when shot wildly and at random are not things to be played with, and as they rowed, the fear of death in their hearts, came another arrow—wide but only a yard to starboard; then came another short and astern.

"We're out of range," said Carlin. They let the boat drift a moment. Another arrow came, but well astern.

Then with a yell as if the silent devil in the soul of him had spoken at last, Rantan sprang to his feet and shook his fist at the figure on the beach.

Then they dropped the anchor and took up the rifles. The boat was out of arrow range, but the bushes were still a clear target for the rifles.

Like artists who know their limitations, the two gunmen turned their attention from the single figure on the beach to the greater target, and Dick, who on seeing the boat draw off beyond range, stood without shooting any more, victorious for the moment but waiting.

He saw the anchor cast over, he saw the boatmen taking up their positions again, he saw the thready tubes of the guns and knew that the firing was about to recommence, then, bending, he seized an arrow and clasping it with the bow in his left hand, rushed into the water. Swimming with his right arm, he headed straight for the boat.

Dick in the water was a fish. To get close to the boat, and, treading water or even floating, loose the arrow at short range, was his object. He was no longer a man nor a human being, but implacable enmity, reasonless energy directed by hate.

Rantan and Carlin had fired before they saw what was coming, a head, an arm half submerged and a bow skittering along the water. Carlin's jaws snapped together, he tried to extract the cartridge case from his gun, fumbled and failed.

Rantan, less rattled and quicker with his fingers, extracted and reloaded, aimed and fired and missed.

"Fire, you damned fool:" he said to the other, but the game was lost—Carlin was at the anchor rope, the memory of the four dead men on the beach slain by the poisoned arrows of Karolin had him in its grip as it had the other, who with one last glance at the coming terror dropped his gun and seized an oar.

They were beaten, put to flight—if only for the moment.

THE RETURN TO THE KERMADEC

As they rowed making for the schooner with the light of the westering sun in their eyes, they could see the head of the swimmer as he made back for the shore, and away on the beach near the trees they could see the great gulls congregated around the forms of the four dead men, a boiling of wings above the reef line and against the evening blue of the sky.

Predatory gulls when feeding on a carcass do not sit and gorge, they are always in motion more or less, especially when they are in great numbers as now. Far at sea and maybe from a hundred miles away guests were still arriving for the banquet spread by death—late comers whose voices went before them sharp on the evening wind, or came up against it weak, remote and filled with suggestions of hunger and melancholy.

"God's truth," said the beachcomber, spitting as he rowed.

They were coming on towards the ship and it was the first word spoken.

They had defeat behind them, and even if it were only momentary defeat, ahead of them lay explanations. How would the remainder of the crew take the killing of Sru and his companions? There was also the fact that they had lost four divers.

The *Kermadec* was close to them now but not a soul showed on her deck, not even Le Moan, who on sighting the returning boat had slipped into the galley where she sat crouched in a corner by the copper with eyes closed as if asleep.

She had told the fellows below that she would warn them on the return of the boat. She had forgotten her promise, her mind was far away, travelling, circling in a nebulous world like a bird lost in a fog, questing for a point to rest on. She knew well that though the boat was returning, this was not the end of things. To-morrow it would all begin again, the destroyed canoes, the implacable firing from the boat; the face of Rantan as he pushed off all told her this. Crouching, with closed eyes, she heard the oars, the slight grinding of the boat as it came alongside and the thud of bare feet as Carlin came over the side on to the deck. No voices.

The beachcomber had taken in the situation at a glance, the crew were down below, smoking or sleeping, leaving the schooner to look after herself. It was just as well—down there they would have heard nothing of the distant firing, seen nothing of the killing. He knew kanakas, knew as well as though he had been told that as soon as he and Rantan had pushed off, the crew had taken charge of the foc'sle.

Leaving Rantan to tie up, he went below to the cabin for some food, where, a moment later, the mate joined him.

In a few minutes, their hunger satisfied, they began to speak and almost at once they were wrangling.

"Shooting up the lagoon—well, you've shot it up and much good it has done us," said Carlin. "I'm not against killing, but seems to me the killing has been most on their side. What's the use of talking? It will take a year at this game to do any good and how are you to manage it from the boat?"

"To-morrow," said Rantan, "I'll move the ship up, anchor her off that village and then we'll see. Chaps won't come swimming out to attack a ship, and we can pot them from the deck till they put their hands up. We've no time to wipe them all off, but I reckon a few days of the business will break them up and once a kanaka is broken, he's broken."

Carlin without replying got into his bunk and stretching at full length, lit his pipe; as he flung the Swedish match box to Rantan, a sound from the deck above like the snap of a broken stick, made him raise his eyes towards the skylight. Rantan, the box in his hand paused for a moment, then the sound not being repeated, he lit his pipe.

Throwing the box back to the other he came on deck.

The deck was still empty, but the spear that had been leaning against the rail was gone. Rantan did not notice this, he came forward passing the galley without looking in and stopped at the foc'sle hatch to listen.

One of the strange things about sea-going kanakas is their instinct to get together in any old hole or corner out of sight of the deck, the sea, the land and the sky, and in an atmosphere that would choke a European, frowst.

The fellows below were just waking up after a catnap and the fume of Blue Bird, the old tobacco of the old Pacific days sold at two cents a stick, was rising from the hatch mixed with the sound of voices engaged in talk; they had heard nothing of the firing, if they had they would not have bothered; they had no idea of the fate of Sru and his companions, if they had they would not have much cared. Time was, for these men, the moment; unspeculative as birds they took life with a terrible light-heartedness scarcely human in its acceptance of all things: blows or bananas, the righteousness or the rascality of the white man.

Rantan rapped on the hatch and called on them to tumble up. Then when he had them all on deck, the sunset on their faces and fear of what he might say to them for leaving the schooner to take charge of herself in their hearts, he began to talk to them as only he knew how.

Not a word of abuse. The natives of this island were bad men who had treacherously killed Sru and his companions who had landed to talk with them. In return, he, Rantan, had killed many of them and destroyed their canoes. To-morrow he intended to bring the ship further up towards the village, and with the speak-sticks kill more of them. Meanwhile the crew could go below and enjoy themselves as they liked, leaving one on deck to keep watch on the weather. There was no danger from the beach as all the canoes had been destroyed. Then he dismissed them and went aft.

THE MIND OF KANOA AND THE RISING MOON

The crew, numbering now only six, and deprived of the leadership of Sru, watched Rantan go aft and disappear down the saloon hatch, then they fell to discussing the fate of Sru and his companions. The lost men were from Soma, of the remainder two were from Nanuti in the Gilberts, the rest were Paumotuans hailing from Vana Vana and Haraikai. The loss of the others did not affect them much, nor did they speculate as to the possibility of their own destruction at the hands of the natives of Karolin; they had little imagination and big belief in Rantan, and, having talked for a while and chosen a man to keep watch, they dived below. Then dark came and the stars.

Kanoa was the man chosen, a pure Polynesian from Vana Vana, not more than eighteen, slim and straight as a dart, and with lustrous eyes that shone now in the dusk as he turned them on Le Moan, the only living creature on deck beside himself.

He had been watching Le Moan for days, for weeks, with an ever-increasing interest. She had repelled him at first despite her beauty, and owing to her strange ways. He had never seen a girl like her at Vana Vana nor at Tuta Kotu, and to his simple mind, she was something more than a girl, maybe something less, a creature that loved to brood alone and live alone, perchance spirit; who could tell, for it was well known at Vana Vana that spirits of men and women were sometimes met with at sea on desolate reefs and atolls, ghosts of drowned people who would even light fires to attract ships and canoes and be taken off just as Le Moan had been taken off by Pete'son, and who always brought disaster to the ship or canoe foolish enough to rescue them.

Sru had kicked him for speaking like this in the foc'sle. After Pete'son had been left behind at Levua, supposedly killed by Tahaku and his followers, Kanoa, leaning on his side in his bunk and pipe in mouth had said: "It is the girl or she that looks like a girl but is maybe the spirit of some woman lost at sea. She was alone on that island and Pete'son brought her on board and now, look—what has become of Pete'son?" Upon which Sru had pulled him out of his bunk and kicked him. All the same Kanoa's mind did not leave hold of the idea. He was convinced that there was more to come in the way of disaster, and now, look, Sru gone and three men with him!

But Kanoa was only eighteen and Le Moan for all her dark beauty and brooding ways and mysterious habits was, at all events, fashioned in the form of a girl, and once in a roll of the ship Le Moan slipping on the spray-wet deck would have fallen, only for Kanoa who caught her, almost naked as she was, in his arms, and she was delicious.

Ghost or not there began to grow in him a desire for her that was held in check only by his fear of her. A strange condition of mind brought about by the conflict of two passions.

To-night close to her on the deserted deck, the warm air bringing her perfume to him and her body outlined against the starlit lagoon, he was only prevented from seizing her in his arms by the thought of Sru and his companions dead on the reef over there; dead as Pete'son, dead as he—Kanoa—might be to-morrow, and through the wiles of this girl so like a spirit, this spirit so like a girl.

He felt like a man swimming against the warm current that sweeps round the shoulder of Haraikai, swimming bravely and seeming to make good way, yet all the time being swept steadily out to sea to drown and die.

Suddenly—and just as he was about to fling out his hands, seize her and capture her in a burning embrace, mouth to mouth, breast to breast, and arms locked round her body—suddenly the initiative was taken from him and Le Moan, gliding up to him, placed a hand upon his shoulder.

Next moment she had pressed him down to the deck and he was squatting opposite to her, almost knee to knee, love for the moment forgotten.

Forgotten even though, leaning forward and placing her hand on his shoulder, she brought her face almost in touch with his.

"Kanoa," said Le Moan, in a voice just audible to him above the rumble of the reef, "Sru and the men who were with him have been slain by Rantan, and the big red man, not by the men of Karolin. To-morrow you will die, I heard him say so to the big man, you and Timau and Tahuku and Poni and Nauta and Tirai." She told this lie with steady eyes fixed upon him, eyes that saw nothing but Taori, the man whose life she was trying to save. No wonder that love dropped out of the heart of Kanoa and that the sweat showed on his face in the starlight. It was the first time that she had spoken to him more than a word or two, and what she said in that swift dear whisper passed through him like a sword. He believed her. His fear of her was the basis of his belief. He was listening to the voice of a spirit, not the voice of a girl.

He who a moment ago had been filled with passionate desire, felt now that he was sitting knee to knee with Death.

Such was the conviction carried by her words and voice that he would have risen up and run away and hidden, only that he could not move.

"Unless," said Le Moan, "we strike them to-night, to-morrow we will all be killed."

Kanoa's teeth began to chatter. His frightened mind flew back to Vana Vana and the happy days of his youth. He wished that he had never embarked on this voyage that had led him to so many strange passes. Strike them! It was easy to say that, but who would dare to strike Ra'tan?

He was seated facing aft and he could see the vague glow of the saloon skylight golden in the silver of the star-shine. Down below there in the lamplight Ra'tan and the red bearded one were no doubt talking and making their plans. Strike them! That was easily said.

Then, all at once, he stopped shivering and his teeth came together with a click. The light from the saloon had gone out.

He touched Le Moan and told her and she turned her head to the long sweep of the deck, empty, and deserted by the vanished light. It was as though the power of the after guard had suffered eclipse. Rantan and the other would be soon asleep, if they were not asleep now, helpless and at the mercy of the man who would be brave enough to strike.

Le Moan turned again and seizing Kanoa by the shoulder whispered close to his ear.

"Go," said she; "tell the others what I have said, bring them up, softly, Mayana, softly so that *they* may not hear, they need lift no hand in the business. I will strike; go!"

He rose up and passed towards the foc'sle hatch whilst Le Moan, going into the galley, fetched something she had hidden there—the head of the spear which she had broken off from the shaft, the spear Carlin had brought on board as a trophy, and the snap of which he had heard as he lay in his bunk whilst Rantan had been lighting his pipe.

She sat down on the deck with the deadly thing on her knee, poisoned with argora. A scratch from it would be sufficient to destroy life almost instantaneously, and as she sat brooding and waiting, her eyes saw neither the deck nor the starlight, but the vision of a sunlit beach and a form, Taori. Taori for whom she would have destroyed the world.

The sea spoke on the great reef loud to windward, low to leeward; you could hear within the long rumble and roar of the nearby breakers the diminuendo of the rollers that smoked beneath the stars, ringing with a forty-mile mist the placid ocean of the lagoon.

The moon was rising. She could see the gleam of its light on the binnacle where the Godling lived that had always pointed away from Karolin, on the port rail and on the brass-work of the skylight. Then, roused by a sound soft as the sifting of leaves on a lawn, she turned and behind her the deck was crowded.

The crew had come on deck led by Kanoa, and the stem of the schooner swinging towards the break with the tide, the level light of the moon was on their faces.

NIGHT, DEATH AND PASSION

She made them sit down and they sat in a ring on the deck, she taking her place in the middle.

Then she talked to them respecting what she had already told to Kanoa, telling them also that the men of Karolin were not enemies but friends, that Rantan and the red-bearded man though fair-spoken were indeed devils in disguise, that they had killed many of the men of Karolin, killed Sru and his companions and intended on the morrow to kill Kanoa and the rest. And they sat listening to her as children listen to the tales about ogres—believing, bewildered, terrified, not knowing what to do.

These men were not cowards; under circumstances known and understood they were brave, weather could not frighten them nor war against kindred races, but the white man was a different thing and Rantan they feared even more than Carlin.

They would not move a hand in this matter of striking at them. It would be better to take the boat and land on the reef and trust to the men of Karolin if they were trustworthy as Le Moan had reported.

Poni, the biggest and strongest of them, said this and the others nodded their heads in approval, and Le Moan laughed; she knew them and told them so, told them that as she had saved them by overhearing Rantan's plans, she would save them now, that they had nothing to do but wait and watch and prepare their minds for friendship with her people when she had finished what she intended to do.

Then she rose up.

As she stood with the moonlight full on her, a voice broke the silence of the night. It came from the saloon hatchway, a voice sudden, chattering, complaining and ceasing all at once as if cut off by a closed door. They knew what it was, the voice of a man talking in his sleep. Carlin on his back and seized by nightmare had cried out, half awakened, turned and fallen asleep again.

The group seated on the deck, after a momentary movement, resumed their positions. There is something so distinctive in the voice of a sleep-talker that the sound, after the first momentary flutter caused by it, brought assurance. Then, prepared at any moment to make a dash for the boat, they sat, the palms of their hands flat on the deck and their eyes following Le Moan, now gliding towards the hatch, the spear head in her left hand, her right hand touching the port rail as she went.

At the hatch she paused to listen. She could hear the reef, and on its sonorous murmur like a tiny silver thread of sound the trickle of the tide on the planking of the schooner, and from the dark pit of the stairway leading to the saloon another sound, the breathing of men asleep.

She had never been below. That stairway, even in daylight, had always filled her with fear, the fear of the unknown, the dread of a trap, the claustrophobia of one always used to open spaces.

Lit by the day it frightened her, in its black darkness it appalled her; yet she had to go down, for the life of Taori lay at the bottom of that pit to be saved by her hands and hers alone.

Kanoa, amongst the others, sat watching. The mind of Kanoa so filled with fear when she told him that his death was imminent, the mind of Kanoa that had lusted for her, the mind of this child of eighteen to whom light and laughter had been life and thought, a thing of the moment, was no longer the same mind.

The great heroism he was watching, this attempt to save him and the others, had awakened in him something perhaps of the past, ancestors who had fought, done great deeds and suffered—who knows—but there came to him an elation such as he had felt in the movements of the dance and at the sound of music. Rising and evading Poni who clutched at his leg to hold him back, he came to the rail, stood for a moment as Le Moan vanished from sight and then swiftfooted but silent as a shadow, glided to the saloon hatch and stood listening.

Holding the polished banister rail, and moving cautiously, step by step, Le Moan descended, the spear head in her left hand. As she came, a waft from the cabin rose to meet her in the darkness—an odour of humanity and stale tobacco smoke, bunk-bedding and bilge.

It met her like an evil ghost, it grappled with her and tried to drive her back; used as she was to the fresh sea air, able to scent rain on the wind and change of weather, this odour checked her for a moment, repelled her, held her and then lost its power; her will had conquered it. She reached the foot of the stairs and before her now lay the open doorway of the cabin, a pale oblong beyond which lay a picture.

The table with the swinging lamp above it, the bunks on either side where the sleeping men lay, clothes cast on the floor, all lit by the moon-gleams through the skylight and portholes.

From the bunk on the right hung an arm. It was Carlin's; she knew it by its size. She moved towards it, paused, looked up and stood rigid.

Above Carlin, now on the ceiling, now on the wall, something moved and danced; a great silver butterfly, now at rest, now in flight, shifting here and there, poising with tremulous wings.

It was a water shimmer from the moonlit lagoon entering through a porthole, a ghost of light; it held her only for a moment, the next she had seized the hand of the sleeper and driven the spear point into the arm. Almost on the cry of the stricken man, something sprang across the table of the cabin, seized Le Moan by the throat and flung her on her side. It was Rantan.

Up above Kanoa, standing by the opening of the hatch, listening. The reef spoke and the water trickled on the planking, but from below there came no sound. Moments passed and then, sharp and cutting the silence like a knife came a cry, a shout, and the sound of a furious struggle. Then, fear flown and filled with a fury new as life to the newborn, Kanoa plunged down into the darkness, missed his footing, fell, rose half stunned and dashed into the cabin.

Carlin, naked, was lying on his face on the floor, dead or dying; Rantan, naked, was at death grips with Le Moan. She had risen by a supreme effort, but he had got her against the table, flung her on it and was now holding her down, his knee on her thigh, his hands on her throat, his head flung back, the flexor muscles of his forearms rigid, crushing her, breaking her, choking the life out of her, till Kanoa sprang.

Sprang like a tiger, lighting on the table and then in a flash on to Rantan's back, breaking his grip with the impact and freeing Le Moan. He had got the throat hold from behind, his knees had seized Rantan's body and he was riding him like a horse. The attacked man, whooping and choking, tried to hit backwards, flung up his arms, rose straight, tottered And crashed, but still the attacker clung, clung as they rolled on the floor, clung till all movement ceased.

It was over.

The silver butterfly still danced merrily on the ceiling and the sound of the reef came through the skylight, slumberous and indifferent, but other sound or movement there was none till Le Moan, stretched still on the table, turned, raised herself on her elbow and understood. Then she dropped on to the floor. Ran- tan lay half on top of Carlin and Kanoa lay by Rantan.

Kanoa's grip had relaxed and he seemed asleep. He roused as the girl touched him; the fury and wild excitement had passed, he seemed dazed; then recovering himself he sat up, then he rose to his feet. As he rose Rantan moved slightly, he was not dead and Le Moan kneeling on the body of Carlin seized the sheet that was hanging from the bunk, dragged it towards her and handed it to Kanoa.

"Bind him," said Le Moan, "he is not dead, let him be for my people to deal with him as they deal with the dog-fish."

As they bound him from the shoulders to the hands a voice came from above. It was the voice of Poni who had come to listen and who heard Le Moan's voice and words.

"Kanoa," cried Poni, "what is going on below there?"

"Coward!" cried Le Moan, "come and see. Come and help now that the work is done."

"Ay," said Kanoa the valorous, "come and help now that the work is done."

Then, kneeling by the bound figure of Rantan, he gazed on the girl, consuming her with his eyes, rapturous, and unknowing that the work had been done for Taori.

Taori, beside whom, for Le Moan, all other men were shadows, moving yet lifeless as the moon-born butterfly still dancing above the corpse of Carlin.

MORNING

When the firing had ceased and the boat had returned to the ship the wretched people hiding amongst the mammee apple had come out and grouped themselves around Aioma and Taori. Taori had saved them for the moment by his act in swimming out to attack the boat; he was no longer their chief, but their god, and yet some instinctive knowledge of the wickedness of man and of the tenacity and power of the white men told them that all was not over.

Amongst them as they waited whilst Aioma and Katafa distributed food, sat two women, Nanu and Ona, each with a dead child clasped in her arms. The child of Nanu had been killed instantaneously by a bullet that had pierced its neck and the arm of its mother. Ona's child, pierced in its body, had died slowly, bleeding its life away and wailing as it bled.

These two women, high cheeked, frizzy-headed and of the old fierce Melanesian stock which formed the backbone and hitting force of Karolin, were strange to watch as they sat nursing their dead, speechless, passionless, heedless of food or drink or what might happen. The others ate, too paralysed by the events of the day to prepare food for themselves, they yet took what was given to them with avidity, then, when dark came, they crept back into the bushes to sleep, whilst Dick, leaving Katafa in charge of Aioma, left the trees and under cover of the darkness came along the beach past the bodies, over which the birds were still at work, until he was level with the schooner.

She showed no lights on deck, no sign of life but the two tiny dim golden discs of the cabin portholes.

Taking his seat on a weather-worn piece of coral, he sat watching her. Forward, close to the foc'sle head, he saw now two forms, Le Moan and Kanoa; they drew together, then they vanished, the deck now seemed deserted, but he continued to watch. Already in his mind he foresaw vaguely the plan of Rantan. To-morrow they would not use the boat, they would move the schooner, bring her opposite the village and then with those terrible things that could speak so loudly and hit so far they would begin again—and where could the people go? The forty-mile reef would be no protection; away from the trees and the puraka patches the people would starve, they would have no water. The people were tied to the village.

He sat with his chin on his clenched fists staring at the schooner and the two evil golden eyes that were staring him back like the eyes of a beast.

If only a single canoe had been left he would have paddled off and, with Aioma and maybe another for help, would have attacked, but the canoes were gone—and the dinghy.

Then as he sat helpless, with hatred and the fury of hell in his heart, the golden eyes vanished. Rantan had put out the light.

With the rising moon he saw as in a glass, darkly, little by little and bit by bit, the tragedy we have seen in full. He saw the grouping of the foc'sle hands as they came up from below, he saw them disappear as they sat on deck. Then he saw the figure of Le Moan, her halt at the saloon hatch and the following of Kanoa, he heard the scream of the stricken Carlin.

Lastly he saw the crowding of the hands aft, Carlin's body being dragged on deck and cast overboard into a lather of moonshine and phosphorus, and something white carried shoulder high to forward of the galley where it was laid on deck.

Then after a few moments lights began to break out, lanterns moved on the deck, the portholes broke alive again and again were blotted out as the cabin lamp lit and taken from its attachments was carried on deck and swung from the ratlins of the main for decorative purposes. The moon gave all the light that any man in his sober senses could want, but the crew of the schooner were not sober, they were drunk with the excitement of the business, and though nominally free men they felt as slaves feel when their bonds are removed. Besides, Rantan and Carlin had plotted to kill them as they had killed Sru and the others. On top of that there was a bottle of ginger wine. It had been stored in the medicine locker—Peterson, like many other seamen, had medical fancies of his own and he believed this stuff to be a specific for the colic. It had escaped Carlin's attention, but Poni, who acted as steward, had sniffed at it, tasted it and found it good.

It was served out in a tin cup.

Then, across the water came the sound of voices, the twanging of a native fiddle, and now the whoop- whoop of dancers in the hula dance songs, laughter against which came the thunder of the moonlit sea on the outer beach and an occasional cry from the gulls at their food.

Dick, rising, made back towards the trees; his heart felt easier. Without knowing what had occurred, he still knew that something had happened to divide his enemies, that they had quarrelled, and that one had been killed; that, with Sru and his companions, made five gone since the schooner had dropped anchor.

Lying down beside Katafa, whilst Taiepu kept watch, he fell asleep.

At dawn Taiepu, shouting like a gull, came racing through the trees whilst the bushes gave up their people. They came crowding out on the beach to eastward of the trees and there, sure enough, was Le Moan, the schooner against the blaze at the Gates of Morning, and the boat hanging a hundred yards off shore.

Kneeling on the sands before Taori, glancing sometimes up into his face, swiftly, as one glances at the sun, Le Moan told her tale whilst the sun itself now fully risen blazed upon the man before her.

Dick listened, gathered from the artless story the sacrifices she had made at first, the heroism she had shown to the last, but nothing of her real motive, nothing of the passion that came nigh to crushing her as Katafa, catching her in her arms, and, pressing her lips on her forehead, led her away tenderly as a sister to the shelter of the trees.

Then the mob, true to itself and forgetting their saviour, turning, raced along the sands, boys, women and children, till they got level with the waiting boat shouting welcome to the newcomers.

Poni in the stern sheets rose and waved his arms, the boat driven by a few strokes reached the beach and next moment the crew of the *Kermadec* and the people of Karolin were fraternizing—embracing one another like long-lost relatives.

And now a strange thing happened.

Dick, who stood watching all this, deposed for a moment as chief men are sometimes temporarily deposed and forgotten in moments of great national heart movements, saw in the boat, the naked, bound figure of Rantan lying on the bottom boards.

He came closer and the eyes of Rantan, which were open, met the eyes of Taori. Rantan was a white man.

There was no appeal in the eyes of Rantan—he who knew the Islands so well knew that his number was up; he gazed at the golden brown figure of Taori, gazed at that face so strange for a kanaka, yet so truly the face of an islander, gazed as a white man upon a native.

For a moment it was as though race gazed upon kindred race disowning it, not seeing it, mistaking it for an alien and lower race and from deep in the mind of Dick vague and phantom-like rose trouble.

He did not know that he himself was a white man, blood brother of the man in the boat. He knew nothing, yet he felt trouble. He turned to Aioma.

"Will he die?"

"Ay, most surely will he die," said the old fellow with a chuckle. "Will the dog-fish not die when he is caught? He who killed the canoes, the children, is it not just that he should die?"

Dick inclined his head without speaking. He turned to where Nanu and the other woman were standing, waiting, terrible, with their dead children still clasped in their arms.

"It is just," said he, "see to it, Aioma," and turning without another glance at the boat he walked away, past the shattered canoes, past the half-picked bones, through the sunlight, towards the trees.

Aioma, no longer himself, but something more evil, came towards the boat making little bird-like noises, rubbing his shriveled hands together, stroking his thighs.

The tide was just at full ebb, the old ledge where the victims of Nanawa were staked out in past times for the sharks to eat was uncovered and only waiting for a victim. It lay halfway between the village and the reef break and in old times one might have known when an execution was to take place by the fins of the tiger sharks cruising around it. This morning there were no sharks visible.

Rantan was reserved for a worse fate; for, as Aioma, standing by the boat, called on the people to take their vengeance, the woman Nanu, still holding her dead child in her arms stepped up to him followed by Ona.

"He is ours," said Nanu.

Aioma turned on her like a savage old dog—he was about to push her back amongst the crowd when Ona advanced a step.

"He is ours," said Ona, glancing at the form in the boat as though it were a parcel she was claiming, whilst the crowd, reaching to the woods, broke in, speaking almost with one voice.

"He is theirs, he has slain their children, let them have him for a child."

"So be it," said Aioma, too much of a diplomat to oppose the mob on a matter of sentiment, and curious as to what gory form of vengeance the women would adopt. "So be it, and now what will you do with him?"

"We will take him to the southern beach with us. We alone," said Nanu.

"We would be alone with him," said Ona, shifting her dead child from her right to her left arm as one might shift a parcel.

"But how will you take him?" asked the old man.

"In a canoe," said Nanu.

"Then go and build it," said the canoe-builder. "What foolishness is this, for well you know the canoes are broken."

"Aioma," said Nanu, "there is one little canoe which is yet whole, it lies in the further canoe-house, so far in that it has been forgotten; it belonged to my man, the father of my child, he who went with the others but did not return. I have never spoken of it and no one has seen it, for no one goes into the canoe-houses now that the great canoes are gone."

"Then let it be fetched," said Aioma. He stood whilst a dozen of the crowd broke away and racing towards the trees disappeared in the direction of the canoe-houses. Presently the canoe, a fishing outrigger, showed on the water of the lagoon, two boys at the paddles. They beached it close to the boat, the dead children were lashed to the gratings with strips of coconut sennit, Rantan, raised by half a dozen pairs of hands, was lifted and placed in the bottom of the little craft, and the women, pushing off, got on board, and raised the sail.

The steering paddle flashed and the crowd stood watching as the canoe grew less on the surface of the water, less and less, making for the southern beach, till now it was no larger than a midge in the lagoon dazzle that, striking back at the sun, roofed Karolin with a forty-mile dome of radiance.

H. de Vere Stacpoole

THE VISION

Now when Katafa led Le Moan away into the shelter of the trees, Le Moan, with the kiss of Katafa warm upon her forehead, knew nothing, nothing of the fact that Katafa was Taori's, the dream and treasure of his life, beside whom all other living things were shadows.

And Katafa knew nothing, nothing of the fact that

Taori was Le Moan's—was Le Moan; for Le Moan had so dreamed him into herself that the vision of him had become part of herself inseparable forever.

Ringed and ringed with ignorance, ignorance of their own race, and the affinity between them, of the fact that they and Taori formed amongst the people of Karolin a little colony alien in blood and soul, of the fact that Taori was their common desire, they went between the trees, Katafa leading the way towards the house of Uta Matu, above which Nan on his pole still grinned towards the schooner, grinned without nodding, maybe because the wind that had moved him had ceased.

Katafa, taking the sleeping mat used by her and Taori, spread it on the floor of the house, then she offered food, but Le Moan refused, she only wanted sleep. For nights she had not slept and the kiss that Katafa again pressed upon her brow seemed to her the kiss of a phantom in a dream as she sank down and died to the world on the bed of the lover who knew nothing of her love.

It was still morning.

Outside in the blazing sun the people of Karolin went about their business, mending the wall of the house that had been broken, preparing food for the newcomers, rejoicing in the new life that had come back to them. Whilst in the lagoon the anchored schooner swung to her moorings, deserted and without sign of life, for Dick had decided that no one should board her till he and Aioma led the way, that is till the morrow, for there were many things to be attended to first.

Le Moan had brought him not only a ship, but six full-grown men, a priceless gift if the men were to be trusted.

Aioma, who had held off from the business of fraternizing, watching the newcomers with a critical eye, believed that they were good men. "But wait," said Aioma, "till they are fed, till they have rested and slept amongst us; a good-looking coconut is sometimes rotten at the core, but these I believe to be good men even as Le Moan has said; but to-night will tell."

405

At dusk he came to Taori, happy. Each of the new men had taken a wife; incidentally, in the next few days each of the newcomers, with one exception, had taken from four to six wives.

"Each has a woman," said the direct Aioma. "We are sure of them now, they are in the mammee apple, all except one who is very young and who says that he has no heart for women."

He spoke of Kanoa. Kanoa brooding alone by the water's edge, sick with love and desire. Love that was even greater than desire, for the deed of Le Moan that had stirred in him the ghosts of his ancestors, had raised the soul of Kanoa beyond the flesh where hitherto it had been tangled and blind.

Meanwhile Le Moan slept. Slept whilst the dusk rose and the stars came out, slept till the moon high against the Milky Way pierced the house of Uta Matu with her shafts.

Then sleep fell from her gradually and turning on her elbow she saw the moon rays shining through the canes of the wall, the little ships ghostly on their shelves and through the doorway the wonderful world of moonlit reef and sea.

Nothing broke the stillness of the night but the surf of the reef and a gentle wind that stirred the palm fronds with a faint pattering rainy sound and passed away across the mammee apple where men and women lay embraced, who the night before had not known even of each other's existence.

Before the doorway, sheltered from the moon by a tree shadow, all but their feet that showed fully in the light, two forms lay stretched on a mat—Taori and Katafa. They had given up their house to the saviour of Karolin, taken a mat from one of the women's houses, and fallen asleep with only the tree for shelter. Le Moan, not recognizing them, still dazed with sleep, rose, came to the doorway and looked down.

Then she knew.

Taori's head was pillowed on Katafa's shoulder, her arm was around his neck, his arm across her body.

THE CASSI FLOWERS

If the sea had risen above the reef destroying the village and sweeping the population of Karolin to ruin whilst leaving her untouched, Le Moan would have stood as she stood now, unmoved before the inevitable and the accomplished.

Her world lay around her in ruins and the destroyers lay before her asleep.

She had feared death and dreaded separation, but she had never dreamed of this—for Taori, in her mind, had always stood alone as the sun stands alone in the sky.

A spear stood against the tree bole and the pitiless hand that had killed Carlin could have seized it and plunged it into the heart of Katafa, but if the sea had destroyed her world as this girl had destroyed it, would she have cast a spear at the sea? The thing was done, accomplished, of old time. Her woman's instinct told her that.

Done and accomplished, without any knowledge of her, in a world from which she had been excluded by fate.

Moving from the doorway she passed them, almost touching their feet. To right and left of her lay the tumbling sea and the lit lagoon, before her the great white road of the beaches and the reef. She followed the leading of this road with little more volition than the wind-blown leaf or the drifting weed; with only one desire, to be alone.

It led to the great trees where the canoe-builders had been at work. Here across the coral lay the trunks felled by Aioma, filling the air with the fragrance of new-cut wood. One already had been partly shaped and hollowed, and resting on it for a moment, Le Moan followed its curves with her eyes, felt the ax marks with her hand, took in every detail of the work, saw it as, with outrigger affixed and sail spread to the wind, it would take the sea, sometime—sometime—sometime.

The ceaseless breakers casting their spindrift beneath the moon lulled her mind for a moment till trees, canoe, reef and sea all faded and dissolved in a world of sound, a voice-world through which came the chanting of stricken coral and, at last, pictures of the wind-blown southern beach.

The southern beach, sunlit and gull-flown, a beached canoe, a form—Taori.

It was now and now only that the pain came, piercing soul and rending body, crushing her and breaking her till she fell on the coral, her face buried in her arms, as though cast there by the sea whose eternal thunder filled the night.

The night wind moved her hair. It was blowing from the village and as it came it brought with it a vague whisper from the bushes and trees and now and again a faint perfume of cassi. Perfume, like music, is a voice speaking a language we have forgotten, telling tales we half understand, soothing us now with dreams, raising us now to action.

The cassi flowers were speaking to Le Moan. After a long, long while she moved, raised her head and, leaning on her elbow, seemed to listen.

Close to her was a pond in the coral—a rock pool filled with fresh water such as existed on the southern beach and a fellow of which lay in the village close to the house of Uta Matu.

Dragging herself towards it she leaned on her arms and looked deep down into the water just as she had been looking into the pool that day when raising her eyes she found herself first face to face with Taori.

The cassi flowers were speaking to Le Moan, their perfume followed her mind as it sank like a diver into the pool's moonlit, crystal heart. Their voices said to her:

"Taori is not dead. Whilst he lives do not despair, for who can take his image from you and what woman's love can equal yours? Peace, Le Moan. Watch and wait."

Presently she arose, returning by the way she came. She drew towards the house of Uta Matu and passed the figures on the mat without glancing at them. Then in the house she lay down with her face to the wall. When the dawn aroused Katafa, Le Moan had not moved; one might have fancied her asleep.

VENGEANCE

Rantan, when they cast him in the fishing canoe, could see nothing but the roughly shaped sides, bright here and there where the scale of a palu had stuck and dried, the after outrigger pole, the blue sky above the gunnel and the heads of the crowd by the waterside.

By raising himself a little he might have glimpsed the two dead children tied to the outrigger gratings, but he could not raise himself, nor had he any desire to do so.

He knew the islands, he had heard what passed between Aioma and the women, and as they carried him from the boat to the canoe, he had seen the dead children tied on the gratings. What his fate was to be at the hands of Ona and Nanu he could not tell, nor did he try to imagine it.

All being ready, the stem of the canoe left the beach, the two women scrambling on board as it was waterborne. Nanu sat aft and Ona forward, trampling on Rantan's body with her naked feet as she got there. The paddles splashed and the spray came inboard striking Rantan on the face, but he did not mind; neither did he mind the heat of the steadily rising sun, nor the heel of Ona as she dropped her paddle for a moment and raised the sail.

Sometimes he closed his eyes to shut out the sight of Nanu, who was steering, her eyes fixed on the sail; sometimes on the beach ahead, never or scarcely ever on Rantan.

Sometimes he could hear Ona's voice. She was just behind his head holding on to the mast and trimming the canoe by moving now to the left or right—her voice came calling out some directions to the other and then sharp as the voice of Ona came the cry of a seagull that flew with them for a moment, inspecting the dead children on the gratings till the flashing paddle and the shouts of Nanu drove it away.

And now as the sun grew hotter, a vague odour of corruption filled the air, passed away with the back draught from the sail yet returned again, whilst the murmur of the northern beach that had died down behind them became merged in the wash of the waves on the southern coral.

Then as the place of their revenge drew close to them and they could see the deserted shacks, the long line of empty beach and the coconut trees in their separate groups, Nanu seemed to awake to the presence of Rantan. She glanced at him and laughed, and steering all the time, with side flashes of the paddle pointed him out to Ona whose laughter came from behind him, shrill, sharp and done with in a moment.

Truly Rantan wished that he had never embarked on this voyage, never seen Peterson, never left him for dead away there on Levua; bitterly did he repent his temerity in coming into Karolin lagoon and his stupidity in trying to shoot it up.

Sometimes, long ago, he had amused himself by imagining what might be the worst fate of a man at sea, shipwreck, slow starvation, death from thirst, from sharks, from fire. He had never imagined anything like his present position, never imagined himself in the hands of two women of the Islands, whose children he had been instrumental in murdering, two women who were taking him off to a desolate beach to do with him as they pleased. He could tell the approach of the beach by the face of Nanu and the outcries of Ona. Sometimes Ona would give his body a kick to emphasize what she was saying, which was Greek to Rantan. So sharp was her voice, so run together the words, that her speech was like a sword inscribed with unintelligible threats.

Now Nanu was half standing up, Ona was hauling the sail, the paddles were flashing, the sands close. They brought the stem of the canoe on to the shelving sand, and, on the bump and shudder, dropping their paddles, they jumped clear, seized gunnel and outrigger and beached her high and dry.

Then seizing their victim by the feet and the shoulders, they lifted him from the canoe and threw him on to the sand. He fell on his face, they turned him on his back and then left him, running about here and there and making preparations for their work.

The tide was running out and the wind, that had slacked to due west, bent the coco palms and brought up from all along the beach the silky whisper of the sands, the rumour of twenty miles of sea beating on the southern coral and the smell of sun-smitten seaweeds and emptying rock pools.

Rantan, who had closed his eyes, opened them, and turning his head slightly, watched the women; Nanu who was collecting bits of stick and wood to light a fire and Ona who was collecting oyster shells. There were many oyster shells lying about on the beach and Ona, as she went, picked and chose, taking only the flat shells and testing their edges with her thumb.

Rantan knew, and a shudder went through him as he watched her carrying them and placing them in a little heap by the place where Nanu was building her fire.

A big brown bird with curved beak and bright eyes sweeping in the air above them would curve and drift on the wind and return, making a swoop towards the beached canoe and the objects on the outrigger gratings, and the women, busy at their work, would shout at the bird and sometimes threaten it with a paddle which Ona ran and fetched from the canoe. Not till vengeance had been assured would the dead children be cast to the sharks. The shark was the grave and burial-ground of Karolin.

When everything was ready they turned from the fire and came running across the sand to their victim.

Rantan, lying on his back with eyes closed and mouth open, had ceased to breathe.

Never looked man more dead than Rantan, and Ona, dropping on her knees beside him with a cry, turned him on one side, turned him back, cried out to Nanu who dashed off to the fire, seized a piece of burning stick, rushed back with it and pressed the red hot point of it against his foot. Rantan did not move.

410

Then furious, filling the air with their cries, with only one idea, to rub him and pound him and to bring back the precious life that had escaped or was escaping them, they began to strip him of his bonds, tearing off the coconut sennit strips, the sheet, unrolling him like a mummy from its bandages, till he lay naked beneath the sun—a corpse that suddenly sprang to life with a yell, bounded to its feet, seized the paddle and flung itself on Nanu, felling her with a smashing blow on the neck, turned and pursuing Ona chased her as she ran this way and that like a frightened duck.

Few men had ever seen Rantan. The silent, quiet, sunburnt man of ordinary times was not Rantan. This was Rantan, this mad figure yelling hatred, radiating revenge, mad to kill.

Rantan robbed of his pearl lagoon, of his ship, of his prospect of wealth, ease, wine and women—by kanakas; Rantan whom kanakas had bound with a sheet and dumped into a canoe; Rantan whom two kanaka women—women!—women, mind you—had trodden on, and whom they had been preparing to scrape to death slowly inch by inch with oyster shells, and bum bit by bit with hot sticks.

This was the real Rantan raised to his n^{th} power by injuries, insults, and the escape from a terrible death.

Ona dashed for the canoe, maybe with some blind idea to get hold of the other paddle to defend herself with, but he had the speed of her and headed her off; she made for the rough coral of the outer beach but he headed her off; time and again he could have closed with her and killed her, but the sight of her frizzy head, her face, her figure, and the fact that she was a woman, filled him with a counter rage that spared her for the moment. He could have chased her forever, killing her a thousand times in his mind, had his strength been equal to his hatred; but he could not chase her forever, and, suddenly, with a smashing blow he brought her to ground, beat the life out of her and stood gasping, satiated and satisfied.

Only for a moment. The sight of Nanu lying where he had felled her brought him running. She had fallen near the heap of oyster shells, the fire that she had built was still burning, the stick which she had pressed against his foot was close to her. She had recovered consciousness and as she lay, her eyes wide open, she saw him stand above her, the paddle uplifted, and that was the last thing she saw in this world.

He came down to the water's edge and sat, squatting, the paddle beside him and his eyes fixed away over the water to where the schooner was visible, a toy ship no larger than the model of the *Rarotonga*, swinging to the outgoing tide.

Beyond the schooner the trees that hid the village were just visible.

He was free, free for the moment, but still in the trap of the lagoon.

Free, but stripped of everything; absolutely naked, without even shoes.

He was thinking in pictures; pictures now vague, now clear ran through his mind, the shooting up of the lagoon, the figure of Dick swimming off towards him and Carlin as they were firing from the boat, the fight in the cabin, the killing of Carlin—and again Dick.

Dick as he had come and stood looking at him (Rantan) as he lay bound and helpless. His hatred of the kanakas and the whole business seemed focused in Dick, for in that bright figure and noble face lay expressed the antithesis of himself, something that he could not despise as he despised Sru, the Karolin people, even Carlin.

He loathed this creature whom he had only seen twice and to whom he had never spoken—loathed him as hell loathes heaven.

Then Dick dropped from his mind.

He was still in the trap of the lagoon. He turned his head to where behind him on the sands lay the two dead women, then he turned his eyes to the beached canoe where lay the two dead children strapped to the gratings. The waves spoke and the wind on the sands, and the bo'sun bird returning with a mate swept by, casting its shadow close to him.

Rantan shouted and picking up the paddle threatened the bird just as the women had done, then he sprang to his feet.

He must get out, get out with the canoe, dear off before the kanakas had any chance of coming across. They had no canoes, but they had the ship's boats and if they came and caught him, it would be death; he could get drinking nuts from the trees, but first he must untie those cursed children from the gratings. He turned towards the canoe and as he turned something caught his eye away across the water.

The merry west wind had blown out a bunt of the schooner's hastily stowed canvas in a white flicker against the blue. Were they getting sail on the schooner?

He turned and ran towards the trees. He could climb like a monkey, and heedless of everything but drinking nuts and pandanus drupes, he set to work, collecting them. A mat lay doubled up near one of the deserted shacks; he used it as a basket and between the trees and the canoe he ran and ran, sweating, with scarcely a glance across the water—his only idea the thirst and hunger of the sea which he had to face, the terror of torture and death that lay behind him. There was a huge fig tree, the only one on Karolin, and a tree bearing an unknown fruit in form and colour like a lemon. He raided them, tearing branches down and stripping the fruit off. Before his last journey to the canoe he flung himself down by the little well, the same into which Le Moan had been gazing when she first saw Taori, and drank and drank—raising his head only to drink again.

Reaching the canoe for the last time he threw the fruit in and took a glance across the water to the schooner. The wind had taken advantage of the clumsy and careless work of the crew and the size of the bunt had increased. In his right senses he would have known the truth, but terror had him by the shoulder and seizing the gunnel he began to drive the canoe into the water. The falling tide had left her almost dry, the outrigger interfered with his efforts, getting half buried in the sand. He could not push her out and at the same time keep her level with the outrigger lifting. He had to run from side to side pushing and striving, till at last the idea came to him to spread the mat under the outrigger. That made things easier. He had her now nearly waterborne; throwing in the paddle he prepared to send her out with a last great push, and, running through the shallow water, scramble on board.

Such was the state of his mind he had not recognized that the bodies of the two babies tied to the gratings were a main cause in the tilting of the canoe to port and his difficulty in keeping her on a level keel; nor did he now, but he recognized that he could not put to sea with those terrible bodies tied to him.

He set to work to untie them, but Nanu and Ona, as though provisioning this business, had done their work truly and well—the spray and the sun had shrunk the coconut sennit bindings and the knots were hard as bits of oak. He had no knife, and his hands were shaking and his fingers without power.

A gull swooped down as if to help him and he struck at it with his fist; the sweat poured from him and his knees were beginning to knock together.

The tide was still falling, threatening to leave the canoe dry again; he recognized that and, leaving the bodies untied, raced round to the starboard side, seized the gunnel and pushed her out. On board he paddled kneeling, and using the paddle now on one side, now on the other; making straight out, the lose sail flapping above him, his knees wet with crushed pandanus drupes, gulls following him swooping down and clanging off on the wind.

Then, far enough out, he gave the sail to the breeze that was blowing steady for the break. He was free, nobody could stop him now. Wind and tide were with him, so were the lagoon sharks, who guessed what was tied to the gratings and the gulls who saw.

A royal escort of gulls snowed the air above the flashing paddle and the bellying sail as the canoe, driving past the piers of the opening took the sea and the outer swell, steering dead before the wind for the east.

Little by little the gulls fell astern, gave up the chase, swept back towards Karolin, leaving the man and the dead children and the canoe to the blue sea and the wind that swept it.

Rantan steered. He was used to the handling of a canoe and he knew that, alone as he was, he could do nothing but just keep the little craft before the wind. Where the wind blew he must go and with him his cargo, the fruit at his feet and the forms tied to the grating.

Once with a dangerous and desperate effort he tried to untie them, but his weight thrown to port nearly capsized him. Then, giving the matter up and steeling his heart, he steered before a wind that had now shifted, blowing from the north.

At sunset it was blowing dead from the north and all night long it blew till the dawn rose and there before Rantan, breaking the skyline, palm tops showed and the foam of a tiny atoll singing to the sunrise.

The break was towards the north and the wind brought him through it into the little lagoon, not a mile broad, and on to the beach.

Springing on to the sand and looking wildly around him he saw nothing—only the trees, not a sign of life, only the trees in their beauty, the lagoon in its loveliness, the sky in its purity. Blue and green and the white of coral sand, all in the fresh light of the forenoon Paradise.

Having looked around him, listened and swept the sea with a last glance, he turned to the trees, cast himself in their shadow and leaving the canoe to drift away or stick, fell into a sleep profound as the sleep of the just.

He was saved—for the moment. Freed from Karolin, he had not done with Karolin yet. He had sailed for twenty hours before a five-knot breeze. Karolin was just that distance away below the horizon to the nor'-nor'-west.

BOOK III

LE MOAN WILL KNOW

The dawn that showed Rantan the tiny atoll awakened Aioma who had fallen asleep thinking of the schooner.

Dick had promised that to-day they would board her and the canoe-builder in him craved to get to work, and the boy—the boy wanted to sail her, to feel the wind settling in the great spaces of her canvas, to feel her heeling to it like a tilted world, to feel her answering the helm; the canoe-builder wanted to explore her above and below, examine the fastenings of her timbers; her masts and rigging.

Aioma was very old. He might have been a hundred. No man could tell, for Karolin the clockless kept no account of years. He was too old for fighting, having lost the quickness without which a spear- or dub-man is of no account as a fighter; but he was not too old for fun.

Whip-ray fishing was fun to Aioma—a sport that, next to conger killing, is the nearest approach to fighting with devils; so also was shaping heavy logs to the form of his dream, for Aioma dreamt his canoes before he shaped them, the breaking of Rantan's joints and the staking him on the reef for sharks to devour would also have been fun had not the women claimed the victim to torture him as they pleased.

Aioma, in fact, was as young as he ever had been and as potent in all fields except those of war and love. He came to the water's edge and stood looking at the schooner. He had dreamt that, walking on the sands of the beach with Taori they had looked for the schooner and found her gone. But she was there right enough, her spars showing against the blaze in the east.

The gulls knew that she was deserted, they flew above her in the golden morning and lighted on her rails and spars whilst the ripple of the tide past her anchor chain showed the living brilliancy of light on moving water.

The canoes and dinghy being destroyed they would have to get off to her in the boat.

For a moment the old man stood looking at the bones of the broken canoes and the planks of the poor old dinghy; the fishing fleet of Karolin had gone just as the fighting fleet had gone, yet the gods had made compensation, for there lay the schooner, a thing more potent than all the fleets of Karolin combined, and there lay her boat, a fine four-oared double-ender, carvel built, white painted, a joy to the eye.

Yesterday at odd times he had examined her outside and in; this morning as his eyes swept over her again, new thoughts came to him and a new vision.

Canoes, what were they beside these things, and why build canoes any more, why hollow and shape those vast tree-trunks over which they had been labouring for long weeks when here to their hands lay something better than any fleet of canoes? If Taori wished to attack those men on the northern island, why not attack with the schooner, a whole fleet in one piece, so to speak?

As he stood pondering over this new idea, Dick, who had awakened early, came towards him from the trees accompanied by Katafa.

"Taori," said the canoe-builder, "we will go to her (the schooner) you and I; she is ours and I want no other hand to touch her or foot to rest on her till we alone have been with her for a space. Help me." He laid his hand in the gunnels of the boat as he spoke and Dick, as eager as the other, calling to Katafa to help them, went to the opposite side; between them they got her afloat and tumbled in.

Aioma had learned to handle an oar in the dinghy; the heavy ash sweep was nothing to him and as the boat made across the glitter of the lagoon, Katafa, her feet washed by the little waves on the sand, stood watching them.

Dick had not asked her to accompany him. It was as though the schooner had come between them as a rival—a thing, for the moment, more desirable than her.

She was feeling now what she had felt before only more vaguely. She had always distrusted the little ships, those models born of the pocket knife and ingenuity of Kearney, those hints of an outside world, a vague outside world that might some day break into their environment and separate her from Dick.

This distrust had been built up from the cannon shot of the *Portsey* that had smashed her canoe, from the schooner that had come into Palm Tree lagoon with its cargo of Melanesians and it joined with a vague antagonism born of jealousy.

When Dick fell into contemplation of the ship models and especially that of the schooner, he seemed to forget her more completely than even when he was fishing.

Fishing, his mind would be away from her no doubt, but it would still be close; brooding over the little ships and especially the schooner, his mind would be far away. She could tell it by the look in his eyes, by his expression, by his attitude.

And now that this apotheosis of the model schooner was handed to him by the fates as a plaything, the distrust and antagonism in the mind of the girl became acute.

It was almost as though another woman had put a spell upon him alienating him from her. As a matter of fact this was the case, for the schooner was the gift of Le Moan.

*

As the boat came alongside the *Kermadec*, the gulls left her, drifting off on the wind. Swinging with the tide, her stem was towards the break, the water rippling on the anchor chain which could be followed by the eye through the crystal clear water to where the anchor held in the lagoon floor. The copper sheathing was clearly visible with a few weeds waving from it, fish hung round the stern post and the secret green, the ship-shadow green—the green that is nowhere but in sea water alongside a moored ship—went to Dick's heart as something new, yet old in memory, a last touch to the wonder and enchantment of the hull, the towering masts, the rigging outlined against the 'diamond-bright blue of the sky.

Tying the boat to the chain plates he scrambled on board followed by the other. Then he stood and looked about him.

His feet had not rested on the deck of a ship since that time when as a tiny child he stood on the deck of the *Rarotonga*, Kearney about to hand him into the shore boat, Lestrange waiting to receive him. So many years ago that time had taken away everything from memory, everything but a vague something that was partly a perfume: the smell of a ship in tropical waters, tar, wood, cordage, all intensified by the tropical sun and mixed with sea scents in one unforgettable bouquet.

He swept the deck with his eyes and then looked aloft. The strange thing was that not only did he know all the important parts of the standing and running rigging, but he knew each part by its name, and by its English name; the only remnants of the language of his childhood were here, attached to the down-hauls, the topping lifts, the halyards, the blocks, taught by Kearney and held tightly to his mind by the model; and Aioma, the old child, voracious in sea matters as the child that once was Dick, knew them too, nearly all, taught to him on the model by Dick.

Master and pupil stood for a moment in silence, looking here, looking there, absorbed, taking possession of her with their minds. Then the pupil suddenly clapping his hands began to run about swinging on to ropes, poking his head here and there, now into the galley, now down the foc'sle hatch.

"It is even as it was in my dream," cried he, "but greater and more beautiful, and she is ours, Taori, and we will take her beyond the reef—*e manta Tia kau*—and we will fill her sails with the wind; she will eat the wind, there will be no wind left for canoes in all the islands." As he chattered and ran about, every now and then his face would turn to port as though he were looking for something. It was the obsession of the outrigger. You will remember that even in his dream when *half an inch high* he had helped to work the model across the rock pool, the dream ship had developed an outrigger; it was so now. The outrigger had so fixed itself in his mind, owing to ancestral and personal experience, as part of the make-up of a sailing craft that Aioma could not escape from the idea of it.

There was something wanting. Reason told him that there was nothing wanting, that the schooner had beam and depth enough to stand up to the wind and sea without capsizing—all the same every now and then, when facing the bow, he was conscious that on his left-hand side there was something wanting, something the absence of which as a stabilizer made him feel insecure.

Dick, having glanced at the compass in the binnacle, of which he could make nothing, turned his attention to the wheel. He had never seen a wheel of any sort before and he had no idea of the use of this strange contrivance. Kearney's ships were all rigged with tillers. Aioma was equally mystified.

"Le Moan will know," said he, "and the men she brought with her. But look, Taori."

He was standing by the saloon hatch and pointing down. He was brave enough on deck, but, like Le Moan, the interior of the schooner daunted him. He had never gone down stairs in his life, nor seen a step, neither had Dick.

The peep down the stairway, the mat below, the vague light through the saloon doorway fascinated Dick without frightening him, and, leaving the other to keep the deck, he came down cautiously, step by step, pausing now and then to listen.

In the saloon he stood looking about him at the handiwork of a civilization of which he knew nothing. The place was in disorder, nothing had been put straight since the fight that still existed in evidence. Bunk-bedding was tossed about, a water bottle lay smashed on the floor by the clothes that once had belonged to Rantan and Carlin. He noticed the telltale compass and the attachments of the swinging lamp, that had been brought on deck, the chairs, the door of the after cabin, the glass of the skylight and portholes, the table on which Rantan had held down Le Moan, the rifles in the rack and the two rifles used by the beachcomber and his companion standing in a corner cleaned and waiting for the deadly work which Le Moan had frustrated.

The smell of the place came to him. The vague odour of sandalwood from the cargo piercing bulkheads and planking, the smell of stale tobacco smoke, fusty bunk-bedding and the trade schooner smell that hinted of cockroaches and coconut oil gone rancid. It seemed part of the place and the place after the first few moments began to repel him.

What came to him through the sense of smell and sight was in fact a waft from the closed spaces of the cities of which he knew nothing, from the men who labour and construct and live and trade crowded like ants under roofs, shut out from the sun and stars and winds of God.

He drew slowly back as though the environment were clinging to him and holding him—but in his hand there was a rifle. Close to him, in the corner by the door, he had seized hold of it. His piercing sight had taken in the shape of the thing used by Rantan in the boat, the thing that spoke so loud and killed at such a distance, and now, seeing the death-dealer so close to his hand, he could not resist it.

He brought it on deck where Aioma was waiting for him and they examined it, but could make nothing of it.

"Let it be," said the canoe-builder, resting it against the coaming of the skylight. "Le Moan will know, or some of those men she has brought with her."

He looked round. Something was troubling his mind. Knowing nothing of the use of the steering wheel he was looking for the tiller.

Dick looked about also. On boarding the schooner he had noticed the absence of a tiller, the most striking object on the deck of the model, but other things had so seized him that he put the question by for the moment.

"No matter," said Aioma, "I know not how we will steer (*accoumi*) when the sails are given to the wind, but Le Moan, she will know."

THE THREE GREAT WAVES

The schooner had two boats, the four-oar and a smaller one black painted, battered by rough usage, but still serviceable. Later that day Aioma brought both boats on to the beach for an overhaul.

The remains of Sru and his companions had been dragged by the women to the outer coral and cast at low-tide mark for the sea to dispose of them. Nothing spoke of the tragedy but the remains of the canoes, the planking of the broken dinghy and the ship swinging idly at her moorings.

It was late afternoon and the crew, released from their wives for a moment, sat round whilst Aioma worked. Le Moan sat close to him but apart from the others, amongst whom was Kanoa.

The eyes of Kanoa might wander here or there, towards the canoe-builder, towards the lagoon, towards the schooner, but they always returned to Le Moan, who sat unconscious of his gaze listening to the talk of the old man and the answering words of Poni, whose dialect was the closest to that of Karolin.

Aioma had taken Le Moan off to the schooner that afternoon when he went to fetch the second boat.

It was not really the boat he wanted. His object was to get the girl on board alone with himself so that she might teach him the secret of the tiller and other things so that he might teach Taori. He was not jealous of Taori on land, he had supported him in every way as ruler, but in sea matters and in the mysteries of construction it was just a little hard that he, Aioma, should be less in knowledge than Taori or be condemned to learn with him from the mouth of a girl.

So, not stealing a march on Taori, but at least not awakening him, as the whole village slept in the heat of early afternoon, Aioma had pushed off with the girl and Kanoa, who, being unmarried, was drowsing close under the shelter of a tree.

Leaving Kanoa to keep the boat they had boarded the schooner alone.

Here the girl had explained the mystery of the wheel, the binnacle, in which dwelt a spirit prisoned there by the white men, the winch for getting up the anchor chain. She told him she alone had been able to steer the schooner and she showed him the compass card whose spear head always pointed in one direction no matter how the ship lay.

She did not know how it told the white men where to go, but she thought it must be friendly to Karolin as it had always pointed away from it. If they had obeyed it, they would not have been killed nor the children of Nanu and Ona, nor would Nanti have been wounded (the boy first shot by Carlin and whom Taori had carried off on his back amongst the trees).

"What of that," said Aioma, "children are children, and Nanti will take no hurt. He is already running about and the hole in his thigh will fill up— What of all that, beside the *ayat*?" Yet still his respect for the thing in the binnacle increased, and he followed with his eyes the pointing of the spear head. Why, it was pointing in the direction in which Marua (Palm Tree) lay! Marua, the island of the bad men, who some day—some day would raid Karolin, according to Taori.

He put this matter by in his mind to mature, and then he turned to the last unexplained mystery, the rifle leaning against the saloon skylight just as Dick had left it. She could explain this, too. She had seen Peterson using a rifle for shooting at bottles and her keen eyes had followed everything from the taking of the cartridge from the box to its insertion in the breech, to the act of firing and extraction.

She went to the galley where Carlin had placed the spare ammunition to be handy, and returned with a half full box of cartridges, and, obeying direction, Aioma did everything that Peterson had done. The recoil bruised his shoulder and the noise nearly deafened him, but he was unhurt, neither was the village alarmed owing to the distance, a few birds rose on the reef and that was all. But it was great. The noise delighted him and the smell of the powder. Then leaving the rifle on deck they returned to the beach towing the second boat.

He was talking now as he worked, telling Poni and the others that life on Karolin was not going to be all beer and skittles for them, that as they had joined the tribe and taken wives they would have to work; to work in the paraka patches and in the fishing and to help man the schooner. "For," said Aioma, "there are things to be done beyond the reef, away over there," said he straightening himself for a moment and wiping his brow and pointing north, "where lies Marua, an island of tall trees, and evil men who may yet come in their canoes—no matter. It is not a question for you or for me, but for Taori."

"What you set us to do we will do," said Poni. "We are not beach crabs, but men, Aioma. What say you, Kanoa?"

Kanoa laughed and glanced at Le Moan and then away over the lagoon.

"I will work in the paraka patches and at the fishing," said he, "but the work I would like best would be the work of measuring myself against those evil men you speak of, Aioma—that is the work for a man."

As he spoke the reef trembled and the air shook to a long roll of thunder, an infinite, subdued, volume of sound heart-shaking because its source seemed not in the air above them, but in the earth beneath them and the sea that washed the reef.

The wind had died out at noon, the outer sea was calm and the lagoon, mirror-bright, was making three inch waves on the sand; the tide was at half flood.

Aioma looked about him, the others had risen to their feet and Poni, leaving them, had run on to a higher bit of ground and was looking over the outer sea.

Through the windless air came the outcrying of gulls disturbed and then in the silence following the great sound that had died away, came another silence. The voice of the rollers on the outer beach had almost ceased.

"The sea is going out," cried Poni, "she is leaving us, she is dying—she has ceased to speak!"

As his voice reached them, they saw the water at the break swirling to an outgoing tide: an outgoing tide at half flood!

Led by Aioma they reached the higher ground, stood and gazed at the sea. The vast blue sea glittering without a touch of wind showed like a thing astray and disturbed. Its rhythm had ceased, swell met counter swell, and the Karaka rock spoke in foam; the wet coral showed the fall of the receding tide, and away to eastward white caps on the flawless blue marked the run of the north-flowing current checked for a moment in its course.

The village, disturbed by the vast rumour from the heart of things and answering to the call of Poni, came crowding out from the trees—the women had caught up their children, the boys and young men had seized spears and bows. They glanced to right and left; a woman cried out; then dead silence fell on them. Every eye was fixed on Aioma.

He was standing on a higher piece of coral, mute, motionless, as if carved from rock, his eyes fixed on the troubled waters. Taori might be their chief, but the wisdom of Aioma they knew of old, and seeing him undisturbed, they remained calm, waiting.

The voice of Poni broke the silence:

"She is coming back."

The flood was returning, the swirl at the break had ceased and a wave broke on the coral of the outer beach; the line of white caps died away, the Karaka rock ceased to spout, moment by moment the sea resumed her lost rhythm as breaker on breaker came in filling the air again with the old accustomed sound.

A great sigh went up from the people. All was over.

Yet Aioma did not move.

Dick, who had followed with the others, stood beside Katafa. He noticed that the schooner was swinging back to her old position, the incoming tide setting her again bow to the break, that the sea had regained its accustomed appearance, and that the lagoon was filling. All was right again.

Yet Aioma did not move. He stood with his eyes fixed to the far north. Then, suddenly, he turned and sprang from the rock.

"To the trees—to the trees!" He was no longer a man, he was a whirlwind, he rushed on the people with arms outspread, and, turning, they broke and ran.

"To the trees—to the trees!"

A hundred voices caught up the cry, the groves echoed it in a flash, the beach and coral stood empty, the people had taken to the trees; some to the near trees, some racing along the reef sought the great trees of the canoe-builders.

It was not climbing, as we know it. These people, like the people of Tahiti, could literally walk up a tree, bodies bent, hands clinging to the trunk and feet clutching at the bark.

Katafa could climb like this; Dick, less expert but a good climber, followed her, making her go first, seizing before he left the ground a child that held on to his neck. The child was laughing.

Fifty feet above the ground they clung and looked.

From east to west across the sea stretched a line of light, lovely and strange and infinite in length, swift moving, changing in brilliancy yet ever brilliant. Ever advancing, whilst now from tree top to tree top came the cry, shrill on the windless air:

"Amiana—amiana!—the wave—the wave!"

It met the Karaka rock and a great white ghost of foam rose towards the sun. A few seconds later came the boom of the impact followed by the clanging of the reef gulls rising in clouds and spirals; it passed the rock, re-forming, forward sweeping, bearing straight for the reef; a mound of sea towards which the shore waters rushed out as it checked, curved, paled and burst in thunder on the reef, sweeping houses to ruin and flooding into the lagoon.

The trees held though the foam dashed thirty feet up their trunks. Aioma unterrified, with one thought only, the schooner, could see from his eerie that she was safe. Broken by the reef the great wave had not harmed her. But now and again came the cry caught from tree top to tree top.

"Amiana—amiana! The wave—the wave!"

The duplicate, the glittering brother of the first long line of light, was moving as swiftly towards them across the sea. Again the Karaka spouted and the gulls clanged out, again the great green hill of water sucked the shore sea to it, curved, crested and broke to the roar of miles and miles of reef.

The bones of the houses broken by the first great comber could be heard washing amidst the tree roots below and from the canoe-builders' grove came the crash of a great tree, a matamata, less secure a refuge than the slender-stemmed coconuts. It had fallen lagoon-ward and the people on it, unkilled, were climbing along it back to shore when yet again came the cry:

"*Amiana—amiana!* The wave—the wave!"

It was the third great wave, bright like a far glittering bar of crystal, scintillating with speed, sweeping through distance as the others had swept towards the reef and lagoon of Karolin.

But now, after the first outcry, the people in the treetops no longer awaited the coming of the danger in silence.

Their spirit suddenly broke. The sight of this third dazzling apparition was too much. What had they done to the sea that she should do this thing to them? Their houses were gone, the trees were beginning to go; the trees would be destroyed and the reef itself would follow them, for what could withstand the enmity of the sea or the night that sent these vast glittering waves unleashed across her, one following on another—with how many more yet to come!

So as the third great wave drew back in silence for its blow against the land, the voice of Karolin was heard, a lamentable voice against the crying of the gulls; children and women and youths and some of the newcome kanakas joined in the cry, but not Le Moan or Katafa, nor Dick. Not Aioma, who, sure of his beloved schooner, found now time and words to comfort his weaker brethren when the comber crashing in spindrift and thunder left the trees still unbroken and a silence through which his voice could be heard.

He called them names that cannot be repeated, but which heartened them up, then he told them that the worst was over and to look at the sea.

Yes, the worst was over. No fourth brilliant line of light showed like the sword blade of Destruction sweeping over the blue, only a greater heave of the swell lifting the inshore green into breakers, horses of the sea resuming their eternal charge against the long line of the reef.

THE SECOND APPARITION

Dick was the first person down, followed by Katafa.

He nearly stepped on the spinous back of a great fish, a fish such as he had never seen before, larger than a full-grown man and tangled amongst the bushes and the trees.

The ruin was pitiable. Gone were the great canoe- houses, their thatch and ridgepoles floating in the lagoon water, gone the houses of the village, and all their humble furniture, mats and bowls and shelves, knives, implements and ornaments.

Gone were the little ships and each single thing that Dick and Katafa had brought from Palm Tree; gone was Nan, grin and post and all.

The house of the Uta Matu which, despite its walls of cane and roof of thatch, was in fact a public building, the canoe-houses which were a navy yard—three great waves had washed away all visible sign of the past of Karolin; but the people did not mourn, they were alive and the trees were saved, and the wreckage in the lagoon could be collected and rebuilt into new houses. There were three hours yet before sunset and led by Aioma the salvage hunting began, knives were recovered from cracks in the coral and mats that had wrapped themselves round tree trunks, canes and ridgepoles from the near water of the lagoon; the rainy season was far off and in that sultry weather being roofless was little discomfort; a week or more would put the houses up again, the only serious loss was in the paraka patches, washed clean out. But there was paraka growing on the southern beach, which the waves had not affected, and there was the huge fish of which the sea had made them a present.

Not one of them asked why this thing had occurred, or only Dick of Aioma and Aioma of his own soul.

"I do not know," said Aioma, "only as I stood there I knew in my mind that the sea had not ceased to speak, then I saw the far waves and called to the people to climb the trees."

Of the little ships, not a trace could be found. They had gone forever to some port beyond recall. Dick, to whom these things had been part of his existence, bound up in his life, left Aioma and sat apart by himself brooding as the dusk rose.

The heat had dried up the moisture that had not drained off into the lagoon and the sleeping mats were spread near to where the house of Uta Matu had once stood, but Dick had no heart for sleep.

Not only were the little ships gone, but everything he and Katafa had brought from Palm Tree. But it was the loss of the ships that hurt.

They were his earliest recollection, they were his toys; they had never ceased to be his toys, he who could kill so well and fight so bravely had never tired of them as playthings, playthings sometimes used in play, sometimes forgotten, but always remembered again. Then they were more than that; who can tell how much more, for who can see into the subliminal mind or tell what dim ghosts hiding in the under mind of Dick were connected with these things—Kearney surely, Lestrange and the men of the *Rarotonga*, perhaps. Palm Tree and his life on that enchanted island, certainly.

It was as though Fate, in taking his toys, had cut a cord attaching him to his past and the last remnant of civilization. How completely the hand of Fate had done its work he was yet to know.

The stars showed through the momentary gauze of dusk, and then blazed out over a world of night.

Le Moan, who had refused a mat, was nowhere to be seen. She had slunk away into the tree shadows, where, sitting with her back to a tree bole, she could, unobserved, see the reef and the figure of Dick seated brooding, Katafa's form on the mat where she had lain down to wait for Dick, the foam lifting in the starlight and the sea stars beyond the foam.

What the cassi flowers had said still lingered in the mind of Le Moan.

In that mind so simple, so subtle, so indefinite, so wildly strong, had grown since the night before an energy, calm, patient, sure of itself: a power so large and certain that the thought of Katafa did not even stir jealousy; a passion that could not reason but yet could say, "He is mine, beside me all things are nothing—I want only time."

Katafa had ruined her imaginary world only to create from the ruins this giant whose heart was determination.

Amidst the trees Kanoa, resting on his elbow, could see Le Moan as she sat, her head just outlined in the starlight.

The mind of Kanoa formed a strange contrast to that of the girl. In his mind there was no surety, no calm. Though he had rescued Le Moan, his heart told him that her heart was far from him, she had no eyes for him and though she did not avoid him, he might have been a tree or a rock, so little did his presence move her—and yet, if only she would look at him once, give him recognition by even the lifting of a finger, all his weakness would be turned to strength, his longing to fire.

426

Presently as the moon rose high, Le Moan's head sank from sight. She had lain herself down and the lovesick one, turning on his side, closed his eyes.

Dick, rising and straightening himself and stretching his arms, turned to where Katafa was waiting for him; he made a step towards her and then stood, his eyes fixed across the northern sea.

Cutting the sky from east to west, bright in the light of the moon lay a cloud, a long thready cloud.

No, it was not a cloud, it was too low. It was different it swelled and contracted, rose and sank.

He called to Katafa and his voice roused Kanoa, whose voice brought Poni from the mammee apple.

In a minute the village was awake and watching this new prodigy, wondering, doubting, the women calling one to the other till the voice of a man rang out:

"Gulls."

A murmur of relief went up from the women.

Gulls, only gulls. Thousands of gulls flying in line formation—and then the murmur checked and died out.

What was driving the gulls?

A storm coming from the north? No, the sky to the north was stainless and to these people who could smell and feel weather, there was no sign of storm.

"Look!" cried Kanoa.

The formation had altered; sweeping round from the east in a grand curve, the great moonlit line was shortening moment by moment till now it had contracted, showing only the van of the oncomers, who were heading for Karolin through the night sky like a spear towards a target.

The sound of them could now be heard, a steady winnowing sound, the pulse-like beat of ten thousand wings, whilst all along the reef from windward and leeward came the crying of the gulls of Karolin.

The crying of the burgomasters and skuas, the frigate birds and the great southern gannets, the laughing gulls and the Brandt's cormorants, all rising like a challenge to the newcomers from whom came no response other than the steady throbbing of the wings.

The gulls of Karolin knew, knew that of which the human beings were ignorant—knew that away beyond the sea line some great home of the sea fowl had vanished beneath the waves as Kingaman island and Lindsay island have vanished in the past, as many a Pacific island will vanish in the years to come. Knew that this was an army of invasion, a fight for a home and fishing rights. Knew that the waters of Karolin and the breeding places were insufficient for themselves and the strangers, knew that the moment which all nations and all wild herds and flocks must face, had come, and then as though actuated by one single mind, rose in a vast ring-shaped cloud and swept away south.

Swept away south beneath the moon whilst the van of the invaders now nearly above the reef swerved and turning due west, was followed by the whole line in what seemed, at first, level flight. Then rising and curving in a grand curve like that of a spiral nebula it broke into voice, a challenge that was answered from the south.

"Look!" cried Aioma.

The Karolin birds were returning, drifting like a curl of smoke. A wind seemed blowing them lazily through the sky, a wind seemed molding them and the invaders, till, in the form of two great vortex rings, they overhung the lagoon: a moment and then clashing in battle, they broke, reformed, and broke again, snowing dead and wounded gulls beneath the moon. The storm of their cries filled the night from reef to reef—now they would be dark against the moon, now away like blown smoke.

Sometimes the battle would drift towards the southern beach only to return gliding towards the northern. It was truly the battle that drifted, not the birds.

Just as a flock flies like one bird, moving here, heading there, under the dominion of a common mind, so these two great flocks fought—each not as a congregation, but as an individual; till, of a sudden and as if at the sounding of a trumpet, the combat broke, the storm ceased, the clouds parted, one still circling above the reef, the other drifting away southeast beneath the moon.

Southeast to find some more likely home, to die in the waves, to split up into companies seeking shelter in the Paumotuan atolls—no man could say, or whether the birds of Karolin were the victors or the strangers from the north. Wanderers lost forever to sight as their home sunk beneath the waves.

WHAT HAS HAPPENED TO THE REEF?

Three weeks' work had recreated the houses broken by the great waves, and put a top knob to the work of the builders. Nan had been recovered. A boy found him cast up in the sand near the break. A new post for him was cut, and Karolin, no longer godless, was itself again. But Aioma was not happy.

The sea when it had swept the reef had not disturbed the tree trunks felled and partly shaped, or had only altered their position slightly as they lay waiting for the canoe-builders to resume work; but Aioma had lost heart in the business. He had come to the conclusion that the schooner was better than any fleet of canoes, and all his desires were fixed on her.

Yet still something called him to the shaping of the logs, the voice of the Unfinished Job perhaps calling to the true workman, or maybe just the voice of habit—all the same he did not turn to it. He was under the spell of the schooner. Pulled this way and that he was unhappy. It is hard to give up a life's vocation even at the call of something better, and he would sit sometimes squatting on the sands, his face turned now to the object of his passion, and now towards the trees that talked to him of the half-born canoes.

Meanwhile in his mind there lay side by side and growing daily, a great curiosity and a great ambition.

The curiosity had been born of the battle of the gulls.

"What," asked he of himself, "has happened to the reef of Marua (Palm Tree)?" He knew Marua, he had been one of the fighters in the great battle of long years ago when the men of the north of Karolin had pursued the men of the south and slain them on Palm Tree beach. He had seen the reef and instinct told him that the invading gulls of three weeks ago had Come from there.

They were seeking a new home. Why? What had happened to the reef, or what had driven them from the reef?

Had the great waves of the same day, those three great waves that he still beheld scintillating in his mind, had they destroyed the reef? But how could that be, since they had not destroyed Karolin reef? The whole thing was a mystery and beside the curiosity that it excited, there lay in his mind the great Ambition, to take the schooner into the open sea and sail her there.

The lagoon, great as it was, was too small for him, besides, it was dangerous to the west with shoals and banks.

No, the outer sea was the place for him and there came the rub—Katafa.

Katafa had a horror of the vessel. She would not go on board it and well he knew that Taori would not go any distance from Karolin without Katafa, and he (Aioma) greatly daring, wished to go a long way, even as far as Marua, to see what had happened to the reef.

429

There you have the whole tangle and you can see how the curiosity and the ambition had grown together whilst lying side by side in his mind.

There was also a scheme.

Katafa would not object to Taori going out in the schooner a little way, and Taori would not mind leaving Katafa for a little time. And, thought the cunning Aioma, once we are out beyond there I will tell him what is in my mind about the gulls and the reef and he will want to go and see; it is not far and the colour of the current will lead us as it always has led the canoes, and the light of Karolin in the sky (*ayamasla*) will lead us back; besides, I will take with me Le Moan, who can find her way without eyes. Cooking this scheme in his mind he said nothing for some days till one evening, getting Taori and Katafa alone with him, he broached the idea of taking the *ayat* out a little way and to his surprise there was no resistance to it on the part of Katafa.

She had seen Dick's face light up at the suggestion. His trouble on account of the lost toys had affected her as though the loss had been her own, and she would say no word to mar this new pleasure, she would even overcome her hatred of the schooner and go with him, if he asked her.

But he did not ask her, he knew her dislike of the ship and the idea of taking her along never occurred to him.

"Then," said Aioma, "to-morrow I will get all things ready with water and fruit, for it is a saying of Karolin that no canoe should ever pass the reef without its drinking nuts lashed to the gratings—one never knows."

"Aie," said Katafa. Then she checked herself and turned away whilst Dick and the old man finished their talk.

**

They had several names for the sea in Karolin, names to suit its moods in storm and calm; one of these names spoke volumes of past history, history of sufferings endured by canoe men through the ages— The Great Thirst.

The sea to the people of Karolin was not an individual, but almost a multitude; the sea of calm, the sea of storm, the sea that canoe men encountered when blown off shore with the last drinking nut gone—The Great Thirst.

Katafa had known of it all her life. Once she had nearly sailed into it, and the words of Aioma about the water for the *Kermadec* recalled it to her. She shivered, and as the others talked, she scarcely heard their voices, contemplating this new terror which had arisen above her horizon.

But she said nothing, neither that night nor the next day when the casks were being brought on shore to be filled, when the nuts and pandanus fruit were being brought down to the boat by the women, many of them wives of Poni and the others of the crew.

Aioma had told Poni about the coming- expedition and the men of the schooner were not only willing to take their places on board again, but eager. Maybe they were tired for a moment of their wives, or just craving for something new—however that may be, they went aboard that night to make preparations for a start on the morrow, leaving their wives on the beach to look after themselves—all but Kanoa.

Kanoa did not go on board. He had had enough experience of that schooner, he did not want to set foot on her again; besides, he wanted to be left behind for his courage was growing and with it the determination to have it out with Le Moan.

So when the others were putting off, Kanoa was not with them. He had gone off along the beach towards the great trees, determining to hide till the schooner was beyond the reef. She was due to go out at dawn or a little later with the ebb tide and he would hide and watching till her topmasts were visible beyond the coral he would come back to the village to find Le Moan.

He would pretend that he had gone fishing on the reef and so had lost the schooner. As he sat down by the great logs of the canoe-builders and watched the stars looking out above the foam, he saw himself returning to the village, the sun in his face, the hateful vessel gone and Le Moan waiting for him.

Kanoa thought in pictures. Pictures suggested to him pictures. He did not know, neither did he picture the fact that Aioma, having decided to take Le Moan with him as a sort of navigating instrument, the girl was at that moment on board of the schooner, asleep, waiting for the dawn, dreaming, if she dreamed at all, of Taori.

MAINSAIL HAUL

The dawn rose up on the shoulder of a southeast wind, warm, steady, and breezing the gold of the lagoon water.

Gulls flew about the schooner on board of which Dick and Aioma had slept so as to be ready for an early start.

Now could be heard Aioma's voice calling up the hands from the foc'sle and now Katafa, watching from the shore, could hear the sound of the winch heaving the anchor chain short.

Poni, who had been chief man under Sru, knew all the moves in the game. He watched the mainsail set and the fore, the gaskets taken off the jib; talking to Aioma and explaining things, he waited till the canvas was set and then gave the order for the anchor to be got in.

Le Moan watched as Poni, taking the wheel, let the mainsail fill to the wind that was coming nearly dead from the south, whilst the schooner, moving slowly against the trickle of the ebb, crept up on the village and then turning south in a great curve made for the break on the port tack.

Le Moan could see Katafa far away on the shore backed by the trees of the village, a tiny figure that grew less and less and less as the Gates of Morning widened before them and the thunder of the billows loudened.

The sun had lifted above the sea line and the swell and the wind whipped the spray across the coral of the southern pier whilst Aioma, hypnotized, half terrified, yet showing nothing of it all stood, his dream realized at last.

Oh, but the heart clutch when she heeled to starboard and he recognized that there was no outrigger to port—for the outrigger is always fastened to the port side of canoes—no outrigger to port for the crew to crawl out on and stabilize her by their weight, and when she heeled to port the terror came lest the outrigger should be run too deep under.

There was no outrigger, he knew it—but, just as in the dream ship, he could not get rid of the obsession of it.

Moreover, now that the canvas was raised, now that the wind was bravely filling it, the enormousness of the size of those great sails would have set his teeth chattering had he not clenched his jaws.

To take a ship out of Karolin lagoon with the ebb running strong and a south wind, required a cool head and a steady nerve on the part of the steersman. The great lagoon emptying like a bath met the northerly current, the outflowing waters setting up a cross sea. There was also a point where steerage way was lost and it all depended how the ship was set for the opening as to whether she would broach to and be dashed against the coral.

But Poni was used to lagoon waters and the schooner safe in his hands came dead for the centre of the opening; then the ebb took her, like an arrow she came past the piers of coral, met the wash of the cross sea, shook herself and then to the thunder of thrashing, cleared the land and headed north.

"She will eat the wind," Aioma had once said, "there will be no more wind left for canoes in all the islands"; and now as Poni shifted the helm and the main boom stuttered and then lashed out to port, she was eating the wind indeed, the wind that was coming now almost dead aft. The smashing of the seas against her bows had ceased: with a following swell and a following breeze, silence took them—silence broken only by the creak of timber, block and cordage.

Le Moan looked back again. Almost behind them to the sou'-sou'west Karolin lay with the morning splendour on its vast outer beach whose song came faint across the blue sea, on the tall palms bending to the wind, on its gulls forever fishing.

Her eyes trained to great distances could pick out the thicker tree clumps where the houses lay and near the trees on a higher point of coral something that was not coral; the form of a girl, a mote in the sea dazzle now perceived, now gone.

Le Moan watched till the reef line was swallowed by the shimmer from which the trees rose as if footed in the sea. She had stirred no hand in the whole of this business: her coming on board had been at the direction of Aioma, the fate that threw her and Taori together even for a few hours whilst separating him from Katafa was a thing working beyond and outside her, and yet it came to her that all this was part of the message of the cassi flowers, something that had to be because of her love for Taori, something brought into existence by the power of her passion—something that united her forever with Taori.

The mind of Le Moan had no littleness, it was wanting in many things but feeble in nothing; it was merciless but not cruel, and when the sun of Taori shone on it, it showed heights and depths that had only come into being through the shining of that sun. For the sake of Taori she had sacrificed herself to Peterson, for the sake of Taori she had destroyed Carlin, for the sake of Taori she would sacrifice herself again, she who knew not even the meaning of the word "unselfish" or the meaning of the word "pity."

She could have killed Katafa easily, and in some secret manner—but that would not have brought her Taori's love, and to kill the body of Katafa, of what use would that be whilst the image of Katafa endured in Taori's mind.

Katafa was a midge whose buzzing disturbed her dream, it was passing, it would pass.

She turned to where Aioma, who had recovered his assurance and stability of mind, had suddenly flung his arms round Dick, embracing him.

There was something of the schoolgirl in this old gentleman's moments of excitement and expansion, something distinctly feminine in his times of uplift. No longer fearing capsize, free now of the obsession of the outrigger and glorying in the extraordinary and new sensations crowding on him, he remembered the gulls, the reef of Marua and his scheme.

"Taori," cried Aioma, "the canoes I have built, nay the biggest of them, are to this as the chickens of the great gull to their mother. Let the wind follow us till the going down of the sun and we will see Marua."

Dick, for the first time, looked back and saw the far treetops of Karolin. They seemed a vast distance away.

He thought for the first time of Katafa. She had said no word asking him to limit the cruise. Aioma had only suggested taking the ship beyond the reef and the provision of water and fruit had only been taken as a precaution against the dangers of the sea. She had dreaded the business but had spoken no word, fearing to spoil his pleasure, and sure that he would risk nothing for the love of her. But she had reckoned without his youth and the daring which God had implanted in the heart of man; she had reckoned without the extraordinary fascination the schooner exercised upon him and of which she knew next to nothing. She had reckoned without Aioma.

A thread tying his heart to the distant shore twitched as though at the pull of Katafa.

"But Marua is far," said he.

Aioma laughed. "The canoes have often gone there," he replied, "and what are they to this? Besides, Taori, it is no idle journey I wish to make, for it is in my mind that it was from the reef of Marua those gulls came that fought the gulls of Karolin, they were seeking a new home. Why?"

"The gulls only know," replied Dick, "and then there are the bad men whom some day I mean to slay, but not now, for we have not enough men, not a spear with us."

"We have the speak sticks of the papalagi," said Aioma, "and I can use them. Le Moan taught me, but the bad men are out of sight; in this business we need not draw nearer to Marua than we are now from Karolin, or only a little. It is the reef I wish to see and what may walk on it, for gulls do not leave their home just because

434

the wind blows hard or the sea rises high. They have been driven, Taori, and what has driven them—greater gulls, or some new form of man—who knows? But I wish to see."

Dick pondered on this. He had only intended to sail the schooner a short way, to feel her moving on the outer sea, to handle her; with the eating had come the appetite, with the handling of power the desire to use it. He had no fear about getting back, Karolin lagoon light would lead them just as it had led him and Katafa, and his mind was stirred by what Aioma had said about the gulls.

What had happened to drive them away from their home? He had never thought of the matter before in this light, thinking of it now he saw the truth in the words of the other, and having a greater mind than the mind of the canoe-builder, he linked the great waves with the business more definitely than the latter had done.

"Aioma," said he, "the great waves that broke our houses drove the gulls."

"But the waves," said Aioma, "came before the gulls."

"But the gulls may have rested on the water and come after," said Dick, "the waves may have broken the reef as it broke our houses."

"But the reef of Karolin was not broken," said Aioma.

"The waves may have been greater at Marua," replied Dick, "and have grown smaller with the coming."

"I had thought of the waves," said Aioma; "well, we will see; if the reef of Marua is broken, it is broken; if greater gulls are there, we will see them."

Dick looked back once again. The treetops of Karolin so far off now showed only like pins' heads, but the lagoon glow in the sky was definite; ahead could be seen the north-flowing current. Like the *Kuro Shiwo* of Japan, the *Haya e amata* current to the east of Karolin showed a blue deeper than the blue of the surrounding sea; but the *Kuro Shiwo* is vast, many miles in breadth, sweeping across the Pacific from Japan, it comes down the coasts of the Americas—a world within a world, a sea within a sea. The *Haya e Amata* is small, so narrow that its confines can be seen by the practiced eyes of the canoe men, and from the deck of the schooner its marking was clearly visible to the eye that knew how to find it; a sharp yet subtle change of colour where the true sea met its river.

Dick could see it as plain as a road. With it for leader and the lagoon light of Karolin for beacon, they could not lose their way. Then there was Le Moan, the pathfinder who could bring them back even though the lagoon light vanished from the sky.

The weather was assured.

Le Moan had taken the wheel from Poni, who wanted to go forward. She, who had brought the schooner to Karolin was, after Aioma and Dick, the chief person on board; in a way she was above them, for neither Dick nor Aioma had yet learned to handle the wheel.

Forward, by the galley, stood the rest of the crew and Dick's eyes having ranged over them, turned to Aioma.

"Yes," said he, "we will go and see." He turned to the after rail. The treetops had vanished, the land gulls were gone, but Karolin still spoke from the great light in the sky that like a faithful soul remained, above all things, beautiful, assured.

VOICES OF THE SEA AND SKY

Kanoa, dreading another voyage in the schooner and hating to be parted from Le Moan, hid himself amongst the trees of the canoe-builders.

He was nothing to Le Moan. Though he had saved her from Rantan, he was less to her than the ground she trod on, the sea that washed the reef, the gulls that flew in the air; for these she at least felt, gazed at, followed with her eyes.

When she looked at Kanoa, her gaze passed through him as though he were clear as a rock pool. Not only did she not care for him but she did not know that he cared for her.

Worse than that, she cared for the sun-like Taori. This knowledge had come to Kanoa only the other day.

Sitting beneath a tree, Reason had stood before him and said, "Le Moan does not see you, neither does she see Poni nor Aioma, nor any of the others—Le Moan only sees Taori, her face turns to him always."

As he lay now by the half-shaped logs waiting for the daylight that would take away the schooner, Reason sat with him telling him the same story, the sea helping in the tale and the night wind in the branches above.

It was night with Kanoa, black night, pierced by only one star—the fact that Taori was going away, if even for only a little time. The perfume of the cassi flowers came to him, and now, with the perfume, a far-away voice calling his name.

It was the voice of Poni. The men were going on board the schooner and Poni was collecting the crew.

Again and again came the call, and then the voice ceased and the night resumed its silence, broken only by the wash of the reef and the wind in the trees.

"They will think I have gone fishing," said Kanoa to himself, "or that I have gone on a journey along the reef, or perhaps, that the sea has taken me, but I will not go with them. I will not leave this place that is warm with her footsteps, and on all of which her eyes have rested; the place, moreover, where she is."

He closed his eyes and presently, being young and full of health, he fell asleep.

Dawn roused him.

He could see the light on the early morning sea. The sea grew luminous and the gulls were talking on the wind, the stars were gone, and the ghost of Distance stood in the northern sky blue and gauzy above the travelling sea that now showed the first sun rays level on the swell.

Then Kanoa rose up and came towards the village beyond whose trees the day was burning.

A woman met him and asked where he had been.

"I have been fishing," said Kanoa, "and fell asleep."

He came through the trees till the beach tending towards the break lay before him and the lagoon. The schooner under all plane sail was moving up towards the village and turning in a great curve, but so far out that he could not distinguish the people on deck. He watched her as she came up into the wind and lay over on the port tack. He watched her as she steered, now, close-hauled and straight, for the Gates of Morning, and then he saw her meet the outer sea.

She was gone. Gone for a little time at least; gone and he was left behind, free in the place Le Moan had warmed with her feet, on every part of which her eyes had gazed, and where, moreover, she was living and breathing.

The women had parted with their new husbands the night before. There was no crowd to watch the vessel go out, only Katafa, a few boys and a couple of women who were dragging in a short net which they had put out during the night, using the smaller of the schooner's boats which Aioma had left behind. The women stood for a moment with their eyes sheltered against the sun, then they returned to their work whilst Katafa, leaving the beach, came on to the high coral and to the very point of rock where Aioma, standing, had seen the approach of the giant waves.

She had scarcely slept during the night. Taori was going away from her, nor far or for any time, but he was going beyond the reef. To the atoll dweller the reef is the boundary of the world—all beyond is undecided and vague and fraught with danger;

the comparative peace of the lagoon waters gives the outer sea an appearance of menace which becomes fixed in the mind of the islander and even a short trip away from the harbour of refuge is a thing to be undertaken with precaution.

But she had said nothing that might disturb Dick's mind on her account or spoil his pleasure or mar his manhood. Even had the business been visibly dangerous and had Dick chosen to face it, she would not have held out a hand to prevent him. This was a man's business with which womenfolk had nothing to do. So she ate her heart out all the night and stood waving to him as the boat pushed off and watched the *Kermadec* leave the lagoon just as she was watching it now out on the sea, sails bellying to the wind and bow pointing north.   .

She watched it grow smaller, more gull-like and more forlorn in the vast wastes of water and beneath the vast blue sky. On its deck Le Moan was watching Karolin and its sinking reef just as on the reef Katafa was watching the ship and its disappearing hull, dreaming of wreck, of disaster, of thirst for her beloved one, dreaming nothing of Le Moan.

She watched whilst the morning passed, and the schooner still held her course. "She will soon turn and come back," said Katafa, as the distance widened and the sails grew less, and as the hull sank from sight she strained her eyes thinking that she saw the sails broaden as the ship, tired from going so great a distance and remembering, turned to come back to Katafa.

But the mark on the sky did not broaden. Vaguely triangular and like a fly's wing it stood undecided in the sea dazzle, it seemed to wobble and change in shape and change back again, but it did not increase, and one moment it would be gone and the next it would say "Here I am again, but see how much smaller I have grown I" Then it vanished, vanished for a long time, only to reappear by some trick and again to vanish and not to return.

The sea had taken the schooner and its masts and spars, its sails, its boat; everything that was mirrored only last evening in the lagoon the sea had taken and dissolved and made nothing of. The sea had taken Poni and Timau and Tahuku the strange kanakas; the sea had taken Aioma, and—the sea had taken Taori.

Oh, the grief! The pain that like a knife cut her heart as she gazed on the sea, on the far horizon line above which the speechless sky stood crystal pale sweeping up to azure. He had gone only a little way, soon to return, storms would not come nor would the wind change, nor would it matter if it did change.

Nothing could keep him from coming back. He had food with him in plenty, water in abundance, he had Poni and Timau and Tahuku and Nanta and Tirai; he had Aioma the wise and he had Le Moan—Le Moan the pathfinder.

Nothing could keep him from coming back and yet the heart of Katafa failed her before that speechless sky and that deserted sea whose meeting lips had closed like the lips of silence upon her lover. Her happiness, so great, perhaps too great, had been cut apart from her for the moment; it stood aside from her never to join her again till Taori came back from what the gods might be doing to him beyond that deserted sea, beneath that speechless sky.

The waters that from all those desert distances drew the voice of indifference and fate that she heard at her feet in the thunder of the breakers, the sky, robbed of speech, yet filled with the ever-lasting complaint of the questing gull.

Someone drew near her. It was Kanoa.

Katafa, who was a friend of all the world, was a friend to Kanoa. She had watched him as he sat apart from the others, noticed his melancholy and spoken to him, asking the reason.

"I am thinking of my home at Vana Vana," had lied Kanoa, "of the tall trees and the village and the reef, of my young days and my people." His young days! He who was still a boy!

"But you will return," said Katafa.

"I do not wish to return," said Kanoa, "I am as one lost at sea, who has become a ghost, and whose foot may no more be set in a canoe and whose hand may no more hold the paddle." Then Katafa knew that he was in love, but with whom she could not tell, nor had she time to watch and find out, being busy.

As he drew near her now, she turned to him, and for a moment almost forgot Dick in her anger.

"Kanoa," said she, "where have you been in hiding? They have gone without you; they called for you and you did not come, and they could not wait. You were wanted to help them in the raising of the sails and the work with the ropes—where have you been in hiding?"

"I have been fishing," said Kanoa.

"And where are the fish?" asked Katafa.

"Oh, Katafa," replied Kanoa, "I hid because I could not leave Le Moan, who is to me as the sun that lights me, who is my heart and the pain in my heart, my eyes and the darkness that blinds them when they see her not. I go to find her now to say to her what I have never said and to die if she turns her face from me."

"And how will you go to find her now?" asked Katafa. "Have you then the wings of the gull and know you not that she has gone with the others?"

"She has gone with the others!"

"She has gone with the others."

Kanoa said nothing. He seemed to wither, his face turned grey, and his eyes sought the distant sea. He, too, had watched the schooner disappear, rejoicing in the fact that she was gone with Taori leaving him (Kanoa) to find his love. And now Le Moan was gone—and with Taori. But he said nothing.

He turned away and lay down with his face hidden in his arms and as Katafa stood watching him, her anger turned to pity.

She came and sat beside him.

"She will return, Kanoa; they will return: he whom I love and she whom you love. They are gone but a little way. It is because they have gone from our sight that we grieve for them. Aioma said they would go but a little way—aie, but my heart is pierced as I talk, Kanoa, my breast is torn; they have gone from our sight and all is darkness. I will see him no more. I will see him no more."

Then, as on the night of the killing of Carlin, the man in Kanoa rose up and cast the boy away; saying not a word about his suspicions of the passion of Le Moan for Taori, he turned to comfort the wildly weeping Katafa.

"They will return," said he, "Aioma is with them and they can come to no harm—they will return before the sun has found the sea or maybe when he rises from it we will see them sailing towards Karolin. Peace, Katafa, we will watch for them, you and I. Go now and sleep and I will wait and watch, and if I see them I will come running to you, and when I sleep you can wait and watch and so with our eyes we will draw them back to us."

Katafa, whose tears had ceased, heaved a deep sigh. She rose and stood, her eyes fixed on the coral at her feet. Weary from want of sleep, she listened to the words of Kanoa as a child might listen, then, without looking once towards the sea, she passed away towards the trees.

Kanoa stood, his gaze fixed on the sea line, and from then through the hours and the days the eyes of the lovers watched and waited for the return of those who had gone "but a little way."

ISLANDS AT WAR—THE OPEN SEA

Something beside curiosity and the spirit of adventure had made Dick decide to push on towards Marua (Palm Tree).

The truth is Marua was calling to him. He wished to see it again if only for a moment. The hilltop and the groves and the coloured birds sent their voices across the sea to Karolin just as Karolin had sent its appeal across the sea to Katafa when Katafa had lived at Palm Tree.

As a matter of fact those two islands were forever at war in the battle ground of the human mind. In the old days natives of Karolin had gone to live on Marua, and Karolin had pursued them and brought them back, filling their minds with regret and longing and pictures of the great sea spaces and free sea beaches of Karolin. In the same way natives of Marua had gone to live on Karolin and Marua had pursued them and brought them back, filling their minds with regret for the trees, the hilltop and the blue ring of the lagoon.

Between Dick and Katafa there was only one faint suspicion of a dividing line, something that might increase with the years and make unhappiness the difference between Marua and Karolin: the null of the two environments so vastly different, the call of the high island and the call of the atoll, of the land of Dick's youth and the land of the youth of Katafa.

It is extraordinary how the soul of man can be pulled this way and that way by things and forms that seem inanimate and yet can talk—aye, and express themselves in the most beautiful poetry, strike in their own defense through the arms of men, follow without moving though the pursued be half a world away, and inspire a love as lasting as the love that a man or woman can inspire.

The love of a range of hills, what battles has it not won, and the view of a distant cloud, to what lengths may it not raise the soul of man—heights far above the plain where philosophy crawls, heights beyond the reach of thought.

With the suggestion of Aioma, the concealed longing in the mind of Dick began to show itself. He forgot Katafa; he forgot the bad men who had taken possession of Marua, old days began to speak again and the sound of the reef, so different from the voice of Karolin reef, to be heard.

He watched Le Moan at the wheel, and noticed how her eyes followed the almost imperceptible track far to starboard where the water colours changed. She was steering by the current as well as by the sense of direction that told her that Karolin lay behind. He did not know the speed of the schooner, but he had travelled the road when coming to Karolin with Katafa and he knew that soon, very soon, the hilltop of Marua must show.

He went forward and gazed ahead—nothing. The land gulls had been left behind and in all that sea to the north there was nothing. He came aft to find Poni again at the wheel, and as he came he crossed Le Moan who was going forward; she did not look at him and he scarcely looked at her. Le Moan, for Dick, was the girl who had saved them by killing Carlin and fighting with Rantan till he was overcome; but to him, personally, she was nothing. So cunningly had she hidden her heart and mind that not by a glance or the least shade of expression had she betrayed her secret to him. Kanoa only suspected—but he was her lover.

Aioma was squatted on the deck near the steersman, eating bananas and flinging the skins over his shoulder and the rail.

"Aioma," said Dick, "there is no sight of Marua yet, but soon we will see it lifted to the sky, with the trees—it calls to my heart. You have seen it?"

"I was one of those who chased Makara and his men to Marua," said Aioma, "we fought with them and slew them on the beach; aie, those were good times when Uta Matu led us and Laminai beat the drum— *taromba*—that is only beaten for victory, and will never be beaten again, since it went away with Laminai and has never returned. Tell me one thing, Taori. When you came to Karolin with Katafa, you made friends with the women and children, and Katafa told them a tale, how the canoes of Laminai had been broken by a storm, and all his men lost, and how the club of Matu was found by you on the reef of Marua and the gods had declared you were to be our chief. I was on the southern beach at that time and did not hear the tale, but the women and children took it without any talk, glad to have a man to lead them.

"Tell me, Taori, was that all the tale? I never asked you before and I know not why I ask you now."

"Aioma," said Dick, "there was more than that. Laminai and his men came through the woods of Marua and there was a great fight between them and me. I slew with my own hands Laminai and another man. Then, taking fright, all his men ran away and they fought with each other in the woods—many were killed, and then came the big wind from the south and the men who were trying to leave Marua were dashed on the reef, not one being left."

Aioma forgot his bananas. Some instinct had told him that there was more in the story of Katafa than revealed by her to the women, but he had not expected this.

So Laminai, the son of Uta Matu, had been slain by Taori, and his men put to flight; the storm had destroyed them before they could put away, but it would not have destroyed them only for Taori.

He looked up at Taori, standing against the line of the rail, his red-gold head against the patient blue of the sky, and to Aioma it seemed that this journey they had embarked on was no trip to view the outer beach of Marua—that they had been deluded by the guardians of Karolin and the ghosts of the Ancient, drawn to sea to meet the vengeance of the dead Uta Matu, of his son, and the men slain by the hand and will of Taori.

That thunder from the heart of the sea, those waves from nowhere, the prodigy of the gulls, all these were portents.

"Taori," said he, "now that you have told me, I would go back. My heart misgives me and if I had known that Laminai fell by your hand I would not have come; I love you as a son, Taori, you fought for the women and children of Karolin against the white men, but you do not know Uta Matu the king, whose son you killed, whose men you put to flight."

"But Uta Matu is dead," said Dick, "he has no power."

"You do not know Uta Matu," said Aioma, "nor the length of his arm, nor the power of his blow. You have not seen his eyes or you would not say those words. Let us return, Taori, before he draws us too far into his grasp."

"When I have seen what I wish to see, I will return," said Dick. He had no fear of dead men, nor of living men either, and for the first time his respect for Aioma was dimmed. "I will return when I have seen what we came to see. I am not afraid."

Aioma rose and straightened himself.

"I have never known fear," said he, "and I do not know it now. It was for you I spoke. Go forward then, but this I tell you, Taori, there are those against us who being viewless we cannot strike, whose nets are spread for us, whose spears are prepared."

"Aioma," said Dick, "no net can hold me such as you speak of. Nets spread by the viewless ones are for the spirit—*Ananda*—not the body. My spirit is with Katafa, safe in her keeping, how then can Uta Matu seize it?"

"Who knows?" said Aioma. "He is artful as he is strong, and Le Juan who is dead with him is more artful still, and, look, we have the child of Le Juan's daughter with us—Le Moan. Aie! had I thought of all this I never would have brought her."

"How can she hurt us?"

"It is not she. It is Le Juan, the wicked one, whose blood is in her."

To Aioma, as I have said before, people were not dead as they are with us, only removed to a distance, and though he might speak of Spirits, he spoke of people removed out of sight, yet still potent.

He did not believe that Uta Matu could use a real net or spear against Dick, but he did believe that the dead king of Karolin and his witch woman could, in some way, stretch through the distance to lay nets and strike with spears. Ghostly spears and nets not meant for the body, but the man.

If you could have pierced deeper into the mind of Aioma you would have found the belief—never formulated in words—that a man's body was just like the shell of a hermit crab, a thing that could be thrown off, crept out of, discarded. Uta Matu when called into the distance had discarded his shell, but the man and his power remained—at a distance.

"I fear neither Le Juan nor Uta Matu," said Dick, and as he spoke the air suddenly vibrated to the dang of a bell.

WE SHALL NOT SEE MARUA AGAIN

It was the ship's bell.

Tahuku had struck it in idleness, just as a child might, but the unaccustomed sound coming just then seemed to Aioma a response to the words of the other. But he said nothing. Taori had chosen his path and he must pursue it.

At noon the northern horizon still showed clear and unbroken by any sign of land, yet still the wind blew strong and still the schooner sped like a gull before it.

Tahuku, who had been cook and who knew where the stores were kept, prepared a meal; and whilst the crew were eating, Aioma took the place of the lookout in the bow. Nothing—neither land gull nor trace of land. Nothing but the never ending run of the swell bluer from the southern drift that showed still the contrast of the deeper blue.

A road leading nowhere.

The canoe-builder came up to where Dick was standing in the bow.

"Taori," said Aioma, "we have not lost our way, there runs the current and there Karolin still shows us her light, we have come faster than the big canoes of forty paddles and so have we come since morning, yet Marua is not in sight."

It was late afternoon, and Aioma as he spoke skimmed the sea line from west to east of north with eyes wrinkled against the light.

"No cloud hides it," went on the old man like a child explaining a difficulty, "it is full day, yet it is not there—to our sight."

Dick, as perturbed as Aioma, said nothing. He knew quite well that by now Marua should have been high on the horizon. They had been travelling since morning, how swiftly he could not tell, but with great speed, seeing that they had with them the wind and the current; also the sky stain made by Karolin was now very vague, vague as when he had viewed it from Marua.

"Where then is it gone?" went on the old fellow, "or how is it hidden? Has Uta Matu cast a spell upon us or has Marua been washed away?" Then turning as if from a suddenly glimpsed vision: "Taori —we may sail till the days and the nights are left behind us with the sun and the moon and the stars, but Marua we shall not see again."

Dick still said nothing. He refused to believe that Uta Matu had the power to put a spell on them and he refused to believe that Marua had been washed away by those waves that did little more than smash a few houses at Karolin. All the same he was disturbed. Where then was Marua?

Poni, who was standing near them with Le Moan who had heard what Aioma said, suddenly struck in, in his sing-song voice.

"Surely we passed an island when Pete'son commanded this ship and we were running on this course, an island that would be about here, but is not here anymore—and you remember the great waves that came to us at Karolin and the gulls who sought a home? All these things have just come together in my head as it might be three persons meeting and conversing. Well then, Aioma, it is clear to me now that this island you seek is gone beneath the sea. At the time of the gulls and those great waves, I said to Timan, that somewhere an island had gone under just as Somaya which lay not far from Soma went under in the time before I started to sail in the deep- sea ships. One day it was there and the next day it was not, and there were the big waves just like those that came to Karolin. Marua, you called this island; well, Aioma, you may be sure that Marua has gone under the sea."

And now strangely enough Aioma, so far from accepting the support of this statement, turned upon the unfortunate Poni who had dared to bring experience and common-sense with him to the bar.

"Gone under!" The scream of laughter with which Aioma received this suggestion when it had percolated down into the basement of his intelligence made the faces of the others turn as they stood about near the foc'sle head discussing the same subject.

"Gone under!" What did Poni mean by such silly talk, did he not know that it was impossible for an island to sink in the sea? Sink like a drowning man! No, the great waves had knocked Marua to pieces, either that or Uta Matu had veiled it from their sight . . . and so the talk went on and all the time the sun was falling towards the west and Le Moan's palms were itching to feel again the spokes of the wheel and the kick of the rudder; for a plan had come into the mind of Le Moan, a plan put there maybe by Uta Matu, who can tell; or Passion, who can tell? But a perfectly definite plan to take the wheel, steer through the night and put the schooner absolutely and fatally astray: Put her away from Karolin so far and so much to the east that the lagoon light would be no guide and a course to the south no road of return.

The plan had come to her, fallen into her head, only just now; it was indefinite, but cruelly straight like the flight of an arrow, and in one direction—away from Karolin.

Great love is an energy that, born in mind, has little to do with mind. It is a thing by itself, furiously alive, torturing the body it feeds on and the mind that holds it. Hell is the place where lovers live. Even when they escape from it to heaven as in the case of Katafa, it is always waiting to receive them back, as also in her case.

To Le Moan, dumbly suffering, the message of the cassi flowers telling that Taori was hers by virtue of the power of her passion for him, had suddenly lost all significance. He was here now by the power of the wheel of the ship over the rudder. She could take him away, now, to be always with him—take him away forever from Katafa, steer him into the unknown. And yet the knowledge of this physical power and the determination to use it brought her no ease. She would be dose to him, but of what avail is it to a person suffering from the tortures of thirst if he is close to water yet may not drink. All the same she would be close to him.

As she watched the sun so near its setting she dwelt on this fact as a bird on the egg it is hatching, and brooding, she listened whilst Aioma urged that they should

446

turn back at once, and Dick countered the suggestion asking for more time. He had it in his mind to hold on till sunset, till night came to cut them off in the quest. Well knowing in his mind that Marua was no more, that the reef and lagoon and hilltop, the tall trees and coloured birds had all vanished like a picture withdrawn, either gone beneath the sea as Poni said or devoured by the waves as Aioma held—well knowing this in his mind, his heart refused to turn from the quest till turned by darkness.

He would never see Palm Tree again. Like grief for a person lost, the grief of this thing came on him now. He knew now how he loved the trees, the lagoon, the reef, and he recalled them as one recalls the features of the dead. He could not turn till darkness dropped the veil and said to him definitely, "Go back."

He was standing with this feeling in his mind when a sound made him turn to where Aioma had suddenly taken his seat on the edge of the saloon skylight with body bent double and head protruding like the head of a tortoise. He seemed choking. He was laughing.

Aioma, like Sru, had a sense of humour, and a joke, if it were really a good joke, took him like the effect of a dose of strychnine. Sure now that Marua had been swallowed by the sea, the catastrophe, having made itself certain and obtained firm footing in his mind, suddenly presented its humorous side. He had remembered the "bad men." They were swallowed with Marua, he could see them in his imagination swimming like rats, screaming, bubbling—drowning—and the humour of the thing skewered him like a spear in the stomach.

BOOK IV

E HAYA

The sun touched the sea line, the blazing water leaping to meet him, and then in a west golden and desolate, in a sea whose water had turned to living light, he began to drown.

Dick watched as the golden brow, almost submerged, showed a lingering crescent of fire and then sank, carrying the day with it as Marua had sunk carrying with it his youth and the last visible threads connecting him with civilization.

He turned. Le Moan had taken the wheel.

The sails that had been golden were now ghost white and a topaz star had already pierced the pansy blue where in the west the new moon hung like a little tilted boat.

"To the south," cried Aioma. "*E Haya*—to the south, Le Moan, to Karolin now that we have seen there is nothing to be seen, to the south; to the south, for I am weary of these waters."

Le Moan, dumb and dim in the starlight now flooding the world, spun the wheel; on the rattle of the rudder chain came the thrashing of canvas and the schooner bowing to the swell lay over on the port tack—due east.

Aioma glanced towards the moon but Le Moan reassured him.

"The current is fighting us," said she, "and I would get beyond it. Have patience, Aioma, the way is clear to me."

He turned away satisfied and lay down on deck. Dick who had brought up some blankets from below to serve as a sleeping mat, lay down by him, and the kanakas, all but Poni and Tahuku, went to their bunks in the foc'sle.

Aioma, lying on his face with his forehead on his arms, heard the rattle of the rudder chain and knew that Le Moan was edging now to the south. She would steer all night with the help of Poni, and sure of her and sure of Karolin showing before them at daybreak, he let his mind wander, now to the canoe-building, now to the spearing of great fish, till sleep took him as it had taken Dick.

Le Moan, steering, could see their bodies in the starlight, and beyond them Poni and Tahuku seated close to the galley, their heads together talking and smoking, heedless of everything but the eternal chatter about nothing which they could keep up for hours together, whilst the schooner under the hands of the steersman was heading again due east.

An hour after midnight the wind shifted, blowing from the west of south. Poni came aft to see if Le Moan wanted anything, food, water, a drinking nut— she wanted nothing; as she had steered all that night long ago towards Karolin, she steered now, tireless, wrapt in herself, without effort.

As the dawn showed in the eastern sky she altered the course to full south and handed the wheel to Poni.

She had done her work, *e Haya*, steered they forever now they would never raise Karolin—so far to the west that even the lagoon light would be all but invisible.

The first sun ray brought Aioma to his feet, he saw Poni at the wheel and Le Moan lying near him fast asleep like a creature caught back into darkness now that her work was done. The sunrise to port told him that the ship was heading south, then he came forward and looked.

The southern sea showed no sign and the southern sky no hint of the great lagoon. Not a bird's wing appeared.

He roused Dick, who came forward and they stood whilst the canoe-builder pointed to the south.

"There is nothing," said Aioma— "yet we have come all the night and she is never wrong—not even the light in the sky. Yet by now the trees should have shown."

Dick, gazing into the remote south at the blue and perfect and pitiless sky, unbroken at the sea line, unstained above it, drew in his breath; a cold hand seemed placed on his heart. Where then was Karolin?

"Who knows," said Aioma, "it may show when the sun is higher. Let us wait."

They waited and watched whilst the sun rose in the sky, but the sun revealed nothing that the dawn had not shown—nothing save away to the westward unseen by them and so faint as scarcely to be seen, a pale spot in the higher blue—the light of Karolin.

Aioma came running aft. He shook Le Moan and roused her from her sleep and she came forward and stood in the bow, sheltering her eyes against the light.

"It is not there," said she; "I can see nothing with my eyes nor in my mind—the power has gone from me, Aioma, it has been taken from me in my sleep."

Aioma struck his head with the flat of his hand, then he turned to her as she stood there with the lie on her lips, close to, almost touching Dick, who stood, his hand on the rail, scarcely breathing.

"Gone from you," cried the canoe-builder, "taken in sleep, aie, what is this! We are adrift and astray, gone! And who could take it but Uta Matu. Taori, we are lost, we are in the hands of the viewless ones; their nets have taken us. I told you this, yet you would not put back. Never more shall we see Karolin."

Dick did not move. He saw again the figure of Katafa as she stood on the beach when they were leaving, that loved figure from which he had parted with scarcely a thought, so full was he of the schooner and the dream of sailing her on the outer sea. Katafa who even then was watching for him away beneath that tiny stain on the western sky, grown so faint now as to be almost invisible.

Even last night when sure of return, his heart had longed for her, he had dreamed of her; by a thousand little threads, each living, she had joined herself to his very being, and he would never see her again!

"Never more shall we see Karolin." He turned to the desolate south, to the west, to the east; then, heedless of the others, a savage in his grief, he cast himself on the deck, his face on his arms as if to hide himself from the hateful sun.

AIOMA CURSES THE WIND

"Never more shall we see Karolin."

The words of Aioma were repeated by

the sky, by the sun, and the sea. Never more would he see Katafa, hear her voice, feel her arms about him. The hard hot deck beneath him, the sun beating on his back, the sounds of the sea on the planking and the groaning of the timbers all were part of his misery, of the awful hunger that fed on his heart.

He loved her as a man loves a woman, as a child loves a mother, as a mother loves a child. He who had killed men and dared death was, in fact, still a child; passionate, loving, ignorant of the terrors that life holds for the heart of man, of the grief that kills and the separation that annihilates. He had never met grief before.

Le Moan watched him as he lay. She knew. He was lying like that because of Katafa, she had lain like that on the coral because of him.

By declaring that vision had returned to her, by seizing the wheel and steering for Karolin, she could have brought him to his feet a well man—only to hand him over to Katafa.

She could not do that.

Her heart, pitiless to the world, was human only towards him; she had braved the unknown and she had braved death to save his life, but to save him from this suffering she could not speak three words.

Aioma watched him absolutely unmoved. If Dick had been wounded by a spear or club, it would have been different, but mental anguish was unknown to the canoe-builder and you cannot sympathize with the unknown.

Then as Dick struggled to his feet and stood with his hand on the rail, dazed and with his face turned again to the south, the old man recommenced his plaint with the insistency of a brute, whilst the wind blew and Poni at the wheel kept the ship on her course south, ever towards the hopeless south.

"No," said Aioma, "never more shall we see Karolin. Uta has us in his net. Never more shall I shape my logs (he had dropped that business before leaving Karolin) or spear the big fish by night whilst the boys hold the torches (*upoli*), and the great eels will go through the water with none to catch them. It is this *ayat* that has brought us where we now are to confusion and a sea without measure, and this wind, which is the breath of Le Juan, and may her breath be accursed. Well, Taori, and so it stands, and what now? Shall we go before the wind or counter it— seek the south *e Haya* where nothing is, or the east *e Hola* where nothing is?"

Dick turned his face to the canoe builder. "I do not know, Aioma, I do not know. It is all darkness." His eyes turned to Le Moan and passed her, falling on Poni at the wheel, and the sea beyond.

Aioma had told him that he was taking Le Moan as a pathfinder, but Dick had troubled little about that, scarcely believing in it. He had trusted to the current and the light of Karolin as a guide. They were gone, but it was the words of Aioma that removed the last vestige of hope.

He trusted Aioma in all sea matters and when Aioma said that they were lost, they were lost indeed. Palm Tree vanished, Karolin gone, nothing but the sea, the trackless hopeless sea and the words of Aioma!

Urged by a blind instinct to get away from the sight of that sea, that sky, that pitiless sun, he left the deck and came down the steps to the saloon where he stood, a strange figure, almost nude, against the commonplace surroundings; the table, the chairs, the bunks with their still disordered bedding, the mirror let into the forward bulkhead, a mirror so old and dim and spotted that it scarcely cast a reflection.

He looked about him for a moment, moved towards the bunk where Carlin had once slept, and, sitting down on the edge of it, leaned forward, his arms resting bn his knees, his head bowed; just as his father had sat long, long years ago when Emmeline had vanished into the woods to return bearing a child in her arms—bearing him, Taori.

Just as his father had sat all astray, crushed, helpless and lost, so he sat now, and for the same reason.

Up on deck Poni at the wheel turned to the canoe-builder.

"And what now, Aioma," said Poni, "since Le Moan knows not where to go, where go we?" As he spoke the mainsail trembled, rippled, and flattened again.

The canoe-builder turned aft. The breezed-up blue, beyond a certain point, lay in meadows and a far glitter spoke of a great space where there was no wind.

"The wind is losing its feathers," said Poni with a backward glance in the direction towards which the other was looking.

As he spoke the mainsail trembled again as though a shudder were running up it and the boom shifted to the cordy creak of the topping lifts.

Yes, the wind was losing its feathers, dying, jaded, exhausted; again the mainsail flattened, shivered and filled only to flatten again, the wobble of the bow wash began to die out and the schooner to lose steerage way.

The breath of Le Juan was failing and Aioma who had cursed it saw now the calm spreading towards them, passing them, taking the southern sea.

Poni left the wheel.

There was nothing to steer. A ship is only a ship when she is moving, and the schooner, now a hulk on the lift of the swell, lay with a gentle roll on the glassy water—drawing vague figures upon the sky with her trucks, complaining with the voice of block and cordage whilst the canoe-builder standing with his eyes on the north, felt the calm: felt it with a sixth sense gained from close on a century of weather influence; measured it, and knew that it was great. Great and enduring because of its extent, complete and flawless as a block of crystal placed by the gods on the face of ten thousand square miles of sea.

He remembered how he had cursed the wind, and turning to speak to Le Moan, found her gone.

Le Moan following Dick to the saloon hatch had stood for a moment listening.

Unable to hear anything below, she waited till Aioma's back was turned and then cautiously began to descend the steps of the companion-way; cautiously, just as she had come down those steps that night to attack the white men single-handed and save, at the risk of her life, the life of Taori.

Reaching the door of the saloon, she saw him half seated on the bunk's edge, his elbows on his knees and his face in his hands whilst above him, now on the ceiling, now on the wall, glimmered and glittered and danced the same water shimmer that had danced above the sleeping Carlin. Only now it was a butterfly of gold.

The ripples sent out by the roll of the schooner on the sea surface gave it its tremor, the roll its extent of flight, the sunlight its gold.

It fluttered now, sweeping down as if to light on Dick, and now it was flying on the ceiling above him. It seemed a portent, but of what she could not tell, nor did she heed it after the first glance.

Crossing the floor, she came to him, sat down beside him, and rested her hand on his shoulder.

Dick turned to her. Like the child that he was, he had shuddered and sobbed himself into a state where thought scarcely existed above the sense of despair. He turned to her, the touch of a woman's sympathy relaxing the numbing grip of Disaster, yet not for a moment releasing him. Then casting his arms around her neck, he clung to her for comfort as a child to its mother.

Clasping her arms around his naked body, her lips on his throat, her eyes closed, in Paradise—heedless of life and death and dead to the world, Le Moan held him, flesh to flesh, soul to soul, for one supreme moment her own. That she was nothing to him was naught, that grief not love had thrown him into her arms was naught, she held him.

To Le Moan whose soul was, in a way, and as far as Taori was concerned, greater than her body, marriage and its consummation could have given little more—if as much. She held him.

Above them danced the golden butterfly that no man could catch or brutalize; a thing born of light, of the sea, of chance; gold by day that had been silver by moonlight, elusive as the dreams that had led Carlin to his death and the love that had led Le Moan to destroy him.

Then, little by little, the world broke in upon her, her arms relaxed, and rising, half blind and groping her way, she found the door, the steps, the deck, where Poni stood released from the wheel, and Aioma by the rail.

HE HAS TURNED HIS FACE FROM THE SUN

The ocean is a congregation of rivers, the drift currents and the stream currents; rivers, some constant in their flow, some intermittent and variable; some wide, as in the case of the Brazil current which at its broadest covers four hundred and fifty miles; some narrow as in the case of the Karolin-Marua drift, scarcely twenty miles from east to west. The speed of these rivers varies from five miles a day to fifteen or thirty, as in the case of the Brazil current, or from ten to a hundred and twenty miles a day as in the case of the Gulf Stream.

Sometimes these rivers, lying almost side by side, are flowing in opposite directions, as in the case of the north running Karolin-Marua current and the southerly drift that had now got the schooner in its grasp; and each one of these streams of the sea, from the Arctic to the Antarctic, has its own peculiar people, from the Japanese swordfish of the *Kuro Shiwo* to the Gambier turtles on the Karolin-Marua.

Left without wind the schooner drifted, her sails casting vast reflections on the glassy swell; sometimes, away out, a slight disturbance on the water would show where a sleeping turtle had suddenly submerged, and over-side in the ship's shadow, fucus and jelly-fish floating fathoms deep could be seen drifting with the ship. Nothing else. Neither shark nor albacore nor palu nor gull spoke of life across or beneath that glacial sea.

The sun sank in a west of solid gold and the stars took the night, the sails showing black against the brilliant ceiling.

Dick, who had come on deck before sunset, stood by Aioma at the after rail. He seemed himself again, but he had not eaten that day; a fact that disturbed the canoe-builder, who had turned from dark thoughts and misgivings to a sort of cheery fatalism. Aioma was alive and there was food and water on board for a long time and the wind might blow soon or the drift—he sensed a drift—take them somewhere. He had a feeling also that his curses had closed the mouth of Le Juan; he had eaten well, and his belly was full of ship's food and bananas, so his sturdy nature refused depression.

"Of what use," he was saying, "is a man without food? A man is the paraka he eats and the fish . . . Go and eat, Taori, for without food a man is not a man."

"I will eat to-morrow," said Taori, "I have no heart for eating now."

Away forward crouching in her old place Le Moan listened to the creak of the ship as it moved to the swell and watched the stars that shone on Karolin.

The faithful unbreakable sense born with her as truly as the power of the water-finder is born in him, or the power of the swallow to find its southern nest, told her just where Karolin lay; away on the starboard beam to the north, now dead aft as the schooner turned to some gentle swirl of the current, now a bit to port, now back again to starboard.

She could see the figures of Taori and Aioma in the starlight and she could hear the voices of Poni and the others from the foc'sle, the creak of the timbers and the creak of the main boom as it moved to the rocking of the swell. She too had not eaten that day.

She had done her work and she had received her reward. With his body in her arms and her lips on his neck, she had drunk him as a creature dying of thirst might drink long delicious draughts from a poisoned well; for he had clung to her not in the passion of love, but of misery, and he had let her hold him as a comforter not as a lover, and she knew that till the stars fell dead and the sun ceased to shine that never would he be closer to her than that.

This knowledge had come to her from the very contact with his body, from the clasp of his arms about her neck. He had told her unconsciously and without speech more than he could have ever have told her in words. He was Katafa's.

He was forever out of her reach, sure and certain instinct told her that, yet he was near her and she could see him—they were together.

Only a little before sundown Aioma had said to her, "Le Moan, maybe since the wind has gone the spell of Uta Matu has ceased to work. Shut your eyes, turn, and see if you cannot get a view again of where Karolin lies; is the sight of it still gone from you, Le Moan?"

"It is still gone," she had answered him, "and even if it were with me, of what use, for there is no wind?"

She had told the lie looking him in the face and seeing only Taori.

It was no little jealousy that made her lie; she had no jealousy towards Katafa whom Fate had bound to Taori before she had seen him. He had not chosen Katafa in preference to her; perhaps that was why her heart held no jealousy. All the same to bring him back, to take the wheel and steer him into the arms of Katafa—she could not.

To save his life she could easily have died for him, to give him back to joy and love was impossible.

The night passed and the sun rose on another day of calm, and still the schooner drifted, the variable current setting her back sometimes, sometimes leading her a bit more south. Truly it was a great calm as Aioma had predicted and it fell on Taori, as on the sea, like the hand of death. He scarcely ate at all; he had fallen away from himself, his mind seemed far away, he scarcely spoke.

As men who have never met the microbes of disease fall easily victims and die when other men only fall ill, Taori, who had never before known grief, in the language of Aioma, turned his face from the sun.

On Karolin men had often died like that, of no disease—because of insult, because of a woman, sometimes just for some reason that seemed trivial. It is one of the strangest attributes of the kanaka, this power of departing from the world when life becomes unendurable, too heavy or even just wearisome.

"He has turned his face from the sun," said Aioma to Poni one morning—the fourth morning of the calm—and Le Moan who was nearby heard the words.

It was on that same morning that the breeze came, a light air from the north strengthening to a steady sailing wind, and almost on the breeze came the call of the look-out who had climbed to the cross-trees.

"Land!"

Just a few palm tree tops to the southeast, the trees of a tiny atoll, so small that it cast no lagoon reflection; and Aioma who had climbed to see came down again whilst Poni, who had taken the wheel, put the ship to the southeast taking his position from the sun not far above the eastern skyline.

Presently the far-off treetops could be seen from the deck, but Dick as Poni steered, and after a glance at the distant trees, lost interest.

He had turned his face from the sun.

WHAT HAPPENED TO RANTAN

When Rantan awoke from sleep it was morning. He had slept the clock round. He awoke hungry and full of vigour, and coming out from amongst the trees he stood for a moment by the edge of the little lagoon above whose sapphire waters the white gulls were flighting against a sky new-born and lovely and filled with distance and light.

The canoe lay where he had left it, high-beached now, for the tide was out. The bodies that had been tied to the gratings were gone, the gulls had done their work, and nothing showed but the coconut sennit bindings hanging brown like rags and moving to the breeze.

Close to the northernmost of the trees lay a little pond from which he had drunk before lying down; the trees stretching from the pool ran in a dense line for a quarter of a mile, pandanus, coconut palm, bread fruit, and a dense growth of mammee apple, shading beach and reef to a spot where the naked reef took charge. The rest of the ring of the atoll showed few trees, just a small clump or two of fifty-foot palms, wand-like and feathery against the blazing blue.

There was food here, enough of a sort, but he had neither knife nor fire nor fishing line. He was naked.

When they had bound him and kept him and flung him in the canoe to take him to the southern beach of Karolin, he had not bothered about the fact that he was naked—it had not troubled him at all till now. Now that sleep had restored him to himself, the fact of his nakedness came to him as a sudden trouble making him forget for the moment everything else, even food.

The trouble was entirely psychical. The climate of the beach was so warm that he did not require clothing as a protection, and there was shade enough to shelter him from the sun if he were too warm. All the same, his nakedness lay on him like a curse. He felt helpless, part of his environment that had clung to him for forty years was gone from him and without it he was all astray; naked as a worm he felt useless as a worm, ready to flinch at anything, without initiative, without power.

Dick had never known the need of clothes, he had never worn them. It was different with Rantan.

The absence of shoes he felt less, though without them he was condemned to keep off the rough coral and keep to the beach sands.

He came along the sands towards the canoe. Had you been watching him and had he been clothed in purple and fine linen you still would have said to yourself "There is something wrong about that man, why does he walk like that?"

When he reached the canoe he looked in at the remains of the fruit all squashed and gone bad from the sun; then, turning to the gratings he began to unfasten the strips of coconut sennit that had tied the bodies of the children.

The birds had pulled the bodies to pieces, not even the little bones were left and the bindings hung lax; his fingers were not trembling now as they had trembled on Karolin when trying to untie the knots; he had plenty of time to work in and bit by bit the fastenings came undone.

Then the gulls, if they had bothered to look, might have seen a strange sight: Rantan trying to make himself a loin cloth.

Why?

He had neither real decency nor shame in his composition, there was no one to see him in his nakedness but the gulls. Why then did he trouble?

Trouble he did and the result was scarcely worth his trouble. Then, and still without eating, he turned to and cleared the rotting pandanus and other fruit out of the canoe—he could not swill her out as he had nothing with which to hold water, but she had brought in a long piece of weed tangled on the outrigger; the sun had dried it, but he wet it again in the lagoon water and used it as a sort of mop.

Having cleaned her and seen that the mast, sail and paddles were all right, he came back to the trees, plucked some pandanus drupes and began to eat.

As he sat down to the food, he made to hitch up his left trousers leg, a habit he had. Before leaving the canoe to come back to the trees he had tried to put his hand in his pocket. In this way and in other ways and incessantly his vanished clothes spoke to him, reminding him that he was naked, worm-naked on the face of the world.

He ate, staring at the lagoon as if hypnotized by its blueness, and as he ate, pictures travelled before his mind's eye, pictures of Karolin lagoon and the two dead women he had left on the southern beach, and then, as a bird hops from one branch to another, his mind left Karolin and lit on the deck of the *Kermadec* and from that on to the sands of Levua in whose woods he had slain Peterson.

All his troubles had started from the killing of Peterson. It was just as though Peterson had been following him, stripping him steadily and bit by bit of everything down to his very clothes: of the schooner, of the pearl lagoon, of his sea chest, of the few dollars he had saved, of his hat, his shoes, his trousers, his shirt, his coat—everything. He tried to put away this idea but failed.

It was now only nine o'clock in the morning of a day that would not end at sunset, of a blue and blazing day that, with night intermissions, would last for months and months—for the rainy season was far off. And he was out of trade tracks.

He stood up, looked about him, and then walking carefully, picked his way on to the rough coral above the outer beach. Here on a smooth spot he stood looking over the sea to the northeast.

Nothing.

Karolin, with fabulous treasure in its blue heart, lay somewhere over there, lost, so far that even the lagoon light did not show.

He turned to the southeast. Somewhere there lay the Paumotus.

Should he push off in the canoe and try to reach them?

Since waking this morning there had fallen upon Rantan a double obsession, the paralysing sense of his nakedness and now the feeling that somehow in some way Peterson was following him—following him wearing the seven-league boots of bad luck. He believed neither in God nor in ghosts, but he believed in luck—and his luck had been frightful and it had dated from the killing of Peterson.

This double obsession cut the ground from under the feet of his energy, so that the idea of escape in the canoe entered his mind only to leave it again. He came back to the trees, lay down in their shadow and now the gulls began to talk to him.

The little island had two voices, the endless sound of the breakers and the unending complaint of the gulls; sometimes it would be just a voice or two, sometimes clamour—always indifference, voices from a world that knew nothing of man.

The dead women he had left lying on Karolin beach were not further beyond the pale of things than he who had slain them, and it came to Rantan as he lay there that he was shut out; no one knew of his fate, he was of no manner of interest to anything that surrounded him; to the wind, to the sunlight, to the trees, to the gulls. If he were to drop dead on the sands, he would become an object of interest to the predatory gulls, but alive he was of interest to nothing.

This was not a passing thought; it was kept alive in his mind by his nakedness. His mind had been stripped of its clothes in the form of living beings and accustomed surroundings, just as his body had been stripped of its clothes in the form of shirt, coat and trousers. The two nakednesses were as two voices perpetually talking together, answering each other, echoing one another.

Then, hypnotized by the murmur of the reef, he drifted off into sleep.

He was on the schooner. She was anchored in Karolin lagoon and the crew were diving for pearls, the deck was strewn with heaps of shells and Carlin was showing him a huge pearl in the palm of his hand. It was the last, they had stripped the lagoon clean, and now it was mainsail haul for 'Frisco, wealth, wine and women. He was down in the cabin, pearls all over the floor and pearls in the bunks, and as the ship rolled, the pearls ran and he chased them about the floor on his hands and knees, and they turned into pebbles as he caught them. Some turned into white mice and ran over Carlin who was lying dead by his bunk, and then Poni shoved his head through the skylight and called down at him: "Caa—caa—caa," and he awoke beneath the trees to the call of a passing gull.

WHAT HAPPENED TO RANTAN (CONTINUED)

He sprang to his feet and came running out on to the sands. For a moment he could not tell where he was, then he remembered.

It was past noon and the tide was beginning to ebb.

He saw the canoe and he stood, stood for a full minute without moving a single muscle—his mind working furiously, no longer diffident, no longer helpless, as though the dream in restoring his old environment had given him strength, renewed courage and daring.

He must clear out of this place, get to the open sea.

The Paumotus were possible, ships were possible, death was possible, but better than this place where nothing was possible, where nothing was but a beach to walk on, blazing sun and jeering gulls.

The ebb was beginning to run, it would take him through the break, he must act at once.

He ran towards the trees and began collecting pandanus drupes and carrying them to the canoe. He climbed like a monkey for drinking nuts, and just as on the Karolin beach he ran, sweating as he came piling the fruit on board; drinking nuts, drinking nuts—he never could have enough of them. Then the last of his frantically collected cargo on board he did what he had also done on the beach of Karolin, flung himself down by the little pool and drank till he nearly burst.

It was all a repetition of that business and only wanted the dead bodies of the women to make the picture complete. Then he came to the canoe.

Here it was the same again. He could not get her off. The dead children no longer weighed down the outrigger, but he had stowed his cargo badly and that did the business; the outrigger was bedded in the sand. He laboured and sweat rearranging the fruit, then at last she began to move; he pushed and drove, the lagoon water took her to amidships—another effort and she was water-borne and he was on board working with a single paddle and getting her farther out.

He was free.

A weight seemed gone from his soul, he no longer felt his nakedness; the power of movement, the escape from the beach and the new hope that lay in the open sea, were like wine to his spirit. It was a move in a new game and daring whispered to him that he would yet beat Peterson.

Working with the paddle from side to side, he got her farther and farther out, and the break lay before him now and beyond the break beckoned the sea.

He had turned sideways to take a last derisive look at the prison house of the trees and beach when—aye, what was that? Water ran over his knees as he knelt to the paddling, water that moved with a slobber and chuckle beneath the nuts.

The canoe was leaking. The sun must have done this business yesterday, craftily, whilst he was asleep. She had been bone dry when he stowed the fruit and now the stuff was awash or nearly so.

The mat sail was brailed ready to be broken out when clear of the lagoon. He looked at it, then his eyes fell again to the interior of the canoe—the water had risen higher still: this was no ordinary leak that immersion would caulk, there was nothing to be done but to return and try to mend it on the beach.

He began to paddle, making frantic efforts to turn the canoe's head and bring her ashore. He was too late, the ebb had her like a leaf and though he turned her head, it was only to make her float broadside to the spate of the tide.

The only chance was to try and hit the beach near the break.

He worked like a giant.

Only a few minutes before his heart had rejoiced at his escape, now, with the prospect of certain death from drowning in the outer sea, the beach seemed to him the most delectable place in the world.

But he could not reach it. The nearer the break the swifter the ebb; the lagoon water had him like a swiftly running river; the canoe twisted and turned to his efforts but he could not alter the line of its travel sufficiently to hit the beach.

Then, flinging the paddle away he rose, held on to the mast, plunged over the side and struck out for the shore.

When he reached it and stood up, the canoe was gone, swept to sea to be submerged and tossed on the swell.

His last possession had been taken from him. Schooner, money, pearls, clothes and lastly the canoe, all were gone; he had nothing in the world—save the loin cloth made from the bindings of the dead children.

But he was not thinking of that. His life had been saved. He had almost touched death and now as he looked on the oiling current, he saw a shark fin shearing along as though the shark that had missed him was blindly hunting for him.

He came back to the trees, hugging the life that had been spared to him and sat down to rest, Death sitting opposite to him—cheated.

This business brought things to a crisis with Rantan; though robbing him of his last possession, it still had given him a sense of winning a move, and truly, though his luck had been dreadful, there had been an undercurrent of good luck. He had escaped from Le Moan that night, he had escaped from Nanu and Ona who had him bound hand and foot, he had escaped from the sea coming to this atoll, and he had escaped from the leaking canoe and the shark. His mind took a turn. He felt that he was meant to live, he was sure that now he would be rescued. A ship would come.

And at this thought that seemed clothed in surety, the man's soul blazed up against Karolin. If she were only a ship with the right sort of people on board, he would find Karolin for them and they would rip the floor out of that lagoon and the hearts out of the kanakas that lived by it.

And the right sort of people would be on that ship and she would come—she would come. He knew it.

WHAT HAPPENED TO RANTAN (CONTINUED)

He fell asleep on the thought and for days and days he hugged it, and every day a dozen times he would go to the flat space on the coral and look over the sea for the ship.

One morning he saw something dark on the beach near the break; it was the canoe, the tide had taken her out only a little way and the sea had played with her, submerged as she was, returning her to the lagoon where the full flood had beached her. The water had drained out of her with the ebb and there she was and there he found her, pulling her up higher just for something to do. He found the crack that made the leak, it was quite small and he might have plugged it, but there was no paddle and anyway he would not have used her—he was waiting for the ship that was sure to come.

Rantan had, like most sailors, the full use of his hands, and he longed to use them, but he had no tools or anything to work on; near the trees and close to the mammee apple there was a patch of coarse grass and the idea came to him to make something out of it. Once in Chile he had escaped from prison by making a grass rope and the idea came to him now to make another; anything was better than sitting in idleness, and it seemed a lucky thing to do, for not only had he escaped from the Chilean prison by means of the rope, but he had come on a streak of good luck when free. So, gathering grass, he sat down to weave his rope.

The business was a godsend to him.

He limited the work to a few hours a day so as not to cloy himself, and he would look forward to the work hours as men look forward to a smoke.

Whilst he worked at it, he wove his thoughts into the rope, his desires, dreams and ambitions all were woven into it, the killing of Peterson went in, and the memory of the dead women on Karolin beach, his hatred of the kanakas and of the red-headed one who had come and looked at him, Dick.

As a woman weaves into her knitting her household affairs and so on, the busy fingers of Rantan wove into his rope visions of ripping the pearls out of Karolin lagoon, of hunting the kanakas to death, of drinking bars and loose pleasures to be had with the pearl money—truly, if an inanimate thing could be evil, it was evil, for it held Rantan's past. The amount of grass being limited, he sometimes knocked off work for a couple of days; and the days became weeks and the weeks went on and on till one morning, when the grass being nearly finished and the rope almost long enough to hang a man with a six-foot drop, Rantan, coming to his lookout, sighted a ship.

Away towards the north she lay so far that he could only tell she was of fore and aft rig and making either for or away from the atoll. Ten minutes showed her bigger—she was coming for the atoll. She was The Ship.

Then Rantan danced and sang on the smooth bit of coral and shouted to the gulls, and he came down to the sands and ran about on them like a dog in high spirits; he shouted to the canoe and abused her and called her filthy names, then back again to see how the ship was growing and back again to the sands to cut more capers.

She grew.

Returning to his lookout post for the fourth time, she seemed to have suddenly shot up in size as if by magic. Now he could see her clearly, her make and size and the patch on her foresail. He took a breath so deep that his chest stood out above his lean belly like a barrel. God! she was the *Kermadec!* The *Kermadec* or a sister ship, her twin image; the eye of a sailor told him that, the patch on the foresail he knew—he had helped to put it there.

He turned and came running on to the sands.

White men must have come into Karolin lagoon and made friends of the kanakas—the women would have been found dead on the beach, the canoe gone. It was all plain.

They would know that with the wind blowing at that time the canoe would have come in this direction; he was being searched for, either to be clubbed to death by kanakas or hanged by whites.

There lay the canoe on the beach and his footsteps on the sand.

He looked round. There was no mark of a campfire to give him away, nothing but the canoe, the footsteps, the fruit skins and coconut shells he had left lying about, and the rope.

He started to clear up, casting the skins and shells amongst the bushes. Then, diving into the bushes he hid there listening—waiting, sweating, the rope coiled by his side.

THE BATTLE AND THE VICTORY

The island grew.

Poni at the wheel, his eyes wrinkled against the sun, steered; Aioma beside him, Le Moan near Aioma and Dick forward near the galley. Dick had taken his seat on the deck in a patch of shadow and now he was leaning on his side supporting himself with his elbow. The sight of this island that was not Karolin had completed the business for Dick.

For four days he had scarcely touched food and for four days Le Moan had watched him falling away from himself. It was like watching a tree wither.

There was a vine on Karolin that would sometimes take a tree in its embrace just as ivy does, grow up it and round it and cling without doing the tree any injury; but if the vine were cut away from the tree, the tree would die.

It seemed to Le Moan that Taori was like the tree and Katafa the vine.

She was right.

Seldom enough, yet every now and then you find in this wilderness of a world, amidst the thorns of hate and the poison berries of passion and the dung of beasts and the toadstools of conjugal love, a passion pure and unselfish like the love of Katafa and Taori. Who moreover, above most other mortals, stood apart in a world there was no room for little things—where the sky was their roof and the ocean their floor and storm and war and cataclysm, halcyon weather, and the blaze of a tropic sun their environment, where the love that bound them together had, woven into it—after the fashion of the rope of Rantan—their past.

The thousand little and great and beautiful and terrific things that made up their past, all these were woven into the passion that bound them together.

To cut this bond, to separate them forcibly one from the other, was death.

In hot climates, in the tropics where the convolvulus grows so rapidly that the eye can all but see it grow, people can die quickly of love. Death grows when released with the fountain speed of the rocketing datura and the disruptive fury of corruption.

Dick cut away from Katafa was going to die. It was not only the cutting away, but the manner of it, that made his case hopeless.

Not only was he cut away from Katafa, but he was also divorced from his environment. His universe had consisted of Palm Tree and Karolin, the sea that held them, the sky above them: Katafa—nothing more.

Then Palm Tree had vanished and Karolin had been taken from him and nothing was left but the great vacant world of the sea, that and the grief for the loss of Katafa.

He was going to die. He was dying. His very strength was killing him.

You sometimes find that—find that the power of a powerful man can be turned in against itself by grief or by disaster or disease.

He was going to die, as Aioma said, and Le Moan knew it.

He was dying because Katafa had been cut away from him.

The sound of the bow-wash and the sound of the sea as it washed past the counter, and the creak of rope and spar, kept saying all this.

"Taori is dying because Katafa is no more with him—no more with him . . ."

Meanwhile the island grew.

And now Aioma, cheered by the sight of this bit of land, began talking to Poni in a high-pitched voice. But Le Moan did not hear or heed what he said.

So, Taori was going to die. And it was for this that she had taken him away from Katafa. She had taken him away to have him to herself and he was turning into a dead man. To save him from death she had given herself up to Peterson, to save him from death she had killed Carlin and risked being killed by Rantan, and yet he was going to die.

She could hear now the faint and far-away breathing of the surf on the reef ahead mixed with the words of Aioma to Poni; and now harsh and complaining and sudden and near came the call of a gull; a land gull, flying as if racing them.

"Taori is dying because of Katafa—Katafa— Katafa," cried the gull, and Le Moan following the bird with her eyes let her gaze sweep back to the deck where Taori was lying, half leaning, the sun upon his bare back where the vertebrae showed and the ribs.

And louder now came the breathing of the surf on the reef, heavy like the breathing of a weary man.

"All life is weary and full of labour," sighed the surf, "and there is no more joy in the sun—and Taori is going to die because of Katafa."

"Katafa," creaked the cordage to the foam that went sighing aft.

The wind freshened and the main sheet tautened and the great sail bellied hard against the blue, the schooner lifting to the swell crushed into it with great sighs and long shudders like the sighing and shuddering of a dying man, and the atoll leaped larger to view, the palm trees standing clear of the water above the coral and the visible foam.

"The palm grows, the coral waxes, but man departs," whispered the wind, repeating the old rede of the islands; and now the lagoon showed through the break and Le Moan, watching and knowing that there, should they enter that lagoon, Taori would find his last home beneath the palm trees, scarcely knew of the terrible battle raging in the darkness of her mind— knew only that she was all astray, helpless, useless, pulled this way and that between two opposing forces great as the powers of life and death; whilst louder now came the sound of the surf, louder and deeper and more solemn, till once again she was on the beach of Karolin, the stars were shining, the little conch shells whispering and chirruping to keep the evil spirits away, for Uta Matu the king was dying and his breathing came from the house like that.

Then, suddenly, with the cry of a dreamer awakened from some terrible dream, flinging out her arms to thrust away the dark spirit that had all but seized her soul and the body of Taori, Le Moan flung Poni from the wheel, seized the spokes and the schooner, checking, turned, her canvas thrashing and clawing at the wind.

Turned—the island wheeling to the port quarter and the main boom flogging out with Aioma and Poni hauling at the sheet; turned and held, close hauled and steering for the west of north.

"Karolin," cried Le Moan, "Aioma, the sight has come to me—the path is plain."

"Karolin!" cried Aioma. "Taori, the spell is broken, we are free and the net of Le Juan tom asunder and the spears of Uta blunted."

WHAT HAPPENED TO RANTAN (CONCLUSION)

Safe hidden amongst the bushes he listened. It would take a full hour yet before the schooner could make the break, yet he listened as he lay, his rope beside him, his mind active as a squirrel in its cage.

They would search the atoll, they would hunt amongst the bushes—yet they might miss him.

Should they find him! His dark mind took fire at the thought, wild ideas came to him of escaping into the lagoon, boarding the schooner, seizing a rifle and turning the situation. He was a white man, a match for a hundred kanakas if only he could get a foothold above them, a rifle in his hands. In this he was right, as he had slain the women who had him safely bound, so had he the possibility in him to meet this last attack of fate, free himself, and dominating and destroying, make good at last.

Time passed, the reef spoke and the wind in the trees, but from the outer sea came nothing. He peeped through the bushes, getting a view of the reef line to northward. By now surely the topmasts of the schooner ought to show close in as she must be, yet there was nothing.

He came out of the bushes like a lizard, stood erect and then came cautiously towards the higher coral where his outlook post was; literally on hands and feet he crawled, inch by inch, till the sea came in view and then he crawled no longer. He stood erect.

Far off on the breezed-up sea the schooner close-hauled was standing away from the island.

Rantan could scarcely grasp the fact before his eyes. She had been making for him and now she was standing away.

She had not been searching for him, then. Was she after all the *Kermadec* or had he been mistaken?

Her shape, her personality, that patch on the sail—well what of that? Other ships had patched canvas besides his schooner. He had surely been mistaken.

As she dwindled dissolving in the wind, his hungry eyes followed her.

How fast she was going, faster than the *Kermadec* could sail close-hauled.

He watched her till she was hull down, till her canvas showed like a midge dancing in the sea dazzle, till it vanished taken by the round world into the viewless.

Then he came back to the trees.

Just as the ship had gone from the sea, so had his dream ship gone from his mind, taking hope with her, leaving him to his utter nakedness. He went to the old canoe that he had abused and vilified in his hour of triumph; the sun had enlarged the crack, the forward outrigger pole had worked loose with the tossing in the swell, there was no paddle.

Yet she could talk to him, telling him of Nanu and Ona and their dead children, and of Carlin and Peterson, and beyond that of Soma and Chile and many a traverse to the beginning of that great traverse of his life.

He wished to be done with it all.

With the going of hope, the fact of his nakedness had seized him again.

It had never quite left him; the feeling of being without clothes had tinged even his dreams, he had fought against it and put it by, but it always returned, and now that hope had departed it was back and in a worse form. For now if he did not fight it hard, it was taking the form, not of discomfort and a sense of want, but of uneasiness, the terrible excitable uneasiness that the stomach can produce when disarranged— stomach fear.

He fought it down, returned to the trees and found that his worry about the ship and his own position had quite gone; he was worrying about nothing, for he was at grips with something new, something born of his naked skin and his stomach that had been feeding on uncooked food for so long, something that had been making for him for weeks, something that threatened to rise to a crisis and make him run—run—run.

Dropping to sleep that night he was brought awake by something that hit him a blow on the soles of his feet; twice this happened and when he slept he was hunting for his clothes, and when he awoke it was to face another blue day, a day lovely but implacable as a sworn tormentor.

He walked the beach in his nakedness.

The gulls had begun to jeer at him now. Up to this they had left him severely alone, treating him with absolute indifference, but they had found him out at last; they were laughing at him all along the reef, talking about him and every now and then rising above the trees to look at him.

This idea held for a little and then passed, and he knew that he had been the victim of a delusion.

The gulls were quite indifferent to his presence.

Now amongst the trees and close to the waterside stood a gigantic soa with rail-like branches projecting like limbs across the sand and one big branch standing at right angles from the trunk some fifteen feet up.

Lying now amongst the tree shadows, and listening to the gulls' voices that had become normal, and the long roll of the unending breakers and the whispering movements of the robber crabs, Rantan fixed his eyes on this branch and saw himself in fancy swinging from it at the end of a rope, free of all his trouble, naked no longer. The rope he had woven and which was lying amongst the bushes had tied itself to the branch in his imagination.

He saw himself rising, hunting amidst the bushes and coming out of them with the rope in his hand; climbing the tree, fixing the rope to the limb, making the noose in the free end, placing the noose round his neck, dropping—kicking the air—dangling.

At noon a great gull sweeping across the lagoon from the leeward to the windward beach, seeing the dangling figure, altered its line of flight as if deflected by a blow, and a high-going burgomaster, seeing the deflected flight of his brother in hunger, circled and dropped like a stone to where Rantan was dangling and dancing on the wind. A naked figure yet capable, had the schooner put in, of boarding it by night, seizing command by treachery, sailing north and sweeping Karolin, for such is the power of the White Man. But Rantan was dead, slain by the action of Le Moan in putting the schooner about. This was the third time she had sacrificed herself for the sake of Taori, the third time that she had countered danger and death with love.

THE GREEN SHIP

Le Moan steered. Tireless and heedless of time as when she had brought the schooner first to Karolin, she kept the wheel all that day and through the night, giving it over to Poni for short intervals, whilst Dick slept.

She had given life back to him and it was almost as though she had given him her own life, for the world around her had become as the world wherein ghosts move; disembodied spirits, not dead but no longer connected with earth.

Before setting eyes on Taori, she had lived on the southern beach of Karolin, lonely, cut off with Aioma and the others who had no interests beyond the interests of the moment; as she lived so might she have died neither happy nor unhappy, without pity and without love or care for the morrow or thought of the past.

Then Taori had come, not as a man but as a light greater than the sun, a light that struck through the darkness of her being, bringing to birth a new self that was his—that was he.

She had braved death and the unknown—everything—only to find herself at the end face to face with death, and death saying to her "He is mine—or Katafa's."

Like the woman who stood before Solomon, she had to choose between the destruction of the thing she loved and the handing of it to a rival to be lost to her forever, to see its arms clinging to another, and its love given to another, and its life becoming part of the life of another; and she chose the greater sacrifice, not because she was Le Moan, a creature extraordinary or supernormal, but just because at heart she was a woman.

A woman, acting, when brought to the great test, less as an individual than as a part of the spirit of womanhood. The spirit changeless through the ages and unalterable. The spirit so often hidden by the littleness of the flesh, so seldom put to the heroic test, so absolutely certain in its answer to it. For when a woman really loves she becomes a mother even though she never may conceive or produce a child.

Aioma, who had slept through the night on his belly on the deck, spread like a starfish, awoke as the sun was rising.

Poni was at the wheel—Le Moan had gone below. The cabin had no fears for her now, and she had said to Poni, just as the sun was rising and pointing into the west of north, "You will see the lagoon light there."

Dick, by the galley, was still sleeping, Tahuku and Tirai were the watch.

The beauty of that sunrise on that blue and lonely sea, beyond word or brush, was unseen by Aioma.

"It will be over there," said Poni, pointing ahead. "It does not show yet" Aioma went forward and stood looking into the northwest No, it did not show yet nor would it show till the sun was twice its diameter above the horizon. Aioma, listening to the slash of the bow breaking the water and fanned by the draught from the head sails, having swept the sky found his eye caught by something far across the sea and right in their course. It looked at first glance like a rock but at once his bird-like eyes resolved it into what it was—a ship, an *ayat*, but with no sail set.

The canoe-builder glanced back along the deck past the sleeping figure of Dick to the figure of Poni at the wheel, then he turned his eyes again upon the far-off ship, and now in the sky to the north above and beyond the ship lay something for which he had been on the lookout—the lagoon light of Karolin, almost imperceptible, but there just in the position where Le Moan had said it would be.

The something he had waited and longed for, but spoiled, almost threatened, by this apparition of a ship.

Aioma wanted to have nothing more to do with ships; this traverse in the schooner had turned him clean back towards canoes; for days past, though he had said no word on the matter, all his ancestors had been hammering at the door of his mind shouting, "Aioma, you are a fool, you have forsaken the canoes of your forefathers for this *ayat*, and see how it has betrayed you, and why? Because it is the invention of the white men, the cursed papalagi who have always brought trouble to Karolin. If we could get at you, Aioma, we would stake you out on the reef for the sharks to eat. You deserve it."

He had said nothing of this because Aioma never confessed to a fault.

Well there was another *ayat*, blocking the way to Karolin and sure to bring trouble.

Civilization and trouble had come to be convertible ideas in the mind of this old gentleman who although he did not know the English word that represents greed, brutality, disease, drink, and robbery dressed in self- righteousness, had sensed the fact that the white man always brought trouble.

Well, there it was straight before him heading her off from Karolin. What should he do? Turn and run away from it? Oh, no. Aioma, who had fought the big rays and who was never happier than when at grips with a conger, was not the person to turn his back on danger or threat, especially now with Karolin in view.

This thing lay straight in his path, as if daring him, and he accepted the challenge; they had the speak sticks, there were eight of them not including Le Moan and if it came to a fight—well, he was ready.

Without rousing Dick, he called the fellows up from below, pointed out the ship and then stood watching as she grew.

Now she stood on the water plainly to be seen, a brig with canvas stowed as if in preparation for a blow. If any canvas had been set it must have been blown away by the wind, for she showed nothing but her sticks as she lay rolling gently to the swell.

Tahuku, who had the instinct of a predatory gull coupled with the eye of a hawk, suddenly laughed:

"She is empty," said Tahuku, "she has no men on her. It is a dead turtle, Aioma you have called on us to spear."

Aioma hit by the same truth ran and roused Dick, who on waking sprang to his feet. He was renewed by sleep and hope, a creature reborn and as he stood with the others he scarcely noticed the ship, his eyes fixed on the light of Karolin.

Poni at the wheel called Le Moan and she came up from below and stood watching whilst the brig, now close to them, showed her nakedness and desolation beneath the burning light of morning.

Old-fashioned, even for these days, high-pooped, heavily sparred and with an up-jutting bowsprit, her hull of a ghastly faded green rolled with a weary movement to the undulations of the swell, revealing now the weed-grown copper of her sheathing, now a glimpse of the deserted deck. There were no boats at the davits and as the current altered her position, giving her a gentle pitch, came a sound faint against the wind, the clapping of her deck-house door.

Aioma turning, ran aft and stood beside Poni at the wheel giving him directions. The canoe-builder, urged by his ancestors and his hatred of the *papalagi*, had evolved an idea from his active brain and Dick, who had let his eyes wander from the brig to the far-off light of Karolin, heard suddenly the thrashing of canvas as the steersman brought the schooner up into the wind.

Aioma was going to board the *ayat*. He was shouting directions to Tahuku and the others—they ran to the falls, the boat was lowered, and in a moment he was away, shouting like a boy; scrambling like a monkey when they hitched on to the broad channel plates he gained the deck and stood looking round him.

Aye, that was a place! Bones of dead men picked clean by the birds lay here and there, and a skull polished like a marble rolled and moved and rotated on the planking to the pitch of the hull, the clicking of the lax rudder chain, and the clapping of the deckhouse door.

He had brought his fire-stick with him and its little bow, from the deck of the schooner. They watched him as he stood looking about him. Then turning, he darted into the deck-house.

He was there a long time, perhaps ten minutes, and when he came out a puff of smoke came after him. Holding the door open, he looked in till another puff of smoke garnished with sparks, hit him in the face, then having done a little dance on the deck and kicked the skull into the starboard scupper, he dropped into the boat and came back to the schooner, singing.

The boat was hoisted in, the schooner put on her course and the smoking brig dropped far astern, but Aioma, still flushed with his work and victory, heeded nothing.

He sat on the coaming of the saloon skylight singing.

He sang of the bones of the dead men and the skull he had kicked and the *ayat* he had fired and the cursed *papalagi* whose work he had destroyed; then, with a great whoop he curled up and went asleep, undreaming that the *papalagi* might yet have their revenge, and Dick, to whom Aioma and the ship astern flaring horribly in the sunlight were as nothing, watched from the bow the steady growing beacon of Karolin in the sky.

H. de Vere Stacpoole

There was Katafa.

His soul flew ahead of the schooner like a bird, flew back and flew forward again calling on the wind, and the wind, nearing, strengthened, so that a little after midday the far treetops of the southern beach came to view and now, faint and far away, the song of the great atoll.

Birds flew to meet them and birds passed them flying towards the land and as the sun began its downward climb to the water, the break began to show away on the port bow and Le Moan, pushing Tahuku, who was at the wheel, aside, prepared to take them in.

For only Le Moan knew the danger of the break when the tide was ebbing as now.

The waters were against them. It seemed the last feeble effort of fate to separate Dick from the being he loved.

The vast lagoon was pouring out like a river, it was past full spate, but the swirl was enough, if the helmsman failed to drive them on the coral.

Now they were in the grip of it, the schooner bucking like a restive horse, now steady, now making frantic efforts to turn and dash out to sea again—Aioma in the bow crying directions, Le Moan heeding him as little as she heeded the crying of the gulls.

Now they had stolen between the piers. The break on either side of them seemed immensely broad and the grand sweep of the outgoing water lit by the westering sun showed with scarcely a ripple to where it boiled against the piers: gulls in flight above it showed as in a mirror, yet it was flowing at a six- knot clip.

The schooner with every sail drawing seemed not to move, yet she moved, turning the mirror to a feather of foam at her cut water and a river of beaten gold in her wake. The piers dropped astern, the current slackened, the lagoon was conquered and lay before them a blaze of light from the beach sands to its northern viewless barrier.

Katafa was sleeping. She who slept scarcely at all by night and whose eyes by day were always fixed towards the sea, was sleeping when the voice of Kanoa roused her:

"They come, Katafa, they come!"

Raising herself on one hand, she saw the sunset light through the trees and the form of Kanoa making off again to the beach his voice drifting back to her as he ran:

"They come, Katafa, they come!"

Then where the whole village was waiting, she found herself on the sands, the lagoon before her and on the lagoon the schooner bravely sailing in the sunset blaze, the sails full and now shivering as, curving to her anchorage, the wind left them and the rumble of the anchor chain running out came across the water, rousing her to the fact that what she saw could not be, that what she saw was a ship, but not the ship that had taken Taori away, the ship she had watched and waited for till hope was all but dead and life all but darkness. It could not be. It could not be that she should return like this, so sure, so quietly, so real, the dream ship that held her heart and soul, her love, her very life.

The boat putting off now was a phantom, surely, and Taori as he sprang on the sands and seized her in his embrace was unreal as the world fading around her, till his lips seized her up from twilight to the heaven of assurance.

"Taori has come back," cried the women, forgetting him as they turned to the men who were standing by the boat—unheeding Le Moan who stood, her work done, a being uncaring, seeing nothing, not even Kanoa, crouched on the sands half dead with the beatitude of the vision before him.

ARIPA! ARIPA!

"Listen!" said the wind.

From her place amidst the trees where Le Moan had settled herself like a hare in its forme she heard the silky whisper of the sands and the voice of the beach and the wind in the leaves above bidding her to listen.

Far-away voices came from the mammee apple where the men of the schooner and their wives were making merry, and now and then, the faintest thing in the world of sound, a click and creak from Nan on his post above the house where Taori lay in the arms of Katafa.

To Le Moan all that was nothing. She had banded death in exchange for Taori, all her interest in life, all her desires. She had not even the desire to destroy herself. The fire that had been her life burned low and smouldered; it would never blaze again.

"Listen!" said the wind.

Something moved amidst the trees—it was Kanoa: Kanoa, his heart beating against his ribs, his hands outstretched touching the tree boles.

474

She saw him now as he came towards her like a phantom from the star-showered night, and she knew why he came, nor did she move as he dropped on his knees beside her—all that was nothing now to Le Moan.

Since the night when he had saved her from Rantan, he had been closer to her than the other men of the schooner, but still only a figure, almost an abstraction.

To-night, now, he was a little more than that, as a dog might be to a lonely person, and as he poured out his heart in whispers she listened without replying, let him put his arm around her and take her lips; all that was nothing now to her whose heart would never quicken again.

*

The wind died, day broke, and the wind of morning blew.

Joy and the sun leapt on Karolin. Joy for Katafa who came from the house to look at a world renewed, for the women whose husbands had returned, for the men, for the children. Joy for Kanoa, his soul shouting in him, "She is mine, she is mine," and for Aioma, the lust of revenge and destruction alive and dancing in his heart.

"He had killed the green ship; this morning he would kill the schooner; the cursed *ayat*, that he had yet loved so dearly only a week ago, was doomed to die.

He hated it now with an entirely new and delicious brand of hatred and if he could have staked it out on the reef for the sharks to devour, so would he have done.

It had given him the scare of his life, it had all but snapped him away from Karolin, it had caused ancestral voices to rise cursing him for his folly and treachery towards his race; it had brought up visions of the Spanish ship, the brutal whale men, Carlin, Rantan, and the whole tribe of the papalagi, it was theirs and it had got to die.

Besides, it was going to give him the chance to set fire to things. He was still licking his chops over the firing of the green ship and the joy of incendiarism was about to be recaptured.

It was the last blaze up of youth in him. He called the village together and explained matters.

The *ayat* was accursed. His father, Amatu, had explained it all in a dream, commanding him, Aioma, to attend to this matter. The thing had to burn; if it did not bum worse would befall Karolin.

"Burn, burn, aripa, aripa!" cried the boys.

"Aripa!" shrieked the women, the men took tongue and the cry went up like the crackle of flame.

Katafa listened, loathing the schooner. The cry went up from her heart.

Dick stood dumb. Dumb as a man hesitating before cutting away the very last strand connecting him with his past. Dumb as a man about to renounce his race, though of his race and of the civilized world from whence he had sprung he knew nothing—nothing save the fact of the cannon-shot of the *Portsey* long years ago the white-led Melanesians of Palm Tree, the ruffianism of Carlin and Rantan and the rage in his own breast for adventure that had nearly separated him forever from Katafa.

Then, suddenly, he joined in the shout.

"Aripa! aripa! aripa!"

Forgetting his chieftanship he raced with the others to help to push off the boat bearing Aioma to his work.

Then he stood with Katafa watching. Near them and beside Kanoa stood Le Moan.

They watched the canoe-builder clamber on board like a monkey, they saw him dancing on the deck like a maniac insulting the ropes and spars, then they heard the ship's bell go clang-clang, as he made her talk for the last time.

He vanished down the foc's'le and came out escorted by a cloud of smoke, down the hatch of the saloon from whose skylight presently a blue-grey wreath uprose and circled on the faint breeze.

Then he was on deck again and away in the boat, and the schooner was burning fore and aft.

Wreathing herself in mist that cleared now to show two tall columns of smoke rising and spreading and forming spirals on the wind, red flames like the tongues of hounds licking out of the portholes, flames that ran spirit-like about the old tinder-dry deck. The main boom was burning now, the topping lofts were snapped, flames curling round the masts like climbing snakes, and now, like the rumble of a boiler, came the rumble of the fire as it spread in her, breaking through bulkheads, seizing the cargo and splitting the decks.

The sandalwood was burning and the incense of it spread across the lagoon to the white-robed congregation of the gulls wheeling and giving tongue above the reef; burning and blazing till the decks gave utterly and the crashing masts full sheeted in flame like tall men tumbling to their ruin amidst the roar of a burning city.

The flames devoured the smoke and the sun devoured the flames, forty-foot jets that leaped tongue-like sunwards, fell and leapt again. The great conflagration gave no light; it roared, and the consuming wood, pine and deal, teak and sandal filled the air with the sound of bursting shells and the rattle of musketry, but the sun of that blazing day ate the light of the flames so that they showed stripped of effulgence, stark naked; ghosts, cairngorm coloured, wine coloured, spark spangled, illuminating nothing.

And now the port bulwarks, breaking in one piece from the stern to amidships, fell in a blaze and the anchor chain, running out, broke from its attachments and she was adrift miraculously on the flood, now low to the break, now broadside, as the current took her—blazing as she drifted, pieces of her ever going, dipping now by the bow, slipping from sight in a veil of steam as the water rushing in fought the fire and the fire fought the water and was killed. And now there was nothing but driftwood so far out as scarcely to be seen, and a tiny cloud that vanished and a perfume of sandalwood that lingered in the air, ghost-like . . . gone.

THE GREEN SICKNESS

All that remained of her was the boat, the lesser of the two boats which Aioma had saved for the moment.

The island was without a single canoe, and he intended to build one as swiftly as might be for the fishing; that being done he would destroy the boat and so obliterate the last trace of the cursed *papalagi*.

So he set to work and the work progressed, Le Moan helping with the others. She worked at the making of the sail, Kanoa helping her, happy, ignorant of her utter deadness to all things, yet sometimes wondering.

Sometimes this woman he had taken to his heart seemed indeed a spirit or a lost soul as she had seemed to him that time before the killing of Carlin; always she was remote from him in mind, untouchable as the gulls he had chased as a child on Soma. Yet she was his and she let him love her,—and "Time," said the heart of Kanoa, "will bring her arms around me."

Her strangeness and indifference increased his passion. A child and yet a man, he moved now in a wonder world, he was always singing when alone and there was something in his voice that made it different from the voices of the others, so that when the women heard him singing in the groves they said "That is Kanoa."

And despite his happiness in her and his love for her and his embraces, despite the joy of new life that filled Karolin and the beauty of the nights in which Taori and Katafa walked together on the reef, never once did the desire come to Le Moan to destroy herself—all that was nothing to her now.

She had torn out her heart and nothing else mattered, even life.

"And to-morrow or next day," one morning said Aioma, "the canoe will be ready and we will burn the lesser *ayat* as we burned the greater. Ah hai, what is this, the reef is lifting before my eyes—Look you, Tahuku!"

But Tahuku saw nothing. The reef was solid as of old and the sun was shining on it and he said so.

The canoe-builder shut his eyes and when he opened them again the reef had ceased to lift, but he was weary. Bells rang in his ears and his hands were hot and dry and now after a while and towards midday one of the *papalagi*—so it seemed to him—had seized him from behind and tied a band round his head, screwing it so tight that he would have screamed had he been an ordinary man.

He lay on the ground, and as he lay a woman, one of the wives of Poni, came running, panting as she ran.

"I burn, I burn!" cried the woman. "Aioma, my sight is going from me; I burn, I burn!" She fell on the ground and Katafa running to her raised her head.

Aioma turning on his side tried to rise but could not, then he laughed.

Then he began to sing. He was fighting the *papalagi* and killing them, the Spaniards of long ago and the whale men and Carlin and Rantan; his song was a song of victory, yet he was defeated. The white men had got him with the white man's disease. Measles stood on the beach of Karolin, for the green ship with its cargo of labour had fallen to measles and Aioma in boarding it had sealed his doom.

It was Poni who guessed the truth. He had seen measles before—and now, remembering the ship, he cried out that they were undone, that the devils from the green ship had seized them and that they must die.

He had no need to say that.

Aioma lasted only a day, and the lagoon took him; by then the whole population was down, all but Taori, Katafa, Le Moan and Kanoa.

Kanoa had taken the disease at Vana Vana many years ago and was immune; the others, saved, perhaps, by the European blood in their veins, still resisted the disease.

The people died on the coral or cast themselves burning into the lagoon and were seized by the sharks, who knew.

And to Le Moan as she watched them, it was not the green sickness that did the work, but she herself.

She had brought this curse on Karolin. She had brought the schooner and the white men, she had taken the schooner to meet the green ship; it was the mother of her mother, Le Juan, who was reaching through her to slay and slay. Aioma in a lucid interval before he died had seized her by the hands and told her this, but she had no need of the telling of Aioma. She knew. And she watched, helpless and uncaring. She could do nothing, and the people passed, vanished like ghosts, died like flies, whilst the wind blew gently and the sun shone and the gulls fished and dawn came ever beautiful as of old through the Gates of Morning.

THE RELEASE OF LE MOAN

One night, when the disease seemed past and only ten people were left of all those who had watched the burning of the schooner, Le Moan, sleeping by Kanoa, was awakened by Katafa.

Katafa was weeping.

She seized Le Moan by the hands and raising her without waking Kanoa, led her to the house above which Nan still stood frizzy-headed in the moonlight.

In the house on a mat Dick was lying tossing his head from side to side and talking in a strange tongue.

Talking the language of his early childhood, calling out to Kearney whom he had long forgotten, but whom he remembered now.

The green sickness had seized Dick—resisted for days and days it had him at last.

Le Moan stood in the doorway and the moon looking over her shoulder lit the form on the mat, the reef spoke and the wind in the trees, but she heard nothing, saw nothing and for a moment felt nothing.

Taori was lying on the mat talking in a strange tongue, turning his head from side to side.

Then, as a person all but drowned, all but dead, comes slowly back to life and comes in agony, Le Moan began to feel the world come round her once more, the world she had known before she tore her heart out.

Taori was going to die. And the heart she had torn out was back again and the love that had filled it.

Taori was going to die—to die as the others had died and as surely, and as certainly through her who had brought this curse on Karolin and through whom the hand of Le Juan was still striking.

So great was the power of this thought that it fought with and overcame the passionate desire to fling herself on her knees beside him and take him in her arms; so great was its power that it almost drove the thought of him away before the crowding recollections it brought up of her own disastrous history in which she had brought evil to everyone. To Peterson, to Rantan, to Carlin, to Poni, to Tahuku—Tirai, all whom she had touched or come in contact with. To Aioma—and lastly to Taori.

Taori is going to die—*Ai amasu Taori*—the wind sighed it above him, it came mixed with the sobbing of Katafa and the voice of the beach with the rumbling voice of Taori himself, talking, talking, talking, as he wandered on the reef of memory with Kearney in a land that knew not Katafa.

Ai amasu Taori—and she dared not bid him goodbye; to save him she must go, leave him untouched, for the net of Le Juan was not yet torn, nor the spears of Uta blunted.

Even to look at him was fatal, yet she could not tear her eyes away.

Ai amusu Taori—a great breaker on the coral cried it to the night and broke the spell and turned her towards the weeping Katafa.

"Oh, Katafa," said Le Moan, speaking in a voice clear but scarcely above a whisper, "Taori will not die—I go to save him; the nets are spread for him but I will break them, I the daughter of Le Jennibon, the daughter of Le Juan."

Even as she spoke the voice from the house quieted.

"I who have brought this evil." Katafa heard her voice, not knowing what she said, for the change in the voice of the sick man was speaking to her.

Gliding into the house she lay down beside him, her cool hand upon his brow.

Le Moan turned to the beach through the trees. Night rested on Karolin and the moon showed the sands far stretching and filled with the silky whisper of the wind.

Far to the right lay the canoe all but completed, to the left the boat of the schooner. Le Moan came to the boat.

The tide was full, almost touching the keel, it was a light boat, the sands were firm, and evil though it was, it could not resist her. Afloat, with an oar, she drove it out, and raising the sail shipping the rudder, gave the sail to the wind.

The wind was favourable for the break, the ebb was beginning to run, all things were helping her now because she had conquered. Death could do no more against her for she was his.

To the right lay the moonlit sands of the southern beach from which she had sailed that morning with Peterson and with a dread in her heart that she did not feel now; before her lay the widening break with the first ebb racing through it to the sea, a night-flying gull cried above her as the breakers loudened on the outer beach and fell behind her as the wind and tide swept her out to the sea.

Far out, beyond return by drift or chance, she brailed the little sail, unstepped the mast and cast mast and sail to the water, cast the oars to the water, and lying down gave her soul into the hands of that Power through which her mother's people had gained release when, weary of the world, they chose to turn their faces from the sun.

*

Northwest of the Paumotas men talk of a vast atoll island half fabulous, half believed in. Ship masters have sighted a palm line by day reefless because, steer as they will, some sort of current has never allowed them to raise the reef and by night the pearling schooners have heard the breathing of a beach uncharted, and always on the sound a wind has followed blowing them away from the mysterious land.

Karolin—who knows?—the island of dreams, sealed by the soul of Le Moan to the civilization that the children of Lestrange and their child escaped from; a beach that the pleasant sunshine alone lights for me; where Aioma shapes his logs and where I watch, undisturbed by the noise of cities, the freshness we have lost and the light that comes alone through the Gates of Morning.

THE END

www.ingramcontent.com/pod-product-compliance
Lightning Source LLC
Chambersburg PA
CBHW030925020726
47498CB00001B/118